THE ENIGMA OF
GENERAL BLASKOWITZ

THE ENIGMA OF GENERAL BLASKOWITZ

Richard Giziowski

LEO COOPER
LONDON
HIPPOCRENE BOOKS
New York

For information, address:
HIPPOCRENE BOOKS, INC.
171 Madison Avenue
New York, NY 10016

Published in the United Kingdom in 1997 by
LEO COOPER
an imprint of
Pen & Sword Books Ltd.
47 Church Street
Barnsley, South Yorkshire S70 2AS
LEO COOPER ISBN 0 85052 554 3

Library of Congress Cataloging-in-Publication Data
Giziowski, Richard J. (Richard John)
The enigma of General Blaskowitz / Richard Giziowski.
p.   cm.
Includes bibliographical references and index.
ISBN 0-7818-0503-1
1. Blaskowitz, Johannes von, 1883-1948. 2. World War, 1939-1945-
-Atrocities. 3. Germany. Heer—Biography. 4. War criminals-
-Germany—Biography. 5. War criminals—Poland—Biography.
6. Poland—History,—occupation, 1939-1945. 7. Generals—Germany-
-Biography. I. Title.
D804.G4G54   1996   96-42239
940.54'05'0943—dc20   CIP

Printed in the United States of America.

CONTENTS

MAPS

ACKNOWLEDGMENTS

AMONG THE PERSONAL AND INTELLECTUAL DEBTS inevitably accumulated during the course of the research and writing of this book, perhaps the greatest is to my Doktorvator, Dr. Lawrence Walker, for his unfailing historical instinct and gentle but firm guidance of the doctoral dissertation which led to this book. I am indebted also to the late John Mendelsohn of the U.S. National Archives and to Mr. Robert Wolfe, Mr. John Taylor, Dr. Timothy Mulligan and Mr. Fred Purnell, at the U.S. National Archives. I wish also to acknowledge the assistance of Magrit Krewson, Central European Specialist at the Library of Congress. Dr. Richard Sommers and Mr. David Keough at the U.S. Army Military History Institute provided exceptional assistance during the research for this book. I am also indebted to the Archives of Ohio University for making the Cornelius Ryan Papers available to me, and to the staff of the Manuscript Division of the Library of Congress for granting access to me to the John Toland Collection. The author is also indebted to the research staffs at the Widener Library at Harvard University, the U.S. Air Force Historical Research Center at Maxwell Air Force Base (Alabama), the main Research Library of the City of New York at Forty-Second Street, the Archives of the United Nations and the Public Library of the City of Worcester, Massachusetts. Acknowledgment of the kind assistance of the staffs at the Public Archives of Canada, the Imperial War Museum, the Public Record Office, the Churchill College Archives at Cambridge and St. Antony's College Archives at Oxford is hereby made. I owe a particular debt to the trustees and to Ms. Patricia Methven at the B.H. Liddell Hart Centre for Military History at King's College, London, for her unfailing long-term assistance. I would be remiss if I neglected to thank the staffs at Bundesarchiv Militärarchiv, Freiburg im Breisgau, Bundesarchiv-Koblenz and Bundesarchiv Aachen, in addition to the staffs at Generallandsarchiv Karlsruhe, Stadtarchiv Konstanz and the Archiv der

Kameradschaft ehemaliger 114/14er in Konstanz. Thanks also to the staff at the Service Administratif De La Meteorologie in Paris.

I wish to make special mention of the help of my friend Oberstleutnant a.D. Reimar Grundies in many aspects of this biography. Dr. Med Joern Hansen of Kassel painstakingly deciphered some of Blaskowitz's handwritten almost code-like Gothic script. The kindness of Mr. David Irving in opening his personal collection of papers to me and also to Dr. Harold C. Deutsch for sharing both his papers and his vast experience must be made. I was privileged also to be granted a gracious interview and lengthy correspondence with Mr. Telford Taylor who served as the U.S. Chief of Counsel for the Prosecution of Axis Criminality at the Nuremberg War Crimes Trials. Mr. Taylor, Dr. Harold Deutsch, Dr. Lawrence Walker, Dr. Robert Ciottone and Dr. Joseph Holmes each read the entire manuscript and offered numerous suggestions and constructive criticism. Major John Moncure (U.S.A.) was kind enough to read and criticize Chapter II, and to provide helpful questions. My personal gratitude to Mr. Johannes Koepcke Jr. and to Prince Friedrich Biron von Kurland for their gracious hospitality deserves particular mention. Miss Anne Mazur assisted with translations from Polish, and Ulrike Bernhardt with the German. Conrad M. Allen, a good friend, was supportive through the long years of research and writing. Cathy M. and Brian C. Taylor, Barbara J. Fuhr and Richard Baker provided exemplary word processing services without which the completion of this book would have been impossible. Ms. Delores Delude helped keep a voluminous correspondence manageable. No list of my debts would be complete without recognizing the years of encouragement and support of my dear wife Christine. Heartfelt thanks. I wish also to express my gratitude to God for the years of His Grace which made possible the conversion of a dream into the reality of this manuscript. Finally, I must express my admiration to all those who have confronted evil with limited success and without recognition.

I wish to dedicate this biography to my father and mother, and to my Aunt Jenny. To them, as to all of those mentioned above, I owe a great debt. For any errors of fact or interpretation I am solely responsible.

R.J.G.

INTRODUCTION

NÜRNBERG, GERMANY, FEBRUARY 5, 1948: "The Associated Press reported today the suicide of Colonel-General Johannes Blaskowitz of the German Army just hours before his trial as a war criminal was scheduled to begin."[1] The lesser-known, soon-forgotten German general, indicted in the so-called "minor" war crimes trials, reportedly leaped to his death from the top tier of the high catwalks surrounding the prison rotunda. His was the ninth suicide at the Nürnberg jail since war criminals were brought to Nürnberg in November 1945.[2]

The story of another suicide among Nazi war criminals merited only a page thirteen story in *The New York Times*. The post-war world was little interested. Inside the walls of the Nürnberg prison, among the alleged war criminals whose trials began that day, it was quite another matter; many of them believed that Blaskowitz had been murdered by the SS.[3] Among them the story circulated that SS members who had become prison trusties had murdered Blaskowitz.[4]

Could the SS—three years after total defeat in WW II—have murdered Colonel-General Blaskowitz behind the walls of the jail at the *Palais du Justice*? Europe had feared the SS for years and its "mystique" became the basis for stories about a "Fourth Reich" in fiction for years to come; but did SS members kill Blaskowitz before he went on trial for fear of his possible testimony? The SS certainly knew the design of the jail in which he was confined from the days before Nazi Germany's defeat. SS prisoners of war had recently reconstructed the bomb-damaged prison walls while working under Allied guards. The prison commander, U.S. Army Colonel Burton Andrus thought these SS laborers "A dangerous force to be reckoned with."[5]

One prisoner incarcerated at Nürnberg jail that fateful day reported years later that at nine o'clock on the evening of Blaskowitz's death "a tune that we all knew was started by one person and before long others

9

joined in." The singing was loud and clear through the cells of the prison. It was the theme song of the SS: "If all turn against us and become unfaithful and disloyal, we remain steadfast!" Some prisoners did not join in the singing.

In the morning American guards moved many of the prisoners to another wing of the prison with special restrictions. Prince Friedrich Christian zu Schaumburg-Lippe, who witnessed and reported the singing, thought it was a demonstration to honor Blaskowitz, but this is a bizarre interpretation given the long history of hostility between Blaskowitz and the SS.[6] More intriguing is the question of why some prisoners thought that the SS might try to kill Blaskowitz.

Behind the barbed wire of P.O.W. camps and the steel bars of prisons Germans struggled in a kind of civil war that saw beatings, murders and "suicides;" German soldiers found a beating so ordinary an occurrence that it was called a visit of the "Holy Ghost" and spoken of commonly. Many Germans were so indoctrinated into believing the SS omnipotent that they thought any threat by them could be carried out.[7] Doubts lingered; nearly thirty years later, *Altpreussische Biographie*, a famous German publication, stated: "Blaskowitz took his own life in the stairwell of the prison. There is no witness to this event."[8]

The "Report of Death" by the U.S. Army 385th Station Hospital Headquarters, Nürnberg, to the Office of the Chief Counsel for War Crimes, simply reported Blaskowitz's death at 1020 hours 5 February 1948. Death was the result of multiple fractures: ribs, spine, hip, scapula, and severe pulmonary hemorrhaging. There was no mention of either suicide or murder.[9]

The list of countries interested in bringing this virtually unknown German commander to justice was lengthy. The Americans had begun his trial as an indicted war criminal that morning. The United Nations War Crimes Commission Files included charges against him by the Netherlands, Czechoslovakia and Poland. According to the U.N. "C.R.O.W.C.A.S.S." (Central Registry of War Criminals and Security Suspects) List number 8, Poland wanted him for murder.[10]

Curiously, the American War Crimes Group located at the notorious Dachau Concentration Camp, which investigated possible War Criminals, had written in a memo on 27 November 1946 that Blaskowitz, "Prisoner Number 29-6172, is of no interest to the U.S., but of possible

War Crimes interest to the Polish Authorities."[11] Ironic, since Blaskowitz had already been listed in the U.S. Army Central Intelligence Command Registry as "cleared for extradition to Poland as a war criminal" two months earlier. Still more ironic is the fact that the Poles neither obtained nor tried Blaskowitz; instead the Americans finally indicted him.[12]

The inconsistent American position on Blaskowitz may have been what caused a high ranking American OSS (Office of Strategic Services) official who had interrogated Blaskowitz to feel even forty years later that: "I still regret deeply that his treatment by us led to his suicide."[13] Certainly, there were many other factors at work, not the least of which were the charges against him.

The list of charges in the indictment (February 5, 1948) was overwhelming. Blaskowitz was charged with crimes against peace, crimes against enemy belligerents and prisoners of war, crimes against civilians, and common plan or conspiracy to make war.[14] The Associated Press also reported indictment for wartime atrocities in Poland.[15] A list of criminal charges like these evokes the instinctive reaction that the perpetrator must have been an ogre.[16] Considering the shocking list of American charges combined with Polish, Czechoslovakian, and Dutch interest in prosecuting Blaskowitz, it was strange that France, where the Colonel-General spent most of the war, brought no charges against him at all.

Notes to Introduction

1. M.S. #B-800 (Blaskowitz), Record Group 338 (Record Group hereafter cited as: R.G.), Records of United States Army Commands, 1942-, National Archives (National Archives hereafter cited as: N.A.), Washington, D.C.

2. Ibid.; "Blaskowitz Leaps to Death in Jail Before Start of War Crimes Trial," *The New York Times*, 6 February 1948, 13.

3. G.S. Graber, *History of the SS* (New York: David McKay Company, Inc., 1978), 151; Gerald Reitlinger, *The SS: Alibi of a Nation* (New Jersey, Englewood Cliffs: Prentice-Hall, Inc., 1981), 135.

4. Louis Snyder, *Encyclopedia of the Third Reich* (New York: McGraw-Hill Book Company, 1976), 29. Snyder called it "a story of doubtful authenticity...." Snyder apparently takes his cue from John Wheeler-Bennett, *The Nemesis of Power: The German Army in Politics, 148-1945* (New York; St. Martin's Press, 1953), 462., who calls it a "story of very doubtful authority." Richard Brett-Smith, *Hitler's Generals* (San Rafael, California: Presidio Press, 1977), 53. Brett-Smith states: "There seems to be no basis to a story that he was murdered by ex-members of the S.S. working as 'trusties'." Robert Wistrich, *Who's Who in Nazi Germany* (New York: Bonanza Books, 1982), 18-19. Wistrich writes: "Fellow prisoners believed that he had been murdered by SS men, but this has never been substantiated."

5. Burton C. Andrus, *I Was the Nuremberg Jailer* (New York: Coward-McCann, Inc., 1969), 73.

6. Friedrich Christian Prinz zu Schaumberg-Lippe, *Zwischen Krone und Kerker* (Wiesbaden: Limes Verlag, 1952), 423-424.

7. Martin Poppel, *Heaven and Hell: The War Diary of a German Paratrooper*, trans. Louise Willmot (New York: Hippocrene Books, Inc., 1988), 240; Judith Gansberg, *Stalag U.S.A.: The Remarkble Story of German P.O.W.'s in America* (New York: Thomas Y. Crowell Co., 1977), 50-53; Arnold Krammer, *Nazi Prisoners of War in America* (New York: Stein and Day, 1979), 170-173. At one American camp for German prisoners of war "visits of the Holy Ghost" were common. One barracks even had a swastika laid out in small stones on the ground near the entrance. German prisoners were obviously insecure, especially since the American camp directors did not put a stop to the violence. Author's correspondence with Father Rudolf Kittel of Haaren,

Germany, February, 1990.; Leon Jaworski, *After Fifteen Years* (Houston, Texas: Gulf Publishing Company, 1961), 21-49. Murders were common enough for Jaworski to entitle chapter III of his book about American P.O.W. camps for Germans "Murder Among Comrades." Sometimes the nature of the conflict between Nazis and anti-Nazis reached absurd levels in P.O.W. camps. At British P.O.W. camp No.11, for example, in mid-April 1944 the pro-Hitler P.O.W.s wished to drink a birthday toast to Hitler, but were concerned about anti-Hitler P.O.W.s opposing the celebration. The pro-nazis P.O.W.s agreed that it is was a "great pity" that this toast to Hitler's health would have to be made in "*English* beer, but that cannot be helped." WO 208/4202, Public Record Office (hereafter cited as: P.R.O.)

8. *Altpreussische Biographie*, 1975 ed., s.v. "Blaskowitz, Johannes Albrecht," by Gerd Brausch.

9. "Report of Death," Blaskowitz, Johannes, 6850th Internal Security Detachment, OCCPAC and OCCWC 201 Files, 385th Station Hospital, Headquarters, Nurnberg Military Post, National Archives Collection of World War II War Crimes Records, R.G. 238, N.A.

10. United Nations War Crimes Commission Index of War Criminals, 1942-1948, Germans, A-Cz Reel UNWCC/NDX/1, and the following Files: 3628/NE/G/206; 284/P/G/29; 399/Cz/G/Ç8; 423/Cz/G/9; 432/Cz/G/11; 463/Cz/G/13; and, Reel 42/PAG-3/2-1:147.

11. Blaskowitz, Johannes, 201 Personnel File, Dachau Detachment War Crimes Group, R.G. 238, N.A.

12. U.S. Army C.I.C. Central Registry, I.R.R. Files, Subject File, German General Staff Study, Box 14, XE 001893, Vol. IV, Folder (3), R.G. 319, Records of the Army Staff, N.A.

13. Letter from Harold C. Deutsch to the author, dated 10 October 1988.

14. *Trials of War Criminals Before the Nuernburg Military Tribunals Under Control Council Law No. 10*, 15 vols. (hereafter cited as: *T.W.C.*) (Washington: United States Government Printing Office, 1951), 10: 10-48.

15. MS#B-800 (Blaskowitz), R.G. 338, N.A.

16. See for example the novel by Michel Tournier, *The Ogre*, trans. Barbara Brey (New York: Dell Publishing Co., Inc., 1972).

CHAPTER I

EARLY LIFE

INCONSPICUOUS DURING HIS LIFE and nearly unknown since his death, Johannes Albrecht Blaskowitz came from a suitably obscure birthplace. He was born on 10 July 1883, at Paterswalde in the Wehlau district of East Prussia, a small town about thirty miles east of Königsberg on the river Alle, not far from the Frederician battlefield of Gross-Jägersdorf. A tiny hamlet with a population of just over seven hundred people, Paterswalde was sometimes called a "church-village" because for such a small village it had a remarkably large neo-roman-esque Lutheran church. Even thirty years after Blaskowitz's birth, the hamlet had only a train station, a marriage license bureau, a mental institution, a flour mill and a brick works, and fewer than fifteen hundred residents. The Protestant pastor and local bee-master were its most prominent citizens.[1]

The region was an area of historic battlefields. Less than fifty miles to the southwest was Eylau, where Napoleon and the Russians had fought to a draw in 1807. About forty miles to the northeast, at Tilsit, Napoleon and Alexander I had met on a raft in the River Niemen to divide Europe between them.

Paterswalde was dominated by Wehlau, the district capital, located less than three kilometers to the north. Originally founded by the Teutonic Knights, Wehlau is a place almost forgotten by history, except for those scholars who remind us that it was there by the Treaty of Wehlau (1657) that Frederick William, the Great Elector, allied the House of Hohenzollern with Poland against Sweden and was promised in return that he would rule in sovereignty in East Prussia.

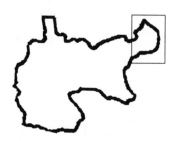

Germany 1914

East Prussia 1914

Wehlau had a population of approximately five thousand residents in 1883, the year of Blaskowitz's birth. It was an old Prussian walled town on the River Pregel and had numerous tanneries, steam engine factories and a copper foundry. There was a large Lutheran church, a town hall, a school, railroad and telegraph stations and paved roads. In July, Wehlau hosted the greatest horse-market in Europe, by far the largest regular "event" of the area.[2]

The district and its capital city knew the difficulties of enemy conquest and occupation. Wehlau and Paterswalde had been occupied by the Russians in 1757 after the battle of Gross-Jägersdorf. The Cossack and Kalmuk troops earned a bad reputation by their atrocities but most of the Russian regular troops behaved well. Napoleon had come to Wehlau in the middle of June 1807 and his troops plundered for two days.[3]

Although local lore undoubtedly contained a stock of tales about the trials of occupation by foreign troops, it is likely that it emphasized the conquest of East Prussia by the Teutonic Knights to a far greater degree. East Prussia was sometimes called the "Ordensland"—"the land of the Order" —to remind everyone of its special status in German history. East Prussia had been conquered by the "Order of German Knights" led by Hermann von Salza early in the thirteenth century. The Crusader State that evolved in East Prussia was ruled by warrior-priests under the Grand Master of the Order. Before the decline of the Teutonic Knights more than fifty castle/churches dominating local roads had been built.

The castle/churches of the Order had the look of fortifications which combined a "sturdy Nordic virility and a deep religiosity." They were an expression of the monastic order of warrior-priests. As one over-wrought account put it,

> It was as though these massive piles exhaled the spirit of the Order. No individual note struck the eye, in accordance with the rule that the individual must submit to the demands of the collective task, the service of God. And everything was considered to be such divine service.[4]

The legends of the Teutonic Knights were kept alive by periodic state celebrations, sometimes with mounted men in armor riding through the streets of Wehlau.[5] It was history permeated by God's mission.

The connection between warriors and religion was long and venerated in Prussia. Even as recently as the wars of Frederick the Great there had been strong bonds in Germany between soldiers and their religion. At Zorndorf, for example, the Prussian drums played "Ich bin ja Herr in deiner Macht" (I am in Your Power, Lord.) to encourage the infantry about to attack the Russians.

The Wehlau district is an area of mixed pine and birch forests whose farms grow wheat and rye. The sandy soils of the region have also produced many famous East Prussian soldiers. Since the 1860's a significant number of these soldiers were sons of the clergy.[6] Prussian protestantism was very "soldierly."[7]

Johannes Blaskowitz too was the son of a minister, Hermann and Marie (Kuhn) Blaskowitz. The Reverend Blaskowitz was a local luminary because of his position as pastor. Due to his eloquence in delivering fire and brimstone sermons, he was known popularly throughout East Prussia as "Thundering Blaskowitz."[8] Both father and son were devout believers throughout their lives. When he was born his father wrote next to his name in the church birthbook: "And see, I hold you in My hands."[9]

The Blaskowitz family did not have a tradition of military service. Blaskowitz's grandfather had been a head forester in East Prussia. The family had originally come from Slovenia and reportedly had not been Germanized for very long. Young Blaskowitz ("Hans" by family members), had three sisters: Margarete, Hildegard ("Hilde"), and Ellinor ("Ellen").[10] The household practiced a quiet piety. Hans learned at a very young age that he had to put into action what he believed and what he had learned in his heart was right.

His early life was clearly not a pastoral idyll. One week before his third birthday his mother died.[11] For the next several years little Hans was cared for by his father and a very kindly nanny named Frau Weichaus.[12] His father later remarried and Louise (Steiner) Blaskowitz became stepmother to Hans.

Less than two years later, in March of 1888, during the mourning period for Kaiser Wilhelm I, there was a spell of unusually cold weather and heavy blizzards followed by sudden hot weather. The entire area was flooded and connections with the outside world severed.[13]

After attending elementary school until 1892 and then a year studying with a private tutor young Blaskowitz went off to cadet school at Koeslin in 1894 at the age of ten, to lighten the family's financial burden.[14] Education at home was common among aristocrats and soldiers but a private education was beyond the means of a simple pastor's family. Fortunately, the monarchy often subsidized school fees for cadets with Blaskowitz's background. And with this help Blaskowitz entered into his path in life.

Entrance into a Prussian cadet school meant admission into the cadet corps of Imperial Germany.[15] And it meant immersion into an exclusively military atmosphere at an impressionable age. Some critics said that the "almost monastic system" had a "narrowing effect upon the mind" and was "fatal to freedom of thought and development of character."[16] There is no doubt that the junior cadet schools typically were based on a Roman or Spartan model of severity; institutional discipline was supplemented by the cadets themselves. If reports are credible, the cadets did not hesitate to inflict beatings on their classmates to implant their own concepts of manliness, obedience, self-denial, honor, and esprit de corps. It was thought to be the price to be paid for wearing the king's blue coat and the uniform with the yellow cord.[17] The cadets sometimes even spent the Christmas holidays at the Academy.

In one sense, the Cadet Corps amounted to a nursery school for the Central Cadet School in Berlin. Blaskowitz had begun to study at *L'école de Mars* when he entered Koeslin Cadet Academy, which was located close to Kolberg, near the Baltic Sea.[18]

It is doubtful, however, that Hans could have foreseen when he put on the royal coat at age ten that he would wear a uniform for the rest of his life; and everything which that entailed. From cadet's uniform to that of Royal Prussian officer to commander in the "Republican" *Reichswehr* of the Weimar era and to soldier in the army of the Third Reich, he passed through dramatic epochs in his nation's history, but never as a civilian.

In Imperial Germany officers wore the uniform except when they went to bed. It was a breach of regulations for an officer to appear in public except in uniform.[19] In any case, few officers would have wished to be seen in public in such apparel for it was taught that civilian clothes lacked honor. One former officer recalled being told by his instructor: "'An officer always wears [his] uniform. Mufti is less "honorable dress," even in peacetime!'"[20]

Wearing the King's colors meant entrance into a world distinctly different from civilian Germany. Nobles had always dominated the officer corps and the outlook of the aristocracy was the pervading, exclusive standard for all officers. Embodying an almost medieval concept of honor, officers were trained to be sensitive to any offense and to feel superior to every civilian. They were taught a "contempt for everything civilian beneath the grade of a privy councillor or a first secretary."[21] Recognition of this in Germany dated at least to the Napoleonic era when reformers thought the cadet schools "were really nurseries of class prejudice ...."[22] But little changed. In most situations the officer's unique status remained obvious. When an officer walked along the sidewalk, everyone moved aside. Under no circumstances did officers "queue up" before a theater box office; civilians moved aside making a place at the head of the line. Upon entering a restaurant they were served first.[23]

Restrictions as well as privileges defined an officer's behavior. Regulations prohibited an officer from carrying an umbrella or a parcel, even for a lady. Officers could not marry without the permission of their superior officers. Nor could they vote or engage in any kind of business for profit. Officers could not even be subpoenaed to court without the permission of a superior officer.[24] It was a life separated from civilian Germany by a great gulf. At age ten, however, it is likely that putting the uniform on meant to young Blaskowitz what it meant to many other cadets; on holidays they could go home and proudly show off their uniform to their friends.[25]

Such proud displays to friends had typically been earned at the price of discipline and regimentation. At the junior cadet schools the young cadets were typically "enrolled in a 'company' as well as a class." Cadets were drilled throughout the day, beginning with the morning order to fall to the knees: "Attention! Pray!;" ending with the order at night: "Attention! Go to Sleep!" Cadets even paraded to meals. It was a harsh existence for young boys.[26]

There were compensations. Already in these years of his youth Blaskowitz was making friends who became life-long comrades in arms. Among his schoolmates at Koeslin were the future Field Marshal Günther von Kluge and Generaloberst Paul Hausser.[27]

Three years at Koeslin cadet school were followed by five years at the Central Cadet Corps school at Gross Lichterfelde near Berlin.[28] The Berlin Cadet Academy was the most important and recognized Army cadet school in Imperial Germany. Originally founded in 1717 by King Frederick William I it had been one of the special projects of Frederick the Great. The famous soldier-king had built numerous buildings for the academy in 1775 and had dedicated them "to the pupils of Mars and Minerva."[29] Frederick, whose army was the only one in modern history with a truly Roman discipline, seemed to have applied the same principle to his cadet school. The underlying theme appears to have been the ancient Roman axiom: "Few men are brave; many become so through care and force of discipline."[30]

Frederick's influence was tangible at the academy; even a century after the great king's death the cadets still retained the Frederician privilege of preceding all other troops in any march past the King. Cadets marched beneath the flag used when Frederick was a cadet and the flag still had Frederick's initials stamped upon it. It was undoubtedly a source of pride to cadets.[31]

The Central Cadet Academy which Blaskowitz attended from 1897 until 1901 was a complex of twenty-year old buildings which had been built specifically for the cadets. Located in the southwestern Berlin suburb of Lichterfelde between the more famous suburbs of Charlottenburg and Potsdam, the academy was connected to downtown Berlin by suburban trains. According to one description the academy appeared from a distance to be "not a single institution, but a newly-created city."[32] In other ways it must have seemed a world distinct unto itself, and in a way, it was.

The academy was a complex of eighteen buildings of different sizes laid out in a rectangle about twice as long as it was wide. The entire school was surrounded by a brick wall with iron fencing on top. The area enclosed by the buildings was open to the sky and served as a drill area and cadet parade ground. The various buildings included barracks, classroom buildings, a church and an administration building. Behind the classroom building but in its own wing was the "Field Marshal Hall, the great room of the corps where paintings of the Prussian Field Marshals hung."[33] Here also— displayed in a glass case—was Napoleon's sword, donated to the academy by Marshal Blücher.[34]

Gross Lichterfelde had more than one thousand students who lived in plainly furnished apartments which had sleeping quarters for eight cadets next to a common living room. Junior cadets were supervised by senior cadets with regular army officers who were lieutenants and captains in charge of education and training.

The creed taught there emphasized discipline, courage and loyalty to comrades, thereby making virtues out of military necessities. Discipline was stern and the education at Gross Lichterfelde was one of "military austerity and simplicity." Some observers even described it as a "monastic school." Emphasis was placed upon development of a "sense of decency and comradeship." This included "a strict sense of duty, punctuality and cleanliness." Inculcation of a sense of "élan" also had a high priority, as did also the implanting of the virtue of soldierly dignity.[35]

The curriculum was based on that of the civilian *Realgymnasium*, emphasizing modern languages, mathematics and history, although the academic standards were less demanding than in civilian schools.[36] Sports, too, were emphasized. It was "Prussian discipline in its most insistent and sophisticated form...," according to one source, but attempted at its best to inculcate a "definite philosophy and attitude, a flexibility which is unfathomed by those who visualize Prussianism only in its unbending form." It recognized the desirability of "expressing uncompromising opinions up to the moment of an order's delivery." The cadet was educated to acknowledge authority, "but only after argument had been exhausted."[37] Admitted into the caste system of the Prussian-German officer as a mere boy, he would prove in the unfolding of his life that a caste mark its children indelibly.

Typically, cadets began their day at half-past five in summer and six in winter, had twenty minutes to dress, turn out of their rooms, form on parade and march to breakfast. Breakfast was followed by a half-hour's study of class lessons, cleaning of weapons and then morning roll call. Classes began at 8 A.M. and continued until 1 P.M. with a twenty minute break at 11A.M. At one o'clock cadets fell in by companies on parade, were read the orders of the day and then marched to lunch.[38]

Moving by companies into the great mess hall where a thousand were fed at a time, cadets stationed themselves in front of tables arranged in parallel lines. The order was given by the senior cadet at each table for "prayer" and after a silent grace cadets sat and ate.[39] Along the upper wall of the long wood paneled side of the mess hall there was a royal gallery; the King might appear on any given day to observe the cadets.

Afternoons were taken up with fencing, riding, dancing or gymnastics except on Wednesdays and Saturdays when cadets were marched to the drill-ground for battalion drill. At half-past five students were obligated to go to their rooms until 8 P.M. for studying. At 8 P.M. dinner was served and cadets were free from after dinner until 9:30 P.M. when they went to bed; lights out was at ten. On Sundays dinner was at noontime and most cadets had the day to themselves but were not permitted to leave the academy.[40]

It may seem surprising that cadets practiced both fencing and dancing. Swordsmanship had long been recognized as endowing young men with speed and strength while "dancing brought elegance and dignity to carriage and movement." [41] Nothing was overlooked for improving the officer's appearance; it was also indispensable at social events. At Lichterfelde Blaskowitz especially enjoyed fencing, riding and gymnastics. But he did not neglect his studies. His performance on his academic studies was superior. In recognition of this he was selected for the prestigious "Prima" course. The selection marked him as a man with a future in the highest command circles.[42]

This sort of education had immediate results with young Hans, for he later spent three years at the Army Gymnastics Institute and eventually qualified as an interpreter of French and a beginner in the English language. He maintained a life-long appreciation for physical culture and practiced Swedish drill and light athletics until his last days. He was an enthusiastic horseback rider and hunter for much of his life.

The more subtle results of this education revealed themselves throughout his lifetime, perhaps most significantly in the idea of "duty." Prussian discipline trained men to unquestioning obedience of orders but, it was not merely *kadavergehorsamkeit*, ("Blind obedience"); training aimed at inculcating a deep sense of duty that prompted action (*Pflichtgefuhl*).[43] On the entrance to one of the main buildings at Gross-Lichterfelde was a statement which expressed the ideal: "Prussian obedience is a voluntary decision, not a slavish compliance."[44]

Blaskowitz's education had been "royal." No slogan had greater currency in the army than "Für Kaiser und Vaterland". The Prussian War Minister, General Karl von Einem, had reputedly stated that he "liked a soldier loyal to his King, even if he were a bad shot better than a less loyal one, no matter how good a shot ...." According to one source this gave officers two souls: "One class-conscious and exclusive in regard to everything plebeian around him, and the other servile to his superior and to the court."[45] The idea of a duality of soul is perhaps a most suggestive insight into Blaskowitz's nature. In Blaskowitz's case, however, he learned to be servile to God and obedient to his King.

The King personally reinforced the "royal" nature of the education at Gross-Lichterfelde by meeting each senior cadet just prior to graduation and granting a ritual interview. The senior cadets were assembled in the Field Marshal Hall and stood at attention in a single line. The King, dressed in full uniform and accompanied by his entourage, entered the room and stepped in front of each cadet. The cadet took two steps forward, announced his name, his father's occupation and the regiment to which he hoped to be assigned.

> On one occasion the king spoke to each man, recalling the good services his ancestors had performed for former Prussian Kings; 'Ah, yes, your grandfather was a young hero at Jena and Leipzig ....' In 1888 William I spoke to the assembled cadets, saying, 'I am glad to have met you, even if only en *passant*. You were educated at the expense of the state; be thankful for it when you are in the army. Do your duty, hold high the honor of the army; only then will you be the standard bearers of honor.[46]

Clearly, from the military viewpoint, the military education at Gross-Lichterfelde Cadet Academy was a success. Of the cadets who were there with Blaskowitz, one later became a field marshal and commander-in-chief of the German Army (Walter von Brauchitsch). There were four other field-marshals (Fedor von Bock, Ernst Busch, Günther von Kluge, and Erwin von Witzleben), five colonel-generals

(Nikolaus von Falkenhorst, Hermann Hoth, Adolf Strauss, Paul Hausser and Kurt von Hammerstein-Equord), and numerous generals. Purely from the military perspective, this was a remarkable group of fellow-cadets.

Foremost at Gross-Lichterfelde was military education; but pomp and pageantry had their place as well. The cadets not only went on maneuvers with the Guards from the Potsdam garrison, but also took part in their parades.

Graduation from the Cadet Academy in 1901 was followed by entrance into the Army at Osterode, East Prussia, in Infantry Regiment 18, the "Grolman" Regiment.[47] Entering the army was usually marked by a rite of passage. In the Imperial Army there was a semi-religious ceremony in which officers swore an oath upon the national flag and on the sword of the regimental commander. The oath pledged loyalty to the King and not to the constitution. In fact very few officers read the constitution; the Kaiser himself once said "quite frankly that he had never read it."[48] It was an oath which proved benign in its results. Oaths would not always prove so fortuitously benign in Blaskowitz's life.

Not very far from his birthplace, Osterode was nevertheless very different from tiny Paterswalde. Headquarters for the XX German Corps, Osterode was a garrison town. In addition to Blaskowitz's own regiment the 72nd Infantry Brigade and Field-Artillery Regiment 18 were based there. Out of a population of fourteen thousand residents there were twenty-three hundred officers![49] Osterode was similar to many other towns east of the Vistula River; professional isolation and monotony contributed to a "soul-killing boredom" in towns such as Osterode. Soldiers commonly called such places *Drecknester*, ("shitholes").[50]

A railroad junction town on Lake Drewenz, Osterode was Blaskowitz's home from March 1901 until 1904 except for time spent at Officer's Candidate School. It was a critical time in his career since no officer candidate was commissioned without the approval of the regiment's colonel. This usually meant the unofficial approval of other regimental officers, frequently involving heavy social drinking in the officer's mess hall.[51] There was also a "careful investigation" into the family background to ascertain that social attitudes and associations were "acceptable." Any suspicion that even slightly "reformist" views were held by family members was sufficient ground for exclusion from the officer corps.[52] A few months with the troops was followed by assignment to Officers' Candidate School at Engers near Koblenz.

At Engers Blaskowitz was evaluated as "satisfactory" in gymnastics, marksmanship, fencing and horseback riding, and "good" at conduct, initiative and training. The evaluation continued:

> He is physically and mentally rather well put together. He has shown consistent attentiveness and eagerness to learn and has yielded good results in his scientific endeavor. In all other subjects he did rather well too, especially in practical training, where he showed great enthusiasm and the ability to reach fast decisions. His character is very mature for his age. He is conscientious, reliable and dutiful.[53]

The following month, January, 1902, he was favorably evaluated at the Grolman Infantry Regiment. The evaluation was superior: "His talents are ample, his military instinct and endeavor are unusually smart ...." Significantly, the evaluation added: "His leadership had a two fold significance: it was the moral as well as the military performance that was striking."[54] The evaluation was to prove profoundly insightful.

Young Blaskowitz was commissioned as a second lieutenant in January of 1902, with his patent dated July 10,1900. Commission as an officer amounted to admission to "an order which had a mission."[55] Blaskowitz devoted his life to this order, the army, and to its mission.

He was with his regiment from 1902 to 1904. He spent the next three years at the Army Gymnastics Institute in Berlin, initially as a student, then as an assistant instructor. Regrettably little is known about these important years of Lieutenant Blaskowitz's life. Nothing is recorded, for example, about when he met Fraulein Anna Riege, but it is established that they were married on April 17, 1906, when Blaskowitz was twenty-three years of age.[56]

Blaskowitz's bride came from a middle class background. Her father was an architect, a Baltic German from Libau in Russia.[57] The marriage of a young officer such as Blaskowitz to a middle class bride fit squarely into a long-standing pattern in Imperial Germany. A second lieutenant's pay in the Prussian Army was then equivalent to only about forty pounds per year, making it almost impossible for him to live "without some small additional private income, more especially in Berlin."[58]

Moreover, promotion rates for officers stagnated in the beginning of the twentieth century in Germany. Second lieutenants had to wait an average of eight to ten years before receiving promotion to first lieutenant, then another four to six years before promotion to captain. Officers typically remained captains for ten years.[59]

As a result, officers had not only to find wives who had socially acceptable backgrounds, but who also had private sources of income. Indeed, army regulations concerning marriage required proof of an annual income of at least 2,500 marks more than the officer's salary. Either the officer or the bride could provide the income.[60]

Married officers were expected to invite superior officers, comrades and subordinates to dinners on an ever more lavish scale. Failure to do so ran the risk of having an unfortunate entry mark on their personal record. Some officers owed their careers more to their excellent dinners than to professional ability.[61]

Marriages beginning in this way do not always end well, but the Blaskowitzes were fortunate; theirs was a lasting and very happy union.[62] In 1907 a daughter, Annemarie, was born. Four years later a son, Hans Junior was born.[63] In 1907 Blaskowitz returned to his Regiment at Osterode in East Prussia. The year was spent in study and training for the War Academy (*Kriegsakademie*) in Berlin under the direction of the later famous Field Marshal, August von Mackensen. Mackensen served as Blaskowitz's superior and tutor.[64]

Blaskowitz was particularly fortunate to have Mackensen as his tutor. Descended from Scottish immigrants originally named Mackenzie, Mackensen was a non-noble son of an estate-manager. He served in the first Death's Head Hussar Regiment during the Franco-Prussian war of 1870-1871 and received a field commission. Tall, handsome and an excellent horseman, he became an officer without ever having attended military school. He served as tutor in military history to the future Kaiser Wilhelm and then as adjutant to General Alfred von Schlieffen, chief of the great General Staff, without ever attending the *Kriegsakademie*. Then followed his appointment as "General Adjutant to the Kaiser." Blaskowitz was eminently fortunate to have a tutor with Mackensen's experience and personal connections.[65]

Mackensen tutored Blaskowitz for the rigorous competitive entrance examination required for admission into the War Academy. A mere 130 candidates were accepted annually.

Only three of the forty candidates from the Osterode garrison successfully passed the exams for the Army Staff College in Berlin. Lieutenant Blaskowitz was one of them, so he spent the next three years at the War Academy (1908-1911), where the course of studies was so stringent that four out of five of those who had been admitted from all over Germany failed to finish the three year course.

At the War Academy Blaskowitz was initiated into the elite of the officer caste of the Imperial Army, the Great General Staff. Located on the Dorotheenstrasse in a single building, the War Academy was where General Staff officers were trained. Staff officers were supposed to be superior to line officers in their ability and education, the *creme de la creme* of the officer-corps. The broad vertical red stripe on the sides of a General Staff officer's trouser legs conspicuously marked him as a mentally and professionally superior military man.[66]

Theoretically the War Academy provided a superior general education as well as an excellent military one. In addition to universal history, logic, philosophy and literature, the curriculum emphasized military education: History of war, tactics, fortifications, staff duty, the art of sieges, field fortifications and military administration. "A General Staff officer was expected to be a highly competent military technician ...." He was educated to work in the background, "shunning the limelight and subordinating himself unquestionably to the common interest." This was a very narrow, specialized education.[67] Classes were conducted from October to the first of June with students assigned to active duty with the troops during the summer months.

It may be useful to draw upon a description of the German officer's mental approach to his work written in November, 1940 by the American military attaché to Germany. "The trained German officer who has been given or assumes a mission, always proceeds to carry afoot with the following logic: (A) An estimate of the situation: (B) a decision: (C) a general plan simply expressed."

The report notes that German officers apply this rule "habitually" to every task whether it involved a military assignment or the purchase of a suit of clothes, a two weeks annual leave or dinner conversation. If an officer is without a mission from higher authority he assigns himself a mission for the day. "He approaches each day's tasks as he would a battle, so that in the end he will approach battle as he would a day's task." Such a practice made German officers as thoroughly professional as possible. The report continued:

> We may say that no German officer or noncommissioned officer is ever without a mission. If a superior should direct him to state his mission (and this is frequently done) he is prepared to answer immediately and without hesitation with a clear statement of his mission, his estimate and his plan. This leads to the habit of logical thought and decision, both of which are necessary to real accomplishment.
>
> Even the meal in officer's mess has prescribed procedures and topics of discussion with "talking shop," criticism of individuals, or mentioning women by name ruled out. The purpose of conversation is to aid digestion. The commanding officer directs the conversation (announces his mission) and officers are expected to contribute to the conversation. "When this type of meal is over, every officer returns to his task refreshed both mentally and physically."[68]

It is not difficult to picture Blaskowitz fiting into such a world. Thirty years after leaving the War Academy, his daily practice was still to have such meals with his officers.[69]

By no means were his years of early manhood without joy; he spent some time in the social life of Imperial Berlin attending salons and social functions.[70] Soldiers, especially officers, were the darlings of newly Imperial Berlin; all doors in society were open to them. It was not coincidental that "lovelorn Berlin ladies, really identified with popular singers who sang 'Forget me not, my darling Guard officer.'"[71] Among the wealthy Berlin families a "dinner was not considered a really successful affair, unless a couple of cavalry officers graced it with their uniforms and gave it a "'chivalrous' character by their presence."[72]

Almost overnight Berlin had become a *Weltstadt*, a "world city;" by 1910 it had over two million residents.[73] It was an arrogant, nationalistic city in which a public opinion poll had recently named Field Marshal Helmuth von Moltke as the "greatest thinker" of the nineteenth century.[74] In many ways Berlin still reflected old Prussia when it was "not a state that had an army but an army that had a state."[75] The Emperor constantly wore a military uniform in public; everywhere there were victory columns and statues of generals, troops and artillery were frequently paraded. Military bands often played martial music, sometimes accompanied by the firing of real artillery.[76]

Graduation from the elite War Academy in Berlin in 1911 was followed by reassignment to his regiment, but this proved impossible for his family. The climate of East Prussia was unhealthy for his daughter and especially for his infant son. It was also difficult for Blaskowitz himself since he suffered from a chronic illness of the ears and nose. He requested and received a transfer to Infantry Regiment 170 at Offenburg, an old imperial city in the Black Forest in Baden, where the family moved in 1912. However, the change in climate was too late to save their only son; Hans Junior died in 1912. It must have been a difficult loss to endure. Fortunately, the move came soon enough to help in the recovery of their daughter, who was seriously ill with pleurisy and tuberculosis.[77] Promotion to first lieutenant came at this time.

In December, 1913, his last official evaluation before World War I referred to him as "a good horseback rider, gymnast and educator." He also enjoyed fencing, but he soon had no time for any of these endeavors.[78] In February 1914 he was promoted to Captain. The following month he was transferred to Rastatt in Baden where he took command of the 10th Company in Infantry Regiment 111. His wife and daughter moved to Rastatt with him. Six months later, Imperial Germany and its Austro- Hungarian ally were suddenly at war with much of the rest of Europe. The regiment was mobilized on 2nd August. On 6th August a parade was held in field service order in the new grey-green field uniforms. The troops marched from the parade to the front.[79]

Notes for Chapter I

1. E. Uetrecht, ed., *Meyers Orts und Verkehrs Lexikon Des Deutschen Reichs* (Leipzig: Bibliographisches Institute, 1912-1913), 453; *Heimatbuch des Kreises Wehlau* (Leer, Gerhard Rautenberg, 1975), 68, 408-409. Paterswalde today is in Kaliningrad Oblast in Russia and is named "Bol'shaya Polyana."

2. Joseph Thomas, ed., *Lippincott's Gazetteer of the World* (Philadelphia: J.B. Lippincott Company, 1893), 2786; Filipa Sulimierskiego *et. al., Slownik Geograficzny Krolestwa Polskiego* (Warsaw: Wieku Nowy-Swiat, 1882), 264-265; *Heimatbuch des Kreises Wehlau*, 100-101, 114-115, 136-141.

3. Christopher Duffy, *The Army of Frederick the Great* (London: David & Charles, 1974), 181, Emil Johannes Guttzeit, *Ostpreussen in 1440 Bildern* (Ostfriesland: Verlag Gerhard Rautenberg, 1972), xxxv.

4. Gotz von Selle, *German Thought in East Prussia* (Marburg: Elwert Grafe, 1948), 7-9; Franz Ludtke, *Ordensland* (Berlin: Verlag Erwin Kintzel, 1943), 110-111. Field Marshal von Manstein's English Defense Counselor uses the term "soldier monks." Reginald Paget, *Manstein: His Campaigns and His Trial* (London: Collins, 1951), 2.

5. *Heimatbuch des Kreises Wehlau*, 182-183.

6. Karl Demeter, *The German Officer Corps in Society and State: 1650 - 1945*, trans. Angus Malcom, Intro. Michael Howard (London: Weidenfeld and Nicholson, 1965, 22.; Reinhard Stumpf, *Die Wehrmacht-Elite: Rang und Herkunftsstruktur der Deutschen Generale und Admirale 1933-1945* (Boppard am Rhein: Harold Boldt Verlag, 1982), 264.

7. MS#B-351 (Seemueller), R.G. 338, N.A.

8. "Blaskowitz, Johannes Albert," by Gerd Brausch. This is apparently an early, edited version of the article referred to in introduction endnote 8; the information about the Reverend Blaskowitz does not appear in the published edition. Copy in author's possession; Gert Steuben, "So blieb er ohne Marshallstab," *Das Neue Blatt*, 24 Februar 1953, 11-12, *Collection Koepcke*.

9. Herr Schrader, "Feierlichkeit Anlassich der Beisetzung des Generalobersten Johannes Blaskowitz am 14 Februar 1948 in Bommelsen," *Collection Koepcke*, copy in author's possession. A somewhat shorter version may be found in Msg 1/1814, BA/MA.

10. NOKW 141, Records of the United States Nuernberg War Crimes Trials: United States of America v. Wilhelm von Leeb et al. (Case XII), November 28, 1947-October 28, 1948, Microcopy M-898, Roll 28, R.G. 238, N.A. Blaskowitz Interrogation, June 17, 1947, Military Intelligence Division, Military Intelligence Division hereafter cited as: M.I.D., Military Intelligence Service, Military Intelligence Service hereafter cited as: M.I.S., Who's Who Branch, 1939-1945, R.G. 165, Records of the War Department General and Special Staffs, Entry 194, N.A.; "Blaskowitz, Johannes: History of Life," Biographic Files, United States Army Military History Institute, hereafter cited as U.S.A.M.H.I., Carlisle Barracks PA. O.C.M.H. Collection; First Canadian Army Intelligence Summary Number 231, 16 Feb. 1945; Public Archives of Canada, hereafter cited as: P.A.C., Ottawa, Ontario, R.G. 24, Records of the Department of National Defense;, Vol. 10,655, File 215C1.023.; Bundesarchiv-Militärachiv Freiburg im Breisgau, Bundesarchiv hereafter cited as: BA/MA, Pers 6/20, BA/MA;Hellmuth Rossler, *Biographisches Wörterbuch zur Deutschen Geschichte*, Vol. 1, (Munich: Francke Verlag, 1974), 294. *Biographisches Wörterbuch* refers to Blaskowitz as the son of the head forester of an old East-Prussian protestant minister family." See also: *Altpreussisches evangelisches Pfarrerbuch von der Reformation bis zur Vertreibung im Jahre 1945. Biographischer*, Vol. 1, Hamburg: N.P.), 129.

11. *Altpreussische Biographie*, 1975 ed., s.v. "Blaskowitz, Johannes Albrecht," by Gerd Brausch.

12. Froese, Ernst, "Meine Begegnung mit Hans Blaskowitz," *Wehlauer Heimatbrief*, (Hanover: Rudolf Meitsch, 1980), 7.

13. *Heimatbuch des Kreises Wehlau*, 139.

14. *Mitteilungsblatt für Zentral Kartei des Königliche Preussischen und Königliche Sachischen Kadetten*, N.d., Nr. 42.; Blaskowitz Interrogation, 5 June 1945, First Canadian Army Intelligence Periodical No. 4, vol. 10,655, File 215C1.023, R.G. 24, P.A.C.

15. Henry Barnard, *Military Schools and Courses of Instruction in the Science and Art of War in France, Prussia, Austria, Russia, Sweden, Switzerland, Sardinia, England, and the United States)*, rev. ed.,(New York: Greenwood Press, 1969), 310.

16. Henry Vizetelly, *Berlin Under the New Empire*, 2 vols. (New York: Greenwood Press, Publishers, 1968), 1: 394.

17. Ibid., I: 398-399. Steven Clemente, *For King and Kaiser! The Making of the Prussian Army Officer, 1860-1914* (New York: Greenwood Press, 1992), 116.

18. *Stammliste des Königliche Kadethauses Cülm-Cölsin (1 June 1776-1 Nov.1907)* (Berlin: Herman Walter Verlags-buchhandlung, 1907), 2: 373.

19. J. H. Morgan, *Assize of Arms: The Disarmament of Germany and Her Rearmament(1919-1939)* (New York: Oxford University Press, 1946), 119.

20. Wilhelm Neckar, *The German Army of To-Day* (East Ardsley, England: E.P. Publishing, Ltd., 1973), 185.; Charles Messenger, *The Last Prussian: A Biography of Field Marshal Gerd von Rundstedt, 1875-1953* (London: Brassey's 1991), 84. Rundstedt, for example, never felt comfortable out of uniform and called civilian clothes a "funny disguise."

21. Vizetelly, *Berlin Under the New Empire*, 1: 335.

22. Daniel Hughes, *The King's Finest: A Social and Bureaucratic Profile of Prussia's General Officers, 1871-1914* (New York: Praeger, 1987), 62.

23. Morgan, *Assize of Arms*, 119.; James Gerard, *My Four Years in Germany* (New York: George H. Doran Company, 1917), 75-78.

24. Ibid.; Vizetelly, *Berlin Under the New Empire*, 1: 335.

25. Vizetelly, *Berlin Under the New Empire*, 1: 400.

26. Morgan, *Assize of Arms*, 138.; U.S. Adjutant General's Office, Military Information Division, *Military Schools of Europe and Other Papers selected for Publication* (Washington, D.C.: Government Printing Office (1896), 68-75. See also:John Moncure, *Forging the King's Sword: Military Education Between Tradition and Modernization: The Case of the Royal Prussian Cadet Corps, 1871-1918* (New York: Peter Lang, 1993), 99.; Martin van Creveld, *The Training of Officers: From Military Professionalism to Irrelevance* [London: MacMillan, 1990], 22-34.

27. Karl-Hermann Freiherr von Brand and Helmut Eckart, *Kadetten Aus 300 Jahren deutscher Kadetten Korps*, 2 vols.(Munich: Schild-Verlag GmbH, 1989), 1: 245-250.

28. Morgan, *Assize of Arms*, 138.

29. Vizetelly, *Berlin Under the New Empire*, 1: 389; Barnard, *Military Schools*, 312.

30. Christopher Duffy, *The Military Experience in the Age of Reason* (New York: Atheneum, 1988), 53. Duffy is quoting Flavius Vegetius Renatus's *De Re Militari* (A.D. 385-450?) which he states was "absorbed so completely by the age of reason that he became effectively an eighteenth century author."

31. Vizetelly, *Berlin Under the New Empire*, 1: 394.; German Bülle' "Das Königliche Preussische Kadetten Korps," *Deutscher Soldatenkalender*(1962), 210.

32. Rudolf Lehmann, *The Leibstandarte*, trans. Nick Olcott (Winnipeg, Canada: J.J. Fedorowicz Publishing, 1987), 1: 2. Today Hauptkadetten Anstahlt Gross Lichterfelde is German Police Abschnitt #45 Headquarters. There is little evidence of its former glory. The only reminders are some street names in the area: Kadettenweg, Moltke Strasse, Manteuffelstrasse, Roonstrasse and Gardeschutzenweg. Most of the area is private homes.

33. Ibid., 1: 2-6.

34. Vizetelly, *Berlin Under the New Empire,*1: 388-389; Barnard, *Military Schools,* 313.

35. D.J. Goodspeed, *Ludendorff: Genius of World War I* (Boston: Houghton Mifflin Company, 1966), 12.; Heinz Guderian, *Panzer Leader,* trans. Constantine Fitzgibbon (Washington, D.C.: Zenger Publishing Co., 1979), 16-17; Donald G. Brownlow, *Panzer Baron: The Military Exploits of General Hasso von Manteuffel* (North Quincy, Massachusetts: The Christopher Publishing House, 1975), 27; Guenther Blumentritt, *Von Rundstedt: The Soldier and the Man,* trans. Cuthbert Reavely (Long Acre, London: Odhams Press Ltd., 1952), 17.; Paget, *Manstein,* 2.

36. Hughes, *King's Finest,* 62; Barnard, *Military Schools,* 317-318, 397, Clemente, *King and Kaiser,* 96-97.

37. Kenneth Macksey, *Guderian; Creator of the Blitzkrieg* (New York: Stein & Day, 1976), 4-5.

38. Vizetelly, *Berlin Under the New Empire,* 1: 390.

39. Barnard, *Military Schools,* 314; Lehmann, *Leibstandarte,* 1: 5.

40. Vizetelly, *Berlin Under the New Empire,* 1: 390-391.

41. Duffy, *Military Experience in the Age of Reason,* 51.

42. "Blaskowitz, Johannes Albrecht," by Gerd Brausch. This is a manuscript version. See notes 8 and 11.; Moncure, *King's Sword,* 175.

43. Grover Cleveland Platt, "Place of the Army In German Life: 1880-1914," (Ph.d dissertation, State University of Iowa, 1941), 118.

44. *Die Tradition: Informationen Für Militäriasammler,* Juli 1992 ed., s.v. "Das Königlich Preussische Kadetten Korps."

45. Platt, "Place of the Army in German Life," 130.; Franz Carl Endres, *The Social Structure and Corresponding Ideologies of the German Officers' Corps Before World War,* trans. S. Ellison (Works Progress Administration, New York, 1937), 44.

46. John Moncure, "The Royal Prussian Cadet Corps, 1871-1918: A Prosopographical Approach," in Bela Kiraly and Walter Scott Dillard (eds.), *The East Central European Officer Corps 1740-1920s: Social Origins, Selection, Education, and Training* (New York: Columbia University Press 1988), 66.

47. *Geschichte des Infanterie Regiments von Grolman (1 Posenschen)* (Berlin: Ernst Siegfried Mittler and Sons, 1913), 2: 11.

48.Endres, "Social Structure And Ideology," 32;Platt, "Place of the Army In German Life," 32, 139.

49. *Meyers Lexikon,* 429. In 1914 Osterode was headquarters for Hindenburg and Ludendorff during the battle of Tannenberg.

50. Dennis Showalter, *Tannenberg: Clash of Empires* (Hamden, Connecticut: Shoe String Press, 1991), 107-108.

51. Morgan, *Assize of Arms*, 139-140; Vizetelly, *Berlin Under the New Empire*, 1: 329.

52. Platt, "Place of the Army In German Life," 78-79.

53. Pers 6/20, BA/MA

54. Ibid.

55. G. Sprung, "The Mentality and Ethos of the German Army," *The Army Quarterly*, 56 (April, 1948),57.

56. Friedrich-Christian Stahl, "Johannes Blaskowitz," *Bädisches Biographien*, (Stuttgart, 1987), 1: 41.

57. NOKW 141 M-898/28/0163, R.G. 238, N.A.; Pers 6/20, BA/MA Anna-Melita-Elizabeth Reige was born on 27 September 1879 in Libau on the Baltic Sea. Her father was deceased at the time of the marriage. Libau is in modern Latvia, but it was part of the Russian Empire at the time.

58. Vizetelly, *Berlin Under the New Empire*, 1: 333.

59. Hughes, *King's Finest*, 82.

60. Ibid., 94-104. Blaskowitz's wife Anna seems to have fit into the category of officer's wives with a non-noble background of some wealth. Almost forty years after their marriage she still had a bank account with 15,000 Deutsche Marks and their daughter Anna Marie had a similar account of 10,000 Marks. Blaskowitz Fragebogen, 20th October 1945, Biographical Data Personnel Folders Series, R.G. 238, N.A., Clemente, *King and Kaiser*, 163-164.

61. Endres, "Social Structure and Idealogy," 29.

62. Report of Interrogation No. 5554 (Unknown German-undated), Records of the Judge Advocate General (Army), General and Administrative Records, 1944-1949, case 110 (5554), R.G. 153, N.A.; Written information received from Mr. Nikolaus von Mach, Germany, August 8, 1992. Mr. von Mach served closely with Blaskowitz on Blaskowitz's staff from 1942-1944. He had known Blaskowitz personally since 1932 and called him "uncle." Copy in author's possession.

63. NOKW 141, M-898/28/0161, R.G. 238, N.A.

64. Blaskowitz Interrogation Report, 5 June 1945, First Canadian Army Intelligence Periodical. No. 4, vol. 10,655, File 215C1.023, R.G. 24, P.A.C. Field Marshal Mackensen was later the unofficial head of the Schlieffen Society, and was one of the officers who had the courage to protest publicly the murders of Generals Von Schleicher and Von Bredow on 30 June 1934.

65. During World War I, Mackensen was promoted to Army Group Commander and Field Marshal and received the coveted "Pour-le-Merit" and the "Schwar-

zer Adler-Orden" (Prussian Order of the Black Eagle). Showalter, *Tannenberg*, 177-178.; MS# B-351 (Blumentritt), R.G. 338, N.A.

66. Theodore Schwan, *Report on the Organization of the German Army* (Washington, D.C.: Government Printing Office, 1894), 68.; Arden Bucholz, *Moltke, Schlieffen and Prussian War Planning* (New York: Berg, 1991), 140.

67. Barnard, *Military Schools*, 330-334; Nicholas Reynolds, *Treason was no Crime: Ludwig Beck, Chief of the German General Staff*, (London: William Kimber, 1976), 21-23. Beck was a classmate of Blaskowitz at the *Kriegsakademie*; Corelli Barnett, ed., *Hitler's Generals* (New York: George Weidenfeld & Nicolson Ltd., 1989), 176.; Bucholz, *Prussian War Planning*, 141.

68. U.S. Military Attaché, Berlin, Report #17,717, November 18, 1940, "German Military Leadership," 2016-1329-3 U.S.A.M.H.I., The Army War College Collection. This continues to be the case in the Bundeswehr. See: Gerd Niepold, *Battle For White Russia: The Destruction of Army Group Centre, June 1944*, trans. Richard Simpkin & Robin Carnegie (London: Brassey's Defense Publishers, 1926), 274-276.; Such training, in the estimation of military historians, was of "immense value to them in battle; [it gave them] relentless clarity of purpose, the absolute will to win." Max Hastings, *Overlord: D-Day, June 6, 1944* (New York: Simon and Shuster, 1984), 32.

69. David Pryce-Jones, ed., *Paris In the Third Reich: A History of the German Occupation, 1940-1944* (New York: Holt, Rhinehart and Winston, 1981), 255-256; Duffy, *Military Experience, in the Age of Reason*, 80-82.

70. Blaskowitz Interrogation Report, 5 June 1945, First Canadian Army Intelligence Periodical No. 4., vol. 10, 655, File 215C1.023, R.G. 24, P.A.C.

71. Bruce Gudmundsson, *Stormtroop Tactics: Innovation in the German Army, 1914-1918* (New York: Praeger, 1989), 11.

72. Endres, "Social Structure and Ideology", 8.

73. Gerhard Masur, *Imperial Berlin* (New York: Basic Books, Inc., 1970), 132; Elaine Hochman, *Architects of Fortune: Mies Van Der Rohe and the Third Reich* (New York: Weidenfeld & Nicolson, 1989), 29.

74. Masur, *Imperial Berlin*, 122.

75. Ibid., 119.

76. Vizetelly, *Berlin Under the New Empire*, 1: 78, 2: 329.

77. Pers 6/20, BA/MA.

78. Ibid.

79. Walter Goerlitz, *Paulus and Stalingrad: A Life of Field-Marshal Friedrich Paulus with Notes, Correspondence and Documents from His Papers* (New York: Citadel Press, 1963), 9.

CHAPTER II

THE GREAT WAR

"MAKE WAR OFFENSIVELY ...," Napoleon advised.[1] Strategists who devised Germany's plan for World War I heeded his advice. Attack was the basis of German strategy in World War I as envisioned in the so-called "Schlieffen Plan." By this plan a strong right wing would attack in the north of France and sweep all opposition aside while the German left wing in the south remained on the defensive.

Blaskowitz's regiment made up a part of the German army's left wing and fought first at Mulhouse in Alsace with the 28th Division. Mulhouse had been annexed to Germany in 1871 but was treated by the Germans as occupied enemy territory throughout the 1914-1918 war. This old imperial city was along the path of the "Plan 17" offensive, as the French attack plan was called.

Gaining combat experience first in defensive fighting around Mulhouse, Blaskowitz's regiment was in action throughout August and September 1914 at scattered battlefields in Alsace: Petite Pierre, Flirey, Mortagne and Saarburg.[2] According to regimental records, Blaskowitz was awarded the Iron Cross Second Class on 26 September, probably as a result of his conduct in the battle near the French town of Pont-a-Mousson on that date.

The area was an historic battleground, going back to 58 BC when Caesar defeated the German chieftian Ariovistus. In 1914 the fighting was so violent and severe that villages such as Flirey, Regnieville and Réménoville were completely destroyed. Today the only reminder of these towns are roadside signs, e.g., Regnieville "village detruit." Worse still, the fighting was indecisive. Thirty years later to the month

Blaskowitz would be fighting in this area again, commanding a defeated and retreating army group.

The French attacks in Alsace-Lorraine were soundly defeated. The French fought with courage and daring, but little skill. And they presented excellent targets in their red and blue uniforms. By mid-August they had lost 300,000 men without results.[3] The attacks ceased and French soldiers were transferred north to frustrate the main German attack. The fighting in August and September resulted in the failure of German strategy, but left the Germans deep in northern France. The failure of the Schlieffen Plan caused the contending armies hastily to withdraw units from the south, from the German left wing, and transfer them to the northwest, in a frantic rush to outflank the enemy. The opposing armies did not succeed in outflanking each other but only ended in extending the front from Switzerland to the English Channel. Historians now refer to these flanking and counter-flanking movements as the "Race to the Sea." Blaskowitz's regiment was among those withdrawn from the south and sent north.

Withdrawn from combat in Alsace at the end of September, Blaskowitz's regiment had been sent by train to Mons, from which it marched to Lille (in France) and engaged in the fighting there.[4] Just across the border from Belgium, Lille had been an entrenched camp defended by eleven forts in the Franco-Prussian war in 1870. It fell quickly to the German onslaught in 1914. Lille was not far behind the section of the front where Captain Blaskowitz fought for the next several months. Despite its closeness to the front the Allies refrained from shelling it and it became a favorite resort for German officers on leave from the front. In late-October 1914, after fighting near Lille for almost two weeks, he advanced south and west with his regiment.[5]

The regiment passed through Hulluch and Loos along the higher ground north and west of Arras, a fortified town that was the hub of a radius of roads, waterways, and railways situated at a gap in the hills southwest of Vimy Ridge.[6] Arras, which had been militarily significant since the days of the Romans, lacked strategic value for its own sake, but was sought as a gateway to Paris.[7] It was overlooked to the north by Vimy Ridge (elevation 476 ft.) and to the northwest by a higher (elevation 541 ft.) spur which runs east-west and is named Nôtre Dame de Lorette Ridge after a sixteenth century church which stood on its eastern end. Geographically the entire area is where the northeastern European plain meets the western European coastal lowlands. Much like a breaking wave from the east with finger-like spurs running westward, the higher ground of Artois dominates the lower plain of the Pas de Calais to the north and the Picardy region to the south. The Nôtre Dame de Lorette spur itself overlooks the area for miles to the south, east and west. In peacetime it had been a place of pilgrimage with a spectacular view. In a war where the position of the forward artillery observer was crucial, a ridge such as Nôtre Dame de Lorette was often the scene of bitter, bloody combat.

An ancient gallic legend declares that victory in every war goes to the conqueror of this chain of ridges. The Lorette spur was the center of a prolonged and bitter battle from October 1914 to June 1915. Fighting over possession of Vimy Ridge lasted into 1917. Before the struggle for these ridges was completed, the French unofficially re-named them the "crests of sacrifice."[8]

In late October, Blaskowitz and his 111th Infantry Regiment advanced onto Nôtre Dame de Lorette Ridge, where it overlooks the town of Ablain St. Nazaire. Ablain is twelve kilometers northwest of Arras on the south slope of the Nôtre Dame de Lorette Ridge. The German and French armies came to bloody grips with each other all along the ridge and the western end of Ablain. Possibly because of the legendary significance of the ridge, but more probably due to its tactical and strategic importance, the fighting was incredibly vicious, the carnage very heavy. Before the fighting shifted elsewhere on the western front this part of Artois became a huge charnel house. The fighting "must be counted as the prototypical trench slaughter of the Great War."[9] Blaskowitz himself was wounded for the first time by artillery fire on November 1. He suffered only a minor head wound, and remained in command of the 10th Company.[10]

During the third week of November Blaskowitz's regiment took up positions in the ruins of Nôtre Dame de Lorette Chapel.[11] It must have been eerie, fighting in the shattered remnants of a holy place turned fortress. Later, the regiment was transferred into the town of Albain St. Nazaire in the valley. The town was quickly transformed into a defensive bastion while the fighting raged indecisively on the ridge. By late autumn the French and the Germans were temporarily deadlocked, sharing the ridge almost equally, both unable to force the other from their desperate grip on the heights.[12]

During this early fighting, the armies slaughtering one another began to seek shelter by digging crude trenches which eventually reached from Switzerland to the English Channel. Quite early Blaskowitz ordered the men of his 10th Company to dig a rear line of trenches: he believed he might have been the first to have had such a second defensive line in readiness.[13] It did not take long for the trenches dug into the ridge and along its sloping hillside on the western edge of Ablain St. Nazaire to become elaborate. Trench warfare turned infantrymen into laborers: digging trenches and installing barbed wire.[14] By 1918 the grim story circulated among the troops that the war "will be finished when all the dirt in France has been shovelled into sandbags .... Then they'll have to quit, or fall through."[15] Nor did it take long for the soldiers of the 28th Division—to which Blaskowitz's regiment was attached—to find colorful, sometimes grim names for the trenches much as had the English and French soldiers. The open field between the woods on the heights of the ridge was called the "Meadow-of-Death." The woods were nicknamed the "True-Hero's Woods." Doubtless they were well-named. As the trenches made their way down the south side of the ridge toward Ablain, they were called after their most prominent features: The "Dangling Ellipse" and "Crow's Feet Hollow." The trench then passed along the western end of Ablain to the deep ravine of the Souchez River which separates Lorette Ridge from Vimy Ridge to the southeast. The trenches there incorporated the cellars of the buildings in west Ablain into the defense line.

It was in these cellars that the 9th and 10th companies of Blaskowitz's regiment fought after being moved there from the chapel on the ridge. Both companies were under Blaskowitz's command, a measure neces-sitated by the shortage of officers resulting from the high casualty rate. This western trench was part of a position the troops called "The Pulpit." It began mid-way up the slope and from the air looked much like a pulpit.[16] It was protected by barbed wire, numerous machine guns and innumerable hidden batteries of artillery, every obstacle that the German military art could create. By 1915 the position was a "honeycomb of dugouts, reinforced with concrete, capable of withstanding all but the highest caliber shells.[17] One historian described the position as "patently and ingeniously fortified ...."[18]

The late October and early November rains in the area made the combat conditions miserable. An artilleryman stationed not far from Ablain noted on 1 November, "Rainy November days follow, and all rather alike." On 10 November: "It is pouring with rain ...." Finally, on 15 November: "The first snow is falling: icy wind and stormy weather."[19] Nevertheless, the fighting continued unabated. The French winter assaults in Artois, according to one military analyst's later view, "afforded costly proof that against the Germans' skill in trench fighting, Joffre's 'nibbling' was usually attrition on the wrong side of the balance sheet."[20]

The fighting was very much a "Storm of Steel" as Ernst Jüenger romantically described it. Despite the great masses of artillery and ammunition, however, the fighting often came down to hand-to-hand combat between infantry. One infantryman from the 113th Infantry Regiment fighting alongside Blaskowitz's regiment on the Nôtre Dame de Lorette ridge described some of the combat his comrades had experienced in storming a French position: "One had killed a French-man with a pick-axe, another had strangled an officer, and a third had crushed the skull of a *Poilu* [French soldier] with his rifle butt."[21] It was savage, cruel fighting at its most horrible.

In infantry fighting a "new" weapon became prominent, the grenade. Since the trenches were so deep and narrow, it was nearly impossible to use rifles and bayonets in trench fighting and generally these weapons were slung on the infantryman's back in bandolier and the fighting was done with knives and other hand-to-hand weapons, especially grenades. The term "bombing parties" for attacking squads originated in this brutal trench combat.[22]

In many French infantry companies almost half of the men were "bombers" rather than riflemen.[23] One *poilu* who fought in the trenches at Nôtre Dame de Lorette from the autumn of 1914 until the fall of 1915 thought that the "grenadiers" dominated the fighting, especially after mid-December when the French and German lines were "inex-tricably entangled." "The enemy," he wrote, was "always invisible, but frequently nevertheless striking with shot, grenade or shrapnel anyone who lives in a manhole."[24]

On 8 December the French under General Ferdinand Foch opened the battle that later became known as the First Battle of Artois. It proved to be the first of several serious French disappointments in Artois.[25] From mid December until the end of January the carnage continued almost without pause. Trenches were attacked repeatedly, captured, then lost and recaptured, sometimes changing hands many times. Artillery duels were frequent and often "extremely violent." Gains and losses were measured in yards and casualties.[26]

Christmas was foggy and silent for most of the day until the German artillery shelled the French trenches opposite Blaskowitz's men. A localized German attack in the evening was repulsed by the French defenders.[27] Perhaps in retaliation for this bombardment, French artillery rang in the New Year at midnight with a barrage directed against the German lines. There was heavy artillery fire on New Year's day but nothing out of the ordinary for this sector.[28] Local French attacks continued in January.

The fighting escalated in mid-January. On Thursday, 14 January 1915, Blaskowitz and his 9th and 10th Companies were scattered in the cellars and trenches of the west Ablain "Pulpit." There was a steady rain. One of the war volunteers, a soldier named Rensch, described the events which took place around six P.M.

> It was boring. All we could do is clean our uniforms, clean our guns of dirt and rust and after that, all we did was lie in the make-shift beds, made from pieces of wood that we found. We had just taken an afternoon snack when the orderly officer announced sharply and bluntly: 'The enemy has taken the key positions of the Seventh Company, they have lost their trenches and we have to go and get them back.[29]

Under Blaskowitz's command, the 9th and 10th Companies scurried onto the counter-attack. Advancing in small groups by leaps and bounds toward the gate-keeper's house at the edge of the meadow where the French had captured a section of trench, several men were hit by French fire. The *poilus* had put sandbag barricades at the ends of the trench section which they had seized. Initially Blaskowitz's troops used grenades and then leaped into the trench where the fighting became hand-to-hand with bayonets. The French were thrown out of the trench into the flank where more German infantry awaited them.

The attacking French troops were reportedly part of the third battalion of the elite Alpine troops, but they quickly gave up the struggle after a brief but fierce fire fight. Twenty-four *poilus* were taken prisoner. The remaining trenches were also cleared of the French. According to the regimental historian, the bodies piled up in heaps, some dead soldiers were left with bayonets still plunged into their chests.

German infantry and pioneers worked into the night to close gaps in the trenches and erect new barbed wire. The dead and wounded were removed, those killed were buried in the local cemetery. Food was brought into the trenches and guard was stood throughout the night—as on every other night.[30] The nights were often worse than the days. The stress and strain of the silence, isolation and fear during the night could make it seem that time itself had been killed and moved no longer.

Another German infantryman has described these nights with a kind of universality:

> This endless and terribly exhausting round of night guards was endurable in fine weather and even in frost. They were a positive torture when it rained, as it usually does in January. When the wet penetrated first the ground sheet, pulled over your head, the coat and tunic, and trickled, hour after hour, down your skin, there resulted a state of depression that was impervious even to the cheering sounds of the relief coming toward you.[31]

Rain was an "implacable enemy" under these conditions. A soldier's great-coat, normally weighing seven pounds, often absorbed twenty pounds of water in the rain. Standing guard duty at night, clothing became stiff as cardboard with ice in freezing cold air. From the 25th of October 1914 until 10 March 1915 there were only eighteen dry days.[32] In December alone six inches of rain fell in Artois, the rainiest December since 1876. The trenches filled with water and turned into mud. Rifles jammed up in the mud but the fighting continued with bayonets.[33] The troops in the trenches, dirty and caked with mud, were nicknamed *Frontschwein* (front-pigs).[34]

On Friday morning, 15 January 1915, it was raining moderately with a strong southwest wind. The temperature reached forty-four degrees Fahrenheit, milder than normal for the season, but still thoroughly miserable.[35] The white chalky soil had already turned to mud. Nevertheless, the previous day's fighting continued on Nôtre Dame de Lorette and in Ablain St. Nazaire. This time Blaskowitz did not triumph unscathed.

The assault by the French infantry began at approximately 10 A.M. It was not preceded by the usual artillery barrage so the French attack achieved some surprise, and therefore, some success. The Germans spent the afternoon preparing to counter-attack. A shortage of grenades made the preparations difficult, but a plan was developed to attack both flanks of the trench which the French had occupied in the morning attack, meanwhile shelling the trench in advance with mortars. One unit of Blaskowitz's Ninth Company, led by Lieutenant Ruckert, attacked jointly with the Tenth Company under Blaskowitz and the Eleventh and Twelfth Companies under Major Forster.

When the Germans counterattacked, good progress was made despite the lack of surprise. Many of the defenders only lifted their rifles above the trench, pointed in the general direction of the German attack, and fired, never actually exposing themselves or really taking aim. Much of the defensive fire went over the attacker's heads, inflicting few casualties.

Nevertheless, Lieutenant Ruckert's unit from the Ninth Company began to falter just as the attack reached the French trench. The unit had run out of grenades. In self-sacrifice, Lieutenant Ruckert shouted "Germany, Germany, above all and over everything!" and leaped into the enemy trench! Vicious hand—to—hand fighting using rocks and bayonets—grenades had been used up—raged in the trench until twilight. The French *poilus* who could retreat began to flee. "Death had a field day," recorded the regimental history.

Among the dead was the valiant Lieutenant Ruckert. His body in the trench had more than a dozen bayonet wounds. Captain Blaskowitz was lightly wounded in the chest by a grenade but he stayed with the troops. One hundred Frenchmen were taken prisoner that day.[36]

The grim drama in which Blaskowitz had participated on 14 and 15 January merited only a single line in the "Official Reports of War Operations" by the French: "At Nôtre Dame de Lorette ... the enemy re-occupied a portion of the trenches lost to us Jan. 14." The official German announcement was much more "expansive": "The enemy's attacks on our positions ... were repulsed. In a counter-attack our troops captured two trenches and made prisoners of the occupants."[37]

Following the day's combat another rainy and miserable night with temperatures hovering just above freezing was spent repairing the recaptured trench. Greetings on the morning of 16 January included a heavy French artillery barrage but no infantry attack followed.[38] Some units of the regiment were temporarily relieved and rested briefly. Rest and relief was often little improvement over the trenches. As Ernst Juenger wrote:

> It was not much better when the company was in reserve. Our quarters then were small mud huts covered with branches of fir trees .... Many a time one walked in a puddle inches deep. Though up to now I had known rheumatism only by name, it was not many days before I felt it in every joint through being always wet to the skin.[39]

It is perhaps beyond comprehension that armies could stay in the trenches throughout the winter without disintegrating simply through exposure to the elements. Additionally, the stench of the dead filled the air in the trenches and the rats there grew fat from eating the corpses.[40] The Germans often found it too dangerous to remove the bodies of the fallen so they were frequently buried in the floor of the trench.[41] For similar reasons, in the French trenches on Nôtre Dame de Lorette, the *poilus* incorporated the corpses of the fallen into the trench walls, sometimes utilizing a protruding limb as a hanger for their equipment.[42] Sometimes, in sections of "No Man's Land" where the fighting had gone on for months, such as at Nôtre Dame de Lorette, bodies dating from the first fighting dried out, turned black, and assumed the appearance of mummies, adding another element of the macabre to the battlefield.[43] As if these sufferings were not enough, the appearance of trench foot added new miseries to the soldier's life. Rheumatism and pneumonia increased misery and kept some out of the trenches.[44]

Blaskowitz fell seriously ill from a sinus infection, but he remained with his unit.[45] He had already demonstrated physical courage in the battles where he had led the 9th and 10th Companies of his regiment. He displayed endurance in the face of unending torture by the elements of nature in the trenches through the winter. He was not a man to seek an excuse to avoid difficulties; twice wounded he had nevertheless stayed with his regiment. Years later he would also demonstrate moral and civil courage.

During March the Nôtre Dame de Lorette battlefield became the scene of "the most violent conflict on the French front."[46] The fighting was virtually ceaseless with the same trenches repeatedly changing hands, with a variable number of casualties and captured, a few mortars and machine-guns lost or taken, each success heralded, each failure minimized. On 7 March for example, after an attack the previous day in which the Germans seized the first two lines of French trenches, the French counter-attacked from their third trench line only fifty yards away. The counter-attack was preceded by a French artillery barrage so fierce that the attackers could clearly see Germans blown into the air by the explosions. The assault went in and furious fighting raged all night long. If French reports are accepted 3,000 German corpses were counted on the battlefield during the "impressive silence" the next morning. "Everywhere the Germans lay, many falling with rifles clasped in their stiffened hands as if about to fire again.[47] The fighting nevertheless resumed with renewed ferocity the following day.

The focus of the fighting had been on the heights of the Nôtre Dame de Lorette spur, but Blaskowitz and his 10th Company in the cellars of Ablain had been subjected to intense suppressing fire by French heavy artillery, alternating with mortar and machine gun fire, throughout the first week of March. Tenth company had lost three dead and nine wounded. Combat continued throughout the month, casualties mounted; gains and losses were measured in meters. Brief lulls in the desperate fighting taking place solely to reorganize for another attack or to prepare a counterattack. On some days fighting raged all day without any trenches changing hands. On other days there were "only" artillery bombardments. Early in March the Germans regained the crest of the ridge, only to lose it again near the month's end. The regimental historian later described the entire battle as a "Dance of Death."[48]

That month Blaskowitz was awarded the Iron Cross First Class, one of many decorations he was to receive in the Great War.[49] His regiment was stuck in the fighting around Ablain St. Nazaire and Nôtre Dame de Lorette, but by then Blaskowitz was very sick with a chronic sinus infection. It was not a glorious illness, but it was nevertheless quite serious. On 10 April he was sent home on sick-leave and admitted into a sanatorium in Baden-Baden where he stayed for treatment until nearly mid-May.[50]

Although he did not know it, he had seen the last of his regiment. The regiment and the division were known thereafter as the "Conquerors of Lorette" by official order, but the French advanced yard by yard across the ridge during heavy fighting in the second Battle of Artois in the spring. Except for the last few easternmost yards of the ridge, Nôtre Dame de Lorette was finally lost in June 1915, after determined attacks by the French 70th Division under General Petain. The French called it "one of the most important tactical victories ... won by French arms in Northern France.[51]

French "trumpeting" of their triumph may have "partially hid the realization of defeat from the Allied peoples."[52] The truth was that the French had once again woefully underestimated the strength of the German defense and had repeated their earlier experience of failure. The few hundred yards of territory gained had been won after "murderous losses."[53]

Blaskowitz's regiment had been involved in some of the most ferocious bloodletting of the early part of World War I. From October, 1914, to May, 1915, his division's regiments were spent one after the other on the plateau of Nôtre Dame de Lorette. In the course of these winter and spring battles his own regiment was almost completely destroyed; by May 10th its first battalion had only three officers and 272 men. The pre-war strength of the regiment was approximately 3,300 officers and men, but by May 1915, 32 officers and 1,737 men were casualties—about a 54% casualty rate.[54] As if this were not already disastrous, the fighting worsened, and casualty rates soared as the war continued.

After recovering his health in the sanatorium, Blaskowitz was transferred to command a company in the Third Jäger Regiment in the newly formed elite Alpine Corps. Later, he was made a battalion commander under his old tutor, Field Marshal von Mackensen, and served in the battles in the Dolomite Alps in northern Italy and subsequently in the victorious Serbian Campaign. Allied intelligence rated the Alpine Corps as "one of the best German units."[55] In its 1917 evaluation Allied intelligence stated: "The discipline and firmness of the commanding officers makes the Alpine Corps an elite body, of genuine combat value."[56] The discipline and training of this elite unit became Blaskowitz's personal standard; "the training ... received in this new arm stood him in good stead for his later work as an instructor."[57]

Tactical training in elite divisions such as the Alpine Corps was kept at a state-of-the art level. By mid 1916 they were truly elite troops; close copies of the stormtroopers Ernst Jüenger later made famous in his writings. These assault troops were the first to use combined arms tactics.[58]

Elite units such as the Alpine Corps were often employed in the most deadly situations and so was Blaskowitz's battalion. At the beginning of June it was sent to Verdun.[59] Blaskowitz's battalion took part in the heaviest fighting at the village of Fleury. Before the battle was over Fleury had completely disappeared leaving only a "white smear" visible from the air.[60] Blaskowitz's battalion was almost completely wiped out, although he himself had been transferred just before the battle to a staff position with the Headquarters of X Army Corps in Galicia.

After only seven months with X Corps he was shifted again. Blaskowitz was surprised when he was suddenly transferred to the general staff of the 75th Baden Reserve Division in mid-October, 1916.[61] The division was stationed in Galicia. The transfer was clearly not a step up. The 75th Baden Reserve Division was rated as "Third Class" by the Allies.[62] Blaskowitz's appointment, however, was as chief-of-staff, which was virtually a promotion from battalion commander.

In the next several months he attended, in rapid succession, several wartime training courses for officers, including a course for "shock-troops," another called the "Leadership Course," and also the "Artillery Plotting School" and "Chemical Warfare School" courses. By 1918, he attended a brief "general course" and another "Leader Course."[63] Between the courses taken in 1917 and those in 1918, however, he returned to the 75th Baden Reserve Division, which had moved to Courland, and participated in the famous assault on Riga under General Oscar von Hutier.[64] Blaskowitz had obviously been trained in Hutier's famous infiltration tactics in the course for "shocktroops."

It was while serving as the First General Staff Officer in the 75th Baden Reserve Division that Blaskowitz found his home in the trenches—as did so many other World War I soldiers. As he later revealed: "he liked it because he met all the officers of the Division and followed a grand comradely existence."[65]

Blaskowitz had encountered that phenomenon of World War I combat which permeated the armies of all the combatants and which the Germans summed up in the phrase: "Ich habe ein Kameraden," (I have a comrade). It is not surprising that Blaskowitz found comradery as a staff officer.

He revealed through his behavior at this time, however, that he was not an entirely typical officer. In the German Army there was a great social gulf between officers and enlisted men which later revealed itself in the chaos of 1918. Many men blamed their officers for all the deaths, casualties and defeat. Blaskowitz, however, ignored these usual social boundaries and befriended his orderly, Johannes Koepcke, from their first meeting in April 1916. It was an unlikely friendship between an East Prussia officer and a farmer from north-central Germany, but it proved to be devout, durable and deeper than death. Koepcke followed Blaskowitz to each of his assignments for the rest of the war.

In 1917 the war entered its third year. To many it seemed endless. One German artilleryman wrote:

> You think a lot about the war; it was actually intended only to be a sort of intermezzo in one's life, and now it will soon have lasted three years, and sometimes everything seems like a bad dream, but one that we have to dream for years and years.[66]

The collapse of Russia in 1917 and the experience of victory in the east meant the transfer of the division to the Western Front in December of that year for the push to "Final Victory." However, this late in the war morale had deteriorated among some of the German troops. The will to conquer was disintegrating. A German soldier's slogan sardonically echoed the decline in morale in a kind of gallows-humor: "We'll conquer until we're all dead."[67]

Blaskowitz's division was not immune from the contagion of decay. The division reportedly lost forty men as deserters during the train trip from Russia to France.[68] In order to counter such pessimism, the High Command encouraged confidence asserting that behind Bruchmueller's drumfire barrages the Germans would "waltz" to victory (Feurwalz). It would be the "Hindenburg flat race."[69]

From December through February the division trained in France, taking part in maneuvers supported by tanks and also in mock-combat against simulated tanks. At the end of March it went into the line in Picardy, near Chauncy.

The German High Command began its long awaited "Victory Offensives" on 21 March in a series of battles called the *Kaiserschlacht*, the "Emperor's Battle," desperately gambling on victory before the Americans could turn the tide with their numerical superiority. The attack on 21 March in the Somme region was a tactical, but not a strategic success. A similar attack at the end of April in Flanders had comparably limited results, as did a third attack on the Chemin Des Dames at the end of May. The German High Command hastily organized a fourth attack for early June. It was an assault across the Matz River (near Montdidier) aimed toward Paris in early June and Blaskowitz's 75th Baden Reserve Infantry Division took part.

The offensive was code named "Gneisenau-Yorck" and the assault force was the Eighteenth Army, commanded by General von Hutier. His artillery commander was the famous "Durchbruch" Bruchmueller" (Breakthrough Mueller). Eighteenth Army had twenty-four Divisions while the defending French Third Army had only thirteen. Bruchmueller had six hundred batteries of artillery against half that number of French batteries.[70] Bruchmueller's preliminary bombardment was approximately 750,000 rounds of high explosive shrapnel, phosgene, mustard gas and diphenylchlorasine. There were great expectations for the attack.

It was launched on 9 June, but lacked the critical element of surprise since the Allies had expected the assault for the previous five days, learning of it through prisoners and deserters. They greeted it with an artillery barrage ten minutes before the German attack began, catching the German troops massed in their jump-off positions, and inflicting numerous casualities.[71] It was not a good omen.

During the first attack on 9 June, and for the next two days, the attackers had some success, advancing eight miles the first two days. It was a battle in which tanks and air support figured heavily, and in many ways it had more in common with the *blitzkrieg* of World War II than the battles of 1916.[72] On 12 June Blaskowitz's division reported taking French prisoners from nine different divisions, as well as destroying sixty-six tanks, mostly by firing over open artillery sights.[73] Then it was learned that the French had over seventy more tanks poised to attack the German flank.[74] The next day the French counterattack forced the German High Command to call off the attack.

At the headquarters of General Charles Mangin, who commanded the French counterattack, officers beamed with joy. One French officer was overheard to exclaim: "They are killing Boches in swarms ...."[75] At the German High Command Headquarters the Kaiser was in low spirits and ate nothing but chocolate mousse.[76] Blaskowitz's reaction is regrettably undocumented. In any case, he stayed with his division during the bitter defensive fighting which ensued.

The division suffered serious losses in the Battle of the Matz, was disorganized and according to the Allies had poor morale.[77] The last attacks with a genuine prospect of "Final Victory" had failed. Blaskowitz's division had advanced to the Matz River, forty miles from Paris, just short of Compiègne, but the tide had turned and the Germans were thrown onto the defensive by the Allied counterattack. It was the closest, but the last approach to final victory; it did not alter the unfavorable strategic situation.[78] The battle was a turning point; Germany had lost the initiative.[79]

Reaction in the army set in mercilessly. The German army in the field was already disintegrating by the summer of 1918, and Blaskowitz's division was no exception. Indeed, by the last year of the war discipline had deteriorated so much that senior officers regularly referred to the army as a "militia."[80] It was too late to restore discipline by 1918. As one junior officer wrote: "Not all of the army was in revolt. Most of the men simply wanted to get home." He continued: "Only a small proportion of the army had gone berserk. Too many hardships and too much suffering temporarily transformed some German soldiers into stupid and dangerous crackpots."[81] A revolution began. Collapse followed; not victory.

Shortly before the armistice was signed, Blaskowitz was transferred again, this time to the Lorraine Front where he was to have been liaison officer to the 37th Hungarian Infantry Division. He went there with his faithful friend and orderly, Koepcke. The war ended, however, before the division went into action.

Germany abruptly collapsed into revolution. Only a short time earlier "Final Victory" had seemed to some to be within reach. The shock of defeat and revolution was profound.Many Germans blamed the army. Princess Evelyn Blücher described her observations of the atmosphere in Berlin:

> It is a pitiful sight to watch the death-throes of a great nation. It reminds me of a great ship slowly sinking before one's eyes, and being swallowed up by storm-driven waves. I feel intensely for Germany and her brave long-suffering people, who have made such terrible sacrifices and gone through so much woe, only to see their idols shattered and to realize that their sufferings have all been caused by the blundering mistakes and overweening ambition of a class of 'supermen.'[82]

The war was over. Germany was defeated and humiliated. More difficult times followed for both Blaskowitz and the fatherland. On 11 November the Armistice was signed and Germany's armies marched homeward across territory conquered at the cost of so much blood. One soldier wrote:

> The yearning to return home and to see once again wife, children and parents overshadows the terrible conscience of a lost war. Everything is still like a heavy dream. Neither the past nor the future is clearly comprehensible. We sway about in a semi trance. One day it will become clearer.[83]

Lieutenant Walter Karpowski's thoughts may have represented the feelings of many other retreating German soldiers when he wrote: "[A] sense of bitterness arises: ... all for nothing, all for nothing .... That's what rises in the soldier's ears as they tramp wordlessly along, stupefied and dejected at the same time."[84] Defeat and revolution was an abrupt turning point in the lives of many Germans.

Imperial Germany's collapse in November, 1918 occurred when Blaskowitz was thirty-five years old. Slightly more than five feet eight inches tall and weighing just less than a trim one hundred and thirty pounds, he was obviously physically fit. His blondish-brown hair and blue eyes combined with his fresh healthy complexion and winning smile to make a pleasant if not overwhelming impression. His nose had broad nostrils and he had a heavy square jaw. He had clearly led a healthy and toughening life. His evident good health reflected his love of athletics, hunting, horseback riding and Swedish drill.[85]

General Günther Blumentritt, who served with Blaskowitz for many years, described him as "rigorously just and high-minded" with a "strong spiritual and religious turn of mind."[86] This may possibly be attributable to the enduring influence of his father. A man of "obviously sharp wits,"[87] Blaskowitz was later officially described by Field Marshal Gerd von Rundstedt as "physically and mentally very capable."[88] Although obviously able to be very serious-minded, Blaskowitz had a good sense of humor and could be considered both "humorous and human."[89] Franz Halder, later Chief of the General Staff, thought that Blaskowitz had God as his "orientation and his guiding principle. He was blessed with warmth of heart, but his mind was strict, righteous and thoroughly immersed in complete devotion."[90] Perhaps Rundstedt's characterization of Blaskowitz as an "honorable man" and Ulrich von Hassell's later classifying Blaskowitz as one of the "excellent people" among the army leaders suffice to depict him as a man.[91]

As a soldier, Blaskowitz was a "representative of the old Imperial Army," a "decent and respected pillar of the old school."[92] Field Marshal Kesselring later judged Blaskowitz to be one of a group of "well-edu-cated General Staff officers with an outstanding insight into practical conditions."[93] At least one observer considered Blaskowitz a "particu-larly good leader"[94] with unquestionable organizing ability[95] and "more than average administrative capacity."[96]Although a colonel who served with him much later regarded Blaskowitz as a "splendid fellow and soldier, indeed a cavalier,"[97] he was more nearly a simple "upright, straight forward soldier."[98] But in 1918 he was only one officer in a defeated, and rapidly disintegrating army.

The defeat of Germany in the Great War and the subsequent reduction of her army to the tiny force of 100,000 men dictated by the Versailles Treaty, caused doubts to enter Blaskowitz's mind "as he did not know whether he would be, as he so strongly desired, one of the chosen few of the hundred thousand army."[99] As another officer wrote: "[N]o one knew anything about his own future."[100] It was undoubtedly a time for soul-searching. Blaskowitz was unsuited by either education or experience to enter any civilian profession. Dis-missal from the army would have meant an abrupt and total reorientation of his life; a difficult task in the best of times. Although he held several medals, including the Iron Cross First Class and the House Order of Hohenzollern, he had "not had a brilliant career by any means to this point in time."[101]

Undistinguished by accomplishment, he may have thought himself destined for historical anonymity; yet he was selected to remain with the small army of the Weimar Republic, Germany's new government. His selection meant some personal security for the next few years. Germany had little security.

Notes for Chapter II

1. David Chandler, *The Campaigns of Napoleon: The Mind and Method of History's Greatest Soldier* (New York: MacMillan Publishing Co., Inc., 1966), 145.

2. Kriegstagebuch Infanterie Regiment 111, III Battalion, July 31, 1914-March 3, 1915, No. 9, Generallandsarchiv Karlsruhe. Generallandsarchiv Karlsruhe hereafter cited as: G.L.A.K.

3. Gudmundsson, *Stormtroop Tactics*, 2.

4. Kriegsrangliste (I) des Infanterie Regiment 111, vol. 13, no. 17, left and right pages, G.L.A.K.

5. Ibid.

6. Alexander McKee, *The Battle of Vimy Ridge* (New York: Stein and Day, 1967), 14.

7. Ibid.

8. After the First World War, France built a National Memorial and Cemetery on Nôtre Dame de Lorette Ridge. It is testimony to the severity of the fighting that there are 20,000 individual graves and another 20,000 unknown dead in eight ossuaries. See Rose E.B. Coombs, *Before Endeavors Fade: A Guide To the Battlefields of the First World War* (London: Plaistow Press Magazines, Ltd., 1976), 66, 70. When the year-long battle finally ended the writer Will Bird walked around the plateau, which the French troops had called, "La Butte de la Mort" [the Hill of Death]. According to one source: "When Will Bird, with his sensitive writer's perception, first saw the carnage on the Lorette Spur, it made his flesh crawl: he had never before seen so many grinning skulls. Here was a maze of old trenches and ditches littered with the garbage of war: broken rifles, frayed equipment, rusting bayonets, hundreds of bombs, tangles of barbed wire, puddles of filth, and everywhere rotting uniforms, some French blue, others German grey, tattered sacks now, holding their own consignment of bones." Pierre Berton, *Vimy* (London: Penguin Books, 1986), 77. It may have been under the inspiration of the fighting on the Nôtre Dame de Lorette ridge that the Kaiser related his favorite war story to his entourage in April 1915, about a "violet blue slope-blue with the coats of the dead Frenchmen ..." Walter Goerlitz, ed., *The Kaiser and His Court. The Diaries, Notebooks and Letters of Admiral Georg Alexander von*

Muller, Chief of the Naval Cabinet, 1914-1918 (New York: Harcourt,Brace, Inc., 1961), 72.

9. Douglas Porch, "Artois, 1915," *Military History Quarterly* 5, no.3 (Spring 1993): 42.

10. Kriegsrangliste (I) des Infanterie Regiment 111, vol. 13, no. 17, left and right pages, G.L.A.K.

11. *Schlachten des Weltkrieges.* Vol. 17: *Loretto* (Berlin: Gerhard Stallings, 1927), 50.

12. C.R.M. Cruttwell, *A History of the Great War, 1914-1918* (Chicago: Academy Chicago Publishers, 1991), 162.; Tonie and Valmai Holt, *Battlefields of the First World War: A Traveller's Guide* (London: Pavilion Books, Ltd., 1993), 88-89.

13. Blaskowitz Interrogation, 8 Sept. 1945, Schuster Interrogation Files, R.G. 165, N.A.

14. Gudmundsson, *Stormtroop Tactics*, 82,; Eric Leed, *No Man's Land: Combat & Identity in World War I* (London: Cambridge University Press, 1979), 91-92.

15. Stanley Weintraub, *A Stillness Heard Round the World: The End of the Great War: November 1918* (New York: E.P. Dutton, Truman Talley Books, 1985), 3.

16. Theodore Zahn, *Das Infanterie Regiment Markgraf Ludwig Wilhelm (3. Badisches) Nr. 111 in Weltkriege 1914-1918* (Wiesbaden: Matthias Grünewald Verlag, 1936), 81-83; George Allen, *The Great War, vol. 4, The Wavering Balance of Forces* (Philadelphia: George Barrie's Sons, 1919), 29. The map here confirms the accuracy of the map printed in Zahn.

17. "French Preparing for A New Offensive," *The New York Times*, 15 May 1915, 8.

18. Allen, *Great War*, 28. Part of this defense line is the Eglise d'Ablain Saint-Nazaire which is a conserved battle ruin whose shell and gun-pocked walls bear testimony to the savage fighting there in 1914 and 1915.

19. Herbert Sulzbach, *With the German Guns: Four Years on the Western Front 1914-1918*, trans. Richard Thonger (Hamden, Connecticut: Archon Books, 1981), 38-40.

20. B.H. Liddell Hart, *The Real War 1914-1918* (Boston: Little, Brown and Company, 1964), 118.

21. Stephan Westman, *Surgeon with the Kaiser's Army* (London: William Kimber, 1968), 58.

22. Francis Reynolds, ed., *The Story of the Great War* (New York: P.F. Collier & Son, 1916), 5: 1324; Gudmundsson, *Stormtroop Tactics*, 35.

23. Richard M. Watt, *Dare Call It Treason* (New York: Simon and Schuster, 1963), 85.

24. Henri René, *Lorette: Une bataille de douze mois, octobre 1914 octobre 1915* (Paris: Librairie Academique, 1916), 76-79, 84.

25. John Terraine, *The First World War, 1914-1918* (London: Leo Cooper, 1983), 47. Joffre later admitted that "the results obtained were very poor ...."

26. See for example: "German War News, *The Times* (London), 21 December 1914, 7.; "Advance on Both Flanks." *The Times* (London) 6 January 1915, 3.

27. "Intermittent Artillery Fighting." *The Times* (London), 26 December 1914, 6.

28. Kriegstagebuch Infanterie Regiment 111, III Battalion, 25.12.14 & 1.1.15, 88 & 91, G.L.A.K.

29. Zahn, *Infanterie Regiment 111*, 94.

30. Ibid., 94-95.

31. Ernst Juenger, *The Storm of Steel: From the Diary of a German Storm-Troop Officer On the Western Front*, trans. Basil Creighton (London: Chatto & Windus, 1930), 7.

32. John Ellis, *Eye-Deep in Hell: Trench Warfare in World War I* (Baltimore: Johns Hopkins University Press, Paperback ed., 1989), 44-45, 48, 51.

33. Modris Eksteins, *Rites of Spring: The Great War and the Birth of the Modern Age* (Boston: Houghton Mifflin Company, 1989), 102.

34. Ibid., 146.

35. The weather report is based upon the author's correspondence with the "Service central d'exploitation de la météorologie," in Paris and upon the "Bulletin international du Bureau central météorologique de France" for Friday 15 January 1915.

36. Zahn, *Infanterie Regiment 111*, 95; Kriegsrangliste (I) des Infanterie Regiment 111, Vol. 13, No. 17, left and right pages, G.L.A.K.; Kriegstagebuch Infanterie Regiment 111, III Battalion, 15 January 1915, G.L.A.K.

37. "Official Reports of War Operations," *The New York Times*, 17 January 1915, 3.; "Appreciable Results," *The Times* (London), 18 January 1915, 8.

38. Zahn, *Infanterie Regiment 111*, 95.

39. Juenger, *Storm of Steel*, 8.

40. Leed, *No Man's Land*, 18.

41. Sven Hedin, *With the German Armies in the West*, trans. H. Walterstorff (London: John Lane, 1915), 323.

42. Porch, "Artois, 1915," 49-50.

43. "French Bayonets Won Fierce Battles," *The New York Times*, 25 March 1915, 2.; Porch, "Artois, 1915," 50.

44. Eksteins, *Rites of Spring*, 103.

45. Kriegsrangliste (I) des Infanterie Regiment 111, vol. 13, no. 17, left and right pages, G.L.A.K.

46. "Kaiser Holds A War Council Close To Lille," *The New York Times*, 19 March 1915, 1.

47. "Fierce Night Combat Costs Germans 3,000," *The New York Times*, 9 March 1915, 2. The III Infantry Regiment history admitted to 1800 casualties in XIV Corps between 3/3/1915 and 6/3/1915; Zahn, *Infanterie Regiment III*, 106.

48. Zahn, *Infanterie Regiment III*, 101-103.; "All-Day Fighting Near Arras," *The Times* (London), 10 March 1915, 10.; "Official Reports of War Operations: Germany," *The New York Times*, 19 March 1915, 2.

49. NOKW 2439, Blaskowitz, T-1119/31/0410, R.G. 238, N.A.; Blaskowitz also received the following decorations from the states of Imperial Germany: Prussia, Order of the Red Eagle Third Class with Swords, Wound Medal in Black; Bavaria, Bavarian Military Service Order Fourth Class with Swords; Baden, Order of the Golden Lion with the Knight's Cross; Brunswick, War Service Cross; and, Oldenburg, Cross of Frederick-August First Class. From Austria-Hungary he received the Military Service Cross Third Class and from the Ottoman Empire the Order of the Iron Halfmoon. Reichswehrministerium, Heere-Personalamt, ed. *Rangliste des deutschen Reichsheeres nach dem Stande von 1 Mai 1930* (Berlin: E.G. Mittler and Son, n.d.), 111.

50. Kriegsrangliste (I) des Infanterie Regiment 111, vol. 13, no. 7, left and right pages, G.L.A.K.

51. "Won Lorette Hills By 13-Day Fight," *The New York Times*, 25 May 1915, 3.

52. Crutwell, *Great War*, 165.

53. B.H. Liddell Hart, *History of the First World War* (London: Book Club Associates, 1973), 196. The French, however, may simply have been trying to "put a good face on it ...." It had been a Pyrrhic victory. In the May-June attacks the French had 102,000 casualties. The French estimated German losses at 80,000, but Berlin admitted to less than 50,000. The military historians Douglas Porch and Leonard Smith have regarded the results of the French Artois offensives as "disastrous" for the French, tracing the psychological transformation of the French Army which climaxed in the 1917 mutinies to the Artois offensives, especially the failed assaults in the Third Battle of Artois in the autumn of 1915 when French units broke off attacks on the last few yards of Nôtre de Lorette on their own initiative (after another 48,000 casualties. They consider it the beginning of the end of the "sacrificial elan" of the French Army. Conversely, the Germans in Artois began by the spring of 1915 to develop flexible small-unit defensive and counter-attack infiltration tactics which culminated in the mis-named "Hutier Tactics" employed so successfully at Riga, Caporetto and the Western Front in the spring of 1918.

Porch, "Artois, 1915," 50-51. Prior to the Third Battle of the Artois Joffre had told his men "Your èlan will be irresistable." The shrewd *poilus* began to conclude otherwise. Terraine, *First World War*, 92. See also: Timothy Lupfer, *The Dynamics of Doctrine: The Changes in German Tactical Doctrine During the First World War* (Fort Leavenworth, Kansas: Combat Studies Institute, U.S. Army Command and General Staff College, 1981), 2-7.; For the tactical failure of the French artillery in the Second and Third Battles of the Artois see: Bruce Gudmundsson, *On Artillery* (Westport, Connecticut: Praeger, 1993), 51-52.

54. United States War Department, General Staff, *Histories of 251 Divisions of the German Army Which Participated In the World War (1914-1918)* (Washington: Government Printing Office, 1920), 375. The French conquest of Nôtre Dame de Lorette in 1915 thus eventually confirmed the old legend that whoever held the Nôtre Dame spur would win any battle in the area; In ante-bellum German war games it was held that losses on this scale were "equivalent to complete destruction..." of the unit. Bucholz, *Prussian War Planning*, 88.

55. Ibid, 11.; Lieutenant Friedrich Paulus, later Field Marshal Paulus of Stalingrad, served as Adjutant to the 111th Infantry Regiment until this time and was coincidentally transferred to the Alpenkorps where he served as a staff officer to the 2nd Jaeger Regiment. Paulus and Blaskowitz were life-long friends. Goerlitz, *Paulus*, 9.

56. United States War Department General Staff, *Histories of 251 Divisions*, 375.

57. Blaskowitz Interrogation Report, 5 June 1945, First Canadian Army Intelligence Periodical No. 4, vol. 10,655, File 215C1.023, R.G. 24, P.A.C.

58. Gudmundsson, *Stormtroop Tactics*, 130. Combined arms tactics is the integrated use of infantry, artillery, air support and perhaps armour together to achieve victory. See: Jonathan House, *Toward Combined Arms Warfare: A Survey of 20th- Century Tactics, Doctrine, and Organization* (Fort Leavenworth, Kansas: Command and General Staff College, 1985).

59. United States War Department General Staff, *Histories of 251 Divisions*, 327.

60. Alistair Horne, *The Price of Glory: Verdun, 1916* (New York: Penguin Books, 1978), 300. The "white smear" was the result of the nitrate-tainting of the ground by the concentrated high explosives.

61. Blaskowitz Interrogation, 5 June 1945, First Canadian Army Intelligence Periodical No. 4, vol. 10,655 File 215C1.023, R.G. 24, P.A.C.; NOKW 141, Blaskowitz, Records of the United States Nuernberg War Crimes Trials: United States of America v. Wilhelm von Leeb et. al. (Case XII), November 28, 1947-October 28, 1948, M-898/28/0161, R.G. 238, N.A.

62. United States War Department General Staff, *Histories of 251 Divisions*, 526-7.

63. NOKW 141, Blaskowitz, M-898/28/0161, R.G. 238, N.A; Kriegstagebuch 75 Reserve Infanterie Division, Rangliste des Stabes, G.L.A.K.

64. Ibid.

65. Blaskowitz Interrogation, 5 June 1945, First Canadian Army Intelligence Periodical No. 4, vol. 10,655, File 215C1.023, R.G. 24, P.A.C.

66. Ellis, *Eye-Deep In Hell*, 190.

67. Weintraub, *Stillness Heard Round the World*, 3.

68. United States War Department General Staff, *Histories of 251 Divisions*, 527.

69. Randal Gray, *Kaiserschlacht 1918: The Final German Offensive* (London: Osprey Publishing Ltd., 1991), 17-18.

70. Joseph Gies, *Crisis 1918* (New York: W.W. Norton & Co., Inc., 1974) 175-176.; Herman von Kuhl, *Der Weltkrieg, 1914-1918* (Berlin: Wilhelm Kolf, 1929), 2:361. Von Kuhl claimed thirteen divisions were involved in Eighteenth Army's attack. Asprey says eleven first-line divisions backed by seven reserve divisions. See: Robert Asprey, *The German High Command At War: Hindenburg and Ludendorff Conduct World War I* (New York: William Morrow and Company, Inc., 1991), 429. Herbert Essame agrees with Asprey's estimate. See: The Marshal Cavendish Illustrated Encyclopedia of World War I, 1982 ed., s.v. "Matz,The."

71. "Report of the Marshal Commander in Chief of the French Armies of the North and North-east [Pétain] on the Operations in 1918: The Defensive Campaign (March 21- July 16, l918), Part V, The Battle of the Matz, June 5-30, 1918," trans. Louis Pendleton, the U.S. Army War College, September, 1931, U.S.A.M.H.I.

72. Martin van Creveld, *Command in War* (Cambridge, MA: Harvard University Press, 1985), 183.; Gray, *Kaiserschlacht 1918*, 15.; During the entire month of June the German air arm had 487 victories for 150 losses. John Morrow, *The Great War In the Air* (Washington: Smithsonian Institution Press, 1993), 302.

73. Kriegstagebuch 75 Reserve Infanterie Division, Rangliste des Stabes, G.L.A.K.; Kriegstagebuch 75 Reserve Infanterie Division, 12 June 1918, G.L.A.K.; Heinz Guderian, *Achtung Panzer! The Development of Armoured Forces, Their Tactics and Operational Potential*, trans. Christopher Duffy (London: Arms and Armour Press, 1992), 96.

74. Rod Paschall, *The Defeat of Imperial Germany: 1917-1918* (Chapel Hill, North Carolina: Algonquin Books, 1989), 157.; John Toland, *No Man's Land: 1918, The Last Year of the Great War* (Garden City, New York: Doubleday & Company, Inc., 1980), 292-293. George Patton watched the battle.

75. Marquise De Foucault, *A Chateau at the Front, 1914-1918*, trans. George Ives (Boston: Houghton Mifflin Co., 1931), 293.

76. Toland, *No Man's Land*, 293

77. United States War Department General Staff, *Histories of 251 Divisions*, 527.

78. Erich von Ludendorff, *Ludendorff's Own Story*, 2 vols. (New York: Harper & Brothers, Publishers, 1919), 2: 272.

79. Terraine, *First World War*, 170-171.; H. Essame, *The Battle For Europe, 1918*, (London: B.T. Batsford, 1972), 76-77.; Crown Prince William wrote in his memoirs that "in those days of June, 1918, the fate of the war hung by a hair." William, Crown Prince of Germany, *My War Experiences* (New York: Robert McBride & Co., 1923), 326.; See also: Winston Churchill, *The World Crisis* (New York: Charles Scribner's Sons, 1927), 4: 183.

80. Gudmundsson, *Stormtroop Tactics*, 145; Ellis, *Eye-Deep in Hell*, 181; Ludendorff, *Ludendorff's Own Story*, 2: 216.

81. Fritz Nagel, *Fritz: The World War I Memoirs of a German Lieutenant*, ed. Richard Baumgartner (Huntington, West Virginia: Der Angriff Publications, 1981), 106.

82. Princess Evelyn Blücher, *An English Wife in Berlin* (London: Constable, 1920), 253.

83. Weintraub, *Stillness Heard Round the World*, 387.

84. Ibid., 385.

85. Blaskowitz Interrogation CCPWE #32/DI-43, 28 July 1945, Records of U.S. Theaters of War, World War II, R.G. 332, N.A.; Blaskowitz Interrogation Report, 5 June 1945, First Canadian Army Intelligence Periodical. No. 4, vol. 10,655, File 215C1.023, R.G. 24, P.A.C.; Blaskowitz, Johannes: 201 Personnel File: Detention Report, Office of the Chief of Counsel for War Crimes, R.G. 238, N.A.

86. MS#B-308 (Zimmermann), R.G. 338, N.A.

87. Blaskowitz Interrogation Report, 5 June 1945, First Canadian Army Intelligence Periodical. No. 4, vol. 10,655. File 215C1.023, R.G. 24, P.A.C.

88. NOKW 141, Blaskowitz, M-898/28/0161, R.G. 238, N.A.

89. Blaskowitz Interrogation CCPWE#32/DI-43, 28 July 1945, R.G. 332, N.A.

90. Franz Halder, Eidesstattlich Erklärung, undated, circa 1947, *Collection Koepcke*, Copy in author's possession.

91. "Re: von Rundstedt," John Toland Papers, Series 2, "Adolf Hitler," Ro-Rz Folders, Franklin Delano Roosevelt Library, Hyde Park, New York; Ulrich von Hassell, *The Von Hassell Diaries: 1938-1944; The Story of the Forces Against Hitler Inside Germany, As Recorded by Ambassador Ulrich von Hassell, a Leader of the Movement* (Garden City, New York: Doubleday & Company, Inc., 1947), 80.

92. MS#B-308 (Zimmermann), R.G. 338, N.A.; Brett-Smith, *Hitler's Generals*, 44.

93. MS#P-031a (Kesselring), R.G. 338, N.A.

94. Kurt Hesse, "Collapse of the German Western Front 1944," No File Indicated, R.G. 165, N.A.

95. Blaskowitz Interrogation Report, 5 June 1945, First Candian Army Intelligence Periodical. No. 4, vol. 10,655. File 215C1.023, R.G. 24, P.A.C.

96. Ibid; "German Commanders in the West: No. 3, Blaskowitz;" Weekly Intelligence Summary No. 8, Records of Allied Operational and Occupation Headquarters, World War II, General Staff G-2 Division Intelligence Reports, 1942-45, R.G. 331, N.A.

97. Blaskowitz File, M.I.D., M.I.S., Who's Who Branch, 1939-1945, Entry 194, R.G. 165, N.A.

98. Blaskowitz Interrogation CCPWE#32/DI-43, 28 July 1945, R.G. 332, N.A.; See also: Kurt Lang, "Bureaucracy in Crisis: A Role-Analysis of German Generals Under Hitler" (M.A. Thesis, University of Chicago, 1952), 278-279.

99. Blaskowitz Interrogation Report, 5 June 1945, First Canadian Army Intelligence Periodical. No. 4, vol. 10,655. File 215C1.023, R.G. 24, P.A.C.

100. Adolf von Schell, *Battle Leadership* (Columbus, Georgia: The Benning Herald, 1933), 87.

101. Blaskowitz Interrogation Report, 5 June 1945, First Canadian Army Intelligence Periodical. No. 4, vol. 10,655. File 215C1.023, R.G. 24, P.A.C.; See: J. Nothaas, *Social Ascent and Descent Among Former Officers in the German Army and Navy After the World War*, trans. A. Lissance (New York: Works Progress Administration, 1937), passim.

CHAPTER III

DEFEAT: WEIMAR DEMOCRACY

GERMANY, NOVEMBER 1918: "A world has come to an end ...,"[1] observed Walter Gropius, Germany's premier architect. And so it had indeed. Revolution broke out in Germany; the Kaiser abdicated and fled to Holland. On the Unter-den-Linden in Berlin, the crowds sang the "Internationale."[2]

Revolution was anathema to Germany's professional officers. Nationalistic and conservative at heart, the officers were repulsed by the revolution, especially by its left wing. There was ample precedent for their feelings. General Albrecht von Roon had felt similarly in 1861 when he spoke of an earlier flirtation with liberal democracy, with parliamentary "Revolution":

> There is nothing worse for Prussia than its absorption into the doctrinaire swindle. Out of the mud-bath of a new revolution Prussia can emerge with new strength; in the sewer of doctrinaire liberalism she will rot without redemption.[3]

The abdication of the Kaiser and his flight to the Netherlands suddenly deprived the officer corps of the "spiritual and ideological centre on which its whole existence rested."[4] The special relationship of the officer with the monarchy was finished. The centeredness of the officer was shaken violently—more violently perhaps than in four years of war—and thrown off balance. For four years of war there had been news only of victories in both east and west. Suddenly there was defeat and disconnection. It was a profound shock; many officers found it

63

impossible to adjust to the changes. In October and November 1918 staff officers had been crying "at the thought that the invincible German Army had been defeated." Few had had the slightest idea that defeat was possible.[5]

Ludwig Beck, later Chief of the Great General Staff, was then a major at the Headquarters of Army Group Crown Prince and expressed what many officers experienced emotionally when he wrote,

> What we all without exception have lived through during the last weeks is so enormous that one often believes one is still dreaming. At the most difficult moment of the war the ... long prepared revolution has attacked our rear .... I do not know of any revolution in history that has been undertaken in so cowardly a manner .... It is poisonous if the people in the rear, most of whom never heard a shot, ... fabricate a contrast between officer and private soldier. And it is the worst thing they can do, to undermine the authority of the officer; it leads directly into anarchy .... For an officer like myself and many thousands who live through this, the decline of our army is something dreadful ....[6]

Beck knew that defeat was inevitable but nevertheless argued from his heart that "we could have held a shorter line ... if we had had the whole-hearted support of the home front. We could thereby have forced the enemy to decide whether to make peace right away or extend the war to 1919 ...."[7] Along with so many others Beck found it impossible to admit defeat in the field and anticipated the claim that the army had been stabbed in the back.

Germany's armies retreated to the fatherland. The variety of experiences which some other officers of Blaskowitz's rank had exemplified the division and chaos in the Germany to which Blaskowitz returned. Captain Erhard Milch, later a Luftwaffe Field Marshal, for example, marched the men of his squadron across the border from France into Aachen. In his diary he wrote: "Into Germany—not one of the swine welcomes us back—only the little children wave." His contempt for the revolutionaries was boundless. At the town hall, Milch met a revolutionary council of soldiers, sailors and workers with red armbands. He told them: "I would advise you to get rid of your red arm bands if you value your lives. There's a division loyal to the Kaiser not far behind, shooting every revolutionary they lay hands on."[8]

Mutual recrimination was the order of the day. Soldiers blamed the revolutionaries for the betrayal and stab-in-the-back while revolutionaries blamed officers for all the costs and losses of the war. In the streets of many German cities crowds surrounded officers, spat at them and tore the epaulets from their uniforms. Many officers were insulted and humiliated. Others were attacked, beaten and even killed.[9] On 15 November Count Harry Kessler, in Berlin, thought it remarkable when he saw an officer at Potsdamer Platz wearing his epaulets.[10] Some officers even had their epaulets torn off while still in occupied enemy territory.[11]

Captain Heinz Guderian, subsequently a famous tank commander, wrote to his wife Gretel from Munich: "Our beautiful German Empire is no more." He continued bitterly,

> Villains have torn everything to the ground... All comprehension of justice and order, duty and decency, seems to have been destroyed. The Soldier's Council still suffers from teething troubles ... and makes ridiculous regulations ... I only regret not having civilian clothing here in order not to expose to the jostling mob the clothes which I have worn with honour for twelve years.[12]

Across Germany there were a wide range of responses to the return of the defeated Army. In some towns along the Rhine there were "seas of flags and bunting." Banners welcoming the troops were sometimes accompanied by military bands playing loudly. In Cologne, on the other hand, revolutionaries stood next to the army general reviewing the marching troops and the band stayed silent. People lined the streets and watched in silence. Only the cacophony of the hob-nailed boots on the pavement interrupted the silence. Crunch-crunch-crunch, was the only music.[13]

On 11 December troops returning from the Western Front were greeted in Berlin by Germany's new Chancellor, Friedrich Ebert. Cavalry troops with lances from which pennants flew, accompanied by a military band playing "Deutschland über Alles," were the first troops to pass in review at the Brandenburg Gate. "I salute you," Ebert declared, "who return unvanquished from the field of battle."[14] Many embittered Germans who could not accept defeat as a reality seized this "official" explanation of the lost war—an explanation whose acceptance later grew to gigantic proportions. The seeds of the stab-in-the back legend were officially sown in fertile ground. Other seeds—seeds of hate—were sown also.

One observer who noticed the soldier's eyes felt they

> were hidden in the shadows ...[and] ... looked neither to the right nor to the left ... those thin faces, impassive under their helmets, those bony limbs, those ragged clothes covered with dirt! They advanced step by step and around them grew the void of great emptiness .... But here was their home, here warmth and fellowship awaited them—then why did they not cry out with joy? .... These men did not belong to us at all .... These men had come from a totally different world! Suddenly I understood .... Their home was the front—That was their homeland .... Yes, that is why they could never belong to us. That is the reason for this stolid spectral return .... They would always carry the front in their blood ....[15]

In Berlin Chancellor Ebert held a meeting in December 1918 at the Berlin Philharmonic Hall to appeal to officers to support the new government including its latest edict that all epaulets, medals, and insignia of rank be removed from uniforms. From the audience a twenty-five year old pilot in full uniform, wearing captain's stars and Germany's highest military decoration, the Pour le Mérite, walked onto the platform as an unscheduled speaker. The man was Hermann Goering. He expressed powerful emotions eloquently when he said:

> For four long years we officers did our duty and risked our lives for the Fatherland. Now we come home, and how do they treat us? They spit on us and deprive us of what we gloried in wearing. I will tell you this, that the people are not to blame for such conduct. The people were our comrades... for four long years. No, the ones who have stirred up the people, who stabbed our glorious army in the back.... I ask everyone here tonight to cherish a hatred, deep and abiding hatred, for these swine who have outraged the German people and our traditions. The day is coming when we will drive them out of Germany.[16]

In the meantime Germans lived in the "dreamland of the armistice period."[17] It might have been more reasonably called a "fool's paradise."[18] It was a time of unrealistic hope that the defeated fatherland would receive a "realistically" generous peace. In this interim the struggle within Germany over the nature of the new Fatherland continued. Naturally soldiers and officers were involved in the up-heaval.

In early 1919 in Barvaria the "Red Terror" ruled. The worst fighting was in Munich, but in Nuremberg then Captain Albert Kesselring witnessed the storming of the General Headquarters at the *Deutschherrn* Barracks by an armed mob. He called it the "most humiliating moment" of his life.[19] Kesselring had been ordered to Nüremberg to assist in the army's demobilization, an assignment similar to Blaskowitz's in Hanover.

Incidents such as that experienced by Kesselring were not uncommon. Even more common was the experience of another captain, Erwin Rommel, later famous as the "Desert Fox." Ordered in March 1919 to Friedrichshafen on Lake Constance to command Internal Security Company Number Thirty-two, he found his troops were mutinous Red sailors who "jeered at his medals and refused to drill." Rommel whipped them into military shape. In the following spring he was using fire hoses like machine guns against revolutionaries attacking the Gmund Town Hall. [20]

In the fall of 1918 in this atmosphere of defeat, revolution and despair, Captain Blaskowitz and his faithful aide-de-camp returned from France to Offenburg. Blaskowitz sent his aide-de-camp home with his horses in the chaotic conditions of revolution which existed in Germany.[21] He then reported for duty to Hanover, headquarters of X Army Corps, where he worked on army demobilization until the Autumn of 1919.[22] All around him chaos reigned and events moved quickly.

It is not known whether Blaskowitz's role in demobilizing the army at Hanover involved any dramatic episodes such as those experienced by Milch, Kesselring or Rommel. Hanover had been temporarily taken over in November 1918 by a revolutionary council, but there is no record of Blaskowitz's personal experiences in these events. What is known, however, is that the defeat of the fatherland which Blaskowitz experienced was followed on 30 April 1919, by the death of his father.[23] Blaskowitz regularly visited his parents' grave in the cemetary at Paterswalde for the rest of his life.[24]

During a visit to East Prussia in 1919 with one of his sisters, Blaskowitz spoke to a group of soldiers there, impressing them with his knowledge and his careful reflections upon events. He made it clear that he had not lost faith in Germany or the German soldier despite the lost war. He impressed his audience with his belief that justice would ultimately prevail. Such convictions must have been refreshing at such a difficult time when so many others were despondent.[25]

In June the Treaty of Versailles was signed, two months later the Weimar Republic's constitution was proclaimed. For Blaskowitz the defeat of the fatherland and the death of his father may have seemed like lines of parallel grief. Worse still, humiliation was on the horizon. Food shortages, chaotic transport, and shortages in the coal and electricity supply were bad enough. They were compounded by "strikes, dissension and uncertainty." The mood of Germany was one of "gloom and vexation."[26]

In the fall of 1919 Captain Blaskowitz was transferred to Stuttgart where he was assigned as a General Staff officer to the headquarters of the Fifth Military District.[27] Stuttgart had been an important Spartacist center since the summer of 1918 when it had acted as a collection point for Army deserters.[28] Undoubtedly sensitive to the "humiliation" of Germany and especially of the army, in Stuttgart he probably witnessed the continued humiliation of the new Weimar government, so pathetic in its weakness, during the events of the following year.

On 13 March 1920 a right-wing revolution nominally headed by Wolfgang Kapp, supported by two brigades of troops marked for demobilization led by Hermann Ehrhardt, seized Berlin. President Ebert asked the army chief of staff for assurance of army support. General Hans von Seeckt replied that, "he would never permit Berlin to be presented with the spectacle of their soldiers fighting each other with live ammunition."[29] Without army support Ebert and his ministers had no choice but to flee. A convoy of cars left Berlin at five A.M. for Dresden.

Ebert and his colleagues traveled to Dresden but found the atmosphere in the local army commander's office inhospitable and continued their flight to Stuttgart. Lacking the united support of the army high command, Ebert issued a proclamation to the working class calling for a general strike to defend the Republic.[30] In Stuttgart Blaskowitz's commanding officer, General von Bergmann, declared his support for the Ebert government and his opposition to the putschists led by Kapp.[31]

Coincidentally, Blaskowitz was well situated to view the government's pitiable weakness. Although his reaction to these events is unknown, it is clear that other officers had strong emotions. Guderian, for example, wrote to his wife about the "cowardice, stupidity and weakness of this lamentable government."[32] However critical of the government, most officers nevertheless did not support the putsch.[33] Five days later, 18 March, the Kapp Putsch collapsed amid the general strike and the government returned to Berlin. It had not been an interlude which increased the government's prestige. As Count Kessler observed in his diary: "It all smacks more of farce than history."[34]

Ironically the success of the general strike encouraged the most radical socialists, the Spartacists, to attempt once again to seize the government. But Ebert turned to the army and the *Freikorps*, irregular volunteer troops, mostly combat veterans, to put down this "revolution." Western Germany, especially the Ruhr cities, had been taken over by an "army" of fifty thousand socialists inspired by the Bolshevik success in Russia. Though less extreme, the situation was similar in central Germany.[35] Regular army units took part in crushing the revolt in Central Germany and Blaskowitz took part in the fighting although nothing more is known than these few skeletal facts.[36] Whatever his role in suppressing the uprising, it is clear that his superiors were pleased with him. On 1 January 1922 he was promoted to major.[37]

Nothing is known of Blaskowitz's view of the new German government at Weimar in its early years. Many professional officers in the *Reichswehr*, however, seem to have remained monarchists throughout the period of Weimar democracy. Ludwig Beck, for example, despised the Weimar government for its instability and its humiliation of the army through the Versailles Treaty and probably remained a monarchist at heart as did many officers.[38]

The Weimar government not only was an object of hostility to the left wing but was perhaps even more hated by the right-wing. One anonymous history professor later recalled:

> I remember one day when Ebert came to visit our town, ... and all along the streets that his car was to travel, the shopkeepers hung out underwear from their windows. There were a few flags that the

authorities had put up, of course, but all along the President's path, he had to see the shopkeepers' underwear.[39]

Weimar democracy seems to have been thought of as a foreign government imposed by the victors of the Great War. The military provisions of the Versailles Treaty were commonly considered humiliating. "Heerlos, Wehrlos, Ehrlos" (disarmed—defenseless—dishonored) was one of the catch-phrases of the interwar years.[40] Defeat, revolution and inflation were to make these traumatic years indeed for Germany. The inflation was so severe that "all previous ideas concerning the worth of money were destroyed. All money seemed worthless; the money of one day would buy nothing the next."[41] The mark tumbled from 64 to the dollar to 4.2 trillion to the dollar. The price of a meal rose while it was eaten. A sum of money adequate to purchase dinner one day was barely enough for a cup of coffee the next day.[42]

By 1924 the country seemed to be relatively more stable than in the beginning of the decade. Blaskowitz was transferred to garrison duty at Ulm on the Danube where he commanded the 3rd infantry battalion of the 13th Infantry Regiment. In 1926 he was promoted to the rank of Lieutenant-Colonel. The following year he became Chief of Staff of the Fifth Infantry Division at Stuttgart; promotion to Colonel came the next year. After a brief period as Commander in Baden in 1930 he was made a regimental commander at the beginning of December 1930.[43]

The new assignment, command of the 14th Infantry Regiment, proved to be the happiest of Blaskowitz's life.[44] The regimental garrison was located at Constance on Lake Constance, where Germany, Austria and Switzerland meet. Constance is an old Roman fortification established in 41 A.D. by the Emperor Claudius on the lake shore where the Rhine River begins to flow northward. It is an area of unusual scenic splendor: the striking beauty of the water contrasts charmingly with the snow-capped Alpine peaks to the south. Mild climate and plentiful sunshine make the area most pleasant. Blaskowitz loved the out of doors. Hiking and enjoying nature were great pleasures to him.[45] His assignment at Constance was his good fortune.

The 14th Infantry Regiment, nicknamed the "Sea Hares," was an old, traditional southwestern German military unit and one might think an East Prussian soldier would find the relocation and different mentality of this part of Germany alien to his ways. Blaskowitz proved to be a welcome surprise. The regiment found him quite to its liking. One of the regiment's junior officers later stated "[H]e could actually lead the 'Seehasen' as a person and as a soldier. The men from East-Prussia usually are cut from a different wood, a more strong and durable and harder wood."[46]

Blaskowitz found a home here. For his part, although he was an East Prussian by birth, "he felt himself in no way an East Prussian and his accent and vocabulary showed him to be saturated in the life of the happier Southwestern parts of the Reich." He compared the "dour, stolid, cold and uncivilized East of Germany unfavorably with the happier, less hard and more tutored life of the richer and more gracious West [of Germany]."[47] He was an unusually cultured man among German officers despite his Spartan upbringing.[48] He loved classical music, opera and the arts.[49] It was not long after his assumption of command of the regiment that Blaskowitz's personal qualities— "warmth, dedication, courage and faith"—were recognized. Within a few years he would be given the honorary title of "Father of the Regiment."[50]

These last years of the Weimar Republic were the final quiet time in Blaskowitz's life and it was a time when the most private parts of his personality revealed themselves. Approaching fifty years of age in 1930 when he became commander of the "Sea Hares" in Constance, he had, according to those who knew him well at that time, developed a "winning charm and pleasant manner that was heartwarming ...." One source said that "the one category that was most impressive about his character was the fact that he was completely incorruptible about the duties ... and ... ethics of a soldier."[51]

Together with his wife Anna, Blaskowitz opened his home to the officers under his command. On one occasion he invited two junior lieutenants to lunch on Sunday. By this time he had assumed a fatherly role toward many junior officers. After he had lunch with Lieutenants Gaudig and Michelly he announced to them: "I will retire now for a brief nap. You go ahead and make yourselves comfortable. Afterward we will have coffee together."[52]

Very much a traditional soldier, Blaskowitz was nevertheless very "modern" in his down-to-earth open manner with younger subordinates.[53] The lesson of the "mistake of distance" between high-ranking officers and enlisted men in the German Army which had proved so explosive in November 1918 had been fully digested by officers such as Blaskowitz.[54] Or perhaps he was only following the fatherly example that had been set for him by Field Marshal MacKensen at the Osterode Garrison during his early days in Infantry Regiment 18.

These were halcyon days for Blaskowitz. At a time when relations between the army and the government and press were sometimes troubled in other parts of Germany, Blaskowitz was always able to maintain good relations—a challenge to which his predecessor had not always been equal.[55] He had the facility for speaking brilliantly, saying just the right words at the right time.[56]

Within the regiment, matters went along with equal smoothness. Although he could be stern and demanding of his subordinates he seems to have had that indefinable leadership characteristic of being able to inspire devotion and loyalty among his men. As one of them wrote later: "We felt his heart underneath his sternness." It may have been during this time that he began to acquire a reputation as being "clever but good natured."[57]

Middle age was a time in Blaskowitz's life when the full fruits of his youthful endeavors became apparent in his character. During his years as a cadet and a junior officer there had been dramatic changes in the nature of German Army officers. The finest traditions of Prussia were represented until the reign of Wilhelm II by officers who were an "unostentatious lot," thoroughly loyal to their King, and profoundly earnest about their careers as military men. As a class, army officers

> ...lived simply, avoided lavish display, and prided themselves on being representatives of those Prussian traditions of frugal, pious, and sober living that had brought the Kingdom intact through the ordeal of the Seven Years' War ...Economy, piety, solid and sober conduct in private life were the hallmarks ... [of this tradition].[58]

In the "Gilded Age," during the rule of Wilhelm II, wealth had become perhaps too important a factor among officers and changes in values had transformed the officer corps. Blaskowitz came from the older, more solid traditions, which were silently but irrevocably passing into history. In a lifetime of dramatic and dynamic change followed by the cataclysmic and accelerated metamorphosis of the officer corps, Blaskowitz was a stable factor representing the best of the old traditions.

During the last years before Hitler came to power there is no evidence of turmoil in Blaskowitz's relationship with the world. He followed the simple non-political path prescribed for soldiers and looked neither to the left nor to the right.

Reflecting retrospectively on the last half-decade before Hitler attained power—years of political turmoil and economic depression—Blaskowitz admitted to following the typical non-political path of German officers.He "had no contact ... with the fermenting national socialist movement or, indeed, with any political life, being glad of having a job to do and of being cut off by official duty from the world around." He described his life as "Musschränke," a word which gives the keynote to the man's character and means "the box whose containing walls are made of don'ts and duty." Especially at Constance "away from the toil and turmoil of contemporary German life," he lived "as on an island," and was "not interested in politics and ... happily content just to be in the army."[59] Though he apparently wished only to be exclusively a soldier "politics" became an ever more frequent invader into Blaskowitz's non-political world.

In the turmoil of 1932 it seemed to some in Germany that the Nazis might try to seize power through violence. Blaskowitz, who was then commanding the 14th Infantry Regiment declared to his officers: "If the Nazis commit any stupidities, they will be opposed with all our force, and we shall not recoil from the most bloody conflicts. In particular, it is believed that the army and police are absolutely in the position to cope alone with these fellows...."[60] He explained the general political situation in the following way to his officers:

> The parties are Germany's misfortune. By their selfishness ... they prevent any stable and useful work of the government, which today is more essential than ever to lead us out of this misery. Therefore, the government must be freed from the chains of parliamentarianism, to be able to work independently, supported by the confidence of the president and the power of the Reichswehr. Both instruments of power symbolize most clearly the idea of German unity and are particularly suitable, on account of their position above party, working solely for the good of the state, to have a steadying effect:

73

they thus form the only basis for a government such as we need now. Brüning was not able to follow the president completely on this road that he intended to take for a long time, and in the end, Brüning became again more or less dependent upon the parties. Therefore, he had to go. Undoubtedly the N.S.D.A.P. has smoothed the path of Schleicher's policy in many ways. But its demand to exercise complete power is contradicted by the need of having a government above party. Therefore, it will be treated exactly like the other parties ....[61]

Like many Germans of the Weimar Era, Blaskowitz was apparently disgusted with the unending party struggles, constant changes of government and repeated crises. He seems to have felt, as did most *Reichswehr* officers, no rejection of the constitution and the Republic in principle but was more concerned with "the reality of the State." The prevalent view among *Reichswehr* officers was that "the State ought to be 'strong' and hierarchical in structure." Accordingly, the state should put national interest—the restoration of genuine sovereignty and the destruction of the limitations of the Versailles Treaty—above all else.

In this the Weimar Republic failed. The *Reichswehr* officers, however, applied the same standard of judgment to the right-wing parties and disapproved of them as well. Conservative if not reactionary, and powerfully nationalistic, they sought a Germany restored to strength.[62]

German soldiers tend to be conservative and traditional in their outlook. The views of many professional officers in the Weimar years echoed the thoughts of an earlier Chief of the General Staff, Alfred Count von Waldersee, who wrote in his diary in 1878: "how deeply I despise the national- liberal parliamentary majority, which does not get beyond theoretical verbiage and is pulling back the country further and further every year ...."[63]

Indeed the commander and most influential soldier of the *Reichswehr* in the Weimar era, General Hans von Seeckt, set the tone for the army. In 1923 he told the Chancellor that parliament was the "cancer of the time." It was not a coincidence that Seeckt was never present when the anniversary of the constitution was celebrated, because on these occasions "his duty unavoidably kept him away from Berlin."[64]

In Constance, far from the centers of power, Blaskowitz tried to remain apolitical. It is a measure of his success that when Schleicher was dismissed as Reich Chancellor in December 1932, Blaskowitz's wife Anna went to a neighbor to ask for an explanation of the political situation, pleading that she was unequipped to form any political opinions since her husband never spoke to her about politics. According to the neighbor's husband, despite frequent and intimate interaction with Colonel Blaskowitz, he was not able, at any time, to detect the slightest hint of sympathy for the fast-rising National-Socialist movement.[65]

Absence of political discussion in Blaskowitz's conversation—even with intimate friends—is perhaps less surprising than it might appear to be at first glance. During his formative years as a young Royal Prussian Army Officer, his opportunities for social chatter had most likely been limited to off-duty hours at officers' clubs. At such clubs officers with plenty of firm political convictions engaged, nevertheless, in little discussion. "Officers knew what they thought about the German political scene, but they seldom talked about it because they were in essential agreement on all points." Their political views were "beyond discussion." Besides, it was contrary to tradition to "talk politics."[66] Talk at officers' clubs had been "nothing but insipid stories about women, horses, dogs and the chances for promotion."[67] It was second nature to omit politics from conversation.

In the border garrison at Constance life went on much as it always had for both the garrison and Blaskowitz. On 1 November 1932 he was promoted to brigadier general. When the local officers offered their congratulations the General responded quietly in his humble manner: "Don't fuss about it so much, it is nothing but a symptom of old-age."[68]

Personal modesty and private perceptivity together made Blaskowitz an attractive personality along the lines of the old axiom that "still waters run deep." During the years at Constance he was privately, but "greatly impressed with the need of an eventual settlement of western territorial questions such as those of the Ruhr and Eupen-Malmédy." He was "dissatisfied with the size and equipment of the 100,000 man army ...," inadequate even to defend Germany. In these years, "he was daily impressed with the unemployment situation in Germany and the generally poor economic conditions."[69]

It is not surprising, then, that his ideas coincided to some extent with Hitler's publicly proclaimed goals to make Germany strong, to eradicate Germany's humiliation by the Versailles treaty, and to end her deplorable weakness during Weimar democracy. Hitler cunningly appealed to all Germans along such "national" lines of thinking and feeling. He indeed seemed to strengthen Germany, changing much from the very day he took office. It was called the "Nazi Revolution."[70]

Notes for Chapter III

1. Hochman, *Architects of Fortune*, 46.

2. John Wheeler-Bennett, *Hindenburg: The Wooden Titan* (New York: St. Martin's Press, 1967), 207.

3. F.L. Carsten, *Essays in German History* (London: The Hambledon Press, 1985), 198.

4. F.L. Carsten, *The Reichswehr and Politics: 1918-1933* (Berkeley, University of California Press, 1973), 8.

5. WO 106/5421, P.R.O.

6. Carsten, *Reichswehr and Politics*, 9.; Reynolds, *Beck*, 30.

7. Reynolds, *Beck*, 29-30.

8. David Irving, *The Rise and Fall of the Luftwaffe: The Life of Field Marshal Erhard Milch* (Boston: Little, Brown and Company, 1973), 10-11.

9. One of the more gruesome examples took place in Dresden when a crowd threw a Lieutenant Colonel von Klüber into the Elbe River, then fired on him and wounded him. When he tried to climb out they cut off his hands. See; Hans Schröder, *A German Airman Remembers*, trans. Claud Sykes (London: Greenhill Books, 1986), 202.

10. Harry Kessler, *In the Twenties: The Diaries of Harry Kessler*, trans. Charles Kessler (New York: Holt, Rinehart and Winston), 1971, 13; Schell, *Battle Leadership*, 83. See also: Ernst Udet, *Ace of the Iron Cross*, ed. Stanley Ulanoff, trans. Richard Reihn (New York: Ace Books, 1970), 96-97.

11. Schröder, *German Airman*, 204.

12. Macksey, *Guderian*, 23.

13. Weintraub, *Stillness Heard round the World*, 390-391.

14. Otto Friedrich, *Before the Deluge: A Portrait of Berlin in the 1920's* (New York: Harper & Row, Publishers, 1972), 30.

15. Weintraub, *Stillness Heard Round the World*, 405-406.

16. Friedrich, *Deluge*, 31; Leonard Mosley, *The Reich Marshal: A Biography of Hermann Goering* (New York: Dell Publishing Co., Inc., 1974), 66-67; Nigel

Jones, *Hitler's Heralds: The Story of the Freikorps, 1918-1923* (London: John Murray (Publisher's, Ltd., 1987), 13.

17. James Diehl, *Paramilitary Politics In Weimar Germany* (Bloomington, Ind.: Indiana University Press, 1977), 47.

18. Macksey, *Guderian*, 26.

19. Albert Kesselring, *The Memoirs of Field-Marshal Kesselring*, trans. Lynton Hudson (London: William Kimber, 1953), 18-19; Kenneth Macksey, *Kesselring: The Making of the Luftwaffe* (New York: David McKay Company, Inc., 1978), 28-30.

20. David Irving, *The Trail of the Fox* (New York: Avon Books, 1978), 26.

21. Johannes Blaskowitz telegram to Johannes Koepcke, Offenburg to Bommelsen, Germany, 1 December 1918, *Collection Koepcke.* Copy in author's possession.

22. NOKW 2439, T-1119/31/0408-0411, Nuernberg War Crimes Trials Records-NOKW, R.G. 238, N.A.; Blaskowitz Interrogation, CCPWE #32/DI-43, 28 July 1945, R.G. 332, NA.

23. *Altpreussische Biographie*, 1975 ed., s.v. "Blaskowitz, Johannes Albrecht," by Gerd Brausch.; Jones, *Hitler's Heralds*, 22. Blaskowitz's step-mother, Luise Steiner, died on November 28, 1927 at Görlitz.

24. Froese, "Meine Begegnung Mit Hans Blaskowitz,"

25. "Porträts grosser Soldaten," *Kampftruppen*, NR.3 (June 1967): 94.; Msg 1/1814, BA/MA.

26. Carl Zuckmayer, *A Part of Myself*, trans. Richard and Clara Winston (New York: Carroll & Graf Publishers, Inc., 1966), 183.

27. *Bibliotheca Rerum Militarium Quellen und Darstellungen zur Militärwissenschaft und Militärgeschichte.* Vol. 15. *Stellenbesetzung im Reichsheer vom 16 Mai 1920, 1 Oktober 1920, 1 Oktober 1921* (Osnabrück: Biblio Verlag, 1968), *11.; NOKW 2439, Blaskowitz, T-1119/31/0410, R.G. 238, N.A.; Pers 6/20, BA/MA.*

28. J.P. Nettl, *Rosa Luxemburg* (New York: Schocken Books, 1969), 451-452.

29. Carsten, *Reichswehr and Politics*, 79.

30. Craig, *Germany, 1866-1945* (New York: Oxford University Press, 1978), 430; Wheeler-Bennett, *The Nemesis of Power*, 78.

31. Gordon Craig, *The Politics of the Prussian Army: 1640-1945* (Oxford: Clarendon Press, 1955), 379; Carsten, *Reichswehr and Politics*, 34.

32. Macksey, *Guderian*, 34.

33. Schell, *Battle Leadership*, 85.

34. Kessler, *Diaries*, 119.; Albert Seaton, *The German Army, 1933-45* (New York:, St. Martin's Press, 1982), 11

35. Waite, *Vanguard of Nazism*, 168-182.

36. Stahl, "Johannes Blaskowitz," 1: 41.

37. NOKW 141, M-898/28/0161-0164, R.G. 238, N.A.

38. Reynolds, *Beck*, 179.

39. Friedrich, *Deluge*, 168.

40. John Keegan, *Six Armies In Normandy: From D-Day to the Liberation of Paris, June 6th-August 25th, 1944* (New York: Viking Press, 1982), 243.; Matthew Cooper, *The German Army, 1933-1945; Its Political and Military Failure* (New York: Stein and Day, Publishers, 1978), 117.

41. Schell, *Battle Leadership*, 88.

42. John Putnam, "West Germany: Continuing Miracle," *National Geographic*, Vol. 152, No.2, August 1977, 158.; Hedda Adlon, *Hotel Adlon: The Life and Death of A Great Hotel* (London: Barrie Books, 1958), 139.

43. NOKW 141, M-898/28/0161-0164, R.G. 238, N.A.

44. "Blaskowitz, Johannes Albrecht;" Gustav Seiz, "Durch Kreuz-Zur Krone," *Der Seehase*, Easter, 1955. *Der Seehase* is the newspaper of the veteran's association of the 114th and 14th Infantry Regiments located at Constance. Correspondence and copies of *Der Seehase* in author's possession.

45. Herr Schrader, "Feierlichkeit Anlassich der Beisetzung des Generalobersten Johannes Blaskowitz am 14 Februar 1948 in Bommelsen," *Collection Koepcke.* Copy in author's possession. A somewhat shorter version may be found in Msg 1/1814, BA/MA.

46. Seiz, "Durch Kreuz-Zur Krone."

47. Blaskowitz Interrogation Report, 5 June 1945, First Canadian Army Intelligence Periodical No. 4, Vol. 10,655, File 215C1.023, R.G. 24, P.A.C.

48. Wilhelm Scheidt, "Biography Report [Blaskowitz]," 22 October 1945, Biographical Data Personnel Folders Series, R.G. 238, N.A.

49. Written information received from Mr. Nikolaus von Mach, Germany, August 8, 1992. Mr. von Mach was a close friend of Blaskowitz from 1932-1948.; Written information from Dr. Edward Hay, Königsdorff, Germany, August 24,1992. Dr. Hay was Blaskowitz's personal adjutant for part of 1941-1942 and 1943-1944, and spoke with Blaskowitz daily.

50. Seiz, "Durch Kreuz-Zur Krone."

51. "Personalveränderungen in der Konstanzer Garnison," *Bodensee-Rundschau*, February 1933. File No. SII/9240; Stadtarchiv Konstanz, Constance, Germany; Hellmuth Gaudig, "Im Gedenken an Generaloberst Blaskowitz," *Der Seehase*, 1976.

52. Gaudig, "Im Gedenken an Generaloberst Blaskowitz."

53. "Personalveränderungen in der Konstanzer Garnison."

54. "Extract From a Manuscript Study on the Subject of 'The German Reichswehr.'" No Report Number, No Report Date, M.I.D. 2016-1304/1, R.G. 165, N.A.

55. Personalveränderungen in der Konstanzer Garnison.; Seiz, "Durch Kruez-Zur Krone."

56. Ibid.

57. Ibid.; Hanns Möller-Witten, *Mit dem Eichenlaub zum Ritterkreuz* (Rastatt: Erich Pabel Verlag, 1962), 221.

58. Platt, "Place of the Army In German Life," 92.

59. Blaskowitz Interrogation Report, 5 June 1945, First Canadian Army Intelligence Periodical No. 4, Vol. 10,655, File 215C1.023, R.G. 24, P.A.C.

60. Hans Rothfels, ed., "Ausgewählte Briefe von Generalmajor Helmuth Stieff," *Vierteljahrshefte für Zeitgeschichte*, 2 (1954): 296-7.

61. Ibid.

62. Wilhelm Deist, *The Wehrmacht and German Rearmament* (Toronto: University of Toronto Press, 1981), 18-19.

63. Carsten, *Essays*, 199.

64. Ibid., 204.

65. Hans Gies, "Eidesstattliche Aussagen zur Anklage gegen Generaloberst Blaskowitz," 22 January 1948, Bundesarchiv-Militärarchiv MSg 1/1814, BA/MA.

66. Platt, "Place of the Army In German Life," 108.

67. Enders, "Social Structure and Ideology," 28.

68. Gaudig, "Im Gedenken an Generaloberst Blaskowitz."

69. Blaskowitz Interrogation, 9 November 1945, Biographical Data Personnel Folders Series, R.G. 238, N.A.

70. David Schoenbaum, *Hitler's Social Revolution: Class and Status in Nazi Germany, 1933-1939* (Garden City, New York: Anchor Books, 1967), passim.

CHAPTER IV

NAZI PEACE YEARS

BERLIN, 30 JANUARY 1933:

> The day passes like a dream. Everything is like a fairy tale. At seven o'clock Berlin resembles a swarming beehive. And then the torchlight procession begins .... Hundreds and thousands and hundreds of thousands march past our windows in never-ending uniform rhythm.
> The rising of a nation!
> Germany has awakened![1]

These were the thoughts of Dr. Joseph Goebbels, Hitler's Propaganda Minister, on the day the dictator became Chancellor of Germany. General Blaskowitz, who had been transferred to Berlin to become Inspector of Arms and Services, first met Hitler that very day.

Hitler had a hypnotic affect on many Germans, but apparently not upon Blaskowitz. Nevertheless, he was favorably impressed with Hitler as a person of "unusual talents." He thought Hitler "grasped things with unusual rapidity, saw the point quickly and was very alert and well informed on all technical matters. He also had oratorical ability ... [but] had no ability to judge people ... [such as] Ribbentrop and Bormann.[2] The irony in Blaskowitz's remark about Hitler's inability to judge people is striking. The Führer's opinion of him determined the course of much of the remainder of Blaskowitz's life and perhaps even his death. In the future Hitler's opinions would determine the course of Germany's future, but the dictator initially proceeded cautiously when it came to the German Army and its commanders.

On 3 February, Hitler met unofficially with the leading generals and admirals at General Kurt von Hammerstein's apartment at No.14

81

Bendlerstrasse. Although it is not recorded that Blaskowitz was present, it was noticed that Hitler was nervous until the dinner-party ended and he gave a speech in which he said:

> There are two possible ways of overcoming our desperate situation: Firstly, seizing by force new markets for our production; secondly, obtaining new *Lebensraum* for our population surplus. A peace loving public cannot stomach objectives like these. Thus, it must be prepared for them ....Democracy is a utopia, it's impossible. You won't find it in either industry or the armed forces, so it's not likely to be much use in such a complicated institution as a state. Democracy is the worst of all possible evils. Only one man can and should give the orders.[3]

It was a clever address, calculated to appeal to men who understood orders and respected authority.

Hitler's political genius kindled popular enthusiasms long dorment in guilt-and-shame-ridden Weimar Germany. He harnessed a passionate idealism and nationalism, and, on the darker side, provoked a virulent anti-semitism, for his own purposes. He restored pride and inspired a sense of power in many. "But to those not under his spell ...," there was a "bone-chilling" element to Hitler's charisma.[4] In the next weeks and months, a real revolution took place. Walter Goerlitz, an eminent German historian, observed and later wrote:

> Hitler had mastered the art of giving hope back to the hopeless, and, more important, of providing illusion to a people that wanted illusion almost more passionately than they wanted anything else. Hitler had accumulated a capital of love and reverence that made him a popular idol ....[5]

Hans Bernd Gisevius, a conspirator against Hitler, but not one of the inner circle and generally hostile to Germany's military leaders, described the mood of Germany at that time this way:

> Seldom has a nation so readily surrendered all its rights and liberties ... as did ours in those first hopeful, intoxicated months of the new millennium .... The lost war, continual unrest, the inflation ... unemployment ... all these things and a great deal more preyed upon the souls of sixty million people. And then it suddenly appeared that the pressure was relaxing. All distress of mind ... and misery of

body was to be exchanged for work, bread, and a good livelihood
....[6]

Nevertheless, Germany's new leader moved cautiously where the army was concerned. He flattered the *Reichswehr* leaders publicly, such as in his speech in the Reichstag on 23 March 1933 when he said:

> The protection of the frontiers of the Reich and thereby of the lives of our people and the existence of our business is now in the hands of the *Reichswehr*, which, in accordance with the term imposed upon us by the Treaty of Versailles, is to be regarded as the only really disarmed army in the world. In spite of its enforced smallness and entirely insufficient armament, the German people may regard their *Reichswehr* with proud satisfaction. This little instrument of our national self-defense has come into being under the most difficult conditions. The spirit imbuing it is that of our best military traditions.[7]

In the highest army leadership circles Hitler began to make some converts. By July 1933, Wilhelm Keitel, later a field marshal, appeared to be "fascinated" with Hitler. Keitel felt that Hitler "was a man who was determined to bring about an era which would lead us out of the deplorable conditions then prevailing." He agreed strongly with Hitler that the Versailles Treaty was a "dirty shame!"[8]

Blaskowitz later admitted that he, too, privately "more or less sympathized with the upward trend of events initiated by the new regime."[9] However, he did not reveal his "sympathy," not even to his intimates, but instead kept it strictly personal. He later admitted his recognition of the "necessity for a strong man, for a leader, for someone who appreciated the needs and necessity of a large German army ...." Despite his confessed sympathy for "a strong man" and the "upward trend of events," Blaskowitz refused even retrospectively to offer an opinion of National- Socialism.[10]

Although he had "a certain antipathy toward the Nazis on religious lines ...,"[11] General Blaskowitz was "basically neuter" in his orientation toward the Third Reich.[12] As a professional soldier he obeyed the orders of the government even if it were a Nazi government. His attitude appears to have been similar to that of the architect Ludwig Mies Van Der Rohe who was asked how he could design buildings for the Nazis when he did not share their politics: "Michelangelo was not a religious man" [sic] ..., he responded; "Yet he worked for the pope!"[13]

As Inspector of Arms and Services, Blaskowitz was responsible for the supervision of the service schools and training of officer cadets as well as inspection of ordnance. He had an enormous amount of work to do, but he found it fulfilling since rebuilding the army was one of his main ambitions. He worked in the *Reichswehr* Ministry in Berlin directly under Army commander General Werner von Blomberg. This period was a time which he enjoyed.[14] Germany soon began to rearm at a feverish pace and Blaskowitz was busy with his small role in the rearmament program.

Building four new schools for officer cadets, selecting teaching staffs and general supervision of the schools was a full-time job. Teachers were especially hard to find in the circumstances surrounding the Army's rapid expansion. There was little spare time in which to contemplate politics even if the inclination had been present.

Blaskowitz had thus far had a "fairly typical career."[15] In 1936 the French, who observed the German military both closely and anxiously, published a study of the German Army which summarized Blaskowitz the following way: "All of this, of course, is nothing outstanding and is not in any way an unusual career."[16] Nor had Blaskowitz acquired influence or special prestige within the officers' corps."[17] Now, however, his career and professional life took a straight road upward.[18]

Along the upward road, however, events took place which later assumed greater significance than was obvious at the time they transpired. On 30 June of 1934 Hitler moved ruthlessly against a party faction led by Ernst Roehm, commander of the storm troops, and had him killed in the famous "Night of the Long Knives." Roehm's "Storm Troopers," or SA, a potential Party rival to the Army, was thereby decapitated. Retired generals von Schleicher and von Bredow were also executed. Most Germans applauded. Only Blaskowitz's old tutor, Field Marshal von Mackensen, protested, to no avail.

A great many officers privately admired Hitler's successes and his nationalism, particularly as the Führer often expressed it publicly through adulation of things military. Simultaneously, the same officers detested Hitler's followers, especially the SA, Hitler's "Storm troopers." Some officers called them "Brown Dirt," and welcomed their decapitation. Erich von Manstein, for example, embodied the "curious paradox of approval of Hitler and disapproval of the Nazis." He found the appearance, behaviour and manners of the Party pretentious and offensive. He detested the greed and arrogance of the "village Hitlers" on the local level. Hitler, on the other hand, had initiated the restoration of German greatness. According to General Siegfried Westphal, there was a "general tendency to place all unpleasantness and misdeeds" at the door of the Party. Frequently one heard: "The Führer knows nothing about it, you can be sure." Perhaps the passage of time "would dispose of the Nazi crudities."[19]

The similarity of Blaskowitz's feelings to those attributed above to Manstein and Westphal is verified by Franz Halder, who later recalled meeting Blaskowitz quite by chance in a train compartment in 1933. Halder remembered that Blaskowitz "expressed his dismay and strict abhorrence of the violence and the ostentatious and ballyhoo propaganda put forth by the National-Socialist movement." He was "very distressed about its leadership." Halder was "convinced from this moment on, that Blaskowitz was part of the political opposition, as far as his thoughts were concerned."[20]

The Führer encouraged the acceptance of the dichotomous perception that generals such as Manstein, Westphal and Blaskowitz had developed. Speaking frankly to his assembled generals on 10 September 1934, on the last day of the Nazi Party Day ceremonies at Nuremberg, Hitler declared:

> I know that you reproach me for a number of faults in the Party. You are quite justified for doing so. But please remember that Germany's intelligentsia failed to support me during the years of struggle, and that this leaves me to work with inferior assistants for the time being. Rest assured that I am going to reorganize the Party. Just as it takes years to develop a good officer corps, however, it will take a long time to perfect a corps of Party leaders.[21]

Among the generals Hitler's candor was on target, convincing and was received approvingly. Hitler had planted the seeds of the myth that he was without sin, despite the sinful actions of his underlings.

Those officers who thought the Army's sole rival had been eliminated did not have to wait long to discover their error. In the next few years Hitler promoted Himmler's SS as the new and more dangerous competitor. By late 1935 evidence was discovered that the Gestapo had been "conducting systematic and extensive inquiries into the political views of Army officers ...." Some generals soon believed that the SS was "assembling dossiers on them." Hidden microphones were discovered in Army headquarters in Munich in 1938. When General von Blomberg was retired the safe in his office was found to be wired with microphones connected to Gestapo headquarters.[22] The SS was profoundly more threatening to the Army than Roehm's SA. Hitler had outmaneuvered his generals the same way he had his foreign enemies. Germany was becoming a police state for the generals as well as for the "man on the street." The SS threat was not obvious, however, as early as 1934.

When Germany's President, Paul von Hindenburg, died on 2 August 1934, Hitler assumed the office, simultaneously continuing as Chancellor. He immediately issued orders that the army take a new oath of loyalty. Ominously, the oath read:

> I swear by God this holy oath, that I will render to Adolf Hitler, Leader of the German Nation and people, Supreme Commander of the Armed Forces, unconditional obedience, and I am ready as a brave soldier to risk my life at any time for this oath.[23]

Speaking in the evening, *Generaloberst* Ludwig Beck described the day as "the blackest of my life."[24] General Guderian wrote to his wife that it was "an oath heavy with consequence! Pray God that both sides may abide by it equally for the welfare of Germany. The army is accustomed to keep its oaths. May the army be able, in honour, to do so this time."[25] Traditionally in Germany such oaths were taken in solemn public ceremonies, before family, friends, comrades and the assembled regiment. For many Germans such an oath, was the "positive embodiment of their honour."[26] There is no record of Blaskowitz's reflections upon the meaning of the oath, but there can be no doubt that an oath sworn to God was profoundly meaningful to so deeply religious a man as Blaskowitz.

Hitler's announcement of the first of a series of rearmament measures was made in 1935. When seven new corps' headquarters were later created for the expanding army, Blaskowitz was appointed commander of the Second Military District at Stettin, a position which he held until 1938. He remembered this time also as "happy, because the political party had given him work to do." Despite his lack of involvement in politics, he was so busy as a military man that although he was, "an ardent huntsmen, [he] gave up hunting completely in order not to waste time on non-essentials." "I have the strongest belief in the permanency of the German militarist soul ...," he declared. The Army was "the school for the German nation, so necessary for the good of the whole." He did not consider that a trained army was potentially an offensive weapon.[27] As he admitted later, the "rearmament of Germany was welcomed by me."

All officers of the army shared this attitude and, therefore, had no reason to oppose Hitler. Hitler produced the results which all of us warmly desired."[28] Clearly, Germany must be able to defend itself; perhaps even more especially so when the issue was the border problem with Poland. But that question could only be addressed later.

It was during this period that Blaskowitz achieved his masterpiece, development of the training ground at Gross Born, near Neustettin, where two divisions, "like two small towns of 30,000 men could be drilled and prepared in the German military traditions."[29] Ever since his days with the Alpine division, he had been a superb trainer of troops, and it is understandable that this duty and time was so satisfying for him.

Command of the Second Military District, headquartered at Stettin on the Baltic Sea, provided Blaskowitz with new insight into Germany's situation. Many defensive fortifications and anti-tank ditches were built along the "Polish Corridor" which separated East Prussia from the rest of Germany. On one occasion Blaskowitz had to arrange transport by sea for troops being transferred from East Prussia to Germany since they could not cross the corridor. The absurdity of this procedure made Blaskowitz feel that the problem with Poland had eventually to be solved, "no matter by what means. ..," although Germany, he thought, would not be strong enough to solve it by force before 1945 when the army should be fully rebuilt.[30] In the meantime, there was much taking place in Germany that brought satisfaction to the professional soldier.

The restoration of German prestige had European implications felt personally by soldiers such as Blaskowitz. In 1934 Blaskowitz was sent to Hungary and again in 1938 to Sweden—both times to act as Germany's representative at each country's army maneuvers. He also visited Rumania with Hermann Göring. However pleasant such duties may have been, they nevertheless contributed to the frantic pace kept by soldiers during these years. Such a pace kept them narrowly occupied, a fact undoubtedly welcome to both Himmler and Hitler.

Another gratifying duty was a speech he delivered on Sunday, 17 March 1935, at the dedication ceremony for a World War I memorial in Bommelsen, Germany, where his devoted friend and World War I aide-de-camp, Johannes Koepcke, made his home. During the 1920's and 1930's, Blaskowitz had visited Koepcke at least annually and the wartime friendship had deepened. Koepcke stood at Blaskowitz's side when Blaskowitz gave the speech and old comrades from the 75th Reserve Infantry Division were in the audience. Speaking of the pains of grief and loss borne by the surviving family members of deceased veterans, he said:

> God has meant this life of ours, everyone's life, to be filled and to have a purpose. And when, tonight, you will pray and have your own private conversation with God, then you will be able to find peace and not bitterness, and you will be able to overcome your painful memory. You will be able to say, in your own heart: 'God has given, and God has taken. His name lives forever!'

Blaskowitz had clearly been favorably impressed by Hitler's positive achievements. Revealingly, he continued; speaking about Germany in defeat and in the present and said

> [T]he whole nation was held together by grief and endurance, by pain and strain, by love and compassion the whole nation became one family. When the pain and misery did not seem to be bearable anymore, God was close. He gave us our new leader who was able to unify us ... and to make Germany into one community of people, who gave us self-respect and renewed our soul ....

Suggesting that "we need no longer be ashamed of ourselves ..., no longer feel guilty ... for now we have reappeared from the ashes and are going to start a new nation ...," Blaskowitz continued:

> The sorrow and woe of the years after the war is gone. We know where we are going. Toward a new future. God has been with us and He is no longer removed from us. We have God on our side.[31]

Many Germans were enthusiastic about their "Leader" in the mid

1930's. In fact his string of successes was impressive: repudiation of the Versailles Treaty, re-armament, withdrawal from the League of Nations, return of the Saarland, and achievement of "full employment." Indeed many Europeans admired Hitler at that time and it appeared that Nazism and Fascism might be the "wave of the future."

In March of 1936 Hitler boldly sent army units to reoccupy the Rhineland and his daring proved a ringing success.[32] Hitler's series of triumphs had made so great an impression upon Europeans that in the Olympic Games of 1936, held in Berlin, even the big French delegation marched past Hitler in the opening ceremony with their right arms raised in the Nazi salute. One German wrote: "Had I not seen it for myself I would scarcely have believed it, because in German families at that time the use or non-use of the 'German greeting' amounted to a confession of faith."[33] Even Winston Churchill remarked that although he hated Nazism, he hoped that if ever England lost a war, it would "find a champion as indomitable [as Hitler] to restore our courage and lead us back to our place among the Nations."[34] David Lloyd George expressed even more extravagent sentiments.

In March of 1938 Austria was annexed in a bloodless triumph after favorable results in a plebisite. German tanks decorated with flags and flowers were greeted along the march routes to Vienna by Austrian World War I veterans who pinned their decorations to their chests and saluted as the tanks passed.[35] But again Hitler's Army commanders had urged caution upon the Führer just as they had when Germany reoccupied the Rhineland. Again Hitler was vindicated in his gamble.[36] In Austria there was "just one great outburst of joy from everybody, give or take a few panicky Jews and other guilt-stricken gentlemen," commented Hermann Göring.[37]

Greater triumph followed in September of that year at the Munich Conference where Europe's great powers handed over the Sudetenland. Hitler's prestige soared. By this time he was already shouting in his speeches: "the miracle of our times [is] that you have found me—that you found me among so many millions! And that I found you is Germany's fortune."[38] General Blaskowitz's reaction to the Austrian *Anschluss* and the occupation of the Sudetenland was "one of pleased surprise that these two questions, both of which he construed as being justly settled in Germany's favor, were solved without bloodshed."[39]

While Hitler had enjoyed these successes, troubled relations with his own army reached a crisis early in 1938. It seems that Blaskowitz knew nothing of this impending crisis and was unprepared for the shock.[40] Indeed, "outside of Berlin, the number of prominent military men who before February 1 [1938] had even heard of the furor could be counted on the fingers of a single hand."[41] Nevertheless, General Blaskowitz was ordered to Berlin for an address by Hitler at 2 P.M. on 4 February in the main assembly hall of the War Ministry.[42]

Hitler's speech to the generals was a brilliant performance; his ability as an actor and speaker had been honed by repeated rehearsals. He combined truths, half-truths and clever lies to convincingly explain that the Third Reich's top two soldiers had been dismissed and resigned respectively. The Army's top two officers, Hitler alleged, had broken their officer's code of morality in a most disgraceful and odious way. Field Marshal Werner von Blomberg and Colonel General Werner Freiherr von Fritsch both departed under circumstances reflecting unfavorably upon the honor of the Army according to Hitler, who explained: "After such sorrowful experiences, I must consider anyone capable of anything."

Hitler announced the appointment of Walter von Brauchitsch as Army Commander and his own assumption of the post of War Minister.[43] Furthermore, Generals Wilhelm von Leeb, Günther von Kluge, and Maximillian von Weichs were retired and numerous other high-ranking officers transferred to different positions. On 1 November, Rundstedt also retired. In fact, it was a virtual decapitation of the army by the Nazi leader, the result of an ignominious intrigue begun by Himmler, Heydrich and Göring which Hitler exploited. Few army men realized it at the time.

The departure of Colonel-General von Fritsch meant that the Army, the last remaining non-Nazi bastion, could no longer resist Nazi domination. Strong reactions among the generals might have been expected and the Nazi leaders themselves feared a "general's strike" or mass resignations.[44] The accusations of homosexuality against Fritsch and the allegations that Blomberg's new wife had been a prostitute, however untrue, nevertheless shocked the officer corps into a temporary psychic paralysis. "The majority of officers averse to Nazism were like rudderless ships amidst swift currents." Although a few understood what had transpired, many others did not comprehend it for a long time.[45]

The German generals, therefore, did not react with unity. Referring to Hitler's speech, one of the generals whispered into the ear of another: "After hearing him talk, I could almost believe it."[46] Some generals apparently still did not comprehend the tale or the intrigues behind it. Guderian's reaction, for example, was that, "For the majority [of generals present at the speech], the true state of affairs remained obscure."[47] The later Field-Marshal Erich von Manstein related that the generals'

> ...attitude was due to ignorance of the true facts of the case, their inability as decent soldiers to believe the State leadership capable of such a base intrigue, and the practical impossibility in such circumstances of carrying out a *coup d'état*.[48]

Despite many difficulties, some of the generals began to work quite actively for von Fritsch's rehabilitation. Old Field Marshal von Mackensen, for example, repeatedly protested vigorously in writing to Hitler, demanding Fritsch's reinstatement. Hitler did not reply. Divisions of opinion among the generals became obvious.

General Blaskowitz was not among these who supported General von Fritsch actively. He "held to a reserved course of action."[49] This despite the fact that Blaskowitz "knew General von Fritsch very well personally."[50] Blaskowitz apparently did support Fritsch privately. He visited Fritsch at his home in Achterberg, not far from Koepcke's home, in the spring of 1938. "Thank God one can speak here!" said Fritsch. "Or do we have to watch for microphones here too? Let's be safe and not sorry ...." And he put the coffee-warmer over the telephone.[51] Regretably, but understandably, no record was kept of the conversation. Only the preceding fragment remains to tantalize us. Clearly, however, Blaskowitz had to realize, if he had not realized it previously, that his beloved Germany had become what historians would later call a "surveillance society."[52]

William Shirer, an American journalist living in Germany, described Gestapo spies as everywhere.

> No one, if he were not foolish, said or did anything that might be interpreted as 'anti-Nazi' without first taking precautions that it

was not being recorded by hidden SD microphones or overheard by an SD agent. Your son or your father or your wife or your cousin or your best friend or your boss or your secretary might be an informer for Heydrich's organization; you never knew and if you were wise nothing was taken for granted.[53]

After his experience at the hands of the Nazis Fritsch clearly took nothing for granted.

When von Fritsch was exonerated by his trial, he was appointed honorary Chief of Artillery Regiment No. 12 at the Gross-Born parade grounds near Schwerin in Pomerania, an area under Blaskowitz's command. The ceremonies took place on 11 August 1938. In the evening, General Blaskowitz gave a large party in von Fritsch's honor.[54] Apparently, General Blaskowitz was in sympathy with von Fritsch but was determined not to become involved in a dispute which was political in nature—certainly not at a time when a clash with Czechoslovakia was imminent.

The attention of the German generals to the von Fritsch crisis and trial had certainly been diverted when Hitler successfully ordered the march into Austria on 12 March 1938.[55] The trial itself was interrupted and resumed in a very different atmosphere after the successful *Anschluss*. Although numerous generals still considered tending their resignation, Hitler defused the threat by announcing on 28 May 1938, in a speech delivered by Brauchitsch at Barth, that an "unavoidable clash with Czechoslovakia loomed in the near future."[56] Hitler, addressing the generals, appealed to them "not to abandon the flag at so critical a time ...."[57] It was a very successful appeal.

Lack of unity within the *Generalität*, the ranking army generals, was evident not only with regard to the von Fritsch case but existed also in fundamental military questions.Blaskowitz was a conservative and traditional soldier and he took a strong stand in the debate over the role of armor in the new German Army. His position, along with such notable officers as Generals Ludwig Beck, Ritter von Leeb and Gerd von Rundstedt, opposed the development of tanks as a nearly independent weapon as advocated by generals such as Guderian and Hermann Lutz.[58] General Blaskowitz soon had the opportunity to express his views on the role of the tank directly to Hitler.

During the training exercises of August, 1938 the role of the tank within the German Army was under study and the General was one of those appointed to criticize the maneuvers. During the exercises, Hitler was present and witnessed an "awful muddle" resulting from "inept orders from the commander and staff of Panzer Regiment 1."[59] Although Blaskowitz passed quite lightly over the errors,[60] he did seize the opportunity to speak to Hitler.

The General explained his view that tanks were really a heavy infantry support weapon and not appropriate for an independent combat role. It was a view he shared with General Beck and other generals. Hitler disagreed completely and returned to Berlin "in an agitated state of mind." Although General Blaskowitz had an outstanding reputation in the Army, Hitler thought of him from then on as "a general with no capacity to lead tank units."[61] Hitler was not one to easily forget such disagreements; he would remember Blaskowitz.

In November of 1938, General Blaskowitz was promoted and transferred from the command of Military District II at Stettin to Dresden, where he became commander of the Third Army Group.[62] He made his permanent home there with his wife. Dresden was so close to the Czech border that it was obviously part of the staging area for any action by the Reich against Czechoslovakia. Hitler was not satisfied with the occupation of the Sudetenland agreed to at Munich that autumn. It proved to be only a matter of months before the occupation of the rest of Czechoslovakia took place.

Hitler, however, had given his word at Munich in September 1938, that he would respect the territorial integrity of the rump of Czechoslovakia. Chamberlain had announced "Peace in our time" to the world and many felt that the crisis had passed and they could go home and relax. "Home" now meant Dresden for Blaskowitz.

Dresden was called the "Florence on the Elbe" and was historically a pilgrimage site for devotees of art, opera and classical music. The long-time capital city of the Kings of Saxony, Dresden was famous for its baroque and rococo architecture and its legendary art collections as well as the city's symphony orchestra—the Dresdener Stadt Kapelle—which dated back to 1548.

It is perhaps not surprising then that Blaskowitz—a music lover—and his wife decided to make their permanent home in Dresden. The Blaskowitzes purchased a "sizable mansion" on Heideparkstrasse #8 in

Neustadt on the outskirts of the city in a neighborhood of upper middle class residences. A fashionable brick-stucco and wood house with a mansard roof, surrounded by a garden, the home had been built only about fifteen years earlier and clearly reflected wealth and prestige. Their daughter, Annemarie, had moved out on her own in 1935, but it was the last home the family ever knew together.[63] Even while the Blaskowitzes moved into their new home the pace of events moved on yet more rapidly.

Blaskowitz officially took over command of Army Group 3 at Dresden on 10 November 1938. It must have been a chaotic day to take over a new command because in the middle of the night demonstrations against the Jews had broken out all over Germany. It was called *Kristallnacht,* the "Night of Broken Glass." Jews were assaulted, their homes, businesses and synagogues burned or vandalized and windows broken everywhere. The pogrom began at 2 A.M. in Dresden but it is unclear if it continued throughout the day. Neither is it known what time Blaskowitz actually took command. In such circumstances it is uncertain whether he bore any particular responsibility for failing to take action to stop the pogram.

What is known is that nowhere in Germany did any general order out troops to end the pogrom. One source said; "The top army leadership had played deaf and blind. The meaning of this is clear." Decent Germans could not expect protection from "horrible excesses." The "cowed middle class stared at the Nazi monster like a rabbit at a snake. A general psychosis had been created under which the population was reduced to absolute submission ...."[64] "Arrests" and "excesses" became words frequently heard in Germany.

On the other hand, it is understandable that no officer schooled in the *Reichswehr's* traditions was willing to risk the inevitable civil war if the troops were called out. Since many of the enlisted men and junior officers by this date undoubtedly had Nazi sympathies, for the generals to have called out the troops against the legally constituted government would have required reliance upon an instrument of doubtful reliability in a matter of questionable utility.

Officially, the riots of *Reichskristallnacht* had been spontaneous. Goebbels issued a statement that the pogrom was "the justified and understandable indignation of the German people at the cowardly assassination of a German diplomat." Reichmarshal Göring added: "No Jew had a hair of his head touched .... Thanks to the outstanding discipline of the German people, only a few windows were broken in the riots."[65]

These were lies. The episode was a disgrace. As one thoughtful German wrote in his diary; "I am most deeply troubled about the effect on our national life, which is dominated ever more inexorably by a system capable of such things."[66]

Before very much thought could develop along these lines in Germany, people's attention was focused once again upon what Neville Chamberlain had described as "a quarrel in a faraway country between people of whom we know nothing."[67] On Monday, 13 March 1939, the German Air Force was placed on alert. On the following day Air Fleets commanded by Generals Kesselring and Hugo Sperrle moved to designated air fields in the vicinity of the Czechoslovakian border. There was talk of a "spring maneuver and parade over Prague ..."[68] Europe was again in crisis.

Notes for Chapter IV

1. Joseph Goebbels, *My Part In Germany's Fight*, trans. Kurt Fiedler (New York Howard Fertig, Inc., 1979), 208.

2. Blaskowitz Interrogation, CCPWE #32/DI-43, 28 July 1945, R.G. 332, N.A.

3. David Irving, *The War Path: Hitler's Germany 1933-1939* (New York: The Viking Press, 1978), 28-29. The dinner was organized by Blomberg.

4. John Toland, *Adolf Hitler*, (Garden City, New York: Doubleday & Company, Inc., 1976), 362.; Joachim Fest, *Hitler*, trans. Richard & Clara Winston (New York: Harcourt, Brace, Jovanovich, Inc., 1974), 417-448.

5. Walter Goerlitz, *History of the German General Staff: 1657-1945*, trans. Brian Battershaw (New York: Frederick A. Praeger, Inc., 1957), 273.

6. Friedrich, *Deluge*, 390; Hans Bernd Gisevius, *To the Bitter End*, trans. Richard and Clara Winston (Westport, Connecticut: Greenwood Press, Publishers, 1975), 93.

7. Adolf Hitler, *My New Order*, ed. Raoul de Roussy de Sales (New York: Octagon Books, 1973), 155.

8. Gene Arnold Mueller, "Wilhelm Keitel: Chief of the Oberkommando Der Wehrmacht, 1938-1945," (Ph.d Dissertation, University of Idaho, 1972), 1977.

9. Blaskowitz Interrogation, 9 November 1945, Biographical Data Personnel Folders Series, R.G. 238, N.A.

10. Blaskowitz Interrogation Report, 5 June 1945, First Canadian Army Intelligence Periodical No. 4, vol. 10,655, File 215C1.023, R.G. 24, P.A.C.

11. Blaskowitz Interrogation CCPWE #32/DI-43, 28 July 1945, R.G. 332, N.A.

12. Taylor, *Sword and Swastika: Generals and Nazis in the Third Reich* (New York: Simon and Schuster, 1952), 248.

13. Hochman, *Architects of Fortune*, 283. Michelangelo's spirituality and religion evolved as he aged and his anti-clerical remarks may have actually been made in piety. Mies Van Der Rohe was in error.

14. Blaskowitz Interrogation Report, 5 June 1945, First Canadian Army Intelligence Periodical No. 4, vol. 10, 655, File 215C1.023, R.G. 24, P.A.C.; "Blaskowitz, Generaloberst," 17 June 1947, M-1019, Roll 6, R.G. 238,

N.A.; Robert J. O'Neill, *The German Army and the Nazi Party, 1933-1939* (New York: James H. Heineman, Inc., 1966), 219 + 232.

15. "German Commanders in the West: No. 3, Blaskowitz," 13 May 1944, Supreme Headquarters Allied Expeditionary Force [SHAEF] Weekly Intelligence Summary No. 8, R.G. 331, N.A.

16. Berthold Jacob, *Das neue deutsche Heer und seine Führer: Mit einer Rangliste des deutschen Heeres und Dienstalterliste* (Paris: Editions du Carrefour, 1936), 105. Interestingly, the French publication then proceeded to point out General Ulex, a division commander under Blaskowitz was a "very capable man of the artillery who we are expecting to be outstanding in the future."

17. Taylor, *Sword and Swastika*, 248.

18. *Altpreussische Biographie*, 1975 ed. s.v. "Blaskowitz, Johannes Albrecht," by Gerd Brausch.

19. Paget, *Manstein*, 9-11.; Siegfried Westphal, *The German Army in the West* (London: Casell & Company, Ltd., 1951), 5-6.

20. Franz Halder, Eidesstattlich Erklärung, undated, circa 1947, *Collection Koepcke*, Copy in author's possession.; Johannes Koepcke, Eidesstattlich Erklärung, 18 December 1947, Bommelsen, *Collection Koepcke*, Copy in author's possession.

21. Weichs Interrogation, SAIC/FIR/55, 12 October 1945, Entry 179, G-2 Intelligence Division, Captured Personnel and Material Branch, Enemy P.O.W. Interrogation File, 1943-45, R.G. 165, N.A.

22. O'Neill, *German Army and Nazi Party*, 181.; Irving, *War Path*, 43-44.

23. O'Neill, *German Army and Nazi Party*, 55.

24. Ibid.

25. Guderian, *Panzer Leader*, 34.

26. O'Neill, *German Army and Nazi Party*, 58.

27. Blaskowitz Interrogation Report, 5 June 1945, First Canadian Army Intelligence Periodical No. 4, vol. 10,655, File 215C1.023, R.G. 24, P.A.C.

28. Blaskowitz, 3706-PS, *Nazi Conspiracy And Aggression*, 8 vols. (Washington: United States Government Printing Office, 1946), 6: 417, *Nazi Conspiracy and Aggression* hereafter cited as: *N.C.A.*

29. Blaskowitz Interrogation Report, 5 June 1945, First Canadian Army Intelligence Periodical No. 4, vol. 10,655, File 215C1.023, R.G. 24, P.A.C.

30. Blaskowitz Interrogation, 9 November 1945, Biographical Data Personnel Folders Series, R.G. 238, N.A.

31. Blaskowitz Fragebogen, 16 February 1947, 201 Personnel File, R.G. 238, N.A.; "Einweihung des Ehrenmals für die im Weltkrieg Gefallenen auf dem

Friedhofe zu Mommelsen [sic] am Heldengedenktage," 17 March 1935, MSg 1/1814, BA/MA.

32. O'Neill, *German Army and Nazi Party*, 128-130. Hitler made this daring move against the advice of Fritsch and Blomberg. It doubtlessly enhanced his opinion of his "intuition."

33. Alexander Stahlberg, *Bounden Duty: The Memoirs of a German Officer 1932-1945*, trans. Patricia Crampton (London: Brassey's, 1990), 79.

34. William Manchester, *The Last Lion: Winston Spencer Churchill*, vol. 1, *Visions of Glory, 1874-1932* (Boston: Little, Brown and Company, 1983), 1: 871.

35. Guderian, *Panzer Leader*, 50-51.

36. Wilhelm Keitel, *The Memoirs of Field-Marshal Keitel*, ed. Walter Goerlitz, trans. David Irving (New York: Stein and Day, 1966), 58.

37. David Irving, *Göring: A Biography* (New York: William Morrow & Co., Inc., 1989), 209.

38. Rudolf Binion, *Hitler Among the Germans* (New York: Elsevier, 1976), XV.

39. Blaskowitz Interrogation, 9 November 1945, Biographical Data Personnel Folders Series, R.G. 238, N.A.

40. *Trial of the Major War Criminals Before the International Military Tribunal; Nuremberg 14 November 1945—1 October 1946*, 42 vols. (Nuremberg, Germany: 1947-49), 12: 201.

41. Harold C. Deutsch, *Hitler and His Generals: The Hidden Crisis, January-June 1938* (Minneapolis: University of Minnesota Press, 1974), 277.

42. Ibid., 263; NOKW 2608, T-1119/33/01250, R.G. 238, N.A.

43. Deutsch, *Hitler and His Generals*, 262-265. Brauchitsch thought that his "first task was the rehabilitation of my predecessor, Colonel-General Fritsch." Brauchitsch Interrogation, 20 October 1945, M-1270, Roll 2, R.G. 238, N.A. Brauchitsch was inconsistent and hesitant in this matter as in so many other issues. It was perhaps Brauchitsch's influence, however, which allowed *Militär Wochenblatt* (1938, No. 13, 818) to publish the article, "Anniversary and a Day to Devote to Memory" commemorating Fritsch's fortieth anniversary as a soldier. The article ended with the declaration: "We hope that this upright soldier and talented leader will be ours for a long time and will be well." It was signed Wtz (Wetzell?).

44. Deutsch, *Hitler and His Generals*, 259-260.

45. O'Neill, *German Army and Nazi Party*, 172.

46. Gisevius, *Bitter End*, 243.

47. Guderian, *Panzer Leader*, 48-49. This public statement of Guderian's in his published memoirs stands in contradiction, however, to statements he made, under interrogation on October 4, 1945. He then admitted that the Fritsch-

Blomberg crisis made the position of the army weaker and that "This became particularly clear at the time of the removal of Blomberg and Fritsch; which was a disgraceful episode from every standpoint. On that occasion, Guderian felt the Army chiefs should have threatened a mass resignation if Hitler persisted." Recorded by the interrogator, Harold C. Deutsch and checked by Lt. Ford. Guderian Interrogation, 4 October 1945, M-679, Roll 1, General Records of the Department of State, R.G. 59, N.A.

48. Erich von Manstein, *Lost Victories*, ed. and trans. Anthony G. Powell (Chicago: Henry Regnery Company, 1958), 78-79.

49. Wheeler-Bennett, *Nemesis of Power*, 371. Though not an entirely reliable source, Curt Reiss suggested that Blaskowitz supported Hitler albeit with reservations. See: Curt Reiss, *The Self-Betrayed: Glory and Doom of the German Generals* (New York: G.P. Putnam's Sons, 1942), 29.

50. Blaskowitz Interrogation, USFET-MISC, 8 September 1945, R.G. 165, N.A.

51. Gert Steuben, "So blieb er ohne Marshallstab," *Das Neue Blatt*, 24 Februar 1953, 11-12, *Collection Koepcke.*

52. Robert Gellately, "Surveillance and Disobedience: Aspects of the Political Policing of Nazi Germany," in Francis Nicosia and Lawrence Stokes (eds.), *Germans Against Nazism; Nonconformity, Opposition and Resistance in the Third Reich* (New York: Berg/Oxford; 1990), 15-31.; Telephone communication "monitoring" was extensive in Germany throughout the Nazi era. Under the direction of the innocuously named "Research Office" in Berlin, offices for wiretapping telephones were established in fifteen major German cities and in 1942-3 in fifteen further major European cities in Nazi-controlled Europe under the cover name "Research Offices A." Donald C. Watt, "Introduction," in David Irving, ed., *Breach of Security* (London: William Kimber, 1968), 22-23.

53. William Shirer, *The Rise and Fall of the Third Reich* (New York: Simon and Shuster, 1960), 273.; See also: Adlon, *Hotel Adlon*, 235-236.

54. Taylor, *Sword and Swastika*, 160; W.E. Hart [pseud.], *Hitler's Generals* (Garden City, New York: Doubleday, Doran & Company, 1944), 33-35. Fritsch's gratitude to Blaskowitz was expressed clearly in his speech that evening. See "Rede am 11.8 abends im casino vor etwa 5—600 offizieren," Nachlass Fritsch, AL 277813-4, Imperial War Museum. Parties for retiring senior generals were customary but this one was "as elaborate as military ceremonial could make it." It obviously had attached to it a certain special meaning. Deutsch, *Hitler and His Generals*, 409-411.

55. Deutsch, *Hitler and His Generals*, 343.

56. Ibid., 402-405.

57. Ibid., 405.

58. Hart, *Hitler's Generals*, 16.

59. Macksey, *Guderian*, 73.

60. Ibid.

61. Nicolaus v. Below, *Als Hitlers Adjutant 1937-45,* (Mainz: V. Hase & Koehler Verlag, 1980), 116.

62. NOKW 141, M-898/28/0161, R.G. 238, N.A.; NOKW 2439, T-1119, Roll 31, Frames 0408-0411, R.G. 238, N.A.; "Blaskowitz, Johannes: History of Life," Biographic Files, O.C.M.H. Collection, U.S.A.M.H.I.; "Blaskowitz, Generaloberst," 17 June 1947, M-1019, Roll 6, R.G.238, N.A.; Pers 6/20, BA/MA.

63. Letter from Oberst Zumpe, Director, Army Museum of the German Democratic Republic, Dresden, to the author, dated 12 May 1989. Letter from Annemarie Blaskowitz dated May 15, 1992. Copies in author's possession.

64. Gisevius, *Bitter End,* 334. Although it may be coincidental, General Erwin Rommel also assumed a new command on 10 November 1938. In this case it was command of the Military Acadamy at Wiener Neustadt. David Fraser, *Knight's Cross: A Life Of Field Marshal Erwin Rommel* (New York: HarperCollins Publishers, 1993), 130-132. A summary analysis of my personal collection of German documents reveals that the following were also "coincidentally" transferred into new positions on the morning of 10 November 1938: Fedor von Bock, Karl Hollidt, Hermann Hoth, Walter Model, Hans Reinhardt, Helmut Stieff, Adolf Strauss, Kurt von Tippelskirch, Walter Warlimont, and Erwin von Witzlelen. Witzlelen became Commander of 2nd Army Group; Strauss, Commander of II Army Corps; Reinhardt, Commander of 4th Panzer Division; Model, Chief of Staff of IV Army Corps; Hoth, Commander of XV Army Corps; Hollidt, Commander of 9th Infantry Division; and, Bock, Commander of First Army Group. If these twelve men in key roles were "coincidently" assuming new positions on the morning of *Kristallnacht* it would appear appropriate to consider new research into this matter. In his pioneering 1952 M.A. Thesis Kurt Lang isolated the most significant eighty-four German Officers in the 1933-1945 period (See Chapter 11, note 92). The above twelve officers are all on Lang's list and constitute almost 15% of it. If the top six army commanders who were retired seven months earlier in the wake of the Fritsch Crisis are added to the total here it would suggest that the Army was not only decapitated seven months earlier in 1939 but also cleverly outmaneuvered at the time of *Kristallnacht.* Further complicating the situation of the Army at the time of *Kristallnacht* was the feverish rate of Army expansion. On 10 November 1938, for example, the 4th Panzer Division and the 1st, 2nd, and 3rd Light Mechanized Divisions were activated, a circumstance serving to absorb all of the attention of the newly appointed commanders and their staffs. See: Leo Niehorster, *German World War II Organizational Series* (Hannover: Leo Niehorster, 1990), I/1: 58,84,98

& 112. Perhaps, therefore the Army does not deserve the severe judgment pronounced by Gisevius and others.

65. Anthony Read and David Fisher, *Kristallnacht: The Nazi Night of Terror* (New York: Random House, 1989), 109.; Hermann Graml, *Anti-Semitism in the Third Reich*, trans. Tim Kirk (Cambridge, MA: Blackwell Publishers, 1992), 11-29.; As one German stated: "It's odd that the spontaneous rage happened to burst out ... exactly at the same time all over the Reich." Ruth Andreas-Freidrich, *Berlin Underground: 1938-1945*, trans. Barrows Mussey (New York: Paragon House, 1989), 21.; Ralf Reuth, *Goebbels*, trans. Krishna Winston (New York: Harcourt Brace & Company, 1933), 240.

66. Hassell, *Hassell Diaries*, 14.

67. Telford Taylor, *Munich: The Price of Peace* (New York: Vintage Books, 1980), 8.

68. U.S. Military Attaché, Berlin, Report #16,517, March 18, 1939, "Air Force Participation in the Annexation of Bohemia-Moravia to Germany," M.I.D. 2657-II-90/176, R.G. 165, N.A.

Generaloberst Blaskowitz *(Bundesarchiv-Militärarchiv)*

Frau Anna Blaskowitz and daughter Annemarie *(Collection Koepcke)*

Ruins of the church on the Notre Dame de Lorette
Ridge overlooking Ablain St. Nazaire where Captain
Blaskowitz took part in heavy fighting in 1914 and
1915. *(Imperial War Museum)*

Blaskowitz as a Reichswehr officer at Thomashof, Bommelsen. *(Collection Koepcke)*

Blaskowitz with Field Marshal
August von Mackensen
(Collection Koepcke)

Blaskowitz and Koepcke at
Church in Bommelsen, Germany
(Collection Koepcke)

Blaskowitz and Koepcke at the dedication speech for
World War I memorial in Bommelsen, Germany, 17
March 1935 *(Collection Koepcke)*

Blaskowitz and Hitler review a regiment at District of Pomerania Day Parade in Stettin, 12 June 1938. *(Ullstein Bilderdienst)*

Second Army Corps maneuvers at Gross Born Training Grounds in Pomerania on 19 August 1938. From left: Blaskowitz, Hitler, Generalobersten V. Rundstedt (half visible), V. Brauchitsch, and Major Schmundt, Army Adjutant to Hitler. *(Ullstein Bilderdienst)*

Hitler and Blaskowitz near the front by Lodz, Poland, 14 September 1939 *(U.S. National Archives)*

German victory parade in Warsaw, Poland, 5 October 1939.
From left: Schmundt, Keitel and Blaskowitz
(U.S. National Archives)

Generaloberst Blaskowitz and
Governor General Hans Frank,
20 April 1940
(U.S. National Archives)

Generaloberst Blaskowitz *(Bundesarchiv-Koblenz)*

Generaloberst Blaskowitz with Knight's Cross to the Iron Cross, 13 July 1940
(Bundesarchiv-Militärarchiv)

Generaloberst Blaskowitz with Army Group G Chief of Staff, Lieutenant General Heinz V. Gyldenfeldt, probably in France, 1944 *(Bundesarchiv-Koblenz)*

Generaloberst Blaskowitz *(Bundesarchiv-Koblenz)*

Generaloberst Johannes Blask-
owitz as Commander of Army
Group H, 28 January 1945
(Bundesarchiv-Militärarchiv)

Generaloberst Blaskowitz under
guard during his exercise period
after his arrest at Apeldoorn,
Netherlands, by the Canadian
Army, 14 June 1945
(Public Archives of Canada)

Surrender of German Army in
the Netherlands, 5 May 1945.
On right: Blaskowitz and Gen-
eral Reichelt. On left: Canadian
Lieutenant General Charles
Foulkes
(Public Archives of Canada)

Captive German leaders in the summer of 1945. Seyss Inquart is at left in third row; Blaskowitz is third from right in fourth row. *(AP World Wide Photos)*

Blaskowitz, Koepcke and the Bommelsen Trumpet Choir at Thomashof in Bommelsen, 7 September 1947 (*Collection Koepcke*)

Blaskowitz at Nuremberg prior to being handed his indictment as an alleged war criminal *(U.S. National Archives)*

Blaskowitz pleading "not guilty" at the Palais du Justice, Nuremberg *(U.S. National Archives)*

Palais du Justice Prison, Nuremberg *(U.S. National Archives)*

CHAPTER V

DRESS REHEARSAL IN CZECHOSLOVAKIA

PRAGUE: 15 MARCH 1939: "After hasty but simple orders and no long previous planning, General Blaskowitz led the German troops in the occupation of Bohemia."[1] It took a mere six hours for General Blaskowitz's troops to cross the border and to occupy Prague.[2] Blaskowitz received only a few hours notice of the invasion. Hitler had decided upon it after bullying the Czech president throughout the night. President Hacha conceded the German occupation after Goering threatened to bomb Prague.

Asked later about the morning of the invasion, Blaskowitz admitted the affair was impromptu.

> No, I had no idea of the invasion of Bohemia. When I drove out in the morning, my chauffeur asked me how long we would be on the road and for how many days he should prepare. I told him we would be back by evening so I had no presentiment of what was really happening.[3]

While it may be true that Blaskowitz may not have known this was the day the invasion would actually take place, the preparations for the troops had been made in advance.

Officials in London may have been better informed about Germany's plans to invade Czechoslovakia than Blaskowitz claimed to have been since British Intelligence learned on 13 March of German plans through a high ranking German Intelligence official code-named "A-54." The Czechs were able to burn their intelligence service Archives before the Germans entered Prague. Some Czech officers escaped to Britain.

Britain could do very little.[4] When the British Ambassador telephoned Hermann Goering to protest—Goering was in Berlin deputizing for Hitler, who had gone to Prague—Goering "professed well-feigned surprise that Britain should get worked up over 'such a trifle.'"[5]

The occupation met no Czech resistance, the biggest obstacle was the raging snowstorm on the country roads. It was really only a matter of assembling, equipping and marching the troops.[6] At least one anti-Nazi recognized it as "March madness."[7] It was the last of the *Wehrmacht's* "*Blumenkriege*," or "flower wars." The Czechs, however, responded to the occupation by Blaskowitz's troops with "silence and despair" instead of flowers.[8]

In this atmosphere, General Blaskowitz, sporting a "Hitler" mustache, became Military Commander of this part of dismembered Czechoslovakia. It was a command that lasted only three weeks. These three weeks, however, were filled with potential for crises.

When the first motorized column entered Prague at 9 A.M., having previously occupied the airport at Ruzyne, it was greeted by stunned silence from men on their way to work who apparently had not learned of the occupation and were astonished to see the grey-green uniforms. In the heavy snowstorm, no sounds were heard until the soldiers entered Wenceslas Square at the center of Prague. Small groups of waiting Czechs greeted them with whistles and raised clenched fists. Larger numbers of people in the Square were weeping and at 9:30 A.M., sang the National Anthem.

The soldiers kept excellent discipline and responded only by raising their arms in the Nazi salute when isolated Germans in the crowd shouted their welcome. Hastening to the Hradschin Castle, which towers over Prague and which was home to both Bohemia's kings and the Czechoslovakian president, German troops took up positions with armored cars and light artillery. Other detachments occupied key points in the city.

As the day wore on, announcements were broadcast by loud-speakers into the streets to help ease away the "bewilderment and dejection" of the crowd. The mood became more lively, the crowds more excited, agitated and hostile.[9] Little flags of the Czechoslovak Republic appeared in button-holes and loud, prolonged whistling and jeering of the German troops began, followed by volleys of snowballs being thrown at the tanks and armored cars. Platoons of Czech police kept the crowds from "springing at three of the armored cars and their embarrassed operators."[10] Both sides deserved credit for exercising restraint and allowing this potentially explosive situation to be defused.

The new German commander of the city imposed an 8 P.M. curfew and announced that all cafes, wine shops and liquor establishments were to be closed. It was a prudent safeguard against an incident facilitated by drunkenness on either side. Coincidently, it also made it easier for the Gestapo to begin its first round of arrests, mainly of German political emigres and Jews.

In the afternoon the Czech President returned to the Hradschin from Germany, where he had signed the Czech capitulation in the small hours of that morning. The German guards, who had replaced the Czech legionnaires formerly on duty, gave him the full military honors due a head of state. It was not until 7 P.M. that Hitler arrived, but within an hour his personal standard, displaying a huge swastika, was raised on the ramparts of the citadel.[11]

Entering the Hradschin Castle through the main gate, both General Blaskowitz and Hitler walked past a series of cast-iron statues on the stone columns between the iron fencing. One of the statues depicted two mythical giants locked in struggle. Legend has it that whoever controls Prague—symbolized in the Hradschin—controls all of Europe. High drama indeed!

Hitler and Blaskowitz both moved into the Hradschin Castle but for the Fuehrer the stay would be brief and filled with official activity. He issued a decree establishing a German Protectorate over Czechoslovakia. General Blaskowitz was named Military Governor of Bohemia—which included Prague—with Konrad Henlein, the Sudeten German leader, named as Civil Governor.[12] He met with several Czech leaders, including Hacha and the Lord Mayor of Prague, "to whom he promised the city a 'long period of peace and cultural development.'"[13]

Hitler then turned and entered the great banquet hall, "lit by countless candles, opened a window and walked out onto the balcony ...." Snow was still falling, it was very cold. "Hitler shuddered, re-entered the banqueting hall and shut the window." The dictator walked to a table set with Prague hams, cold meats, game, cheeses and Pilsner beer. In "an uncharacteristic impulse he raised a mug of beer and emptied it at a draught, grimaced and burst out laughing." It was the only time he was seen to drink alcohol; as if to celebrate his bloodless victory.[14] By 5 P.M. the next day, the dictator departed from Prague in his open automobile, flanked by armored cars and trailed by SS troops in black uniforms.

Blaskowitz too had a busy day. Calling for a meeting with the Cabinet Ministers of the former Czech state, the General utilized the occasion to set the tone for the military occupation which he headed in Bohemia. In a short speech, he assured the ministers that he:

> ...had the fullest understanding for the present position of the Czechs. They might be assured that he met them in a spirit of soldierly honesty, and he expected from the new government a genuine readiness to cooperate with him in establishing peaceful, just, and happy conditions in which all racial groups could live.[15]

It was clearly a statement of studied moderation designed to put the Czechs at ease. He had told the Czech leaders simply that he would act correctly and asked them to reciprocate in "our mutual interests."[16] Blaskowitz proved that he meant this through his actions during the next few weeks. One observer described Blaskowitz's relationship with the Czech leaders as discharged "with perfect military courtesy."[17]

Blaskowitz lived in the same part of the Hradschin Castle as Czech President Hacha and they met and talked frequently during the three weeks that Blaskowitz was Military Commander in Bohemia. In fact, Blaskowitz described his relations with Hacha as "extremely cordial."[18]

General Blaskowitz "moved about freely in the country without any security measures." He traveled around Bohemia to "see how the situation developed ...,"[19] visiting, for example, the Skoda Armaments factory at Pilsen on 31 March.[20] He utilized his visit to the Skoda works to deliver a speech to the German workers.[21] He attempted to work for reconciliation of Germans and Czechs, telling the German workers, "Let's go and meet the people of Czechoslovakia and let's not show them anger and hate, but instead treat them as human beings."[22]

As far as the General could see, the Czech government stayed in power and "everything went on as usual." Important governmental decisions, however, were submitted to him for his approval. His main duty was the disarmament of the Czech Army and the transfer of its war material to the Reich.[23]

Blaskowitz thought it was his "purpose to avoid all friction and difficulties in order to make it possible to transport all war material to Germany easily." "Part of the troops which marched into Bohemia were sent home gradually, because it was immediately to be seen that life would go on without great difficulties." He "refused to interfere with President Hacha in any way." Blaskowitz later stated that he only said, "Peace and order has to be maintained. Everything else is a matter for the Czechs to decide ...." In the General's "personal opinion, one should have left the Czechs alone as much as possible and interfere[d] as little as possible."[24] As Military Governor of Bohemia, Blaskowitz "acted with moderation toward the conquered people until replaced by Himmler and his Gestapo."[25] But the General's stay in Prague was not destined to be without further complications.

Although his speech to the Czech cabinet was intended to ease tensions and despite the exemplary conduct of the army—not a single case of misbehavior by German soldiers was reported[26]—Prague continued to be a powder keg. The Luftwaffe, grounded by the snowstorm on the day of the occupation, had flown continuously in squadrons over Prague on March 16, obviously intimidating the Czechs, but by no means lessening tensions.

Neither did Heinrich Himmler's presence in Prague serve to reduce tensions; quite the contrary. It was reported that on the first day and night of German control in Prague, 5,000 people on the Gestapo Black List were arrested.[27] Jewish owned shops were closed and the first concentration camp was set up in Milovice, sixteen miles outside of Prague. On the main street of Prague itself, four Jews jumped from windows in suicide leaps, one after the other in rapid succession. The Jew-baiting which marked the occupation of Vienna the previous year, however, was missing. In this strained atmosphere it would have taken only a small spark for large scale violence to break out. Germany's "Army Day," 19 March, could easily have provided the circumstances for such an incident.

"Army Day" in Germany traditionally meant parades in all Army garrisons. The previous year the German Army had paraded for the first time in Vienna with Hitler present before a cheering, adulating crowd of Viennese. The parade in Prague this year proved strikingly different.

All possible preparations were taken to avoid an incident. Buildings along the parade route were hung not only with the Nazi swastika, but in equal number with the red, white and blue flag of the Czech Republic. Prague's police lined the curb up to the review stand where Blaskowitz was to review his troops and take their salute. At the stand itself, brownshirted SA troopers reinforced the police. The review stand was also decorated with the Nazi and Czech flags as well as with the German Army colors. Although neither Hitler nor President Hacha were on the review stand, Blaskowitz and all other members of the Czech Protectorate's leadership were there voluntarily, including General Jan Syrovy, Minister of Defense in the last Czech cabinet and former Chief-of Staff of the Army.

Ten thousand German troops paraded past the review stand at Wenceslas Square: tanks, armored cars, tractor-drawn artillery, anti-aircraft guns rolled by and parachutists and infantry marched past for two hours until the parade ended at noontime. A bomber group flew overhead. According to one source, there appeared to be more troops than spectators.[28] The crowd took its cue from Czech general Syrovy, who entered the review stand with a stiff exchange of salutes with the German officers and then stood "impassive and obviously unhappy for the two hour parade."[29]

It was a bitter day for the Czechs and a day of restraint for the Germans. The parade took place between lines of silent Czechs. Czechs did not boo or hiss and Germans avoided any further provocations except the Nazi salute. Neither the Czech nor the German National Anthem was played—the only music was military marches. The silent parade march was an extraordinary expression of both the German determination to dominate Prague and the sullen grimness of the Czechs. Perhaps more than anything else it spoke of the determination of both parties to avoid further violence.[30]

The parade ended at noon, the crowd peaceably dispersed and many of the German soldiers received leave. They wandered through Prague in small groups without incident. The tension abated somewhat, but it was evident that it had not disappeared when, at the Church of St.

Mary that night, the service closed with worshipers singing the hymn of St. Wenceslas, the patron saint of Prague; it was the prayer sung for protection at times of national danger.[31]

The remaining immediate tensions in Prague apparently focused for the next several days on protest demonstrations around the Tomb of the Unknown Soldier on Vitkov Hill. Crowds stood around the tomb in the evening. Photographs of two Czech patriots, Dr. Jan Masaryk and General Milan Stefánik, were put on the monument and citizens placed "simple bunches of snowdrops which have been arranged in the shape of a heart ... [before the tomb]."[32] The Czech's deep patriotic feelings seemed to be focused upon this spot.

General Blaskowitz removed the fuse from this powder keg by having the photographs quietly removed and replaced with a large swastika dominating the scene. He and Czech General Syrovy publicly laid a wreath on the Unknown Soldier's grave. In the evening crowds of Czechs still gathered but they placed no more flowers.[33] Thereafter, German soldiers were ordered to salute when passing the Tomb of the Unknown Soldier.[34]

Confrontation had taken place with quiet dignity and mutual respect; bloodshed had been avoided. While both sides should be commended for their tact, Blaskowitz in particular proved a successful soldier/diplomat. There were yet more "complications" for General Blaskowitz, but these were with his own countrymen rather than with the Czechs.

The *Wehrmacht* had experienced no difficulties at all during the occupation and had only two men wounded, but special SS units that participated in the invasion "did become involved in a number of clashes and excesses."[35] "For the first time, several atrocities were revealed which had been committed by an SS regiment."[36] When he learned of the atrocities, General Blaskowitz ordered a court martial in order to establish the guilty parties, but no action followed. Blaskowitz then turned the matter over to Keitel in the *OKW*, but Hitler shelved the case, to the disgust of the army officers.[37] Future events had been foreshadowed.

Before this problem became the dominant issue in the Czech occupation, Blaskowitz was transferred outside the Protectorate. As early as 20 March, Baron Constantine von Neurath, a veteran diplomat and former Foreign Minister of Germany, had been appointed "Reich Protector of Bohemia-Moravia." Czech opinion apparently felt that in the circumstances the appointment of Neurath was about as favorable as anyone could hope.

On 5 April, Blaskowitz met Neurath at the Woodrow Wilson train station in Prague and accompanied him to the Hradschin castle in a motorcade.[38] German Army Commander Walther von Brauchitsch and General Blaskowitz attended a dinner given by Neurath at the castle that very evening where the Army officially turned over the governmental power to the "Reich Protector." In his speech Neurath declared: "The Hapsburgs failed, but Chancellor Hitler succeeded—that is the happiness of both nations and the peace of Europe and the world."[39] Despite the "happiness" Neurath found upon his arrival in Prague, General Blaskowitz was probably quite ready to leave the Protectorate.

The General later declared that even then he did not give any thought to German foreign policy, as "tradition has raised an iron barrier between politics and the army." Though this was certainly true and while Blaskowitz was both a traditionalist and exclusively a soldier, he did confess to having some personal reflections. He admitted for the first time that he had some "private thoughts upon this rape of a foreign land but refused to give voice to them."[40] His austerity of temperment, his taciturnity, fell clearly within the code of the Prussian officer. Like Guderian, if he did not agree with a disgraceful action he would not make a case "in justification of evil inflicted on a non-German people."[41] Whether Blaskowitz accepted Hitler's "military" argument that it was necessary to "eliminate the aircraft carrier in the midst of Germany ..."[42] is unknown. He again reiterated that it was not his fault nor was it his business to look into the why and wherefore.[43] Many years later Blaskowitz admitted that:

> ...his reaction to Hitler's further occupation of [the remainder of] ... Czechoslovakia, in direct violation to his word at Munich, was to hold his breath waiting for a world-wide explosion, at the failure of which to ensue he was greatly surprised .... what amazed him the most was that Hitler dared to do such a thing at a time when, militarily speaking, it was a bluff which could not have been carried out, because Germany was not then able to wage a successful war.[44]

It was simply a matter of duty for the General. Duty would call again quite soon and Blaskowitz would respond with greater enthusiasm, even at the risk of a European-wide war, prompted by the planned revenge upon Poland. Although he thought that France and Great Britain "would not repeat the mistake which they had made by not declaring war when Germany invaded the whole of Czechoslovakia after the Munich agreement," he thought it nevertheless a "sad necessity."[45]

Within months Hitler had taken steps to solve the "Polish Question." World War II was on the horizon. For the moment Hitler seemed to have triumphed. Another German general—one who evidently saw Hitler much more clearly than Blaskowitz—reputedly characterized the dictator quite caustically: "Hitler is a swine—but a lucky one!"[46] He had been very lucky indeed.

Perhaps, however, the final word was spoken by Jan Masaryk, the Czech Minister in London. He reputedly remarked, "The Czechs will at any rate give Germany a stomach ache."[47]

Notes for Chapter V

1. Blaskowitz Interrogation Report, 5 June 1945. First Canadian Army Intelligence Periodical. No.4, vol. 10,655. File 215C1.023, R.G. 24, P.A.C. Colonel General List led the troops which occupied Moravia. Blaskowitz's statement regarding lack of "previous planning" and "hasty but simple orders" should be understood advisedly since Hitler had toured the Sudeten fortifications with a number of officers not including Blaskowitz about the middle of December 1938. During lunch at the inn of a small Sudeten town, Hitler "startled his audience" by repeating earlier expressed intentions of occupying Bohemia and Moravia and indicating that the *Wehrmacht,* the new name of the *Reichswehr* should adopt "all necessary measures to avoid ... tactical complications ...." Surprisingly, Hitler said these critical things very openly, "without even troubling to exclude from the room the employees of the inn." Wilhelm Keitel interpreted this as an order and in the areas bordering Bohemia and Moravia, a system of "'accelerated readiness to march'" was adopted in which troops were prepared to march on twelve hours notice. Warlimont Interrogation, 22 September 1945, Department of State Poole Special Interrogation Mission, M-679, Roll 3, Frames 0680-0684, General Records of the Department of State, R.G. 59, N.A.

2. *Neue Tag,* 26 June 1944, Cited in Blaskowitz File, M.I.D., M.I.S., Who's Who Branch, 1939-1945, Entry 194, R.G. 165, N.A. Germany invaded the Czech state at the same time as Poland and Hungary seized other parts of Czechoslovakia.

3. Blaskowitz Interrogation, 8 September 1945, Schuster Interrogation Files, R.G. 165, N.A.

4. C. Amort and I.M. Jedlica, *The Canaris File* (London: Allen Wingate, 1970), 39-45; F.H. Hinsley, Thomas, Ransom and Knight, *British Intelligence In the Second World War,* 5 vols. (London: Her Majesty's Stationery Office, 1979-1988), 1: 58.

5. Irving, *Göring,* 245.

6. Taylor, *Munich,* 955.

7. Gisevius, *Bitter End,* 336.

8. Taylor, *Munich,* 955.

9. Leo Geyer von Schweppenburg, *The Critical Years* (London: Allan Wingate, 1952), 183.

10. "German Troops Occupy Prague," *The Times* (London), 16 March 1939, 16.; "Reich Occupation Has Clear Sailing," *The New York Times*, 16 March 1939, 18.; "Hitler In Prague, Sets Up Nazi Government; Weeping Czechs Boo His Army, Snowball Tanks," *The New York Herald-Tribune* (late ed.), 16 March 1939, 1.

11. "Reich Occupation Has Clear Sailing," *The New York Times*, 16 March 1939, 18.; "Hitler In Prague, Sets Up Nazi Government; Weeping Czechs Boo His Army, Snowball Tanks," *The New York Herald-Tribune* (Late ed.), 16 March 1939, 1.

12. "The Reich's New Provinces: Civil Governors Named," *The Times* (London), 16 March 1939, 16.; "Hitler's Residence in Prague: His New Administrators", *The New York Herald-Tribune*, 16 March 1939, 3.

13. "Hitler Receives Czechs," *The New York Times*, 17 March 1939, 5.

14. Andre Brissard, *Canaris: The Biography of Admiral Canaris, Chief of German Military Intelligence in the Second World War*, trans. and ed. Ian Colvin (New York: Grosset & Dunlap, Publishers, 1973) 130-131.; *Keitel Memoirs*, 81.

15. "Round-up in Prague: The Gestapo At Work," *The Times* (London), 18 March 1939, 11.; Vojtech Mastny, *The Czechs Under Nazi Rule: The Failure of National Resistance, 1939-1942* (N.Y.: Columbia University Press, 1971), 54-55.

16. "Hitler Receives Czechs," *The New York Times*, 17 March 1939, 5.

17. Willi Frischauer, *The Nazis At War* (London: Gollancz, 1940), 200-201.

18. Blaskowitz Interrogation, 25 October 1945, Biographic Data Personnel Folders Series, R.G. 238, N.A.

19. Blaskowitz Interrogation, 25 October 1945, Microcopy M-1270, Roll 1, R.G. 238, N.A.

20. "Prague Atmosphere Tense With Rumors," *The New York Times*, 2 April 1939, 44.; Blaskowitz did have a security guard of the SS *Das Reich* engineering battalion inside the Hradschin and on official visits such as to the Skoda Works. Otto Weidinger, *Das Reich 1934-1939*, trans. Bo Friesen (Winnipeg, Canada: J.J. Fedorowicz, Publishing, 1990), I: 83.

21. Hans Umbreit, *Die Militärische Besetzung der Tschechoslowakei und Polens* (Stuttgart: Deutsche Verlags-Anstaltt, 1977), 55.

22. Johannes Koepcke Sr., "Ein Grab in Bommelsen," undated, unpublished, *Collection Koepcke*. Copy in author's possession. See also Msg 1/1814, BA/MA.

23. Blaskowitz Interrogation, 25 October 1945, M-1270, Roll 1, R.G. 238, N.A.

24. Ibid.

25. William D. Bayles, *Caesars in Goose Step* (New York: Harper & Brothers Publishers, 1940), 258.; Vojtech Mastny, who was a minister in the Czech government, later wrote that "Blaskowitz handled the subdued adversary with tact." Mastny, *Czechs Under Nazi Rule*, 55.

26. "Round-Up In Prague: The Gestapo At Work," *The Times* (London), 18 March 1939, 11.; Mastny, *Czechs Under Nazi Rule*, 55.

27. "Planes Drop Leaflets," *The New York Times*, 17 March 1939, 5.

28. "Army Day In Prague," *The Times* (London), 20 March 1938, 13.

29. "Germans Parade In Silent Prague," *The New York Times*, 20 March 1939, 3.

30. Ibid.

31. Ibid.

32. "Future Czech Government," *The Times* (London), 27 March 1939, 11.

33. Ibid.; Shiela Grant Duff, *A German Protectorate: The Czechs under Nazi Rule* (London: MacMillan & Co., Ltd., 1942), 71.; Victor Mamatey and Radomir Luza, eds., *A History of the Czechoslovak Republic, 1918-1948* (Princeton: Princeton University Press, 1973), 301.

34. Mastny, *Czechs Under Nazi Rule*, 54-55. After Blaskowitz's departure Czechs began to leave wreaths ribboned in black crepe at the King Wenceslaus statue during the night. The SS stopped it. See: John Raleigh, *Behind the Nazi Front* (New York: Dodd, Mead & Co., 1940), 137-138.

35. Warlimont Interrogation, 22 September 1945, M-679/3/0680-0684, R.G. 59, N.A.

36. Warlimont Interrogation, 3 July 1945, M-679, Roll 3, R.G. 59, N.A.

37. Ibid.; Warlimont Interrogation, 22 September 1945, M-679/3/0680-0684, R.G. 59, N.A. Warlimont was interrogated twice on this subject and had somewhat different recollections. When interrogated on July 3, 1945 at Seventh Army Interrogation Center he stated that Blaskowitz turned the matter of the court martial over to the *OKW* and that Hitler shelved it. When interrogated on September 22, 1945 at Oberursel by Harold Deutsch, he declared that "in spite of the most energetic efforts of General Blaskowitz and the *OKH*, it was impossible to introduce a court martial procedure ...." Keitel promised to report on the cases to Hitler but the result of any such report was unknown to Warlimont. In fact, Hitler may not have learned of the report since it is likely that Keitel did not present it to him as he liked to refrain from reporting "difficult" matters to Hitler.

38. Umbreit, *Militärische Besetzung*, 58-59.; Hans Umbreit, Rolf-Deiter Müller and Bernard Kroener, *Das Deutsche Reich und Der Zweite Weltkrieg*, vol.5, *Organisation und Mobilisierung Des Deutschen Machtbereichs* (Stuttgart: Deutsche Verlags-Anstalt, 1988), 25.

39. "Protector Takes His Post In Prague," *The New York Times*, 6 April 1939, 8.

40. Blaskowitz Interrogation Report, 5 June 1945. First Canadian Army Intelligence Periodical No. 4, Vol. 10,655. File 215C1.023, R.G. 24, P.A.C.

41. Macksey, *Guderian*, 76.

42. Ibid., 77.; Günther Blumentritt, "Polish Campaign 1939" B.H. Liddell Hart Papers, King's College, London, L.H. 9/24/53.

43. Blaskowitz Interrogation, 5 June 1945, First Canadian Army Intelligence Periodical. No. 4, vol. 10,655. File 215C1.023, R.G. 24, P.A.C.

44. Blaskowitz Interrogation, 9 November 1945, Biographical Data Personnel Folders Series, R.G. 238, N.A.

45. Ibid.

46. "Portrait of a General Dated 3.12.41", G-2 Regional File (Intel.) 5990, R.G. 165, N.A. The general in question was the later Field Marshal Ewald von Kleist. As can be easily imagined, Kleist's acid tongue did not endear him to the Nazis. According to a Colonel Hoeffner "Kleist was unpopular with the highest authorities, and therefore Zeitzler [his chief of staff] got all the glory. Kleist couldn't be given the credit because 'he was no good.'" WO 208/4169, P.R.O.; Pierre Galante, *Operation Valkyrie: The German Generals' Plot Against Hitler*, trans. Mark Howson and Cary Ryan (New York: Harper & Row, Publishers, 1981), 61.

47. Neville Henderson, *Failure of a Mission: Berlin, 1937-1939* (New York: G.P. Putnam's Sons, 1940), 222.

CHAPTER VI

THE POLISH CAMPAIGN

ON 1 JUNE 1939, General Blaskowitz received an order from *OKH* to prepare for an attack on Poland.[1] Shortly before, Blaskowitz had been appointed commander of Eighth Army. It was an historic command since it had been Eighth Army that had won the Battle of Tannenberg in 1914. Hitler had opposed his assignment to command an army, but army leaders had successfully supported Blaskowitz. "Hitler did not think Blaskowitz was qualified to have extraordinary tasks put in front of him, he thought him to be of mediocre qualifications."[2]

The Führer had not forgotten Blaskowitz's disagreement with his own ideas on the role of tanks, and possibly remembered his attempts to bring the SS perpetrators of atrocities in Czechoslovakia to trial. Nevertheless, Hitler did not have his way this time and General Blaskowitz received a command for the approaching Polish campaign.

Only two weeks after receiving orders to prepare an attack on Poland, General Blaskowitz was hard at work. His order of 14 June 1939, to Third Army Group, began:

> The Commander-in-Chief of the Army has ordered the working out of a plan of deployment against Poland which takes into account the demands of the political leadership for the opening of war by surprise and for quick success.[3]

He continued:

> The operation, in order to forestall an orderly Polish mobilization, is to be opened by surprise with forces which are for the most part armored and motorized .... The initial superiority over the Polish

frontier guards and surprise, ... are to be maintained by quickly bringing up other parts of the Army, as well as by counteracting the marching up of the Polish Army.

Accordingly, all units have to keep the initiative against the foe by quick action and ruthless attacks.[4]

General Blaskowitz probably looked forward to the Polish Campaign. Indeed, he later admitted as much when he declared: "I myself ... believed that these ... questions, outstanding among which was the question of the Polish Corridor, would have to be settled by force of arms."[5] He added significantly: "A war to wipe out the political and economic loss resulting from the creation of the Polish Corridor and to lessen the threat to ... East Prussia ... was regarded as a sacred though a sad necessity."[6] General Blaskowitz apparently felt that the very existence of the Polish Corridor was such a stain upon German honor, that it had to be rectified even at the risk of general European war.

In expressing these deep sentiments he might have been speaking for virtually the entire officer corps. General Keitel, for example, spoke of the same subject in this manner:

> An American simply cannot understand our desperation after the Treaty of Versailles. Just think: unemployment, national disgrace. Let me say it bluntly in all honor—the Treaty of Versailles was a *dirty shame*! And that is what every decent German had to feel. Just imagine ripping the heart out of Prussia to give Poland a corridor to the sea! Every decent German had to say, '*Down with the Treaty of Versailles*, by any means, fair or foul!'[7]

Throughout the *Reichswehr* period, German soldiers could only contain their furious resentment and anger, and vehemently insist that someday Germany would regain the Corridor.[8] The famous World War I commander Hans von Seeckt, the man who literally formed the *Reichswehr*, undoubtedly had the Corridor in mind when he announced: "Poland's existence is unbearable."[9] As long as Poland and the Corridor existed, the German Reich was "defenseless and dishonored."[10]

The *Reichswehr* was obsessed throughout the Weimar period with the idea of defense against a Polish invasion of eastern Germany, sometimes in concert with a French attack in the west. Beginning with the Army war games in 1923 and continuing through those of 1932, the Army leadership analyzed German defenses against attack by Poland and her Allies, and in each case the outcome suggested was catastrophic for the Fatherland.[11] Little wonder, then, that most officers thought the lands lost to Poland a legitimate cause for war.[12]

Speaking about his own viewpoint and that of his fellow generals, Blaskowitz elaborated:

> We hoped that the Polish question would be settled in a peaceful fashion through diplomatic means, since we believed that this time France and England would come to the assistance of their ally. As a matter of fact we felt that, if political negotiations came to naught, the Polish question would unavoidably lead to war, that is, not only with Poland herself, but also with the Western Powers.[13]

Blaskowitz had completed all of the necessary preparations for his army by mid-July. On 1 August he wrote a letter to his old friend Johannes Koepcke. He informed Koepke that he had prepared himself "physically and spiritually" by climbing the Grossglockner peak in the Alps and by reading books, "mostly those of spiritual value." He added, "God only knows, I will be most urgently and most seriously involved in heavy performance of duty soon ...." Then, "I am looking forward to the action that is coming my way." And finally, "God knows, soon I will not be able to sleep in my own bed anymore."[14]

On 22 August 1939, General Blaskowitz was ordered along with other generals to Hitler's residence in the Obersalzberg to hear Hitler give a speech.[15] The Führer told the assembled generals that he would "give a propagandistic cause for starting the war ... whether it is plausible or not." He demanded the generals, "[h]ave no pity." The Führer wanted them to have a "brutal attitude" and demanded the "greatest severity."[16] He repeatedly referred to "annihilating" the Poles.

Regrettably, General Blaskowitz's reaction to the speech is unrecorded. His later actions, however, reveal that he could have had no insight into the meanings which Hitler and Himmler attached to such terminology. He may even have naively attached a military meaning to these terms since he was so busy with military matters and was soon to begin operations.[17] His ethical and religious beliefs would not have allowed him to act as Hitler demanded. Indeed, Blaskowitz carried a Bible with him into Poland and his last act before going to bed every night was to read from the New Testament.[18]

General Blaskowitz's command of the Eighth Army was a rather humble assignment. Eighth Army had four infantry divisions, two border defense units and part of the SS-*Leibstandarte Adolf Hitler*, then a motorized infantry regiment.[19] The infantry divisions were organized into two corps, the X and XIII, each with two divisions. There were no panzer divisions under his command, and no cavalry for reconnaissance, although Eighth Army did have three Luftwaffe reconnaissance squadrons attached to it.

One formation called an *Einsatzgruppen* was also attached to Eighth Army. Although these "action commandos" later became notorious as death squads, the SS had been careful not to disclose their true purpose to military commanders. Indeed, in its Order of the Day of 9 September, Eighth Army defined the task of the *Einsatzgruppen* as suppression of all anti-Reich and anti-German elements in the rear of the "fighting troops, in particular, counter-espionage arrest of politically unreliable persons, confiscation of weapons, safeguarding of important counter-espionage material, etc."[20]

Eighth Army was comparatively weak and had the limited role of guarding the flank of von Reichenau's Tenth Army.[21] Together with Reichenau's Army and List's Fourteenth Army, Blaskowitz's Eighth Army constituted Army Group South under the overall command of Colonel-General von Rundstedt who had been recalled from retirement due to the outbreak of the war.

General Walter von Reichenau's powerful Tenth Army, the *Schwerpunckt*, the point of main effort of the attack, had orders to advance from Silesia to Lodz and on to Warsaw.[22] Operating from Silesia on Reichenau's northern flank, General Blaskowitz's Eighth Army was to attack from the area of Glogow in the direction of Lodz and to provide Reichenau's army with flank protection, particularly along the banks of the Warta and Bzura Rivers, where Reichenau's northern flank would be at its most vulnerable.

The Central Polish Plain across which Blaskowitz's Army would pass varies from a flat to a rolling plain with many wide valleys. The Warta and Bzura Rivers present the only natural obstacles in what is mostly agricultural country where corn and sunflowers were the main crops (Many small, bitter battles were fought in its vast fields).[23]

The bulk of the Polish Army facing Blaskowitz was under the

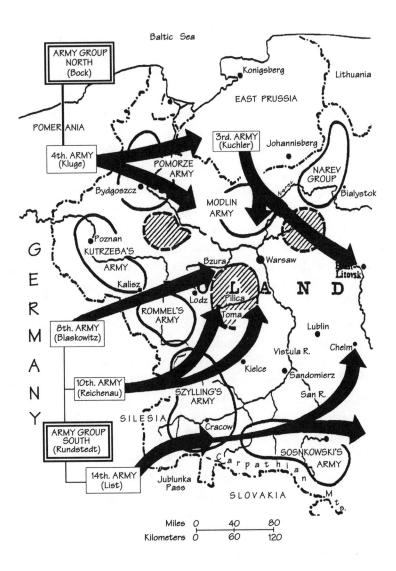

Deployments - September 1, 1939

German Armies   Main Polish Concentrations

Planned German Attacks   Polish Reserves

command of General Kutrzeba and was concentrated around Poznan, just to the north of Blaskowitz's open flank.[24] According to the German *Blitzkrieg* plan, the Poznan Army was to be by-passed. It was potentially a very difficult assignment. With a weak, slow-moving army of only four infantry divisions Blaskowitz was charged with keeping up with Reichenau's motorized army to protect its flank while simultaneously by-passing the Polish Army on his own flank.[25]

The attack began at 4:45 A.M. on 1 September 1939, in favorable weather. In the early morning there was a ground fog which aided the surprise attack.[26] Elements of the *Leibstandarte* seized the intact bridge over the Prosna River just across the border.[27] The shooting had begun; the war had been unleashed. Eighth Army streamed into Poland. The ground was dry, solid and hard packed; made to order for tanks. For the next several days, the daytime heat was oppressive, but the nights were cool. In Poland autumn is proverbially ripe; the Germans called it "Führer's weather."[28]

Polish resistance to the assault of Blaskowitz's Eighth and Reichenau's Tenth Armies was initially feeble and the Poles fell back on the Warta River line to the east. The objective for the second day of the war was the Warta River, the first major obstacle. *Leibstandarte* remained in the vanguard of Eighth Army, followed by X Corps. The Warta line was fortified with concrete pill boxes and the Germans expected strong Polish resistance.[29] In fact, the Poles expected to hold these positions for six months, until English and French attacks in the west brought victory.[30] Polish resistance became much stiffer on the second day of combat and Blaskowitz's lead elements failed to reach the banks of the Warta, creating an awkward situation because Tenth Army to the south had already crossed the Warta and had begun to create a bridgehead on the east bank.[31] Stalled on the west bank, Eighth Army could not protect Tenth Army's flank.

The second night of war was "a nervous one," according to the *Leibstandarte* divisional history: "everywhere on the horizon burning towns; a sky glowing red and colorful fireballs painted a war-like picture."[32] The next day the Germans found an increasing number of demolitions and hastily built obstacles. Polish resistance was stubborn throughout the day and the Warta River was not crossed until 4 September. On that day one of Blaskowitz's division commanders directed an attack on the Warta positions by carefully coordinated infantry, artillery and anti-tank units which successfully seized five undemolished bridges despite the fact that each had been prepared with demolition charges.[33] Eighth Army crossed quickly to the east bank where it engaged in heavy combat during which XIII Corps advanced twelve miles, completely smashing the line of Polish pill boxes.[34]

Unknown to Blaskowitz, he was by-passing General Tadeusz Kutrzeba, the Polish commander of the Poznan Army on his northern flank. On the previous day Kutrzeba had proposed to the Polish High Command that he attack Eighth Army's flank. The Polish High Command, however, rejected the proposal and the Poznan Army withdrew eastward toward Warsaw.[35]

General Kurtzeba described the Polish retreat this way:

> Night had fallen and movement began all over the hitherto dead battlefield .... Our retreat resembled a migration into unknown territory, often without maps and without commanders, our forces wandering into the dark night, whose stillness was broken by the sounds of shots. In this atmosphere of incertitude, disorder was inevitable.[36]

Luftwaffe reports described the Polish withdrawal as "disorderly" and "panic stricken." Polish roads were bombed and railroads smashed; the Polish Poznan Army retreated on foot, cross-country, at night, hiding in the forests during the day. Despite Luftwaffe reports of "complete success," the Polish Army remarkably had not disintegrated as a fighting force.[37]

During the evening of 4 September Army Group South's chief of staff, General Eric von Manstein, in a long-distance telephone call with General Halder, advised him that Eighth Army should pursue the retreating enemy vigorously to try to stop him. Fear of a flank attack from the area of Posen was now without foundation. "Nothing serious was to be expected."[38] Already that morning Army Group South had estimated the Poznan Army as "incapable of launching a heavy attack on the exposed left flank of Eighth Army as it advanced north-eastward."[39] The German High Command, *OKH*, had concluded that the Polish Army had already lost its freedom of action, its only remaining choice was to stand and fight on the west bank of the Vistula River.[40]

The Germans knew that a rapid decision in the war in Poland could come only on the western bank of the Vistula. At all costs the Poles must be prevented from escaping eastward across the Vistula. German troops had to get there before the Poles. A race began along the whole front between the Poles and the Germans to get to the Vistula first. "The Polish retreat was outpaced by the German advance."[41] Polish units were by-passed, isolated, and "destroyed piecemeal" by German infantry units following their vanguard elements. The Polish predicament was swiftly becoming irretrievable. Newsmen began to use the term "Blitzkrieg," meaning "lighting war."

The Eighth Army objective for the next day, 5 September, became a rapid advance northeastward toward Lodz and the Bzura River beyond the city.[42] Blaskowitz nicknamed this area devoid of natural obstacles a "bowling alley" where his troops had to hurry to keep pace with Reichenau's motorized army.[43] He turned his X Corps so that it faced northward to guard his flank while his XIII Corps pushed toward Lodz in very heavy fighting against Polish rear-guard units determined to slow down the Germans.

Blaskowitz had already extended his flank from the German border near Breslau almost as far east as Lodz, nearly 150 kilometers. It was obvious to Army Group South's commander, Colonel-General von Rundstedt, that Eighth Army's flank had to be reinforced. Several Battalions of the IV Frontier Command, a regiment of the 62nd Infantry Division and elements of the 252nd Infantry Division were ordered to cross the Reich frontier and to assume responsibility for the westernmost part of Blaskowitz's flank. These units were named "Group Gienanth" after their commander, General Curt Ludwig Freiherr von Gienanth. This limited measure was followed by further reinforcements the next day, 6 September.

Rundstedt revised Army Group South's estimate of the possibility of an attack on Blaskowitz's flank by the Poznan Army and prepared to meet a Polish attack from the north by releasing the 213th and 221st Infantry Divisions, and inserting them on the flank between Group Gienanth and X Corps. The transfer of these divisions meant that Blaskowitz in effect then commanded three corps, but these new divisions were still too far west to support X Corps in case of an attack from the north. Rundstedt also requested cavalry for Eighth Army once again, for reconnaissance purposes. The High Command did not make any available. On 7 September air reconnaissance spotted a large Polish formation on the flank of Eighth Army.[44] Despite this XIII Corps advanced toward Lodz, simultaneously serving as a flank guard for Tenth Army. X Corps further increased the prolongation of the line it held, particularly along the front of the 30th Infantry Division.[45]

Blaskowitz's chief of staff, General Hans Felber, had wanted to stay in Germany as long as possible after the outbreak of the war so as to utilize the excellent channels of radio communication and "besides, there are bedbugs and fleas ..." over there in Poland, he wrote in his diary.[46] Blaskowitz "led" from the rear, his leadership was reflective and managerial, not heroic. His concern for his troops was exemplary. He spent part of 7 September, for example, visiting wounded German soldiers at a military hospital. He was pleased to find that many soldiers only had arm wounds.[47]

Eighth Army headquarters moved to Gross Wartenburg on 4 September and to Sieradz, near Lodz, on 8 September. Then the next target, the Polish Lodz Army, was heavily attacked.[48]

On 8 September Army Lodz withdrew from the city of Lodz and retreated toward Warsaw. A delegation of citizens offered the surrender of the city to the 17th Infantry Division. Blaskowitz's Order of the Day proclaimed "The enemy is in rapid retreat before Warsaw."[49]

Already on the previous evening Blaskowitz had made his fateful decision. On the evening of 7 September he had issued orders to pursue the retreating Poles in the direction of Warsaw with the aim of cutting off the Polish retreat from the area around Kutno, north of the Bzura River, in the direction of Warsaw.[50] It was an audacious decision aimed at fighting a battle of annihilation west of the Vistula River.

Shortly after Blaskowitz had issued his orders General von Manstein ordered Eighth Army to advance rapidly toward Warsaw, cutting off the Polish retreat north of the Bzura and simultaneously going to the support of the Fourth Panzer Division, which planned to assault Warsaw the next day.[51] Blaskowitz and Manstein had independently conceived the same orders, a tribute to their General Staff training.

Blaskowitz and Manstein had both assumed that the Poles would retreat eastward toward Warsaw. Neither aerial nor ground reconnaissance presented any intelligence to the contrary. Attacks upon Blaskowitz's flank had in fact already begun on 7 September. They were relatively minor, however, and not deemed strong enough to cause Eighth Army to focus its attention upon them. On 8 September the 24th Infantry Division, part of X Corps, had been attacked by Polish units supported by artillery, but the attackers had then disengaged and moved eastward, apparently headed for Warsaw.[52] The opening phase of the campaign in Poland ended with these events. The Germans had every reason to be delighted with their successes, but potential catastrophe waited in the wings.

When von Reichenau's army had smashed the Polish attempts to form a line on the Warta River on 3 September, it was clear to everyone—except perhaps to the Poles themselves—that disaster was imminent for Poland.[53] Even so distant an observer as Count Galeazzo Ciano, Italy's Foreign Minister, could write in his diary on 3 September: "The German advance in Poland is overwhelming. It is not impossible for us to foresee a very rapid finish."[54]

In Warsaw, however, there was definitely no panic at the first German victories. People went to work as usual, streetcars operated, newspapers sold, movie theaters ran films. At the Ali Baba night club, a comedian still presented a skit of Adolf Hitler "[n]ot calculated to please the invaders."[55]

Perhaps Polish disregard of the critical situation of Warsaw had been fostered by the apparently slight impact of Luftwaffe attacks on the capital in the first days of the war. The few squadrons which attacked the city had dropped small bomb loads. Ironically, the first eleven bombs fell on the grounds of the Tworki Lunatic Asylum.[56]

The Warsaw Poles apparently concluded that the Luftwaffe was not a weapon of annihilation which dictated their hasty submission. The truth was that most of the Luftwaffe's planned massive raid was cancelled because the cloud ceiling was only six hundred feet and visibility was limited. Thick fog rolled in later in the day.[57] In Warsaw the Poles continued to trust in their military forces and in the alliance with England and France, rejoicing in the streets when, on 3 September, the Allies declared war on Germany.[58] The population remained composed but days of torment were close at hand. Blaskowitz too, had some difficult days approaching.

During the first days of the attack on Poland, everything had proceeded superbly for all of the German Armies, particularly for Army Group South, and for General Blaskowitz's Eighth Army. Later the General described these early days of the Polish Campaign in terms of a virtual victory march: "We were only held up by the refugees who had been driven out onto the main roads by senseless evacuation orders. We had to chase these people into the fields to open up the roads."[59]

Events went so favorably that General Blaskowitz boldly assumed the initiative and stated later, with characteristic modesty, "I went beyond my actual orders and made a rapid advance. By thus occupying the railroad lines, I brought their entire transport system to a standstill and the Poles had either to attack or proceed on foot."[60] It was at this time that Blaskowitz's army, in the drive through Lodz towards Warsaw, ran into a serious crisis.[61] Indeed, it was the biggest crisis of the Polish Campaign for the *Wehrmacht*.[62]

In the breakthrough battles along the Polish border, General Blaskowitz's Eighth Army had moved south of the Polish Army under General Kutrzeba. The subsequent German advance toward Warsaw left the Poznan Army isolated in western Poland. Its only possible escape routes were eastward toward Warsaw or southward through Blaskowitz's flank toward the Rumanian border. When von Reichenau broke through the Warta River line and advanced on Warsaw, it threatened to cut off the retreat routes of the Poznan Army. Then Blaskowitz's army followed quickly as Reichenau's flank guard, placing its advance elements between Scylla and Charybdis, in this case, between the Poznan Army and Warsaw. The Poles responded just as Blaskowitz had forseen, although the direction of their attack was southward rather than eastward.

Naturally, the Poznan Army tried to break through Blaskowitz's lines. On the night of 9-10 September, in unison with some elements of the Polish Pomorze Army escaping from the north, the Poles heavily attacked the exposed flank of Blaskowitz's Army, attempting to break through southward to Lodz.[63] The ensuing battle was virtually the death knell of the Polish Army, but it threatened for some time to be a "critical" one for the *Wehrmacht*[64] and particularly for General Blaskowitz. Retrospectively, the General admitted: "My flank was very deep and my first [sic] Division was, also, much exposed."[65]

Actually, the Polish blow struck General Blaskowitz's 30th Infantry-Division; it struck with the power of possessed men in a desperate situation. Blaskowitz wheeled his army to face the attack and tried to form a defensive front facing northward. Some army elements actually had to turn about completely and re-trace their march back toward the threatened area. Eighth Army was as much in danger of being taken from the *rear* as from the exposed flank. Blaskowitz appealed to Army Group South for Panzers as reinforcements, but that request was denied.[66] Army Group South had its own ideas about how to counter the developing Polish threat.

Army Group South's commander, Colonel-General von Rundstedt, requested the immediate transfer of the Luftwaffe's top secret 7th Air Landing Division's 16th Infantry Regiment to Eighth Army. These were elite air-landing troops under Colonel Kreysing, who served under General Kurt Student. They were dispatched by JU- 52 transports to the crucial battle area north of Lodz.[67] In the meantime, all available German military police units were thrown into action near Lodz.[68] The 545th anti-tank unit was also rushed to the area north of Lodz to bolster the German defenses.[69] The Poles had sixty-five armored cars and tankettes two and one-half ton, tracked, armored vehicles armed with machine guns.[70]

The German command, including *OKH*, Army Group South and Blaskowitz's Eighth Army had been aware of the potential threat to Eighth Army's flank since the beginning of the Polish Campaign.[71] General Walter Warlimont, who was in Berlin with the Armed Forces Operations Staff, later recalled that, "At first, it was not clear why the main Polish forces were not encountered [by Blaskowitz's army]."[72] General von Manstein noted that "We knew, after all, that the enemy had assembled strong forces in Poznan Province, which had not yet come to light."[73] On 8 and 9 September he told General Hans Felber, Blaskowitz's Chief of Staff, that "he must pay special heed to reconnaissance on his northern flank."[74]

Blaskowitz, charged with the dual task of covering the flank of Reichenau's Tenth Army and blocking the escape route eastward toward Warsaw of the Polish Poznan Army, had given priority to the second task when he was struck in the flank.[75] Referring later to the Polish flank attack, Blaskowitz admitted: "We [had] always considered this [a] possibility."[76]

Blaskowitz was keenly aware of the potential danger to his exposed flank.[77] He had gambled, balancing the risk of an exposed and dangerously thin left flank with the consequent possibility of a Polish breakthrough, if the Poles attacked, against the chance of trapping the Poles in a pocket and blocking its southern and eastern exits. It was bold, daring and risky; he suppressed the counsel of his fears. One German general later described Blaskowitz's decision in the terms of Greek mythology: "one has to grasp the forelock of the Goddess of Luck, because her head is bald in back; ... once Luck has passed you there is no way to reach for it." And indeed, the Goddess of Luck was on his side.[78]

Undoubtedly, Blaskowitz should have watched the Poznan Army more closely. Yet in his defense is the fact that Brauchitsch and Halder had sent to him a teleprinter message on 9 September "to the effect that the enemy was moving them [the Poznan Army forces] off to the east with all the transport he could muster, and that a threat to Eighth Army's deep flank need no longer be feared."[79] Without his own reconnaissance troops he could not confirm this. The crux of the matter was that his army lacked reconnaissance troops.[80] And as the great Moltke had written, "Even a *single* error in the original assembly [deployment] of ... armies can hardly be made good again during the entire course of the campaign."[81]

Only later, after characteristically careful professional study, was it discovered how the Poles had managed to surprise Blaskowitz. In the first days of the campaign the Luftwaffe had successfully interdicted every Polish attempt to move large numbers of troops in the open. Later in the campaign the Luftwaffe smashed Polish attempts to break out of encirclements.[82] In the interim period, however, the Luftwaffe was careless, as Polish General Tadeusz Kutrzeba later explained to his German captors. Despite the fact that Blaskowitz's Eighth Army had three close range reconnaissance Staffeln (squadrons), he said that enemy reconnaissance "reported only the confusion on the main roads by day but not the secret movements of troops by night." Kutrzeba added:

> Our tank formations were deployed almost entirely by night—as we had soon discovered that the enemy Air Force which could fulfil [sic] all its tasks by day without any difficulty—usually discontinued operations by early evening.[83]

Additional weaknesses in German doctrine and training were later studied and corrected. Some of these were related to shortcomings in ground reconnaissance, unsurprising in a "green" army early in a war.[84] These had translated into a shocking blow on Blaskowitz's flank.

Hitler oversaw the battle which resulted when the Polish Poznan Army assaulted General Blaskowitz's flank. He did not, however, intervene in the conduct of the battle with definite orders.[85] The Führer visited Blaskowitz's headquarters on September 12 and the latter briefed him on the conduct of the battle.[86] General Keitel later related that the Führer had critically watched Blaskowitz's Eighth Army operations, "to which he had taken the strongest possible exception."[87] One of Hitler's adjutants recorded an even stronger impression. According to him, "Hitler had seen the mistake made by Blaskowitz and he never forgot it. Hitler was extremely upset about this sloppiness by Blaskowitz."[88]

These reports of Hitler's displeasure with Blaskowitz's conduct of the battle stand in contrast to a witness who reported that Keitel had lavished praise on Eighth Army during this same visit to its headquarters with Hitler. Keitel admitted that Blaskowitz's "army has been endowed with the most difficult task, and *we all* agree on that."[89] The other armies had only to advance, Eighth Army had to advance, simultaneously keeping step with Tenth Army and protecting its flank. And these tasks had to be accomplished with the weakest, least mobile of the German armies in Poland. Far from being anxious about this situation, Hitler's main concern seemed to be Warsaw, and beginning on 13 September he plagued Blaskowitz for estimates on how long it would take to starve the city into surrender.[90]

Hitler apparently became more critical of Blaskowitz after his visit to General Kurt von Briesen, commander of the 30th Infantry Division in the middle of General Blaskowitz's weakly defended flank. Von Briesen had courageously led his division in a counterattack against the furious Polish breakout attempt. In the last hours before the tide of battle turned he had personally led his last reserve battalion into action and had his left fore-arm shot away in the bloody battle.[91]Von Briesen was the scion of an old Prussian-Junker family that had first earned renown in the Napoleonic wars. He would fight to the death before risking dishonor. Von Briesen had lost eighty officers and fifteen hundred men on the battlefield. Coincidentally, his father, a Prussian General, had been killed nearby in November, 1914.[92] Hitler and Keitel visited von Briesen in the schoolroom which served as his command post during the battle and the latter outlined the development of the battle and explained the loss of his forearm. The obviously straight-laced von Briesen impressed Hitler as the embodiment of Prussian generals as he had imagined them during his childhood.[93] Walking away from the command post, Hitler said to General Keitel:

> That is a real Prussian general of the Royal school. You can't have enough soldiers like him. He's a man after my own heart. Before today is over, I want him to be the first divisional commander to get the Knight's Cross. He has saved Blaskowitz's army by his gallantry and drive.[94]

Von Briesen's valor, however heroic, was only one part of Eighth Army's salvation. The most crucial phase of this critical battle was between 9 and 11 September, prior to Hitler's visit and before Rundstedt and Manstein intervened. On 9 September at 2:30 P.M., while Eighth Army advanced at almost breakneck speed toward Warsaw to support 4th Panzer Division, Polish troops attacked the northern flank of General von Briesen's 30th Infantry Division. Initially, Blaskowitz thought it was merely another attack similar to the one two days earlier by Polish cavalry which had struck the German flank only to be followed by a hasty retreat northward, little more than a raid.[95] Almost as soon as the attack had begun, it ceased again.

When 30th Infantry Division resumed its advance again around 4:30 P.M. the Poles renewed their attack, this time with artillery support. Since the 30th Infantry Division was spread thinly along a wide front it lacked concentrated offensive strength and its attempt to renew the advance stalled. During the night alarming reports reached Blaskowitz's headquarters at Lodz; it was suddenly clear that the situation on the Bzura was serious indeed, perhaps potentially catastrophic for the 30th Infantry Division, and possibly for Eighth Army.

The situation was unique during the German campaign in Poland;

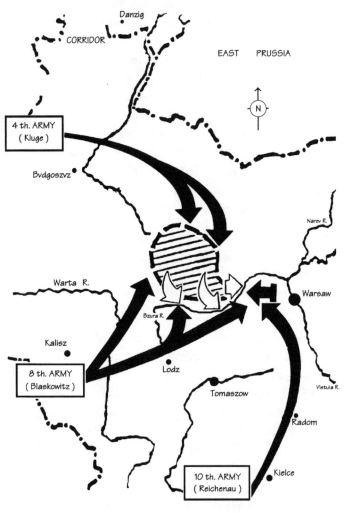

Battle of the Bzura
10-18 September

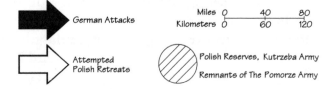

the Poles had a numerical superiority of three to one in infantry, a twofold advantage in artillery, and sixty-five tankettes and armored cars without the Germans in the battle area having any panzers at all.[96] Blaskowitz was not certain of the odds against his troops but had reason to believe the situation very serious. Not only had the 30th Infantry Division's attack been stopped cold, but a Polish deserter had revealed that three Polish divisions equipped with heavy artillery were headed from Kutno toward Lodz. This intelligence was later confirmed.[97]

Blaskowitz realized that the situation of his northern flank was precarious and that the 30th Infantry Division had already suffered heavy casualties and was near exhaustion. Another Polish attack had to be anticipated the following day, 10 September. On the other hand, Manstein had given him orders to advance rapidly to Warsaw to support the 4th Panzer Division. Blaskowitz had no reserves with which to reinforce the 30th Infantry Division and a continued advance would probably stretch the already weakened division beyond the breaking point. Compounding this already complex dilemma, Blaskowitz's headquarters lost radio contact with *OKH* and Army Group South.[98] Blaskowitz's decision had to be made immediately, there was no (precious) time to lose.

At 1:45 A.M. on 10 September Blaskowitz lifted his Order of the Day, stopping the advance toward Warsaw. Moreover, he ordered the 17th Infantry Division to turn one-hundred-twenty degrees and reverse direction toward the battlefield on the Bzura. The 10th Infantry Division was also directed to the Bzura battlefield. The 24th Infantry Division was given a more simple "halt" order. Further west on Eighth Army's flank, the 221st and 213th Infantry Divisions were ordered to accelerate their march eastward so as to link up with X Corps from the west while XIII Corps joined it from the east to form a solid, continuous front facing the Poles to the north.[99]

Army Group South did not yet see the attack on Blaskowitz's flank as anything more than the usual enemy activity. When Rundstedt learned of General Blaskowitz's new orders—which contradicted his own directives to advance rapidly on Warsaw—he nevertheless did not object, even quietly, but continued to stick to his own operational plan.[100] In any case, he was not in radio contact with Blaskowitz at this time.

The Polish attack on Blaskowitz's flank on 10 September not only had a numerical advantage in infantry and light armored vehicles, but the Poles also supported it with heavy artillery and even some fighter planes. As a result, the Poles crossed the Bzura in several places, forcing the Germans to retreat. The Polish attack upon von Briesen's 30th Infantry Division was executed by three Polish infantry divisions and two cavalry brigades. Briesen's troops took a severe beating, gave ground in some places, but managed to hold out against heavy attacks throughout the day, a fabulous performance. The 24th Infantry Division also held, after giving up some ground. There were some critical hours around noontime, but an afternoon lull gave the Germans a chance to reorganize units on the verge of disorder.

Events became more frantic again toward evening, taking a turn for the worse as far as the Germans were concerned. By late evening the situation was reported as "dreadfully serious." Lieutenant General Hans Felber, Blaskowitz's chief of staff, wrote in his diary:

> The evening of 10 September will always be in my memory. I will not forget it because the drama was unprecedented. One series of bad news reports followed another, all night long. It was high drama. We felt like we were hit on the head over and over again.[101]

Throughout the night of 10-11 September Blaskowitz, Felber and the rest of Eighth Army's staff worked feverishly to rebuild the front facing the Poles along the Bzura River. Blaskowitz and his staff had only one and one-half hours sleep that night, but their work helped to save the next day. Miraculous marches, especially by the 24th and 17th Infantry Divisions, made it possible to confront the Poles with a continuous German front on the morning of 11 September.[102]

Eighth Army's execution of Blaskowitz's orders was far from flawless; some units did not receive their orders at all, others misapplied them. The confusion continued to some extent for the next few days and has been the basis of some hard criticism of Blaskowitz's direction of the battle.[103] Nevertheless, Blaskowitz had correctly evaluated the situation despite the lack of reconnaissance reports and contradictory orders from Army Group South. He then issued suitable orders and halted the Polish advance. He had accurately analyzed Eighth Army's predicament and independently executed the proper solution in the midst of the chaos prevalent in battle. He had been fortunate to have the gallant, determined von Briesen as his subordinate at the turn of the tide. He had been even more fortunate that the Polish commanders facing him proved irresolute in their conduct of the battle, but the personal favor that Mars bestowed upon him was perhaps his greatest advantage; Blaskowitz was lucky. Triumph followed.

The reality of the Battle of the Buzra was that there was far more than Poznan Army's four infantry divisions and two cavalry brigades opposing Blaskowitz in the pocket around Kutno. The Poznan Army had been reinforced by the remnants of the Lodz Army, five infantry divisions and one cavalry brigade, and also by the battered but still combat-worthy units of the Pomorze Army, an additional three infantry divisions. In fact, there was a total of twelve Polish infantry divisions and three cavalry brigades, some badly blooded in earlier fighting to the north but still capable of combat, potentially facing Blaskowitz. This force represented more than one-third of the Polish Army.[104] Needless to point out, the failure to locate so large a military force was a major reconnaissance failure responsible for Eighth Army's plight.

Later it became clear that the three Polish Armies disposed of more than sufficient force to break through Blaskowitz's flank but failed to accomplish this because each army attacked separately, sometimes days apart, and at differant locations. Poor communications and faulty leadership—and of course Blaskowitz's countermeasures—resulted in a Polish catastrophe instead of a German disaster.[105]

On 11 September at two o'clock, after all measures for defense had been taken, communications were fortuitously re-established with Army Group South, which then transferred XI and XVI Corps from Reichenau's Tenth Army to Blaskowitz's temporary command. Both of Tenth Army's Corps were then withdrawn from the Warsaw Front, except for a thin screen which remained, and turned west to face the Poles in what was becoming a cauldron at Kutno. The Luftwaffe was also appealed to for maximum support.

Polish attacks against Blaskowitz bogged down on 11 and 12 September and General Kutrzeba withdrew his troops from the attack on Blaskowitz's flank to reorganize them and reorient their attack eastward toward Warsaw.[106] It was already too late.

On 12 September Colonel-General von Rundstedt and General von Manstein also visited Blaskowitz at his headquarters in the Grand Hotel in Lodz. Von Rundstedt assumed direct control of operations and issued orders on Manstein's advice to call up the Army Reserve from the west, two corps from the east from von Reichenau's Tenth Army and also III Corps from the north, giving Eighth Army a total of six corps, all of which were temporarily placed under Blaskowitz's command for the encircling of the Poles. The Luftwaffe flew numerous sorties against the Poles in the meantime. Thus the Polish Army's attempt to smash through the flank of Blaskowitz's Army was itself surrounded in a great cauldron in the bend of the Bzura River centered around the rail and communications town of Kutno.[107]

Blaskowitz's Eighth Army served as the anvil on which the other German armies shattered the Polish Poznan Army and the surviving elements of the Pomorze and Lodz armies. Colonel Kurt Meyer of the *Leibstandarte Adolf Hitler* paid tribute to the Poles' heroism when he wrote: "The Poles proved again and again that they know how to die." Polish attacks were made with "enormous ferocity and desperation" and their losses were gruesome.[108] The Luftwaffe smashed the Poles in the pocket from the air,[109] committing "maximum air strength" against the Poles beginning on 11 September.[110] Every Polish troop movement, every military concentration, was attacked, bridges destroyed, anti-aircraft guns and artillery annihilated. The Kutno cauldron was turned into a Polish graveyard.[111]

One Polish soldier caught in the cauldron later wrote: "we had been attacked by the entire German air force on the Polish front .... Then we knew only that we had to leave this place as quickly as possible if anyone was to survive."[112] After the battle the airport and railroad station at Kutno, which had been completely destroyed, could be identified only by the great craters in the earth where they had stood before the battle.[113] General Kutrzeba declared, "It was Hell come to Earth."[114] The Luftwaffe had efficiently done its deadly work.

Although the final Polish attacks eastward toward Warsaw against XVI Corps initially had some limited successes, even bypassing, overrunning and isolating some German units, the Polish assaults proved to be only "the death throes of a dying army."[115] In the last furious Polish breakout attempt Polish General Skotnicki led a bayonet charge pistol in hand while German senior officers fought as common soldiers. German artillery fired over open sights into swarms of Poles attacking with all of the power of desperation.

After the battle both banks of the Bzura were covered with the dead. Polish dead on the southern bank of the Vistula lay four and five deep. Some had escaped, but the bulk had died on that killing ground. The whole battlefield was a panorama of death and destruction, smashed equipment, dead and wounded men and horses.[116] Although the battle lasted until 19 September, the crisis had passed by 12 September and the Germans had regained the initiative.[117]

General Blaskowitz perhaps deserved the lion's share of the credit for the hard-fought German victory. He was justifiably proud. As his chief of staff wrote, Blaskowitz was "absolutely beaming with joy over our success. I will attest that he has proven to be a terrific leader in a difficult situation."[118]

The Battle of the Bzura was the largest envelopment battle that the Germans had fought up to that time. It was a tribute to the tradition of Count Alfred von Schlieffen, who had directed German military thought along the lines of fighting battles of envelopment.[119] On 19 September 1939, approximately 170,000 Poles who had fallen back on Kutno surrendered.[120] The official communiqué of the Army High Command boasted: "If the Poles captured in the Vistula Battle were lined up in single file ... the line would extend about 125 miles. If the war material taken ... were added ... it would extend to 500 miles."[121] On 20 September *OKW* radioed its congratulations to Blaskowitz for his victory in "one of the greatest battles of all times."[122]

Blaskowitz issued a proclamation almost Napoleonic in grandeur to his troops on 19 September to commemorate the great victory.

> Soldiers of Eighth Army! The ten day battle of the Bzura has been conducted victoriously .... You have conducted yourself gloriously and with utter bravery against the Poles .... Victory ... is yours! With the greatest pride I commend your actions. You bear honorably the same number of the famous Eighth Army of Tannenberg! You have honored the Fuehrer and your Fatherland! Soldiers of the Eighth Army! I am proud of your results. Behind you lie days of greatest efforts! I have known you to fulfill every claim I have boasted of your prowess. I thank you from the bottom of my heart!
> Blaskowitz, General of Infantry[123]

Napoleonic pronouncements aside, Blaskowitz knew that the crisis on his flank had been very serious. Asked about it almost two weeks later, he admitted "If the Poles had had even a third of the number of tanks we used against them, we might still be fighting in front of the Vistula. They could have met our attacks with enough armored strength to hinder our flanking efforts seriously."[124] It was a sober, objective assessment made during the heady days of victory. Blaskowitz was very much the cool analytical soldier that his years of training had aimed to make him. His proclamation of victory can be taken as the end of the second phase of the German campaign in Poland. The third and final phase centered around the assault upon Warsaw.

Warsaw remained the only major surviving Polish bastion and Blaskowitz's Eighth Army was ordered to capture the Polish capital. It was an honorary assignment in recognition of his achievements on the Bzura. Warsaw had been largely an unfortified city at the outbreak of war, but during early September the suburbs were incorporated into the main defense zones. An assault would probably involve "difficult street fighting."[125] Casualties would be numerous.

There had been some panic in the city when the Polish High Command announced it was departing for Brzesc in southeast Poland on the evening on 6 September, but Mayor Stefan Starzynski's stirring radio broadcasts calling upon the citizens of Warsaw to volunteer to dig anti-tank ditches and erect road obstructions were successful.[126] Calm returned. When elements of the Fourth Panzer Army reached Warsaw a couple of days later, the city of 1,300,000, including 400,000 Jews, had begun to gear up for a prolonged defense. In addition to blocking the main streets with wide antitank ditches, the capital's citizens had pushed Warsaw's red tramway cars, cobblestones and earth into position as barricades. More importantly, 37 mm anti-tank guns and 75 mm field guns supported by infantry had been sited at key street corners.[127]

On 8 September tanks from 4th Panzer Division had actually entered the suburbs of Warsaw as the spearheads of Army Group South. Even on the wide boulevards like Grojecka Street, however, the tanks were unable to maneuver and were repulsed by point blank anti-tank artillery with the loss of almost sixty tanks. Clearly, this foreshadowed the diminished effectiveness of tanks in street fighting in World War II and made it obvious to Blaskowitz that, if a determined defense of the Polish capital were attempted, the assault on Warsaw would be dearly paid for in the blood of German infantry.[128] This was precisely the intention of the Polish Army Command in Warsaw.[129]

During the night, German saboteurs put Radio Warsaw out of action and German propagandists began broadcasting on the Warsaw wave length from a station in Katowice, representing themselves to the world as Radio Warsaw. Just before midnight, with bombs exploding and machine guns firing in the background, the Germans with macabre intent played Chopin's Funeral March and then the station went dead.[130] Although other nations may have been fooled temporarily into concluding that Warsaw had fallen, neither Warsaw's residents nor the German panzers planning to attack in the morning were deceived.

German armor made a more determined attack on Warsaw the next day, 9 September, but received another rebuff and withdrew again. Warsaw had gained a temporary respite; the German tanks were pulled out of Warsaw to go to the support of the German forces in the critical Battle on the Bzura. A thin screen of infantry masked the city in the meantime.[131]

Besieged Polish forces in Warsaw used the respite to strengthen the city's fortifications. Tactically important buildings were sandbagged and reinforced with concrete. Barbed wire was laid down. Underground connections between cellars were dug so that strong centers of resistance networks could communicate and be reinforced. City parks had artillery dug into them. Warsaw truly became a fortress.[132]

Von Rundstedt and von Manstein wanted to keep German casualties to the absolute minimum. Accordingly, Rundstedt ordered Blaskowitz to limit the attack on Warsaw to a siege combined with air and artillery assault.[133] For this purpose Blaskowitz had 150 batteries of artillery set up in the suburbs."[134]

On 25 September, Hitler, along with von Brauchitsch and Halder, visited Blaskowitz's Eighth Army Headquarters at Grodzisk, ten miles southwest of Warsaw, to review his plan of attack.[135] Hitler insisted upon the attack on Warsaw so that he could present foreign powers with a *fait accompli*.[136] Blaskowitz, supported by von Brauchitsch, argued passionately that the Luftwaffe bombings obscured artillery targets with smoke and fire and protested that on one occasion incendiaries blown by the wind had landed among German troops. Luftwaffe commander Wolfram von Richtofen tried to dispute their arguments, but the Army men ignored him. Hitler, however, listened to the case each party presented. When Richtofen finished, Hitler turned to him and said just two words: "Carry on!"[137] Then the Führer was briefed on Eighth Army's attack plan:

> The main artillery attack on the fortress will commence early on September 26th. Until then only identified military targets, enemy positions and vital installations such as gas, water, and power stations are being bombarded by ground and air forces. The Thirteenth Army Corps' attack is to begin on September 26th, followed by the Eleventh Army Corps one day later ....[138]

General Blaskowitz revealed his own feeling about the attack on the Polish capital when he later reported:

> What shocked even the most hardened soldier was how at the instigation of their military leaders a misguided population, completely ignorant of the effect of modern weapons, could contribute to the destruction of their own capital.[139]

On four separate days the Luftwaffe had dropped leaflets advising that further resistance was futile and that casualties were the responsibility of the Poles.[140] The resistance continued.

Although he firmly followed orders, Blaskowitz seemed to take little satisfaction in the assault. His sensitivity to the matter of the bombardment of Warsaw was apparent in his defensiveness when he later met the special military commissions of Hungary and Finland and the assistant American military attaché to Berlin, the latter accompanied by two American student officers studying at the *Kriegsakademie*. The group had been granted the unusual privilege of a five-day visit to battlefields in Poland at the end of October, 1939.

In a jointly-authored report the Americans described Blaskowitz as "medium sized, rather thin ..., in perfect physical condition ... and rather cold and abrupt in manner ...." The report continued, stating that Blaskowitz nevertheless did not have an "unfriendly attitude." The general estimate was that Blaskowitz was a soldier of the first order who was "mentally and physically at the height of his power."[141] After lining up the touring soldiers by countries and rank, Blaskowitz

...made a short speech justifying his destruction of WARSAW on the ground that the entire city was fortified and could not be taken economically by ground forces; that the Poles had refused to release their civilian population to a place of safety .... He asked us to look at WARSAW with the eyes and attitude of military men and to examine carefully the Polish defenses in the city.[142]

Blaskowitz then shook hands stiffly with each man and departed. He may have appeared defensive because his assault upon Warsaw had been publicly critized by Lord Milne in the British Parliament and others. Nevertheless, the incident reveals a sensitive nature only partially obscured by his sometimes severe exterior. Blaskowitz obviously had deeper feelings since he permitted General Erwin Jaenecke, one of his subordinate staff officers, to write in his final report on the campaign in Poland: "This city, this beautiful city of long cultural heritage had to be bombarded and destroyed." Claiming that Hitler had been patient, but that Polish resistance made it necessary, it is unusual language for a supposedly cold, soldierly mentality.[143]

During the week of September 10th to 17th, while the Battle of the Bzura had been fought, German air and artillery attacks on Warsaw had not been heavy and the Poles had increasingly fortified Warsaw. Over 30,000 Polish soldiers including General Kutrzeba—defeated at Kutno—had escaped to Warsaw to reinforce the garrison there.[144] Morale among the Polish regular troops was good, ammunition was in ample supply, and the food situation was reported as fair, although the report may have been optimistic.[145] Already on Thursday, 21 September notices had been posted within the beleaguered city ordering butchers to report to military headquarters for allotments of wounded horses to be slaughtered for the "near-starving million inhabitants of the city."[146]

On the 18th the Germans resumed operations against the city with a "heavy and sustained" air and artillery bombardment that continued without interruption until the city surrendered.[147] By 23 September the situation in Warsaw had become grim. Food supplies had reached the shortage point and the bombardment had taken a heavy toll. Many of the city's buildings were destroyed and trees were torn up by exploding shells. One artillery shell alone had demolished a building in Napoleon Square and killed fifty persons. The dead were being buried in public parks and squares, or any of the few remaining green spots. Typhoid fever was thought to be imminent.[148] Nevertheless, the Poles continued to defy the attackers.

Although the artillery bombardment had been proceeding for several days, it achieved a terrible ferocity on Monday, 25 September which the citizens of Warsaw called "Black Monday."[149] It intensified on September 26th and 27th, in combination with massed Luftwaffe bombings. Hitler himself watched the attack for a half-hour from a plane flying above the city at an altitude of nearly 2,000 meters.[150]

According to one observer, "A great pall of smoke and dust lay over Warsaw as again and again fresh squadrons of bombers in close formation like swarms of hornets flew over the city raining death and destruction upon it."[151] Slow JU-52 transport planes plodded over Warsaw with men shoveling incendiary bombs out of the plane doors.[152] The massed artillery pounded the city. The artillery and the bombers each complained that the "dust thrown up by the other obscured targets from view ...."[153] The German infantry assault began on 26 September.

Generals Felber and Blaskowitz observed the bombardment of Warsaw from the front line. Felber then wrote in his diary:

> My only wish was: I hope that this does not happen to our German cities. This side of the war is most horrible. The fateful destruction of cities, their culture and their children. The civilians are to be pitied.[154]

The following day General Kutrzeba met General Blaskowitz at the Skoda Airplane Factory in Rakow, outside of Warsaw, and within an hour signed an agreement for the "unconditional surrender" of Warsaw.[155] Albert Kesselring, Commander of Luftflotte I, which had bombed Warsaw, stated: "Blaskowitz, the commander of the investment troops, could be justifiably proud."[156]

Hitler recognized this himself when he called Blaskowitz to Berlin on 30 September, along with seventeen other military leaders, to receive honors for their "outstanding" leadership in the Polish campaign. The dictator asked the commanders to relay his congratulations to the troops.[157] General Blaskowitz was presented by Hitler with the Knight's Cross to the Iron Cross. Earlier in the campaign, he had already received Clasps to the Iron Cross First and Second Class for his leadership role in crossing the Warthe River.

Hitler privately had a different opinion of Blaskowitz. Within the army Blaskowitz was considered one of its best generals, especially after the battle on the Bzura and the capture of Warsaw. Some of his fellow generals thought that he was "the most accomplished Army commander in Poland," apparently being groomed for the highest leadership roles. But Hitler held the opposite view, probably as a result of his misunderstanding of Blaskowitz's handling of the battle and his "subsequent desire to discredit Blaskowitz, not to mention the eagerness of the others to take credit for the victory."[158]

Hitler's hatred of Blaskowitz and his contention that Blaskowitz's military leadership during the campaign in Poland was flawed may have had its roots in Hitler's distaste for Blaskowitz's deep and sincere Christianity. In any case Hitler considered him "unfit for command," a charge which Halder considered "very much unjustified and [which] reflected ill will." The General Staff then produced an official study of Blaskowitz's leadership in the campaign in Poland and presented it to Hitler, "contradicting Hitler's allegations." This stopped Hitler's tirade against Blaskowitz, but it did not stop Hitler from trying to hurt Blaskowitz.[159]

The American Vice Consul in Warsaw. a Mr. T. Chylinski, watched the Germans enter the city on 30 August as agreed. He thought the "troops were exceptionally well disciplined and behaved well except for some requisitioning of bedding from the Jewish population." There was no celebrating, order was re-established, army field kitchens were brought in to feed the population, fires were extinguished, bomb duds removed, bomb craters filled and electrical and water services restored.[160] Medical support for civilians was brought into the city.[161] The Army, however, only kept control of the city for two weeks of comparative peace and then withdrew. Himmler's men then moved into the city and took control.

About one month after Warsaw surrendered Goebbels drove across Poland to visit Warsaw. He described the drive across the flat Polish countryside "past totally destroyed villages and towns. A picture of desolation."[162] His impressions of Warsaw itself were even more stark:

> Warsaw: This is Hell. A city reduced to ruins. Our bombs and shells have done a thorough job. No house is undamaged. The populace is apathetic, shadowy. The people creep through the streets

like insects. It is repulsive and scarcely describable. Up on the citadel. Here everything has been destroyed. Hardly a stone left standing.[163]

After visiting Marshal Josef Pilsudski's deathbed at Belvedere Castle, Goebbels again drove through Warsaw. He added little to his earlier impressions: "Another drive through the city. A memorial to suffering."[164]

Hitler was delighted with the *Blitzkrieg* victory in Poland and in conversation with visitors to Berlin "went on for hours recapitulating all the phases of the campaign and giving detailed accounts of the prisoners and booty taken."[165] On October 5 Hitler returned to Warsaw to watch the victory parade. Blaskowitz, von Rundstedt, von Brauchitsch and von Reichenau met him at the airport.[166] General Erwin Rommel, in his role as commander of Hitler's escort troops, was also there to greet the Führer.

General Blaskowitz would have preferred that Hitler not attend the victory parade because Warsaw was still in a state of chaos and he could not guarantee the Führer's safety.[167] His fears were well-grounded since the Polish underground resistance had a plan to kill Hitler.

In the last hours before Warsaw's capitulation, the underground had planted two enormous explosive charges under the pavement at the intersection of Jerozlimske Avenue and Nowy Swiat, anticipating Hitler's arrival for just such a parade and knowing that he would almost be compelled to pass through this major intersection in his motorcade. Blaskowitz would likely have been riding in the car behind Hitler and might possibly have fallen victim to the explosion aimed at Hitler. For a number of circumstantial reasons the attempt to kill Hitler was not carried out.

The Polish Army officer in charge of the detonation could not get to the bombsite because the Germans closed the nearby streets to all Poles. The officer at the site had been given authority to act on his own, but only if he were certain that Hitler was there. Because he did not know whether Hitler, Blaskowitz or Brauchitsch was in the lead vehicle, he hesitated, and the cavalcade sped past him at high speed in a few seconds, frustrating the assassination attempt.[168] Blaskowitz probably never knew how close he had come to a common death with Hitler that day.

Elaborate preparations had been made for Hitler to take a salute on the Ujazdovska Aleja, Warsaw's Fifth Avenue, by the six divisions which had captured the city.[169] All possible security precautions had been taken. On the main boulevard armed soldiers stood guard at ten yard intervals, on the rooftops and at intersections mobile machine gun units were set up. Poles were forbidden to come closer than one hundred yards of the parade route.[170] It was the same route Goebbels described as a "monument to suffering."[171]

Generals Blaskowitz and Rundstedt had been directed to supervise the arrangements for the victory march and salute to Hitler. Von Rundstedt found the event most distasteful and acidly described it as "*Affentheater*," or "monkey theater," to SS general Reinhard Heydrich.[172] Blaskowitz was similarly "astringent" in his comments. Reportedly, "neither spared acid comparisons between the meticulous preparations and the work they had done to reach Warsaw at all."[173] Since Hitler himself was the centerpiece of the ceremony it was an inauspicious beginning to the day's events.

Hitler's review stand had been set up across from the Belgian Embassy. The Belgian flag flying there still had shrapnel holes from the fighting. Hitler arrived in his six-wheeled gray Mercedes, escorted by SS guards armed with machine guns. He stepped from the first car and was greeted by a monocled General von Reichenau. "Fuehrer," Reichenau said, "I give you Warsaw."[174]

The SS guards quickly took their prearranged positions on both sides of the review stand and the parade began, led by a divisional band playing suitably martial march music. The infantry made a most favorable impression:

> They goose-stepped in an ardent, clashing rhythm which shook their bodies from head to foot. The steel helmets jumped from chin straps and banged heavily on the soldier's heads each time they smashed a nail-studded boot on the pavement.[175]

The parade lasted nearly three hours, Hitler saluting file after file of the grey-clad troops. As each division passed, its commanding general dismounted his horse and joined the Fuehrer on the review stand. By the end of the parade the steel-helmeted, mostly monocled generals, "stiff as ramrods, eyes flashing pride," surrounded their Fuehrer, and, according to one observer, resembled a Napoleonic painting in modern martial dress.[176]

Later in the day Hitler, Blaskowitz and Kesselring were together and discussion naturally turned to the assault on Warsaw. Blaskowitz asserted that the artillery bombardment had been primarily effective in forcing Warsaw to surrender while Kesselring pointed out that "Polish prisoners were terrified to the marrow of the Stukas and that the targets in Warsaw devastated from the air were proof positive of our share [the Luftwaffe] in the victory."[177] Kesselring claimed that a "tour of the city made this plain."[178]

It was probably also on this day that Blaskowitz made another *faux-pas* in Hitler's eyes. Hitler, extremely proud of the Waffen SS, asked the General how the SS unit *Leibstandarte Adolf Hitler* had fought during the Polish Campaign, perhaps anticipating a flattering description of the merits of the Praetorian Guard that bore his name. But Blaskowitz was no sycophant. Replying with candor rather than cunning, the General told Hitler "that it was an average unit, still inexperienced, with no unusual qualifications."[179] In a single statement he had probably displeased Hitler, angered Himmler and made Sepp Dietrich, who commanded the *Leibstandarte*, furious with rage.[180] Yet another, more serious *faux pas* followed later that day.

Hitler had ordered that a field-kitchen be set up at Warsaw airfield where he could meet the commanders of the troops which had participated in the victory parade.[181] Blaskowitz, apparently thinking that the "occasion warranted a gala display, had extra benches and tables arranged in the hangars, the tables being laid with paper tablecloths and decorated with flowers."[182] Although Hitler's personal pilot, Lieutenant General Hans Baur, warned the major in charge of the airplane hangar of Hitler's preference for simplicity in his personal style, the major insisted that Hitler could not be asked to sit at an uncovered table.[183]

Hitler arrived at the airport around 4 P.M. and was promptly surrounded by admiring officers and soldiers. Cheers for the Fuehrer repeatedly rang out. Hitler spoke to a group of news correspondents:

> Gentlemen, you have seen for yourselves what criminal folly it was to try to defend this city. The defense collapsed after only two days of intensive effort. I wish only that certain statesmen in other countries who seem to want to turn all of Europe into a second

Warsaw could have the opportunity to see, as you have, the real meaning of war.

John Raleigh, a *Chicago Tribune* correspondent who was present that day, later wrote that he doubted that any of those who had heard Hitler, "grasped the significance behind the Fuehrer's words ...," that "they held the poison sword of a terrible prophecy ..."[184]

When he saw the covered tables decorated with the bowls of late fall flowers he asked to know who had ordered it. "He wanted to know whether a war was going on or a state dinner was being scheduled."[185] He turned and walked away from the tables snubbing von Brauchitsch's attempts to get him to change his mind.[186] Instead, he joined the troops at the field kitchen outside where he "swallowed a few spoonfuls of soup and chatted to the men around him ...."

According to one general present, "It was a patent attempt to demonstrate his 'attachment to the popular masses,'" as well as a "snub which ... inevitably set one thinking."[187] Hitler then flew back to Berlin with his entourage. According to Kesselring, "From that moment on, as later became evident, Blaskowitz was regarded with suspicion."[188]

Only two days earlier the Nazi Party newspaper, *Völkischer Beobachter* had prominently announced General Blaskowitz's promotion to the rank of colonel-general.[189] His picture was featured that very day on the front page taking the victory salute in Warsaw.[190] His photograph never appeared again in the Nazi paper. He would not be promoted to field marshal at all, the sole colonel-general from 1939 who was not promoted to field marshal. Hitler would not even keep a promise made to him earlier in the day.

During the parade, Hitler had told Blaskowitz, "Your command will be one of the first to be transferred to the West."[191] Accordingly, a few days later, Blaskowitz ordered his staff westward to Germany in anticipation of transfer to the western front. He himself went by automobile from Warsaw to Dresden and then to Duesseldorf and on to Eisenach. But in Eisenach he was stopped suddenly on the street and told to contact his chief of staff, General Hans Felber, in Frankfurt. When Blaskowitz telephoned Felber he was informed that he was to surrender the Army command and that his successor would be his recent subordinate, General Maximilian Freiherr von Weichs.[192] He himself should return to Lodz in Poland. He arrived in Lodz between the 10th and 15th of October.[193] Much had obviously transpired since the day of the victory parade in Warsaw.

Germany had plunged ever more deeply into unreality.[194]

Notes for Chapter VI

1. *I.M.T.*, 4: 415.

2. Below, *Als Hitlers Adjutant*, 205; David Irving, *Hitler's War*, 2 vols. (New York: The Viking Press, 1977), 1: 5.

3. *I.M.T.*, 4: 425.

4. Ibid., 426.

5. 3706-PS, *N.C.A.*, 6: 41.

6. Ibid.

7. G.M. Gilbert, *The Psychology of Dictatorship* (New York: The Ronald Press, 1950: reprint ed., Westport, Connecticut: Greenwood Press, 1979), 209.; Morgan, *Assize of Arms*, 305.

8. Gaines Post, *The Civil-Military Fabric of Weimar Foreign Policy* (Princeton, N.J.: Princeton University Press, 1973), 98-100.

9. Robert M. Citino, *The Evolution of Blitzkrieg Tactics: Germany Defends Itself Against Poland, 1918-1933* (Westport, Connecticut: Greenwood Press, l987), 9.

10. Ibid., 93.

11. Ibid., 79-94, 147-191; Deist, *Wehrmacht and German Rearmament*, 14-16. Germany's ability to defend herself against Poland exclusively improved through this period.

12. Citino, *Evolution of Blitzkrieg Tactics*, 50; *I.M.T.*, 4: 413-414.

13. *I.M.T.*, 4: 415.

14. Blaskowitz to Koepcke, 1 August 1939, *Collection Koepcke*, Copy in author's possession.

15. NOKW 2608, T-1119/33/0150, R.G. 238, N.A.; Jodl Interrogation, 28 October 1945, M-1270, Roll 8, R.G. 238, N.A. According to Colonel-General Alfred Jodl the meeting was specifically attended by Hermann Goering and Generals Keitel, List, Reichenau and Blaskowitz. Others such as Kesselring and Rundstedt were in attendance.

16. *I.M.T.*, 2: 290-291. The later Field Marshal von Bock told Fabian von Schlabrendorff later in the war that in this speech Hitler had included a

warning that "things would happen which would not have the approval of the German generals ...." Hitler reportedly stated ominously that "liquidations" for "political reasons" including "extermination" of the Polish clergy and upper classes, would be entrusted to the SS, since he did not want to "burden the Army." "All he asked was that the generals not interfere with these matters, but concentrate exclusively on military tasks." It appears, however, that Bock's memory was faulty and that Hitler spoke these words at a later date. Norman Rich suggests the conference of 12 September as the time these words were spoken. Fabian von Schlabrendorff, *The Secret War Against Hitler*, trans. Hilda Simon (New York: Pittman Publishing Corporation, 1965), 111-112. See also: Norman Rich, *Hitler's War Aims*, 2 vols. (New York: W.W. Norton & Co., 1973-74), 2: 74.

17. Paget, *Manstein*, 18-19.

18. Report of Interrogation No. 5554 (unknown German- undated), Case 110 (5554), R.G. 153, N.A.

19. Klaus Maier, Horst Rohde, Bernd Stegemann and Hans Umbreit, *Germany and the Second World War*, vol.2, *Germany's Initial Conquests in Europe*, trans. Dean McMurray and Ewald Osers (New York: Oxford University Press, 1991) 2: 92.

20. Heinz Höhne, *The Order of the Death's Head: The Story of Hitler's SS*, trans. Richard Barry, (New York: Ballantine Books, 1977), 337.

21. Taylor, *Sword and Swastika*, 284; MS #C-065c (Greiner), R.G. 338, N.A.

22. Taylor, *Sword and Swastika*, 282.

23. James Lucas and Matthew Cooper, *Hitler's Elite Leibstandarte SS, 1933-1945* (London: Macdonald and Jame's, 1975), 55.

24. Blumentritt, *Rundstedt*, 46.

25. James Weingartner, *Hitler's Guard: The Story of the Leibstandarte SS Adolf Hitler, 1933-1945* (Nashville: Battery Classics, N.D.), 32.; T-312/37/7545292-298, R.G. 238, N.A.

26. Ibid., 32-33.

27. Lehmann, *Leibstandarte*, I: 92.

28. James Lucas, *Das Reich: The Military Role of the 2nd SS Division* (London: Arms and Armour Press, 1991), 30.; F.T. Csokor, *A Civilian in the Polish War*, trans. Philip Owens (London: Secker & Warburg, 1940), 21.

29. Lucas and Cooper, *Hitler's Elite Leibstandarte SS*, 55.

30. Jaenecke, Erwin, "Die Armee Blaskowitz im Polenfeldzug," T-312/37/7545292-298, R.G. 238, N.A.

31. Weingartner, *Hitler's Guard*, 33.

32. Lehmann, *Leibstandarte*, I: 95. Major General Herbert Loch, commander of

the 17th Infantry Division, to which *Leibstandarte* was attached, complained that the "wild shooting and burning of villages" by the *Leibstandarte* destroyed needed troop shelters and obstructed lines of march. Weingartner, *Hitler's Guard*, 33.

33. T-312/37/7545292-298, R.G. 238, N.A.

34. Ibid.; Rolf Elble, *Die Schlacht an der Bzura im September 1939 aus deutscher und polnischer Sicht* (Einzelschriften zur Militärischen Geschichte des Zweiten Weltkrieges, 15; Freiburg, 1975), 78.; Weingartner, *Hitler's Guard*, 33.

35. Steven Zaloga and Victor Madej, *The Polish Campaign 1939* (New York: Hippocrene Books, 1985), 119.

36. "The Luftwaffe in Poland (September 1939)." German Translation No. VII/33, Maxwell Air Force Base Historical Research Center (Alabama).

37. Ibid.; Maier, Rhode, Stegemann and Umbreit, *Germany and the Second World War*, vol. 2, *Germany's Initial Conquests in Europe*, 106-107.

38. Elble, *Die Schlacht an der Bzura*, 79.

39. Robert Kennedy, *The German Campaign in Poland (1939)*, (Washington, D.C.: Department of the Army Pamphlets No. 20-255, 1956), 85.

40. Maier, Rhode, Stegemann and Umbreit, *Germany and the Second World War*, vol. 2, *Germany's Initial Conquests in Europe*, 106.

41. Cajus Bekker, *The Luftwaffe War Diaries*, trans. and ed., Frank Ziegler (Garden City, New York: Doubleday & Company, Inc., 1968), 45-46.

42. Elble, *Die Schlacht an der Bzura*, 80.

43. Jaenecke, Die Armee Blaskowitz im Polenfeldzug," T-312/37/7545292-298, R.G. 238, N.A.

44. Möller-Witten, *Mit dem Eichenlaub zum Ritterkreuz*, 215.

45. Kennedy, *German Campaign in Poland*, 85-86, 100-101.; Maier, Rhode, Stegemann and Umbreit, *Germany and the Second World War*, vol. 2, *Germany's Initial Conquests in Europe*, 107.

46. "Auszug aus Briefen und Tagebuchaufzeichnungen wahrend des POLENKRIEGES" (Felber), T-312/37/7545689-99; Kennedy, *German Campaign in Poland*, 88, 100. Kennedy gives the dates as 6 and 7 September.

47. Ibid.

48. Ibid.

49. Lehmann, *Leibstandarte*, I: 100.; Elble, *Die Schlacht an der Bzura*, 84.

50. Elble, *Die Schlacht an der Bzura*, 81-83.; Möller-Witten, *Mit dem Eichenlaub zum Ritterkreuz*, 215.

51. Ibid.

52. Ibid.

53. Addington, *Blitzkrieg Era*, 76-77.

54. Galeazzo Ciano, *The Ciano Diaries: 1939-1943*, ed. Hugh Gibson (New York: Doubleday & Company, Inc., 1946), 140.

55. "All Citizens Called to Aid of Warsaw," *New York Post*, 6 September 1939, 1,12.

56. Csokor, *Civilian in the Polish War*, 29.

57. Williamson Murray, *German Military Effectiveness* (Baltimore: The Nautical & Aviation Publishing Co., 1992), 109.; Bekker, *Luftwaffe War Diaries*, 27,34-35.

58. Herbert Drescher, *Warschau und Modlin im Polenfeldzug 1939: Berichte und Dokumente* (Pforzheim: N.P., 1991), 35.; Zaloga and Madej, *Polish Campaign*, 122.

59. Blaskowitz Interrogation, USFET-MISC, 8 September 1945, R.G. 165, N.A.

60. Ibid.

61. Warlimont Interrogation, SAIC/FIR/11, 24 July 1945, WO 208/3151, P.R.O.

62. Richard Humble, *Hitler's Generals* (Garden City, New York: Doubleday & Company, Inc., 1974), 36.

63. Ibid.; Addington, *Blitzkrieg Era*, 77-78.

64. Manstein, *Lost Victories*, 56.

65. Blaskowitz Interrogation, USFET-MISC, 8 September 1945, R.G. 165, N.A.

66. Addington, *Blitzkrieg Era*, 55-56.; 78.

67. Bekker, *Luftwaffe War Diaries*, 55-56.; Kurt Student, *Generaloberst Kurt Student und seine Fallschirmjäger: Die Erinnerungen des Generaloberst Student*, ed. Hermann Götzel (Friedberg: Podzun-Pallas-Verlag, 1980), 66-67.

68. Andrew Mollo, *To The Death's Head True*, (London: Thames/Methuen, 1982), 66.

69. Elble, *Die Schlacht an der Bzura*, 143.; Kennedy, *German Campaign in Poland*, 102.

70. Zaloga and Madej, *Polish Campaign*, 91, 133.

71. Manstein, *Lost Victories*, 55-56.

72. Warlimont Interrogation, SAIC/FIR/11, 24 July 1945, WO 208/3151, P.R.O.

73. Manstein, *Lost Victories*, 55.

74. Ibid., 56. Manstein is silent in these memoirs regarding his orders to Eighth Army on the evening of 7 September urging Blaskowitz to hasten toward Warsaw.

75. Ibid.

76. Blaskowitz Interrogation, USFET-MISC, 8 September 1945, R.G. 165, N.A.

77. Möller-Witten, *Mit dem Eichenlaub zum Ritterkreuz*, 216.

78. Ernst Kabisch, *Deutscher Siegeszug in Polen* (Stuttgart: Union Deutsche Verlagsgesellschaft, 1940), 136.

79. Manstein, *Lost Victories*, 56.

80. B.H. Liddell Hart Papers, King's College London, LH 9/24/53, This is the opinion of Günther Blumentritt.; Murray, *German Military Effectiveness*, 231. It would seem at first glance, to have been natural to have used the *Liebstandarte* element for reconnaissance but this unit was generally thought to be insufficiently trained, rather more a liability than an asset, and merited only return to a reserve. Charles Messenger, *Hitler's Gladiator: The Life and Times of Oberstgruppenführer and Panzer Generaloberst Der Waffen SS Sepp Dietrich* (London: Brassey's Defence Publishers, 1988), 74. Rundstedt had recognized the weakness before the 1939 campaign and requested the transfer to Eighth Army of some of the cavalry regiments assigned to duty on the "West Wall." Instead the SS *Leibstandarte* was given to Eighth Army. Rundstedt regarded it as a unit "not fully qualified for combat" at the time. MS#B-847 (Rundstedt), R.G. 338, N.A. See also: Lehmann, *Leibstandarte*, I: 76, 101-104.

81. Daniel Hughes, ed., *Moltke On the Art of War: Selected Writings*, trans. Daniel Hughes and Harry Bell (Novato, California: Presidio Press, 1993), 91.

82. Williamson Murray, *Strategy For Defeat: The Luftwaffe, 1933-1945* (Secaucus, New Jersey: Chartwell Books, 1986), 33.

83. "The Luftwaffe in Poland (September 1939)," German Translation No. V11/33, Maxwell Air Force Base Historical Research Center (Alabama).; Paul Deichmann, *German Air Force Operations in Support of the Army*, ed., Littleton Atkinson, U.S.A.F. Historical Division (New York: Arno Press, 1962), 78.

84. Murray, *German Military Effectiveness*, 111-112, 230-238.

85. Cooper, *German Army*, 178.

86. Peter Hoffmann, *Hitler's Personal Security* (Cambridge, Massachusetts: The M.I.T. Press, 1979), 138.

87. Keitel, *Memoirs*, 94.

88. Below, *Als Hitlers Adjutant*, 205.

89. "Auszug aus Briefen und Tagebuchaufzeichnungen wahrend des POLENKRIEGES" (Felber), T-312/37/7545689-99, R.G. 238, N.A., Emphasis added.

90. Irving, *Hitler's War*, I: 18.

91. Keitel, *Memoirs*, 95.

92. Irving, *Hitler's War*, I: 18. the Poles claimed 1500 men taken as prisoners

from the 30 Infantry Division alone. Zaloga and Madej, *Polish Campaign*, 133.

93. Samuel Mitcham, *Hitler's Legions: The German Army Order of Battle, World War II* (New York: Dorsett Press, 1985), 64.

94. Keitel, *Memoirs*, 95.; Von Briesen's impression upon Hitler was deep enough for the Führer to mention it in his famous speech of 6 October to the Reichstag.

95. "Entwicklung der Krise bei 8. Armee und ihre Behebung in der Zeit vom 9.-11.9.39." (Felber), T-312/37/7545678-88. R.G. 238, N.A.; Möller-Witten, *Mit dem Eichenlaub zum Ritterkreuz*, 216.

96. Möller-Witten, *Mit dem Eichenlaub zum Ritterkreuz*, 216.; Zaloga and Madej, *Polish Campaign*, 133. German estimates were a *four* to one Polish Infantry superiority.

97. "Entwicklung der Krise bei 8. Armee und ihre Behebung in der Zeit vom 9.-11.9.39" (Felber), T-312/37/7545678-88, R.G. 238, N.A.

98. Ibid., Elble, *Die Schlacht an der Bzura*, 141-142.

99. Ibid.

100. Möller-Witten, *Mit dem Eichenlaub zum Ritterkreuz*, 217.

101. "Auszug aus Briefen und Tagebuchaufzeichnungen wahrend des POLENKRIEGES" (Felber), T-312/37/7545689-99, R.G. 238, N.A.

102. Ibid., Elble, *Die Schlacht an der Bzura*, 141-142.

103. Nikolaus von Vormann, *Der Feldzug 1939 im Polen; Die Operation des Heeres* (Weisenburg, 1958). For a summary of Vormann's critique see; Möller-Witten, *Mit dem Eichenlaub zum RitterKreuz*, 219-221.

104. Kennedy, *German Campaign in Poland*, 102.

105. Jaenecke, "Die Armee Blaskowitz im Polenfeldzug," T-312/37/7545292-298.

106. Zaloga and Madej, *Polish Campaign*, 134-135.

107. Manstein, *Lost Victories*, 56-58; Addington, *Blitzkrieg Era*, 78-79.

108. Lehmann, *Leibstandarte*, I: 113.

109. Humble, *Hitler's Generals*, 36.

110. Bekker, *Luftwaffe War Diaries*, 54.

111. Deichmann, *German Air Force Operations in Support of the Army*, 105.

112. Kazimierz Wierzynski, *The Forgotten Battlefield*, trans. Edmund Orden (New York: Roy Publishers, 1944,), 165.

113. Raleigh, *Behind the Nazi Front*, 218.

114. Deichmann, *German Air Force Operations in Support of the Army*, 105. See also: Majer, Rhode, Stegemann and Umbreit, *Germany and the Second World War*, vol. 2, *Germany's Initial Conquests in Europe*, 117.

115. James Lucas, *Battle Group! German Kampfgruppe Action of World War Two* (London: Arms and Armour Press, 1993), 24.; Lucas and Cooper, *Hitler's Elite Leibstandarte SS*, 60-61.

116. Ibid.

117. Elble, *Die Schlacht an der Bzura*, 144.

118. "Auszug aus Briefen und Tagebuchaufzeichnungen wahrend des POLENKRI-EGES" (Felber), T-312/37/7545689-99, R.G. 238, N.A.

119. Jehuda Wallach, *The Dogma of the Battle of Annihilation: The Theories of Clausewitz and Schlieffen and Their Impact on the German Conduct of Two World Wars* (Westport, Connecticut: Greenwood Press, 1986), 249-252.

120. Ibid.; Manstein, *Lost Victories*, 57.

121. "Poles Still Resist Nazis In 4 Sectors," *The New York Times*, 22 September 1939, 6.

122. T-312/45/7557562-3, R.G. 238, N.A.

123. Raleigh, *Behind the Nazi Front*, 214-215.; T-312/37/7545799, R.G. 238, N.A.

124. Ibid., 103.

125. Blaskowitz Interrogation, USFET-MISC, 8 September 1945, R.G. 165, N.A.

126. Zaloga and Madej, *Polish Campaign*, 139.

127. Ibid.

128. Ibid.; Bryan Perrett, *A History of Blitzkrieg* (New York: Stein and Day Publishers, 1983), 79; Blaskowitz, "Die Einnahme von Warschau," T-312/37/7545279-289, R.G. 238, N.A.

129. Blaskowitz Interrogation, USFET-MISC., 8 September 1945, R.G. 165, N.A.

130. Nicholas Bethell, *The War Hitler Won: The Fall of Poland, September 1939* (New York: Holt, Rhinehart and Winston, 1972), 113-114.

131. Ibid., 114; Zaloga and Madej, *Polish Campaign*, 139.

132. Blaskowitz, "Die Einnahme von Warschau," T-312/37/7545279-289, R.G. 238, N.A. This is the General's official final report about the battle of Warsaw.

133. Manstein, *Lost Victories*, 59.

134. Blaskowitz Interrogation, USFET-MISC, 8 September 1945, R.G. 165, N.A.

135. Taylor, *Sword and Swastika*, 336.

136. Ibid.; Manstein, *Lost Victories*, 59; Addington, *Blitzkrieg Era*, 79.

137. Bekker, *Luftwaffe War Diaries*, 58.; Richtofen had suggested to the Chief of Air Staff that Warsaw should be ruthlessly destroyed since it would only be a "customs station" in the future. The suggestion had been rejected at the

time. "German Bombings of Warsaw and Rotterdam," German translation No. VII/132, Maxwell Air Force Base Historical Research Center (Alabama).

138. Blaskowitz, "Die Einnahme von Warschau," T-312/37/7545279-289, R.G. 238, N.A.

139. Ibid.; Irving, *Hitler's War*, 1: 19.

140. Bekker, *Luftwaffe War Diaries*, 54.

141. U.S. Military Attaché, Berlin, Report #D-16,955, October 31, 1939, "Major Military Operations: Visit to Polish Theatre of Operations," M.I.D. 2016-1297/64, R.G. 165, N.A.

142. Ibid.

143. Jaenecke, Erwin, "Die Armee Blaskowitz im Polenfeldzug," T-312/37/7545292-298, R.G. 238, N.A. Ironically, at this very time the American military attaché at Berlin praised cold-bloodedness by saying, "the man who combines inspiring leadership with skillful generalship and a logical, cold-blooded mind has the qualities of a great soldier." U.S. Military Attaché; Berlin, Report #17,717, November 18, 1940, "German Military Leadership," 2016-1329-3, The Army War College Collection, U.S.A.M.H.I.

144. Bethell, *The War Hitler Won*, 138-139.

145. Kennedy, *German Campaign in Poland*, 110.

146. "Defiant Warsaw Still Repels Foe," *The New York Times*, 21 September 1939, 6.

147. Kennedy, *German Campaign in Poland*, 110-112.

148. "Warsaw Buries Dead In Parks. Typhoid Strikes," *Chicago Sunday Tribune*, 24 September 1939, Sec. 1, 7.

149. Zaloga and Madej, *Polish Campaign*, 140.

150. Hans Baur, *Hitler At My Side*, trans. Lyndel Butler (Houston, Texas: Eichler Publishing Corporation, 1986), 120.

151. Walter Schellenberg, *The Labyrinth: Memoirs of Walter Schellenberg*, trans. Louis Hagen (New York: Harper & Brothers Publishers, 1956), 57-58.

152. Macksey, *Kesselring*, 64.; Bekker, *Luftwaffe War Diaries*, 58.

153. Ibid (Macksey).

154. "Auszug und Briefen aus Tagebuchaufzeichnungen wahrend des POLENKRIEGES" (Felber), T-312/37/7545689-99, R.G. 238, N.A.

155. Taylor, *Sword and Swastika*, 337.

156. Kesselring, *Memoirs*, 47; The American edition of these memoirs, substantially shorter than the British Edition, also contains this comment. Albert Kesselring, *Kesselring; A Soldier's Record*, trans. Lynton Hudson (New York: William Morrow & Co., 1954), 43.

157. "Reich Calls Ciano In Peace Offensive," *The New York Times*, 1 October 1939, 1 & 48.

158. Wilhelm Scheidt, "Biography Report [Blaskowitz]" 22 October 1945, Biographical Data Personnel Folders Series, R.G. 238, N.A.; Samuel Lewis, *Forgotten Legions: German Infantry Policy, 1918-1941* (New York: Praeger, 1986), 70-71.

159. Franz Halder, Eidesstattlich Erklärung, undated, circa 1947, *Collection Koepcke*, Copy in author's possession.

160. T.H. Chilinski, Vice Consul, November 13, 1941, "Poland Under Nazi Rule," M.I.D. Regional File, 1922-1944, Entry 77, R.G. 165, N.A.

161. Möller-Witten, *Mit dem Eichenlaub zum Ritterkreuz*, 219.

162. Joseph Goebbels, *The Goebbels Diaries: 1939-1941*, ed. and trans. Fred Taylor (New York: G.P. Putnam's Sons, 1983), 37.

163. Ibid.

164. Ibid.

165. Paul Schmidt, *Hitler's Interpreter*, ed. R.H.C. Steed (New York: The MacMillan Co., l951), 164.

166. Below, *Als Hitlers Adjutant*, 211.; Hoffman, *Hitler's Personal Security*, 140.

167. Blaskowitz, "Die Einnahme von Warschau," T-312/37/7545279-289, R.G. 238, N.A.

168. Jan Nowak, *Courier From Warsaw* (Detroit: Wayne State University Press, 1982), 60-61.

169. Manstein, *Lost Victories*, 61.

170. Raleigh, *Behind the Nazi Front*, 202. Raleigh was the *Chicago Tribune* correspondent and had been invited to the parade.

171. Goebbels, *Goebbels Diaries: 1939-1941*, 37.

172. Hart, *Hitler's Generals*, 58-59; Brett-Smith, *Hitler's Generals*, 18.

173. Ibid.

174. Raleigh, *Behind the Nazi Front*, 204.

175. Ibid., 205.

176. Ibid., 206.

177. Kesselring, *Kesselring*, 42.

178. Ibid. At least one other observer thought both Blaskowitz and Kesselring were wrong and vividly argued that the mortars had done the most damage. He wrote, "The greatest results were achieved by our 30.5 cm. mortars, the noise of which for many days was the voice of Warsaw. The mortars spoke incessantly, one battery after another, showering a hot rain of metal over Poland's capital, bursting in windows and tearing out window frames and

doors. Watching by night we saw curves of coloured fire flashing gracefully toward Warsaw. The earth quivered and our eardrums seemed about to split. Looking to Warsaw we saw columns of smoke soaring languidly, as if from mighty cigars. In all directions, long smoky tongues of fire spurted up every second. In the heavens the clouds were as red as blood." Bethell, *The War Hitler Won*, 139.

179. Blaskowitz File, M.I.D., M.I.S., "Who's Who Branch, 1939-1945," R.G. 165, Entry 194, N.A.; Blaskowitz Interrogation, CCPWE#32/DI-43, 28 July 1945, WO 208/3154, P.R.O.

180. Although there is no proof that Himmler learned of Blaskowitz's indifferent evaluation of the *Leibstandarte*, it was a fact that he was embittered that the SS field units had not been specially commended for their part in the campaign in Poland. See Reitlinger, *SS*, 127. Hitler had an "intense" interest in his namesake military formation. "During the Polish Campaign Hitler had marked on a map in the Reich Chancellery the simple notation Sepp,' to reveal to him at a glance the location of his' Leibstandarte." Weingartner, *Hitler's Guard*, 35.

181. Manstein, *Lost Victories*, 61.

182. Kesselring, *Kesselring*, 43.

183. Baur, *Hitler At My Side*, 120.

184. Raleigh, *Behind the Nazi Front*, 210.; Irving, *Hitler's War*, I: 30.

185. Baur, *Hitler At My Side*, 120.

186. Kesselring, *Kesselring*, 43.

187. Manstein, *Lost Victories*, 61.

188. Kesselring, *Kesselring*, 43.

189. "Blaskowitz, Kluge und Reichenau zu Generaloberst befordert," *Völkischer Beobachter* (Norddeutsche Ausgabe), 4 October 1939, 2. See also "Promoted to Rank of Colonel General in German Army," *The New York Times*, 3 October 1939, 12.

190. "Generaloberst Blaskowitz in Warschau" (Photo), *Völkischer Beobachter* (Norddeutsche Ausgabe), 6 October 1939, 1.

191. Blaskowitz Interrogation, 25 October 1945, M-1270, Roll 1, R.G. 238, N.A.

192. Weichs had commanded XIII Corps in Eighth Army.

193. Blaskowitz Interrogation 25 October 1945, M-1270, Roll 1, R.G. 238, N.A.

194. Friedrich Reck-Malleczewen, *Diary of a Man in Despair*, trans. Paul Rubens (London: The MacMillan Company, 1970), 93.

CHAPTER VII

OCCUPIED POLAND 1939

ON 3 OCTOBER the occupation troops in defeated Poland were officially organized into an over-all command called *Oberost*, High Command East.[1] Colonel-General Gerd von Rundstedt was appointed "Commander-in-Chief in the East." Von Rundstedt vehemently disliked the assignment. He knew that a civil governor was to be appointed in Poland, and that conflict between the military and civilian governors was inevitable.[2] Efforts to change von Rundstedt's assignment were sent out immediately from the small manor house in southwest Warsaw in which his staff was quartered. They were soon successful.[3] On 15 October General Adolf Heusinger arrived from *OKH* with the "welcome news" that von Rundstedt and his headquarters were to be sent to the west.[4] Von Rundstedt was temporarily transferred to Lodz where he turned over *Oberost* to Blaskowitz and moved on to command of Army Group A on the Rhine. Rundstedt was awarded the Knight's Cross—which Blaskowitz had already been granted on September 30th—while Blaskowitz received the position of *Oberost*.

General of Infantry Curt Liebmann served as the transitional military chief in Poland between the departure of von Rundstedt and Blaskowitz's return to Poland. In late October the commandant of Warsaw, General Neumann-Neurode told Liebmann about a meeting he had held in Warsaw with subordinate officers to discuss alleviating conditions in Warsaw for the Poles.

The meeting had only begun when an uninvited SS officer interjected that he understood from his orders that the population was not to be helped at all. Quite the contrary, upper class citizens and the intelligentsia were to be allowed to die. The common man was to be permitted to live solely to work for his new German masters. General Neumann-Neurode told General Liebmann that he wished in these circumstances to resign; Liebmann said he had not heard of any such orders and would resign himself if such were the case.[5] The incident proved to be a clue to the future for both Poland and Blaskowitz.

Blaskowitz spent most of the first days of November organizing his staff and official headquarters in Lodz and then in moving to Spala, a Czarist hunting lodge half-way between Lodz and Warsaw.[6] Spala had also been the summertime residence of the Polish President during the interwar years and was rather isolated from the public. He chose it deliberately because of its inaccessibility, which made it easier for him to avoid "political" surveillance.[7] Spala had its own rail station and line connection as well as a small airfield despite being located in the middle of a forest. Some barracks were built for the troops. Blaskowitz thought it possible to "move about without attracting too much attention."[8] In his view, "it came as an advantage that I had some privacy."[9]

The move was a prophylactic measure since his staff had learned of fundamental changes in the administration of defeated Poland around 15 October.[10] A civil governor was to be appointed for Poland which would henceforth be called the "General Government." The Army Commander's authority was to be restricted to purely military matters; he would have authority only over the small number of troops remaining in Poland. Administration of civil matters and police duties were not his responsibility, but instead were allotted to the civil governor. Clearly, it was an arrangement likely to "cause the greatest tensions between the Commander in Chief and the Governor General." This was the impression, at least, of Major-General Rudolf Langhaeuser, a member of the General's staff.[11]

Conflict was indeed likely between Blaskowitz and the civil governor of the General Government since Blaskowitz "was not one deliberately to toady ...,"[12] and was "acutely aware of the ethical responsibility of the German soldier."[13] Indeed, Colonel-General Blaskowitz's character made a conflict with the Governor-General probable. Hitler's plans for Poland—carried out by his Governor-General—virtually guaranteed the inevitability of a clash.

Hitler had revealed his intentions for Poland to General Eduard

Wagner in a conference held in mid-October. On 18 October, Wagner had informed Halder about the conference with the Führer:

> We have no intention of rebuilding Poland .... Assembly area for future German operations. Poland is to have its own administration. Is not to be turned into a model state by German standards. Polish Intelligentsia must be prevented from establishing itself as a new governing class. Low standard of living must be conserved. Cheap slaves .... The administration in Poland will have complete authority except on military matters. Only one supreme authority: Governor-General. Total disorganization must be created! No cooperation of Reich Government agencies! The Reich will give the Governor-General the means to carry out this devilish plan.[14]

It was probably also General Wagner who reported Hitler's summary instruction to Hans Frank, whom he had chosen to be Poland's Governor-General: "Other people to whom such territories are handed, would ask: 'What would you construct? I will ask the opposite'"[15] It was indeed a devilish plan, and quite in contrast to Colonel-General Blaskowitz's more traditional ideas. The Colonel-General held the same ideas concerning the occupation of Poland as he had in Prague. His "opinion was to let things get settled again." He wanted the populations evacuated during the hostilities to be given a chance to return home. Industry was to be revived. Finally, "in general, everything should be done that was possible and that with the least possible number of troops, I would safeguard peace and order."[16]

With the appointment of a civil governor and the drastic reduction of his own responsibility, the General's attitude was that his responsibility was solely military but that any conditions which threatened military security and made it necessary for Germany to keep more troops in Poland than really essential was a matter of his "legitimate interest ...."[17] He would soon find that the new Governor-General provided plenty of reason for concerns along these lines. As a member of his staff later wrote, "we soon had to realize that ... [Poland] was now made an object of trial and exploitation on the part of dilettantism and arbitrariness."[18] He continued by noting that, although the new Governor-General "promised to make the country a flourishing province, practice had a different aspect."[19] This last thought was a classic understatement. The Governor-General was notorious.

Hans Frank, lawyer, one-time member of the Reichstag, Minister of the Reich without portfolio, long-time supporter of Hitler, although not a member of Hitler's inner circle, was appointed Governor-General in a decree promulgated by Hitler on 12 October 1939.[20] He was directly subordinated to the Führer himself.[21] His power in the Government General would be vast, his attitude central for the rump Polish state. Nevertheless, von Rundstedt mockingly called him the "King of Poland," "Stanislaus the little."[22] Similarly, Germans fond of puns called Poland "Frankreich."

It had not originally been Hitler's intention to appoint a civil governor in Poland. General Keitel had supported the establishment of a traditional military government. After a short visit to Poland, however, Frank had visited Hitler and "cursed the Wehrmacht for its weak and inefficient military administration, and on the strength of this, was at once installed in his new office by Hitler."[23] Nor was this a lone incident. When Frank was visited by Goebbels, on Thursday, 2 November 1939, at Frank's residence, the latter recorded Frank's comments and his own thoughts: "At Frank's house in the evening, he tells me of his problems. Principally with the Wehrmacht, who are pursuing a milksop-bourgeois policy, rather than a racially-aware one. But, Frank will get his way."[24] "Frank's way", as Goebbels saw it, and as he and Frank had discussed, (that afternoon during a visit to the Lodz Ghetto) was clear. In the Ghetto, as Goebbels wrote, "These are no longer human beings, they are animals. For this reason, our task is no longer humanitarian but surgical. Steps must be taken here, and they must be radical ones, make no mistake."[25]

Frank was critical of the *Wehrmacht* in Poland—and indirectly of Blaskowitz—but he felt no compassion at all for the Poles themselves. He later suggested that when their usefulness was exhausted, "then, for all I care, mincemeat can be made of the Poles and Ukrainans and all the others who run around here—it does not matter what happens."[26]

On 17 October, Frank visited Hitler before leaving for his new position as Governor-General in Poland. He told Hitler that "the military administration in Poland was by no means sufficient, and that it would be necessary for him to go at once with his civilian administration."[27] General Keitel, who witnessed this scene, remarked shortly after the meeting that Hitler had stated that the soldiers were lucky if they were separated from the administration. Then he added prophetically, "the two administrations cannot exist."[28]

It was a moment in which Hitler's reported gifts of prophecy were self-fulfilling. The issue on which the clash would focus would be the status and treatment of the Jews in the General Government. In mid-December, Frank would inform his staff about his position in this matter: "I want to say to you quite openly ... that we shall have to finish the Jews, one way or another."[29] Few others knew this at the time.

Most foreign visitors were forbidden by the German government to visit occupied Poland. Even the representatives of an American relief mission were refused permission to go to Poland to supervise distribution of relief aid.[30] Nevertheless, reports of conditions in Poland reached the west. One report to British government circles succinctly described Poland's fate:

> Hate and murder. Plunder of property and treasure. SS, Gestapo and Pgs [Parteigennossen] all busy enriching selves. In Rumppolen Poles literally becoming slaves of feudal Nazis. Girls and women used for concubines en masse. Country laid waste ....[31]

An 8 December report which originated in Estonia and reached the American military attaché in Berlin corroborated the above report and added: "The Polish people are being terrorized by German SS troops against the wishes of the German Army. Considerable friction is known to exist between the Army and the party troops."[32] Indeed, as early as Christmas 1939 the American military attaché in Berlin reported that there had been a "constant flow of reports from Poland that there is considerable friction between the SS units and the German Army." He continued: "The main source of complaint has been the ruthless methods used by the SS to establish control over the inhabitants." Noting that the army was restricted to "normal garrison duties in occupied territory" the attaché added:

> The Polish people ... seemed to hold the personnel of the German Army in much higher regard. The treatment received from the Army was considerate and much regret was expressed when the Army relinquished control and the methods of the SS were imposed.

The report concluded: "Friction exists between the SS and the

German Army, the seriousness of which is not yet fully known. The Army deprecates the methods used by the SS in Poland."[33]

The accuracy of the report by the U.S. military attaché in Berlin is proven by a letter from a German General Staff officer who visited Colonel-General Blaskowitz in Poland and who wrote to his wife describing his visit on 21 November 1939. Helmuth Stieff described Warsaw dramatically:

> The city and its inhabitants are doomed to die. This situation is so sad and incorrigible that one cannot have a free minute to relax. The horror follows everywhere. You see ladies that held high positions and prestige in society sell themselves in the street to our soldiers for a piece of bread.[34]

He continued:

> But this is not the worst. The worst is that there is a high degree of shameful actions and looting, murder, organized and without regrets, that is being executed by our very own people. The things that I have seen done by Germans to the Polish are so incredible that I cannot call these people anything but evil and inhuman. Germany does not deserve to be called by its name. Germans have begun to be sub-human. I am ashamed to belong to the German race.[35]

He concluded this letter by mentioning his visit to Generaloberst Blaskowitz.

> I have spent almost an hour with Blaskowitz. He poured his heart out to me and told me about his concern and worries. He felt deeply about the situation. He especially was concerned about the goings on at OB-east.[36]

Even ordinary enlisted men who abhorred the atrocities they had witnessed were going A.W.O.L.(Absent Without Official Leave) to make reports about the horrors to Blaskowitz personally. He pleaded with Stieff to bring the matter to the attention of the army high command.[37]

Stieff's characterization of Blaskowitz as a man tormented by what he saw and learned of the atrocities in Poland confirmed the impression of another visitor six weeks earlier, even before Blaskowitz had been appointed *Oberost*. Wilhelm Canaris, Chief of the Abwehr, secret intelligence, had visited him then and described him as "extremely upset and concerned about the lack of discipline among the soldiers and higher ranking officers."[38]

It was no wonder that the general was worried about the "goings-on" in High-Command East: he had much about which to worry almost from the very beginning of the attack on Poland. There had been outrageous offenses against mankind and the laws of war common to civilized nations.

On 10 September, when the campaign in Poland was less than two weeks old, General Halder noted in his diary that members of the SS had "herded Jews into a church and massacred them." He noted also that a court martial had taken place and that the SS men involved in the massacre had received a sentence of one year in a penitentiary, but that General von Küchler had not approved of the sentence and had demanded a more severe punishment.[39] When the matter was finally resolved in court, a German military judge granted "extenuating circumstances" to the SS officer guilty of the crime because "as an SS man, particularly sensitive to the sight of Jews, and hostile to the attitude of Jewry to Germans, he, therefore, acted quite thoughtlessly in youthful rashness."[40] Punishment was fixed at three years. The sentences were eventually dropped under amnesty and neither of the perpetrators served a day in prison for the crime.[41]

On the same day that General Halder had made this diary entry, Hitler's favorite actress and film producer, Leni Reifenstahl, witnessed twenty-two Jews being shot. She was so upset that she could not continue filming and reported this incident to an officer who forwarded the report to General von Manstein. Though an investigation was ordered, similar incidents continued to take place.[42]

On 18 September, General Wilhelm List, who commanded the Fourteenth Army, issued an order prohibiting looting, rape, burning of synagogues and the shooting of Jews.[43] Two days later, however, Major Schmidt-Richtberg, who served as the staff intelligence officer to General List, referred to "further reports about unrest in that army area arising from the partly illegal measures taken by the Special Purpose Group [Einsatz Gruppe] of Brigadier General Woyrsch. (Mass shootings, especially of Jews)." The reports stated that "It was especially annoying to the troops that young men, instead of fighting at the front, were testing their courage on defenseless people."[44] The *Einsatz Gruppe* under Udo von Woyrsch "behaved with such unparalled bestiality that it was thrown out of the operational area."[45]

Colonel-General Blaskowitz and Colonel-General von Rundstedt had apparently learned in advance that Hitler planned to pardon those who were guilty of such atrocities. On 10 October they visited Halder to complain, but it was to no avail. Halder listened to them, but took no action.[46]

The German campaign in Poland had aroused some members of the High Command and the rank and file against the SS but Heinrich Himmler—leader of the SS—had also been aroused by Army attempts to bring SS men to trial for atrocities committed during the military campaign. Himmler persuaded Hitler to order that such attempts should not be permitted to hamper the SS in any way. On 17 October, a "Decree relating to a Special Jurisdiction in Penal Matters for Members of Police Groups on Special Tasks" freed the SS from army legal jurisdiction and placed them under special SS courts.[47]

As a German historian later wrote: "Hitler's order of 17 October 1939, turned the East ... into the Wild West of the Reich, where law and order counted for little."[48] The SS had a free hand in Poland. Hitler's decree was not at all surprising; during the campaign in Poland, the SS leader for the conquered regions of Poland had operated from Hitler's private headquarters train.[49]

In a special "Jewish Decree," Hitler additionally directed that "all penal procedures against members of the armed forces who had committed acts of violence against Jews in Poland were to be discontinued and closed."[50] The net result of these decrees was that the Army and the SS went their own ways in Poland, since the Army Commander, Walter von Brauchitsch, issued a supplementary directive which permitted prosecution of crimes by Army men in most cases.[51]

Hitler's intentions to destroy Poland and Polish Jewry had been questioned on 12 September in Hitler's private train by Admiral Wilhelm Canaris, head of the Counter-Intelligence. Canaris told General Keitel that he had learned that "extensive executions were planned in Poland and that particularly the nobility and the clergy were to be exterminated." He added that, eventually, "the world would hold the *Wehrmacht* responsible for this." Keitel told him that this decision had been made by Hitler himself and that the Führer had told him that "if the *Wehrmacht* did not want any part in these occurrences, it would have to accept the SS and the Gestapo as rivals."[52] Hitler also told one of his adjutants that "it did not matter what the German troops occupying Poland were doing, as long as they were present. They did not have orders to see to it that law and order were maintained. Hitler said laissez-faire was all right."[53]

"Laissez-faire" may have been to Hitler's liking but it revolted some in the military. After witnessing the events in Poland, General Hans Oster was moved to write about Hitler: "[He is a] mad criminal who is engaged in destroying everything that is sacred to me as an officer, as a human being, as a Christian, and as a German."[54] Some officers were so shocked by what they learned about the atrocities that the military opposition to Hitler which had mounted prior to the Munich Conference "flared-up" again.

Halder later explained this "flare-up" of the opposition to Hitler this way:

> It was a question of certain disagreeable events which took place toward the end of the Polish campaign, which had been committed by the SS without our knowledge, but of which we learnt [sic] and to which we give [sic] the name "the Polish atrocities."[55]

Hitler's insistence on a campaign in the west and the reports of atrocities in Poland led Halder to characterize that time as one in which "the whole atmosphere was charged with tension ...."[56]

The tension-filled atmosphere was apparent even to experienced observers in Germany. Wallace Deuel, Chief of the *Chicago Daily News* Berlin bureau from 1934 to 1941, who was distinguished for his news dispatches, "With the German Army in Poland," described the events in Poland as a "rape," "carried out by the party in opposition to the wishes of most of the generals who know what is going on in Poland—and most of them do not—and in spite of the fact that Poland is ... [under armed forces protection]."[57]

Despite the wide range of the SS atrocities some army leaders were slow to realize that Poland was being devastated according to Hitler's plan. Interrogated on precisely this point after the war, General Halder stated:

A. It was, according to our opinion, a series of single acts by the SS in which they illegally and senselessly killed many people.

Q. Why do you say single acts? Didn't you know these acts were committed according to plan?

A. We did not have the impression and the proof of that at that time. I am giving you a picture of that time. Of course, later when we learned about the regime, Frank, we saw some connection between these single acts, but at that time, they appeared to us as single acts, we thought of no other possibility.[58]

Although an occasional isolated army commander was sufficiently shrewd to suspect that the SS atrocities were the result of a planned operation,[59] it does not appear that Colonel-General Blaskowitz was among them. Harold Deutsch, the distinguished historian, wrote that "This soldier of literal mind knew only that Hitler had decreed a division of powers; he had little notion of the implications."[60]

It took time for this strict soldierly mentality to realize fully that the atrocities were part of Hitler's plan for Poland.[61] Perhaps naively, he began his command at *Oberost* on 26 October with an order of the day in which he admonished his troops that "the Eastern Army must concern itself with purely soldierly assignments and is freed of all that has to do with administration and internal politics."[62]

Already in September during the campaign he had clashed with the SS. One source reports that he had then issued court martial orders of a "group" of SS men for the murder of 450 Jewish civilians, but the SS were "amnestied almost immediately."[63] Ulrich von Hassell, a German diplomat connected with the anti-Nazi opposition, wrote in his diary on 19 October that Blaskowitz had "wanted to prosecute two SS leaders—including that rowdy Sepp Dietrich—for looting and murder."[64] As commander of Eighth Army during the campaign, he may also have learned of atrocities committed by the "Brandenburg" Division in Wloclawek.[65] According to one source, the "iron-spined" Blaskowitz "found all the Death's Head units loathsome and was ... horrified by their excesses ...."[66] He may also have heard stories of army regimental commanders ending SS atrocities by force of arms.[67]

Those atrocities which were reported to him troubled him so much that he took the unusual step of sending one of his adjutants; von Perbundt, to privately inform his friend Koepcke of the nature of his personal situation and of Nazi rule in Poland. As Military Commander in Poland, his relations with the SS—especially with SS Police *Obergruppenführer* Krueger—who had once been Goebbel's expert in street fighting—were very strained.[68]

His relations with Governor Frank were no better.[69] General Blaskowitz had strictly limited powers as Military Governor. The SS and the SD "were in many respects independent of Hans Frank's civil administratration and absolutely independent of Colonel-General Blaskowitz, the military governor."[70]

In the chaos of competing governmental agencies which the Nazis had created in occupied Poland, Colonel-General Blaskowitz's conception of his role as military commander in Poland was that his responsibility was strictly military, in light of Frank's appointment to head the civil government. Nevertheless, any events or condition that threatened military security or caused Germany to keep more than the minimum numbers of troops necessary in Poland "were subjects of legitimate interest to him."[71]

Blaskowitz believed that it was his responsibility to maintain order only in the areas occupied by the army; responsibility for the other parts of Poland rested with the General Government. "Beyond that he tried to keep his troops strictly segregated from the Poles, since contacts with the Poles only caused trouble and increased the distrust." He disagreed strongly with Frank's criticism that his troops were not "harsh enough" in maintaining order.[72] A clash with Governor General Frank and with the SS was inevitable.

During the autumn Blaskowitz received reports from his unit commanders that the SS was engaging in "large scale raids which gathered in Jews and certain Polish elements."[73] Although he did not know for certain what was done with the Jews he believed that they were sent to the Warsaw Ghetto, which he described as a "giant collecting camp for Polish Jews."[74] He issued the "strictest possible orders that all [army] troops were to refrain from any activities of this kind ...."[75] Men who violated the order were to be court-martialed.[76]

Blaskowitz assigned to a member of his staff at Spala, General-Major Langhaeuser, the task of combatting these atrocities, "first by means of complaints and protests to the Governor General and the Higher SS and Police Commander [Krueger], then through an appeal to the Army

High Command ..., always without any success.[77] Langhaeuser also used a "special channel through ... Admiral Canaris, to bring the events in the General Government to the attention of the *Wehrmacht* High Command and of Hitler."[78] Colonel-General Blaskowitz and his staff at *Oberost* believed that "the Army High Command lent its fullest support to our protests, and presented them in the most express manner to the *Wehrmacht* High Command and the *Reichsführer SS*."[79] The "Army High Command" meant the Army Commander-in-Chief, Colonel-General von Brauchitsch.

Von Brauchitsch had been a member of the elite of the old imperial army. He had entered the select Third Guard-Grenadier Regiment in Berlin in 1900 and served in a succession of elite regiments. In World War I, during the crucial battle at Verdun in August, 1916, the venerated Ludendorff personally had nominated von Brauchitsch to receive the Iron Cross medal of the House of Hohenzollern for his outstanding bravery in combat.[80] An exceptional leader in "questions concerning training,[81] a "thoroughbred aristocratic old-Prussian, and deeply religious," Brauchitsch's temperament was "more thoughtful than energetic in nature." But, "around Hitler and the Nazi-milieu, he was of course not assertive enough, not robust enough ...."[82]

Usually a "cautious and conscientious man ...,"[83] Brauchitsch's Chief of the General Staff, Franz Halder, admitted that "Brauchitsch was just too relenting, too fastidious."[84] "He added, "I will admit that General von Brauchitsch was perhaps not a strong enough personality ...."[85] Field Marshal Milch of the Luftwaffe incisively characterized von Brauchitsch—perhaps more accurately than any of his other colleagues:

> He did not have a strong character. He did not speak up—he was the silent type. He didn't press his own ideas with Hitler. He told Hitler what he thought and Hitler would contradict him: he would try again very politely, and then when he got the impression that Hitler would not follow his ideas, he dropped it.[86]

The British military attaché to Berlin succinctly described von Brauchitsch as "a sound soldier with an East Prussian background, but with no outstanding personality or strength of character."[87] He was simply too "weak-willed" repeatedly to confront Hitler with ideas contrary to those of the Führer.[88]

Although von Brauchitsch "left no doubt that he considered Hitler undesirable,"[89] he could not forcefully stand up to the dictator. His hesitating character was probably also further restrained by the fact that he was indebted to Hitler for the financial assistance that had made his divorce and remarriage possible.[90] His second wife, Charlotte Schmidt-Ruffer was an admirer of Hitler, and habitually reminded him of "how much we owe the Fuehrer."[91] Indeed, the very circumstances of his marriage compared with the causes for his predecessor's dismissal likely increased his insecurity vis-à-vis Hitler since the Führer had known about the liaison before the divorce took place.[92]

Handicapped as von Brauchitsch was in his relationship to Hitler, he was nevertheless the one man upon whom Blaskowitz had to rely to present his protests of SS atrocities in Poland to Hitler. It was reliance upon a straw man who proved to be both clumsy and ineffectual. What Blaskowitz did not know was that von Brauchitsch had consented to the creation of the dual military and civilian administrations in Poland despite his knowledge that this foreshadowed further persecution of the Jews and the Poles. Von Brauchitsch wished only to keep the Army from active involvement in the "dirty work."[93] Although he learned of the SS atrocities, his ability to take protests to Hitler was compromised by his indebtness to the Führer. Nevertheles, von Brauchitsch provided the only avenue for Blaskowitz's protests to reach Hitler. And von Brauchitsch did make an effort in his own fashion.

As early as mid-September von Brauchitsch "had at the daily conferences already complained about interference by the police in occupied Polish territory."[94] At the end of September he approached Keitel and "complained about police actions which occurred in Poland, and he requested a change in policy from Hitler."[95]

Hitler, who was behind the policies pursued by the SS in Poland, would not have changed his policy in any event since it grew "logically" from his racial politics. He was, however, particularly incensed with von Brauchitsch at the end of September because of the general's actions with regard to the death of General Freiherr von Fritsch, who had been killed on September 22 in action in Poland.

Von Brauchitsch had infuriated Hitler by issuing orders honoring von Fritsch and even personally delivering the eulogy at the state funeral.[96] Hitler had resented von Fritsch since the struggle to remove him from command. During the eulogy von Brauchitsch had called von Fritsch an "extraordinary, blameless man ...."[97] Von Brauchitsch's actions had "provoked Hitler's extreme indignation."[98]

Von Brauchitsch added fuel to the fires of Hitler's anger when they met at the Congress Hall in the Reich Chancellery on 5 November 1939. Von Brauchitsch presented Hitler with a memorandum detailing his opposition to the proposed attack on France. The general asserted that the infantry in Poland had been "over cautious and insufficiently attack-minded." Discipline had been very lax and reminded him of 1917—there had been drunken orgies and bad behavior in troop trains and at railway stations.[99]

Hitler predictably flew into a rage, making continued conversation impossible. The dictator apparently took von Brauchitsch's accusations as a slur upon National Socialist education of youth and was "deeply offended."[100]

As a result of this meeting, Hitler refused in the next few weeks to even see von Brauchitsch.[101] As one of Hitler's later field marshals wrote, it was "a quite impossible situation ...."[102] In Berlin, wild rumors circulated that:

> General von Blomberg, one time Commander in Chief of the Armed Forces, is reported to have been shot; Generals von Hammerstein (once Chief of Staff), Stülpnapel, Rundstedt, Brauchitsch and Blaskowitz, are reported in various degrees of disfavor ranging from concentration camps to merely being replaced. Young von Hammerstein ... states that his father is out "hunting." The "hunt" has lasted several weeks.[103]

Indeed, Hitler's fury continued to rage about von Brauchitsch. The following day, at a meeting attended by generals Schmundt, Keitel and Jodl, Field Marshal Göring, and Hitler's adjutants, von Below and Puttkamer, Göring said to Hitler: "My Fuehrer, why don't you divorce yourself from these—Brauchitsch and Halder?" Hitler replied, "I can't do that now right after the Polish victory."[104]

In these astounding circumstances—with Hitler and von Brauchitsch temporarily not talking with each other—Blaskowitz took the only action possible to a decent, honorable soldier. He informed his Commander-in-Chief in writing on 16 November of the horrible torture of Poland. Clearly there could have been little in the memorandum that was strikingly new to von Brauchitsch; only two days earlier, Major General Kurt von Tippelskirch had told him all that he needed to know. Von Tippelskirch, Chief Intelligence officer at *OKH*, had told von Brauchitsch of mass executions in Poland and that "women and children were put into large graves."[105] The Army Commander-in-Chief's reaction was unfortunately not recorded, but he did at least forward Blaskowitz's written protest to Hitler through his adjutant.

Major Curt Siewert, von Brauchitsch's adjutant, passed the memorandum, which itself has disappeared, to Gerhard Engel, Hitler's Army adjutant. Engel submitted it to Hitler that very day. The memorandum expressed Colonel-General Blaskowitz's extreme alarm about illegal executions, his worries about maintaining troop discipline under those circumstances, the failure of discussions with the SD and Gestapo and their assertions that they were only following SS orders. The report was of a "highly objective nature."[106]

Hitler's reaction was predictably explosive. The methods of the army leaders were "salvation army" methods; their ideas "childish." "This was no way to conduct a war." He admitted to "never having trusted Blaskowitz and having nursed an aversion to him for a long time." Hitler concluded by asserting that "Blaskowitz could not command an army, [and] was not actually suited to do so and should be removed."[107]

Engel informed von Brauchitsch of Hitler's hostile reaction to Blaskowitz's report. Blaskowitz never learned of Hitler's response or received any other official response.[108] He submitted his first report on atrocities after only three weeks in office as *Oberost*, it was clear that he was a man of conscience, as well as a man of duty; a soldier of the old Prussian tradition who retained a sense of his own dignity and decency—qualities not subject to Hitler's or anyone else's command. His actions were reminiscent of the old Prussian General F.C. Saldern, who had refused to execute an order of Frederick II, declaring that "Your Majesty may send me to attack the enemy batteries, and I will readily obey. But to act contrary to my honor, oath and duty is something which my will and conscience do not permit me to do."[109] Whether from conscience or duty, having had no official response to his first memorandum, he began to draft another; meanwhile, complaints from officers in his command continued to arrive at Spala.

Blaskowitz's first memorandum was apparently neglected by Hitler despite his anger about it because he had a more important priority. He wanted to attack France immediately, but faced strong resistance from his generals. The Führer must have known that von Brauchitsch's opposition to the proposed offensive in the west represented the unanimous opinion of the senior commanders on the Western Front.[110] Clearly, Hitler's suspicions against the Army had been aroused.[111] He became determined to have his own way and to strengthen the political attitude of the officer corps prior to the offensive against France.

To this end, army officers were required to attend a series of lectures given by Goering, Goebbels, and Ley, climaxing with a speech by Hitler on 23 November. The speeches of his underlings followed the theme that the Luftwaffe generals and Navy admirals were completely reliable, "but the Party cannot place unconditional trust in the good faith of the army generals."[112]

The culminating speech was given by Hitler himself on 23 November, 1939, at the Reich Chancellory to most of the Army generals and ranking officers of the Navy and Luftwaffe. Possibly because the speech was intended to convince the Army leadership on the Western Front of the successful prospects for the western offensive, or perhaps out of spite, Blaskowitz was not invited and did not attend.[113] The speech made obvious, however, that the Führer had not forgotten him, although he was not specifically named.

Hitler began his address by recounting his political successes since 1919, and especially since his takeover of power in 1933. Expressing his Social Darwinist creed, he warmed up his vocal cords: "Fight and fight again. In fighting I see the fate of all creatures. Nobody can avoid fighting if he does not want to go under."[114] Referring to the recent victory in Poland, he continued: "Basically I did not organize the armed forces in order not to strike. The decision to strike was always in me."[115] Arguing in favor of his plan to attack France, he addressed von Brauchitsch's arguments eloquently:

> I was most deeply pained when I heard the opinion that the German Army was not individually as capable as it should have been. The infantry in Poland did not accomplish what one might have expected from it. Lax discipline. I believe that troops must be judged on their relative value in comparison with the opponent. There is no doubt that our armed forces are the best.[116]

Perhaps ironically, he added: "I must pay the present leadership the compliment that it is better than it was in 1914."[117] Repeating his determination to attack France, he warned his audience:

> The military conditions are favorable. A prerequisite, however, is that the leadership must give from above an example of fanatical unity. There would not be any failures if the leaders of the people always had the courage a rifleman must have. If, as in 1914, the commanders suffer a collapse of nerves, what should one demand of the simple rifleman?[118]

He concluded with a threat:

> With the German Soldier, I can do everything if he is well led. Internal revolution is impossible ... I shall not recoil before anything and shall annihilate everyone who is opposed to me ... No capitulation to the outside, no revolution from above.[119]

Reaction from the Army leaders was mixed. General Walter Warlimont felt that Hitler had "upbraided them for being beset by fears and held them up as doubters who were always tugging at his coat sleeves."[120] The later Field Marshal von Manstein wrote that:

> ...his speech constituted a massive attack not only on the O.K.H., but on the Generals of the army as a whole, whom he accused of constantly obstructing his boldness and enterprise .... It was the most biased speech I have ever heard Hitler make.[121]

Guderian was stung by the slur on the Army's honor and eventually went to Hitler himself to obtain redress, but, getting nowhere with the dictator, left quite depressed.[122] Von Brauchitsch felt that the whole purpose of the conference had been to disprove what he had told Hitler on 5 November, to undermine him, and to demand the offensive in the west.[123] Nevertheless, he had to sit through a second Hitler speech that day and then returned to Army Headquarters at Zossen, outside of Berlin. In the evening von Brauchitsch was ordered to see the Führer again. He returned to the Reich Chancellory with General Halder at about 8 P.M.[124]

General Halder waited outside Hitler's office while General von Brauchitsch met again with Hitler. The meeting proved to be yet another lecture by Hitler. He told von Brauchitsch that he knew the "spirit of Zossen," "the stiff-necked attitude of the General Staff, which kept it from falling in with the Führer."[125] The generals of the Army, he stated, were the last remnants of an old fashioned trend of ideas whose limitations had already been proved in the First World War. "In Poland we had shown that we had not yet grasped the spirit of the times, and we were still being chivalrous ...."[126]

> The Führer "blamed the leaders of the Army for having opposed all his successful actions, instead of thanking him for having created the new Army, frequently against the opposition of the Army High Command, which alone had made the success in the Polish campaign possible. He demanded whole-hearted agreement with his ideas and unconditional obedience."[127]

He ended this final lecture by declaring that the German people supported him and that "the idea of a revolution would destroy those who played with such ideas."[128]

Von Brauchitsch offered Hitler his resignation but it was refused.[129] Matters became even more difficult for him when only a few days later he received a second report from Blaskowitz about further events and atrocities in Poland. Hitler had just told him that the army's "chivalry" in Poland must stop, but the memorandum from Blaskowitz arrived on 27 November 1939, just four days after Hitler's tirade.

Colonel-General Blaskowitz expressed his horror of conditions in Poland in a language that was without precedent in German military history. Unfortunately, only part of the memorandum has survived but it nevertheless forcefully expresses Blaskowitz's torment about the outrages the SS was practicing. He began by explaining that under Frank's authority, the situation in Poland had deteriorated, but at least the regular army soldiers refused to participate in the SS cruelties and executions. Indeed, the troops referred to the SS as an "execution command," and asserted that "the special police has done nothing but spread horror and fear ... [and] for the soldiers to see that this is done in the name of the German Army is inconceivable."[130] Indignantly demanding that these things be corrected, he continued:

> It must be said that the situation needs to be changed. Because if it is not drastically changed and rectified, there will be an insurrection, there will be no chance to do right by the occupied land and its residents, to be in peaceful coexistence with the citizens of Poland and to make them useful to our own nation. There is no way

that we can continue to use force, brutality and bestial actions in order to secure the order and tranquility that is said that we are striving for.[131]

The Army and the civilians, Blaskowitz argued, want to see "order and mutual respect restored." For this to happen, it was of "eminent importance that the population be nourished adequately and properly." The Polish people must be given the goods they need and their economy should be given a chance to prosper.[132] This was indeed strong language but the timing of this second protest proved particularly inopportune.

While it is true that growing rumors of the SS atrocities in Poland contributed to the rekindling of differences between the generals on the one hand and Hitler and the SS on the other hand, more sensational issues, especially the *Frauenerlass*,[133] or "woman's order," temporarily assumed center stage. The *Frauenerlass* was a decree by Himmler to the effect that war was a form of bloodletting in which the "best blood" was often lost. Therefore, to replace this loss it was the duty of married women, whose husbands were at the front, not to deny themselves to members of the SS.[134] Another issue was the suppression of religion in the armed forces. It seemed that since no one could or would do much about the atrocities in Poland, attention turned to other issues.[135]

As for the hope that Colonel-General Blaskowitz had placed in General von Brauchitsch, it appeared that General von Tippelskirch's earlier assessment of him held true. He felt that it was impossible to initiate action on the part of the Army Commander [von Brauchitsch] on the situation in Poland. He was too old, raised in Prussia and unable to envision revolution ...."[136] Von Brauchitsch, according to one unsubstantiated rumor, apparently by order of Hitler, forbade further reports on atrocities.[137] If this were indeed the case, it provides new insight into the disgust, outrage and disapprobation Colonel-General Blaskowitz felt toward the SS atrocities in Poland. For Blaskowitz to have attempted to submit reports on the "Polish atrocities," even after orders not to do so, was extraordinary disobedience, tantamount to mutiny. Yet this was apparently what he attempted to do through his Luftwaffe liaison officer, Major General Karl Henning von Barsewisch. According to von Barsewisch's account, Colonel-General Blaskowitz spoke to him this way in November, 1939:

Barsewisch, I cannot get through to higher places by the official channels of the Army. Please try the G.A.F. [German Air Force] channel .... General Jaenecke ... [Blaskowitz's Deputy Chief of Staff] will hand you documents concerning revolting atrocities of the SS all over the Eastern Territories. Fly to Berlin, this disgrace must be wiped out.[138]

Blaskowitz, traditional soldier that he was, clearly still believed that Hitler was not responsible for the crimes in Poland and that everything would change if only the Führer knew of these horrors.[139] It was a delusion that was soon to be removed.

General Jaenecke presented von Barsewisch with a bundle of papers one to one and one-half inches thick: complaint reports, witness depositions and interrogations. The latter found the contents "so shocking" that he worked out a very sharply worded memorandum about them, demanding punishment of the SS and their replacement by troops with more sense of honor.[140]

Von Barsewisch submitted the massive protest document to Luft-waffe General Erhard Milch in Berlin "with a view of getting through personally to the Führer—still believing that it was a matter of excesses by subordinate commands and that Hitler did not know about them."[141] Milch examined the material, locked it up, and forbade Barsewisch from further talk or writing about it, "adding that the Führer himself had forbidden any interference with the doings of the SS." Von Barsewisch's reaction was reserved: "I inwardly detached myself from a regime which I had suddenly come to recognize as criminal." He reported the failure of his mission to Blaskowitz upon his return to Poland, and also that his confidence in the political leadership had been shattered.[142]

As November turned into December, this revelation must have been a shock indeed to Colonel-General Blaskowitz. Undoubtedly the Colonel-General's thoughts were very complex: did Hitler really know about the atrocities in Poland? Could Milch be relied upon to have told the truth? Old ideas of duty and conscience compelled Blaskowitz to take no chances that Milch could be in error. He determined to send a complete report of the barbarous conditions in Poland—with five copies in case one was "locked-up"—to General von Brauchitsch in Berlin.[143]

Ironically, while Blaskowitz was in the process of sending yet another report to Berlin, Hitler was meeting on 5 December with Frank and Goebbels. The later had just returned from a speaking tour in German enclaves in Poland. After entering into his diary for that day his feeling that Hitler looked "wonderful," was in the "best of moods," and totally shared his opinion on the Jewish and Polish question. Goebbels added, "We must liquidate the Jewish Danger. But it will return in a few generations. There is no panacea against it. The Polish aristocracy deserves to be destroyed." Frank, Goebbels explained, "has an enormous amount of work to do and is framing a series of new plans."[144]

Three days later, 8 December 1939, General Jaenecke, Blaskowitz's Deputy Chief of Staff and Quartermaster- General, flew to Berlin with six copies of the new report.[145] After his arrival at *OKH*, showing it to officers there, and relating some personal recollections, "hell broke loose among the officers."[146] Helmuth Groscurth, an intelligence officer at *OKH* asked the obvious question: "Why does nobody interfere with these ongoing conditions?"[147]

Most regrettably the document which so excited the officers at the Army High Command that day has not survived; it is, however, possible to reconstruct its essential content and flavor to some degree. According to Colonel-General Blaskowitz's own account of the memorandum, it contained a list of all the reports by his officers of incidents of unrest and of arrests in the East. In his list he detailed the "arrests of Jews, the forming of Ghettos, and the resulting local unrest.[148] Governor General Frank, he explained, "had begun arrests of different kinds in different cities, arrests which had been carried through with his own police force. As a consequence there was unrest in the entire territory where this took place ...." Even the troops who did not participate because of his orders not be take part, were nevertheless negatively affected.[149] Objecting to the raids upon the Jews and their deportation by the SS, the report specified three grounds on which the objections were based: (1) that the discipline of his own troops was endangered by the SS activities; (2) that the security of the country was endangered since the population became restive; and, (3) that production was inhibited since the population would not work if it saw purposeless destruction.[150]

The tone of the language used in the report may be surmised from two sentences, recalled by different sources. Von Hassell noted in his diary that the memorandum "contained a sentence to the effect that, judging from the conduct of the SS in Poland, it was to be feared they might turn upon their own people in the same way."[151] The memorandum concluded with these most dramatic and forceful words: "Law, property and life are, in these circumstances, concepts which have ceased to exist."[152] It was language without precedent in German military history; language previously considered to be outside the vocabulary of a German officer.

Blaskowitz felt that he could only submit such a memorandum at all in the context of making a case against Frank's policy "from the military standpoint."[153] Since his orders strictly limited his responsibilities as *OB East* exclusively to the military sphere, Frank's policies were not technically within his realm. He could not, however, simply stand by and watch the perpetration of horrors beyond belief.

As his Chief of Staff, General Karl Hollidt, later stated, Colonel-General Blaskowitz gave to the ideas of military security, maintenance of troop discipline, and German interest in Polish war production, a very generous interpretation, specifically so that he could report on the atrocities to higher command in Germany.[154] It seems incredible that it was necessary at all to construct a premise for submitting a report on widespread horrors and atrocities. Nevertheless, it was true. And to have any possibility of being effective, of receiving a real hearing by Hitler, the protest had to be couched in terms of Nazi-self-interest. Wide-sweeping protests argued in ethical and humanitarian terms would receive no hearing at all.

Helmuth Groscurth, the officer at *OKH* whose indignation had been aroused by the Army's inaction over Blaskowitz's report, took the initiative on his own responsibility. Recognizing that many army commanders in the west strictly opposed Hitler's proposed offensive against France and aware that they were also excited by Himmler's notorious *Frauenerlass,* he thought perhaps he could provoke those generals into action against Hitler by further inflaming them through showing Blaskowitz's atrocity reports to them. He believed that the report would arouse them if only they knew about it, so he took it upon himself to inform them. He left for a tour of the Western Front on December 18th.[155]

That very day the divergence between the plans of the Nazi party and the hopes of some opposition generals to limit the war and restore the homeland to traditional order, as well as to bring an end to the atrocities in Poland, was made obvious to informed people—though there were few of these. The Nazi perspective came in a speech in Lodz in occupied Poland given by Dr. Robert Ley, head of the German Labor Front, when he said,

> The German race, that is our Faith ...! It has higher rights than all others. A German laborer is worth more than an English lord. We have the divine right to rule and we shall assure ourselves of that right.[156]

Ley continued, expressing the ruthless determination of the Nazis: "We know the issue; it is to be or not to be." Expanding on this: "We want to be hard in this war. We are going to forget the arch-evil, our good-nature, and will be hard and relentless in battling for our demands."[157]

The newspaper *Boersen Zeitung* echoed Ley's speech: "General equal rights of peoples and nations is the same liberal fallacy as the twaddle of human rights. There is a law of nations, but no rights of nations. And not every people has a national or imperial mission."[158]

Quite in contrast to the aims of Ley and the Party were those of Groscurth upon his arrival the following morning, 19 December, at the headquarters of Wilhelm Ritter von Leeb's Army Group C at Frankfurt am Main. A deeply religious, practicing Catholic and very much a traditional German soldier, von Leeb was aghast at the revelations of horrors practiced in Poland. He immediately contacted Halder, asserting that the atrocities in Poland were "outrageous and not in accord with the values and norms of a cultivated nation such as Germany."[159]

Groscurth also visited Generals von Witzleben, von Rundstedt and von Bock during the next few days to spread news of the atrocities and to provoke reaction by the generals. Although Groscurth felt that the responses had been positive everywhere, he may have overestimated his impact.[160] Other than von Leeb's letter to Halder, the results were bureaucratic and stunted, and too limited to have long range results. In the short term a bee's nest had been disturbed but no *coup d'état* against Hitler took place.

The very same day that Groscurth had aroused General von Leeb's indignation about the atrocities in Poland and provoked his statement to Halder, the first "official" recognition of disagreement between the Nazi Party and the army appeared publicly. The official German News Agency issued a communiqué which was, according to newspaper accounts, "couched in terms that are usually employed only in connection with diplomatic conferences between representatives of sovereign powers."[161] According to the press announcement, Frank and Blaskowitz met the previous day in Poland with their assistants and had reached agreement on all matters:

> Discussion of various questions connected with administration of the occupied territory and their settlement resulted in a most complete agreement of views between the military authorities and those of the Government General.[162]

Naturally, a discerning reader would have reasoned that there had been significant disagreement. *The New York Times* concluded that the reports of the German Army's objections to Frank's ruthless policies had real substance. A struggle between the party and the army was being waged in earnest in Poland. Predicting that the party would prevail, the *Times* pointed out that party bosses had won the previous struggles with the Army and that, "All generals who dared stand in their way have been eliminated."[163] A warning such as this was probably news to the *Times'* American readers but not to Germans. Events unfolded in Poland and Germany that month in a way that made the *Times* seem prescient. The conflict in Poland would not disappear quietly as the Nazis would have liked but instead escalated publicly to a fever pitch.

Already on 3 December, Count Raczynski, the Polish Ambassador to Britain, had given Foreign Secretary Lord Halifax a written protest charging that human life had "become the sport of ferocious and bestial hangmen in Poland." He accused the Germans of wholesale shootings of leading citizens, as well as widespread seizure of private property. "The soil of Poland under German domination," he declared, "has become the soil of martyrdom."[164]

Polish exiles who had escaped to the west reported that in Warsaw, Catholic priests were being driven through the streets, being forced to clean and sweep them. Prominent rabbis had their beards cut, Jewish children were forced to wear armbands with the Star of David. Warsaw's 160,000 Jews were driven into a ghetto.[165]

It was inherent in Nazi propaganda techniques not only to deny revelations like these but also quickly to assume the offensive. At the end of December, the German Foreign Office released a book calculated to overawe excited critics of the Nazi regime in Poland. Profusely illustrated with starkly gruesome photos, *The New York Times* called it one of the "most revolting records ever printed," surpassing the imagination of "the most sadistic writers of horror tales." Accusing the Poles of 5,437 murders of German nationals, the Nazis claimed it proved that the Polish Government had a well prepared anti-German plan.[166] In January 1940 an enlarged English translation was published with claims of Germans dead and missing raised to 58,000.[167] If Nazi propagandists hoped that world opinion would be diverted by accusations such as these, they were disappointed. Neither would Blaskowitz be diverted behind the scene.

By 21 December, von Brauchitsch had digested the report on atrocities in Poland which Blaskowitz had sent to him on 8 December. Just four days before Christmas, von Brauchitsch told Blaskowitz that he had examined the report, had lengthy conversations with General Keitel and been given assurances that the "necessary steps would be taken by *OKW*, in order to guarantee that this kind of situation would be remedied." Von Brauchitsch also signed an order which read:

> I expect complete cooperation and immediate remedial action to change the situation. The military officer and also every soldier is called upon to respond with high integrity and straight-forward moral behavior, with sure and energetic steps and—if there is no alternative—with the use of weapons in order to restore the esteem and respect of the German nation abroad.[168]

Having received an order like this one, Blaskowitz's confidence in his ability to deal satisfactorily with the SS horrors in Poland must have been cautiously restored. He went home to Dresden for his Christmas leave from duty for about two weeks.[169] He may have been unaware that the moment was unique. Neither before nor afterward was there so large a consensus among Army commanders against the Führer's policies.[170] The anger about the *Frauenerlass*, outrage over events in Poland and opposition to the plans for attack in the west seemed to have united the generals. But the unity was more apparent than real, more fluid than firm. Von Hassell wrote in his diary that Christmas day:

> Gogo Nostitz, very depressed, told about absolutely shameless actions in Poland, particularly by the SS. Conditions there as regard to sanitation defied description, especially in the Jewish district and in the resettlement areas. The shootings of hundreds of innocent Jews was the order of the day. Furthermore, an increasingly insolent attitude was adopted by the SS toward the Army, which they did not salute but jeered at and undermined.
>
> Blaskowitz had written a memorandum describing all this quite frankly. It also contained a sentence to the effect that judging from the conduct of the SS in Poland, it was to be feared they might later turn upon their own people in the same way. Blaskowitz, as a matter of fact, had executive powers only in case of a 'revolt.' Otherwise, he had nothing to say outside the military sphere. Frank was carrying on like a megalomaniacal pasha. Perhaps we may hope that the behavior of the SS will be the quickest way to enlighten the Army.[171]

"Enlightenment" was not fully possible in the Army. Blaskowitz was by no means alone in attributing the horrors not to Hitler but instead to the dictator's underlings. There was discussion of plans for a *coup d'état* in opposition circles but no action followed. It is unlikely that Blaskowitz learned anything about the hopes some placed in a coup d'état or about the part his memoranda had played in exciting opposition circles, but he did learn that his latest memorandum had become well known, at least among commanders in the west. On 5 January 1940, before returning to Poland, he met with the Army commander, von Brauchitsch, and asked why his report had been made known in the west.[172] It was only one unanswered question in a field of unknown dimensions.

Notes for Chapter VII

1. Taylor, *Sword and Swastika*, 359.

2. Gienanth, General d. Kavallerie a.D. Curt Freiherr von, "Niederschrift der Un-terredung des Herrn General d. Kavellerie a.D. Curt Freiherr von Gienanth am 7 Dezember 1952 mit Dr. Freiherr von Siegler," Institut für Zeit-geschichte, ZS-237, hereafter cited as IFZ, ZS-237.

3. Blumentritt, *Rundstedt*, 53.; NOKW 141, M-898/ 28/0161-0164, R.G. 238, N.A. According to Höhne, Rundstedt felt so strongly that he actually submit-ted his resignation. Höhne, *Death's Head*, 344.; Messenger, *Last Prussian*, 94-95.

4. Manstein, *Lost Victories*, 63.; Messenger, *Last Prussian*, 95.

5. "General der Infanterie Curt Liebmann," undated, MSg 1/1669, BA/MA.

6. Blaskowitz Interrogation, 25 October 1945, I.W.M.; MS#P-031b (Lang-haeuser), R.G. 338, N.A.

7. Blaskowitz Interrogation, 7 September 1945, XL 19048, Records of the Office of Strategic Services, R.G. 226, N.A.

8. Ibid.

9. Blaskowitz Interrogation at Nuremberg, 25 October 1945, I.W.M.

10. MS#P-031b (Langhaeuser), R.G. 338, N.A.

11. Ibid.

12. Brett-Smith, *Hitler's Generals*, 51.

13. Möller-Witten, Hanns, "Generaloberst Blaskowitz," *Deutscher Soldatenkalen-der: 1958* (Munich-Lochausen: Schild Verlag, 1958), 172-173.

14. Franz Halder, *The Halder Diaries: The Private War Journals of Colonel-General Franz Halder*, ed., Arnold Lissance, 2 vols. (Boulder, Colorado: Westview Press, 1976), 1: 106-107. This was originally published in eight volumes but all of these are collected here between two covers. A more recent edition ed-ited by Charles Burdick and Hans-Adolf Jacobsen has also been used for this research. See note 46.

15. Halder Interrogation, 26 February 1946, M-1270, Roll 6, R.G. 238, N.A.

16. Blaskowitz Interrogation, 25 October 1945, I.W.M.

17. Blaskowitz Interrogation, 13 September 1945, XL 19048, R.G. 226, N.A.

18. MS#P-031b (Langhaeuser), R.G. 338, N.A.

19. Ibid.

20. *I.M.T.*, 18: 135-137; *I.M.T.*, 5: 78.

21. Ibid., His powers as Governor-General existed alongside of a special position in Poland for Himmler established by secret decree and which placed Frank and Himmler frequently at odds in the General Government.

22. Messenger, *Last Prussian*, 94.; WO 208/4170, P.R.O.

23. Warlimont Interrogation, S.A.I.C./FIR/3, 3 July 1945, R.G. 332, N.A.; Warlimont Interrogation, 28 May 1945, 134008, R.G. 226, N.A.

24. Goebbels, *Goebbels Diaries: 1939-1941*, 36.

25. Ibid.

26. *I.M.T.*, 19: 425.

27. Warlimont Interrogation, 16 October 1945, M-1270, Roll 21, R.G. 238, N.A.

28. Ibid.; Rich, *Hitler's War Aims*, 86.

29. Toland, *Hitler*, 703.

30. James R. Lovell, U.S. Assistant, Military Attaché, Berlin, Report #D-17,031, Dec. 22, 1939, "Dissention between the Wehrmacht and the SS.," M.I.D., 2016-1297-75, R.G. 165, N.A.

31. Papers of Sir Malcolm Noel Christie, Chris 1/35, Churchill College, Cambridge University.

32. U.S. Military Attaché Berlin, Report #17,128, March 1, 1940, "Major Military Operations," M.I.D., 2016-1297-3, R.G. 165, N.A.

33. This quotation and most of this paragraph are based upon the report of Captain John R. Lovell, Assistant U.S. Military Attaché, Berlin, Report #D-17,031, Dec. 22, 1939, "Subject: Dissention between the Wehrmacht and the SS," M.I.D., 2016-1297-75, R.G. 165, N.A.

34. H[ans] R[othfels], ed., "Ausgewahlte Briefe von Generalmajor Helmuth Stieff," *Vierteljahrshefte Für Zeitgeschichte* (1954), 298-300.

35. Ibid.

36. Ibid.

37. Helmuth Krausnick and Hans-Heinrich Wilhelm, *Die Truppe des Weltanschauungskrieges: Die Einsatzgruppen der Sicherheitspolizei und der SD, 1938-1942*, vol. 1: *Die Einsatzgruppen vom Anschluss Österreichs bis zum Feldzug gegen die Sowjetunion: Entwicklung und Verhältnis zur Wehrmacht* (Stuttgart: Deutsche Verlags-Anstalt, 1981), 97.

38. Helmuth Groscurth, *Tagebucher eines Abwehroffiziers: Mit weiteren Dokumen-*

ten zur Militäropposition gegen Hitler, ed. Helmut Krausnick and Harold C. Deutsch (Stuttgart: Deutsche Verlags-Anstalt, 1970), 216.; Already on 20 September, before the assault on Warsaw, Blaskowitz had been concerned about military discipline, respect, obedience and responsibility. See his order of that day in this regard: T-175/474/2997028, R.G. 238, N.A.

39. NOKW 3140, T-1119, Roll 38, R.G. 238, N.A. (Diary Entry dated 10.9.39). Three historians have numbered the victims as fifty in this case. Raul Hilberg, *The Destruction of the European Jews* (New York: New Viewpoints, 1973), 126; Gerald Reitlinger, *The Final Solution* (New York: A.S. Barnes & Company, Inc., 1961), 33; Max Hastings, *Das Reich: The March of the 2nd SS Panzer Division Through France* (New York: Jove Books, 1986), 13-14; See also: Walter Goerlitz, *History of the German General Staff: 1657-1945*, trans. Brian Battershaw (New York: Frederick A. Praeger, Inc., 1957), 359. See also: Küchler Interrogation, 8 October 1947, M-1019, Roll 39, R.G. 238, N.A.

40. *I.M.T.*, 22: 290; Hastings, *Das Reich*, 13-14. Stein reports the date of the massacre as 19 September. See: George H. Stein, *The Waffen SS: Hitler's Elite Guard At War, 1939-1945* (Ithaca, New York: Cornell University Press, 1966), 271.

41. Hilberg, *Destruction of the European Jews*, 126; Stein, *Waffen SS*, 271.

42. Reitlinger, *Final Solution*, 34.

43. Hilberg, *Destruction of the European Jews*, 126; Albert Seaton, *The German Army: 1933-45* (New York: St. Martin's Press, 1982), 119.

44. 3047-PS (Canaris Diary Fragments), *N.C.A.*, 5: 771.

45. Harold C. Deutsch, *The Conspiracy Against Hitler in the Twilight War* (Minneapolis: The University of Minnesota Press, 1968), 179.

46. Franz Halder, *The Halder War Diary, 1939-1942*, eds., Charles Burdick and Hans-Adolf Jacobsen (Novato, California: Presidio Press, 1988), 69.; Messenger, *Last Prussian*, 91, 96.

47. Stein, *Waffen SS*, 30.

48. Gerhard Hirschfeld, ed., *The Policies of Genocide: Jews And Soviet Prisoners of War In Nazi Germany*, (Boston: Allen & Unwin, 1986), 79.; Helmut Krausnick, Hans Buchheim, Martin Broszat and Hans-Adolf Jacobsen, *Anatomy of the SS State*, trans. Richard Barry, Marian Jackson and Dorothy Long (New York: Walker and Company, 1968), 248-254.

49. Ronald Lewin, *Hitler's Mistakes* (London: Leo Cooper, 1984), 132.

50. Lattman Interrogation, 8 December 1947, M-1019, Roll 40, R.G. 238, N.A. Dr. Erich Lattmann was Generalrichter of the Army Legal Department in Berlin. Lattmann stated that General Brauchitsch then issued a supplementary directive which directed that members of the armed forces who "had committed excesses against Jews in Poland in order to enrich themselves or

seeking their own individual advantage were not included in Hitler's Jewish decree." Lattmann added that "Practically this Army directive covered all trials in this connection...."

51. Ibid.

52. 3047-PS (Canaris Diary Fragments), *N.C.A.*, 5: 769.; Lahousen, "The Relationship Between Canaris and Keitel", 25 October 1945, M-1270, Roll 11, R.G. 238, N.A. Questioned about this at Nuernberg, Keitel responded that he "did not recall this visit at all. But, from Lahousen's testimony, it appeared ... that I had repeated what Hitler had said and had passed on these orders, as he put it." Keitel added: "I know that the Commander-in-Chief Army, who then directed the military operations in Poland had, at the daily conferences, already complained about the interference by the police in occupied Polish territory." *I.M.T.*, 10: 516. See also: Deutsch, *Conspiracy Against Hitler*, 180-181.; Karl Abshagen, *Canaris*, trans. Alan Brodrick (London: Hutchinson and Co., Ltd., 1956), 143-151.

53. Below, *Als Hitlers Adjutant*, 211.

54. Kurt Sendtner, "Die deutsche Militäropposition im ersten Kriegsjahr," *Die Vollmacht des Gewissens* (Frankfurt am Main: Alfred Metzner Verlag, 1960), 167-68.

55. Halder Interrogation, 26 February 1946, M-1270, Roll 6, R.G. 238, N.A.

56. Ibid., 3.

57. Walter Deuel, *Hitler and Nazi Germany: Uncensored* (n.p.: 1941), 4 & 12. In a conference between Army General Wagner and SS Deputy Leader Reinhard Heydrich on September 19, 1939 the army had attempted to maintain military jurisdiction in Poland until early December. Heydrich demanded: "Clean up, once and for all: Jews, intelligentsia, clergy, nobility." The Army's counter-demands were, "Clean up, after withdrawal of army, and transfer to civil administration. Early December." NOKW 3140, (Halder Diary, 19.9.39), T-1119, Roll 38, R.G. 238, N.A. Hitler vetoed the Army proposals in the conference of October 17. See note 128. See also: Deutsch, *Conspiracy Against Hitler*, 183-184.

58. Halder Interrogation, 26 February 1946, M-1270, Roll 6, R.G. 238, N.A. As early as 21 September, *Reichsführer SS* Himmler had issued a letter to all leaders of the SS *Einsatzgruppen* mentioning a planned objective which was to remain secret. Hirschfeld, ed, *Policies of Genocide*, 78.

59. General Boehm-Tettelbach was one of those who came to this conclusion quite early. Charles Sydnor, *Soldiers of Destruction: The SS Death's Head Division, 1933-1945* (Princeton: Princeton University Press, 1977), 42-43.

60. Deutsch, *Conspiracy Against Hitler*, 185.

61. Ibid.; Helmuth Krausnick, "Hitler und die Morde in Polen: Ein Beitrag zum

konflikt zwischen Heer und SS um die Verwaltung des besetzten Gebiete," *Vierteljahrshefte Für Zeitgeschichte*, 11 (April, 1963), 203-204.

62. Martin Broszat, *Nationalsozialistische Polenpolitik: 1939-1945* (Stuttgart: Deutsche Verlags-Anstatt, 1961), 31.

63. John Lukacs, *The Last European War: September, 1939-December 1941* (Garden City, New York: Anchor Press/Doubleday, 1976), 279; Hassell, *Hassell Diaries*, 79.

64. Hassell, *Hassell Diaries*, 79; Blaskowitz Interrogation CCPWE #32/DI-43, 28 July 1945, R.G. 332, N.A. In this interrogation, Blaskowitz admitted only that he "had differences" with Sepp Dietrich because his unit had "acted too independently."

65. Messenger, *Hitler's Gladiator*, 76.

66. Sydnor, *Soldiers of Destruction*, 43.

67. Hans Rothfels, *The German Opposition to Hitler: An Assessment*, trans. Lawrence Wilson (Frankfurt am Main: Fischer Bücherei, 1958; repr., London: Oswald Wolff (Publishers) Ltd., 1970), 66.

68. Reitlinger, *SS*, 133.

69. Blaskowitz Interrogation CCPWE#32/DI-43, 28 July 1945, R.G. 332, N.A.

70. Reitlinger, *SS*, 132.

71. Blaskowitz Interrogation, 7 September 1945, XL 19048, R.G. 226, N.A.

72. Blaskowitz Interrogation CCPWE#32/DI-43, 28 July 1945, R.G. 332, N.A.

73. Blaskowitz Interrogation, 7 September 1945, XL 19048, R.G. 226, N.A. Although Himmler made every effort to keep actions against the Jews secret, he could at times be candid. Addressing the *Leibstandarte* SS on September 7, 1940, Himmler stated, "Very frequently the member of the Waffen-SS thinks about the deportation of these people here. These thoughts came to me today when watching the very difficult work out there performed by the Security Police, supported by your men who help them a great deal. Exactly the same thing happened in Poland in weather 40 degrees below zero, where we had to haul away thousands, ten thousand, a hundred thousand; where we had to have the toughness—you should hear this but forget it again—to shoot thousands of leading Poles." *I.M.T.*, 3: 582.

74. Blaskowitz Interrogation CCPWE#32/DI-43, 28 July 1945, R.G. 332, N.A.

75. Blaskowitz Interrogation, 7 September 1945, XL 19048, R.G. 226, N.A. See for example Blaskowitz's orders as early as 26 September 1939. T-175/474/2997029, R.G. 238, N.A. Interestingly this order is found among the papers of Heinrich Himmler!

76. Despite General Blaskowitz's strict orders to restore discipline by severe punishment of infractions this could not be accomplished immediately. In the 12th Infantry Division, for example, which was stationed in Poland from Sep-

tember to December 1939, there were 160 offenses against military discipline, mostly traffic violations, theft and absence-without-leave involving drunkenness. See: Omer Bartov, *The Eastern Front, 1941-1945, German Troops and the Barbarisation of Warfare* (New York: St. Martin's Press, 1986), 27-29. Bartov also points out that 30.2% of the junior officers in the 12th Infantry Division were members of the Nazi Party. Ibid., 49. He additionally reminds readers that the troops were subjected to thorough-going propaganda, even in the military newspapers.

As early as 22 October 1939 the 'Information Sheet for the East Prussian Army' described the Jewish refugees encountered by German troops in Poland as 'the vermin of peoples' who 'wizzed to and fro like irksome flies over a carcass, still conducting business in this death and misery.' The Wehrmacht, of course, had nothing to do with this 'death and misery,' for, as the paper asked rhetorically, 'have we beaten up even one single person, just because he was a Pole? Ibid.

77. MS#P-031b (Langhaeuser), R.G. 338, N.A. Blaskowitz described Langhaeuser as "very excitable" to Halder in his report of 8 December. Halder, *Halder Diaries*, Arnold Lissance, ed., 1: 153.

78. Ibid, 39.

79. Ibid.

80. *Deutsche Allgemeine Zeitung*, Berlin, 4 October, 1941, G-2 Regional File (Germany) 5910, R.G. 165, N.A.; See also: Von Brauchitsch Interrogation, Undated, M-679/1/0207-0212, R.G. 59, N.A.; Wolf Keilig, ed., *Das deutsche Herr 1939-1945, Gliederung, Einsatz, Stellenbesetzen* (Bad Nauheim, 1957), 43. See especially: "Die Generalität des Heeres im 2. Weltkrieg, 1939-1945," 43.

81. William Geffen, ed., *Command and Commanders In Modern Warfare: The Proceedings of the Second Military History Symposium, U.S. Air Force Academy, 2-3 May 1968* (Office of Air Force History, Headquarters USAF, and U.S. Air Force Academy, 1971), 193 & 202. This symposium was attended by Professors Harold C. Deutsch, Charles V.P. von Luttichau, Peter Paret and Generals Walter Warlimont, Leo Freiherr Geyr von Schweppenburg, Hasso von Manteuffel, Erich von Manstein, Franz Halder and Adolf Heusinger. The quotations above are taken from the Commentaries of Generals Halder and Heusinger respectively.

82. Günther Blumentritt, "Stellungnahme zur dem buch 'Offiziere Gegen Hitler,'" Unpublished essay of November, 1946, papers of Sir John Wheeler-Bennett, St. Antony's College Archives, Oxford University.

83. Milch Interrogation, 17 October 1946, M-1019, Roll 47, R.G. 238, N.A. Milch was privately even more critically caustic in his assessment of von Brauchitsch's lack of qualities. Imprisoned with von Brauchitsch after the war in England, Milch's diary entry for October 21, 1945 mentions von

Brauchitsch in strong condemnation: "His brain does not go beyond a toilet-bowl and his combination of conceit and aristocracy is unbearable." "Auszuge Aus Privatem Tagebuch Des GeneralFeldmarschall Milch," Microfilm DJ-59, I.W.M.

84. C.S.D.I.C.(U.K.), S.R.G.G. 1350, WO 208/4170,P.R.O. This quotation is taken from a conversation Halder had with General Müller-Hillebrand on 9 September 1945, while a British P.O.W. Since the material was secretly monitored and recorded it is unusually candid and revealing. This judgment of Halder's is supported by that of General Siegfried Westphal, *The German Army In the West* (London: Cassell and Company, Ltd., 1951), 7.

85. Geffen, ed., *Command and Commanders*, 193.

86. Milch Interview, September 24, 1971, T-1, John Toland Papers, Series 2, "Adolf Hitler," Franklin Delano Roosevelt Library, Hyde Park, N.Y.

87. Mason-MacFarland Papers, MM28, I.W.M. See also the assessment of the American military attaché, Colonel Truman Smith. "The German Army is in good military hands under Brauchitsch's leadership. Whether he is strong and clever enough politically to guide the Army through this confused political period through which it is passing, is considered by me as rather doubtful." "General von Brauchitsch," March 25, 1938, Report No. 15,715, G-2 Regional File (Intel.), 5990, 2016-1108-12, R.G. 165, N.A.

88. Alan F. Wilt, "*Das Oberkommando des Heeres* during World War II: An appraisal." (Unpublished Paper delivered to the Western Association for German Studies Convention at Madison, Wisconsin, 1 October 1983), passim. The author is indebted to Professor Wilt for his kindness in providing a copy for this study.

89. "The Political and Social Background of the 20 July Incident" Consolidated Interrogation Report, 10 September 1945, Berlin District Interrogation Center, R.G. 332, N.A.

90. Lammers Interrogation, 29 May 1945, M-1270, Roll 25, R.G. 238, N.A.

91. Deutsch, *Hitler and His Generals*, 229.

92. Ibid., 230.; Harold C. Deutsch, "German Soldiers in the 1938 Munich Crisis," in Francis Nicosia and Lawrence Stokes, eds., *Germans Against Nazism: Noncomformity, Opposition and Resistance in the Third Reich* (New York: Berg, 1990), 307.

93. Klaus-Jürgen Müller, *Das Heer und Hitler: Armee und Nationalsozialistiches Regime, 1933-1940* (Stuttgart: Deutsche Verlags-Anstalt, 1969), 428.

94. *I.M.T.*, 10: 516 (Keitel's testimony).

95. Keitel Interrogation, 10 September 1946, M-1019, Roll 34, R.G. 238, N.A. Von Brauchitsch thought the date was the beginning of October. *I.M.T.*, 20: 573.

96. Report of Alexander Kirk, U.S. Chargé d'Affaires, Berlin, October 2, 1939, G-2 Regional File (Intel.), 5590, R.G. 165, N.A.

97. "Gedenkrede des Oberbefehlshabers des Heeres," *Völkischer Beobachter* (Norddeutsche Ausgabe), Berlin, Mittwoch, 27 September 1939, 2.

98. Donald Detwiler, ed., *World War II German Military Studies*, 24 vols. (New York: Garland Publishing Co., Inc., 1979), 7: 6. The reporter here was Helmuth Greiner, who was custodian of the War Diary in Hitler's Headquarters at the time. See MS#C-065d.

99. Keitel, *Memoirs*, 101-102; Halder, *Halder Diaries*, Lissance, ed., I: 45.; MS#C-065d (Greiner), in Detwiler, *World War II German Military Studies*, 7: 10. According to Greiner's account von Brauchitsch forwarded "extensive documentary evidence in defense of his statements ... a few hours" later.; Interview of Admiral von Puttkamer, October 23, 1970, John Toland Papers, Series 2, "Adolf Hitler," F.D.R. Library. According to von Puttkamer's testimony von Brauchitsch forwarded to Hitler the next day a single minor report of indiscipline on a troop train. Warlimont reported that the evidence supporting von Brauchitsch's claim "was delivered within the hour." Warlimont interrogation, 20 September 1945, XL 28058, R.G. 226, N.A. Keitel admits only that he saw a single such document. Keitel, *Memoirs*, 102. This was doubtless a very difficult experience for von Brauchitsch. One informant reported: "The discussion was heated. Von Brauchitsch almost had a complete breakdown afterwards." Groscurth, *Tagebucher*, 224.

100. Warlimont Interrogation, 20 September 1945, XL 28058, R.G. 226, N.A.; Warlimont Interrogation, OI-IIR/22, 28 December l945, R.G. 165, N.A.,; MS#C-065d (Grenier), in Detwiler, *World War II German Military Studies*, 7: 11; Deutsch, *Conspiracy Against Hitler*, 228.

101. MS#C-065d (Grenier), 11., in Detwiler, *World War II German Military Studies*. Von Brauchitsch "did not see Hitler later for several weeks." Von Brauchitsch Interrogation, 19 November 1945, M-1270, Roll 2, R.G. 238, N.A. Von Brauchitsch reported the precise figure of four weeks in a subsequent interrogation: Von Brauchitsch Interrogation, 20 October 1945, M-1270, Roll 2, R.G. 238, N.A. Halder, remembered this period as lasting two weeks. Halder Testimony, *Trials of War Criminals*, 10: 856.

102. Manstein, *Lost Victories*, 87.

103. War diary, November 17, 1939, U.S. Naval Attaché, Berlin, M-975, Roll 3, R.G. 38, Records of the Chief of Naval Operations, N.A.

104. Interview of Admiral von Puttkamer, October 23, 1970. John Toland Papers, Series 2, "Adolf Hitler," F.D.R. Library;

105. Groscurth, *Tagebucher*, 232.

106. Gerhard Engel, *Heeresadjutant bei Hitler: 1938-1943, Aufzeichnungen des Ma-*

jor Engel, ed. Hildegard von Kotze (Stuttgart: Deutsche Verlags-Anstalt, 1974), 67-68.

107. Ibid.

108. Blaskowitz Interrogation, 18 February 1946, M-1270, Roll 1, R.G. 238, N.A.; Blaskowitz Interrogation, 25 October 1945, M-1270, Roll 1, R.G. 238, N.A.

109. Christopher Duffy, *The Army of Frederick the Great* (London: David and Charles, 1974), 196; Christopher Duffy, *The Military Life of Frederick the Great* (New York: Atheneum, 1986), 334.

110. Warlimont, *Inside Hitler's Headquarters*, 58.

111. Deutsch, *Conspiracy Against Hitler*, 260-261.

112. Ibid; Guderian, *Panzer Leader*, 85.; Heinz Guderian, *Erinnerungen eines Soldaten* (Heidelberg: Kurt Vowinckel, 1951), 76.

113. NOKW 2608, T-1119/33/0150-0151, R.G. 238, N.A.

114. Paul Sweet, *et. al.*, eds., *Documents on German Foreign Policy 1918-1945*, hereafter cited as: *D.G.F.P.*, Series D., Vol. 8, *The War Years*, 439-446.

115. Ibid.

116. Ibid.

117. Ibid.; Deutsch, *Conspiracy Against Hitler*, 262.

118. Sweet, ed., *D.G.F.P.*, Series D, 8: 439-446.

119. Ibid.

120. Warlimont, *Inside Hitler's Headquarters*, 58-59.

121. Manstein, *Lost Victories*, 88.

122. Guderian, *Panzer Leader*, 85-88.

123. Von Brauchitsch Interrogation, 13 November 1945, M-1270, Roll 2, R.G. 238, N.A.

124. Halder, *Halder Diaries*, Lissance, ed., 1: 56; *I.M.T.*, 20: 575.; Brauchitsch Interrogation, 19 November 1945, M-1270, Roll 2, R.G. 238, N.A.

125. Halder, *Halder Diaries*, Lissance, ed., 1: 56, 150.

126. *Trials of War Criminals*, 10: 857; Peter Hoffmann, *The History of the German Resistance: 1933-1945*, (Cambridge: M.I.T. Press, 1977), 143.

127. Franz Halder and Generalmajor Müller-Hillebrand Interrogation Report, 7 August 1945, W.O. 208/4178, P.R.O.; Vice-Admiral Kurt Assmann, "Hitler and the German Officer Corps," *United States Naval Institute Proceedings*, 82, (May 1956), 519.

128. *Trials of War Criminals*, 10: 857.

129. Brauchitsch Interrogation, 19 November 1945, M-1270, Roll 2, R.G. 238,

N.A.; Assmann, "Hitler and the German Officer Corps," 519.; *I.M.T.*, 20: 575.

130. Groscurth, *Tagebucher*, 426.

131. Ibid., 426-427.

132. Ibid., 427.

133. Halder and Müller-Hillebrand Interrogation Report, 7 August 1945, W.O. 208/4178, P.R.O. The term is Halder's.

134. Hoffman, *History of the German Resistance*, 151. Goerlitz, *German General Staff*, 367; Roger Manvell and Heinrich Fraenkel, *Himmler* (New York: Warner Books, Inc. 1972), 99.

135. Hoffmann, *History of the German Resistance*, 151.

136. Groscurth, *Tagebucher*, 232.

137. Barsewisch, Colonel Karl Henning von, "My Political Attitude," July 15, 1945, Manuscript in the collection of H.R. Trevor-Roper's Private Papers. Professor Trevor-Roper, The Lord D'Acre of Glanton, has kindly granted me permission to cite papers from his collection.

138. Ibid.

139. Hitler deliberately fostered the belief of his own "Leadership without Sin," contrasted with the "evil doings of his underlings, unknown to him." See: Ian Kershaw, *The "Hitler Myth:" Image and Reality in the Third Reich* (New York: Oxford University Press, 1990), *passim*, esp. 83-104. "If only the Führer knew about that!" is perhaps the best single phrase characterizing the relationship between the Germans and Hitler." Eberhard Jäckel, *Hitler in History*. (Hanover, New Hampshire: University Press of New England, 1984), 90.

140. Barsewisch, "My Political Attitude," July 15, 1945, H.R. Trevor-Roper's Private Papers.

141. Ibid.

142. Ibid.

143. General Blaskowitz was interrogated on numerous occasions in the post-war period. In four of these interrogations he referred to this memorandum, twice dating it "December, 1939", once calling it "toward the end of the year and once "around Christmas time." Blaskowitz interrogation, 18 February 1946, M-1270, Roll 1, R.G. 238, N.A.; Blaskowitz Interrogation, 25 October 1945, I.W.M., Blaskowitz Interrogation, 7 September 1945, XL 19048 R.G. 226, N.A.; Blaskowitz Interrogation, CCPWE#32/DI-43, R.G. 332, N.A. Additionally, the German diplomat, Ulric von Hassell, mentioned this memorandum in his diary entry for Christmas day, 1939. Hassell, *Hassell Diaries*, 100. The following also refer to this December memorandum. See: Reitlinger, *SS*, 134.; G.S. Graber, *History of the SS* (New York: David McKay Company, Inc., 1978), 150-151. In his memorandum of 15 February 1940,

Blaskowitz stated: "From the great number of transgressions and offenses by the Police, SS and Administration, which have come to the knowledge of Commander in Chief East (Oberost) *after 9 December*, a few significant cases are herewith listed ...." (Emphasis added). No. 3011, R.G. 238, N.A. See also note 140 in which von Barsewisch describes the protest document as "1 1/2 inches thick," and therefore obviously *not* No. 3011.

144. Goebbels, *Goebbels Diaries, 1939-1941*, 60.

145. Groscurth, *Tagebucher*, 236; Krausnick, *Truppe des Weltanschauungskrieges*, 98.

146. Groscurth, *Tagebucher*, 262.

147. Krausnick, *Truppe des Weltanschauungskrieges*, 98.

148. Blaskowitz Interrogation, 25 October 1945, I.W.M.

149. Blaskowitz Interrogation, 18 February 1946, M-1270, Roll 1, R.G. 238, N.A..

150. Blaskowitz Interrogation, CCPWE#32/DI-43, 28 July 1945, R.G. 332, N.A.

151. Hassell, *Hassell Diaries*, 100.

152. Von Pfuhlstein Interrogation, 19-21 April 1945, C.S.D.I.C. (U.K.) G.R.G.G. 286, W.O. 208/4177, P.R.O.; Also found at the National Archives under the following citation: XE 001893, Vol. II of 4, R.G. 319, N.A.; Von Pfuhlstein saw these words at the end of one of Blaskowitz's memoranda of protest but could not be certain as to the date of the memorandum. These words quoted above may also have concluded the missing memorandum of 18 November or the incomplete memorandum of 27 November. Since, however, von Pfuhlstein was on Colonel-General Ritter von Leeb's staff at that time, it is likely that he saw the memorandum of 8 December when it was circulated in the West by Groscurth on 18 December.

153. Blaskowitz Interrogation, 7 September 1945, XL 19048, R.G. 226, N.A.

154. Krausnick, *Truppe des Weltanschauungskrieges*, 97.

155. Hoffmann, *History of the German Resistance*, 147; Deutsch, *Conspiracy Against Hitler*, 281-282.

156. "Nazi 'Divine Right' To Rule Asserted," *The New York Times*, 19 December 1939, 3; Otto D. Tolischus, *They Wanted War*, (New York: Reynal and Hitchcock, 1940), 314-315.

157. Ibid.

158. Ibid.

159. Krausnick, *Truppe des Weltanschauungskrieges*, 98.

160. Deutsch, *Conspiracy Against Hitler*, 281-283; Hoffman, *History of the German Resistance*, 147-149. The later Field Marshal Manstein many years afterward denied that news of the atrocities had a role in strengthening military opposition to Hitler in the Fall of 1939: "'Within my own Army Group

Command, we had only learned that General Blaskowitz had taken steps against criminal acts of the SS in Poland and as a result had been removed from his position as Commander in Chief of German occupation forces.'" Geffen, *Command and Commanders*, 186. The numbers of military men who actually learned of the Blaskowitz memorandum was limited and so, therefore, were results of the indignation about the atrocities.

161. "Polish Row Ended By Nazis and Army: Military and Civil Authorities Are Believed to Have Clashed Over Latter's Ruthlessness," *The New York Times*, 20 December 1939, 12.

162. Ibid; Tolishus, *They Wanted War*, 316-319.

163. Ibid.

164. "Poland Protests German Horrors," *The New York Times*, 3 December 1939, 48.

165. "Exiles, Released By France, Arrive," *The New York Times*, 24 December 1939, 4.

166. "Nazi Documents Charge 'Massacre' of German Nationals by the Poles," *The New York Times*, 31 December 1939, 8.

167. Hans Schadewaldt, comp., *Polish Acts of Atrocity Against the German Minority in Poland*, 2 ed. (Berlin: Völk und Reich Verlag; New York: German Library of Information, 1940).

168. Krausnick, *Truppe des Weltanschauungskrieges*, 98-99.

169. NOKW 2608, T-1119/33/0150-0151, R.G. 238, N.A.

170. Christian Streit, *Keine Kameraden: Die Wehrmacht und die sowjetischen Kreigsgefangenen, 1941-1945* (Stuttgart: Deutsche Verlags- Anstalt, 1978), 318-319, N. 135.

171. Hassell, *Hassell Diaries*, 100.

172. Groscurth, *Tagebucher*, 3.

CHAPTER VIII

OCCUPIED POLAND: 1940

THE ATTENTION WHICH BLASKOWITZ'S REPORT RECEIVED thanks to Groscurth also attracted the interest of those who viewed it in a very different light. Although Blaskowitz originally sent six copies of the report to Berlin—including one which went to Himmler[1]—the SS leader in Poland, Walter Kruger, apparently learned of it only by chance. He complained of this to Himmler:

> [The] ... work by the Security Police in the East-Provinces is extremely demanding and full of conflict. Names did not have to be mentioned necessarily, but there should have been mention of the activities of the reactionary opposition, those things should not be kept in the dark.[2]

The SS, especially Himmler, would neither forget Blaskowitz, nor would they give up their pursuit of him.

Blaskowitz, fortified with von Brauchitsch's order, returned to Poland after spending his Christmas holiday in Dresden. He passed the order on to his subordinate commanders on 11 January 1940.[3] The stage was set for confrontation between the Army and the SS; between Blaskowitz's traditionalism and Himmler's radicalism. Army troops had orders to shoot if need be and the SS would certainly return fire; civil war appeared to be on the horizon. The apparent immanence of civil war was, however, a fleeting mirage in the wintry landscape of Poland.

Nature itself, in the form of the winter weather, had brought SS activities to a virtual standstill that January.[4] There were no shooting incidents between the Army and the SS in the immediate wake of the von Brauchitsch order being passed to the army commanders in Poland.

There were a number of cases in which "local army officers ordered their men to load their guns, and without any resistance from their own troops, forced the security Police to withdraw under threat of armed conflict."[5] But no shooting incidents took place. Unknown to the participants, the tide of events had turned.

Although Blaskowitz could not know it, his support was already waning with Franz Halder, who had perhaps been the most important support for Brauchitsch's flexible backbone. In spite of his stiff bearing and cold, disciplined appearance Halder was a deeply emotional man under great stress. By January 1940 he had begun to reverse his previous support for Blaskowitz, as well as for the anti-Hitler opposition. Early in January, Halder told General von Leeb that the "brutal excesses against Poles seemingly have stopped." He was more candid with his adjutant who had raised the matter of the atrocities: "My poor little Nolte, what do you want? There are much more urgent matters to consider and many other disgusting things that are happening. We cannot do anything about them *now*."[6]

Little more than a month later, on 13 February, Halder would be heard to say, "The conditions in Poland will be forgotten soon because there is really nothing to them."[7] The truth was that he had been outraged upon hearing of SS atrocities in Poland, but that he was also impressed by Hitler's victories and seduced by the possibilities of glory to be won by a victorious campaign in the west.[8] By 13 January, when Groscurth again raised the issue of the atrocities in Poland, Halder answered that the Nazi "revolution was still in progress ... and nothing could be gauged by the traditions that are sacred to us."[9] When Blaskowitz sent Major Langhaeuser, one of his staff officers, to Halder four days later to report on disturbing events in Poland, he returned depressed,[10] apparently due to Halder's failure to support Blaskowitz. Groscurth found Langhaeuser's report, "devastating."[11]

Blaskowitz had visited von Brauchitsch the same day, bringing evidence of the atrocities in Poland with him, but departed feeling both disappointed and despondent. Blaskowitz knew that von Brauchitsch was personally repulsed by the SS crimes in Poland, but nevertheless von Brauchitsch refused to show the incriminating documentation to Keitel or Hitler. Blaskowitz could not understand how von Brauchitsch could be so weak.[12] Typically, von Brauchitsch reversed his position a few days later and sent the documents to Keitel who sent them on to Himmler.[13]

Blaskowitz must have begun to conclude that not all officers strongly supported the position he had taken against SS atrocities. Perhaps he was trying to bolster Halder's fading support the next day, 18 January, when he reported his disgust to Halder, who recorded in his diary, simply, "Blaskowitz—officers too weak: do not stand up for unjustly persecuted."[14]

Nevertheless, in his Berlin office, Goebbels was furious with the army officers. On 25 January he complained to Halder, then wrote in his diary:

> The Wehrmacht leadership is still not totally committed to the racial struggle. We must constantly prod them along. Now they are even intending to build cinemas for the Polish officers. But I kick up a fuss and the Major-General responsible was sacked immediately.[15]

Goebbels may have learned of this incident six days earlier when he had visited Posen to give a speech. Called a "flight into publicity" by some onlookers, Goebbels' speech dealt with the debate between Hitler and some of his generals about whether or not to attack the west. In his speech Goebbels quoted Frederick the Great as saying to his generals who refused to follow him: "Then I will continue the war alone!"

Five days later von Brauchitsch published an article prominently featured in *Völkischer Beobachter*. The article proclaimed, "the German Army's determination to follow Frederick's example and his strategy of attack."[16] Von Brauchitsch had collapsed under pressure and agreed to the attack in the west. He had been under pressure to drop his opposition to the attack proposed by Hitler, but he had also come under pressure from the SS. He had been visited the previous day by Himmler concerning Blaskowitz's allegations of SS atrocities in Poland.[17]

Regrettably, little is known about this meeting. Himmler could be assumed to have arranged it for more than simple "social" reasons. The two men agreed to meet again about ten days later. Their first meeting, on 23 January, may have been necessary because of Blaskowitz's protest memoranda or perhaps because Himmler had learned of von Brauchitsch's order to restore the esteem of the German nation "with the use of weapons" if necessary, but more likely due to the fact that the horrors of SS policy in Poland had finally exploded publicly on the world scene.

On the previous day, Papal broadcasts from the Vatican proclaimed that in occupied Poland the Nazis enforced the "cynical suppression of all but the merest suggestion of religious worship," and declared that Poland had become a land of "horror and inexcusable excesses committed on a helpless and homeless people."[18] Winston Churchill, never one to allow a propaganda opportunity to pass, picked up the theme in one of his famous wartime broadcasts, "A Time to Dare and Endure," delivered on 27 January at the Free Trade Hall in Manchester. After reviewing Nazi atrocities in Czechoslovakia, Churchill continued: "But everything that is happening to the Czechs pales in comparison with the atrocities which, as I speak here this afternoon, are being perpetrated upon the Poles. In German-occupied Poland, the most hideous form of terrorism prevails."[19] After detailing incidents of random shootings of Poles, Churchill explained that Nazi policy "became more discriminating," persecuting especially Poland's natural leaders: nobles, landowners and priests. "It is estimated that upwards of fifteen thousand intellectual leaders have been shot. These horrible mass executions are a frequent occurrence." He added that, "Famine stalks not only amid the ruins of Warsaw, but far and wide throughout that ancient country," and called upon England to draw inspiration from this fate and to *work harder to destroy Nazism.*[20]

Hitler may have learned of Churchill's speech the next day, and this could have been the cause of his burst of rage to Colonel-General Wilhelm Keitel at *OKW.* According to Jodl, the Führer had spoken "indignantly" about "derogatory remarks made by senior officers concerning measures taken by us in Poland."[21]

Perhaps Hitler had only then learned of Blaskowitz's report, or possibly it had to do with remarks by other officers. It is certain, however, that Goebbels had not missed Churchill's speech that Saturday. On Monday he noted in his diary that:

> The campaign of lies about Poland is becoming fiercer from day to day. Churchill has spoken and added new fuel to the fire. I now prepare for a counter-strike. I will have Greiser come from Posen and Frank from Cracow. They must now speak to the foreign press.[22]

That very day (January 29, 1940), Arthur Greiser, German Governor of Poznan, the district the Nazis called the Warthegau, addressed foreign correspondents at the Propaganda Ministry in Berlin. Greiser reminded the newsmen that seven thousand Germans living in Poland—including four hundred children—had been found massacred and mutilated by the advancing army during the September campaign. It was a crime, he charged, "that cultured European nations cannot understand and should have never tolerated."[23] He told how his own father had been mistreated by the Poles following the last war. "Despite this, he said, he was not actuated by petty vengeance but solely by the desire to reconstruct and build up his district ...."

This did not mean, however, that German authorities were using "velvet gloves;" on the contrary, "energetic measures" were employed. Denying that Poles were being expelled from the Warthegau and being driven into the Government General, he asserted that the only Poles who were leaving were those who wished to go. "Moreover, he insisted, Polish peasants, artisans and laborers now were far happier under German rule and leadership than they had been under the Polish and they loved to be back in the Reich."[24]

Greiser's claim that the Poles "loved to be back in the Reich" was discredited by his admission that night that the Catholic Vicar of Poznan had been executed because he had encouraged Poles to take up arms and fire on German troops during the war. His claims were shown for what they were, however, by the headlines to the lead article in *The New York Times* the next day: "Nazis Admit 'Firm' Polish Policy; Cardinal Sees National 'Disaster:' *Even General Blaskowitz Balks at Tactics Held Aimed at Virtual 'Racial Extermination'*—Situation Growing Worse, Says [Cardinal] Hlond."[25]

Clearly, Goebbels "counter-stroke" had miscarried. *The New York Times* devoted several pages to a report by the Polish Cardinal Hlond to the Vatican which was then released by Pope Pius to the Press; it was devastating. Hlond concluded his report this way, "This is a true extermination, conceived with diabolic evil and executed with a cruelty without equal."[26]

Claim and counter-claim in the foreign press, however, was not public knowledge in Germany or in German occupied countries. It is doubtful that Blaskowitz knew that he had made front-page headlines in *The New York Times.* Whether Hitler learned of this or not is unknown, but he may have learned of it through Goebbels, who was often informed in such matters. Or he may have read it himself, since he was an avid reader of foreign press clippings in translated versions.[27]

Ironically, since the Nazis were still sensitive to foreign opinion in January of 1940, it was probably the very publicity that he had received which shielded Blaskowitz. Removing him at this time would have been an admission to the world that controversies and clashes existed in German leadership circles about Nazi policy in Poland. The attention which the foreign press had focused on the plight of the Jews and Poles, combined with Nazi sensitivity (at this date) to foreign public opinion, forced a temporary halt in the atrocities in Poland.[28]

The combination of worldwide publicity of the SS atrocities in Poland and the disquiet among some Army generals resulted in another conference between von Brauchitsch and Himmler on 2 February. It was apparently an attempt by both men to resolve tensions between the Army and the SS about numerous issues so the meeting lasted from four o'clock in the afternoon until 7 P.M. Agreement was reached that Himmler would publish an "explanatory comment" to the birthrate decree; a comment presumably suitable to army sensitivities. There was some discussion about a "Decree on channeling of complaints;" probably inspired by Blaskowitz's repeated complaints to the Army command about SS misbehavior in Poland. Himmler denied that SS men were pledged to inform on the Army. He claimed that SS leaders who were responsible for the mistakes had been punished.[29] Then came the direct discussion of the "alleged immoral and terrorist actions."[30]

> Himmler declared that the SS mission is to carry out ethnical policy. A difficult mission. Mistakes have been made. Has learnt [sic] of five cases from Report of High Command East [Blaskowitz's Report of December 8, 1939?], and asks for information on all other cases. His intention is to carry out his complex task in as considerate manner as possible and with a minimum of bloodshed. He wants good relations with the Army. Denies any intention whatever to set up an Army beside the Army.[31]

Himmler was obviously lying; he wanted to avoid a confrontation with the Army.[32] A showdown with the Army generals was not part of his plan at this time, so he attempted to manipulate von Brauchitsch with a mixture of promises, apologies, lies, and even with something of an offensive against the conduct of Army officers in Poland—tactics clearly designed to keep von Brauchitsch off balance.

When asked specifically about atrocities near the Polish towns of Schetz and Ostrow, he did not hesitate to respond by raising the question of whether, as he claimed, Army troops were getting additional food by slaughtering cattle. He also asserted that some Army officers "took their meals with Polish landowners every day."[33] The very idea that Himmler could question the Army's honor must have thoroughly disarmed a man like von Brauchitsch. As a final touch, Himmler promised that he would investigate the cases mentioned earlier.[34]

Naturally, Himmler had no intention that there should be a genuine investigation. When von Brauchitsch later inquired about the investigation, he was told that "the case showed quite another picture. That means nothing ever happened."[35]

Von Brauchitsch, on the other hand, collapsed nearly totally. The understanding that seems to have been reached between Himmler and the Army commander appears to have amounted to "disregard the past and pursue actions to prevent anything in the future."[36] The revocation of von Brauchitsch's forceful order of 21 December—permitting the "use of weapons" to stop atrocities—was implicit in this understanding.

Himmler certainly left the meeting feeling satisfied that he had at least stalled the Army protests—if not feeling completely triumphant. Walter Huppenkothen, an SS minion of Himmler's, thought disgustedly that Blaskowitz had deliberately seen to it that his memoranda had been passed around *OKW*, where they raised eyebrows under the general title of "Gestapo-horrors." He believed that Blaskowitz had seen to it that his memoranda had also been circulated among the Army commanders in the west.[37] Whether Himmler felt the same way as Huppenkothen did about Blaskowitz when he left the conference that day cannot be proven. That he would later feel that way and remorselessly seek revenge on Blaskowitz—short of murder—was a fact.

In the meantime, however, Colonel-General Blaskowitz was not idle. On 6 February he prepared another memorandum on the situation in Poland which he planned to report verbally to von Brauchitsch during the Army commander's planned visit to *Oberost* headquarters at Spala on 15 February.[38]

While Blaskowitz spent the day writing another memorandum of protest, Hans Frank was giving an interview to a journalist with *Völkischer Beobachter* who had told him that von Neurath had plastered the walls of Czechoslovakia with red posters announcing the execution of seven Czech students. "If I ordered posters to be stuck on the wall each time we shoot seven Poles," jeered Frank, "the forests of Poland would not be large enough to provide the paper!"[39]

The next day, 7 February, 1940, von Brauchitsch made his position on the atrocities in Poland clear to all the commanders. Referring in his message to the

> ...'difficult situation' of 'resolving political differences,' some 'regrettable violations and encroachments' had been committed, and that not 'all political and administrative offices and officers had administered with the necessary tact and understanding their difficult procedures' which in turn had led to 'various rumors(!)'

Von Brauchitsch continued, suggesting that after several meetings with Himmler, it was understood that both the Army and SS agreed to see that "the regrettable situation be remedied." He concluded with a warning that "criticism, meant to undermine and jeopardize the unity and efficiency of the troops" should be avoided and "punished or prevented."[40]

Von Brauchitsch then quoted the Hitler order of 17 October:

> For the security of the German land, solutions have been ordered by Hitler that allow for measures to be taken to deal with the political task of securing our people's future existence. It is inevitable that some of these measures will involve very drastic actions. Actions that will be directed toward the Polish population and that will be unusual.
>
> The process of these actions has, of necessity, been a very swift one, and it has been necessary to implement them with cruelty and brutality.
>
> Yet, I have requested that political offices involved in the implementation of these actions should exercise sound judgement and care while in the process of carrying out what is necessary, for it is expected that some of these actions will damage the spirit and

sense of decency as well as the sense of manhood in the troops, which is why some actions should be kept secret and concealed from the troops.[41]

Von Brauchitsch raised no objections to Hitler's order despite almost certain knowledge of what it meant in practice. He remained immobile in the satisfaction that the Army was not involved in carrying out these horrors. He did not anticipate the damage that would result to his own people, but instead circulated the above declaration to his army commanders—including Blaskowitz.

Probably with the intention of defusing still further the tension between the Army and the SS, von Brauchitsch went to Blaskowitz's headquarters at the old czarist imperial hunting lodge in Spala, Poland on 15 February. He could not have found his reception very much to his liking since Blaskowitz had not been persuaded by von Brauchitsch's declaration to ignore the atrocities in Poland and took no satisfaction in the mere fact that the Army was not an active participant in the execution of the horrors. On the contrary, Blaskowitz had prepared yet another report on the "gestapo horrors" and intended to present it verbally to von Brauchitsch.

After presenting the usual reports pertaining to troop morale, supply, and salvage of war booty, Blaskowitz got to the heart of the business of conditions in Poland. He began by making it clear that he was aware of the attention which the SS atrocities in Poland had received in the world news media.

> Enemy propaganda is furnished with material more effective than can be imagined throughout the world. The propaganda hitherto broadcast by the foreign senders, is only a diminutive fraction of the actual events. We must take into consideration that the outcries abroad will increase, and will thus cause most serious political prejudice against us, since the atrocities really happened and can in no way be refuted.

Addressing the whole question of Nazi policy in Poland he boldly stated:

> It is a mistake to massacre some 10,000 Jews and Poles, as is being done at present; as this, as far as the mass of the population is concerned, will neither eradicate the idea of a Polish state, nor will

the Jews be exterminated. On the contrary, the manner in which these massacres take place, causes the greatest harm, complicates the problems, and renders them much more serious than they would have been if the matter had been dealt with more deliberately and methodically.

Having just referred to "the greatest harm," he now explained that worse would befall the Army and indeed the German people:

> We need hardly again point out the part to which the Wehrmacht is subjected by being forced to watch these crimes inactively; the esteem in which they hitherto were held by the Polish population, has greatly decreased and will never be restored.

> The worst result, however, which will arise for the German people from this situation, is the immeasurable brutalization and moral depravity, which will very soon spread like a plague among valuable German men. If high officials of the SS and police demand atrocities and brutalities and praise them in public, then soon the brutal man will rule. Surprisingly quickly, like-minded persons and people of poor character will come together, as is the case in Poland, in order to find, in violence, an outlet for their bestial and pathological instincts. There exists hardly any possibility of restraining them, as they quite rightly feel themselves authorized officially and justified to commit every outrage. The only possibility to ward off this plague, would be to apprehend the guilty and their followers and put them immediately under military control and jurisdiction.[42]

Referring to a report of General Wilhelm Ulex, one of his subordinate commanders, Blaskowitz stated,

> The atrocities of the Police Forces ... show a quite incomprehensible lack of human and moral feelings, so that one can almost speak in this case of bestiality.[43]

Continuing by citing another report of a subordinate, this time Major von Tschammer und Osten, who was his liaison to Hans Frank, Blaskowitz alluded to a specific list of atrocities given later in his report:

> The interrogation of a staff-sergeant, of a non-commissioned officer, and of a corporal of the Infantry Regiment 414 ...prove what brutalities these beasts were capable of. The attitude of the troops toward the SS and the Police, alternates between abhorrence and hate. Every soldier feels disgusted and is repulsed by these crimes, which

are being committed in Poland by members of the Reich and representatives of the Supreme Power. He cannot understand that such things, especially as they are committed under his protection, if one can put it thus, are possible without punishment.[44]

Coming back to his theme of protest against these atrocities, Blaskowitz forcefully asserted that even the SS should have understood that: *"The idea that the Polish people can be intimidated and kept down by terror, will certainly prove to be wrong. The capacity for endurance which this nation commands is much too great."* Concluding, he summed up by returning to his responsibility as *Oberost* to guarantee the military security of occupied Poland. "There can be no doubt that these activities endanger the military security and the economic exploitation of the East in an irresponsible manner and to no purpose whatsoever."[45] There followed a gruesome list of thirty-three incidents of atrocities; it was a devastating indictment in a language outside the traditional vocabulary of German officers. Indeed, the moral thunder of the language suggests that Blaskowitz's memorandum may actually have been written by Admiral Canaris, but Blaskowitz's signature is at the bottom line.[46]

Blaskowitz's repeated protests, some of which were circulated by Groscurth without his prior knowledge, combined with rumor and international media coverage, created a furor within the upper levels of the officer corps. The Anti-Nazi *Abwehr* officer, Dr. Hans von Dohnanyi obtained SD (Sicherheitsdienst-Security Service) Reports and SS films of massacres in Poland and submitted them to sympathetic officers.[47] Even von Reichenau joined the ranks of those angry with the SS; at Hitler's headquarters no *Wehrmacht* officer would shake the hand of an SS Leader.[48] Reichenau, often inaccurately described as a "Nazi General," even composed a memorandum including complaints against the SS, though he did not send it on to Hitler.[49]

In addition, many officers who opposed the SS actions had not protested in writing because they thought things would change when administrative services in Poland were given to local officers.[50] According to one source the officer corps openly showed its grievance and aggravation and this kept the pressure on von Brauchitsch to do something to alleviate the situation.[51]

While von Brauchitsch considered what to do, it became yet more clear that the conflict between the Army and the SS about the horrors in Poland was becoming critical to the Regime. Goebbels thought it "absolutely essential" that a "big campaign against the atrocity accusations regarding Poland" be pushed hard by his ministry. Interestingly, he noted that the *Wehrmacht* High Command had expressed a desire to "sponsor lectures for the home front." He wrote that "The *Wehrmacht* should look after its own business. In any case, "its ossified ... generals are the worst people to speak to the masses."[52] Doubtless for Goebbels, Blaskowitz was one of the army's "ossified generals."

Blaskowitz was a soldier, seeking only traditional military justice in Poland. Nevertheless, his pursuit of justice had caused others with different goals to become his enemies. The Governor-General of Poland, Frank, had had his fill of Blaskowitz by this time and decided to get rid of him.

On 13 February, Frank visited Hitler at the Reich Chancellery to demand Blaskowitz's dismissal.[53] The military "commanders, he said, had no instinct, they were obstructing his job and the job of his department." Frank wanted the power of the Army in occupied Poland reduced "especially since the military had an aversion of the party and its ideas and actions. Hitler listened silently, but then he had a fit of anger."[54]

For his part, Blaskowitz had dutifully included in his memorandum of 15 February to von Brauchitsch, a statement characterizing the relationship between the Army and Frank. "There has been no change in the relationship between the Governor General and the Police ...," he began. "Attempts are being made to create the impression as though everywhere the best relationship existed with the *Wehrmacht*. More caution is being observed ...."[55] In other words, nothing really fundamental had changed.

Blaskowitz had thought of Frank as a "party usurper" of what had originally been Army territory in Poland and personally had an extremely bad relationship with Frank.[56] On several occasions, Blaskowitz had reprimanded and scolded Frank in an almost schoolmasterly manner.[57] This, in turn, led to Frank's temperamental outbursts.[58]

The two men met on 22 February to attempt to resolve their conflict harmoniously.[59] At the meeting, Frank admitted and lamented the "executions of women, children and the elderly in public ... without the knowledge and against the decision of the leadership!" He insisted that a "radical change" in policy would take place and that these "gruesome actions" would be remedied. Courts would be established and trials held to reduce the "psychological outrage" of public executions. He promised that "a Polish community of the people will be reality sooner or later."[60] Yet, even by 2 March, it was obvious to Blaskowitz that Frank would not keep his promises.

On that day, another meeting was held at which, according to Blaskowitz, Frank "expressed criticism in the harshest of forms, in front of a large number of officers ... concerning actions of the army." Blaskowitz described Frank's comments at the meeting as an

> extraordinary embarrassment to the officers present ... and it created the impression that there is a deep conflict between the Governor-General and the O.B. East. You personally have attacked in the most aggressive form, the actions of the army ....[61]

It was clear that relations between the Army and Frank were strained to the breaking point.

Meanwhile, the pressure on von Brauchitsch had continued to build. He resorted to an idea first suggested to him by von Bock on 8 February. Bock's idea had been to open communications between the SS and the Army by inviting Himmler to address a gathering of Army commanders on the subject of "events in the East."[62] Although he had initially rejected the idea himself, von Brauchitsch ordered General von Tippelskirch to visit Himmler on February 20th to suggest that the SS leader speak to Army commanders so that "higher officers [would] be given the opportunity to see the other side—Himmler's side—[of the atrocities in Poland]."[63]

It seems as if Himmler saw this proposal as a threat—at least at first—and possibly as a "humiliating and utterly impossible situation." He attacked General von Leeb as "hopeless, he would never meet with General Georg von Küchler, who had called the SS a disgrace; Generals Blaskowitz and Ulex were out of the question."[64] Von Tippelskirch cleverly presented it instead as an opportunity to convince skeptics in the Army of the worth of his policies, to change their minds. He even said that the generals were not so much opposed to the brutal actions, but rather that they feared the deleterious effects upon the morale of the soldiers who witnessed such horrors. Von Tippelskirch asserted that von Brauchitsch was not concerned about any orders that Himmler issued, but worried only about the way they were executed. Reluctantly at first, then with enthusiasm, Himmler agreed to deliver a speech to the assembled generals.[65]

While Himmler prepared to deliver his speech, Goering announced on 29 February a new policy for the "East." The guiding rule of thumb should be that all actions should be to strengthen Germany's war potential. All squabbling between subordinates must cease.[66] Poles were to be utilized in the war industry. Even Himmler had to follow this decision—at least for the time being.

On 13 March 1940, at Coblenz, von Brauchitsch had ordered a conference of Army commanders and their deputies. Blaskowitz was there with his three principal generals. The meeting began as many other conferences, with a talk by von Brauchitsch on general questions of supply and equipment. The matter of the pending offensive in the west was not mentioned. That evening, Himmler appeared and delivered a half-hour speech. Some of the generals in the audience had only an inkling of what had been going on in Poland, up to this point.[67]

Himmler did not mention Poland or Blaskowitz's memoranda, but referred only to "occupied areas."[68] It was quite clear to Blaskowitz, however,—especially since Poland was the only "occupied area"—that Poland was what Himmler meant.[69] Himmler's speech was not clearly thought-through and was filled with inconsistencies and awkward explanations.[70] The speech addressed questions of race and nationality and the creation of the "Great-German Reich." The difficulties involved in incorporating such areas into the Reich, he continued, presented problems. The notes for his speech expressed the "problems" this way:

> Executions—of the leading members of the resistance—very drastic but necessary—been present myself—no wild accusation by subordinates—none by me. Know exactly what is going on.[71]

Aggressively defending his terrorist policies he climactically stated: "In this gathering of the highest officers of the Army, I suppose I can speak out openly: I am doing nothing that the Fuehrer does not know."[72] This seemed clear enough, but he continued:

> [I]n things not easily understood or explainable, he would be

willing, before the German people and the world, to take full responsibility for the Führer, because it should not be that Hitler be brought into connection with these things.[73]

Blaskowitz's reaction to Himmler's attempt to convince the generals of the necessity for the SS horrors was typically straightforward: "I was not convinced, and I don't think many others were."[74] Indeed, Himmler's vigorous defense of SS policies had not convinced many that night. During the informal conversations at dinner and later in the evening "most of the generals expressed themselves in a strong, negative sense." Blaskowitz later recalled that his own commanders and "even common soldiers welcomed the position he had taken ... and on numerous occasions told him so."[75]

The reality of it, however, was that no generals had raised an open protest, not one had publicly disputed with Himmler.[76] Private consolation, appreciated though it obviously was by Blaskowitz, did not amount to public vindication. The protest memorandum "awoke no echoes."[77] Quite the contrary; General von Weichs, for one example, concluded that "even high officers were totally unable to do anything against the brutalities perpetrated by Party organizations."[78]

Himmler "hated him" on account of his courageous memoranda and opposition to SS policies.[79] There could, perhaps, be no more dangerous enemy in the Third Reich than Himmler. Himmler's hatred pursued Blaskowitz at every turn until the final days of the Reich's disintegration.

Himmler did not speak personally to Blaskowitz that evening, and the latter returned to Poland with his commanders.[80] It must have been clear to him that he could expect no support from von Brauchitsch or Halder. Expressions of sympathy from his peers had no practical effect. Hitler was obviously satisfied to let the SS execute his policies in Poland while the Army stood aside and did not interfere. For Blaskowitz, an honorable man tormented by the knowledge that the atrocities continued, the separation of the army from the SS policies was ambiguous at best.

The atrocities would continue. Himmler made this clear only two days later in a speech to SS concentration camp commanders in Poland. "All skilled workers of Polish origin are to be utilized in our war industry: then all Poles will disappear from the face of the earth." He continued: "The hour is drawing closer when every German will have to stand the test. For that reason, the great German nation should understand that its most important task right now is to exterminate all the Poles."[81] Himmler's intentions in Poland could not be mistaken.

Four days later Robert Ley, head of the Nazi "German Labor Front," made a speech, the point of which—though possibly coincidental—could not be mistaken. Speaking to the district propaganda chiefs he declared that "the army was good for nothing, that in Poland, the SS have done everything. The Army, he said, simply was not schooled enough in the ways of National Socialism, but still clung to the principles of Christianity."[82]

When Dr. Johannes Popitz, Hitler's Finance Minister, met with von Brauchitsch to discuss the "necessity of wresting power from the talons of the black pirates" (SS)..., von Brauchitsch gave Popitz the "impression of an inwardly broken man."[83] No doubt, von Brauchitsch had been broken; hereafter he would be little more than a backdrop figure to great, often tragic events.

Blaskowitz was not broken; perhaps his religious convictions helped him through this difficult time. Within three weeks he would again be complaining to Halder about events in Poland. Halder would simply note in his diary: "High Command East is still trying to exercise some sort of military rule. Frictions over Police activities and failure to inform the army."[84] Halder would soon be writing, "Take Blaskowitz out."[85]

Blaskowitz was locked into his personal struggle with Frank.[86] This high-level struggle was waged privately while the public face was one of harmony. On 21 April Blaskowitz and Frank attended a performance of Mozart's "The Marriage of Figaro" together at the German Theater in Blaskowitz's honor. An evening reception followed at Frank's castle.[87] To all appearances their relationship was at least satisfactory. In reality, of course, it was quite different.

By the Spring of 1940 meetings were held in mutual disrespect if not contempt.[88] The meeting held only two days after the public pomp at the German theater was a prime example of the shared ill-will. Blaskowitz had lunch with Frank and took General Jaenecke, one of his commanders, with him. Blaskowitz was surprised and not at all pleased to find *Waffen SS* Brigadeführer Gottlob Berger had been invited to attend. Berger reported to Himmler a few days later that:

"Both Colonel-General Blaskowitz and General Jaenecke were not pleased at all that I was invited. Jaenecke could not contain his anger and frustration .... He was very sarcastic." Berger found Frank's speech "very weak" with "no substance to it." Blaskowitz's response, however, was very good, showed insight and substance and a high level of awareness." Blaskowitz "did not hesitate to be aggressive, assertive and outright critical, undisguised and sharp." Berger thought that "this man Blaskowitz knows what he is doing, has great understanding and superior power of analysis." Berger, who could be counted on to be hostile to Blaskowitz, left the meeting "convinced ... that it was in actuality Blaskowitz who was in command and who did most of the controlling.[89] Himmler apparently felt he had cause to fear Blaskowitz's regaining control in Poland, perhaps on the basis of a *de facto* alliance with Frank which could be a serious obstacle in the way of SS plans for Poland. He decided to increase his efforts to have Blaskowitz removed from Poland.[90]

In the light of Berger's impressions it is not surprising that even in April of 1940 Blaskowitz had not given up his losing struggle for the restoration of justice in Poland. The report that he had made to von Brauchitsch had finally to be re-submitted in Berlin. Blaskowitz did this in person, an obvious act of lone defiance, on 24 April 1940. He "appeared at Keitel's office with two red-bound folders and protested to Keitel about the activities of the SS in his area. Keitel's reply was that it was strictly SS business and no concern of his."[91]

Blaskowitz nevertheless left the two folders with Keitel, who clearly wanted nothing to do with them. In a few days they appeared in the out tray of the desk of one of his adjutants, Ottomar Hansen. The first folder was a report with annexes, by the troops, on SS atrocities they had seen. The second folder was a file of photographs of atrocities. When Hansen examined them he became so disturbed that he could think of nothing else. He noticed that Keitel had not initialed them to indicate he had seen them so he passed them back to Keitel but again they were returned to his desk unsigned. He brought the folders personally to Keitel to demand his signature. First flying into a rage, Keitel finally signed the files. Hansen decided to seek a transfer to a front-line unit.[92]

Transfer to the front was one way of escaping the poison behind the lines. For his part, Blaskowitz repeatedly expressed his wish to be transferred to a combat command at the front. It had to be better than occupation duty in Poland. But even at the front it must have been impossible to avoid thoughts similar to those voiced by Canaris on September 8, 1939, when he said, after learning of the plans for exterminations in Poland: "A war waged in defiance of every ethical consideration can never be won! There is still a divine justice made manifest in this world."[93] Thoughts similar to these were very possibly recurrent and haunting to a religious man like Blaskowitz.

Times of crisis, when pressure to conform is greatest, are perhaps the times when character is most important. During such times human frailties or strengths emerge, traits formed in youth and adolescence. During Blaskowitz's childhood in East Prussia his father had been nicknamed "Thundering Blaskowitz" for his fire and brimstone sermons. He had also sometimes been called "Thundering Conscience."[94]

It is not surprising then, that Generaloberst Blaskowitz had the courage of conviction more common to men of the cloth than to soldiers.[95] For a short time he had attempted to act as if he had been Hitler's conscience in the belief that the Führer would put a stop to the evils being committed if only Hitler knew about them. The reality was far more stark.

It is not surprising, either, that after learning of Hitler's responsibility for atrocities, that he did what was possible to protest, to reduce and evade such evils. It was his duty as a Christian and as a soldier. However risky, he could do no less. He understood duty.

Notes for Chapter VIII

1. "The report was addressed to General Brauchitsch but copies of it went, to Blaskowitz's certain knowledge, to [General] Fromm, [General] Keitel, and Himmler. Hitler, also, received the report at some later date, Blaskowitz is not sure when." Blaskowitz Interrogation, 7 September 1945, XL 19048, R.G. 226, N.A.

2. Walter Kruger to Heinrich Himmler, 10 January 1940, T-580, Roll 219, R.G. 238, N.A.

3. Krausnick, *Truppe des Weltanschauungskreiges*, 98.

4. Blaskowitz Interrogation, 7 September 1945, XL 19048, R.G. 226, N.A.; Blaskowitz Interrogation, 25 October 1945, I.W.M.

5. Graml, *Anti-Semitism in the Third Reich*, 158-159.

6. Krausnick, *Truppe des Weltanschauungskrieges*, 100.; See also: Heidemarie Gräfin Schall-Riaucour, *Aufstand und Gehorsam: Offizierstum und Generalstab im Umbruch. Leben und Wirken von Generaloberst Franz Halder, Generalstabschef 1938-1942* (Wiesbaden: Limes Verlag, 1972), 13-21.; Barnett, ed., *Hitler's Generals*, 101,; Hoffmann, *History of the German Resistance*, 80-84.

7. Streit, *Keine Kameraden*, 53.; Barnett, ed., *Hitler's Generals*, 110.

8. Klaus-Jürgen Müller, *The Army, Politics and Society in Germany; 1933-1945* (New York: St. Martin's Press, 1987), 38-39.; Barnett, ed., *Hitler's Generals*, 112.; Cooper, *German Army*, 186-187.; Deutsch, *Conspiracy Against Hitler*, 285.

9. Hoffmann, *History of the German Resistance*, 151; Deutsch, *Conspiracy Against Hitler*, 285.

10. Groscurth, *Tagebucher*, 242.

11. Ibid.

12. Müller, *Das Heer und Hitler*, 443.

13. Halder Interrogation, 26 February 1946, M-1270, Roll 6, R.G. 238, N.A.

14. Halder, *Halder Diaries*, Lissance, ed., 2: 180.

15. Goebbels, *Goebbels Diaries, 1939-1941*, 103; Hassell, *Hassell Diaries*, 109. The often well-informed Hassell entered into his diary that day: "lieutenant colonel from Blaskowitz's staff visited me. He poured out his heart about the

whole miserable situation, especially about the shameful conditions in Poland. Blaskowitz was weak, he said; he had drawn up a memorandum, to be sure, but afterward he had failed to send it on to Hitler." Even members of Blaskowitz's own staff were uninformed of his staunch courage and activity in the atmosphere of intrigue and danger in Nazi Europe, where knowledge might be deemed sufficient cause for death at the hands of the Gestapo or SD.

16. "Nazi Chiefs Emphasize Offensive; Reported Rift Now Believed at End. Brauchitsch's Views Coincide With Hitler's in Stress Upon Frederick the Great's 'Totalitarian' and Aggressive Methods," *The New York Times*, 25 January 1940, 1.

17. Krausnick, *Truppe des Weltanschauungskrieges*, 99.

18. Winston Churchill, *Blood, Sweat, and Tears*, (New York: G.P. Putnam's Sons, 1941), 225.

19. Ibid.

20. Ibid.

21. 1811-PS, Jodl Diary, 28 January 1940, T-84/268/000550, R.G. 242, N.A. According to Heinz Linge, Hitler's valet, the Führer had Churchill's speeches translated into German and read them immediately. *Cornelius Ryan Papers*, German, Linge, Heinz, Hitler's Court File, Box 66, 25, Ohio University Archives, Athens, Ohio.

22. Goebbels, *Goebbels Diaries, 1939-1941*, 106.

23. "Reports Heard In Berlin," *The New York Times*, 30 January 1940, 1 & 9.

24. Ibid.

25. "Nazis Admit 'Firm' Polish Policy; Cardinal Sees National 'Disaster'", *The New York Times*, 30 January 1940, 1. (Emphasis added). See also note 21.

26. "The Text of Cardinal Hlond's Report to the Vatican," *The New York Times*, 30 January 1940, 8-9.

27. Interview of Admiral Karl von Puttkamer, May 20, 1958, by Cornelius Ryan at Düsseldorf, Germany. *Cornelius Ryan Papers*, Von Puttkamer, Karl File, Box 27,20. Ohio University Archives, Athens, Ohio.

28. Adalbert Ruckerl, *The Investigation of Nazi Crimes: 1945-1978. A Documentation*, trans. Derek Rutter (Heidelberg: C.F. Muller, 1979), 18.; Reitlinger, *Final Solution*, 51.

29. Müller, *Das Heer und Hitler*, 446. At the end of January von Brauchitsch sent his personal representative, a Major Kossmann, to Poland to investigate the allegations of atrocities. Kossmann's "devastating" report may have contributed to the need for a second meeting with Himmler.

30. Krausnick, "Hitler und die Morde in Polen," 205.

31. Halder, *Halder Diaries*, Lissance, ed., 1:211-212.

32. Stein, *Waffen SS*, 31.

33. Halder, *Halder Diaries*, Lissance, ed., 1: 1-212; Krausnick, *Truppe des Weltanschauungskrieges*, 99-100.

34. Halder Interrogation, 26 February 1946, M-1270, Roll 6., R.G. 238, N.A.; Krausnick, "Hitler und die Morde in Polen," 205, N.47.

35. Ibid. (both cited sources).

36. Krausnick, *Truppe des Weltanschauungskrieges*, 100.

37. Krausnick, "Hitler und die Morde in Polen," 205.

38. NO 3011, R.G. 238, N.A.; This well known document survived the war while—most regrettably—Blaskowitz's other memoranda of protest did not endure. It is entirely conceivable, given the critical ear with which later verbal testimony must be received, that Blaskowitz would not have been believed had this document not been found. Ironically, the document, usually called simply NO 3011 as above, was found in the Records of Heinrich Himmler's office. See: N.A., T-175/237/725985-726011 (Records of the Reich Leader of the SS and Chief of the German Police), Part III. It will be referred to hereafter by the usual citation: NO 3011.

39. Jacques Delarue, *The Gestapo: A History of Horror*, trans. Mervyn Savill (New York: William Morrow & Co., Inc., 1964), 191.

40. Krausnick, *Truppe des Weltanschauungskrieges*, 103.

41. Ibid., 103-104.

42. No. 3011, R.G. 238, N.A.

43. Ibid.

44. Ibid.

45. Ibid.

46. Deutsch, *Conspiracy Against Hitler*, 186-7.; Historians have debated the meaning of Blaskowitz's protest for years. A careful reading supports the author's interpretation. Referred to repeatedly in general studies of the German Resistance to Hitler (e.g. Deutsch, *Conspiracy Against Hitler*, 185-186.; Hoffmann, *History of the German Resistance*, 147, 151) it nevertheless has been the basis of judging Blaskowitz an "opportunist" (Leon Poliakov, *Harvest of Hate: The Nazi Program for the Destruction of the Jews in Europe* (Westport, Connecticut: Greenwood Press, 1971), 42.), "excluding any invocation of general humanitarian or moral principles." Hilberg, *Destruction of the European Jews*, 127., states: "the general was not outraged by the idea of drastic action, but only by the amateurish way in which the SS attempted to deal with such a massive body as 2,000,000 Jews." For a more recent example see Omer Bartov, *The Journal of Modern History*, Volume 63, No. 1, March 1991. Bartov writes that Blaskowitz demanded that the army be kept out of

the SS crimes but agreed not to do anything to prevent SS atrocities "as long as the military did not have to get their own hands dirty. In this sense, Blaskowitz was actually legitimizing murder ...." See also Bartov: *Hitler's Army: Soldiers, Nazis, and War in the Third Reich* (New York: Oxford University Press, 1991), 65-67.

47. Eberhard Bethge, *Dietrich Bonhoeffer: Theologian, Christian, Contemporary,* trans. Eric Mosbacher et al. (London: Collins, 1970), 576.

48. Höhne, *Death's Head,* 348.; Reitlinger, *SS,* 135.

49. Reitlinger, *SS,* 135-136.

50. Manfred Messerschmidt, *Die Wehrmacht im NS-Staat: Zeit der Indoktrination* (Hamburg: L.R.V. Decker's Verlag, 1969), 392.

51. Krausnick, *Truppe des Weltanschauungskrieges,* 105.; Somehow Blaskowitz's old mentor from imperial times, Field Marshal von Mackensen, had learned of the atrocities and personally wrote to protest them to Brauchitsch on 14-2-40. Müller, *Das Heer und Hitler,* 449.

52. Goebbels, *Goebbels Diaries: 1939-1941,* 119-120.

53. Höhne, *Death's Head,* 348.; Broszat, *Nationalsozialistische Polenpolitik,* 75.

54. Broszat, *Nationalsozialistische Polenpolitik,* 75, n.2.

55. NO 3011, R.G. 238, N.A.

56. Broszat, *Nationalsozialistische Polenpolitik,* 75.

57. ZS-237, IFZ.

58. Broszat, *Nationalsozialistische Polenpolitik,* 75, n.5.

59. T-501/212/000192, This is a letter of 8.3.40 from Blaskowitz to Frank.

60. Krausnick, *Truppe des Weltanschauungskrieges,* 100.

61. T-501/212/000192-3. R.G. 238, N.A.. See the Halder Diary entry for 10 March 1940: "Report on friction between Governor-General and High Command East." Halder, *Halder Diaries,* Lissance, ed., I: 269.

62. Krausnick, *Truppe des Weltanschauungskrieges,* 100.

63. Ibid., 105.

64. Ibid.; Richard Breitman, *The Architect of Genocide: Himmler and the Final Solution* (New York: Alfred A. Knopf, 1991), 107-108.

65. Krausnick, *Truppe des Weltanschuungskrieges,* 105; Müller, *Das Heer und Hitler,* 450.

66. Müller, *Das Heer und Hitler,* 450-451.

67. This information is according to General Dittmar immediately after his capture in April 1945. See: Desmond Hawkins, *War Report: A Record of Dispatches Broadcast By The BBC's War Correspondents with the Allied*

Expeditionary Force, 6 June 1944—5 May 1945 (London: Oxford University Press, 1946), 424.

68. Blaskowitz Interrogation, 7 September 1945, XL 19048, R.G. 226, N.A.; Blaskowitz Interrogation CCPWE#32/DI-43, 28 July 1945, R.G. 332, N.A.; Blaskowitz Interrogation, 27 October 1945 Biographical Data Personnel Folders Series, R.G. 238, N.A.

69. Blaskowitz Interrogation, CCPWE#32/DI-43, 28 July 1945, R.G. 332, N.A.; Blaskowitz Interrogation, 25 October 1945, Biographical Data Personnel Folders Series, R.G. 238, N.A.

70. Krausnick, *Truppe des Weltanschauungskrieges*, 105.

71. Ibid.

72. Krausnick, "Hitler und die Morde in Polen," 205; Krausnick, *Truppe des Weltanschauungskrieges*, 105.; Breitman, *Architect of Genocide*, 112.; Müller, *Das Heer und Hitler*, 451.

73. Krausnick, *Truppe des Weltanschauungskrieges*, 106; Hawkins, *War Report*, 424. Interrogated about this speech during the last days of the war, General Dittmar remembered: "Himmler said that it was the most difficult order he had ever been called upon to give, that this policy should be carried out, but that he'd been ordered himself to go ahead with it, and the generals interpreted this as meaning that the policy came from Hitler himself."

74. Blaskowitz Interrogation, 25 October 1945, M-1270, Roll 1, R.G. 238, N.A.

75. Blaskowitz Interrogation, 7 September 1945, XL 19048, R.G. 226, N.A.

76. Frank Tagebuch, 1940, Zweiter Band, April bis Juni, 21 April 1940, T-989/4/335, R.G. 238, N.A.

77. Hoffmann, *History of the German Resistance*, 263.

78. Weichs Interrogation, SAIC/FIR/55, 12 October 1945, Entry 179, G-2 Intelligence Division, Captured Personnel and Material Branch, Enemy P.O.W. Interrogation File, 1943-45, R.G. 165, N.A.

79. MS#B-308 (Blumentritt), R.G. 238, N.A..

80. Blaskowitz Interrogation, 25 October 1945, M-1270, Roll 1, R.G. 238, N.A.

81. *I.M.T.*, 20: 228-229.

82. Hassell, *Hassell Diaries*, 124.

83. Ibid.

84. Halder, *Halder Diaries*, Lissance, ed., 1: 307.

85. Ibid., 1: 287.

86. Ibid., 1: 266.

87. Frank Tagebuch 1940, Zweiter Band, April bis June, 21 April 1940, T-989/4/335, R.G. 238, N.A.

88. Hans von Krannhals, "Die Judenvernichtung in Polen und die 'Wehrmacht,'" *Wehrwissenschaftliche Rundshau*, 15/1965: 571.

89. NO 1325, R.G. 238, N.A. Letter of 27 April 1940, Berger to Himmler. The meeting was most likely that of 22 April 1940 at Krakau Castle. See the Frank Diary for that date. T-989, Roll 4, R.G. 288, N.A. See also T-77/1057/000005-6.

90. Breitman, *Architect of Genocide*, 115.

91. Interview of Generalleutnant a.D. Ottomar Hansen, October 31, 1971, by David Irving. The author is indebted to Mr. Irving for his generosity in pro- viding a copy of this material. The date of 24 April 1940 for re-submission of NO 3011 to Keitel is taken from the document itself. It is consistent with General of Police Kurt Daluege's signature dated 25 April and SS Records of the same date found elsewhere. See: N.A., T-175/237/ 2725984, Records of the Reich Leader of the SS and Chief of the German Police, Part III. Hansen could not remember the exact date of this event, only that it was the cause of his decision to seek a transfer to a front-line unit. The transfer was ob- tained in early May 1940. Mr. Irving concluded that the date was April 1940. See: David Irving, *Hitler's War* (New York: Viking Press, 1977) 1: 78.

92. Interview of Generalleutnant A.D. Ottomar Hansen, October 31, 1971, by David Irving. The notebooks remained in the faithful possession of Herr Hansen until his death in 1993, as verified in correspondence with his son, Generalleutnant Helge Hansen. Written information from Generalleutnant Helge Hansen dated 12 Juli 1993. Copy in author's possession.

93. Abshagen, *Canaris*, 149.; Höhne, *Canaris: Hitler's Master Spy*, trans. J. Brown- john (Garden City, New York: Doubleday & Company, Inc., 1979), 364.

94. Gert Steuben, "So blieb er ohne Marshallstab," *Das Neue Blatt*, 24 Februar 1953, 11-12, *Collection Koepcke*.

95. Johannes Koepcke, "Ein Grab in Bommelsen," undated, unpublished, circa 1950, *Collection Koepcke*. Copy in author's possession.

CHAPTER IX

OCCUPIED FRANCE: 1940

TRANSFERS WERE THE ORDER OF THE DAY for many people associated with the protests of SS atrocities in Poland. On 3 May 1940, Franz Halder was preparing to transfer Blaskowitz. Indeed, Halder wrote in his diary that day that Blaskowitz was to be transferred to Vienna.[1] A couple of days later the transfer orders arrived at Spala. *Oberost* was reorganized as Ninth Army and was to be shifted to Vienna. Part of Blaskowitz's staff remained in Poland and the rest was to be reorganized. One of Blaskowitz's officers who had suffered through the impossible situation in Poland with the Generaloberst wrote, "All those going with Blaskowitz to the new employment breathed with relief over the prospect of leaving behind the hopeless conditions in the Government General."[2] Blaskowitz himself undoubtedly felt great relief, but more likely also a sense of great foreboding about what would happen in Poland when he had departed. There had been ample hints.

A few weeks earlier the SS journal, *Das Schwarze Korps*, had published an article calling the Polish Jews "degenerate subhumans." Another essay referred to the chaos of Poland and credited the SS and police "with trying to bring order to this chaos...," but the article characterized it as a trying task to encounter daily: "filth (Dreck), filth and more filth."[3] Nothing definite was known, however, about SS plans.

In the meantime, Blaskowitz traveled to Vienna only to be given orders to report instead to Trier on the Western Front where the attack on France was imminent. Ironically, he was given command of Ninth Army—an army that would not have existed except by dint of his own efforts. When he had been given command of the occupation troops in Poland in October of 1939, the best combat troops were immediately sent to the west and Blaskowitz was left with occupation troops who were mostly older men known as *Landesschuetzen*. Undaunted, and knowing that he was a superior trainer of troops, Blaskowitz decided to train his men into regular combat divisions. There was skepticism in some quarters about the possibility of achieving this but by May of 1940 his success was so obvious that it had been decided to use these soldiers in the coming offensive against France as Front-line troops. They formed the Ninth Army and were brought to Trier under his command.[4]

Blaskowitz's Army had an attack plan which led it directly to Paris. After occupying Prague in 1938 and taking Warsaw in 1939, it was understandable that his comrades joked with him that "he appeared to have all the luck of a general who would march only on Capitals."[5] It was not to be so.

Though his troops had been in the jump-off position for two days, he was suddenly called to Colonel-General von Brauchitsch "in the middle of the night and was told that Hitler had ordered his removal and replacement by General Strauss."[6] An embarrassed and confused Colonel-General Brauchitsch tried to explain that Blaskowitz had no experience in the west and had not participated in the preliminary moves. Blaskowitz knew through Wilhelm Keitel's younger brother, Bodewin Keitel, who was in charge of the army personnel office, that Hitler had approved his assignment to command Ninth Army. He questioned Brauchitsch, who admitted that Hitler had previously consented, but had changed his mind at the last moment. Though he had no proof, Blaskowitz believed that Himmler had chosen this time to show Hitler the protest memoranda about Poland.[7]

Brauchitsch was too tactful to tell Blaskowitz the whole truth. Hitler had sarcastically called Blaskowitz "loathsome" and told Brauchitsch that Blaskowitz was "intolerable." Someone else had to be given the assignment of commanding the army that Blaskowitz had trained for the campaign in France.[8]

Removed from his command, Blaskowitz did not take part in the campaign against France. Rather, he was placed in the so-called Führer Reserve, a pool of unassigned officers. With no assignment, he went home to Dresden, perhaps to contemplate the wreckage of his military career. What he had done in protesting the atrocities in Poland had been dictated to him by his character; a strong sense of the ethical dimension of life under God as he understood him.[9] But, in a world gone insane, it was almost obligatory for a decent man to suffer.

His actions in Poland had only postponed further SS "actions" which had been hinted at even before his departure. In Kracow on 30 May, Hans Frank met with his police leaders. He explained to them that: "On May 10 we began our offensive action in the West which means that from this day on the whole world's attention will be focused on the ... West, they will shift from what is happening here in the East to what is happening in the West." This was the opportunity, he continued, "to do something fast and drastic right now with those individuals in our hands, that have a reputation of being instigators and participate in insurrection against us." Coming directly to the point, he announced, "'Obviously, this will mean that several thousand Poles will be killed ....'"[10] He called his plan the "A-B Action."

Blaskowitz had not prevented it, he had only delayed it. Ironically, in mid-November, according to German radio and the Warsaw *Zeitung*, Mr. Hoover's American Relief representative in Warsaw would congratulate Frank on the anniversary of his year in office. William Shirer, an American newsman in Berlin, noted this in his diary and added sardonically: "He congratulates him for what he has done for the Poles!"[11]

In Poland, the situation continued to deteriorate. It would not be very long before this story circulated in Poland about the cold-blooded murdering of Jews:

> An SS officer in Poland had executed all but one of a batch of Jews; he then told this last Jew: 'One of my eyes is a glass eye. If you can tell me which is the glass eye, I shall spare your life.' The Jew had one look and guessed correctly, whereupon the officer asked him how he could tell the difference. The Jew replied: 'My Lord, it looked at me so humanly.'[12]

While Poland was transformed into a land where sadism and death reigned in a thousand hells, Blaskowitz was at home in Dresden powerless to do anything—if even he knew. He was not allowed to do the soldiering that was his life. Even after the events he had witnessed in Poland, his one desire was to again be a commander of troops.[13] Nothing could be more understandable in a man whose whole life had been soldiering, especially so in a man who wished to escape the "poison in the rear."

Incredibly, Blaskowitz had been home in Dresden for less than two weeks when the call came. Although he hadn't known it, Halder had had him in mind since early June for an administrative job in France.[14] He was ordered to report to Lille on 9 June.[15]

Blaskowitz reported to Lille in northeastern France as ordered. It is a large city dominated by a massive Vauban fortress still garrisoned by the French Army. Lille was probably familiar to him since it had been in German hands for four years during World War I and was not far from the battlefields in Artois where Blaskowitz had fought. The city calls itself the "Gateway to Paris" on the large city gate which has survived from earlier times; and it is an important city in northern France. It was supposed to be the center for the German occupation of northern France.

The Generaloberst settled down to his work, which involved establishing a military administration for occupied northern France. In the evenings, as was his habit, he dined with one or more of his staff officers, likely discussing anything other than military matters. On the evening of 13 June, however, dinner was interrupted by the news that Paris would be entered the next day. Without losing a moment, Blaskowitz realized that his assignment had been overtaken by events and he gave orders to his staff to begin preparations to move to the "City of Light."[16] It soon became clear, however, that France had completely collapsed and Blaskowitz's assignment was outdated. On 19 June his headquarters were transferred to Compiègne, near Paris.[17] Negotiations with the defeated French were taking place there and Hitler was directing it all.

Compiègne, forty miles northeast of Paris, is well known as the location of a chateau built by Louis XV, where Napoleon seduced his future wife, the teenage Austrian Princess Marie-Louise. It had been occupied by the victorious Germans in 1870, but probably was more famous as the site where, in Marshal Foch's railway coach, Imperial Germany's plenipotentiaries signed the humiliating armistice ending WW I. The French call it *"La ville de l'armistice."* With his sense of drama, Hitler insisted that France's surrender must be signed in that same railway coach in Compiègne. It was the same town that Blaskowitz and the 75th Reserve Division had fallen short of capturing in the last German WW I offensive in June, 1918. Now, twenty-two years later, Blaskowitz entered Compiègne.

He was billeted in the chateau of the Comte de Vienne, an imposing brick and stone structure at No.22 Avenue Thiers, about 6 kilometers from the site of the railway coach, which had been turned into an historical monument. The Comte's son had just been taken prisoner by the advancing Germans.[18] Fluent in French, Blaskowitz greeted the Comte with all "the chivalry of an age long gone."[19] It was clear that Blaskowitz was, in fact, as one of his officers described him, "a splendid fellow and soldier—indeed, 'a cavalier.'"[20] He was truly a "representative of the old Imperial Army ...."[21] Younger Nazi officers acted quite differently.

Blaskowitz was immediately met at the chateau by Generaloberst von Brauchitsch, who told him that he would be commander of the occupying forces in France. The two generals discussed details of Blaskowitz's new assignment. His tasks included securing supplies and equipment in addition to war booty, but most importantly, order had to be re-established and the economy put back onto its feet. More than seven million refugees who had fled the advancing Germans had to be helped to return home. Prisoners of war had to be kept under guard, at least for the time being. The main task was to set up a durable administration for occupied France. The economy was to be directed into a form of modified war economy to serve Nazi interests.[22]

During their discussion the participants learned that Hitler and his entourage would have lunch at the house in which Blaskowitz was billeted. While lunch was being prepared, the two generals continued their discussion. Hitler and his suite arrived and the two generals were called to lunch. Curiously, Blaskowitz was seated opposite Hitler and next to his arch enemy, Heinrich Himmler.

Throughout the meal, Himmler kept an icy silence and watched him "sharply." After lunch the two generals returned upstairs to continue their discussions. Hitler and his party stayed downstairs for another three hours. During this entire time, General Wilhelm Keitel was negotiating the French surrender terms. Late in the afternoon Hitler and his entourage departed.[23]

Two days later, Brauchitsch sent a message to Blaskowitz; "Conditions" made it necessary to appoint another commander for the occupying forces in France. Blaskowitz was again to return to the Fuehrer Reserve. Once more he returned to Dresden, again convinced that Himmler was behind his removal.[24] Though Himmler was probably influential in Blaskowitz's removal it was Hitler who made the decision. Having learned of Blaskowitz's protest memorandum, he "never forgot this uprising of the general against National Socialism: it had the most unfavorable influence on Blaskowitz's further career."[25]

Hitler's vindictive nature became crystal clear to Blaskowitz shortly after the great German victory over France. At 7 P.M. on 19 July at the Kroll Opera House—which served as the Reichstag—Hitler planned to make a great peace offer to England. He also secretly planned to use the occasion to celebrate the monumental victory over France by announcing Goering's promotion to Reichsmarshal and the promotion of a dozen generalobersts to the rank of field marshal, as well as a large number of other promotions and lavish distribution of medals.

Hitler saw to it that Blaskowitz was ordered to attend the ceremony.[26] The dictator could only have wished to humiliate him and perhaps to instruct him through a national spectacle as to what fate awaited those who displeased him. Blaskowitz dutifully watched his colleagues—many of them his juniors—receiving honors. The "appeal to Britain's common sense" in the speech was a failure.[27] So too, Hitler's extravagence in promoting so many only served to devalue the distinction of rank. The Führer, however, also knew that many men are seduced by promotions.

This most recent removal from command and assignment to the "Führer-Reserve," his second in a matter of a few weeks, proved to be a lengthy one. Blaskowitz was home in Dresden from late June until the 25th of October, 1940.[28] He had much time for reflection upon events. Not far from his birthplace in East Prussia, another German entered his own reflections into his diary

> But a Yorck is not given to every generation, and independent
> political action does not lie in the tradition of German Generals.

Fritsch, too, failed to realize that the new times demanded new methods. It cost him his life. He was the last uniform representative of the old Prussian integrity. His death spared him much. At least he did not witness the shameful passivity with which a once-honorable army tolerated the mass-murder campaign of Himmler's S.S. men in Poland. Was there ever anything more horrifying than that?

He continued, suggesting that such atrocities would have been impossible in the Imperial German Army, but that:

> Today, such atrocious crimes are witnessed silently—with disapproval certainly, but still in silence. And no general has summoned up sufficient courage to prevent the honour of the German Army and of the German people from being besmeared in this way. The old Army protected Germany; it looks as though she will perish of the new.[29]

The diarist expressed thoughts that many in Germany may have felt strongly—albeit silently. Few people in Germany knew about Blaskowitz's protests. It was true that some officers had been aroused by the atrocities and learned about Blaskowitz's memoranda, but Himmler defused them with his speech. Some of the opposition heard confused versions of Blaskowitz's protests; indeed, he became the "White hope of the Resistance Circle,"[30] for awhile, but he was in no way a member of the resistance. As he reflected at a much later time: "the German is, was, and always will be a soldier and, therefore, must do as he is told."[31] Nevertheless, this belief had already begun to change within him. He would continue to struggle and to change.

Duty! Obedience! No, the Generaloberst was not a conspirator! "A simple straight forward soldier, he was one of the few ranking Colonel-Generals that the opposition did not even try to enlist," according to historian Harold Deutsch.[32] Courageous, decent and honorable, he was a soldier: a "nur-soldat" [solely and exclusively a soldier]. He could not have been a conspirator. Neither could he be a Nazi.

Some knowledge of his protests did reach a select few in the ranks of the *Wehrmacht*. A Colonel Kohn later gave this nutshell version:

> I was present at that Frank-Blaskowitz affair. They wanted to court-martial him: they went for him pretty hot. He had stood up to Frank and refused to allow any interference in his military affairs.

Whereupon some party circle intervened and Blaskowitz went to see Frank and they came to an understanding. Blaskowitz went home, and the following day he was dismissed! For the sake of keeping up appearances, they said: 'They have come to an agreement'—and snap, they had got rid of him.[33]

Generally speaking, however, knowledge of Blaskowitz's protests of the SS atrocities in Poland and of the penalty he had suffered was very limited. When he was in Dresden from June through October of 1940, assigned to the "Führer Reserve," he probably thought his career was finished; the Nazis had quietly disgraced him for his very integrity. Character was not an attribute in the Nazi perception of the world. At this time, however, the Gestapo did not like to murder prominent people. Many "enemies of the state" were eliminated bloodlessly by removing them from their position, forbidding public appearances, and maintaining silence in the press, a kind of "sanitary isolation."[34] This was Blaskowitz's situation for some months.

Friends and sympathizers began to work behind the scenes for his restoration to a military command. Brauchitsch was "anxious to make up for having left him in the lurch ..." earlier,[35] and would be cooperative in his reappointment. Among the officers at *OKW*, Hitler's personal command staff, the talented Chief of Operations, Alfred Jodl, strongly supported Blaskowitz. He had heard about the Blaskowitz memorandum but had never read it.[36] Jodl took "a most emphatic stand with Hitler ..." and apparently convinced him that Blaskowitz's treatment had been unjust. There was no doubt, Jodl felt, that Hitler had a "particular animosity" against him, probably "due to the notoriety gained by Blaskowitz's critical report on SS atrocities in Poland."[37] Field Marshal Gerd von Rundstedt, the Army's senior officer, also supported Blaskowitz strongly. Rundstedt "esteemed him both as a soldier and a man, defended him at every opportunity and made efforts to get him into positions he could fill."[38] By late October, 1940 this combination was successful and Blaskowitz received an active command.

Although he was undoubtedly happy to be back in command of troops, his new assignment was not quite a plum. He was placed in command of the First Army in occupied France, not exactly a challenging job. He merely occupied territory already conquered.[39]

Blaskowitz's new command—First Army—had its Headquarters at

Nancy. This elegant French provincial town was designed in the eighteenth century, not by a Frenchman, but rather by a dethroned Polish King in exile whose daughter was the wife of Louis XV. The central square is known as Place Stanislas and there are naturally numerous reminders of Poland. It seems somehow appropriate that Blaskowitz again became an active soldier here, after his own temporary exile. He occupied the 18th century castle of the Dukes of Lorraine, on the Place Stanislaus, as his army headquarters. On the main staircase of the castle there was a commemorative plate marking it as the spot from which Marshal Foch had gone into war in 1914. It was there that Blaskowitz met one of his staff officers: Edgar Röhricht.

They had met before in Dresden and Blaskowitz apparently must have trusted Röhricht unreservedly for he was uncharacteristically open in his conversation with him: "There is not much of a chance that you will be honored through your work with me, if the war should continue."[40] That was all the Generaloberst said that day but it was unmistakable.

The conversation was resumed some months later, in January, 1941, after First Army Headquarters had been transferred to Fontainebleau, outside Paris. Blaskowitz made his headquarters there at the villa of the Dolly Sisters, which Rundstedt found "charming" when he visited it.[41] The First Army troops were mostly billeted in the numerous hotels in the area.

Blaskowitz arrived at Fontainebleau after taking Christmas leave at home in Dresden.[42] It is quite a famous place. Napoleon, for example, had bid goodbye to the Old Guard at the Palace of Fontainebleau before going into exile on Elba. The city is surrounded by a forest of ancient oaks and beeches, named the "Bois Le Rois" (King"s Forest), where Louis XIV had hunted. In this forest the conversation begun earlier continued.

Riding horses together in the forest, Röhricht and Blaskowitz sent their horses and escorts ahead in order to speak privately. Röhricht reported his observation that on the Generaloberst's staff were several persons placed there to spy on him. In addition, the telephone was probably bugged. They agreed that it was useless to raise the issue officially.

Blaskowitz finally asked Röhricht's advice on whether or not he should leave the position, quit as army commander. They both agreed that at least during the time the Generaloberst was in a position of some power he was "in position to be useful to the cause and to prevent some of the things concerning the war and the troops that might otherwise be a detriment." He could "change and alter orders when deviant from his conscience ...."[43] Resignation would have been the easy way out. Instead Blaskowitz chose to endure the pain of shame and disloyalty, attempting wherever possible to mitigate evils and salvage the good for another time, another Germany. Clearly then, in assessing Blaskowitz, it must be considered carefully, if he accomplished these aims. But this was not his last "private" talk with Röhricht.

Upon returning from a visit to the Headquarters of the *OKH* at Zossen outside Berlin that fall, Röhricht went to Blaskowitz with fantastic news; Hitler had decided to attack the Soviet Union! The Colonel-General sat at his desk in silence. On top of the desk was a small globe which Blaskowitz turned with a gentle touch and placed his fingertip on Germany. "'Just take a look at this small spot. This is us! And look at the big rest of the world, especially at this colossus of Russia. Isn't it hubris to attack a nation of this size, when you are this small?'"[44] The Germans were "prisoners of our own success story," Röhricht responded. "Since Compiègne, we do not have a single enemy on this continent. But we cannot venture over and beyond the continent." He continued: "But how should we finish this war, this big machine that is still running, how do we stop it now?"[45] Britain would not surrender, now Hitler planned to attack Russia, and the U.S.A. would probably enter the war against Germany, Röhricht reflected. Blaskowitz countered, "And you think that this kind of mathematical madness will yield success?" It was clear that his General Staff training enabled him to foresee defeat with almost mathematical precision. He then reflected on his own place in all of this.

So it seems that we are going to sit here, with the map in front of us, putting little flags here and there, and deciding things that will be of vital importance to our comrades who may die because of this while we are sitting here in safety. In the meantime Hitler lets us train and make fit our troops in the West, then takes them to the East for action, because he knows that the English are not ready to threaten our newly gained coastal power.

He concluded with a pregnant thought: "this time ahead of us will be painful." He asked Röhricht if he wanted a transfer and upon receiving a negative reply he added, "Good, then we stay together, at least for a while. Sorrow and hardship are easier to get by and get over with a friend who shares them."[46]

It was bound to be difficult, commanding an army when surrounded by spies among your own staff. In an atmosphere such as that, everyone suspected everyone else; distrust was the order of the day.[47] The Gestapo and SD had even penetrated the officer corps.[48] One general later stated that "the entire 'Wehrmacht' was watched by spies of both sexes and every suspicious attitude of higher officers was at once reported to the PARTY or the GESTAPO. That was an easy way to put oneself in [the] favor of the 'Almighty PARTY' for a good promotion."[49]

In all of Blaskowitz's experience, in the traditional code of honor of Prussian officers, there was no guide for conduct in a "totalitarian dictatorship that had spies assigned to high-ranking Army officers."[50] Beside the Gestapo there was the usual Army censorship of mail. It had even opened a letter of General Guderian in the Spring of 1940 and Blaskowitz may have learned of such unusual supervision of even senior generals.[51] In speech, in writing, in all actions, caution was essential. Prudence, no longer merely a virtue, became a tool of survival. People simply vanished and relatives and friends were generally too frightened to make inquiries of the Gestapo.[52]

Under Gestapo surveillance, far from the centers of power, Blaskowitz was unable to influence major events. He was not even invited to attend the conference of 27 March 1941 at which Hitler addressed senior commanders on the necessity of waging a race war without pity (against the U.S.S.R.). Nor would he be invited to attend the conferences of 2 February or 14 June, 1941.[53]

He was definitely in a marginal position, his career was side-tracked. He was responsible, in his command of First Army, "for nursing and reviving the battered divisions from Russia and for building his section of the Atlantic Wall."[54] It was a dismal assignment for a professional soldier who had demonstrated more than mere competence in the past. France was a vast training camp for the army where units trained for Russia and exercised coastal defense against the West as a side-line.[55]

The American assistant military attaché to Berlin in January of 1941 was Captain J.R. Lovell. He naturally tried to keep track of senior German commanders and mistakenly placed Blaskowitz on the Lower Rhine at that time. He added: "Blaskowitz is an able commander and he will probably take active part in the next campaign in order to give him an opportunity to win his Field Marshal rank."[56] It was an opportunity and a promotion the Führer would never grant. By July of 1941, foreign diplomats in Ankara, Turkey would report that he was in Limoges, France, where he had been sent in disgrace after being demoted because of his protests about SS atrocities in Poland.[57]

The thoroughness of Blaskowitz's grasp of command and his soundness as a tactician mattered less in his assignment at First Army than his administrative skills and expertise as a trainer of troops.[58] First Army had done an operational study for a possible invasion of Switzerland, but it remained only a study.[59]

In December of 1940, his Army was available to support Hitler's diplomatic pressure on the Spanish dictator, Franco, to allow a German attack on Gibraltar, but no action resulted. In fact, the whole center of gravity in European military matters shifted eastward after Blaskowitz came to the west.

Sometimes events without historical significance reveal more about a person's character than the dramas woven large upon the historical tapestry. Perhaps the following incident, of no great importance, is just such a measure. It was about this time that Blaskowitz remembered the ninetieth birthday of Frau Weichaus, his childhood nanny in the years after his natural mother's death. She still lived in the rectory in Paterswalde. Blaskowitz somehow learned that she had fallen and broken a leg so he decided to try to help her. He took the time to send her a letter and a package of goodies, red wine, and some money.[60]

Blaskowitz passed Christmas holidays at his home on Heideparkstrasse in Dresden.[61] Christmas 1940 may not have been the usual festive celebration for Blaskowitz as it certainly was not for many Germans. The American naval attaché observed that Christmas 1940 had a "touch of forlornness." The butter ration was reduced to an eighth of a pound for the Christmas week. "The playing and singing of the old Xmas carol 'Silent Night, Holy Night,' was tabooed by the authorities this year, the ground no doubt being that it was too akin to religion."[62]

New Year's Eve also appears to have been sad and subdued. In Berlin there was an 11 P.M. curfew.[63] In Germany it was a tradition at New Year's for all churches to ring their bells at midnight and this tradition continued throughout the war. From his home Blaskowitz could have heard the bells ring in the New Year.[64]

Notes for Chapter IX

1. Lissance, ed., *Halder Diaries*, 1: 339.

2. MS#P-031b, (Langaeuser), R.G. 338, N.A.

3. William L. Combs, *The Voice of the SS: A History of the SS Journal 'Das Schwarze Korps'* (New York: Peter Lang, 1986), 130.

4. Blaskowitz Interrogation, 7 September 1945, XL 19048, OSS Records, R.G. 226, N.A.

5. Ibid.

6. Lissance, ed., *Halder Diaries*, 1: 430.

7. Ibid.; Blaskowitz Interrogation, 25 October, 1945., M-1270, Roll 1, R.G. 238, N.A.

8. Franz Halder, Eidesstattlich Erklärung, undated, circa 1947, *Collection Koepcke*, Copy in author's possession.

9. Möller-Witten, "Blaskowitz," 173.

10. Krausnik, *Die Truppe des Weltanschauungskrieges*, 100-101.

11. William Shirer, *Berlin Diary: The Journal of a Foreign Correspondent, 1934-1941* (New York: Alfred A. Knopf, 1941), 566.

12. C.S.D.I.C. Allied Source Interrogation Report: "F" Series, 15 December 1943, Report No. Allied/F/228, R.G. 165, N.A.

13. Blaskowitz Interrogation, 25 October 1945, M-1270, Roll 1, R.G. 238, N.A.

14. Lissance, ed., *Halder Diaries*, 1: 441.

15. Hans Umbreit, *Der Militärbefehlshaber in Frankreich: 1940-1944*, Boppard A.M. Rhein: Harald Boldt Verlag, 1968), 7.; Eberhard Jackel, *Frankreich in Hitlers Europa: Die Deutsche Frankreichpolitik in Zweiten Weltkrieg* (Stuttgart: Deutsche Verlags-Anstalt), 61. Umbreit gives the date of 13 June, while Jackel dates the event as 9 June. Fritz Freiherr von Siegler, ed, *Die Hoheren Dienstellen Der Deutsche Wehrmacht: 1933-1945* (Im Auftrage des Institute fur Zeitgeschichte; 1953), 113. Siegler states 9 June, as does Keilig, *Das deutsche Heer*, 30.

16. MS# B-308, (Blumentritt), R.G.338, N.A.

17. Umbreit, *Militärbefehlshaber in Frankreich*, 7.

18. David Pryce-Jones, ed. *Paris In the Third Reich: A History of the German Occupation, 1940-1944* (New York: Holt, Rhinehart and Winston, 1981), 255.

19. Ibid.

20. Blaskowitz File, M.I.D., M.I.S., Who's Who Branch, 1939-1945, Entry 194, R.G. 165, N.A.

21. MS#B-308, (Blumentritt), R.G. 338, N.A.

22. Umbreit, *Militärbefehlshaber in Frankreich*, 8-9.

23. Blaskowitz Interrogation, 25 October 1945, M-1270, Roll 1, R.G. 238, N.A.

24. Ibid.; Blaskowitz might not have received the position in any case, since the Army Chief of the General Staff, Franz Halder, was opposed to the idea of a "Military commander" in France. See: Deutsch, *Conspiracy Against Hitler*, 188, n38. It was Harold Deutsch who conducted the interrogation 7 September 1945. See also: Umbreit, *Militärbefehlshaber in Frankreich*, 9; Jackel, *Frankreich in Hitlers Europa*, 62-63.

25. Warlimont Interrogation, 28 December 1945, (OI-IIR/22) R.G. 165, N.A.; Warlimont Interrogation, 3 July 1945,(SAIC/FIR/3), N.A., R.G. 332.

26. Otto Schmeidler, Oberstrichter a.D., Eidesstattlich Erklärung, 10 December 1947, Villa Dalfrid, Billdal, Schwaben, *Collection Koepcke*, Copy in author's possession.

27. Irving, *Hitler's War*, I: 160.

28. NOKW 2608, T-1119, Roll 33, Nuernberg War Crimes Trials Records— NOKW. R.G. 238, N.A.; Blaskowitz also gave "approximately November 1st" as the date for return to duty. Blaskowitz Interrogation, 25 October 1945, M-1270, Roll 1, R.G. 238, N.A.

29. Schlange-Schoeningen, *Morning After*, 124-125.

30. Reitlinger, *SS*, 134.

31. Blaskowitz Interrogation Report, 5 June 1945, First Canadian Army Intelligence Periodical No. 4., Vol 10,655, File 215C1.O23, R.G. 24, P.A.C.

32. Deutsch, *Conspiracy Against Hitler*, 185-186. Extensive research in the relevant documents has turned up only a single report of Blaskowitz associated with the opposition and the source must be discounted. Sir Malcom Noel Christie, an independent British traveler who sometimes sent reports to the British Government reported on 11 February 1940 that, associated with former Leipzig Mayor Karl Goerdeler and Generaloberst Erwin von Witzleben, Blaskowitz led a group of generals who planned to seize Berlin and arrest Hitler, Ribbentrop, Himmler and Goebbels. While such a scheme was, in fact, in the wind, there is no evidence corroborating a role for Blaskowitz. See: Papers of Sir Malcolm Noel Christie, Chrs 7/33, Churchill College, Cambridge University. Gerhard Ritter, *The German Resistance: Carl Goer-*

deler's Struggle Against Tyranny, trans. R.T. Clark (Freeport, New York: Books for Libraries Press, 1970), 148.

33. CSDIC (U.K.), PW Paper 12, The German Revolt of July 1944, H.R. Trevor-Roper Papers, *The Last Days of Hitler* Papers, Folder 14.

34. Gisevius, *Bitter End*, 190.

35. Deutsch, *Conspiracy Against Hitler*, 188.

36. *I.M.T.*, 15: 406; Goerlitz, *German General Staff*, 359.; Luise Jodl, *Jenseits Des Endes: Leben und Sterben des Generaloberst Alfred Jodl* (München: Verlag Fritz Molden, 1976), 49-50.

37. Jodl Interrogation, 12 October 1945, R.G. 165. N.A.

38. MS#B-308, (Blumentritt), R.G. 338, N.A.; Friedrich Paulus also remained loyal to Blaskowitz. Goerlitz, *Paulus*, 34.

39. Möller-Witten, "Blaskowitz," 173.

40. Edgar Röhricht, *Pflicht und Gewissen: Erinnerungen eines deutschen General, 1932 bis 1944* (Stuttgart: W. Kohlhammer Verlag, 1965), 168.

41. Messenger, *Last Prussian*, 161. The improbable name of the villa derives from the professional name of a trio of female singers who enjoyed substantial enough success to purchase and re-name the villa. It was quite modern for the time and was the first in Fountainebleau to have a swimming pool.

42. NOKW 2608, T-1119/33/0150-0151, R.G. 238, N.A.

43. Röhricht, *Pflicht und Gewissen*, 171-172. General Edgar Röhricht was captured on 1 April 1945 by the British who described him as "a man of outstanding intelligence and diversified interests." The British comment continued: "Röhricht was closely associated with General Schleicher and Schleicher's assassination showed him the path the Third Reich was taking. General von Thoma welcomed him to the P.O.W. camp as an old anti-Nazi." WO 208/3433, P.R.O. In a January 1946 conversation with B.H. Liddell Hart, Röhricht described Blaskowitz as "one of the ablest generals in the German Army, an essentially honorable man with a clear political line in opposition to the Nazis." He added, "his ability was indisputable." Notes for History, 7 January 1946, Talk with General Röhricht, *B.H. Liddell Hart Papers*, King's College London, LH 9/24/130.

44. Ibid., 172-173.

45. Ibid.

46. Ibid., 174-175; Fortunately for Blaskowitz there were some members of his staff who were opposed to Hitler and the Nazis. Prince Friedrich Biron von Curland, I.D., for example, characterized Röhricht as "very knowledgeable about politics, and [a soldier] who had his reservations, moderate but firm, about the war." Among the other like-minded members of his staff during his years in occupied France was Lieutenant Nikolaus von Mach, who had

served previously under General von Seydlitz, and who had connections with the underground German Resistance. Prince Friedrich Biron von Curland, I.D., later described von Mach as "very innocent," but having "considerable charm." [Private Memoir of Prince Friedrich Biron von Curland, I.D., "Dedicated to My Children," Winters, 1945-46-47, Graciously loaned to the author. Unpublished. Copy in author's possession.] The Prince later admitted that he "had to sweat" sometimes when von Mach talked at length and without hesitation on his opinions. "I was afraid and worried for him. He was young and impulsive." The Prince often had to "calm him down, for he thought it imprudent and under the circumstances useless to show opposition." [Interview of Prince Friedrich Biron von Curland, I.D., 08/08/92, Bad Godesberg, Germany. Copy in author's possession.] After the Stalingrad debacle the Gestapo came looking for von Mach as a witness against the Walther von Seydlitz family. Blaskowitz's staff hid von Mach in the Forest of Amboise until he could escape across Allied lines and be "captured." [Written Information from Mr. Nikolaus von Mach, 08/08/92, Germany. Copy in author's possession.] Another member of Blaskowitz's staff in France was Colonel Johann Bloch von Blottnitz, i.G., who frequently went horseback riding in the morning with von Mach. According to von Mach the colonel "hated Hitler," and on some morning rides shot at trees, announcing, "I wish it were Hitler." He even refused to have the obligatory portrait of Hitler in his office. [Ibid]

47. Willi Frischauer, *The Nazis At War* (London: Victor Gollancz Ltd., 1940), 202-203.; General Leo Geyer von Schweppenburg, for example, wrote "both in staff and when at home on leave I was under constant surveillance." Geyer von Schweppenburg, *Critical Years*, 200; Siegfried Knappe and Ted Brusaw, *Soldat: Reflections of a German Soldier, 1936-1949* (New York: Orion Books, 1992), 186-187.; Naturally what matters is less the presence of Gestapo spies on Blaskowitz's staff, difficult if not impossible to prove, than acceptance of the perception that this was possible. The degree of acceptance, whether correct or not, is perhaps the best measure of the extent to which the Gestapo had succeeded in becoming a "thought police." Robert Gellately, *The Gestapo and German Society: Enforcing Racial Policy, 1933-1945* (Oxford: Clarendon Press, 1992), 21.; Lochner, *What About Germany?*, 216-224.

48. Max Seydewitz, *Civil Life In Wartime Germany The Story of the Home Front* (New York: The Viking Press, 1945), 402-403; *Defeat* (Washington, D.C.: Headquarters Army Air Forces, Office of the Assistant Chief of Air Staff—2, 1946), 44-45. This Intelligence is an admission of General Heinrich—Gottfried von Vietinghoff gen. Scheel. See also: Lauran Paine, *German Military Intelligence in World War II: The Abwehr* (New York: Stein and Day, 1984), 9; Schellenberg, *Labyrinth*, 9; Delarue, *Gestapo*, 318.; Hans-Jürgen Koehler, a Gestapo operative who fled Nazi Germany for his life in 1939, wrote in 1940 that there was "no hidden cranny of German life into which

the tentacles of the Gestapo do not probe." Hans-Jürgen Koehler, *Inside the Gestapo* (London: Pallas Publishing Company, 1940), 9-10. By the summer of 1941 Berliners had become so accustomed to looking over each shoulder while talking to friends in public that the gesture was called the *Berliner Blick* the Berlin glance. Howard K. Smith, *Last Train From Berlin* (London: The Cresset Press, 1942), 198-201; Lochner, *What About Germany?*, 217.

49. MS#B-397 (Groppe), R.G. 338, N.A.; Peter Padfield, *Himmler: Reichsführer SS* (New York: Henry Holt and Company, 1990), 199. According to Padfield the SD kept a file of "giant card indexes," registering personal details of higher ranks of the army. See also: Höhne, *Death's Head*, 183-184.; Delarue, *Gestapo*, 129. A post-war Allied study concluded that the Gestapo Central Card Index contained some five million cards. In addition, the Gestapo maintained a collection of "personal files." WO 208/3023, P.R.O. See also: E.D.S. Report No. 34, IRR Files, XE020493-Gestapo Card Index "A", R.G. 319, N.A.; See also: Rothay Reynolds, *When Freedom Shreiked* (London: Victor Gollantz Ltd., 1939), 197-201.

50. Mueller, "Keitel", 186; See also Albert Speer, *Infiltration*, trans. Joachim Neugroschel (New York: MacMillan Publishing Company, Inc., 1981), 115-116.

51. Macksey, *Guderian*, 113.; Koehler, *Inside the Gestapo*, 36-37.

52. CSDIC Allied Source Interrogated Report: "F" Series, 15 December 1943, Report No. Allied/F/228, R.G. 165, N.A.

53. NOKW 2609, T-1119/33/0156-0157, R.G. 238, N.A.; Seaton, *The German Army*, 168.

54. Blaskowitz Interrogation, 5 June 1945, First Canadian Army Intelligence Periodical No. 4, Vol.10,655, File 215C1.023, R.G. 24, P.A.C.

55. MS#B-516, (Sodenstern), R.G. 338, N.A.

56. James R. Lovell, U.S. Assistant Military Attache, Berlin, Report #17,922, January 27, 1941, "Order of Battle as of January 20, 1941, M.I.D., 2016-1077, R.G. 165, N.A.

57. "Ankara, Turkey," *The New York Times*, 25 July 1941, 6.

58. Alan Wilt, *The French Riviera Campaign of August 1944*, (Illinois: Southern Illinois University Press, 1981), 40.; Weekly Intelligence Summary No. 8, 13 May 1944, Records of Allied Operational and Occupation Headquarters, World War II, General Staff, G-2 Division Intelligence Reports, 1942-1945, R.G. 331, N.A.

59. T-312/25/7532130-7532221, R.G. 238, N.A.

60. Ernst Froese, "Meine Begegnung mit Hans Blaskowitz," 7; Herr Schrader," Feirlichkeit Anlassich der Beisetzung des Generalobersten Johannes Blask-

owitz am 14. February 1948 in Bommelsen," *Collection Koepcke,* copy in author's possession. See also Msg 1/1814, BA/MA.

61. NOKW 2608, T-1119, Roll 33, Frames 0150-0151, R.G. 238, N.A.

62. War Diary, December 25, 1940, U.S. Naval Attaché, Berlin, M-975, Roll 3, R.G. 38, N.A.

63. Ibid., December 31, 1940.

64. There were three churches quite close to Blaskowitz's home and each rang their bells at New Years: the Garrison church, the Martin Luther Church and the Chapel at the Deaconess Hospital Church. Letter from Oberst Zumpe, Director Army Museum of the former German Democratic Republic, Dresden, to the author, dated 12 May 1989. Copy in the author's possession.

CHAPTER X

OCCUPIED FRANCE: 1941-1943

MOST OF THE GERMAN ARMY stood poised to attack the U.S.S.R. by May, 1941. Only Army Group D remained in France. It was made up of Blaskowitz's First Army, General Dollmann's Seventh Army, and the newly formed Fifteenth Army under Freiherr von Vietinghoff.[1] The onslaught followed quickly.

June 22, 1941 was the day the Nazi attack on Russia began; it was code-named "Operation Barbarossa." "The world," Hitler said, "will hold its breath." Blaskowitz was in Fontainebleau with a few of his officers and a single corporal, Helmut Gollwitzer. Naturally the conversation turned to the assault on Soviet Russia. Those present, except for Blaskowitz, were optimistic, the "whole show would be over in two months—one was very certain about this." Blaskowitz, in a moment of uncharacteristic candor, said that it must be "over" within three months at the most. It must be over before winter, since only the Russians could cope with their winters. He even mentioned the fate that had befallen Napoleon.[2] Blaskowitz, of course, had served in Russia during WW I so he had personal experience of Russian winters. Even so, it was a risky conversation. Anyone might have overheard.

Blaskowitz would clearly have preferred an active command in the east, but others would have found "compensations" for being in France—especially during the winter. Occupied France in 1941 was defeated and demoralized. Less than two per cent—some authorities

241

estimate 0.15 per cent—of the population was active in anything even remotely "resistance" oriented.[3]

During the first summer in France, for example, posters titled "Trust the Good German Soldier," which depicted a German soldier holding a smiling child who munched on bread and butter, appeared all over France. Grammar school girls defaced them but they were replaced by second and third copies together with hand-sized announcements that defacing the posters was sabotage, punishable by death. The "resistance" no longer defaced the posters.[4] There was no armed "resistance" at this time, merely "petty acts of rebelliousness or subversion." Even French patriots called the underground movement "the Whispering Resistance."[5]

The arrival of spring, 1942 witnessed an escalation of the resistance. Attempts on the lives of Wehrmacht officers increased. "Sinister black-and-red posters covered the walls of French buildings. "Bekanntmachung"(Notice), they said, "followed by an announcement of the assassination committed and the names of the hostages shot in reprisal."[6]

On the other hand some members of French womanhood were charmingly collaborationist from the very fall of France. General von Briesen, who will be remembered for the loss of his arm and his defensive courage during the pivotal battle of Kutno in Poland in 1939, commanded the same unit in France in 1940. He was the first German general to march into Paris and took the victory salute of the German troops at the base of the Arc de Triomphe. The 30th Infantry Division was placed in charge of the occupation of Paris in July, 1940 but had to be quickly evacuated, "thanks to the disastrous influence upon them, in a bare twenty-four hours, of French womanhood."[7] Perhaps it was a new form of strategy of attrition.

Eighty-five thousand illegitimate children of French women and German soldiers were born as late as 1943.[8] Fraternization and collaboration were widespread indeed. Such diversions, which continued throughout the occupation, were of no interest to the happily married Generaloberst Blaskowitz.[9] They may even have offended his puritanical character.

In January 1942, with the German Armies frozen before Moscow, rumors circulated in France that Blaskowitz's First Army was going to be despatched to the east to help stabilize the front. But they proved to be only rumors.[10] Blaskowitz probably would have preferred to be in Russia. His distaste for occupation duties in France was due to his understandable professional preference for a combat command.

Joseph Goebbels, Hitler's propaganda minister, disliked the occupation for other reasons. After a minor English raid on coastal defenses at Le Havre, he entered into his diary on 1 March 1942: "Undoubtedly the defenses along the French coast did not function properly. Apparently our men have been asleep. I suspect the Fuehrer will take care of that situation." He continued: "The fact is that living in France has never yet been a good thing for occupation troops, I hear things about our occupation forces there that are anything but flattering."[11] This is ironic since it was Goebbels who issued orders after his visit to Paris in July 1940, to "get the wheels of pleasure, activity, and gaiety turning again 'at any cost'...[as] part of the new Europe."[12]

The raid had not fallen in Blaskowitz's zone of responsibility but it definitely drew Hitler's attention to coastal defense and temporarily away from Russia. Neither Hitler nor Blaskowitz knew that the raid on Le Havre was just one of many planned by Churchill after the Germans had attacked the U.S.S.R. On 23 June 1941, Churchill mentioned it to his personal secretary who noted: "The P.M. is now toying with the idea of an armed raid on the French Coast, while the Germans are busy in Russia. Now, he says, is the time "to make hell while the sun shines."[13] The Le Havre raid was only the beginning.

Hitler had turned his gaze toward the west coast of Europe as early as 14 December 1941, when he had demanded coastal defenses "powerful enough to withstand all invasion efforts."[14] This was followed on 23 March 1942, by Directive No. 40, which detailed Hitler's wishes for coastal defense. The dictator's basic idea was that the Army, Navy and Air Force must cooperate closely to see that any enemy "*attack collapses if possible before it can reach the coast, at the latest on the coast itself.*" Hitler demanded: "Enemy forces which have landed must be destroyed or thrown back into the sea by immediate counter-attack."[15] It would become apparent at a later date that the idea of not permitting even a temporary enemy lodgement on the continent was motivated by reason of political prestige as much as military necessity. The dictator ordered further fortification of the coast. It was the real beginning of the myth of the "Atlantic Wall." Hitler's orders were issued none too soon.

On 28 March Allied commandos raided St. Nazaire, just north of Blaskowitz's area of command responsibility, at the junction with Seventh Army. Although the raid was repelled with heavy losses for the Allies, Hitler was alarmed. A flood of orders went to the responsible commanders.[16] This apparently caused Blaskowitz to move his headquarters from Fontainbleau to Bordeaux, an inland port on the Atlantic Coast of France. He described his assignment as "guarding the coastline from the Loire River to the Spanish border."[17]

Bordeaux, center for famous wines, third gastronomic center of France after Paris and Lyon, and an important commercial port, was the capital of French governments which had fled Paris before the advancing Germans in 1870, 1914 and 1940. It had been raided by the Saracens in 731 and by the Vikings in 848, so it was a likely place for an Allied raid, a good choice for his headquarters.

Bordeaux was used as a base for blockade runners, submarines and German navy destroyers. At Merignac Airport, outside the city, the Luftwaffe had stationed the 40th Bomber Wing. In addition, there were airplane engine plants, oil refineries and railroad junctions in or near Bordeaux. From April 1942 until he left Bordeaux in May of 1944 the city was bombed twice by the British and eight times by the Americans, about one attack every ten weeks. The war was never very far away.[18]

Blaskowitz occupied the first apartment at the Hotel Ballande as his personal residence. It seems certain that he chose this abode not because of its beautiful white empire style interior but instead because it had been the residence of the French commander that he replaced and possibly due to its convenient location across the Place Pey-Berland from the mayor's office. It overlooked the city's central square and the Cathedral St. Andrè so the location may have had some symbolic as well as a political significance.[19] First Army Headquarters was set up at the Place de la Bourse and French citizens were required for security reasons to cross the street in passing this building. The Gestapo moved into a chateau across town at 197 Rue de Medoc; it was like a shadow.[20] Blaskowitz did not think that the prospects for an Allied invasion were imminent so he took his annual leave in springtime, home to Dresden.[21]

On 29 May Hitler issued another Directive, No. 42. It was again concerned with the possibility of Allied assaults on the continent. It warned that it might become "necessary in the future to occupy the *whole* of French territory." Hitler, his hands full in Russia, may have thought of Napoleon's experience in Spain and, also, warned against an attack by the Allies in the Iberian peninsula. He demanded immediate preparation of countermeasures.[22] On 9 July, Hitler reassured his officers in writing that "in the event of an enemy landing, I personally will proceed to the west and assume charge of operations there."[23] The dictator, however, concentrated on the east since he probably still thought major landings in the west to be premature.[24] Premature or not, countermeasures had to be prepared. Field Marshal Gerd von Rundstedt, a good friend of Blaskowitz, replaced Field Marshal Erwin von Witzleben at the end of June. Rundstedt submitted a plan called "Illona" as a counter-measure to a projected Allied invasion on the Spanish peninsula.[25] Blaskowitz obviously had a prominent role in both the planning and projected invasion of Spain since the operation was to be carried out by First Army.

Fear of a possible Allied invasion in Spain may have been given a boost by the large scale raid at Dieppe on 19 August 1942. Troop dispositions in France were changed and reserves moved closer to the coast. In the fall even the elite SS Panzer Divisions, *Leibstandarte Adolf Hitler* and *Das Reich* were temporarily concentrated near the coast to repel any invasion.[26] Hitler's eyes had focused with deliberation on the possibility of invasion in the west. This continued to mean Spain as well as France.

In his "Table Talk" at Führer Headquarters, Hitler mentioned Spanish desires to obtain French North African territory. Italy, too, aspired to control North Africa. The dictator continued:

> I must make the Duce understand that, to meet a possible attempt at invasion by the British, I would much prefer to have a quiet and contented France. Were an invasion to be the sign for a general rising in France, it would greatly complicate matters for us.[27]

Planning the German response to an Allied invasion in the Iberian Peninsula dragged on through the Fall and Winter. Blaskowitz's plans to meet such a contingency were "hastily constructed to meet Germany's deteriorating military situation, but it reflected Hitler's efforts to prepare for every contingency."[28] The goals were modest and employed limited numbers of troops. Hitler's interest in the plans varied with his perceptions of the threat, peaking in January and February of 1943 and dropping off until June, when he finally ordered suspension of all operational plans.

Blaskowitz's private thoughts and reflections on these events are difficult to surmise. Interrogated in the post-war years about the events of 1942, he answered that "he was a small man of no account and could form no opinion ... [on the prospects of eventual German victory]."[29] The interrogator, however, deduced that Blaskowitz was unhappy in his work and "the atmosphere in the room was growing more and more dismal as he remembered the past."[30] It was a disastrous time, late 1942 and early 1943, for many Germans to remember.

The soldiers of the *Leibstandarte Adolf Hitler*, stationed in France at the time, for example, spent their time not unlike many other Germans: "Everyone listened intently to the Wehrmacht report from Stalingrad and turned a hopeful ear to the reports from Africa."[31] Both campaigns ended in disaster. Six days of national mourning followed the Stalingrad debacle.

Blaskowitz's taciturnity at this point in his interrogation was not simply the response of a man whose nation had suffered a crushing defeat and who had been unable to prevent it. It was not merely the reaction of a man who feared for his fate at the hands of his captors. It was by then the tried and trained behavior of a man who had become accustomed to fear and suspicion of his own countrymen while impotently enduring the destruction of his homeland. In the fall of 1942, for example, he had been visited for a weekend by an officer, Colonel Professor Dr. Kurt Hesse, who later recalled the conversations he had with Colonel-General Blaskowitz at his weekend house on the coast near Bordeaux.

Blaskowitz had expected an invasion landing "in a short time ..." and planned to meet it with a concentric advance of forces in Belgium and France. First Army, which then had three motorized divisions, would thrust North to meet the invasion. He "judged the strategic possibilities as favorable, because the enemy was not in a position to bring up strong tank units as quickly as needed. He remarked, of course, incidentally—that he realized clearly how the Fuehrer's head-quarters saw the situation."[32]

More revealingly, Hesse's recollection of the conversation added:

> He saw the strengths and weaknesses of German military leadership, but still he expressed himself optimistically over the outcome of the war. As to whether or not this was his real judgment, I shall not attempt to say. In all of his statements, General Blaskowitz was *always extremely cautious.*

Cautious indeed! Blaskowitz had to be careful, since he could not even be certain of the specific dispositions of the officers around him.[33] Times such as these gave new meaning to the old German aphorism, "Talking is silver, silence is gold." Since at least October, 1940 he had lived with the apparent fact that Gestapo spies on his staff were watching his every move, waiting for a mis-step, a wrong phrase. The Gestapo office at 197 Rue du Medoc was after all, very nearby and had a large enough cellar to always have accommodations available.[34] He had to appear to be optimistic about the outcome of the war. Hitler could not tolerate pessimism or pessimists. Especially, the dictator could not endure pessimists that he recognized as realists.

Before 1942 turned into 1943, there were more momentous events in Blaskowitz's command in occupied France. On 8 November, 1942 the Allies landed in North Africa. It was only four days after the collapse of Rommel's position at El Alamein. The end of German-Italian dominance in North Africa was obviously at hand. In Europe the Nazi response was swift; southern France was occupied. The so-called Vichy Regime of Marshal Pètain limited itself to a protest. There was no resistance by the French treaty army.

General Blaskowitz's First Army and General Felber's "Armeegruppe Felber" began to occupy southern France on 11 November.[35] By 27 November the *Wehrmacht* had disarmed and disbanded the French Treaty Army, taken over its arms dumps, and occupied all French military barracks.[36] German troops had expected armed resistance. "This will be no picnic, they had been warned ...." But they were pleasantly surprised to encounter no opposition and reported that the old "Franc-Tireur spirit seemed to be dead."[37] By 10 December, the *Berliner Borsenzeitung* remarked that "eternal France," risen out of the ashes, might be Petain's favorite subject but that sober German observers could see only ashes and moral disintegration which had "not reached its lowest ebb." The "French people were a formless mass with no will power whatever."[38]

The relations between the German Army and the French in the occupied South of France "substantiates what has become, in our own day, a literary and cinematic cliche of the evil German Gestapo officer versus the honorable, duty-bound military officer."[39] The German military claimed that the basically smooth relations with the French would have been better still if not for the terror actions of the SD and the Gestapo, and this was "almost certainly" true.[40]

Nevertheless, relations for the most part were smooth, the German troops "correct" in behavior.[41] The monthly report of the French police commissioner of Chamalieres Royat, for example, confirmed this when he wrote in July, 1943: "everywhere, the good impression left by the propriety of the German military is obliterated by the German police methods that may begin to produce hatred."[42] Month after month the reports of German units stationed in the Clermont-Ferrand area began monotonously with the phrase, "still more hostile."[43] In Bordeaux, on the other hand, the local French population was mostly friendly, especially to the young German sailors, who spent their money freely in the local *maison serieuse* and the innumerable bistros.[44]

French hostility during the occupation did not really challenge either German rule or German exploitation of the French economy for its wartime needs.[45] Indeed, German manpower was so limited that the occupation was successful largely because the French, though generally hostile, were simultaneously cooperative in carrying out German policy in France.[46] French police arrested thousands of people for "Gaullism, Marxism, and hostility to the Regime." A pro-German paramilitary force called the "Milice" had forty-five thousand volunteers, and fought the resistance alongside German regular troops and police.[47] This is without mentioning French cooperation in rounding up the Jews, or French volunteers who fought in Russia.

The resistance did not pose anything approaching a serious threat in 1943. Sixty percent of the war material airdropped by the Allies to the resistance that year was intercepted by the Germans.[48] Twenty-five thousand Russian P.O.W.s were housed in France and many had escaped to join the resistance ranks. In addition, there were Poles who had fought with the French Army in 1940 and many other nationalities in the Resistance Forces.[49] Still, the resistance did not threaten German control. In the first nine months of 1943 "terrorists" attacked only 281 German soldiers, killing but eighty-four of them. Despite this, there was only a single incident of mass reprisal executions in 1943.[50] Different rules than applied in Russia were employed in France. Nevertheless, the partisan movement increasingly added an element of uncertainty and terror.

Blaskowitz placed his relations with the French on a proper basis and was liked and respected by the local civilians.[51] Fluent in French, Blaskowitz was sympathetic to them and demanded correct behavior by his troops. He had a staff officer deliver lectures to his officers on France's role in Germany's war effort. In 1943, according to the officer, France supplied all of the Wehrmacht's winter clothing and forty-six percent of Germany's wheat.

This same officer, Blaskowitz's chief supply officer, observed that the Generaloberst continued to live his old-Prussian lifestyle: "He was very strict and in our opinion, at times, rather petty. He demanded a great deal from his subordinates but also did a lot himself." Further describing Blaskowitz, he continued: "During critiques he spoke wisely and his unrehearsed after-dinner speeches were flavored with a warm understanding of all human and soldierly shortcomings, and with words of honest Christianity, so that it was always a pleasure to listen to him."[52]

Blaskowitz's evangelical Protestantism continued through this period to be a vital force in his life. He carried the *New Testament* with him and always read from it prior to retiring at night. In France, "he insisted on numerous religious field services and was always present himself."[53] Obviously this was not calculated to please the Nazis.

Petty harassments continued. 10 July 1943 was Blaskowitz's sixtieth birthday and his fortieth anniversary as a soldier. Senior officers traditionally had their pictures and a short congratulatory article in the newspapers on such occasions. They could expect a letter from the Fuehrer; Blaskowitz received neither.[54] It was obviously another deliberate snub which Blaskowitz bore with composure, not yielding to the temptations of self-pity.[55] Hitler apparently had not forgotten the general who had protested his race policy in Poland; nor had the dictator forgiven him.

A stream of visitors, eight-hundred in 1943 alone, passed through his headquarters at Bordeaux. In what is perhaps the wine capital of the world the Generaloberst took simple meals and requisitioned only the PX supplies needed for his guests. In September, 1943, for example, he was visited by the Japanese Ambassador Oshima and a naval captain who wished to inspect coastal defenses. The Ambassador, who enjoyed liquor and drinking songs,[56] was one of Blaskowitz's feted dinner guests. When he reported his impressions of German coastal defenses to Japan, Allied Intelligence—"Ultra"—decoded it, providing the Allies with a good picture of German dispositions.[57]

In the spring of 1943, Blaskowitz took his usual two weeks annual leave, but he did not go home to Dresden. Instead, he took his leave in Badenweiler, an elegant spa in the Black Forest in the extreme southwest of Germany, near Freiburg in Baden.[58] He met his wife there for their vacation, a brief respite. They spent their time in Badenweiler visiting with one of Blaskowitz's World War I comrades.

In July *The New York Times* described him as "one of a group of German generals forming a junta with the object of overthrowing Hitler and negotiating peace." He was accurately called a man who had disagreed with Hitler's decision to invade Russia and "to have registered his dissatisfaction with Herr Hitler's 'intuition.'" He was reported as commanding German troops in upper Italy.[59] Such a mixture of fact and fancy!

The New York Times' mixture was simple when compared to the complex conversational mix at Blaskowitz's headquarters. In mid-October the German diplomat, Ulrich von Hassell visited Blaskowitz at Tonart Castle, an English medieval fortress complete with moat, which serve as Blaskowitz's weekend home. Others present included Gregor, the German Consul General at Toulouse, Colonel Gerd Feyerabend, Chief of Staff, and Major von Renteln, who commanded a Cossack Regiment attached to First Army. News had just arrived of the Allied occupation of the Azores Islands when lunch was served.

Major von Renteln was the center of the conversation, which concerned his Cossack troop's fighting experiences. Renteln had been a Russian officer for nineteen years with the Imperial Horse Guards and later fought with the White Russians against the communists. It was an interesting luncheon. After lunch, Hassell, Blaskowitz and Gregor had a "political conversation." Gregor showed them an order from Berlin which stated that conflicts among the Allies were very great, but should be played down in public speeches. Blaskowitz did not comment. Hassell had been told that Blaskowitz had been "'refreshingly optimistic'" in his speeches to his officers and was curious. Himself a member of the opposition to Hitler, he asked Blaskowitz to meet privately with him for conversation. Half-past six was agreed upon for dinner.

The private dinner conversation was "not very successful" according to Hassell, who wrote in his diary:

> He sees things essentially from the soldier's point of view. He hopes for an increasing slump of American interest in the European war and for 'some' military event which will make it easier for us to hold out until a political opportunity shows up. For example, a severe defeat of the Anglo-Americans in Italy. He does not believe a landing will take place in France but if it comes, it will be very bad.[60]

Hassell had heard that Blaskowitz was "refreshingly optimistic" but his thoughts, as revealed in this conversation, could hardly be called "optimistic." There was once again a contrast between the general's public pronouncements and his private thoughts. Public optimism was a requirement for holding his job. Privately he could be more gloomy; the vagueness of his hope for "some" military event that would turn the scales was clear to his General-Staff educated mind, if not so obvious to Hassell. Hassell did not even raise the matter of the anti-Nazi opposition to this soldier, who "sees things essentially from the soldier's point of view."

The fact, apparently unknown to Hassell, was that Blaskowitz had already been approached by a member of his own staff, First Lieutenant Nikolaus von Mach, who was secretly connected with those who plotted against Hitler. Von Mach had spoken privately with Blaskowitz in an attempt to recruit him into what became known later as the 20 July 1944 conspiracy against Hitler.[61] Blaskowitz listened in silence to von Mach's description of plans for revolution and assassination of Hitler, but refused to participate. He explained that as a pastor's son and believing Christian he could not take part in murder, even Hitler's. "Thou shalt not kill." He did not betray the plotters.[62]

At the end of the month Blaskowitz was awarded the German Cross in Silver for his military services.[63] In this fourth year of this war, it was the first award he had received since the Polish Campaign, when many thought he was a sure bet to make the rank of field marshal. It was doubtless little compensation for all that he had endured. He would have preferred a combat command.

As 1943 passed into 1944, Germany's military power was deteriorating rapidly. Many German New Year's parties may have been pervaded by a sort of collective gallows' humor. Blaskowitz's New Year's Eve began with the regular dinner shared with officers of his staff. After dinner he dismissed all of the officers except one who was known throughout the staff as an alleged defeatist.

The officer, who had known Blaskowitz since 1938, was a paymaster who had been arrested in Berlin in December 1941 for remarks he had carelessly made in confidence to a "friend." He had told his "friend" that he had been at the Moscow front that month, only returning to Berlin because of a fractured skull, and that what he had seen in Russia was proof that Germany could not win the war, that the best divisions had been destroyed at Moscow. Those guilty for the misery on the front should be hanged. The soldiers at Moscow were freezing to death, while the SS officers in Berlin wore fur coats. Finally, he claimed to have heard that in Borisov, near Minsk, seven thousand Jews had been killed by Lithuanians on SS orders. The "friend" reported him to the Gestapo.

Blaskowitz had learned of the case and intervened to save the paymaster, arranging for disciplinary action through the Army rather than the Gestapo, and then setting up a transfer to First Army. In the field, Blaskowitz himself acted as presiding officer at the court-martial. The Generaloberst detoured the punishment into simple disciplinary punishment and then fulfilled it by a strong verbal reprimand. The case was closed, the officer served on Blaskowitz's staff well into 1944. They sat up together on New Year's eve until 4 A.M. talking.[64] While they talked the Allied Air Force bombed the nearby Merignac air field and U-boat pens, presumably as a New Year's greeting.[65]

The paymaster told Blaskowitz that the synagogue in Bordeaux was used by the Security Police (SD) as a place of confinement for suspected members of the Maquis, the French Resistance. Under arrest there had been a forty-six year old schoolteacher, about whom the paymaster had learned. He went to the synagogue and bribed the guard with clothing to obtain release of the teacher. Blaskowitz verbally approved of his actions but indicated that he did not want to be connected with the affair.[66]

This was certainly not the typical New Year's Eve conversation of a German general in wartime Europe. It is perhaps not surprising in the light of this conversation that, among the captured papers of one of Blaskowitz's later commands is a monthly report dated 6 December 1944 from Krakau, Poland, on events in the General Government. Blaskowitz had apparently kept track of events in Poland since the time he left. There is no other reason for this record to be found among the records of Army Group G.[67] If this is correct, then it is reasonable to assume that his personal torment about the atrocities in Poland continued long after he could influence events. He knew about the murders in Russia from his paymaster, whom he rescued from the Gestapo.

Blaskowitz was a "one hundred per cent soldier, a military man of the finest Prussian style and principle, yet down to earth and easy to talk to ...", according to Hans Brandner, who served on his staff.[68] He certainly knew about the atrocities in Russia.[69] And he knew about the euthanasia that had been practised by the Nazis within Germany itself, even inquiring about the inmates of the asylum in his birthplace to the Reverend Ernst Froese, a minister from Paterswalde, that he met.[70] Despite this knowledge he knew that he had no influence on these large events, that he could influence events only within his small realm of command, and even there only to a most limited degree.

He did not know, as he retired to bed that New Year's Eve, that it was that very week that the Allies had set up a U.S. Seventh Army planning staff in the Ecole Normale at Bouzareah, in Algiers, to plan the invasion of Southern France. It was to be known to the Allies by the code name "ANVIL," and had a target date of May, 1944.[71]

Saturday, 1 January 1944, New Year's Day, was not pleasant in Bordeaux. It was foggy and cloudy until mid-day, raining in the afternoon, and a mixture of fog and drizzle in the evening with temperatures rising only to 43 degrees Fahrenheit.[72] It was not an auspicious beginning for the new year. On the positive side for the Germans, however, the weather meant that Bordeaux would not be bombed that day as it had been the previous day.

In the evening an old friend from Blaskowitz's days as commander of the 14th Infantry Regiment at Lake Constance came to visit. The conversation naturally turned to the coming year. "Blaskowitz said that night that in this coming new year there would be war in the west."[73]

Notes for Chapter X

1. Seaton, *The German Army*, 175.

2. Hellmut Gollwitzer, "Der Überfall," *Zeit Magazin,*NR.13, 23 March 1984, 30.

3. Werner Rings, *Life With the Enemy: Collaboration and Resistance in Hitler's Europe, 1939-1945* (Garden City, New York: Doubleday and Company, Inc. 1982), 211.

4. Anon., *"All Gaul Is Divided:" Letters from Occupied France* (New York: The Greystone Press, 1941), 51.

5. Peter Leslie, *The Liberation of the Riviera: The Resistance to the Nazis in the South of France and the Story of Its Heroic Leader, Ange-Marie Minicon* (New York: Wyndham Books, 1980), 56.

6. Henri Frenay, *The Night Will End*, trans. Dan Hofstadter (New York: McGraw-Hill Book Company, 1976), 165.

7. Pryce-Jones, *Paris in the Third Reich*, 256; Gerard Walter, *Paris Under the Occupation*, trans. Tonny White (New York: Orion Press, 1960), 37-41.; Umbreit, Müller and Kroener, *Das Deutsche Reich und Der Zweite Weltkrieg*, 5: 69. Von Briesen was killed in Russia in November 1941.

8. Charles Whiting, *'44 In Combat from Normandy to the Ardennes* (New York: Military Heritage Press, 1988), 116.

9. Report of Interrogation No. 5554 (Unknown German, Undated), Records of the Judge Advocate General (Army), General and Administrative Records, 1944-1949, Case 110 (5554), R.G. 153, N.A.

10. Major (a.D) Hellmuth Gaudig, "Im Gedenken an Generaloberst Blaskowitz," *Der Seehase*, Nr. 122, 1976.; In November and December 1941 five German divisions in France were transferred to Russia. Seaton, *The German Army*, 186.

11. Louis P. Lochner, ed., *The Goebbels Diaries: 1942-1943*, ed., trans. and Intro. Louis Lochner (Garden City, New York: Doubleday and Company, 1948), 106.

12. Giles Perrault, *Paris Under the Occupation* (New York: Vendome Press, 1989), 12.

13. John Colville, *The Fringes of Power: 10 Downing Street Diaries, 1939-1955* (New York: W.W. Norton & Company, 1985), 406.

14. Charles Burdick, *Germany's Military Strategy and Spain in World War II*, (Syracuse, New York: Syracuse University Press, 1968), 156.

15. H. R. Trevor-Roper, ed., *Blitzkrieg to Defeat: Hitler's War Directives, 1939-1945.* (New York: Holt, Rhinehart, and Winston, 1964), 112.

16. Burdick, *Germany's Military Strategy and Spain*, 157.

17. Blaskowitz Interrogation, 28 July 1945, CCPWE#32/DI-43, R.G. 332, N.A.

18. Kit Carter and Robert Mueller (Comps), *The Army Air Forces in World War II: Combat Chronology, 1941-1945*, Army Air Force Combat Chronology (Office of Air Force History, Air University, 1973), 136, 179, 226, 242, 246, 286, 302, 375 and 424.; Hinsley, *British Intelligence*, II: 542, Vol. III, Part I: 252: Janusz Pekalkiewicz, *The Air War: 1939-1945*, trans. Jan van Heurck (Dorset, England: Blandford Press, 1985), 293; Wesley Craven and James Cates (eds.), *The Army Air Forces In World War II*, (Office of Air Force History: Washington, D.C., 1983), II: 244.; Martin Middlebrook and Chris Everitt, *The Bomber Command War Diaries: An Operational Reference Book, 1939-1945* (New York: Penguin Books, 1990), 348, 501-502.

19. Pierre Becamps, *Bordeaux sous l'occupation* (Rennes: Ouestfrance, 1983), 8, 166.

20. Jacques Delarue, et. al., "La Gestapo En France," *Historia hors serie* (c. 1972), 9.

21. NOKW 2608, T-1119/33/0150-0151, R.G. 238, N.A.

22. Trevor-Roper, ed., *Blitzkrieg to Defeat*, 121-123. Hitler had considered the occupation of Vichy France as early as 10 December 1940 in Directive No. 19. See 44-46.

23. Ibid., 123-124.

24. Ibid., 124.

25. Burdick, *Germany's Military Strategy and Spain*, 149.

26. Colonel C.P. Stacy, *Six Years of War: The Army In Canada, Britain and the Pacific*, (Ottawa: Queen's Printer and Controller of Stationery, 1955), 406-407.

27. H. R. Trevor-Roper,ed., *Hitler's Secret Conversations: 1941-1944*, (New York: Farrar, Strauss and Young, 1953), 540.

28. Burdick, *Germany's Military Strategy and Spain*, 163.

29. Ibid., 173-174, 180-187. See also: T-312, Roll 25, R.G. 238, N.A.

30. Blaskowitz Interrogation, 5 June 1945, First Canadian Army Intelligence Periodical No. 4, Vol. 10,655, File 215C1.023, R.G. 24, P.A.C.

31. Lehmann, *Leibstandarte*, II: 235.

32. Kurt Hesse, "Collapse of the German Western Front 1944," (CA. August 1945?) R.G. 165, N.A.

33. Ibid. (Emphasis added).; Interview of Prince Friedrich Biron von Curland, I.D., 08/08/92, Bad Godesberg, Germany. Copy in the author's possession. The author wishes to express his deep gratitude for the gracious hospitality and kindness of the Durchlaucht, Prince Friedrich Biron von Curland.

34. Delarue, *Gestapo*, 206.; Beaucamps, *Bordeaux sous l'occupation*, 166.

35. Percy Ernst Schramm, ed., *Kriegstagebuch des Oberkommandos der Wehrmacht (Wehrmachtfuhrungsstab): 1940-1945*, 1: Hans-Adolf Jacobsen, ed., *1 August 1940-31 December 1941*; 2: Andreas Hillgruber, ed., *1942*; 3: Walter Hubatsch, ed., *1943*; 4: Percy Ernst Schramm, ed., *1944-1945* (Frankfurt am Main: Bernard & Graefe Verlag fur Wehrwesen, 1965), 2: 1436.

36. Rings, *Life With the Enemy*, 123.

37. John F. Sweets, *Choices In Vichy France: The French Under Nazi Occupation*, (New York: Oxford University Press, 1986), 173-174.

38. Arvid Fredborg, *Behind the Steel Wall: A Swedish Journalist in Berlin, 1941-1943*, (New York: The Viking Press, 1944), 153.

39. Sweets, *Choices in Vichy France*, 189.

40. Ibid.

41. Ibid., 188.

42. Ibid.

43. Ibid., 190.

44. Dan van der Vat, *The Atlantic Campaign, World War II's Great Struggle At Sea* (New York: Harper & Row Publishers, 1988), 174.; The "most notorious pro-German periodical in all France was based in Bordeaux." Gerhard Hirschfeld and Patrick Marsh, eds., *Collaboration in France: Politics and Culture during the Nazi Occupation, 1940-1944* (New York: Berg Publishers, 1989), 79-80. It seems also, that Bordeaux had an uncharacteristically clever and subtle Gestapo chief from Stuttgart named Dhose who successfully "decimated and disorganized" the local French Resistance throughout the occupation. He was apparently complimented by a rigorously "correct" German Commandant of Bordeaux, a Major-General Hans Knoerzer. Robert Aron, *France Reborn: The History of the Liberation, June 1944-May 1945* (New York: Charles Scribner's Sons, 1964), 378-381.; Robert Aron, *DeGaulle Triumphant: The Liberation of France, August 1944-May 1945*, trans. Humphrey Hare (London: Putnam, 1964), 211-216.

45. Sweets, *Choices in Vichy France*, 192.

46. Ibid., 184-185.

47. Rings, *Life With the Enemy*, 123.

48. Ibid., 274.

49. Ibid., 212.

50. Richard C. Fattig, "Reprisal: The German Army and the Execution of Hostages during the Second World War" (Ph.d. dissertation, University of California at San Diego, 1980), 97-98.

51. Möller-Witten, "Blaskowitz," 173.

52. Report of Interrogation No. 5554 (Unknown German, Undated), case 110 (5554), R.G. 153, N.A.

53. Ibid., Interview of Prince Friedrich Biron von Curland, I.D., 08/08/92, Bad Godesberg, Germany. Copy in author's possession.

54. Ibid. (Interrogation No. 5554).

55. Otto Schmeidler, Oberstrichter a.D., Eidesstattlich Erklärung, 10 December 1947, Villa Dalfried Billdal, Schwaben, *Collection Koepcke*. Copy in author's possession.

56. Hans-Georg von Studnitz, *While Berlin Burns: The Diary of Hans-Georg von Studnitz, 1943-1945*, trans. George Weindenfeld (Englewood Cliffs, New Jersey, 1964), 199.; Blaskowitz File, Entry 194, M.I.D., M.I.S., Who's Who Branch, 1939-1945, R.G. 165, N.A.

57. Hinsley, *British Intelligence*, III, Part 2, 771-775.; Carl Boyd, *Hitler's Japanese Confidant: General Oshima Hiroshi and Magic Intelligence, 1941-1945* (Lawrence, University of Kansas Press, 1993), 185-191.

58. NOKW 2608, T-1119/33/0150-0151, R.G. 238, N.A.

59. "Blaskowitz Is Nazi Chief," *The New York Times*, 31 July 1943, 3; in August 1943 the O.S.S. was still receiving reports that he was in Italy. See: OSS Records, OB 2653, R.G. 226, N.A.

60. Hassell, *Hassell Diaries*, 323-324.

61. Tagesbuchaufzeichnungen Nikolaus von Mach, unpublished, Entry dated "Ende August 1943," loaned to a grateful author. Von Mach kept his diary in Greek letters so that it would be without meaning to most people. Copy in author's possession.

62. Written information from Mr. Nikolaus von Mach, Germany, August 8, 1992. Copy in author's possession. Blaskowitz's Christianity may have been reinforced by the opinion commonly held in his early manhood among soldiers in Germany that although tyranicide had been considered moral in antiquity, "at the present day political murder is universally condemned from the stand point of political morality." See: Fredrich von Bernhardi, *Germany and the Next War*, trans. Allen Powles (New York: Longman's Green, and Co, 1914), 48. Significantly, Bernhardi added: "The man who pursues moral ends with unmoral means is involved in contradiction of motives, and nullifies the object at which he aims, since he denies it by his actions." Failure to report the

conspiracy was high treason and therefore "denotes a basic distaste if not de-
testation for the regime ...." Deutsch, "German Soldiers in the 1938 Munich
Crisis," 306.

63. NOKW 141 Blaskowitz, M898, Roll 28, Frames 0161-0164, R.G. 238, N.A.

64. Report of Interrogation No. 5554 (Unknown German, Undated), Case 110
(5554), R.G. 153, N.A.

65. Carter and Mueller (Comps.), *Army Air Force Combat Chronology*, 424.

66. *Report of Interrogation No. 5554* (Unknown German, undated), Case 110
(5554) RG 153, N.A.

67. T-311/146/7192957, R.G. 238, N.A.

68. Written information from Mr. Hans Brandner, Wängle, Germany, September
15, 1992. Copy in author's possession. Mr. Brandner served on Blaskowitz's
staff for seven months.

69. Written information from Mr. Nikolaus von Mach, Germany, August 8,
1992. Copy in author's possession.

70. Ernst Froese, "Miene Begegnung mit Hans Blaskowitz", 8-9.

71. *Report of Operations: The Seventh United States Army In France and Germany*,
Three Volumes (Heidelberg: Heidelburg Gutenberg Printing Company, May
1946), 1: 1-2.

72. The weather report is based upon the author's correspondence with the "Service Central D'Exploitation De La Meteorologie" in Paris dated 01/04/89.
Copy in author's possession.

73. Hans Gies, "Generaloberst Johannes Blaskowitz," *Der Seehase*, Nr. 93/94,
Konstanz, Dezember 1965, 6.

CHAPTER XI

OCCUPIED FRANCE: 1944

HITLER DID NOT REQUIRE PSYCHIC POWERS to realize that 1944 was the year the Allies would attempt to invade the continent. Nevertheless, as late as November, 1943 there was no overall German plan for defense of the continent against invasion, only local measures.[1] To correct this, Hitler turned to Field Marshal Erwin Rommel. Rommel the "Desert Fox," was assigned in November, 1943 to survey the defenses of German-occupied western Europe. The Führer's favorite in happier times, Rommel was a disillusioned man after his experiences in Africa.[2] Nevertheless, he attacked his new assignment with all of his legendary energy, motivated perhaps by the awareness that the fate of Germany could hinge on the success or failure of the invasion.

Taking with him Admiral Friedrich Ruge and Major General Alfred Gause as Chief of Staff, Rommel began his inspection tour of coastal defenses in Denmark in the beginning of December, 1943. He toured all of Europe's coastline, including not only the Atlantic, but also the Mediterranean coast. On 9 February 1944 at 7 P.M., Rommel and his advisors arrived at Blaskowitz's headquarters in Bordeaux. According to Admiral Ruge, they had barely put their luggage in their rooms at the Hotel Splendide when discussion with Blaskowitz began. Only an experimental strip of coastal defense obstacles was under construction. Rommel was obviously not pleased. In Ruge's words: "Although the Army had received Rommel's constant proposals and suggestions, [this] indicated how uncertain [was] the success of mere advice [Rommel lacked command authority]...."

The conference continued, interrupted at 9 P.M. for a "casual snack."

At 10 P.M. there was a signals report, followed by an engineer's report. It may have been later in the evening when Rommel and Blaskowitz discussed "other" matters, presumably more privately. During 1943 Rommel had learned from Dr. Karl Strölin, Mayor of Stuttgart, of the Nazi extermination of the Jews. Did Blaskowitz know anything of these "rumors?" In response, Blaskowitz asked him, "Why, did Rommel suppose, was he, Colonel-General Blaskowitz, not a Field Marshal?" Blaskowitz then revealed his refusal to condone the SS atrocities in Poland in 1939-40 and his written condemnations of SS atrocities sent directly to Hitler, who had received them contemptuously.[3] It was a depressing ending to an exhausting day, but Rommel departed the next morning promptly at 8 A.M., noting alertly that Blaskowitz's command—First Army—included both Cossacks and Indians from the "Free India" movement. Moreover, "Resistance" strongpoints on the beaches manned by these "volunteer" troops were as much as three and a half kilometers apart.[4] It was not encouraging.

When he reported to the *OKW* a few days later, Rommel merely stated that the center of First Army was too thinly defended. He proposed moving troops from the interior to the coast. Generally, he continued, everything at First Army was in order. Raising a more fundamental issue, Rommel added that in the west the chain of command was "unclear."[5] It was Rommel's opening salvo in his campaign to obtain clear command powers.

On 20 March he visited Hitler at Klessheim and found the dictator in agreement with his views—the invasion must be defeated on the beaches. Therefore, Rommel must have command power over at least part of the armored reserves of OB West—Field Marshal von Rundstedt. In addition, Rommel was given responsibility for the coastal defenses of First and Nineteenth Armies on the Atlantic and Mediterranean coasts, and also for Seventh and Fifteenth Armies on the Channel Coasts.[6]

If this were not sufficiently confusing, there was also the existence of Panzer Armies West, under the command of General Freiherr Geyr von Schweppenberg. This command theoretically controlled armored reserves in the west, but in fact Hitler would not allow them to be moved without his personal consent. Superimposed on Panzer Armies West—Schweppenberg's panzer command, Rommel's Coastal Inspection and Defense Command, and all individual armies (including Blaskowitz's First Army)- was the Commander in Chief West (*Oberbefehlshaber*—OB), Field Marshal Gerd von Rundstedt! Although Rommel's command responsibility was not clear, it potentially conflicted with von Rundstedt's responsibilities and prerogatives.[7] Naturally, this confused picture of the German chain of command becomes even more blurred when the Navy and Luftwaffe are added.

Rundstedt was the German general who most nearly fit the stereotypical Allied preconceptions of German militarism personified. The last member of a military family which had produced soldiers for Germany all the way back to the twelfth century, Rundstedt derived from the oldest Brandenburg nobility.[8] A member of a military caste comparable only to the Japanese Samurai, Rundstedt was the first member of his family to be awarded the field marshal's baton.[9] Nearly seventy years old in 1944, von Rundstedt projected a public image, "almost Roman in its gravity ...."[10] Taciturn, reserved and modest— sometimes wearing the uniform not of a field marshal, but instead that of a colonel in the 18th Infantry Regiment—Rundstedt led a simple life.[11]

Privately, however, Rundstedt had a "bitingly sarcastic" humor, which frequently had Hitler as its object—especially when he had been drinking. Perhaps it was incongruous with the rest of his character, but Rundstedt was a heavy smoker and a legendarily immoderate drinker. He was a keen mimic and his vocabulary was rich with the word "Scheisse."[12] Nevertheless, he was a widely respected soldier of "immense professional competence, sobriety of judgement, complete calm, and, in general, affability and politeness."[13]

Rommel and Rundstedt contrasted in almost every way. Rundstedt was old, tired and militarily orthodox. Rommel was comparatively youthful, energetic and unconventional. Rundstedt commanded from rear headquarters; Rommel led from the front.[14] Conflict was probably inevitable. Rundstedt later wrote that he had hoped that Rommel would replace him as Commander-in-Chief West, but Keitel visited the old field marshal in November, 1943 and explained that this would never take place. The Führer himself thought Rommel's strength and abilities suitable for other tasks; Rommel was seen by Hitler as fitted for "attacks à la Seydlitz at Rossbach, but not for strategic operations."[15]

Despite his claims of respect for Rommel's military qualities, it was obvious that Rundstedt resented Rommel's insertion into the command structure:

> We have shown at Dieppe how to fight against enemy invasion.... We did not need the instructions and preachings from the "greatest commander-in-chief of all times [Hitler] to do this. Neither did we need instructions by Mister Rommel.[16]

Rumor circulating among some German soldiers to the effect that Rundstedt had once referred to Rommel as "the clown who commands the Adolf Hitler circus," may have been known to Rommel.[17] Such knowledge could not have smoothed their relationship. On the professional level, however, Rommel undoubtedly respected Rundstedt, but trusted in his relationship with Hitler when he came into conflict with the old field-marshal. Rommel, after all, was the "*Fuehrer's Marshal.*"[18]

Though not to each other's faces, both field marshals had "pet-names" for the other. Rommel's South German expression for the elderly Field Marshal was "Der Rundstedt." For his part, Rundstedt called the younger Rommel "Marshal Laddie."[19] Favorite nicknames for each other might have partially masked the serious differences in strategic views of how to deal with the coming invasion—differences which were critical—but after operations had begun, these differences were less important since Hitler kept tight control over the operations of both field marshals.[20]

As Rundstedt later admitted: "The pressure from behind," he said, "was always far worse than the pressure in front." Continuing, he declared: "As Commander-in-Chief West, my only authority was to change the guard in front of my gate."[21]

Upset by the increased authority Hitler had granted to Rommel, and not entirely innocent to political in-fighting, Rundstedt countered on the following day, 21 March 1944. He informed Keitel in Berlin that two-thirds of the beach defenses had been completed in First Army's area.[22] Rundstedt, however, did not have much faith in reinforced concrete. He was also realistic about the limited support the Luftwaffe would provide. His main concern was the Army manpower shortage in France.[23] He bombarded Keitel with the manpower shortage problem repeatedly enough for Keitel to react stingingly. Keitel's response was intercepted by Ultra so the Allies eavesdropped on Rundstedt's problem.

Keitel warned Rundstedt by radio on 19 April that *OKW* was well aware of the weakness of First Army and was continually attempting to improve it, but that reinforcements could not be dispatched due to the general situation. Rundstedt would have to transfer troops from other parts of his command to strengthen Blaskowitz's First Army.[24]

Blaskowitz himself had declared First Army's weakness less than two weeks previously in a written report to Rundstedt which was not intercepted by the Allies. Charged with the defense of an 857 kilometer front, Blaskowitz described the First Army zone as an "absolute point of weakness in the defense of the occupied French land, and it will not change." He did not mince his words, adding: "This will not remain a secret to the Anglo-American leadership and investigation. It is probably already known to them."[25] Extreme as this statement appears, it was no exaggeration: First Army had only four infantry divisions on a front of 857 kilometers. And those four divisions were second class units.[26]

On 16 May, Rundstedt signaled his response to Keitel's earlier suggestion. He emphasized the duty to comb out rear echelons to maintain combat units at maximum strength.[27] Clearly, Rundstedt had something in mind. Since Rommel's appointment he had recognized the danger of Army Group B in Normandy acquiring a "preeminent, excessively favored position."[28] He was also familiar with Blaskowitz's manpower shortage at First Army and that of another independent Command—Nineteenth Army—on the Riviera front. Though Rundstedt could not acquire more manpower, he could balance Army Group B's favored status in the north under Rommel with a new southern Army Group. Unified command of the Atlantic (First Army) and Mediterranean (Nineteenth Army) coasts would simplify his command problem and unify command channels in the remainder of France. It would also provide a more important position—army group commander in the south—for his friend Blaskowitz to fill. The arrangement would facilitate Rundstedt's own supervision of the entire theater of war.[29]

Perhaps Rundstedt had these possibilities in mind already in early

March, when the time arrived to formally evaluate his old friend Blaskowitz succinctly:

> Noble, sensitive, extremely valuable person[,] *a live and adaptable National Socialist.* Proven before the enemy. Excellent in fulfillment of his duties. Outstanding instructor of troops. Physically and mentally very capable. Above average. Leave in position.[30] [Emphasis added]

Naturally, the business about Blaskowitz being a "live and adaptable National Socialist," was not exactly true, but was instead something Rundstedt and other generals felt to be mandatory in their evaluations by the spring of 1944.[31] The previous summer the army personnel office had issued the highly ideological book, *What Do We Fight For?*, which was a response to the need for uniform orientation of the officer corps. On 8 January 1944, Hitler had issued an order emphasizing the officer's role in ideological leadership.[32] The handwriting was large and clear on the wall for all to see; it had been clear for a long time. Those who wanted to continue to serve Germany had to receive officially the ideological stamp of approval whether it reflected the truth or not. In protecting his friend and colleague, Rundstedt was also assuring his continued availability as the new army group commander in southern France.

Rundstedt had, in fact, already proposed the creation of an army group in southern France at the end of March. It was to be titled Army Group "G" (Gustav) and would be made up of First and Nineteenth Armies. Blaskowitz was designated by Rundstedt to be commander of Army Group G.[33] *OKW* in Berlin agreed to this arrangement and to Blaskowitz's new appointment about the beginning of April. But even in this agreement, Blaskowitz was snubbed.

In the German Army there is an intermediate status between a Corps and an Army Group ("Heeresgruppe") called an "Armeegruppe." Though the English translation for both "Heeresgruppe" and "Armeegruppe is "Army Group," in German, the status of an "Armeegruppe" is distinctly less than that of a "Heeresgruppe." The "Armeegruppe" is usually a provisional and temporary command. Blaskowitz's new command was designated an "Armeegruppe" rather than a "Heeresgruppe."It was an insult to Blaskowitz, another in a long series of degradations. Rundstedt's chief of staff, Generalleutnant Bodo Zimmermann, explained it this way: "No reason was given for this proviso, but it probably had a close connection with the individual (Blaskowitz) proposed as commander."[34] As another German general wrote: "This was purely a personal matter. Blaskowitz, a fine soldier, was not much liked by Hitler."[35]

In London, news of Blaskowitz's appointment as an army group commander was printed in the London *Daily Express* on 20 May under the headline "Nazis and Generals Make It Up." The article was the usual wartime mixture of truth and misinformation. Reminding readers that Blaskowitz was "easily the most successful individual general in the Polish campaign ...," it continued, asserting that Rundstedt had "undoubtedly" had a hand in Blaskowitz's new appointment: "Without doubt, Rundstedt is the best soldier in the German Army and Blaskowitz is the second."[36] Without complete knowledge of the circumstances of Blaskowitz's new appointment, this was remarkable reporting! The article added: "Readmission to the highest rank of Blaskowitz, however, must have been a considerable pill for the Nazis to swallow."

Further, the story stated that Blaskowitz had once been commander in occupied Poland and had his "stomach turned" by the arrival of the Gestapo. He had protested directly to Hitler in person and verbal insults had been exchanged. Blaskowitz reportedly had called Hitler "a fool, to his face."[37] The last quotation has proved impossible to verify, although it does sum up neatly what Blaskowitz wrote in his memoranda at the time.

Blaskowitz bade farewell to his staff at First Army in his usual way, telling them that he had always tried to know them as people, not merely as soldiers. Significantly, he ended his comments in these words: "God have mercy on our people." He shook hands with each member of the staff and left for Paris.[38]

On 8 May, before actually taking command of Army Group G, Blaskowitz traveled to Paris to meet with the top *Wehrmacht* commanders in France. Admiral Theodore Krancke represented the German Navy at the conference. Field Marshal Sperrle was the Luftwaffe representative. Rundstedt was there as overall commander. Representing the army were Blaskowitz, Rommel, and the chief of Panzer Armies West, General Geyr von Schweppenburg.[39]

Speculation that the meeting re-examined tactics designed to repel the expected Allied invasion went unproven;[40] it was actually to clarify command channels. Cameras recorded the meeting and photographs appeared a few days later in the German language newspapers in Paris.[41] Surprisingly, Blaskowitz's new Army Group G had three of the precious panzer divisions subordinated to it. They were the new 9th and 11th Panzer divisions and the 2nd SS Panzer Division—*Das Reich*.[42] Little else, however, apparently resulted.

British intelligence did not wait until publication of the photograph to learn of Blaskowitz's new assignment. Already on the day of the meeting in Paris it had intercepted and decoded radio intelligence about Blaskowitz's appointment to head Army Group G.[43] Blaskowitz was in command of all German forces in France south of the Loire River.

Under Blaskowitz's command General of Infantry Kurt von der Chevallerie commanded First Army at Bordeaux and General of Infantry Georg von Sodenstern commanded Nineteenth Army at Avignon. Chevallerie was responsible for defending the Atlantic coast and Sodenstern the Mediterranean coast.[44] Blaskowitz established his Army Group headquarters mid-way between them in southwestern France at Rouffiac, a small farming village of about 450 people, about six kilometers from Toulouse. His chief of staff was Generalmajor Heinz von Gyldenfeldt. The staff itself was made up of officers furnished through von Rundstedt.[45]

Throughout the German Army fighting in Russia there was a catch phrase about the soldier's life in France: "Living like God in France." It was based on the Army's collective memory of 1940, but it was no longer entirely true. French civilians addressed soldiers coldly in public if they spoke to them at all. Food was not abundant. Travel alone outside of occupied cities was impossible due to "terrorists." "Even in Toulouse, the officer's messes and the *Soldatenheim* were faced with wire mesh against grenade attack."[46]

A city which in 1944 embodied many of the ambiguities of occupied France, Toulouse is located on a wide bend in the Garonne River within sight of the Pyrenees on a clear day. The old quarter of the city was built out of faded local red brick which gave the city its nickname: "*la ville rose*." Its medieval *Ruelles* provided an ideal maze for an escape route,[47] so it is not surprising that one of the three major escape routes for Allied airmen shot down in Western Europe passed through Toulouse, almost by Blaskowitz's doorstep.[48] Yet, at the same time that Maquisards conspired in the back rooms of bars in Toulouse,[49] and Allied airmen passed secretly through the city, German occupation authorities found the prefect of the city among the most cooperative in southern France.[50]

Blaskowitz kept his headquarters near Toulouse only from mid-May until mid-August, a mere three months, insufficient time to become intimately familiar with the area. But long enough, however, to reveal himself further in the midst of tragedy.

In the meantime, the Generaloberst had his hands more than full with the ultimately impossible task of repelling an Allied invasion in the south of France. As Rundstedt later admitted, "Once the various divisions were stretched along the huge coastal front, there was hardly anything left in the interior." He continued: "Only the armored and parachute divisions contained young men, but there were too few of these to form an adequate fighting force." Most of the troops were over-aged or physically of low quality. "Mixed in among these relics were thousands of Russians (*Ost* Troops) who constituted a menace and a nuisance to operations in France."[51] It was impossible to get more and better troops, so the Germans in France resorted to deception.

An enormous campaign of deception was undertaken to convince the western Allies that a successful invasion was impossible anywhere in France. Intensive propaganda trumpeted the invincibility of the Atlantic Wall. Vast dummy minefields were laid. Maps showing formidable concrete defenses and minefields were passed to the Allies by means of German agents in Paris and Switzerland. Various means were employed to convince the French that reinforcements of old divisions and the arrival of fresh divisions was taking place. All this in the hope that such intelligence would reach England. According to Rundstedt:

> So extensive did these deceptive measures become that it was necessary to keep a list of real and fake divisions at OB West to prevent the staff from becoming muddled. One column showed the facts about the dummy division, its supposed date of arrival and its presumed area of occupation. A second column provided the correct

information. On maps the real divisions were shown in red, while the fake divisions were marked in blue. Even the Japanese Ambassador in Vichy was supplied with some of these false maps designed to lull both him and his government into a sense of security as to the strength of German forces in the West.[52]

Allied intelligence—especially Ultra—retrospectively made the German efforts at deception appear particularly pathetic. Ultra was the secret code name the Allies used to refer to the fact that they had broken many of the German codes used throughout World War II. When the continent was invaded, it was the Germans who were victimized by Allied deception; Ultra provided the Allies with a piercing light with which to see through the fog of war to the "other side of the hill."

The German defenders of the continent did not rely solely on their efforts to deceive the Allies. Naturally, they turned also to steel and concrete fortifications. The more threatened Channel Coast was given priority in construction of fortifications, as it had been in manpower. One German commander aptly described the Mediterranean coast as a "substitute front."[53]

Nevertheless, the Germans had worked in earnest since the end of January—spurred on by both Hitler and Rommel—to fortify the Mediterranean coast. At the beginning of June nearly one thousand permanent fortifications had been built. In addition, almost 62,500 mines had been laid, not to mention miles of barbed wire strung, firing trenches dug, and machine gun nests built. There was also a modest increase in infantry divisions from five in 1943 to seven in 1944.[54] They had also put in anti-aircraft searchlights, radar stations, roadblocks, anti-tank obstacles and prepared demolitions.[55]

The improvement in defenses was dramatic; however, by the day of the Allied landing only one-third of the planned concrete defenses had been finished and almost all of these were in the forward defense zone on the beach. Obstacles in the water were built below the tide-lines. Anti-aircraft and artillery were part of the defenses.[56]

Historians sometimes write about a "South Wall" of France, qualifying it perhaps by the recognition that it really only applied to the "crucial points such as Marseilles, Toulon and the Gulf of Fréjus.[57] The Chief of Staff of Nineteenth Army—Generalleutnant Walter Botsch—

who was directly responsible for defending the Mediterranean Coast, described the construction of defenses as at their "beginning stages." He wrote: "This goes for all the aspects of the construction, the fields, the fortresses and the underwater obstacles."[58]

Summing up his own view of the fortifications of the French Mediterranean coast, and apparently describing the areas other than Marseilles and Toulon, Generaloberst Blaskowitz wrote retrospectively in his direct soldier's manner: "[T]here were, in that sector, hardly any fortified positions worth mentioning ...."[59] It was little more than a "mere system of security and supervision of the coastline."[60] Post-war Allied military analysts described the fortifications on the coast as a "chain of fortifications," but admit that, "In general, the defenses were not deep."[61] Another thin crust of defenses capable of limited resistance with nothing behind them.

It is not surprising, given this state of military affairs in his new command area, that Blaskowitz addressed his new staff at Army Group G in a manner both characteristic of him and reflective of the situation when he first met them on 16 May. After a conference with his chief of staff, he addressed the assembled staff, briefly welcoming them and announcing his expectation that they would work together cooperatively. He explained his view that "bureaucratic work is non-productive and not conducive to success. Emphasis should be on priorities and efficiency rather than protocol." Primary emphasis was support of the troops. This meant constant interaction with them. Co-workers must have sufficient liberty of action—very much in keeping with traditional general staff doctrine.

As if to emphasize his point yet further, he ordered new staff officers to take infantry weapons close combat training "to keep the staff fresh and alert." Finally, he ended the little speech with a statement that he hoped for "noble behavior among officers and in working with subordinate ranks." Straightforward, precise, setting a high standard, pragmatic; vintage Blaskowitz.[62]

His responsibilities occasionally required him to return to his former headquarters in Bordeaux. On one of these visits he invited a small circle of friends to dinner. As was his usual custom, it was the same meal as that of the regular troops, brought directly from the troop's kitchen, but supplemented by fish purchased locally. After dinner, the commandant of Bordeaux played Beethoven sonatas on the piano. After one of these, Blaskowitz remarked to one of his friends: "This was a beautiful half hour. This was good, to forget the war once and for all, at least for a little while."[63]

Responsibility for command of an army group in circumstances that gave little hope for a victorious conclusion of events clearly weighed heavily on the Generaloberst. His own certainty that the strategy which Hitler had dictated for his army group to follow was not the correct one under the circumstances must have imposed a severe strain, not to mention the likelihood that the general continued to be under surveillance.

Strategic options were naturally limited by the geography of the south of France but even so, all of the basic decisions had been made before Blaskowitz assumed command responsibility. Nevertheless it is important to understand the influence of geography before considering the strategic alternatives.

Blaskowitz's territorial responsibility was France south of the Loire River. First Army defended the Atlantic Coast and on the Mediterranean Nineteenth Army defended the coast. The Mediterranean Coast of France consists of three mountain masses cut by two narrow corridors. The mountains from west to east are the Pyrenees, the Massif Central, and the Alps. The western corridor, the Carcassonne Gap, lies between the Pyrenees and the Massif Central along the Aude and Garonne River valleys.

It leads from the Mediterranean Coast generally northwest, past Toulouse, in the direction of Bordeaux. Further east, between the Massif Central and the Alps, lies the second corridor, which leads from the Mediterranean Coast north along the Rhône River valley to the Saone River valley and then northeastward toward southwestern Germany. Julius Caesar recognized the Rhône-Saone Corridor as the great strategic route through France and it had served as an invasion route for the Vandals, Goths, Alamans, Burgundians and Franks.

The coast itself is a long sweeping reverse S-curve between Spain and Italy. The Rhône River forms a broad delta not suitable for landing troops, but the beaches to the east along the Riviera and to the west all the way to the Spanish border are all possible landing sites. The entire western sector is broad beach—good for landings but leading west to the Carcasonne Gap and away from Germany. In the east the beaches are narrow, the coast irregular and mountains come down to the beaches. Passage to the interior is by narrow river valleys.[64] The entire stretch of beach from Spain to Italy had been used as an invasion route by Hannibal and might be used by modern armies.

Since the main theater of Allied operations in France was almost certain to be somewhere along the Channel Coast, the Mediterranean Coast (Nineteenth Army) and the Atlantic Coast (First Army) were of secondary importance. In a sense, Army Group G merely guarded the flank of Army Group B on the Channel.

Nineteenth Army on the Mediterranean Coast was actually a recent creation, dating its formation only from a regrouping of forces in the fall of 1943. The manner in which it should be employed and the strategy it was to follow, was decided during the fall, 1943, and winter, 1944. The lines of debate were similar to those examined previously between Rommel and Rundstedt regarding German strategy in the Channel Coast area. Indeed, it was a debate of classic proportions.

Rommel and Rundstedt argued the opposing sides of the question once again. The debate was not solely about the strategy for Army Group G, but was also about a unified, integrated German plan of defense in the west. The Nineteenth Army commander, General Georg von Sodenstern, first became aware of the debate in August of 1943.

Rommel, who had fought the Allies in North Africa, was keenly aware of their material superiority, especially in the air. He believed that Allied air superiority would paralyze all German movement once the invasion actually began. Supplies and reinforcements not immediately in the invasion area would be impossible to use against the invasion. If the invasion were to be defeated it could happen only in the first forty-eight hours, when the Allies on the beaches were at their weakest. Therefore, all German defensive forces must be moved into the probable landing zones, including especially all panzer formations. Steel and concrete obstacles and fortifications would strengthen the defenders. The invasion must be smashed on the beaches.[65]

Rundstedt's conception of the way to defeat the invasion was the direct opposite of Rommel's ideas. Rundstedt lacked Rommel's experience with Allied air domination and thought along the classic lines of a strategic counterstroke. According to this conception, there simply were not enough troops to defend the entire coastline and still to expect to be able to defeat the enemy where he landed. The enemy would always have local superiority at the assault beach. In addition, the powerful fire of the enemy naval artillery would decisively command the area near the landing. The only possibility was to assemble a mobile reserve—particularly panzers—and to fight a decisive battle of maneuver in the interior on ground chosen by the defender. To fight the decisive battle on the beaches would be a fatal misjudgment.

General von Sodenstern echoed Rundstedt's criticisms of Rommel's plan: "As no man in his senses," he argued, "would put his head on an anvil over which the smith's hammer is swung, so no general should mass his troops at the point where the enemy is certain to bring the first powerful blow of his superior material."[66]

Sodenstern had looked on while the debate over defensive strategy had raged between Rundstedt and Rommel. As recently as August 1943, Rundstedt's plan to fight a defensive battle in the interior of France had dominated German strategy in the west. This began to change as early as September 1943, when the coastal fortifications building program began in earnest. It became apparent to General Sodenstern that there was a divergence of views between Rundstedt and Hitler about how to fight the invasion battles.

Rundstedt's classic mobile counter-attack strategy contrasted with Hitler's opinion that the enemy must be defeated on the beaches or better still on the water before the beaches. Rundstedt's view was widely supported by the various army commanders and their chiefs of staff. Sodenstern thought that Rundstedt intended to fight the battle according to his own ideas, but then Rommel was introduced into the French theater in November of 1943.[67] Definite resolution of the strategy was supposed to be made during the winter or spring.[68] It was, in fact, never resolved at all. Germany fought the invasion without a clear strategy. It fought on the beaches in fortifications with most troops, but it kept a reduced armored reserve in readiness to fight a mobile battle. The battle on the beach was lost and the panzer reserves that intervened were insufficient to turn the tide.[69]

Rommel's strategy was supported to some extent by Hitler, who thought the loss of any French territory—even a temporary beach head—to be politically unbearable.[70] Rundstedt's view was supported by most of his subordinate generals, including Sodenstern and Blaskowitz.

Having made the half-hearted decision to fight the critical invasion battles as close to the landing zones as possible on the Channel Coast, it was not surprising that a similar strategy was applied to the Atlantic and Mediterranean Coasts. General Sodenstern thought it was an ill-conceived strategic decision. In his opinion the decision should have been made to withdraw from the south of France to fight the decisive battle in front of the West Wall. In his view, even a defensive success in the south was meaningless if the Germans were defeated on the Channel Coast.[71]

Blaskowitz essentially agreed with Rundstedt and Sodenstern's views. Recognizing that the prerequisites for a successful coastal defense were lacking, Blaskowitz favored the withdrawal of First and Nineteenth Armies into the interior where they could fight a mobile operational battle, rather than defend a static front.[72] Essentially, however, Blaskowitz had no influence on the decisions that were made—or half-made. He found himself forced to carry out an incorrect strategy against his own accurate inclinations. He would not, moreover, have much time to prepare. The invasion was already imminent.

Between 3:30 and 4:00 A.M. on the morning of 6 June the telephone rang at Army Group G's headquarters at Rouffiac. The Allies had invaded at Normandy. All coastal defense sectors were immediately ordered to full alert.[73] A few days later the alert status order was rescinded and another phenomenon began which led to the decisive weakening of Army Group G. On 8 June, the 2nd SS Panzer Division, *Das Reich*, stationed in the area of Limoges and Toulouse in *OKW* Reserve, was ordered to transfer to Normandy. It would be followed over the next two months by the 9th Panzer Division and the 271st, 272nd, 276th, 277th, 338th and 708th Infantry Divisions and the 341st Assault Gun Brigade. In addition, all anti-tank companies were sent to Normandy. There was even a shortage of *panzerfaust* (bazookas), most of these having also been sent to Normandy. One Army headquarters, two Corps Headquarters and one Panzer Corps headquarters went north too.

Army Group G was gutted by mid-August. It received only the 198th and 716th Infantry Divisions as replacements. The 198th was only in the process of organization and the 716th had been "badly mauled" in Normandy.[74] The former First Army on the Atlantic coast was reduced to a single corps. Nineteenth Army was left with only a single panzer division, which itself was being rebuilt from a cadre brought in from Russia—the 11th Panzer. The infantry divisions which remained were second rate static divisions.

As General von Sodenstern remarked about the transfer of forces from the south of France to Normandy at a time when the Allied invasion of the south was expected daily: "One recognizes the perplexity of a command which to close up one gap, has to tear open another and has trusted to vague hopes of lucky developments in the south of France."[75] There were no "lucky developments" waiting in the wings for the Germans in the south of France. Indeed, if these gloomy developments were not enough, there was already much more to worry Blaskowitz. As was so often the case, there was little that he could do, if anything, to improve the situation.

Since 1943, the Luftwaffe presence in the south of France and in the Mediterranean generally had diminished rapidly as units were ordered home to defend the air over the Reich. The German soldier saw little of his air force for the rest of the war.[76] After the war, even Goering admitted that the Luftwaffe had been defeated by 1 April 1944.[77] So thoroughly defeated was the Luftwaffe by mid-1944 that the best estimates placed German air strength in the south of France at just over two hundred planes.[78] It was a disaster for Army Group G.

Already on 8 May, Rundstedt had reported the interruption of supplies and troop movements by the "systematic destruction" of railways in France.[79] At the end of the month, the whole Bordeaux area had particularly severe supply difficulties as a result of the U.S. Fifteenth Air Force's bombing of viaducts at Nice and bridges and railway installations at Lyon.[80] The French railroad network bordered on collapse.[81] On 25 June both of the airfields near Toulouse were bombed by almost 250 American B-17 bombers.[82] Blaskowitz may have witnessed this attack from his headquarters. That same day 176 B-17's dropped supplies to the French underground. [83]

Allied air mastery was punishing the Germans in France. The oil supply dumps at Bordeaux and Lyon were completely destroyed by bombing on 2 August.[84] Movement by rail and by vehicles on the roads was severely restricted. On Sunday evening, 8 July, however, Allied planes dropped propaganda instead of bombs.

Since the Normandy invasion, the Allies had dropped a German language newspaper called *Nachrichten Für die Truppe* [News for the Troops]. It commented on Field Marshal Rundstedt's replacement in Normandy by Field Marshal Günther von Kluge with an article titled: "Is Blaskowitz Next?" The article clearly suggested that Berlin was considering replacing Blaskowitz since Hitler had replaced elite first-rate leadership (Field Marshals Bock and Leeb) with second-rate generals in 1942 and now was removing remnants of the elite such as Rundstedt and replacing it with third-rate generals.[85] It is not known whether Blaskowitz ever saw the article, but it is remarkable how prophetic it soon proved.

If Blaskowitz could expect little help from the Luftwaffe, he could hope for even less from the Kriegsmarine—the German Navy. The Germany Navy in the Mediterranean was almost non-existent by 1944. It consisted of only seventy-five vessels, the largest of which was a destroyer, a few torpedo and escort boats and approximately ten submarines.[86]

In the air and on the sea then, the contest was grossly unequal. Just over two hundred German aircraft against 4,056 Allied planes; seventy-five small ships versus 2,250 Allied ships and landing craft.[87] Clearly, whatever Blaskowitz would accomplish in the south of France would be achieved solely by the army. The situation of Army Group G was made worse, however, by yet another factor—the French underground—the Maquis.

After the Normandy Invasion on 6 June, Resistance activities increased dramatically. Demolitions of railroad tracks, bridges and highways crippled traffic in the south of France. Security troops were practically unavailable so the coastal defenses were further weakened by withdrawing troops for security services.[88] The communications system of the Army Group, dependent largely on the French postal and telephone network due to inadequate radio communications, nearly broke down completely.[89] Sabotage was rampant. The rail line from Toulouse to Saint-Gaudens, a distance of sixty miles, for example, was cut in thirty-eight places by demolitions.[90] According to one source, from mid-May until the end of July 1944, seven thousand individual attacks were carried out in the south of France, six thousand on French collaborators and one thousand on the Germans.[91]

In the late winter and early spring, the Resistance had been sufficiently emboldened to fight its first pitched battles with the Germans. In March 1944, Communist Maquis lost a battle on the Plateau of Glières, near Annecy, to an estimated ten thousand regular German troops.[92] From mid-June to late July, the Resistance lost another battle in the Vercors near Grenoble.[93] It was clear that the underground could not yet confront the German Army on anything near equality, but it could disrupt the Germans significantly. Even within the immediate region of Blaskowitz's headquarters, there were incidents.

Blaskowitz's headquarters at Rouffiac, did not house all of his staff. The quartermaster detachment, for example, was garrisoned nearby at St. Jean par Castelmauroux. According to one witness, Generaloberst Blaskowitz had given strict orders about correct behavior of troops toward the French population of the region. Relations with French civilians were "very cordial" until one Sunday morning in June when there was "great excitement" among the local population. The bodies of several French civilians had been found in a ditch near the Quartermaster's office. They had been shot.

Rumor circulated that the *Sicherheitsdienst* (SD)—Security Service Branch of the Gestapo—had done it. A telephone call to the SD Office in Toulouse confirmed this. The Army Group G commanding officer refused to send Army troops to bury the bodies. The SD had finally to send two of its own men to perform the burials.

The army wished to impress upon the local French population that it was in no way associated with the SD crimes. A similar incident took place near the city of Albi, where the SD arrested eight to ten French civilians without proper identification papers, took them in a truck to nearby woods and shot them. Again, Army Group G forced the SD to carry out the burials so that the population would know that the Army was not responsible for these atrocities. Relations between the Army and the civilians remained cordial until the Army withdrew.[94]

Blaskowitz was obviously responsible for the conduct of the army. It is clear that he had not changed his beliefs, had not lost his courage, had not accommodated his character since he had been repulsed by SS atrocities in Poland almost five years earlier. Tragic events in France, further atrocities, were again the occasion for Blaskowitz to demonstrate his convictions.

The French Resistance which rose against the Germans after the Normandy Invasion had long been a problem for Blaskowitz. Asked about this after the war, Blaskowitz responded: "Such things are never very pleasant. It led to unpleasant incidents even earlier, but after the invasion it became especially noticeable." Candidly admitting the essence of his military challenge, he continued: "I never had enough troops to fight them effectively. I had 'rolling commandos' set up. These are the best thing in an occupation." Continuing, he added: I organized it on the lines of fire-fighters. If there was a big 'fire,' I sent a strong detachment. These commandos had all to be highly mobile, well armed and, of course, all motorized." The Luftwaffe also cooperated; he could even issue orders from the air against the Maquis. But it was not a complete success:

> After the invasion, of course, the resistance got out of hand. For then there was trouble in every nook and corner. The French could have done nothing on their own; that is absolutely certain.[95]

"Out of hand," described the situation after 6 June in a classic understatement. Army Group Gustav headquarters' Chief of Staff von Gyldenfeldt estimated that Resistance activities rose "200%" in the week after the Normandy invasion.[96] Maquis bands attacked isolated small German garrisons, hoping to slow down the advance of German reinforcements from the south of France to the invasion front. From Berlin the *OKW* responded with an order for the "utmost severity" to be employed in the south: "[T]his lasting source of rebellion must be extinguished." When von Rundstedt passed the order to subordinate units, he urged the troops to use the "sharpest possible measures" to intimidate inhabitants in "bandit-infested regions." Ruthlessness, he advised, was indispensable.[97]

On 7 June, the day before 2nd SS Panzer Division, *Das Reich*, left Toulouse for the battle in Normandy, it received orders from Rundstedt to deploy in the Tulle-Limoges area and to smash the Maquis on its way to the "regular" war.[98] *Das Reich* intended to teach the Resistance a final lesson.

On 10 June, after a sniper shot at one of the *Das Reich* officers, the village of Oradour-sûr-Glane, fifteen miles north of Limoges, was surrounded. The inhabitants were rounded up, the men separated from the women and children. The men were shot, the women and children herded into a church into which the SS troopers then threw grenades and emptied their machine gun magazines. The entire town was then set ablaze and *Das Reich* continued its journey to Normandy. Behind them they left 642 dead French men, women and children.[99] It was one of the worst atrocities in western Europe committed during the war by combat troops, yet no one could possibly have known it from the report sent to Army Group Gustav which said

> Mopping up operations in the region Limoges-Leonhard-Ambazac-Bellac-Rochechouart. Preliminary result: 337 enemy killed, 36 prisoners. Tulle-Seilhac-Vzerche is enemy free.[100]

Blaskowitz apparently learned the truth of what happened only several days later. The French regional Prefect protested to General Schmidt-Hartung, who commanded German Military Government Headquarters 564 in Toulouse. Schmidt-Hartung went to Blaskowitz on 17 June. Blaskowitz could not give orders to the *Das Reich* Division. Although it had been stationed in his region, *Das Reich* remained in *OKW* reserve, then, after 8 June, under the orders of Field Marshal Rundstedt. Repelled by what *Das Reich* had done at Oradour-sûr-Glane, the Generaloberst immediately wrote personally to his old friend and superior commander, reporting what he knew and requesting an investigation.[101]

Blaskowitz had not changed from the man he had been in Poland in 1939-1940. SS actions had repelled him then and continued to repel him. Regrettably, little else had changed. In Poland he had been unable to punish the perpetrators of atrocities; nor could he punish them now. The SS had been under Himmler's disciplinary jurisdiction in Poland and was still under his authority in France in 1944. Rundstedt could only inform the *OKW* and turn the whole matter over to the SS. As far as Rundstedt was concerned, the matter was closed.[102] The *Das Reich* Division went into combat in Normandy.

General Blaskowitz put his thoughts on record in the War Diary of his Army Group and responded to French protests in these words:

> If, in the process of combating terrorism, new methods too severe

for the Western European mind become necessary, we have to remember that the terrorists, with their mask of the peace loving civilian, fighting from the ambush, is a new phenomenon for Western European minds as well.

It is, therefore, the responsibility of French civilians to distinguish themselves from the terrorists ... in a visible and believable way. But that is not all: the French civilian who is not a terrorist and not involved in terrorism has to make sure he takes an active stand against it.[103]

Blaskowitz continued:

What has happened in the past and what is unacceptable in the future is the fact that German troops approach a village that is supposed to be non-terrorist and peace- loving and are received by fighting terrorists. It is up to the peace loving French civilian to make sure that the terrorists among them will be discovered and destroyed before they proceed in their activity against German troops.

The situation we have right now is intolerable and unacceptable: There is no way for the German troops to distinguish between friend and enemy. Much bloodshed could be avoided, bloodshed of innocent French civilians, if the situation could be remedied by making sure that the Germans know who is friend and who is the enemy, who is a peace-loving civilian and who is a terrorist.[104]

Blaskowitz's response to the situation did not end, however, with words; philosophical reflections on the French share of responsibility for tragedies in the German fight against the underground. He took firmly in hand that share of responsibility over which he had some control. He issued a new order to his troops, reminding them that orders for severity, for toughness, had been necessary in the fight against the "Resistance." The troops had responded by following orders, but there had been "incidents."

One of the problems was to distinguish between terrorists and peaceful civilians. "It is inevitable," he continued, "that every so often a person that is innocent will fall victim to being under suspicion and punished in this hard battle that has been started by the terrorists." Blaskowitz then got right to the point: "Yet, we as German soldiers have to keep on trying to fight this battle as cleanly and honestly as possible." Warming to his subject, he continued:

> We have to be sure to be guided by the thought that we are fighting the terrorist, not the innocent civilian, who is frequently himself suffering from the terrorist.
>
> It should not happen that women and children are pulled into this battle, that farms are being burned down, who have never seen a terrorist, or men who have never associated with a terrorist are being shot.
>
> It has to be our major and principle doctrine: we are leading this battle in a decent way, as it is the style and honor of the German soldier to be and conduct himself.[105]

The general's very vocabulary revealed his nature. To speak of fighting "cleanly" and "honestly," "decently," and with "honor" meant something very different than when these words were used in other circles in Nazi Germany. Asked about this order after the war, Blaskowitz admitted that it may have contradicted orders from the C-in-C West and *OKW*, but that he had assumed full responsibility.[106] To Wehrmacht and Waffen SS commanders, the Maquis were partisans who did not enjoy the protection of the Hague convention as prisoners of war, but who were to be executed.[107] Blaskowitz's order meant that Maquis were instead treated as P.O.W.'s and turned over to summary military courts.[108]

It was shortly after the time that Blaskowitz was framing the above orders that British Intelligence received a report that Blaskowitz was supposed to have given orders that "every time terrorists killed a few Germans, ten times as many Maquis were to be killed in the same way on the same spot, and a placard put up with an inscription."[109] The distance separating truth from rumor is sometimes very great.

A little more than a week after issuing his new orders regarding treatment of the Maquis, guerrilla and sabotage activity abated somewhat. Blaskowitz thought the reason might be the effective action of his troops, but speculated that the decreased Maquis activity might also be due to orders from Resistance leaders. By 2 July, however, Rundstedt was warning him that there had been a remarkable increase in French and British radio signals to parachutists in France, just as had been the case before the Normandy invasion. He ordered alert readiness.[110]

The war of nerves approached the breaking point. By late July,

Blaskowitz would be informing Rundstedt that Resistance activity had reached the point where "control over a greater part of the area can no longer be referred to. Only where German troops are in evidence can peace and order be preserved."[111] Even when German troops were present, there was no surplus of either peace or order. The very chain of command in Army Group Gustav was not entirely in "order," though this was not Blaskowitz's fault.

When Blaskowitz was transferred from command of First Army at Bordeaux and made commander of Army Group G, he was followed at First Army by Lieutenant General Joachim Lemelsen, who acted as deputy commander until 2 June when a permanent replacement arrived. Lieutenant General Kurt von der Chevallerie assumed the command on that date. The "Victor of Korosten" and holder of the Oak Leaves to the Knight's Cross, Chevallerie was a leader of proven ability.[112] Arriving four days before the Allies landed in Normandy, and having spent the previous three years in Russia, von der Chevallerie was unfamiliar with his new command to say the least. It was, in fact, soon reduced to a single corps, with the rest sent north to the fighting near Normandy.

"Order" was also upset at Nineteenth Army headquarters at Avignon on 10 June, when General von Sodenstern was informed that he was relieved of duty due to his "reputedly sensitive health" and replaced by Infantry General Friedrich Wiese.[113] It was 1 July before Wiese arrived at Avignon from Russia where he had been since 1941.

A veteran of the Great War, a Freikorps fighter after the war, Wiese had been a policeman in Hamburg from 1919 to 1935, when he rejoined the Army. When the war broke out Wiese had been a lieutenant colonel commanding an infantry battalion. Described by some as "capable and very energetic," Wiese had received rapid promotions throughout the war. One source described him as a "fervent Nazi," a "totally ferocious man" who "might fight to the last cartridge." A personal friend described him as "calm under the most difficult circumstances, although he is no great strategist."[114] He was probably not the man Blaskowitz would have chosen.

Replacement of the two army commanders in the last weeks before the invasion of southern France could not have helped the Germans greatly, but it was only a small part of the larger strategic picture. This picture grew more depressing to German eyes, as each day it became more obvious that the invasion in Normandy had succeeded. It remained only for Blaskowitz to salvage what could be saved in the south of France.

Beginning at the end of June, Blaskowitz repeatedly pointed out to OB West, first von Rundstedt and later von Kluge, that he was no longer in a position to carry out a successful defense in the case of enemy landings in southern France."[115] On 1 July Rundstedt told Hitler that even "security and stability" could not be guaranteed, that it was necessary to "show German uniforms," that defense of the area could not be guaranteed.[116] The army group requested that its static divisions be made mobile so that a mobile tactical reserve could be built up by withdrawing some troops from beach defense. Five days later Rundstedt was relieved from his command and replaced by Field Marshal Günther von Kluge.

OB West agreed with Blaskowitz's evaluation of the situation. Blaskowitz also recommended evacuation of the south of France and withdrawal to the area around Dijon. He proposed to do this prior to any Allied invasion. Again, OB West agreed, but added that the decision belonged to Hitler, "Who could not or would not make up his mind to abandon southern France." Nor would the Führer grant permission to weaken the coastal defense.[117] On 30 July Generaloberst Jodl placed an order before Hitler at his Wolfsschanze headquarters "for possible withdrawal from the coastal sector," an order which was, in effect, a plan to evacuate France. Hitler brushed the order aside stating that it was not yet time for this to take place.[118]

On 1 August, Blaskowitz's operations officer, Colonel Horst Wilutzky, went to OB West to learn about the overall situation in France. From OB West, Wilutzky discussed the situation with General von Gyldenfeldt, Blaskowitz's chief of staff. They all agreed that "there was no military justification for holding German units in southern France any longer."[119] It was the last possible moment for orderly withdrawal. Both Army Group G and OB West, Generaloberst Blaskowitz and Field Marshal Kluge, agreed on this. In spite of their agreement, the Führer ordered Army Group G to stay put.[120]

Three days later Blaskowitz sent a full report to von Kluge. He was aware that Kluge required reinforcements for the Normandy battles and that Army Group G had therefore, to be weakened. But it was his responsibility to indicate that because of the "release of men and weapons its defensive power has become considerably smaller and that a successful defense of the coast is no longer guaranteed."[121]

Blaskowitz could only assume that Hitler's continued refusal to permit withdrawal was attributable to operational, economic and political reasons to which he was not privy as a "mere" army group commander. He was "lacking the necessary insight."[122] General von Sodenstern, who had been replaced by General Wiese as commander of Nineteen Army, was retrospectively sharply critical of Hitler:

> it may be stated that the dilettantism of the German Supreme Command, ...from July on had led to a state of complete bewilderment. One didn't known one's own intentions any longer....[123]

Bewilderment about military strategy was not a new state for many German officers, indeed, for many Germans by 1944. A number of them had formed a group much earlier to take action to bring an end to the chaos. They meant to kill Hitler.

Goebbels, Hitler's propaganda minister, had considered the formation of such a group of officers impossible in Germany. Hitler had thought so too! Speaking about the removal of Mussolini by high Italian officials and military leaders, Hitler, in a short speech on the capitulation of Italy, stated:

> Their idea that they can bring on a 25 of July [removal of Mussolini] in Germany, too, is based on a fundamental error, both as regards to my personal position and, also, with respect to the attitude of my field marshals, admirals and generals.[124]

Goebbels echoed Hitler's sentiments in a speech of his own on 3 October 1943, when he declared, "[T]here is not a soldier in the Wehrmacht, be his position high or low, who prefers cowardly submission to his honor."[125] Not for the first or the last time, both Goebbels and Hitler were wrong. A number of German officers were indeed ready to attempt to remove Hitler.

Field Marshal Rommel was among the conspirators. Three days before the assasination attempt, however, Rommel was gravely wounded by a fighter-bomber attack while traveling in his automobile.

Although Rommel would recover, von Kluge needed a replacement for him. Kluge recommended replacement by a "hard man," a "tough guy," such as Blaskowitz or perhaps Woehler or Hossbach. It might have meant a combat command in a major battle for Blaskowitz, but it was not to be. The job went to SS General Paul Hausser.[126]

On 20th July 1944, while the front in Normandy buckled under Allied attack and Army Group Center in Russia disintegrated under the Russian summer offensive, a group of officers led by Count Claus Schenck von Stauffenberg, attempted to assassinate Hitler at his Rastenberg headquarters. They failed. Hitler survived. Reaction within the ranks of the army was largely critical of the attempt.

Field Marshal Baron von Weichs, for example, wrote into his diary:

> I am sure that a successful coup would have meant total disaster and utter chaos. It seems to be a crazy idea and a deadly thought to assume that such an act might bring peace. I am reminded of the events of 1918, but this one is much worse, since it comes from a segment of the nation's population that was expected by many to act on an exactly opposite line of morale. It is absolutely devastating to hear the names of those that participated. And it is inconceivable how the army, thus deprived of its basic trust and integrity, officer-corps and generals and all, will cope with this shattering situation.

He continued:

> I cannot, for the life of me, understand how two former members of the general staff could conceive such an idea as this, which first of all was criminal and, secondly, was stupid. Moreover, the plans were lacking in thoroughness and depth. There was no certainty as to who was a definite member of the conspiracy when it came down to counting everyone. There was only guess-work about who was behind it and who was not. Even with successful elimination of Hitler, the coup would have failed in its aftermath and it is certain that the German soldier would not have followed the orders of these leaders.[127]

From all over German occupied Europe, high-ranking officers called their superiors to proclaim their loyalty. Sometimes it was truly an expression of loyalty, but at other times, it was the reflex action of a highly developed survival instinct.

General Günther Blumentritt, Chief of Staff at St. Germain, France, where Field Marshal von Kluge had his headquarters, described the scene at High Command West as "chaotic." Teleprints arrived from Germany advising that Hitler was uninjured, that Himmler had taken command of the Replacement Army, that orders issued by the conspirators were invalid. The telephone kept ringing. Bodo Zimmerman, a staff officer, recalled saying: "In the meantime, I've been rung up from all quarters. Everyone asked: 'Where's the Feldmarschal? Where's General Blumentritt? An attempt on the Führer's life; why that's shocking! Salmuth, Blaskowitz, Gyldenfeldt, etc., etc., all rang up."[128]

Blaskowitz sent the mandatory telegram:

> All of us Germans, German men and soldiers, stand before the most vicious and horrific crime with the feeling of horror and dismay, but we stand in awe before Providence that has saved you, our Führer. And we are determined to hold on to you even stronger than before, my Führer! Blaskowitz[129]

It was essential to survival to "ring-up" whether the caller was an ardent Nazi or an anti-Nazi. Especially for someone in Blaskowitz's position. General Dittmar later claimed that in the S.D. (Gestapo) investigation after the attempted assassination, suspect officers were frequently asked, "'What is your attitude toward the shooting of Jews?' A negative answer was often enough to cause the 'extinction' of the officer concerned."[130]

Blaskowitz's attitude was a matter of written record in the office files of the *Reichsführer SS*.[131] He had to be concerned not just for himself, but also for his family. On 23 July, Robert Ley, director of the Nazi Party Bureau, wrote in the Nazi newspaper, *Der Angriff*, that the families of all officers who had plotted against Hitler would be destroyed "root and branch." Ley admitted that this was hard, "but it is necessary in hard times such as these. Whoever betrays us will be annihilated."[132] Although there is no evidence that Blaskowitz ever knew the details of the plot, he had nevertheless to be prudent.

Blaskowitz's troops had powerful reactions to the assassination attempt. One soldier in France wrote into his diary feelings which probably represented those of many others. When he learned of the assassination attempt, Wilhelm Prüller was "speechless." He thought it an "indescribable crime" perpetrated by "swindlers." Chaos would have resulted, the five years of war, the pain and sacrifice, "the lives laid down by millions of Kameraden ..." would have been for nothing. The "front would have melted away ...." "Providence spared the Führer...." Now, there remained the fight to the death. "Victory or death."[133]

Such steadfast resolution was naturally not universal; those who would have wished for the plot's success were understandly less inclined to voice their sentiments. Even some SS units were affected by a phenomenon to which they had previously been nearly immune—shell shock. It was symptomatic of a wholesale collapse in morale. Many troops now had *Heim ins Reich* (Home to Germany) foremost in their thoughts.[134]

A British Intelligence survey of German P.O.W.s completed on 19 July—the day before the assassination attempt—reported that 65 per cent expressed a defeatist outlook; "only the real fanatic" remained convinced of German victory. The defeatists "predominate among the low-grade coastal ... divisions."[135] These divisions made up the majority of Blaskowitz's remaining command by the end of the month. According to the report, German static divisions have "suffered in fighting quality because of softening up during occupation duties."

General Heinz Hellmich, the report continued, "is reported to have said of the 243 Inf.[antry] Div.[ision] that 'the soldiers only fight for fear of punishment.'" The French resistance reported that German morale was low in southwestern France.[136] The report stated that Hitler still had the allegiance of 50 per cent of his soldiers in Allied captivity; 20 per cent "complete devotion," 30 per cent "general approval."[137]

But the German soldier's discipline was not based exclusively upon loyalty. From January to September 1944, the Wehrmacht executed 4,000 of its own men, just over 1,600 for desertion.[138]

Hitler himself would probably not have been surprised by Allied intelligence findings. Toward the end of the war he often denounced his "idiotic General Staff officers" and complained about the German soldier: "The soldier of the First World War was much tougher. Think of all they had to go through, in Verdun, on the Somme. Today, they would run away from that kind of thing," he said.[139]

German troops did not "run" in the south of France despite the accumulation of obvious warnings that the invasion was about to take place. It had been noticed that Free French troops fighting in Italy had been withdrawn and not returned to the fight. This suggested their use in a second landing on French soil in the Mediterranean.[140] German Intelligence also noted the transfer of close support aircraft from the Italian mainland to Corsica.[141]

There were other ominous signs: Allied troops had been photographed from the air in large tent camps in the Oran area of North Africa,[142] four or five additional American infantry divisions had been concentrated at Naples, apparently ready to be embarked.[143] Single Allied submarines were sighted along the Mediterranean coast. Allied tactical planes, squadrons of P-47's and P-38's, Spitfires, B-26 Marauders, Beaufighters and P-51's attacked a variety of targets. Supplementing the sorties of the fighters were heavy bombers and medium bombers: B-25's, B-17's and B-24's.

Military installations, munitions dumps and fuel depots were smashed. Rail lines were cut in numerous places. Then, beginning on 10 August, coastal gun batteries and radar stations became the target. The punishing bombing and strafing was complemented by increased resistance activity by the Maquis.[144] It seemed obviously a repetition of Allied tactics prior to the Normandy Invasion. Undeniably southern France was the next target.

Army Group G, awaiting the Allied invasion, was weaker—dramatically weaker—than the German Seventh Army in Normandy, but nevertheless had much in common with it. No longer the conquering *Blitzkrieg* Army of 1944, it was part of an army that had been wounded grievously by the Russians who had "drawn blood from its main arteries ...." Nevertheless, the German army "could still claim to be qualitatively the best army in the world."[145] It was an "inescapable reality," so far in the war that "when allied troops met Germans on anything like equal terms, the Germans almost always prevailed."[146] The British had been pushed around so much by the Germans early in the war, for example, that at least one high ranking British officer thought that "they began to feel in their heart that they weren't the equals of the Germans."[147]

Since the wars of German unification in the 1860's and 1870's, the German Army had surpassed all other armies in the casualty rates inflicted against its enemies in proportion to its own losses and this was the case again. The "superior professional skill of its officers" and superior "combat savvy and unexcelled courage among the ranks"[148] help account for this. Mastery of coordinated panzers working together was another element of German strength. The effective unit cohesiveness, "Kameradschaft," and desperation to defend the homeland against "unconditional surrender" were also contributing factors.

The superiority of some weapons—particularly the German tank, the 88 mm gun, and the MP 40 machine pistol, played a considerable role, as did mastery of defensive tactics, infiltration, and especially excelling in the quick counter-attack. German junior leadership was markedly superior to anything the Americans or British exhibited.[149] German divisions repeatedly demonstrated an "awesome ability to survive shattering casualties and rebound within weeks as long as an officer cadre remained to train replacements."[150] This capacity would prove critical to the German Army as a whole and to Blaskowitz's command in particular in the second half of 1944.

The German army of 1944, including Army Group G defending the south of France, had "long since passed the peak of its power." It was, however, not an opponent to be treated cavalierly, not even the static divisions. One American general tried to encourage his attacking troops by explaining that the German formation they faced was only a second-rate opponent. In response, a young lieutenant answered: "General, I think you'd better put the Germans on the distribution list. They don't seem to realize that."[151]

Nineteenth Army was stretched along the Mediterranean coast from the Spanish border to Italy, a distance of 650 kilometers. By the time the invasion on the Riviera actually took place, Army Group G had given up two of its three panzer divisions, with *Das Reich* and 9th Panzer going to the Normandy Front and only 11th Panzer Division remaining in the south. The Army Group had also given up six infantry divisions: 271st, 272nd, 276th, 277th, 338th, and 708th. It had also sent to Normandy the 341 Assault Gun Brigade and numerous specialist troops.

Only nine divisions remained, of which two were very weak. The 716th Division had been "mauled" in Normandy and the 198th Division was only being formed—largely from Czechoslovakians—after having suffered very heavy casualties in Russia. Only troops without combat experience were left, older officers unsuitable for combat in Russia and a large number of "*Ost-truppen* of doubtful reliability and allegiance."

General Wiese considered the arms, material and transportation of these divisions "scanty in comparison with those of the divisions on the Russian front." They lacked assault gun battalions, anti-aircraft guns, mobile mortar companies and essential motorization for movement. There were so few troops available that everything was assigned to the main battle line on the beaches with no general reserves available for counterattack.

Even the main defense line, according to Wiese, was really a line of outposts without depth scattered along the coast. Perhaps more critical, however, was the weakness of the Army communication net, which really did not deserve the name since it was "scanty and improvised."[152] Army Group G headquarters at Toulouse was little better in this respect with an experimental prototype radio teleprinter link which lacked mobility.[153]

The weakest division in Nineteenth Army was possibly the 716th Infantry Division, described by its commander, Generalleutnant Wilhelm Richter, as "defeated and badly beaten up in Normandy."[154] Transferred to Perpignan on the southern coast, it was the western-most division in Nineteenth Army. The division arrived there at the end of June and was largely lacking in heavy weapons and fighting vehicles. Richter thought the division "practically useless until re-formed." By mid-August it had received just over five thousand replacements, but "they could not even have stood up to a weak attack."[155]

Unquestionably the strongest and most mobile division was the 11th Panzer Division, the only armored division left in Army Group G by the time of the Riviera invasion. Its commander, Generalleutnant Wend von Weitersheim, played a key role in the survival ordeal of Nineteenth Army over the next several weeks.

A remarkable personality, Wietersheim was born in 1900, the son of a large estate owner, and had joined the Army as a young man near the end of the Great War. From 1924 to 1929 he had been assigned to the Army cavalry school, which he represented as a rider in numerous international competitions—many of which he won. Transferring from the cavalry to the motorized troops in 1934, he began the war in Poland as an adjutant in a panzer division. He had repeatedly distinguished himself in combat and by 1944 had been promoted to the rank of major general in addition to being awarded the Oak Leaves and Swords to the Knight's Cross.

One of his evaluations by a superior officer described him as: "Energetic, lots of drive, knows his own worth, a man who has really put the stamp of his strong character on his division." The evaluation elaborated: "He is not an easy subordinate."[156] It was not only his superiors who found him difficult; if reports are to be believed, Wietersheim was "extremely unpopular and very disliked by his own officers."[157] Wietersheim later claimed that he had realized "long before D-day ... that Germany could not win this war anymore." He did not, however, tell his men of his conviction and kept up the fight. "He was a German officer and war was his business."[158]

The 11th Panzer Division had fought in Russia from 1941 until March 1944, where it was nicknamed "the Ghost Division." It had taken part in many major actions during these years and had been under Wietersheim's command since late 1943. In February of 1944, it had been surrounded by the Russians along with several other divisions at Cherkassy. Although the division broke out, it had been with "appalling losses of life and equipment" and had been sent to Bordeaux to be rebuilt.[159]

The division had been brought up to strength by amalgamation with the 273rd Reserve Panzer Division and then moved to the Toulouse area where it was Blaskowitz's only reserve and sole armored unit at the time of the Riviera invasion. It lacked one battalion of tanks and the usual anti-aircraft battalion, but had a surplus artillery regiment with one heavy rocket projector battery. According to von Wietersheim, the condition of the division was "good" by the time of the Riviera invasion.[160] This was fortunate for Army Group G.

Events moved rapidly from the first day of August, when Blaskowitz's operations officer, Colonel Horst Wilutzky, had gone to Normandy and agreed with Field Marshal von Kluge that withdrawal from the south of France was justified—only to be ordered to stay put by Hitler. Blaskowitz and Kluge did not know it then, but, at noon that day, the best American tank commander—General George Patton—received operational command of the U.S. Third Army and began the breakthrough at Avranches. Patton called it "Touring France with an Army."[161]

That same day in Normandy, General Walter Warlimont was visiting the German Front as Hitler's personal representative. Warlimont met with General Heinrich Eberbach, who suggested that the battle in Normandy must be brought to a close by a German withdrawal through delaying actions to a position behind the Seine River while Army Group G evacuated southern France. Only in this way, Eberbach argued, could the main body of Germans in France be saved, although with heavy losses in material. Warlimont, speaking for Hitler, rejected the scheme as "politically unbearable and tactically impractical."[162] Yet within a couple of days, German soldiers in Normandy could be heard saying: "Guerre Finie ... Allemagne Kaputt. Tommies here tomorrow."[163]

Blaskowitz was unaware of the details of events in Normandy, but knew enough about Patton's Third Army breakout to become "increasingly alarmed over ... communications, which were in danger of being cut off by the advance of the U.S. Third Army toward Dijon."[164] He concluded that the increasing disintegration of the German forces in Normandy made a second Allied landing, this time on the Mediterranean coast, much more likely. Though he knew an invasion was coming soon, Blaskowitz could not be certain of the day or the exact place; the Bay of Genoa was a probable location, offering favorable strategic possibilities.[165] Moreover, there was little he could do to improve his army group's situation anyway.[166]

Whatever he might have attempted would probably have been discovered almost immediately by the Allies, as had been the transfer of divisions to Normandy. Allied Signals Intelligence, especially Ultra, kept a close watch over German moves. On 2 August it knew already of the most recent change in Blaskowitz's army group.

On 2 August, von Kluge in Normandy attempted to guard his open left flank and secure his line of retreat by dividing Blaskowitz's First Army. The Loire River crossings were to be protected by LXXX Corps, while LXIV Corps was to remain behind to guard the Atlantic Coast in the Bordeaux area, with 708th Infantry Division going directly to Normandy. First Army Headquarters went to Fontainebleau a week later.[167] It was virtually the dismantling of the Army as far as Army

Group G was concerned. Before much more time elapsed, Blaskowitz's command would be further reduced.

It was to preserve his army group—what still remained of it—that Blaskowitz gave written notice to OB West on 4 August that his army group could not successfully defend the coast any longer.[168] Hitler rejected the suggestion and its implications. Instead, the warlord ordered a counterattack in Normandy and issued a "stand fast" order to army group G. Within a few days the destiny of the army group appeared to be more clear.

On 7 August, the "systematic, especially heavy air attacks on the transportation links over the Rhône and Var Rivers," Army Group G reported, "point to a landing between these two rivers," and "statements from agents confirm this suspicion."[169] The ever-increasing threat of invasion on the Mediterranean coast was matched by the continued deterioration of the German position in Normandy, where von Kluge was reaching the end of his rope.

On 8 August, Kluge and his chief-of-staff, General Hans Speidel, agreed that it was time to act before time ran out.

> It's time to abandon the South of France, Kluge argued. Why leave the First Army on the Atlantic now that we know the outcome of the war is at stake. Let us put Army Group G on the line Seine-Loire-Gien-Nevers-Gex. Let's abandon Provence.[170]

Hitler refused. It was a dark day for the German Army. In Normandy the commander of the First Canadian Army, which was about to attack, remembered this exact day twenty-six years earlier. On that day, 8 August 1918, the German Army had broken up on the Western Front. It had been called the "Black day of the German Army." "I have no doubt that we shall make August 8, 1944, an even blacker day for the German Army than the same day twenty-six years ago!" he said.[171] It did not quite happen that way, but there can be no doubt that 8 August, 1944 was dark enough to remind both Kluge and Blaskowitz of the earlier war. General Wiese, Nineteenth Army commander, was probably too busy that day to give it very much thought.

Wiese had studied the intensive Allied bombing of the bridges on the Rhône and Var Rivers and combined his study with Intelligence reports of Allied troop concentrations and locations of Allied Air Forces and came to the same conclusion as had Generaloberst Blaskowitz the previous day. The invasion target area must be either the Gulf of Genoa or between the Rhône and Var Rivers on the eastern part of Nineteenth Army's coastal defense responsibility. He could do nothing about a landing in the Gulf of Genoa—it was out of his area—but he could plan against a landing near the Rhône River. He ordered a map exercise on 8 August at Draguignan for all of his generals.

The map maneuver was held in the large hall of garrison headquarters at Draguignan and was attended by Army generals, Army field police commanders, and representatives of the Luftwaffe and Navy. The situation was an enemy assault east of the Rhône River with strong parachute landings in support of the invasion.[172] It was clear that the army was on its own in the "complete absence of naval and air forces." Reserves and heavy artillery too were lacking, as were anti-aircraft and anti-tank guns.[173] It was a depressing picture.

The map exercise revealed the obvious weakness of any attempt to defeat a landing east of the Rhône River: lack of strategic reserves for a counter-attack. Originally it had been Blaskowitz's plan to utilize two panzer divisions in a counterattack, but he now had only the 11th Panzer Division remaining under his command and it was stationed near Bordeaux, obviously too distant to execute a rapid counter-attack.[174] The possibility of a successful counterattack by a single panzer division against a landing bridgehead was in any case, "extremely questionable."[175]

General Wiese, who had ordered the map exercise, made the defensive improvements which were possible. He repeated his request to Blaskowitz to have the 11th Panzer Division moved closer to the Rhône River delta near Avignon where Nineteenth Army headquarters were located. Wiese began to train his own troops in counter-attack. He realized that much of the predicted area of the Allied landing was defended only by *Ost-Truppen*—Russian volunteers in German uniform—and ordered German companies put in between the Russian battalions. He moved one German regiment from the 148th Division from the area around Nice into corps reserve.Nineteenth Army reserves were so few that the army commander could move only a single regiment into reserve! Finally, he ordered an anti-tank gun artillery battalion brought up near St. Raphael.[176]

It was very little and would certainly not stop an invasion. There was, according to Wiese, no doubt that a landing at the weak sector would be successful.[177] Or, as the commander of the LXXXV Corps later stated: "When the invasion finally took place, we were not taken by surprise."[178]

It was simply a matter of awaiting the devastating blow, meanwhile taking small insurance measures to avert a total debacle. If Blaskowitz and Wiese were aware of the origin of the word "debacle"—in the language of Old Provençal—the old language in the province—in the very place they were trying to defend—they could have taken no comfort in it. It means "a sudden disastrous collapse, a rout, ruin." Army Group G had only a few more days to wait for it.

On Thursday 10 August, Army Group G learned almost definitely that the invasion was imminent. Reports from Luftwaffe reconnaissance told of large-scale troop embarkations from Algerian ports. Luftwaffe reconnaissance, which Blaskowitz justly considered "very inferior," had gotten lucky.[179] For weeks the men on Blaskowitz's staff had been making bets on the time and place of the invasion. Blaskowitz himself remained composed, remarking to his officers: "Considering the reconnaissance and intelligence means at our disposal, it must be realized that only [the] landing itself can end any doubts ... about where it is going to take place."[180]

August 12 was an explosive day in the area of Blaskowitz's headquarters near Toulouse and not only because the tension had reached the ignition point. U.S. Eighth Air Force B-17's escorted by P-51 long range fighters from Italy flew to bases in the U.K. and along the way they bombed the Luftwaffe airfield at Francazal near Toulouse.[181] They probably did not realize nearly as well as Blaskowitz did that the Luftwaffe had already been driven from France. They were taking no chances.

That day rumors began to circulate among the local French that 15 August would be the day of the Allied landing.[182] Naturally the Germans picked up the rumor and could not casually dismiss it. The three army divisions east of the Rhône River were placed on "increased alert."[183] By this time, even the average soldier knew "something was up." One wrote to his wife on 13 August: "We will probably not have to wait very long until the invasion takes place. It is believed that the bombardments are a prelude [to the battle] as was the case in Normandy."[184]

In Normandy that day, the German armies commanded by von Kluge were on the verge of being surrounded by the Allies. Kluge desperately wanted to retreat and wanted all of southwest France evacuated. His own armies might form a new defensive front along the Mayenne-Orleans line, if they could link up with a retreating Army Group G. Generaloberst Alfred Jodl, Hitler's chief operations officer, telephoned Kluge from Hitler's headquarters that day: "Your suggestion to transfer the Atlantic and Provence Army Groups to the Loire line has been accepted," telephoned Jodl. "The First Army staff has been given orders to leave Bordeaux." A short time later, however, a second telephone call halted the withdrawal: an invasion was imminent in Provence. Kluge would not get Army Group G.[185]

Time continued to run out. If Army Group G were not permitted to retreat, it would soon be too late. Signs of the invasion mounted. On Sunday, 13 August, two Focke-Wulf pilots flying a reconnaissance mission over Corsica sighted two big convoys of naval craft and transport ships west of the southern tip of Corsica on a course heading due north.[186]

That Sunday afternoon, Hitler finally agreed to the transfer of the 11th Panzer Division to the Nineteenth Army area.[187] The division commander, Generalmajor Wend von Wietersheim, happened to be at Blaskowitz's headquarters at Rouffiac and was personally given a verbal order to move the division eastward to the Rhône delta. Blaskowitz told Wietersheim that a landing was anticipated in the area within the next few days. The 11th Panzer Division began to move that very night. Wietersheim sent a staff officer ahead to General Wiese's headquarters at Avignon where Wiese stated that the invasion was expected within hours. He demanded that 11th Panzer accelerate its march, which was being slowed by Allied air attacks and Maquis activity. By 14 August a command post was established at Remouling; combat elements of the division would not arrive until the evening of 15 August.[188]

The headquarters of the Commander of the Military Government Area—the Army Field Police—was located in the middle of the German army corps sector where the invasion would take place. The commander had scheduled a conference for nine o'clock that morning, 13 August.

He was in turn, also ordered to attend an earlier conference, but did not return until late afternoon, having been delayed by air attacks, destroyed bridges and damaged roads.

The meeting he had planned at his own headquarters had finally been started at 10 A.M. by his second in command. No sooner had it gotten under way than the air raid alarm sounded. Since there was no air raid shelter, the participants scattered into the adjacent open territory. From a wooded hill nearby, Generalmajor Ludwig Bieringer watched the "awful scene of several large scale bombing attacks on Avignon, Orange, Valance and the bridges between them [in the Rhône River delta] almost without any resistance from German defenses."[189]

The conference finally began in the afternoon. The participants were told that the invasion was imminent and could take place as early as 15 August. French civilian vehicles were to be commandeered to evacuate German Army female auxiliaries. Local soldier's clubs were ordered closed. Civilians were to be moved out of the expected combat area. The Army police, mostly overage men with antiquated rifles who had been used to guard industrial plants, were told that they would be part of the defense against the invasion. One district police commander pointed out that "an effective defense of his sector was impossible with the forces at his disposal ... which were absolutely inadequate. The only reply he received was a shrug of the shoulders."[190] As can be easily imagined, the assembled army district police commanders found the meeting very "depressing" to say the least.

That same Sunday, 13 August, Generalmajor Wiese asserted that the actual day of the invasion would be 15 August, based on all those factors previously mentioned which pointed to a landing being imminent. The date "could be recognized from messages of the French resistance movement" so he issued an order which called the invasion imminent, pointing to the air attacks upon gun batteries and radar equipment. The predicted landing sector was from "about the mouth of the Rhône to the Gulf of Tropez." He reminded everyone of the importance of determining and reporting the main points of effort of the enemy attacks, directing that areas not under attack would be "ruthlessly" stripped of forces to transfer them to the fighting. Parachute landings were predicted in combination with seaborne landings.[191]

Monday morning, 14 August was the beginning of what proved to be a very long and difficult week for Blaskowitz and Army Group G. At noon that day he was leading a conference west of Narbonne, where IV Luftwaffe Field Corps had its command post. Generalmajor Wiese was also present. The discussion had to do with problems of defense against the invasion. A telephone message interrupted the meeting. Despite Allied air cover and the slight haze over the Mediterranean, Luftwaffe reconnaissance had again spotted the convoy sighted a few days earlier. The convoy had changed direction to a westerly course in the general direction of Toulon.

Blaskowitz regarded the change of direction as a camouflage measure to deceive the Germans, correctly guessing that the convoy would turn east again at nightfall. 15 August was almost certainly the day of the invasion.[192] Since 11th Panzer Division had already been ordered from Bordeaux to Avignon, and since it was the sole Army Group Reserve, there was nothing more to do but wait. The wait was not lengthy.

Notes for Chapter XI

1. Friedrich Ruge, *Rommel In Normandy: Reminiscences by Friedrich Ruge.* trans. Ursula R. Moessner (San Rafael, California: Presidio Press, 1979), 2.

2. Kenneth Macksey, *Rommel: Battles and Campaigns* (New York: Mayflower Books, Inc., 1979), 160-163; Desmond Young, *Rommel: The Desert Fox* (New York: Harper & Row, Publishers, Inc., 1950), 141-143, 176-182; David Irving, *The Trial of the Fox* (New York: Avon Books, 1978), 406-407.

3. David Fraser, *Knight's Cross*, 150, 536. Based on an interview with Manfred Rommel, Frazer placed this conversation earlier, in 1943. The question of the date aside, the conversation re-affirms the possibilities of discreet communications among officers even fairly late in the war.

4. Ruge, *Rommel In Normandy*, 75-76. Blaskowitz's Cossack troops were probably among those transferred from Army Group North's antipartisan forces, due to their unreliability, in October 1943. See: Earl F.Ziemke, *Stalingrad To Berlin: The German Defeat in the East* (Washington, D.C.: The U.S. Army Center of Military History, 1968), 202-203.

5. Ruge, *Rommel In Normandy*, 77.

6. Seaton, *Germany Army*, 226-227.

7. MS#B-258, (Freiherr Geyr von Schweppenburg), R.G. 338, N.A.; Freiherr Geyr von Schweppenburg, "Invasion Without Laurels," *An Cosantoir: Irish Defence Journal*, December, 1949 (Part I), 575-581; January 1950 (Part II), 2-3.

8. Rundstedt had one son who did not survive him.

9. "German Generals In the East," *Die Weltwoche*, Zurich, 12 September 1941 (trans.), G-2 Regional File (Intel.) 5990, R.G. 165, N.A.; Blumentritt, *Rundstedt*, 13-14.

10. *Fatherland*, (S.H.A.E.F.), No. 29, 3 May 1945, R.G. 331, N.A.

11. Blumentritt, *Rundstedt*, 38; M.S.#B-334., (Blumentritt), R.G. 338, N.A.

12. MS#B-344, (Blumentritt) R.G.338, N.A.; *Fatherland* (S.H.A.E.F.), No. 29, 3 May 1945, R.G. 338, N.A.; 80262 and 69073, OSS Records, R.G. 226, N.A.

13. *Fatherland* (SHAEF), No. 29, 3 May 1945, R.G. 331, N.A.

14. Seaton, *The German Army*, 226.

15. MS#C-069f (Rundstedt), R.G. 338, N.A.

16. Ibid.

17. SHAEF Weekly Intelligence Summary No. 6, 29 April 1944, Records of Allied Operational and Occupation Headquarters, WW II; General Staff G-2 Division Intelligence Reports, 1942-1945, R.G. 331, N.A.; The O.N.I. Weekly, Vol. III, No. 26, 28 June 1944 (Office of Naval Intelligence), 2075.

18. MS#B-344 (Blumentritt), R.G.338, N,A.

19. Ibid.

20. Rundstedt Interrogation, 1 February 1946, vol. 10,661, File 215C1.023 (D41), R.G. 24, P.A.C.

21. Ibid.

22. Bennett, *Ultra in the West*, 51. The entire report was intercepted and decoded by Ultra.

23. Rundstedt Interrogation, 22 June 1945, First Canadian Army Intelligence Periodical No. 5., Vol. 10,655, File 215C1.023, R.G. 24, P.A.C.,; Rundstedt Interrogation 1 February 1946, Vol. 10,661, File 225C1.023 (D4), R.G. 24, P.A.C.

24. Bennett, *Ultra in the West*, 51.

25. T-312/28/7535241-75355244, R.G. 238, N.A.

26. The divisions were the 156th Reserve Division, 708th Infantry Division, 159th Reserve Division and the 276th Infantry Division. T-312/28/7535241, R.G. 238, N.A.; For a brief description of each see: Mitcham, *Hitler's Legions*, 134-136, 201-202 and 309-310.

27. Bennett, *Ultra In the West*, 51.

28. MS#B-308 (Zimmermann), R.G.338, N.A.

29. Alan F. Wilt, *The Atlantic Wall: Hitler's Defenses in the West, 1941-1944* (Ames, Iowa: Iowa State University Press, 1975), 151; Forrest C. Pogue, *The Supreme Command: The European Theater of Operations* (Washington, D.C.: Office of the Chief of Military History, 1954); 178-179.

30. NOKW 141, M-898, Roll 28, R.G.238, N.A.

31. Linnarz Interrogation, 25 February 1944, M-1019, Roll 42, R.G. 238, N.A. Generalleutnant Victor Linnarz worked in the Army Personnel Office and testified to this under oath.

32. Jürgen Förster, "The Dynamics of Volksgemeinschaft: The Effectiveness of the German Military Establishment in the Second World War," in Allan Millett and Williamson Murray, eds., *Military Effectiveness*, 3 vols. (Boston: Allen & Unwin, 1988), III: 207. In April Hitler addressed an assembly of officers, demanding that "every officer had to identify himself with the

'ideas' of national socialism; there could be no such thing as an apolitical officer." Ziemke, *Stalingrad to Berlin*, 311.

33. MS#B-308 (Zimmerman), R.G. 338, N.A.

34. Ibid.

35. Blumentritt, *Rundstedt*, 199.

36. "Nazis and Generals Make It Up," *Daily Express* (London), 20 May 1944, 1. The author wishes to acknowledge his indebtedness to the staff of the British Library Newspaper Library for providing a copy of the *Daily Express*.

37. Ibid., regrettably it has been impossible to trace the source of the reporter's (Morley Richards) information.

38. Ernst Froese, "Miene Begegnung mit Hans Blaskowitz," 9.

39. Ruge, *Rommel In Normandy*, 155.

40. "Nazis and Generals Make It Up," *Daily Express (London)*, 20th May, 1944, 1.

41. "Blaskowitz, Johannes," Entry 194, M.I.D., M.I.S.; Who's Who Branch, 1939-1945, R.G. 165, N.A.

42. Ruge, *Rommel In Normandy*, 155; Hinsley, *British Intelligence*, III, Part 2, 67.

43. Hinsley, *British Intelligence*, III, Part 2: 67-68.

44. Brett-Smith, *Hitler's Generals*, 270.

45. MS#B-308 (Zimmerman), R.G. 338, N.A.

46. Hastings, *Das Reich*, 10.

47. Kedward, *Occupied France*, 52.

48. Rings, *Life With the Enemy*, opposite 208.

49. Hastings, *Das Reich*, 62.

50. Sweets, *Choices In Vichy France*, 183.

51. Rundstedt Interrogation, 1 February 1946,Entry 427 (1954p), R.G. 407, N.A.

52. Ibid.

53. MS#B-516 (Sodenstern), R.G. 338, N.A.

54. Wilt, *Atlantic Wall*, 150-151.

55. "Invasion of Southern France" Office of the Theater Historian, European Theater of Operations, Office of the Chief of Military History, Department of the Army, 16.

56. MS#B-888 (Kniess), R.G. 338, N.A.

57. Jorg Staiger, *Rückzug durchs Rhonetal: Abwehr und Verzögerungskampf der 19. Armee im Herbst 1944 unter besonderer Berücksichtigung des Einsatzes der 11 Panzer-Division* (Neckargemund: Kurt Vowinckel Verlag, 1965), 14.

58. MS#B-515 (Botsch), R.G. 338, N.A.

59. MS#B-800 (Blaskowitz), R.G. 338, N.A.

60. Ibid.

61. "Invasion of Southern France," O.T.H., E.T.O., O.C.M.H., D.O.A., 16.

62. T-311/139/7183434, R.G. 338, N.A.

63. MSg 1814, BA/MA.

64. "Invasion of Southern France," O.T.H., E.T.O., O.C.M.H., D.O.A., 8-9.

65. Gordon Harrison, *Cross-Channel Attack—The United States Army in World War II, The European Theater of Operations,* (Washington, D.C.: Office of the Chief of Military History, Department of the Army, 1951), 253.

66. Ibid.

67. MS#B-276 (Sodenstern), R.G. 338, N.A.

68. Ibid.

69. Harrison, *Cross-Channel Attack,* 258.

70. MS#B-276 (Sodenstern), R.G. 338, N.A.

71. MS#B-516 (Sodenstern), R.G. 338, N.A.

72. MS#B-800 (Blaskowitz), R.G. 338, N.A.

73. MS#A-882 (Wilutzky), R.G. 338, N.A.

74. Ibid; MS#B-800 (Blaskowitz) R.G. 238, N.A. Most of the transfers were ordered by radio and intercepted by Ultra, providing the Allies with an accurate picture of the condition of Army Group G. See: Hinsley, *British Intelligence,* III, Part 2: *passim.*

75. MS#B-516 (Sodenstern), R.G. 338, N.A.

76. Murray, *Strategy for Defeat,* 136-156, 230.

77. Wilbur Morrison, *Fortress Without A Roof: The Allied Bombing of the Third Reich* (New York: St. Martin's Press, 1982), 295.

78. *Seventh U.S. Army Operations Report,* I: 30-37.; Unpublished Paper presented at the Western Association for German Studies Conference at Seattle, Washington, 9 October 1981 and kindly loaned to the author. See: Alan F. Wilt, "The Wehrmacht in Retreat: The Southern France Example," 2.

79. Hinsley, *British Intelligence,* III, Part 2, 113.

80. Ibid.

81. MS#B-696 (Botsch), R.G. 338, N.A.; Morrison, *Fortress Without A Roof,* 296-299, 316-318.

82. Carter and Muller, Comps., *Army Air Force Combat Chronology,* 381.

83. Ibid.

84. *Defeat,* 23-24.

85. "Kommt auch Blaskowitz an die Reihe?" *Nachrichten für die Truppe,* Nr. 83,

Sonnabend, 8 Juli 1944, Band 1, Nos. 1-190, 1; Wesley Craven and James Cate, *The Army Air Forces in World War II,* Vol. III: *Europe: Arguments to V-E Day, January 1944 to May 1945* (Washington, D.C.: Office of Air Force History, New Imprint, 1983), 496. The above was probably dropped by the U.S. Ninth Tactical Air Force "Special Leaflet Squadron," which flew as far south as Toulouse and southeast to Grenoble.

86. Wilt, "Wehrmacht in Retreat;" *Seventh U.S. Army Operations Report,* I: 30.

87. Ibid.

88. MS#A-882 (Wilutzky, R.G. 338, N.A.

89. MS#B-800 (Blaskowitz), R.G. 338, N.A.

90. Wilt, *French Riviera Campaign,* 43; Harrison, *Cross-Channel Attack,* 203-204.

91. Rings, *Life With the Enemy,* 210.

92. Michael J. Bird, *The Secret Battalion* (New York: Holt, Rinehart and Winston, 1964.), *passim.*

93. Michael Pearson, *Tears of Glory: The Heroes of Vercors, 1944* (Garden City, New York: Doubleday Company, Inc., 1979), *passim.*

94. Report of Interrogation No. 5554 (Unknown German-Undated), Records of the Judge Advocate General (Army), General and Administrative Records, 1944 to 1949, Case 110 (5554), R.G. 153, N.A; Efforts to positively identify the "paymaster" in this interrogation have not been entirely successful. Bundesarchiv Aachen ZentralnachWeisstelle attempted to assist in this context but was unsuccessful. Correspondence in author's possession. The *Kriegrangliste Samtlicher Offiziere und Beamten im Offizierrang* (stand 1.2.43) in T-312/26/7532799-803, names Bernard Lüpke as paymaster, as does an unofficial Stellenbestzung (stand 18 October 1942) provided to me by Prince Friedrich Biron von Curland.

95. Blaskowitz Interrogation, 8 September 1945, Schuster Interrogation Files, R.G. 165, N.A.

96. T-311/139/7183659, R.G. 238, N.A.

97. Fattig, "Reprisal," 103.

98. Hastings, *Das Reich,* 103-104; T-311/139/ 7183596-7, R.G. 238, N.A.

99. Hastings, *Das Reich,* 163-182: Reitlinger, *SS,* 400-401; Stein, *Waffen SS,* 276-277. See also: Philip Beck, *Oradour: Village of the Dead* (London: Leo Cooper, 1979), passim.

100. Hastings, *Das Reich,* 186.; T-311/139/ 7183653, R.G. 238, N.A.

101. Fattig, "Reprisals," 109; T-311/139/ 7183353-54, R.G. 238, N.A.; Wilutzky Interrogation, 26 January 1948, M-1019, Roll 79, R.G. 238, N.A.

102. Fattig, "Reprisals," 109; Wilutzky Interrogation, 26 January 1948, M-1019, Roll 79, R.G. 238, N.A.

103. T-311/139/7183353-54, R.G. 238, N.A.

104. Ibid.

105. T-311/139/7183719, R.G. 238, N.A.

106. Blaskowitz Interrogation, 17 October 1947, M-1019, Roll 6, R.G. 238, N.A.

107. Fattig, "Reprisals," 110.

108. Ibid.; Wilutzky Interrogation, 26 January 1948, M-1019, Roll 79, R.G. 238, N.A.

109. L 45593, OSS Records, R.G. 226, N.A.

110. Hinsley, *British Intelligence*, III, Part 2, 202.

111. Wilt, *French Riviera Campaign*, 43.

112. Keilig, *Das deutsche Heer*, 53; John Angolia, *On The Field of Honor: A History of the Knight's Cross Bearers*,(U.S.A.: Clyborne Typographics, 1980).

113. MS#B-276 (Sodenstern), R.G. 338, N.A.

114. "Wiese, Friedrich", Entry 194, M.I.D.-M.I.S., Who's Who Branch, 1939-1945; R.G. 165, N.A.; MS#B-787 (Wiese), R.G. 338, N.A.

115. MS#A-882 (Wilutzky), R.G. 338, N.A.; MS#B-800 (Blaskowitz), R.G. 338, N.A.

116. Dieter Ose, *Entscheidung im Western 1944: Der Oberbefehlshaber West und die Abwehr der Allierten Invasion* (Stuttgart: Deutsche Verlags-Anstalt, 1982), 155.; Blumentritt concurred in this. WO 208/4210, P.R.O.

117. MS#A-882 (Wilutzky), R.G. 338, N.A.; MS#B-800 (Blaskowitz), R.G. 338, N.A.

118. Warlimont, *Inside Hitler's Headquarters*, 444.

119. MS#882 (Wilutzky), R.G. 338, N.A.

120. Ibid.

121. Staiger, *Rückzug durchs Rhonetal*, 21; Wilt, *French Riviera Campaign*, 45.

122. MS#882 (Wilutzky), R.G. 338, N.A.; MS#A-800 (Blaskowitz), R.G. 338, N.A.

123. MS#B-516 (Sodenstern), R.G. 338, N.A.

124. Seydewitz, *Civil Life in Wartime Germany*, 365.

125. Ibid.

126. Ose, *Entscheidung im Western 1944*, 186.

127. Tagesnotizen Feldmarschalle Freiherr von Weichs Aus den Jahren *1943* (Auszug) und *1944* (Vollstaendig), Kriegschauplatz Balkan. Aus den originalnotizen in Gabelsberger Stenographic uebertragen durch Generalmajor a.D. Curt Ritter von Geitner, 1956/57. U.S.A.M.H.I., O.C.M.H. Collection.

128. WO 208/4170, P.R.O.

129. T-311/140/71854630, R.G. 238, N.A.

130. 133036, OSS Records, R.G. 226, N.A.; After 20 July 1944 National Social-ist Leadership Officers (N.S.F.O.) were assigned to army staffs in a role tanta-mount to "official spies." One conversation secretly taped in a British P.O.W. camp in October 1945 between an Oberst Wilck and General Major Bas-senge concerned the lethality of these "N.S.F.O.'s: "Things have gone so far that if anyone says nowadays: 'I hardly believe we can win' he's a dead man before six hours have elapsed. You have no idea to what extent the Officer Corps is spied upon. If you voice an opinion in company of three men whom you don't happen to have known for years, you risk that after eight hours...." WO 208/4169, P.R.O.

131. T-175/474/2997028, R.G. 238, N.A.

132. Sydewitz, *Civil Life In Wartime Germany*, 395.

133. Wilhelm Prüller, *Diary of a German Soldier*, ed., H.C. Robbins Landon and Sebastian Leitner (New York: Coward-McCann, Inc., 1963), 174.

134. Hastings, *Overlord*, 277-278.

135. Paper on Morale of Wehrmacht, 19 July 1944, German Morale, Special Staff P.W.D.-Executive Section, Decimal File, 1944-45, Entry 87, R.G. 331, N.A.

136. Ibid.

137. Ibid.

138. Hastings, *Overlord*, 247.

139. Albert Speer, *Inside the Third Reich*, trans. Richard and Clara Winston (New York: Macmillan Company, 1970), 364.

140.MS#B-421 (Blaskowitz), R.G. 338, N.A.; MS#B-330 (Roettiger), R.G. 338, N.A.; MS#B-516 (Sodenstern), R.G. 338, N.A.

141. MS#B-330 (Roettiger), R.G. 338, N.A.

142. MS#B-421 (Blaskowitz), R.G. 338, N.A.; MS#B-516 (Sodenstern), R.G. 338, N.A.

143. MS#B-516 (Sodenstern), R.G. 338, N.A.

144. Wilt, *French Riviera Campaign*, 71-75.

145. Russell Weigley, *Eisenhower's Lieutenants: The Campaigns of France and Germany, 1944—1945* (Bloomington: Indiana University Press, 1981), 28.

146. Hastings, *Overlord*, 315.

147. Carlo D'Este, *Decision In Normandy* (New York: E.P. Dutton, Inc., 1983), 29-30.

148. Weigley, *Eisenhower's Lieutenants*, 28; Keegan, *Six Armies in Normandy*, 243.

149. Hastings, *Overlord*, 315-316; Keegan, *Six Armies in Normandy*, 241-242.

150. Weigley, *Eisenhower's Lieutenants*, 29.

151. Ibid., 31.

152. MS#B-787 (Wiese), R.G. 338, N.A.

153. MS#A-954 (Zerbel), R.G. 338, N.A.

154. MS#A-875 (Richter), R.G. 338, N.A.

155. Ibid.

156. Generalleutnant (Maj.Gen.) Wend von Wietersheim: Service Sketch, Biographic Files, U.S.A.M.H.I., O.C.M.H. Collection.; "Weitersheim, Wend," Entry 194, M.I.D., M.I.S., "Who's Who Branch, 1939-1945, R.G. 165, N.A.

157. Ibid.

158. Ibid.

159. Mitcham, *Hitler's Legions*, 362-364.

160. MS#A-880 (Wietersheim), R.G. 338, N.A.

161. George S. Patton, *War As I Knew It* (Boston: Houghton Mifflin Company, 1947), 96.

162. Martin Blumenson, *The Duel For France: 1944*, (Boston: Houghton Mifflin Company, 1963), 198.

163. Eddy Florentin, *The Battle of the Falaise Gap*, trans. Mervyn Savill (New York: Hawthorn Books, Inc., 1965), 34.

164. MS#B-421 (Blaskowitz), R.G. 338, N.A.

165. Ibid.

166. Wilt, *French Riviera Campaign*, 75-76.

167. Hinsley, *British Intelligence*, III, Part 2, 236, 247 and 257.

168. T-311/140/7185842, R.G. 238, N.A.

169. Wilt, *French Riviera Campaign*, 75.; T-311/140/7185931, R.G. 238, N.A.

170. Florentin; *Falaise Gap*, 72.

171. Ibid., 60.

172. MS#B-787 (Wiese), R.G. 338, N.A.

173. MS#B-402 (Bieringer), R.G. 338, N.A.

174. MS#A-868 (Blaskowitz), R.G. 338, N.A.

175. MS#A-880 (Wietersheim), R.G. 338, N.A.; The 9th. Panzer Division was put on alert for the move to Normandy on 27 July and moved immediatly, assembling near Alencon on 6 August. Carl Hans Hermann, *Die 9. Panzerdivision, 1939-1945; Bewaffnung, Einsatz, Manner* (Friedberg: Podzun Pallas Verlag, 1976), 150.

176. MS#B-787 (Wiese), R.G. 338, N.A.

177. Ibid.

178. MS#A-888 (Kniess), R.G. 338, N.A.

179. MS#B-800 (Blaskowitz), R.G. 338, N.A.; MS#A-882 (Wilutzky), R.G. 338, N.A.

180. Jacques Robichon, *The Second D-Day*, trans. Barbara Shuey (New York: Walker and Company, 1962), 29.

181. Carter & Mueller, Comps., *Army Air Force Combat Chronology*, 422.

182. Robichon, *Second D-Day*, 30; Wilt, *French Riviera Campaign*, 75; MS#B-800 (Blaskowitz), R.G. 338, N.A.

183. Wilt, *French Riviera Campaign*, 75.; T-311/140/7185931, R.G. 238, N.A.

184. Ibid.

185. Florentin, *Falaise Gap*, 131.

186. MS#A-882 (Wilutzky), R.G. 338, N.A.; MS#B-800 (Blaskowitz), R.G. 338, N.A.; Robichon, *Second D-Day* 30.

187. Robichon, *Second D-Day*, 28; Herrlitz Interrogation, 19 September 1945, CIPIR No. 68. R.G. 338, N.A. Herrlitz, and probably others too, assumed from the transfer of 11th Panzer Division that *OKW* knew the time and place of the Allied invasion in advance of the landing.

188. MS#A-880 (Wietersheim), R.G. 338, N.A.

189. MS#B-402 (Bieringer), R.G. 338, N.A.

190. Ibid.

191. MS#B-696 (Botsch), R.G. 338, N.A.

192. Ibid., MS#B-787 (Wiese), R.G. 338, N.A.; MS#A-882 (Wilutzky), R.G. 338, N.A.; MS#B-800 (Blaskowitz), R.G. 338, N.A.; MS#B-516 (Sodenstern), R.G. 338, N.A.

CHAPTER XII

INVASION AND RETREAT

TUESDAY, 15 AUGUST, was a holy day of obligation to Roman Catholics—the Feast of the Assumption. In Poland, 15 August historically had been "Army Day." In France in 1944, it was definitely not the German Army's day, neither was it Blaskowitz's day.

Just before sunrise, General Heinz von Gyldenfeldt, Blaskowitz's Chief of Staff, was awakened by a telephone call from Nineteenth Army headquarters at Avignon: "The invasion fleet is approaching the coast off Saint Tropez," the Nineteenth Army Chief of Staff, Generalleutnant Walter Botsch, announced, "Therefore, we feel certain that the landings will take place there."[1] Nevertheless, the first news of landings to reach Nineteenth Army headquarters came from Marseilles, far to the west of St. Tropez. The reported "landings" turned out to be only bombing attacks and dummies dropped by parachute as decoys.[2] Within hours, Botsch informed Army Group G headquarters of "Violent air raids and continuous naval bombardment" at several beach sectors near St. Tropez, St. Raphael and Le Dramont.

Another report told of "fierce fighting ... going on twelve miles from Draguignan between Allied paratroopers and the German garrison." Twenty minutes later, LXII Corps informed headquarters of the arrival of two hundred Allied planes.[3] At 11:17 A.M., the Marseilles garrison reported Allied minesweepers in the minefield off the coast. Then, abruptly, Army Group G communications went dead! Telephones, teletype, telegraph would not function.[4] The Maquis had paralyzed communications.[5]

Blaskowitz immediately decided to move the Nineteenth Army units located furthest west on the Mediterranean coast eastward toward the invasion landing area, between Cannes and St. Tropez. Abandoning Rouffiac, Blaskowitz travelled to the headquarters of the IV Luftwaffe Field Corps near Carcassone, where he ordered the previously mentioned westward movement of divisions and continued to move westward himself. During the night he arrived at Avignon, once the home of the Popes in exile, now Nineteenth Army headquarters. Through personal contact with the fighting front, he found that the "German inferiority on the battlefield, both on the ground and in the air" made a counterattack against the already established enemy bridgeheads virtually impossible.[6]

Battle could only be a matter of a delaying action until Hitler agreed to a withdrawal from all of southern France. Even the possibility of a successful withdrawal was not within the army group's control since the southern wing of the Allied armies which had broken through in Normandy was now in a position to cut the army group's line of retreat at Lyon, at the northern end of the Rhône River corridor. The Allied commander of those troops was the U.S. general George Patton, whose daring made the threat a real possibility. Army Group G faced the choice of attempting a breakthrough against Patton or a retreat to upper Italy through the Alps; neither option was desirable.[7] The situation of the army group was already desperate. Geography limited the possibilities.

The entire eastern end of the French Mediterranean coast, where the landing took place, is dominated by flanking geographic features to the east and west. The Alps in the east run from their highest peaks in Switzerland and Italy to the Provence Alps of France, then descend into a massif or highland cut by rivers into numerous deep valleys, which generally run east to west but in one case—the Route Napoleon—run northwest to Grenoble, then to the Rhône corridor near Montelimar. The coastal area itself, the famous Rivièra, is serrated and rocky, dangerous for navigation, with many small deep-water bays and gulfs alternating with little semi-circular sandy beaches of abundant natural beauty.

The climate is usually mild with little rainfall, lots of sun and light winds. The valley hillsides are covered with oaks, pine, chestnut and low scrub growth of juniper, broom and myrtle—the last usually called

"Maquis." It is terrain which favors defensive fighting. Behind the coastal strip is a road net "adequate for military operations" with two main coastal highways, one more inland than the other, each with numerous local secondary roads.[8] West of the landing area the dominant geographic feature is the Rhône River delta leading north to the Rhône-Saone corridor. The delta area itself is unsuitable for an invasion since it is low and frequently swampy, and is criss-crossed by channels of the great river, making employment of tanks impossible.

The actual assault of the parachutists and amphibious assault troops had originally been planned to be simultaneous with the landings in Normandy but had been delayed ten weeks due to shipping difficulties and opposition by Winston Churchill.[9] The Americans had pushed hard for the invasion, code named "Operation Dragoon," while Churchill had preferred a second invasion on the Atlantic coast near St. Nazaire or Bordeaux. When the British Prime Minister finally agreed to the operation on 8 August he said he had been "dragooned" into accepting it.[10] Nevertheless he flew in a Dakota to Corsica on 14 August, boarded the destroyer *Kimberley*, and sailed to within seven thousand yards of the minefields to watch the American assault:

> Here we saw long rows of boats filled with American storm troops steaming in continuously to the Bay of St. Tropez. As far as I could see or hear, not a shot was fired either at the approaching flotillas or on the beaches. The battle-ships had now stopped firing, as there seemed to be nobody there.[11]

What Churchill did not reveal in his memoirs was that even during the hours when he was on board the *Kimberley* watching the invasion, he had access to Ultra, which kept him informed in advance of any moves Blaskowitz might make.[12]

The American view was that the German defense had been caught "'off center' with the bulk of their Divisions far to the west of the assault beaches." The initial German reaction "appeared confused."[13] *The New York Times* headline the next day seemed to sum it up: "Germans caught unaware in South."[14] But it was not true, the Germans had not been unaware; they had been impotent. Everything had gone wrong for them.

In the air, only a single Allied Marauder formation reported meeting anti-aircraft fire—and it was reported as "light." For hours, the Allied pilots saw no evidence of the Luftwaffe. Then, finally, Lightning pilots encountered eighteen Messerschmitt 109's and quickly shot down three and drove off the rest! The Allies dominated the air completely.[15] One source reported that Luftwaffe opposition was so weak that the Allies did not have to subtract much time from strategic bombing to aid the assault forces.[16] It was the same on the sea and it was not much better for the Germans on the ground.

Only one Allied pilot saw German tanks and they were being dive bombed by American Thunderbolts.[17] The *Ost*-Battalions in the landing area—mostly Russians—surrendered without fighting, opening gaps in the already thin German defenses.[18] Perhaps the surrendering Russians explain how British radio correspondent Vaughn Thomas, who landed with the assault troops, could broadcast that the troops who opposed the invaders on the coast—"did not have their heart in this job." "Already many of them are walking down the dusty roads to the prison cages, most of them smiling—glad to be out of it."[19]

Amply endowed with a sense of drama, Thomas reported that American troops now took over the "Luxury villas and grand hotels." The "millionaire's playground" that was the Rivièra quickly filled with "guns, jeeps and bulldozers and with all the various vehicles a modern army can put ashore with high speed."[20] It was not an exaggeration.

On the first day alone, the invaders landed 86,000 men, 12,000 vehicles and 46,000 tons of supplies. Before the day was over, the troops assaulting the beaches had linked up with the parachute and glider troops and firmly established a beachhead.[21] The landing resembled a maneuver.[22] The "major mystery," according to Thomas' broadcast, "is exactly what has become of the Germans."[23]

It was a mystery to some extent to the Germans themselves. In some areas, the Allied attacks moving inland were repelled. In other areas the *Ost-truppen*, mostly Russians, did not fight at all, surrendering instead at the first opportunity.[24] Other sectors, especially around Draguignan, where LXII Army Corps had its headquarters, had an entirely different experience, being surrounded suddenly by Allied parachutists. The Corps headquarters had responsibility for the German defenses in the assaulted beach area; its isolation and the destruction of its communications system meant that in the invasion sector there was no overall local command. The battle broke down into a series of uncoordinated firefights by small groups. There was no continuous line of resistance around the beachhead.[25]

Not a single coordinated German counterattack took place on the first day of the invasion. Instead, contrary to traditional German military doctrine and practice, reinforcements were committed to battle in dribs and drabs, piecemeal, without regard to the tactical situation, as they arrived in the area.[26]

The 242nd Infantry Division tried to do what it could to slow the American advance in the absence of coordinated control by the captured corps headquarters. Hastily erected roadblocks and minor local counterattacks, however, could not drive the Americans into the sea. Appeals were made to Nineteenth Army headquarters for reinforcements. Troops of the 244th Infantry Division were brought up from Marseilles, as well as forces from other divisions, but they totalled only five battalions by the evening of 15 August and even these did not succeed in crossing the Rhône River that day due to the destruction of the bridges by Allied air attacks.

Troops were ferried across under the protection of darkness during the short summer night.[27] It would take the 11th Panzer Division seven full days to get across the River.[28] In the meantime, German troops in the invasion area were without tanks and motorized anti-tank weapons; the latter having all been sent to the Normandy Front. When Blaskowitz wired this information to Germany it was intercepted by Ultra.[29] He was like a wounded prize fighter, "telegraphing" his weakness to his opponent.

German weakness was countered by the Allied strength. The Allies sent "swarms of heavy and medium bombers ... far into southern France to blast bridges, highways and military installations without once seeing a German plane ...." If the reports of The New York Times are to be believed, Flying Fortresses, Liberators and Mitchells were all along the Rhône Corridor.[30] On the ground the invaders consolidated a beachhead seventy-two miles long on the coast and drove as much as twenty miles inland in one place.[31]

German actions on the day after the invasion amounted only to a two battalion attack in the direction of Draguignan to relieve LXII corps headquarters. After initially driving back the Americans, the attack was stopped by an additional American paratrooper airdrop and "smashed up" by air force attacks. The only German attack of the day broke down into a series of scattered individual engagements.[32]

A minor mystery of sorts was explained when the personnel of the German LXII Corps headquarters surrendered and admitted under interrogation that they had learned of the departure of the Allied convoys northward, but that the landing was expected to take place near Genoa. The German commander stated: "In fact, I was informed on the 13th and again later yesterday [14 August] that you would positively attack Genoa today. That is over one hundred miles east of here, so my command was not alerted in its defenses."[33] It was the afternoon of 16 August before Nineteenth Army headquarters learned that LXII Corps headquarters had been captured.[34]

During the next few days, the fighting conducted by the Germans was a series of delaying actions from one defense line to the next.[35] By 18 August part of the armor of the 11th Panzer Division was across the Rhône River only to be stuck in its tracks by a lack of fuel. Fuel was finally brought down river from Lyon, and German resistance stiffened at strong points.[36]

The Allies were unable to take full advantage of the German weakness because of limited Allied supply capacity over the beaches.[37] They required a major port and set out to capture Marseilles and Toulon. In the meantime the rapid advance of American troops left their supplies behind; rations, gasoline and ammunition were supplied by air.[38] Pursuit could not continue indefinitely in this fashion. That it was a matter of "pursuit" had been decided the previous day.

At about noontime, on 17 August, D-Day plus two, remnants of Army Group G headquarters still at Rouffiac received by radio an order from OB West—a long overdue order—to abandon southern France. A preliminary order to Blaskowitz directed the abandonment of southern France up to a line—Orleans—Bourges—Montpellier—making contact with Army Group B retreating from Normandy.

There were exceptions on the Atlantic Coast. The fortresses of the Gironde near Bordeaux and also of La Rochelle were to be reinforced and held indefinitely. The order was impractical since it left part of the Nineteenth Army on the Rivièra. A few hours later however, a new order was received for Nineteenth Army's withdrawal from the Rivièra, again with exceptions. Marseilles and Toulon were to be reinforced and held "to the end." The intention was to deny a port to the Allies. It was essentially the withdrawal which Blaskowitz had asked for repeatedly, most recently on 11 August. The question now was whether the retreat could still be accomplished.[39] Siegfried Westphal, Chief of Staff to OB West, privately thought it doubtful that they could manage to connect with Army Group B.[40] It was indeed a daunting task.

Blaskowitz was faced with a situation of virtually insurmountable difficulty. For centuries soldiers had recognized retreat before a superior enemy as the most challenging military scenario. Napoleon, perhaps the greatest commander there ever was, pointed out that even in a skillfully maneuvered retreat morale was weakened because the chance for victory had been lost:

> Besides, retreats cost always more men and *material* than the most bloody engagements, with this difference, that in a battle, the enemy's loss is nearly equal to your own, whereas in a retreat, the loss is on your side only.[41]

Since Napoleon wrote this, modern technology made the possibilities of disaster in retreat yet more severe. Napoleon had not faced the problems confronting Blaskowitz. A retreating army without an air umbrella becomes a sitting duck for the enemy air force. An army group with its armies as far from each other as the Rivièra and Atlantic Coasts of France could be under a single commander due only to the development of modern radio communications. Blaskowitz's army group, however, had an experimental radio transmission system which was particularly weak when headquarters had to be shifted, as it frequently did during the retreat.[42] Indeed, from 18 August until 1 September, he was unable to contact LXIV Army Corps—what remained of his part of First Army on the Atlantic Coast. He called it a "blind command!"[43]

If these complications were not too much to overcome, there remained the character of most of the retreating divisions themselves; "static" divisions was what they were commonly called. "Static" meant that they lacked their own transportation; they were nearly immobile. Conceived as defensive troops for a geographical district, they were slow moving and would necessarily have to abandon all heavy equipment but nevertheless probably still suffer heavy losses in killed and captured to a mobile enemy such as the Americans.

When the withdrawal order was received by these divisions, such as the 338th Infantry, they commandeered all available French civilian transportation. This helped, but did not overcome the crisis.[44] Supply of these divisions, which were partially equipped with weapons captured on European battlefields, was another nightmare, as was the abandoning of non-mobile anti-aircraft batteries at a time when they were so desperately needed.[45]

In addition to combat troops, there were civilian workers from Organization Todt, Naval and Luftwaffe personnel, border guards, nurses and assorted camp followers. These had to be organized in march groups which were coordinated with divisions. The divisions were then organized into corps. The corps for Nineteenth Army were the IV Luftwaffe Field Corps and the LXXXV Army Corps. The former would retreat along the west bank of the Rhône Corridor and the latter on the east bank. They would retreat northward toward Lyons, where their arrival had to be coordinated with the march of LXIV Corps from the Atlantic Coast through Central France to Lyons. Then they would continue northward toward Dijon, where contact with Army Group B, retreating from Normandy, was presumably to be made. All of this was to be accomplished while the U.S. Seventh Army pursued from the Rivièra Coast and Patton's Third Army threatened to capture Lyons or Dijon before Army Group G got there.

Nineteenth Army had to delay the advancing Americans east of the Rhône River, while simultaneously drawing in its extended right flank along the Mediterranean coast where its units stretched nearly three hundred kilometers westward. These troops and those east of the Rhône were to fall back to Avignon, where they would reorganize into march groups for the retreat northward.[46] The 11th Panzer Division would fight Nineteenth Army's rearguard actions, delaying the Americans by every possible means. That meant not only repelling attacks against the "tail" of the retreating army, but also defense against any attempt to outflank and encircle all or part of Nineteenth Army.[47]

The retreat was organized into phased withdrawals from one line of resistance to the next, each line about twenty-five kilometers from the next line. Movement was at night to avoid air attack. Resistance lines were defended during the day.[48] According to Hitler's orders, demolitions and destruction were to be extensive: "Not one locomotive, bridge, power station or repair shop shall fall into enemy hands undestroyed."[49]

Blaskowitz attempted to strictly control Nineteenth Army in terms of the time element. If the army's retreat were too rapid, it would only have to wait at Lyons and then Dijon for LXIV Corps, retreating from the Atlantic Coast.[50] All of this, naturally, was based on the presumption that Patton's Third Army would not already be at Dijon to "welcome" Nineteenth Army.

The situation of LXIV Corps on the Atlantic Coast was very much in contrast with Nineteenth Army's circumstances. LXIV Corps was composed of the 16th Infantry Division and the 159th Reserve Division, neither of which was a first-class unit, especially after the best combat elements had been left behind to defend the fortresses of Bordeaux-Gironde and La Rochelle.[51] The combat units included a Cossack Regiment and an "Indian" Regiment (British P.O.W. volunteers). The 16th Infantry Division was to serve as the rear guard of the march column, as well as the guard for the northern flank. The 159th Infantry guarded the south flank as well as leading the three groups into which the march column was divided.[52]

Most of the march column itself was composed of men not fit for fighting, older men who had served as field police communications personnel and manned town headquarters units, liaison staffs, field hospital personnel and also Luftwaffe ground personnel. They totalled roughly 100,000 troops, including 2,000 women. The march column had "little or no fighting capacity."

They were ordered to take an indirect, time consuming, circuitous march route through Poitiers and Bourges to Dijon, rather than retreat directly northeast through the Massif Central because "it was completely infested with the Maquis plague."[53] Unable to really defend itself, armed mostly with rifles, they would have been "annihilated" in the Massif Central or the Cevennes and therefore had to take the longer route, further delaying the German withdrawal from France.[54]

Having made these plans at his new headquarters at Avignon, which he shared with Nineteenth Army, Blaskowitz issued them to both Nineteenth Army and LXIV Corps on the morning of 18 August.[55] Naturally this was a simple matter as far as Nineteenth Army went.

"All these matters could be straightened out through personal contacts."[56]

Transmitting the orders to LXIV Corps was a horse of a very different color. Radio communications with LXIV Corps could not be established so it became necessary to improvise. General Edgar Theisen was dispatched by automobile to Toulouse with the mission of stopping at unit headquarters along the way to see that the withdrawal order had been received. The order was to be sent from Toulouse to LXIV Army Corps headquarters by radio and by courier officer. As insurance, a fighter plane was sent from Avignon to Bordeaux with the order to retreat.[57]

Ironically, LXIV Corps did not receive Blaskowitz's command to withdraw by any of these methods, instead receiving it through an order radioed from Berlin to the naval station at Bordeaux.[58] In fact, it seems that the British and Americans received the withdrawal order via Ultra more easily than LXIV Corps. The Allies picked it up when Blaskowitz reported his orders to OB West.[59] Generalmajor Elster, commander of the "tail" of LXIV Corps (Its most westward and slowest march group), unaware of Blaskowitz's communication problems, later described the situation thusly: "I had a wireless transmitter van—I transmitted messages and *screamed* into the ether, so that someone should answer me; but no one answered me at all."[60]

Not all information received in the west was as accurate as Ultra, or as secret. A few days earlier, Swedish correspondents in Stockholm reportedly that Hitler had appointed a new "Brain Trust" to deal with the crisis in France. The leaders Hitler had appointed were "Field Marshals" Rommel, Kluge and Blaskowitz, although no other news of Blaskowitz's "promotion" was reported.[61] The Swedes did not know that Rommel was in the hospital near death. Nor did they know Kluge had committed suicide that day and that Blaskowitz was far from being a recipient of Hitler's trust. Blaskowitz was probably too busy that day to think very often of the Führer's trust.

Blaskowitz and his staff remained at Avignon for a couple of days supervising the execution of its orders and observing carefully the developments in the fighting against the invasion beachhead.[62] General Staff officers were sent to Lyons and Dijon to place the few troops and army staffs there under the orders of Army Group G. Arrangements were made for disposition of the available security troops to keep roads open. Reconnaissance of possible defense lines was begun, and careful observation of the advancing Americans was conducted. Measures for the reception of Nineteen Army in Lyon were taken.[63] Little else could be done since Blaskowitz had no reserves left under his own control.

Fortunately for Nineteenth Army the U.S. Seventh Army used 18 August to consolidate the invasion beaches already seized, to reorganize supply lines and to expand the beachhead modestly. Nineteenth Army Chief of Staff Walter Botsch noticed that day, for the first time, a yawning gap beginning to develop on the northeastern upper flank of the army along the Alps between the Swiss frontier and the Rhône River. East of the Rhône the coastal area had been guarded only by the 242nd Infantry Division and the 148th Infantry Division. Further North at Grenoble was the 157th Reserve Mountain Division, occupying the city and guarding the route through the mountains which ran from the coast northwestward toward Lyon, the so-called "Route Napoleon."

When the Allies landed and expanded their beachhead in the first few days, they had driven between the 242nd Infantry Division on their left (western) flank and the 148th Infantry Division on their right (eastern flank). In the fighting from 15 to 18 August, the 242nd Infantry had been reduced to remnants, then withdrawn into Toulon where it was ordered to resist "to the end."[64] Already on the morning of the 18th, a special Allied assault group, "Task Force Butler," named after Brigadier General Frederick Butler, had moved into the gap and advanced northward.[65] Lieutenant General Botsch realized then that the gap could no longer be closed.[66] It was the first sign of immediate danger threatening the survival of Nineteenth Army.

When Ultra had intercepted Hitler's orders to OB West on 17 August, the Allies learned that both the 148th and 157th Divisions were to withdraw when pressed into the Franco-Italian Alpine mountain passes.[67] Secure in the knowledge that the Germans intended only defensive action on his flank, Seventh U.S. Army Commander Lieutenant General Alexander Patch ordered the Task Force reinforced with the intention of penetrating deeply into the German flank and then springing a trap. Knowledge of German plans made the attempt feasible. One of Patch's officers remarked: "You know, this just isn't cricket."[68]

Botsch became increasingly worried the next day about the gap on the eastern flank. He radioed appeals for Luftwaffe reconnaissance to "all higher headquarters, including the *OKW*." The flights, however, were few in number, the results "scanty" and transmission of the results was delayed and unclear due to poor radio communications.[69] His anxiety was not reduced when he learned that 148th Infantry Division had been ordered to withdraw eastward into the Alpine passes by the commander in chief in Italy, Field Marshal Kesselring. Appeals to stop the American outflanking attempt were radioed to 157th Reserve Mountain Division—the only unit now guarding Nineteenth Army's eastern flank.[70]

The following day, 20 August, General Wiese, alert to the threat to his flank, requested that the 157th Infantry Division be required to defend Grenoble instead of withdrawing into the Alpine passes. It was already too late; most of the division had moved eastward.[71] If it made any difference, Wiese could not even inform Blaskowitz because he had lost radio contact with him.[72]

Blaskowitz and his staff had departed on the 19th for Pierrelatte, a mid-way point in the Rhône Valley between Avignon and Lyons. He had stayed at Avignon long enough to supervise the start of the withdrawal. Pierrelatte was the only communications link the army group had between Avignon and Lyons, but it had switching and relay difficulties, which made any communication "extraordinarily arduous."[73]

Blaskowitz had apparently been aware on 19 August of the 148th Infantry Division's withdrawal eastward into the Alps, but had not learned of the similar withdrawal of the 157th Reserve Mountain Division before moving to Pierrelatte.[74] It appears that he was unaware that 157th Mountain Division had withdrawn until 22 August. Nevertheless, it was apparent that something had gone seriously wrong on the eastern flank. Reports had already reached him that American reconnaissance units had reached Lake Geneva.[75]

On 20 August, when Blaskowitz had moved to Pierrelatte, the situation of Nineteenth Army must have seemed as much in hand as possible. The retreat was underway; units were already streaming northward into the Rhône corridor. Little if any relief might be found, however, merely by entering the corridor. From Avignon to Lyon, where the Rhône River meets the Saone River and then northeastward to Dijon is just over 650 kilometers. It had been an invasion route at least since the time when Julius Caesar had recognized it as a key strategic valley. During the Middle Ages and early modern era castles too numerous to count had been built in the valley. One source claimed that "Each rock carries a fortress, as in the Rhine Valley."

Lyon, the first major destination in the northerly retreat, had been the capital of Roman Gaul, and is two hundred kilometers north of Avignon. It is a journey of some natural beauty in peacetime but perilous in war. The valley is a corridor with a river in the middle; sometimes wide, often narrow, the valley opens and closes "like a series of hourglasses one on top of the other."[76] At one of the narrowest points, the Donzere Gorge, the valley is only a quarter of a mile wide, then opens into the plain of Montelimar for ten miles, only to be constricted narrowly again at the Cross Gorge, usually called the "Gate of Montelimar."

Highways parallel the valley on both the eastern and western sides. Highway 7 on the east bank, also called the *Route Nationale*, was best suited for military traffic. On the west bank Highway 86 is close to the river bank and passes along limestone cliffs broken by steep quarry faces.[77] It is more winding than its eastern counterpart, a straight level road following the old Roman highway, which parallels the only railroad line. In some places on the western bank sharp cliffs drop from the Massif Central more than one thousand meters, while on the opposite eastern side at varying distances from the river, limestone cliffs rise to various heights, sometimes nearly a thousand meters, in their ascent toward the Alps.

Although the Rhône runs north—south, the cliffs on both banks are cut at numerous points by east—west flowing tributaries. Usually swift flowing and wide, the Rhône dries up considerably in the Mediterranean summer, although occasionally swelled by water from torrential downpours in the Alps.

The Germans entering the Rhône Corridor knew it was the only way out of southern France, but they must have been apprehensive at being confined in a funnel, unable to maneuver under air attack or from enemy artillery which had found its way to the dominating heights of either river bank. There was, however, no alternative. Troops in march groups streamed into the corridor on the highways of both river banks.

In the Rhône River delta south of Avignon, on 20 August, German infantry fought a stubborn rear guard action led by the 11th Panzer Division. Road blocks and strong points made up of landmines, anti-tank guns, mortars and tanks slowed the American advance just east of Aix-en-Provence and north of Marseilles.[78] The Germans fought to keep Toulon from being surrounded and to gain time for the troops marching toward Avignon from the west. The entrance to the Rhône Valley had to be kept open at all costs.[79]

On 21 August the German rear guard withdrew to a defense line in front of Arles and Orgon. The U.S. Seventh Army, having made contact with the 11th Panzer Division, was given orders to halt except for reconnaissance units sent ahead to determine if a German armored counter-attack was imminent.[80] Two German tanks had come down Highway 7 supported by infantry and had crashed through an American road block. The U.S. anti-tank gunners bounced several shells off the German tanks "without apparent effect."

American prudence was easily understood. Less comprehensible are the panicky rumors which circulated among the U.S. troops to the affect that one thousand German infantry and one hundred and fifty tanks were seen ready to attack.[81] Clearly, any German counter-attack would have been of only local importance. Even without knowledge gained through Ultra, the Americans might have concluded this from reports of reconnaissance flights by the XII Tactical Air Command.

Prior to 21 August, German motor and rail movement (observed from reconnaissance planes) in the Rhône corridor had been from north to south, as if the Germans intended to reinforce the invasion area. By 21 August, however, the pattern had reversed itself, moving south to north. Traffic from the western Mediterranean coast no longer headed toward the invasion beaches as reinforcements but instead turned north at Avignon. The Germans were in full retreat. Their march columns revealed the poor state of German logistics; even from the air fuel shortages were obvious. Troop carriers trailed tow ropes for troops on bicycles.[82]

Events moved rapidly. That very day French troops who had landed on the assault beaches after the Americans began to make their presence felt by placing Marseilles and Toulon under siege.[83] The Allies needed ports. Perhaps of greater importance that day were events in the gap on the German eastern flank into which U.S. Seventh Army's "Task Force Butler" had advanced.

As recently as the previous day it had not been decided whether the Task Force should advance north to Grenoble or turn west toward the Rhône Valley and occupy the high ground around Montelimar in an attempt to cut the German retreat. At a U.S. Seventh Army conference on 21 August it was decided to attempt to spring the trap at Montelimar, occupying the heights from there to the point where the Drome River entered the Rhône Corridor. VI U.S. Army Corps Commander Lieutenant General Lucien Truscott ordered: "'If humanly possible, create road blocks,' and he added 'you must interrupt all enemy traffic on the main north-south roads in the Rhône Valley.'"[84]

Generaloberst Blaskowitz personally experienced the results of Patch's decision the very next day, although he was unsure of exactly what had hit him. Blaskowitz decided to move north from Pierrelatte to Lyon on 22 August in order to have the army group "exert its influence personally [t]here." In addition, he hoped to re-establish communications with OB West, which had been impossible the last few days.

Traveling the *Route National* on the eastern bank of the Rhône in a command column with an escort, Blaskowitz and his chief of staff found that mere movement "took place under difficulties." The highway was the target of "constant" enemy fighter-bomber attacks. Already "hundreds of disabled vehicles lay burned out on the road, partly obstructing it." Heavy casualties— "unfortunately, often women too—occurred—in the case of large vehicles, such as buses and trucks ...." The methodical Germans had anticipated this and blasted "air shelter holes in the cliffs at regular intervals and along the side of the highway, but they were too few for this situation."[85] The carnage became much worse in the next week.

Passing through the Montelimar Gate where the corridor is quite narrow, Blaskowitz's command column was fired upon from the heights by "considerable machine gun and mortar fire ...." There was also shooting from houses and villages along the route. It was assumed that the Maquis did the shooting. Later, he learned that it had been Maquis in the towns, but that the shooting at Montelimar had been done by advance American units already trying to swing the Montelimar Gate shut on the retreating Germans. "Amid brisk fighting," the vehicles and men of the high command column arrived at Lyon on 22 August.[86]

Blaskowitz and his staff immediately went to work. His orders to the Commander at Lyon, General Dehner, were to use his security troops and whatever else he could scrape together to keep the Lyon—Dijon highway open. He was to "cover" the roads leading through the Alps from Grenoble to Lyon with emergency and flak units. Above all, Lyon itself was to be kept "secure" until Nineteenth Army has passed through the city.

He made arrangements to re-supply the retreating army from supply depots at Lyon. Engineers were ordered to construct road blocks as far northeast as the Jura Mountains. Defensive positions were reconnoitered. Staff officers with similar orders for the commander at Dijon, the Army's next stop northward in the retreat, were despatched.

No communications took place with OB West, now Field Marshal Model, who had replaced von Kluge a few days earlier. No contact could be established with LXIV Corps. The telephone connections to Dijon had been cut by the Maquis. Nevertheless, orders were issued to Generalleutnant Ottenbacher to use security troops to keep the Nevers-Moulins area, especially the Loire crossings, open for the retreat of LXIV Corps. Blaskowitz did not find the lack of communication with OB West or higher headquarters disagreeable; he was able to command his troops without the usual interference from "higher command."[87]

Although Blaskowitz and his staff had obviously accomplished a great deal already by the 22nd, there was clearly no time to take satisfaction in hard-won successes. Major catastrophe—debacle—was a manifestly immediate possibility that day. More precisely, Blaskowitz learned the exact form which the threat of annihilation had taken.

The 11th Panzer Division, situated at Arles, was unaware that the Americans had temporarily halted. Suspicious about the lack of combat pressure and cognizant of its orders to protect the eastern flank of Nineteenth Army during the retreat, 11th Panzer Division's commander sent reconnaissance forces to the northeast where American motorized columns were observed advancing toward Grenoble.[88]

Unknown to the Germans, the Americans, called Amis by the Germans, had already made the crucial tactical decision. A Seventh U.S. Army Command conference had decided to send "Task Force Butler" (then only thirty miles south of Grenoble) west on Highway 93, which ran parallel to the Drome River until the Drome flowed into the Rhône and Highway 93 intersected Highway 7, the *Route Nationale*. By 1700 hours the advance elements reached the Rhône Valley.[89] It may have been these Ami troops that fired upon Blaskowitz and his command convoy on the 22nd.

The German troops were apparently confused and mistook the hostile fire as originating from Maquis, "terrorists," and a small number of Ami parachutists. Consequently they did not pay them the attention they merited on the spot. The Amis immediately took advantage of this lapse to send a fifteen man demolition team to the bridge over the Drome River north of Loriol. The demolition team blew it up in the middle of a German column's passage without a shot being fired.[90] The battle of Montelimar had begun.

On 22 August the Eleventh Panzer Division learned through reconnaisance that American motorized columns were pressing northward across the Durance River toward Montelimar. Since the main body of Nineteenth Army was well south of the Montelimar Gate the Germans were in danger of being annihilated. Highway 7 had to be reopened to German traffic fleeing northward without delay. Orders were issued at 1845 hours to the 11th Panzer Division to throw the Americans out of the Rhône Valley Road.[91]

Over the course of the next week Generaloberst Blaskowitz had no contact with LXIV Corps retreating from the Bordeaux area. In fact this Corps took until 27 August to concentrate its widely scattered units, organize them into march groups, and to march to the Dordogne River just east of Bordeaux. From there it marched north to Poitiers and turned east heading for Dijon. Poitiers was not reached by the rear guard until 30 August.[92] Essentially, the LXIV Corps was on its own throughout the week, dependent upon Nineteenth Army to keep its escape route open at Lyon and then Dijon.

Nineteenth Army had its hands full. It was split into two corps; one marched north on each bank of the Rhône. During this decisive week the IV Luftwaffe Field Corps, commanded by General Petersen, was in charge of those units retreating north on Highway 86 on the western bank of the Rhône amid the increasing danger that French guerrillas would slow its retreat to a crawl in the hilly terrain to the north.[93] On the eastern bank of the Rhone LXXXV Army Corps, commanded by General Kniess, supervised the retreat. The 11th Panzer Division acted as flank and rear guard and did the bulk of the defensive fighting.[94]

There was no defense in the air against the Amis that week. Allied B-25's damaged nine Rhône bridges between 17 and 20 August, but this week belonged to the fighter-bomber; "Jabos" the Germans called them. Crowded columns of retreating troops funneled into a narrow valley, slowed by damaged bridges, were sitting ducks. The U.S. Army Air Force official history called it a "Roman holiday."[95] During the week more than 1,500 vehicles were destroyed and an additional 200 were taken intact. Fifteen hundred horses were killed. Numerous railway cars were destroyed. Three thousand prisoners were captured and one thousand German dead left on the field. One American airman said: "This has been the best day of the war for us."[96]

Brigadier General Gordon Saville, commander of XII Tactical Air Command, describing the "burned and blackened path of slaughter from Montelimar to Livron, called it 'as nearly perfect an example of what to do as one can hope to find.'"[97] Thunderbolts, Seafires and Hellcats strafing the congested roads took an awesome toll. As one German general clinically observed:

> Hundreds of disabled vehicles lay burned out on the road, partly obstructing it. Especially heavy casualties—unfortunately, often women too—occurred in the case of large vehicles, such as buses and trucks, from which people could not alight quickly enough to seek shelter at the time of attack.[98]

In the pocket edition of hell located between Montelimar and Livron that week, cries of "every man for himself," "sauve qui peut," were noticeably missing. There was no panic, no directionless flight; "the troops were firm and solidly in the hands of their officers."[99]

Death and destruction from the air inflicted heavy losses, especially in material, but the question of the army's survival was decided on the ground. Crisis followed crisis in the Rhône corridor. On 22 August at

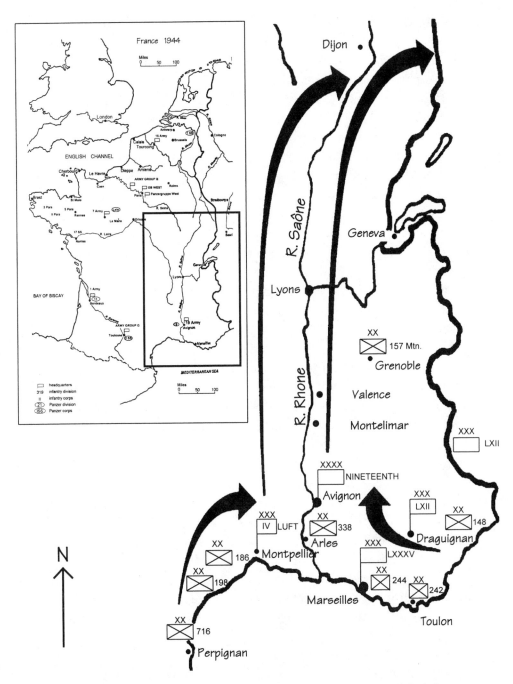

Retreat From Southern France - 1944

2055 hours, the U.S. Seventh Army commander had ordered Task Force Butler urgently: "Your primary mission is to block the Rhône Valley and I expect you to do it .... And when you run out of gas you park your trucks and move on foot." At 0200 hours on the 23rd of August the message was reinforced by another phone call: "interrupt by demolitions that main road ... on the Rhône valley. I don't want a single vehicle to go up that road."[100]

At the southern end of Nineteenth Army the Germans were pursued by the 3rd U.S. Infantry Division, although "pursued" is an overstatement. According to one German officer: "The attacks of enemy infantry supported by tanks, against very weak resistance, became more and more cautious. The tanks risked nothing without the aid of infantry, and the infantry nothing without the tanks."[101] The retreating Germans left behind "unmanned booby-trapped, log road blocks and blown bridges."[102] They were enough to slow the Americans, who had put their real effort into outflanking the Germans with Task Force Butler.

The Americans, under the command of Major-General John Dahlquist, who were attempting to outflank the Germans, were fully motorized and guided by the Maquis. American spearheads reached the Rhône at several points between Montelimar and Livron on the Drome River and succeeded in blowing up the bridges on the Drome. Reinforcements were rushed to support these leading elements. Meanwhile, 11th Panzer Division hastility transfered the preponderance of its rear guard tanks and troops to the threatened flank. "It was a race both won."[103]

Three miles north of Montelimar the Rhône Valley narrows to a width of not over one mile and stays like a funnel for a distance of ten miles to the north. On the eastern side of the valley is the heavily forested area of Marsanne, above which the Rhône Valley widens to admit the Drome River, which widens the valley to a distance of two miles. Two hill masses and a ridge (Hill 430, Hill 294 and Ridge 300), overlook the eastern cliffs north of Montelimar. The hills dominate Highway 7 and the several secondary routes.

American infantry advanced toward Montelimar on the afternoon of 23 August from the chain of hills and ridges north of the city, overlooking Highway 7. Tanks and tank destroyers that were supposed to support the assault on Montelimar had not arrived. The Americans occupied the two hills north of Montelimar, but did not seize either the city itself or Hill 300, just east of the city. It was a critical tactical error. Despite their mistake, from the two hills which they controlled the Amis could fire directly on Highway 7. Ami infantry intended to capture Montelimar and then throw up a roadblock on Highway 7.

The 11th Panzer Division had sent an armored reconnaissance battalion, reinforced by some tanks and an artillery battery, north and east of Montelimar that morning. They occupied Ridge 300. In the afternoon elements of the battalion were attacked by American infantry. It was the "first test of strength." The Maquis, assisting in the attack, were dispersed quickly by the Germans. Then German artillery fire halted the Ami infantry. The German Mark V tanks seemed invulnerable to Ami anti-tank gunfire; it "just bounced off the German tanks." But German 88 mm fire destroyed all the American armored vehicles one by one.[104] The Germans won round one of their fight to survive—round two followed quickly.[105] In the meantime the Germans remained in control of Montelimar and Ridge 300. The trap was not yet locked tight.

During the night, when the Ami fighterbombers were blinded by the darkness and Ami artillery on the heights was least accurate, General Wiese ordered the retreating columns tightly packed at Montelimar to move northward. Other columns moved up from the south. Some Germans slipped through, but by morning the trap was almost fully set. The Yanks had moved additional artillery batteries to the heights at night and effectively blocked Highway 7 in the morning with their fire.[106] Then Mars smiled upon the trapped Germans; there was a way out of the pocket.

On 24 August Ultra signals intelligence intercepted orders from Hitler to the Commander-in-Chief West and to Blaskowitz. All German Forces retreating in France—both from Normandy and from the Rivièra—were directed to form a defense line along the Rivers Seine and Loire towards Dijon. Army Group B was to link up with First Army at Dijon, and in turn, with Nineteenth Army to the Swiss border. Major reinforcements were promised. A bridgehead was to be held around Paris; the city was to be held even if it meant its destruction.[107] This intelligence intercept provided the Americans with an overview of German intentions. German intelligence "luck" that day was more tactical in nature, but it meant survival for the Nineteenth Army.

The Germans captured a copy of the U.S. 36th Infantry Division Operational Instructions. It revealed not only the nature of the American trap, but also the weak spot in the American lines; the hinge or joint where the U.S. 143rd Regiment met the 142nd Regiment. It was at the village of Bonlieu near the Roubion River a few miles east of the Rhône. Since the Roubion connected with the Drome River to the north it provided a secondary route out of the trap if the American line could be pierced.[108] General Wiese ordered LXXXV Corps to use the day to move the 198th Infantry Division into a support position for 11th Panzer Division, which would again lead the attack. The night was utilized to slip more troops out of the pocket northward.[109] Short summer nights meant fewer could escape.[110]

August 25 was an eventful day. Paris was liberated. In the south of France it was no less dramatic.

The Germans executed their attack, but it was unsuccessful. Ultra learned of German intentions to attack, but this does not appear to have helped the Americans since it was too late to change deployments.[112] On the 26th the Germans attacked again, this time cleanly breaking through the American lines and opening up an alternate escape route through which men and machines drove desparately.[113] Mark VI tanks, 70 ton monsters with 88 mm guns (Tiger II) had led the breakthrough. In this ferocious fighting the Allies were reminded of the adage that "he who has not fought the Germans does not know war." German professional officers, at battalion and company level, dazzled their amateur British and American counterparts. The German "might logically be defeated, but he still came onto the field with claws."[114]

During the day and throughout the night German infantry streamed northward through the temporarily open alternate routes. By the morning of the 27th the Americans succeeded in once again sealing the original line, trapping some German troops and capturing abandoned heavy equipment, but elements of the 11th Panzer Division and three infantry divisions had escaped in the meantime. A fourth division escaped up Highway 7 while the trap was open, despite heavy American artillery fire from the heights east of the Montelimar Gate.[115] Some troops were able to cross the damaged bridge at Montelimar to the western bank of the Rhône to join the IV Luftwaffe Field Corps fleeing northward. Engineers had to be dispatched to remove vehicles destroyed by American artillery because so many wrecked hulks were blocking the road.[116] Nevertheless, German movement north out of the pocket kept flowing.

The American VI corps commander, Lieutenant General Lucien Truscott, upon learning through air reconnaissance reports that Germans continued to escape northward, went personally to Major General Dahlquist's command post. When he arrived there he did not waste words:

> John, I have come here with the full intention of relieving you of your command. You have reported to me that you held the high ground north of Montelimar and that you had blocked highway 7, you have not done so. You have failed to carry out my orders. You have just five minutes in which to convince me that you are not at fault.

Dahlquist explained that his infantry had mistakenly failed to take Ridge 300. The trap was finally closed, but four German infantry divisions, one panzer division and numerous mixed elements had escaped.[117]

American "long toms" were very accurate; artillery officers reported later that they had "more target opportunities ... than ammunition to exploit them."[118] For a distance of twenty miles south of Montelimar destroyed guns, trucks, automobiles, wagons and armored vehicles were wrecked bumper to bumper on both sides of the road. There were 7,000 dead horses and uncounted German bodies.[119]

In Lyon Blaskowitz was roughly eight miles north of Montelimar, just far enough to have difficulty realizing the degree of desperation around Montelimar. On 23rd August he radioed orders to General Wiese which read in part:

> The enemy is southeast of Paris, near Sens, advancing toward Troyes. This makes fast retreat necessary .... Every battalion which goes ahead of the Army to Dijon is most valuable, these battalions have to build a flank for the army near Dijon and to the north.[120]

Blaskowitz was worried—naturally—about the U.S. Army passing

Grenoble—getting east of Lyon and cutting off the retreat of both Nineteenth Army and LXIV Corps by reaching Dijon first. His orders were immediately monitored by Ultra.[121] While the Allies appreciated hearing his views, it seems that they were not so welcome at the headquarters of the hard-pressed Nineteenth Army. The Nineteenth Army Chief of Staff later wrote:

> Recognizing the seriousness of the situation, the AOK [Armee Oberkommando] is fully aware that the bulk of the Armee can only escape and be salvaged by means of a quick evacuation from the pocket. The various warnings on the part of higher headquarters were not necessary. The battles raging northeast of Montelimiar [sic] apparently are being totally underated by higher authorities. Unless the enemy forces northeast of Montelimar are kept away from the March Road...the LXXXV A.K. will be doomed.[122]

Wiese decided that Blaskowitz's later request for transfer of the 11th Panzer Division north to Lyon could not be obeyed. The 11th Panzer Division was engaged in heavy fighting with the enemy while two divisions were still encircled. Instead, IV Luftwaffe Field Corps on the western bank of the Rhône was ordered to speed up its withdrawal and to "spare neither men nor horses."[123] If Lyon, only 65 miles north of Grenoble, fell to another Ami outflanking movement, a greater disaster than had already taken place was in the making.

On 26 August orders were finally given by Nineteenth Army to rush 11th Panzer Division northeast toward Lyon—specifically to the area of Valence—from where it would also serve as a flankguard for the army. The infantry and artillery still in the pocket were thought to be able to protect themselves by this time.[124] These measures were implemented not a moment too soon. The 11th Panzer's reconnaissance unit discovered the arrival of the U.S. 45th Infantry Division at the Drome River Valley, a tributary of the Rhône from the east, near the town of Loriol, south of Valence, the following day, 27 August.[125] The bridge over the Drome had already been demolished five days earlier by the Amis, but now the Americans attempted to occupy the area in force.

If the situation was not already beyond mastering, nature itself seemed to throw weight onto the scales against Nineteenth Army's chances to escape. Sudden summertime downpours in the Alps caused the Drome River to flood, beginning at midnight on 26 August. All movement north came to an abrupt halt.[126] It seemed an impossibility in the hot Mediterranean summer, but it had happened. Four fording sites were used to cross the Drome throughout the night. Nevertheless German forces began to build up south of the Drome. By the morning of the 28th German engineers had built an auxiliary bridge over the Drome and the waters had begun to recede. American artillery on the heights east of the Rhône took their toll, but the bulk of the army escaped. The American artillery reported "having a field day ..." once again.[127]

Nineteenth Army's advance elements on the east bank of the Rhône were only sixty miles south of Lyon, but the tail of the army stretched back almost to Montelimar, thirty miles further south. Two divisions remained in the pocket there. On that day staff officers were sent back into the pocket with orders to form the troops there into battle groups and make their way northward to Valence during the night. By this method the bulk of the remaining troops escaped.[128]

While the last troops to escape from the cauldron near the Montelimar Gate were slipping northward, Generaloberst Blaskowitz was also on the move. During the night of 27-28 August Blaskowitz and his staff transferred to Dijon. Before departing Blaskowitz had a lengthy conversation with the commander and the chief of staff of Nineteenth Army. They discussed the situation carefully. According to Generalleutnant von Gyldenfeldt, Blaskowitz's Chief of Staff, "the influence of the Army Group on the command [of Nineteenth Army] was always maintained." Nineteenth Army and Army Group G worked together "in a fine spirit of trust throughout the whole operation ...."[129]

Blaskowitz repeated his orders that combat elements of Nineteenth Army must reach Lyon as soon as possible. Generalleutnant Botsch informed Blaskowitz "about the course of battle, the withdrawal movement and the intentions of the AOK [Armee Oberkommando]." Blaskowitz was told that IV Luftwaffe Field Corps on the western bank of the Rhône had been ordered to accelerate its retreat so as to arrive at Lyon as soon as possible. It was pointed out that the battles around Montelimar Gate had caused "considerable losses of men, weapons and material and would continue to do so."[126]

Upon reaching Dijon on the morning of 28 August Blaskowitz and his staff found a situation approaching panic. Everywhere there was "heavy guerrilla activity." Blaskowitz issued immediate orders for "everybody to stay at his post for the time being." Although local garrison troops lacked combat value, orders were issued to employ them to establish a security line. Alert units were set up from scattered security troops. Road blocks were constructed and all roads placed under reconnaissance. Check points were established to welcome stragglers and assign them to duty stations on the security line. Measures were taken to supply the troops retreating toward Lyon. Improvisation was the order of the day.[131]

Communications from Dijon were possible not only with the retreating Nineteenth Army but also with OB West. Army Group G was able to inform OB West of the details of combat to date and about its plans for future action. *OKW* also called Dijon by telephone to discuss the situation. It seems that Hitler's "High Command" had intercepted American radio communications and learned that Marseilles and Toulon—the two major French Mediterranean ports which Blaskowitz had garrisoned with a full division each to deny the Allies a port—had both surrendered. Hitler had directly ordered that the garrisons hold out to the last bullet, the last man, but the defenders had not fought quite to the last man. Seven thousand Germans surrendered at Marseilles alone with similar numbers at Toulon; both ports surrendered to the French First Army.[132]

According to Blaskowitz's Chief of Staff, "considerable excitement reigned at *OKW* on the subject of the comparatively rapid capture of ... Toulon and Marseilles." When Blaskowitz was questioned about it his reply was in the nature of a reference to his earlier opposition to such measures and his predictions of the futility of such "fortresses."[133] It was a reply clearly lacking in diplomacy. Cold realism was not often well received by either Hitler or his staff at *OKW*. Candor was frequently found abrasive at *OKW*. Neither was OB West spared Blaskowitz's realistic perception.

On 28 August, OB West had ordered Army Group G to hold the line Neufchâteau—Chaumont—Plateau de Langres—Dijon—Swiss Border—as a bridgehead and assembly area. The plan proposed the assembly of a panzer army in the area which would attack northward into the flank of the advancing U.S. Third Army—Patton.

By 28 August Patton's Third Army had advanced as far as Troyes—one hundred miles east of Paris. There were only eighty miles from Patton's tankers to Dijon. The possibility of Third U.S. Army linking up with Seventh U.S. Army advancing up the Rhône Corridor and catching Nineteenth Army and LXIV Corps in the manuever was Blaskowitz's and Hitler's nightmare. It would have made the formation of any front on the western border of the Reich impossible. As a result, Blaskowitz was extremely skeptical of OB West's plan for holding a bridgehead on the Plateau de Langres, assembling a panzer army and counterattacking the enemy's deep flank. Consistent to a fault, Blaskowitz voiced his doubts "with the ranking commands."[134]

First, it was "uncertain" whether the bridgehead could be held with the available troops; second, given the situation in the west, it was doubtful whether the forces required for such a far ranging attack could be assembled. Thirdly, even if panzer forces became available they would most likely be urgently required at critical points on the front to support the hastily constructed defenses. And even if a panzer army could be assembled, where would the troops necessary to exploit the tank's successes be found? "For all of these reasons the intended attack was ... given minimal consideration by Army Group G and its plans were made correspondingly, which was fully justified by the course of events," according to Hans Gyldenfeldt.[135] In fact, Blaskowitz took particular interest in building up a security line from alarm units strengthening it until it could cover the withdrawal of the various retreating formations.

Hitler and *OKW* already planned operational level counter-attacks, but Nineteenth Army's LXXXV Corps still had its hands full with the tactical situation. During 28 August elements of LXXXV Corps on the eastern bank of the Rhône River were still in the narrow Rhône Corridor around Livron, desperately trying to flee northward while American artillery on the eastern heights had an "artillery man's dream," pouring thousands of rounds of mortar fire onto the desperate Germans, blocking the highway "with the debris of destroyed vehicles and trucks."[136] On the western bank of the Rhône IV Luftwaffe Field Corps approached Lyon, pursued by the First French Army. There was still no contact with LXIV Corps.

It was becoming increasingly clear that the Amis were attempting once again to outflank the Germans north and east of Lyon, blocking the Belfort Gap escape route through the Vosges mountains. Simultaneously, the Third American Army threatened to complete the encirclement of Nineteenth Army and LXIV Corps from the north. The Germans moved by whatever means they could find: trucks, cars, buses, horse-drawn carts, bicycles, pushcarts, or afoot. Columns lived off the land, usually marching only at night, hiding by day."[137] Fearful of being cut off by the converging American armies, they lost men and equipment daily to air attack and ambush by the Maquis. By 29 August reconnaissance elements of 11th Panzer Division confirmed Nineteenth Army's re-exposure to the danger of encirclement.[138]

If the tactical situation of Nineteenth Army were not already gloomy enough, rumors began to circulate that day regarding Lyon, the next destination on the retreat. The alarming "news" that Lyon had broken into "revolt" and that there was also fighting east of the city—another Ami encirclement attempt—was supplemented by radio reports that French troops west of the city had been turned back by the anti-aircraft guns of 277th Anti-aircraft Battalion.[139] Anxiety mounted among the Germans as it became increasingly clear that the retreat could not end at Lyon or the Plateau de Langres.

On 30 August advance elements of IV Luftwaffe Field Corps arriving at Lyon were hastily transferred to the east bank of the Rhône where they reinforced the security line after combining with diverse battle groups from 11th Panzer Division. During the day IV Luftwaffe Field Corps began to use most of its arriving troops, however, on the west bank to build a security line there. On the morrow the troops of LXXXV Corps would be rapidly shuffled through the city. The battle weary and battered corps was thus spared from the fighting for a few days, during which it recuperated and reorganized on the march.

30 August saw the beginning of the end of Nineteenth Army's flight. On the ground the escaping Army began to pass through Lyon. Further north Patton's Third Army had turned northeastward, then stopped at Verdun, out of fuel. The Allies had supply problems; Montgomery received most of the gasoline Patton needed. His Third Army remained stationary for five days only seventy miles from the Rhine.[140] They were days the Germans used well, especially Blaskowitz and his command.

"The loss of time is irreparable in war," Napoleon had suggested.

Few things were as important to that master of warfare: "Strategy is the art of making use of time and space. I am less chary of the latter than of the former; space we can recover, time never."[141] The Allied logistical strategy made the German recovery possible. Army Group B, fleeing from Normandy, might link up with Army Group G after all, given this strategic respite in which to recover. Other factors too, worked in the favor of the Germans, especially of Nineteenth Army and LXIV Corps.

On 30 August the American XII Tactical Air Command changed its operations, recognizing that further destruction of rail and highway communications slowed the American buildup and advance more than it hurt the German retreat.[142] "Any bombing in France now within range of medium bombers ... hurts us more than the Germans," stated one officer with XII Tactical Air Command.[143]

The official American army history described the German plight in France accurately:

> During the first few days of September there had been no coherent German defense. Panic infected rear areas. Supply installations were destroyed without orders, fuel depots demolished, ammunition dumps abandoned, ration and supply installations looted by troops and civilians, and reports on the status of supply non-existent. The retreating units had hardly any heavy weapons. Few of the panzer divisions had more than five to ten tanks in working order. The morale of the troops was depressed by Allied control of the air and by the abundance of Allied material ....[144]

The periodic intelligence summary of the Supreme Headquarters Allied Expeditionary Forces (SHAEF) echoed this assessment: "the enemy in the West has had it ...[The German Army is] no longer a cohesive force but a number of fugitive battle groups, disorganized and even demoralized, short of equipment and arms."[145]

It is perhaps not surprising then, that *The New York Times* quoted a diplomat in Switzerland who had recently returned from Germany and reported that "the main topic of conversation in Germany was that the war was lost." What was startling, was the remainder of the diplomat's report

> It was freely predicted that Field Marshal Guenther von Kluge, Nazi commander in the west, and his subordinate, Field Marshal [sic]

Johannes von [sic] Blaskowitz, would fight their way back to the Rhine and lay down their arms after reaching German soil.[146]

Rumors and "topics of conversation" often prove spurious; so it was in this case. There is no evidence that Blaskowitz had considered actions along this line. For his part, Field Marshal von Kluge was dead, having committed suicide several days earlier after having been removed from command and ordered back to the Fatherland.

Half-way across the continent in his East Prussian headquarters at Rastenberg, not far from Blaskowitz's birthplace, Hitler took what measures he could to solve the crisis on the western front. Field Marshal von Rundstedt was re-appointed OB West once again. At Rundstedt's briefing conference the tension was thick about the gap between Army Group B and Army Group G. The retreat of LXIV Corps and Nineteenth Army seemed "painfully slow." The grave urgency felt there was reflected clearly in the Ultra signals intelligence intercepted by the Allies.[147]

During the same week Hitler had exuded confidence in a display undoubtedly intended to impress his admirer, Baron Oshima, the Japanese Ambassador. The course of the war in the west admittedly had been disappointing "because the German effort had been sabotaged by officers who were members of the 20 July conspiracy to assassinate him." It had been necessary to retreat to the "West Wall" but this did not mean defeat. "'From the beginning,' he said, 'we have realized that in order to stabilize the lines it would be necessary to launch a German counterattack.'" Generaloberst Blaskowitz would carry it out with Army Group G. Then he would combine new forces with the veterans for a major attack.[148]

Beyond such public bravado Hitler had a much better grasp of the terrible reality of his position than he had admitted to Baron Oshima. At his staff conference at Rastenberg that first day of September, while orienting Rundstedt to his assignment, he had pointed to Blaskowitz's Army Group and the critical need to link it up with Army Group B to form a new front. Speaking of Blaskowitz, Hitler said:

> 'If he contrives to do that (*i.e. join up Nineteenth Army rapidly with the main body*) then I will make him a solemn apology for everything' *referring to the disfavour in which he had been since his opposition to the occupation policy in Poland in 1939*).[149]

Forgive Blaskowitz and make a "solemn apology?" The Führer was indeed desperate.

Hitler knew that retreat was the most difficult task confronting any general. In December 1942, discussing Rommel's retreats in North Africa at a military conference he had described retreat in a way that applied equally accurately to the predicament facing Blaskowitz:

> Once a unit has started to flee, the bonds of law and order quickly disappear in the course of the flight unless an iron discipline prevails. It's a thousand times easier to storm forward with an army and gain victories, than to bring back an army in an orderly condition after a setback or a defeat. It was perhaps the greatest feat of 1914 that it was possible to bring back the German army after the idiocy of the Marne business, to turn them around again on a definite line and restore them to order. That was perhaps one of the greatest feats. You can do that only with superb, disciplined troops.[150]

Hitler's awareness of the problems involved in a strategic retreat under pursuit by a superior enemy did nothing to help Blaskowitz on 1 September. In fact, his task became more complex that day. A colonel from LXIV Infantry Corps arrived at Dijon as a liaison officer to report on LXIV Corps' position and activities. It was the first contact with LXIV Corps since shortly after the invasion.

Blaskowitz learned that southwestern and Atlantic Coast France—with the exception of major ports such as Bordeaux—had been abandoned according to orders. The retreating troops had been organized into three march groups. There were approximately ninety to one hundred thousand people involved, including civilian and military personnel.[151]

On 1 September the head of the advance march group was near Nevers, about one hundred miles west of Dijon "as the crow flies," but the third march group had only reached Poitiers, 225 miles distant from Dijon by air but substantially further by French highway. The best estimate of the colonel reporting this information was that the advance elements would reach the Dijon area by about 5 September.[152] It would be much later for the "tail" of LXIV Corps. Since the troops of LXIV Corps were desperately needed for the new defense line near the German border, they might arrive too late to help save the western front.

Decisive moments in military history sometimes occur without warning, often in situations demanding improvisation under pressure. Sometimes decisions are made like this one, with dispirited troops marching to the rear in confusion. Tension builds—stamina is drained, brains are strained to the breaking point in weighing the imponderables. Any general's character is tested. Knowledge and efficiency, stoic calm and character master the situation. "This is noticed and sensed by the troops at once and ... is transmitted to them."[153]

Calmly hearing the colonel's report, Blaskowitz considered the circumstances in this manner, as he later explained:

> I myself issued the decisive order to the 19th Army to interrupt its movements and to receive the LXIV A.K. [Army Corps] in the line Autun—Chalons s/S.[Chalons-sur-Saone] In doing this, I was aware of the fact that this would later result in a critical situation on the Doubs River near Besançon. In order to shorten this crisis, instructions were issued to the LXIV A.K. immediately to send all mobile elements ahead to Dijon without delay. The fact that this would worsen the fate of the immobile, and especially the unarmed, columns had to be taken into the bargain, aside from the necessity to reorganize the entire march system of the Corps. The course of subsequent events has justified both arrangements.[154]

In other words, Blaskowitz analyzed the situation quickly and made a deft decision. His long years of training enabled him to rapidly make a very difficult, highly risky decision. LXIV Corps was ordered to reorganize its march groups on the move and to accelerate its pace. The foremost march group was ordered to guard the northern flank for the other groups. Most critically, the available combat elements in each march group were directed to pull out ahead of their groups and to march as rapidly as possible toward Dijon via Autun on the Langres Plateau. Non combat personnel, unarmed and lacking mobility, were left to their fate under orders to proceed eastward without delay.[155]

Nineteenth Army, which had retreated northward through the Rhône Valley to Lyon as hastily as possible, was ordered to apply the brakes, wheel eastward and establish a security line all the way to the Swiss border, retreating slowly before American and French attacks, delaying wherever possible to gain time for the retreating LXIV Corps to reach Autun and the "safety" of German lines. Arriving units would be immediately fed eastward toward Besançon into positions in the security line or to the northeast toward Neufchâteau where a similar security line had been set up. The key, naturally, was to hold the door open between Autun and Chalon-sûr-Saone on the Plateau de Langres while preventing outflanking manuevers to the east at Besançon and to the north at Neufchâteau. The greatest danger was on the flanks.[156] In effect then, Nineteenth Army would try to hold open a large bridgehead west from Dijon for LXIV Corps.

Confusion is normal in battle. Chaos is a component of combat. Combat operations seldom go according to plan. More than two thousand years earlier Hannibal had remarked that "war is dogged by the elements of chance and unpredictable human error."[157] Conscious of this, Blaskowitz left Dijon to pay a personal visit to Nineteenth Army headquarters at Chalons-sûr-Saone to be certain that his orders were clear.

Chalons-sûr-Saone, about 75 miles north of Lyon on the Saone River, is just southeast of Autun, the western entrance to the Plateau de Langres. A strategic location, it has been the historic site of numerous battles. Julius Caesar had campaigned in this area where the Rhône-Saone corridor widens into a broad wooded valley toward Dijon. Caesar had remarked that the Saone River was "so incredibly sluggish that the eye cannot discern the direction of its current."[158] Quite in contrast, the German retreat was anything but "sluggish."

Blaskowitz arrived at Nineteenth Army headquarters that morning, explained the situation and gave orders. General Wiese reacted as might have been expected; a German general obeys orders. But, as he later wrote: "This order had been a severe load for the Army. Every day of freedom of movement would have been necessary to block the Belfort Gap."[159] The Belfort Gap, historic gateway to Germany, was undefended, as was the last fortress in front of it—Besançon. Predictably, much of the remaining combat in the retreat would be about Besançon and—indirectly—the Belfort Gap.

Weise's Chief of Staff, Generalleutnant Botsch, was immediately impressed with the continued danger to the army flank near the Swiss Border. Encirclement by the Americans remained a possibility.[160] The good news, Blaskowitz announced, was that on the northern flank Patton's Third U.S. Army had turned northeast and no longer threatened to combine with U.S. Seventh Army to encircle Army Group G—at least for the time being.[161]

While Patton's Third U.S. Army had been immobilized by lack of fuel the Germans had been very busy. LXIV Corps continued its accelerated retreat eastward toward the bridgehead. Advance elements of the first march group, the 159th Infantry Division, reached Beaune, between Chalons-sur-Saone and Dijon, on 4 September, having suffered heavy losses of men and vehicles to Ami fighter bombers. They were immediately shifted eastward along the Doubs River toward Besançon, to help guard the entrance to the Belfort Gap. They arrived none too soon.[162]

The previous day, Sunday, 3 September, the Germans had tardily evacuated Lyon. The Americans moved into the city within hours, greeted with "hysterical joy by the city's 600,000 residents ...," who promptly began "smothering the soldiers with kisses ...," as well as turning loose "their pent-up vengeance on collaborationists."[163]

In the meantime, Patton's motionless Third U.S. Army to the north was losing its golden opportunity to deliver the *coup de grace*. Patton believed the attack should continue: "This I felt was particularly true against Germans, because as long as you attack them they cannot find the time to plan how to attack you."[164] Perhaps it was coincidental, but it was this very day—3 September—that Hitler's newest orders arrived.

Notes for Chapter XIII

1. Robichon, *Second D-Day*, 224.

2. MS#B-696 (Botsch), R.G. 338, N.A.; Jacob Devers, "Operation Dragoon: The Invasion of Southern France", *Military Affairs*, Vol. X, No. 2, Summer, 1946, 26.

3. Robichon, *Second D-Day*, 224.

4. Ibid.

5. MS#B-800 (Blaskowitz), R.G. 338, N.A.

6. Ibid.

7. Ibid.; MS#A-882 (Wilutzky), R.G. 338, N.A.

8. *Seventh U.S. Army Operations Report*, I: 28-29; "Another Powerful Blow," *The New York Times*, 16 August 1944, 5.

9. Hastings, *Overlord*, 57; Charles B. MacDonald, *The Mighty Endeavor: American Armed Forces In the European Theater In World War II* (New York: Oxford University Press, 1969), 321.

10. Winston S. Churchill, *Triumph and Tragedy* (Boston: Houghton Mifflin Company, 1953), 57-71; MacDonald, *Mighty Endeavor*, 321.

11. Churchill, *Triumph and Tragedy*, 95.

12. Ronald Lewin, *Ultra Goes to War: The First Account of World War II's Greatest Secret Based on Official Documents*, (New York: McGraw-Hill Book Company, 1978), 147.

13. "Invasion of Southern France," O.T.H., E.T.O., O.C.M.H., D.O.A., 184.

14. "Germans Caught Unaware In South," *The New York Times*, 16 August 1944, 1 and 3.

15. "Resistance Slight In South France," *The New York Times*, 16 August 1944, 1 and 3.

16. Morrison, *Fortress Without a Roof*, 331.

17. "Resistance Slight In South France," *The New York Times*, 16 August 1944, 1 and 3.

18. Ibid; MS#B-402 (Bieringer), R.G. 338, N.A.

19. "Some Nazis Glad to Quit As Allies Swarm Ashore," *The New York Times*, 16 August 1944, 12.

20. Ibid.

21. MacDonald, *Mighty Endeavor*, 321.

22. MS#B-402 (Bieringer), R.G. 338, N.A.

23. "Some Nazis Glad to Quit As Allies Swarm Ashore," *The New York Times*, 16 August 1944, 12.

24. MS#B-402 (Bieringer), R.G. 338, N.A.; MS#B-787 (Wiese), R.G. 338, N.A.; MS#B-696 (Botsch), R.G. 338, N.A.

25. MS#B-787 (Wiese), R.G. 338, N.A.; MS#B-516 (Sodenstern), R.G. 338, N.A.

26. MS#B-696 (Botsch), R.G. 338, N.A.; "Invasion of Southern France", O.T.H., E.T.O., O.C.M.H., D.O.A., 184-185.

27. MS#B-696 (Botsch), R.G. 338, N.A.; MS#A-888 (Kniess), R.G. 338, N.A.

28. MS#A-880 (Wietersheim), R.G. 338, N.A.

29. Hinsley, *British Intelligence*, III, Part 2, 274.

30. "No Enemy Planes Sighted," *The New York Times*, 17 August 1944, 3.

31. "Invasion Gaining," *The New York Times*, 17 August 1944, 1.

32. MS#B-696 (Botsch), R.G. 338, N.A.; MS#A-888 (Kniess), R.G. 338, N.A.; MS#B-787 (Wietersheim), R.G. 338, N.A.

33. Jacob Devers, "Operation Dragoon: The Invasion of Southern France," *Military Affairs*, Vol. X, No. 2, Summer, 1946, 7.

34. MS#B-516 (Sodenstern), R.G. 338, N.A.

35. MS#B-787 (Wiese), R.G. 338, N.A.

36. "Invasion of Southern France," O.T.H., E.T.O., O.C.M.H., D.O.A., 185; MS#B-696 (Botsch), R.G. 338, N.A.; MS#A-880 (Wietersheim), R.G. 338, N.A.

37. Thomas Parrish, *The Ultra Americans—The U.S. Role in Breaking the Nazi Codes* (New York: Stein and Day, 1986), 258; Wilt, *French Riviera Campaign*, 115.

38. Craven and Cate, eds., *The Army Air Forces In World War II*, III: 431.

39. MS#B-488 (Gyldenfeldt), R.G. 338, N.A.; MS#B-800 (Blaskowitz), R.G. 338, N.A.; MS#A-882 (Wilutzky), R.G. 338, N.A.; Hinsley, *British Intelligence*, III, part 2: 274 & 334.

40. Siegfried Westphal, *Erinnerungen* (Mainz: V. Hase & Koehler Verlag, 1975), 273.

41 David G. Chandler, ed., *The Military Maxims of Napoleon*, trans. George D'Aguilar, (New York: MacMillan Publishing Company, 1987), 57.

42. MS#A-954 (Zerbel), R.G. 338, N.A.

43. MS#B-800 (Blaskowitz) R.G. 338, N.A.; MS#B-488 (Gyldenfeldt), R.G. 338, N.A.

44. Mitcham, *Hitler's Legions,* 232.

45. MS#A-888 (Kniess), R.G. 338, N.A.

46. MS#B-787 (Wiese), R.G. 338, N.A.

47. MS#A-880 (Wietersheim), R.G. 338, N.A.

48. MS#787 (Wiese) R.G. 338, N.A.; MS#B-488 (Gyldenfeldt), R.G. 338, N.A.; MS#A-882 (Wilutzky), R.G. 338, N.A.

49. Blumenson, *Duel For France,* 286.

50. MS#B-488 (Gyldenfeldt), R.G. 338, N.A.; MS#B-800 (Blaskowitz), R.G. 338, N.A.; There has been a heated debate in military circles about the proper place for a commander—at the front or behind the troops—in the advance, but even so firm an advocate of leadership from the front as General Hermann Balck agrees that retreats must be "led" from the rear. "Conversation with General Hermann Balck" (Battelle Columbus Laboratories Tactical Technology Center, 13 April 1979), 33, NTIS, AD-A160511.

51. Mitcham, *Hitler's Legions,* 53-54, 134-135, and 434.

52. MS#A-886 (Taeglichsbeck), R.G. 338, N.A.

53. MS#B-488 (Gyldenfeldt), R.G. 338, N.A.; MS#A-868 (Blaskowitz), R.G. 338, N.A.

54. MS#B-488 (Gyldenfeldt), R.G. 338, N.A.

55. MS#A-882 (Wilutzky), R.G. 338, N.A.

56. Ibid.

57. MS#B-488 (Gyldenfeldt), R.G. 338, N.A.; MS#A-949 (Theisen), R.G. 338, N.A.

58. MS#B-488 (Gyldenfeldt), R.G. 338, N.A.

59. Hinsley, *British Intelligence,* III, Part 2, 275.

60. WO 208/4169, P.R.O.

61. "Brain Trust Reported," *The New York Times,* 17 August 1944, 5.

62. MS#B-800 (Blaskowitz), R.G. 338, N.A.

63. MS#A-882 (Wilutzky), R.G. 338, N.A.; MS#A-949 (Theisen), R.G. 338, N.A.; MS#B-800 (Blaskowitz), R.G. 338, N.A.; MS#B-488 (Gyldenfeldt), R.G. 338, N.A.

64. Mitcham, *Hitler's Legions,* 178; MS#B-696 (Botsch), R.G. 338, N.A.

65. *Seventh U.S. Army Operations Report,* I: 174.

66. MS#B-696 (Botsch), R.G. 338, N.A.

67. Hinsley, *British Intelligence*, III, Part 2, 274-276.

68. Parrish, *Ultra Americans*, 258-259; Lewin, *Ultra Goes to War*, 147-148; Bennett, *Ultra In the West*, 160.

69. MS#B-696 (Botsch), R.G. 338, N.A.; MS#B-800 (Blaskowitz), R.G. 338, N.A.; MS#B-787 (Wiese), R.G. 338, N.A.; Wilt, "Wehrmacht in Retreat," 5.

70. MS#B-696 (Botsch), R.G. 338, N.A.; MS#B-787 (Wiese), R.G. 338, N.A.

71. Wilt, "Wehrmacht in Retreat," 5.

72. MS#B-696 (Botsch), R.G. 338, N.A. Botsch reports the loss of radio contact as the 19th but it was probably the 20th since Blaskowitz was in Avignon until the 20th, leaving that day for Pierrelatte.

73. MS#A-954 (Zerbel), R.G. 338, N.A.; MS#A-882 (Wilutzky), R.G. 338, N.A.; MS#B-488 (Gyldenfeldt), R.G. 338, N.A.

74. MS#B-800 (Blaskowitz), R.G. 338, N.A.

75. MS#B-488 (Gyldenfeldt), R.G. 338, N.A.

76. "Invasion of Southern France," O.T.H., E.T.O., O.C.M.H., D.O.A., 186.

77. Ibid., 187.

78. *Seventh U.S. Army Operations Report*, I: 174; MS#A-880 (Wietersheim), R.G. 338, N.A.; MS#B-787 (Wiese), R.G. 338, N.A.; Ironically, it was on this very day that Ernst Kaltenbrunner, head of the *Reichssicherheithauptamt* (Main Security Service headquarters) issued a report condemning "non-political" officers as fundamentally hostile to National Socialism, exhibiting a "complete lack of understanding for National Socialism as a Weltanschauung encompassing life in its entirety." Percy Black, *Ernst Kaltenbrunner: Ideological Soldier of the Third Reich* (Princeton, New Jersey: Princeton University Press, 1984), 166.

79. MS#A-868 (Blaskowitz), R.G. 338, N.A.

80. MS#B-696 (Botsch), R.G. 338, N.A.; *Seventh U.S. Army Operations Report*, I: 181.

81. "Invasion of Southern France," O.T.H., E.T.O., O.C.M.H., D.O.A., 212-213.

82. *Seventh U.S. Army Operations Report*, I: 185-186.

83. Devers, "Operation Dragoon," 39.

84. Ibid., 35; *Seventh U.S. Army Operations Report*, I: 196-197; "Invasion of Southern France," O.T.H., E.T.O, O.C.M.H., D.O.A., 200. This document states that the decision was made on the previous day but not issued until 21 August.

85. MS#B-488 (Gyldenfeldt), R.G. 338, N.A.

86. Ibid.; "Invasion of Southern France," O.T.H., E.T.O., O.C.M.H., D.O.A., 201. Confusion reigned to some extent on both sides. The Seventh Army received only one report of an attack by troops on a column of thirty vehicles

which it destroyed. The attack may have been by the Maquis or have been unsuccessful and consequently unreported Army attack. Lower level formations were not eager to report their failures.

87. MS#B-800 (Blaskowitz), R.G. 338, N.A.; MS#A-882 (Wilutzky), R.G. 338, N.A.; MS#B-488 (Gyldenfeldt), R.G. 338, N.A.; MS#A-949 (Theisen), R.G. 338, N.A.

88. MS#-880 (Wietersheim), R.G. 338, N.A.; MS#B-696 (Botsch), R.G. 338, N.A.

89. *Seventh U.S. Army Operations Report*, I: 196.

90. Vincent Lockhardt, *T-Patch to Victory: The 36th Infantry Division from the Landing in Southern France to the End of World War II* (Canyon, Texas: Staked Plains Press, 1981), pp. 31-32.

91. MS#B-696 (Botsch), R.G. 338, N.A.; MS#A-880 (Wietersheim), R.G. 338, N.A.

92. MS#A-960 (Seiz), R.G. 338, N.A.; MS#B-530 (Dernen), R.G. 338, N.A.

93. MS#B-696 (Botsch), R.G. 338, N.A.

94. MS#A-888 (Kniess), R.G. 338, N.A.

95. Craven and Cate, eds., *Army Air Forces*, III: 433.

96. Aron, *France Reborn*, 348.

97. "Destruction of Germans on Rhône Said to Surpass Anything in War," *The New York Times*, 3 September 1944, 1 & 12.

98. MS#B-488 (Gyldenfeldt), R.G. 338, N.A.

99. MS#B-518 (Botsch), R.G. 338, N.A.

100. "Invasion of Southern France," O.T.H., E.T.O., O.C.M.H., D.O.A., 236.

101. MS#A-875 (Richter), R.G. 338, N.A.

102. "Invasion of Southern France, O.T.H., E.T.O., O.C.M.H., D.O.A., 239.

103. Ibid., 240-241.

104. Lockhart, *T-Patch to Victory*, 34.

105. Ibid., 240-242; *Seventh U.S. Army Operations Report*, I: 198; MS#A-880 (Wietersheim), R.G. 338, N.A.

106. MS#B-787 (Wiese), R.G. 338, N.A.; MS#A-880 (Wietersheim), R.G. 338, N.A.; *Seventh U.S. Army Operations Report*, I: 186,199-200.

107. Hinsley, *British Intelligence*, III, Part 2, 371-372.

108. *Seventh U.S. Army Operations Report*, I: 202-203.; "Invasion of Southern France," O.T.H., E.T.O., O.C.M.H., D.O.A., 243; MS#B-516 (Sodenstern), R.G. 338, N.A.; MS#B-787 (Wiese), R.G. 338, N.A.

109. MS#B-696 (Botsch), R.G. 338, N.A.; MS#A-880 (Wietersheim), R.G. 338, N.A.

110. MS#A-868 (Blaskowitz), R.G. 338, N.A.

111. Anton Donnhauser and Werner Drews, *Der Weg der. 11. Panzer Division* (N.P.: 11 Panzer Division, 1982), 152.

112. Hinsley, *British Intelligence*, III, Part 2, 276; *Seventh U.S. Army Operations Report*, I: 202.

113. MS#A-880 (Wietersheim), R.G. 338, N.A.; MS#B-696 (Botsch), R.G. 338, N.A.; *Seventh U.S. Army Operations Report*, I: 203-204.; Donnhauser and Drews, *Der Weg der 11. Panzer Division*, 152.

114. Parrish, *Ultra Americans*, 259.

115. "Invasion of Southern France," O.T.H., E.T.O., O.C.M.H., D.O.A., 243: Devers, "Operation Dragoon," 36; Weigley, *Eisenhower's Lieutenants*, 232.

116. MS#B-696 (Botsch), R.G. 338, N.A.; MS#A-880 (Wietersheim), R.G. 338, N.A.

117. Lucien Truscott, *Command Mission: A Personal Story* (New York: E.P. Dutton and Company, Inc., 1954), 416-417, 430-431.

118. "Invasion of Southern France," O.T.H., E. T.O., O.C.M., D.O.A., 245; *Seventh U.S. Army Operations Report*, I: 206.

119. Devers, "Operation Dragoon," 36.

120. Staiger, *Rückzug durch Rhonetal*, 69.

121. Hinsley, *British Intelligence*, I: 274-276, 375-376.

122. MS#B-696 (Botsch), R.G. 338, N.A.

123. Ibid.

124. Ibid.

125. Ibid.

126. Ibid,; MS#A-868 (Blaskowitz), R.G. 338, N.A.; MS#B-800 (Blaskowitz), R.G. 338, N.A.

127. MS#A-880 (Wietersheim), R.G. 338, N.A.; MS#B-696 (Botsch), R.G. 338, N.A.; "Invasion of Southern France," O.T.H., E.T.O., O.C.M.H., D.O.A., X-XII.

128. MS#B-787 (Wiese), R.G. 338, N.A.; MS#B-696 (Botsch), R.G. 338, N.A.

129. MS#B-488 (Gyldenfeldt), R.G. 338, N.A.; Gyldenfeldt, Blaskowitz and Oberst I.G. Horst Wilutzky, a member of Blaskowitz's staff, each remembered the conversation taking place on 27 August from Lyon. MS#A-882 (Wilutzky), R.G. 338, N.A.; MS#B-800 (Blaskowitz), R.G. 338, N.A. Nineteenth Army's Chief of Staff, Generalleutnant Botsch, recalled the conversation as being on the following day, 28 August, from Dijon. MS#B-696 (Botsch), R.G. 338, N.A. General Wiese is silent on the matter.

130. MS#B-696 (Botsch), R.G. 338, N.A.

131. MS#B-552 (Gyldenfeldt), R.G. 338, N.A.; MS#A-882 (Wilutzky), R.G. 338, N.A.; MS#B-800 (Blaskowitz), R.G. 338, N.A.

132. *Seventh U.S. Army Operations Report*, I: 167; MacDonald, *Mighty Endeavor*, 322; MS#B-488 (Gyldenfeldt), R.G. 338, N.A.

133. MS#B-552 (Gyldenfeldt), R.G. 338, N.A.

134. Ibid,; Wilt, "Wehrmacht in Retreat," 7; Patton, *War As I Knew It*, 118. Patton gives August 26 as the date of the capture of Troyes.

135. MS#-B-552 (Gyldenfeldt), 57; MS#B-800 (Blaskowitz), R.G. 338, N.A.

136. *Seventh U.S. Army Operations Report*, I: 212; Lockhart, *T-Patch to Victory*, 46.

137. "Invasion of Southern France," O.T.H., E.T.O., O.C.M.H., D.O.A., 255.

138. MS#A-800 (Wietersheim), R.G. 338, N.A.

139. Ibid.; MS#B-787 (Wiese), R.G. 338, N.A.; MS#B-696 (Botsch), R.G. 338, N.A.

140. Cooper, *German Army*, 516.

141. David Chandler, *The Campaigns of Napoleon* (New York: Macmillan Publishing Co., Inc., 1966), 149.

142. *Seventh U.S. Army Operations Report*, I: 223.

143. Craven and Cate, eds., *Army Air Forces in World War II*, III: 434.

144. Martin Blumenson, *Breakout and Pursuit* (United States Army in World War II: The European Theater of Operations, Washington, D.C.: Office of the Chief of Military History, 1961), 698.

145. H. Essame, *Patton: A Study In Command* (New York: Charles Scribner's Sons, 1974), 193.

146. "London, Aug. 28 (U.P.)," *The New York Times*, 29 August 1944, 6.

147. Bennett, *Ultra In the West*, 137-139; Hinsley, *British Intelligence*, III., Part 2, 277 & 375-376.

148. Parrish, *Ultra Americans*, 266-267.

149. Warlimont, *Inside Hitler's Headquarters*, 477.

150. Felix Gilbert, ed. & trans., *Hitler Directs His War* (New York: Award Books, 1950), 52.

151. Wilt, "Wehrmacht in Retreat," 7.

152. MS#B-552 (Gyldenfeldt), R.G. 338, N.A.

153. MS#B-685 (Blumentritt), R.G. 338, N.A.;

154. MS#B-800 (Blaskowitz), R.G. 338, N.A.

155. Ibid; MS#B-552 (Gyldenfeldt), R.G. 338, N.A.; MS#A-868 (Taeglichsbeck), R.G. 338, N.A.

156. MS#A-868 (Blaskowitz), R.G. 338, N.A.

157. Essame, *Patton*, 165.

158. Julius Caesar, *The Gallic Wars and Other Writings*, trans. and intro. Moses Hadas (New York: The Modern Library), 25.

159. MS#B-787 (Wiese), R.G. 338, N.A.

160. MS#B-696 (Botsch), R.G. 338, N.A.

161. Staiger, *Rückzug durchs Rhonetal*, 101.

162. MS#B-530 (Dernen), R.G. 338, N.A.; MS#A-882 (Wilutzky), R.G. 338, N.A.

163. "Lyon Kisses Yanks, Mobs Vichy's Men," *The New York Times*, 4 September 1944, 5.

164. Patton, *War As I Knew It*, 134-135.

CHAPTER XIII

"COUNTERATTACK"

HITLER'S "INTUITIVE" STRATEGY revived the earlier scheme for utilizing the bridgehead west of Dijon not only to receive LXIV Corps, but
also as an assembly area for a counterattack on the southern flank of
Patton's Third Army. Hitler selected the 3rd, 15th and 17th SS Panzer
Grenadier Regiments and three new panzer brigades (111th, 112th and
113th) to carry out the attack. These units were to be supplemented
by the *Panzer Lehr* Division, the 11th Panzer Division and the 21st
Panzer Division "if possible." As quickly as possible, headquarters, Fifth
Panzer Army, was to assume command of the counterattack.[1]

Fifth Panzer Army was commanded by newly promoted General der
Panzertruppe Hasso von Manteuffel. Manteuffel had been called to
Hitler's headquarters for appropriate inspiration, then sent to Fifth
Panzer Army to win a great victory. Manteuffel arrived there on 11
September and quickly judged the situation "hopeless."[2] A German
tank commander from the 21st Panzer Division, Colonel Hans von
Luck, met Manteuffel in the Vosges Mountains quite by chance on 9
September. Manteuffel described the situation to him candidly:

> The 6th U.S. Army Group, including the 1st French Army, is
> approaching from southern France and is supposed to join up with
> Patton. The remains of our retreating armies from the Mediterranean
> and the Atlantic coast are ... still holding a wedge that extends as far
> as Dijon, but for how much longer?
>
> "The worst of it is," Manteuffel went on, "Hitler is juggling with
> divisions that are divisions no more. And now" ironically, and with
> a shake of his head, "Hitler wants to launch a tank attack from the

Dijon area to the north, in order, as he likes to put it, 'to seize Patton in the flank, cut his lines of communication, and destroy him.' What a misjudgement of the possibilities open to us."[3]

It was a situation tottering on the edge of the abyss.

When Colonel von Luck found the headquarters of his own unit, the remnants of 21st Panzer Division, he was greeted by the division commander with the news that he had been awarded the Knight's Cross of the Iron Cross. Significantly, when the champagne toast followed, it was not to "Final Victory, but to our all getting home safely after the war."[4]

Blaskowitz was also not optimistic about the possibility of a success-ful counterattack: "The plan's success depended on speed for it was evident that the separation of the two American Armies (Seventh and Third) could not last much longer." He thought that the necessary panzer forces had to be brought up immediately.[5] The question of whether the existing forces could even hold their present positions and receive the LXIV Corps appeared to him to be in doubt.[6] Blaskowitz moved quickly to get offensive preparations under way, possibly because of his realization that speed was the critical factor, or maybe because he found it necessary to react to the "*Fuehrer Befehl* [Hitler Order] with the promptness expected from a German commander not yet completely cleared of the suspicion that attached itself to all general staff officers after the 20 July putsch."[7]

On 4 September Blaskowitz ordered XLVII Panzer Corps (General Luettwitz) into the area of Neufchateau, but on the following day it had to assume a defensive posture against attacks by the XII and XX U.S. Army Corps. It proved impossible for some of the units planned for the attack to be released from defensive battles elsewhere on the front, especially in the First Army area around Metz. Other units designated for the attack failed to arrive due to gasoline shortages.[8] On 7 September the attack was postponed again. On the following day, Blaskowitz was given command of First Army again and his command became a full-fledged Army Group. This did little to bolster the preparations for the attack, however, since most of the units designated for the attack came from First Army anyway.[9]

Perhaps the most positive result of all of this effort for an offensive was the significant reinforcement of First Army during the lull between

August 31st and 5 September. Only a collection of splinter detachments, individual regiments and staffs without troops at the end of August, First Army was now the strongest of all German Armies in the west with a combat strength which OB West estimated as equal to three panzer grenadier divisions, four and one-half infantry divisions, and one panzer brigade."[10] Nevertheless, the seam where First Army met Nineteenth Army—in the area near Nancy—Neufchateau remained "very insecurely" held.[11] Nineteenth Army still had a wide-open northern flank.[12]

During the days when the American Third Army was immobilized and the German First Army was being reinforced in front of it, the German LXIV Corps continued to retreat toward Nineteenth Army, which was pursued in its turn by the American Seventh Army. Blaskowitz took part in directing these events and also in planning the counterattack, but there was much more going on at Army Group G.

On 3rd September—the day Blaskowitz received Hitler's counterattack order and the day prior to the first troops from retreating LXIV Corps arriving at Beaune on the Plateau de Langres, the Generaloberst transferred his headquarters to Geradmer, a mountain resort town northwest of Mulhouse, on the edge of the Vosges Mountains. He described the purpose of the move (at a later date), as for "the clarification of the present defensive power of the Vosges Mountains."[13] It was a simple enough, straight-forward military mission; but it was not uncomplicated. Blaskowitz's friend, Field Marshal von Rundstedt, might have been speaking for Blaskowitz when he spoke of similar situations: "The pressure from behind," he said, "was always worse than the pressure in front."[14] So it was with Blaskowitz.

On 24 August, nine days after the Allied landing on the French Riviéra, Hitler had issued orders charging the responsibility for the construction of lines of defense in the west to Nazi Party functionaries—Gauleiters—(District Leaders) rather than to the Army. In the area of the Vosges Mountains, where Blaskowitz commanded Army Group G, it was the responsibility of *Gauleiter* Adolf Wagner. *Reichsführer SS* Heinrich Himmler, Chief of the Replacement Army since the 20 July assassination attempt, was in charge of "purely military tasks" regarding defense lines in all areas.[15]

Gauleiter Wagner had the authority to mobilize the population for digging and building defensive works. For this purpose the *Organization Todt* (O.T.) was also employed, as were "volunteer" troops from eastern Europe. The construction did not get under way until September and proceeded slowly. Battles were fought west of the mountains as delaying actions to give the workers time to build fortifications. Construction troops sometimes found themselves suddenly part of the front and suffered heavy losses. "Even the construction of strong points in the mountain passes ... did not advance beyond the initial stages and were hardly any use to the withdrawing troops."[16] At least this was the case as reported by a Generalmajor Hans Taeglichsbeck, who was sent by Blaskowitz to study the status of construction efforts.

No clear picture of the details emerges about what happened—Blaskowitz would talk about it only a little after the war. What is known is that Blaskowitz ordered troops to the area of Belfort to "organize and secure the defenses there, to supplement the labors of the *Organization Todt*. Nevertheless, the hastily constructed defenses had very limited value. They had been begun too late.[17] The details, though lost, can be surmised to some degree. Blaskowitz had another clash with the Nazi party—represented by *Gauleiter* Wagner—this time about construction of the defense line.

It appears that Blaskowitz "protested a Himmler order ... for the construction of a defense line that would be under Himmler's command immediately behind the battle front in the Nancy-Belfort sector." *OKW* apparently supported Blaskowitz's authority in this case.[18] Both Himmler—an old adversary—and *Gauleiter* Wagner were angered to say the least. Wagner seems to have taken steps toward revenge behind the scenes and initiated a denunciation by the Party of Generaloberst Blaskowitz.[19] According to one source, "the district commander came down on him hard—that terrible guy from Baden [Wagner] ...."[20]

Although Blaskowitz's denunciation by *Gauleiter* Wagner did not have *instant* results, it nevertheless did not take very long for Blaskowitz to feel an impact. His command authority was limited, much like that of Rundstedt.[21] He was reduced to the role of transmitter of the Fueher's orders. Under circumstances such as these, Blaskowitz nevertheless had to continue the battle.

Pressure from the rear for the proposed counterattack continued, but was temporarily superceded by Allied pressure against the bridgehead being held open for LXIV Corps' retreat, as well as upon the northwestern and southeastern flanks (First Army and Nineteenth Army respectively) of the bridgehead. Blaskowitz's response to the Allied pressure was sheer improvisation.

Retreating Nineteenth Army units and improvised battlegroups had formed a semblance of a "front" from Chalon-sûr-Saone eastward to the Swiss border via Besançon along the Doubs River. The Belfort Gap was at the eastern end of this line and was the strategic hinge of the position as well as the gateway to Germany. Between Besançon and the Swiss border the U.S. Seventh Army sought once again to encircle the Nineteenth Army.

It was at Besançon, a key communications and supply center on the Doubs River, that Nineteenth Army halted its retreat, turned, and made a determined effort to stop the advancing Amis." It was a natural place to stand and fight.[22] "Besançon is a fortress built by nature and improved by generations of military engineers."

Elements of the 11th Panzer Division reached Besançon, early on the evening of 5 September.[23] The following day heavy fighting exploded around Besançon, but, despite this, the first troops from Nineteenth Army reached Belfort that day. Allied intelligence learned through Ultra that "only nine German and half-a-dozen old French tanks and five 88mm guns with 400 rounds between them," had arrived to bolster the German defense. It proved to be enough for the moment.[24] Despite isolated American breakthroughs at several locations across the Doubs River, each breakthrough was contained. The Germans daringly denuded sections of the front temporarily in order to shift troops eastward along the Doubs River toward Besançon and Belfort.

Blaskowitz described the situation later as Nineteenth Army's being "barely able to pull its head out of the noose which is already tied."[25] All along this front, according to Nineteenth Army's Chief of Staff, the situation was "strained to the bursting point."[26] In such critical circumstances it was difficult to realize that developments had tipped the balance temporarily in favor of the defense. The Allies were not only temporarily short of fuel, but also suffered shortages of artillery ammunitions, anti-freeze, tires, winter clothing and overshoes. Allied intelligence sources had dried up along with their gas tanks. German reliance upon the local telephone network in Lorraine instead of radio communications resulted in diminished operational and tactical intelligence. French Resistance sources of intelligence were also much reduced in Lorraine where the loyalties of the population were divided.[27] All of these factors coincided with a German buildup in Lorraine.

On 8 September, German troops around Montbeliard counterattacked the pursuing French I Corps all along the Doubs River just to the west of Belfort and threw back the French. The retreat phase of German operations on this flank ended with this action.[28]

General Wiese later wrote: "It was an enigma to the Army, why the enemy did not execute the decisive assault on Belfort between 8 and 15 September 1944 through a large scale attack." Only later would Wiese learn that the Americans and the French gave the Germans a "breathing spell" because they needed to regroup.[29] During the "breathing spell," the five days between 10 and 15 September, the Germans "organized, built-up and reinforced ...," a real defense line.[30] In the meantime, along the exposed western bridgehead, another crisis was unfolding. Blaskowitz had to face the long anticipated crisis further north on the First Army front.

In the bridgehead the only remaining road from the west passed through Autun after the capture of Chalons-sûr-Saone on 5 September. LXIV Corps, which had been divided into three marchgroups, had rushed its first two marchgroups into the bridgehead by 9 September, but hoped to hold the gateway open for the last marchgroup, Marchgroup Elster—nearly 20,000 Germans. Further complicating the situation, by this date gaps had developed in Blaskowitz's southern flank since troops from IV Luftwaffe Field Corps and LXXXV Corps had been shifted eastward along the Doubs River toward Besançon. Fortunately for the Germans, the pursuing French and Amis had not yet found the gaps which had been thinly screened to some extent by the troops of LXIV Corps who had previously reached the bridgehead.

Blaskowitz obviously wanted to hold the bridgehead until the arrival of the Elster Marchgroup, but on 9 September Nineteenth Army's Chief of Staff reported to Blaskowitz his opinion that another "painful decision" was essential. It was necessary to order those elements of LXIV Corps already in the bridgehead to retreat eastward since they were in danger of being cut off. Any further retreat meant that Marchgroup Elster was "left to its own fate ...." Blaskowitz gave the necessary approval. The majority—between seventy and eighty thousand men, including virtually all of the combat troops—had escaped.[31]

The situation nevertheless remained on the edge of disaster. Some divisions fighting on the southern flank of the bridgehead had been reduced through attrition to a combat strength of a mere twenty men.[32] During the evening of 9 September Autun fell to the First French Army, slamming shut the last escape route open to Marchgroup Elster. It surrendered two days later.[33]

If it seemed pointless to continue to hold the bridgehead, this is nevertheless what Blaskowitz tried to do. The reason was to preserve an assembly area for the long postponed attack on Patton's southern flank. Tanks rolled straight from the factories in Germany to the western front where they were hastily organized into fresh combat units rather than assigned to the old, experienced, but battered panzer divisions. The 112th Panzer Brigade was one of these new units. Equipped with 48 Mark IV tanks and 48 Mark V heavy Panthers, it should have been a formidable force. Unfortunately, from the Nazi viewpoint, the brigade had not had sufficient training time and the "bugs" had not been removed from the new tanks. Both of these difficulties were supposed to be conquered at the front. Nevertheless, 112th Panzer Brigade was a powerful force—on paper. Fifth Panzer Army too, was a mighty force again—also on paper.

Blaskowitz had been ordered by Hitler to hold the growing tank forces behind the front until they could be concentrated into a major striking force of awesome power. He had also been ordered to hold onto the advanced assembly area in the bridgehead. By 11 September Blaskowitz could no longer do both. His troops could not hold the bridgehead without tank support and tank support could not be provided without dispersing the striking force which so far had been gathered.[33] Blaskowitz's hand was forced.

What forced Blaskowitz to act was the advance of the U.S. XV Corps into the loosely held seam where Nineteenth Army linked up with First Army—the area between Nancy and Neufchateau. The Nineteenth Army commander, General Wiese, had no recourse except to request that the 112th Panzer Brigade and the remnants of the 21st Panzer

Division be immediately subordinated to him to restore the front.[35] On 12 September Blaskowitz ordered the Fifth Panzer Army commander, General Manteuffel, to use the panzer elements requested by Nineteenth Army in a "limited counterattack."[36] The attack proved to be an example of command chaos; the sin of which the methodical Germans were supposedly never guilty. Blaskowitz shared the responsibility for this with his "supreme commander" in East Prussia and with his subordinates who "executed" the attack.

Instead of being commanded by an armored staff, as was usually the case, the armored units in the attack were commanded by LXVI Corps, an infantry staff. The two panzer units taking part, 112th Panzer Brigade and 21st Panzer Division, assembled and attacked separately. Neither unit attacked with confidence that the attack would be successful.[37] The 112th Panzer Brigade advanced in two columns, one of which moved westward toward Dompaire, a village southeast of Mirecourt, on the road from Epinal. The other column and the 21st Panzer Division were to advance toward Dompaire by another route. Fuel supplies did not arrive on time for all attacking elements; everything went wrong for the attackers.

The first attack column of the 112th Panzer Brigade collided with the Second French Armored Division at Dompaire, but the French troops had been warned about the approaching Germans by friendly civilians and were prepared in defensive positions on the heights surrounding Dompaire. The German tanks advanced guilelessly on the low ground in the valley.

The American air support officer accompanying the French Second Armored Division radioed the XIX Tactical Air Command and fighter-bombers plastered the Germans with bombs, fragmentation clusters and highly successful rockets in four separate air strikes while the French simultaneously shelled the Germans with tank and artillery fire from the heights. The valley became a killing ground. Only four heavy tanks from the Panther battalion escaped. A rescue attempt by the Mark IV tank battalion resulted in another sixteen destroyed German tanks. The Allied XV Corps commander called it a "brilliant" example of air-ground coordination, and congratulated the air squadron for their "excellent work."[38] At a single stroke the forces so carefully husbanded for the counterattack were lost along with the assembly area for the attack.

Generalleutnant Botsch described the remaining troops as "badly battered weak units and security forces, very poorly equipped with artillery and antitank material and in no position to resist the enemy ...."[39] Blaskowitz had no choice but to request authorization from the Army High Command to allow a retreat to the Vosges mountains.[40] On 13 September he authorized the evacuation of Nancy except for a small bridgehead.[41]

Blaskowitz could not openly abandon Hitler's plan for a massive counterattack against Patton's Third Army's southern flank, but he no longer controlled either the advanced assembly bridgehead area or sufficient armored troops to mount such an attack. By 14 September he had to tell Field Marshal Rundstedt that the proposed offensive by Fifth Panzer Army was impossible. Blaskowitz protected himself from the accusation that he lacked "offensive spirit" by proposing a smaller counter-attack east of the Moselle River.[42] This meant a retreat by Nineteenth Army into the area of Epinal-Remiremont-Belfort. On 15 September he visited Nineteenth Army headquarters to give the retreat order.[43] The following day he received Hitler's assent to his suggestion that Metz be defended.[44]

Blaskowitz thought that Metz could serve as a rallying point for the German armies in headlong retreat, as well as a suitable place to fight defensively in order to gain time for mounting a counter-offensive and for the so-called "West Wall" to be re-armed.[45] It was an excellent recommendation; Metz was a two-thousand year old fortress complex that had not fallen to assault since 641 A.D. It would hold up Patton's Third Army until mid-December.[46] Hitler had not been inclined to follow Blaskowitz's advice, but fortunately for the Nazis, he changed his mind.[47]

By these measures Blaskowitz had secured the defense along his part of the front to the extent that was possible. He also recognized Hitler's personal interest in the counterattack—obvious to all because of Hitler's personal selection of Manteuffel to command Fifth Panzer Army's counterattack. Blaskowitz therefore proposed an attack by the Fifth Panzer Army smaller than that which had Hitler originally proposed.[48] The operation would begin east of the Moselle River in the Epinal area in the direction of Luneville northward toward Chateau-Salins with the object of cutting off the American armor moving eastward.[49] Remarkably, Hitler agreed to the new scheme. On 16 September Blaskowitz received orders from OB West that the attack must begin no later than 18 September.[50]

When the attack was finally carried out on 18 September, it was executed by only three panzer brigades (111th, 112th and 113th Panzer Brigades), one panzer division (21st Panzer) which had only 24 tanks and lacked combat infantry, and the 15th Panzer Grenadier Division. The 112th Panzer Brigade had been decimated in the ill-fated attack of 12 September around Dompaire. The 111th Panzer Brigade had lost eleven tanks and also its company of mobile antitank guns through air attack and mechanical failure before the attack began. The 113th Brigade was reorganizing after having been scattered by an air attack. Its Panther battalion was in the process of detraining when the attack started. The 15th Panzer Grenadier Division had its reconnaissance battalion at the attack point, but still had its rear columns in the First Army zone. As a result, the attack was initially understrength and the additional elements were committed piecemeal as they arrived. It was a formula for failure.

Manteuffel protested that his army was too weak to attempt an attack on this scale, but received orders that he *would* attack on 18 September. Although the orders came from Blaskowitz, he had merely passed them on from *OKW*, Hitler's High Command.[51] A tank commander from the 21st Panzer Division later called Hitler's plan to attack Patton's flank "senseless, unrealistic" and "illusory."[52] And so it was, but Hitler insisted upon the attack.[53]

The assault began at about 7 A.M. on the morning of 18 September. It met with enough initial success to enter the city of Luneville. At noontime Blaskowitz intervened, ordering Manteuffel to "press the attack and take Luneville,"[54] but American artillery forced the Germans back to the outskirts. Fifth Panzer Army had achieved only a limited advance. That night Blaskowitz ordered Manteuffel to continue the attack in the morning "without regard to the losses already suffered or the crippled condition of the 113th Panzer Brigade."[55] He reprimanded Manteuffel for lacking "offensive spirit."[56]

Attacks the next day achieved no further successes. It was the same the following day, 20 September. General Manteuffel called the attack "an outright waste of men and material." Blaskowitz insisted upon the renewal of the attack since it was, "the desire of the German High Command."[57] Manteuffel received a "short homily on tactics and an order to counterattack."[58] Blaskowitz's insistence upon the attack under hopeless circumstances was clearly the result of pressure from Berlin, but the failure of the attacks had other results; it was Hitler's excuse to once again remove Blaskowitz from command.[59]

Hitler had apparently already made up his mind to dismiss Blaskowitz. On 19 September, according to the records of the German Army Personnel Office, "When it became apparent that the retreat actions and measures taken by Army Group G were not in accordance with the way Hitler expected it to be, Hitler ordered Colonel General Blaskowitz ... relieved."[60] On 20 September General Herman Balck and his Chief of Staff, Major General Friedrich von Mellenthin, arrived without prior notice at Blaskowitz's headquarters in Alsace.

They had already been guests at Hitler's headquarters where

> ...in a voice ringing with indignation Hitler severely criticized the way in which Blaskowitz had commanded his forces, and reproached him with timidity and lack of offensive spirit. In fact he seems to have thought that Blaskowitz could have taken Patton's Third Army in flank and flung it back to Reims.

Mellenthin added: "The absurdity of this criticism soon became clear to us."

> He [Blaskowitz] had just extricated his army group from the south of France under extremely difficult conditions, but his offense was that he had quarreled with Himmler, first in Poland and recently in Alsace. Like so many others, Blaskowitz was made a scapegoat for the gross blunders of Hitler and his entourage.[61]

Hitler continued the fruitless attacks for ten more days.[62] Whether Blaskowitz's dismissal had been based upon "not merely a pretext but a cause for fury" in Hitler's eyes was a moot question.[63] Blaskowitz went home to Dresden at this critical time in Hitler's war. According to a source of variable reliability, Mrs. Blaskowitz then wrote a letter to Swiss relatives stating that: "Hans is now at home, planting cabbage."[64] It seems possible given Blaskowitz's character.

Blaskowitz's achievement in the month between the invasion and the failed counteroffensive has been called a "Masterpiece," an "inspiration;" and "well-nigh a miracle" by one general commenting upon it.[65] One military critic called Blaskowitz a "master of evasive tactics."[66] The official U.S. Army history called Blaskowitz's handling of the retreat "skillfull."[67] In a studiously restrained evaluation which has been echoed by other American historians Alan Wilt stated: "General Blaskowitz ... certainly directed his forces in retreat with great skill and imagination."[68] These last are classics of understatement. The British military historian, Bryan Perrett, has praised Blaskowitz's command of the retreat as "expertly" conducted.[69]

Blaskowitz had overseen the retreat of approximately 240,000 men over distances varying between 300 and 500 miles in roughly 28 days before a vastly superior enemy who totally controlled the air.[70] Despite strong enemy pressure roughly two-thirds of the combat troops had escaped, turned around and counterattacked their pursuers, and then proceeded to stubbornly defend the borders of the Reich well into the winter. Establishment of a continuous defensive front in eastern France and the link-up with Army Group B made possible the continued defense of Germany when the war might otherwise have come to an end. It has been called the "Miracle of the West."[71]

Characteristically modest about his own major role in the "miracle," Blaskowitz later objectively analyzed his achievement with a clinical detachment that revealed his general staff training. The Army group had accomplished its mission—"to evacuate Southern France and gain contact with Heeresgruppe B." But:

> Its accomplishment was bought with unnecessarily high losses of personnel and material. Its success was carried by the skillful coordination of the leadership as well as the stubborn determination on the part of the humble German man to place himself protectively in front of home and hearth ....[72]

He continued: "it had been possible for the time being to screen off the southwestern border of Germany, for which the necessary forces would have been lacking otherwise."[73]

This is a classic understatement. Neither does it acknowledge what Blaskowitz did not know; facts which became public knowledge only many years later. Blaskowitz's achievement had been accomplished against an enemy who had advance knowledge of his circumstances and plans throughout the campaign as a result of Ultra signals intelligence intercepts and decodings.[74] His achievement was therefore all the more remarkable.

Hitler's personal prejudices permitted Blaskowitz few opportunities to win the coveted field marshal's baton. Indeed some have accepted Hitler's prejudices as the last word in *military* wisdom. But others recognize the nature of Blaskowitz's achievements and call him the "Field Marshal without baton."[75] Even the Allied victors paid him tribute in April 1945, when, writing about Heinz Guderian and Blaskowitz, it was stated that: "He [Guderian] became Generaloberst, a rank which he holds still, though there can hardly be an officer of high rank in the whole German Army, except possibly Blaskowitz, who more richly deserves to be a Fieldmarshal."[76]

Against his own wishes, Hitler had been forced to employ Blaskowitz time and again because of Blaskowitz's military merit. But the dictator just as frequently removed Blaskowitz because he could not stomach him. The Generaloberst has been criticized for nevertheless continuing to answer the call of duty. Doubtless he did so despite his hatred of Hitler because he loved Germany and the Germans, and because failure to answer the call in war-time was to his mind desertion in the face of the enemy. He served to the bitter end.

Notes for Chapter XIII

1. H.M. Cole, *The Lorraine Campaign* (United States Army in World War II: The European Theater of Operations, Washington, D.C.: Historical Division, Department of the Army, 1950), 190-193.

2. Brownlow, *Panzer Baron*, 122.

3. Hans von Luck, *Panzer Commander: The Memoirs of Colonel Hans von Luck*, (New York: Praeger, 1989), 168-169.

4. Ibid, 169.

5. MS#B-800 (Blaskowitz), R.G. 338, N.A.

6. Ibid.

7. Cole, *Lorraine Campaign*, 192.

8. Ibid, 192-194.

9. Ibid., 193.

10. Ibid., 48.

11. Ibid., 52.

12. MS#B-552 (Gyldenfeldt), R.G. 338, N.A.

13. MS#B-800 (Blaskowitz), R.G. 338, N.A.

14. Rundstedt Interrogation Report, 1 February 1946, Historical Section, Canadian Military Headquarters, Vol. 10,661, File 215C1.023 (D-41), R.G. 24, P.A.C.

15. Trevor-Roper, ed., *Hitler's War Directives, 1939-1945*, 181-184.

16. MS#B-504 (Taeglichsbeck), R.G. 338, N.A.

17. MS#B-800 (Blaskowitz), R.G. 338, N.A.

18. Cole, *Lorraine Campaign*, 46-47.

19. Westphal Interrogation, 17 December 1947, M-1019, Roll 79, R.G. 238, N.A. Siegfried Westphal was Chief of Staff to Commander in Chief, Field Marshal von Rundstedt in September 1944.

20. Schramm Interrogation, 14 July 1948, M-1019, Roll 66. Percy Ernst Schramm kept the War Diary at *OKW*, R.G. 238, N.A.

21. Rundstedt Interrogation Report, 1 February 1946, Historical Section, Cana-

dian Military Headquarters, Vol. 10,661, File 215C1.023 (D-41), R.G. 24, P.A.C.

22. *Seventh U.S. Army Operations Report,* I: 260.

23. MS#A-880 (Wietersheim), R.G. 338, N.A.; MS#B-696 (Botsch), R.G. 338, N.A.; MS#B-800 (Blaskowitz), R.G. 338, N.A.

24. Bennett, *Ultra In the West,* 161.

25. MS#B-800 (Blaskowitz), R.G. 338, N.A.

26. MS#B-696 (Botsch), R.G. 338, N.A.

27. Christopher Gabel, "The Lorraine Campaign: An Overview, September-December 1944," Combat Studies Institute, U.S. Army Command and General Staff College, Fort Leavenworth, Kansas, February 1985, 6-7.

28. *Seventh U.S. Army Operations Report,* I: 268.; Craven and Cates, eds., *Army Air Forces in World War II,* III: 436.

29. MS#B-787 (Wiese), R.G. 338, N.A.

30. MS#A-880 (Wietersheim), R.G. 338, N.A.

31. MS#B-696 (Botsch), R.G. 338, N.A.; MS#B-800 (Blaskowitz), R.G. 338, N.A.

32. MS#B-696 (Botsch), R.G. 338, N.A.

33. Jean de Lattre de Tassigny, *The History of the French First Army,* trans. Malcolm Barnes (London: George Allen and Unwin Ltd., 1952), 146-151.

34. Cole, *Lorraine Campaign,* 198.

35. MS#B-696, (Botsch), R.G. 338, N.A.

36. Cole, *Lorraine Campaign,* 198.

37. MS#B-696 (Botsch), R.G. 338, N.A.

38. Cole, *Lorraine Campaign,* 199-201.; Forrest Pogue, *The Supreme Command,* (United States Army In World War II: The European Theater of Operations, Washington: Office of the Chief of Military History, 1954), 304.; O.P. Weyland, XIX Tactical Air Command Report (U.S. Army: N.P.,N.D.), 30. Photocopy in author's possession.

39. MS#B-696 (Botsch), R.G. 338, N.A.

40. Ibid.

41. Cole, *Lorraine Campaign,* 95.

42. Ibid, 216-217.; MacDonald, *Mighty Endeavor,* 337-338.

43. MS#B-696 (Botsch), R.G. 338, N.A.

44. Cole, *Lorraine Campaign,* 164-165.; Anthony Kemp, *The Unknown Battle: Metz, 1944,* (New York: Stein and Day, Publishers, 1981), 86-87.

45. MS#ETHINT 32 (Blaskowitz), R.G. 338, N.A.

46. Patton, *War As I Knew It*, 164.

47. Cole, *Lorraine Campaign*, 165.

48. Pogue, *Supreme Command*, 304.

49. Cole, *Lorraine Campaign*, 216-218.; MacDonald, *Mighty Endeavor*, 337-338.

50. Cole, *Lorraine Campaign*, 218.

51. Ibid., 219.; Brownlow, *Panzer Baron*, 122-123.

52. Luck, *Panzer Commander*, 172-173.

53. Brownlow, *Panzer Baron*, 120.

54. Cole, *Lorraine Campaign*, 220-221.

55. Ibid., 226.

56. Ibid.

57. Brownlow, *Panzer Baron*, 123.

58. Cole, *Lorraine Campaign*, 229.

59. Ibid, 222 and 229.; MacDonald, *Mighty Endeavor*, 338.

60. T-78/39/6001495, R.G. 238, N.A.; Hans Adolf Jacobsen *et al* eds., *Kriegstagebuch des OberKommando der Wehrmacht (Wehrmachtführungstab), 1940-1945* (Frankfurt am Main: Bernard & Graefe Verlag für Wehrunesen, 1965), IV: 393-394. According to this source Hitler decided to replace Blaskowitz with Balck on 18th September, the day the offensive began.

61. F.W. von Mellenthin, *Panzer Battles: A Study of the Employment of Armor in the Second World War*, trans. H. Betzler, Ed. L.C.F. Turner (New York: Ballantine Books, 1971), 371-372. According to one American post-war view, Blaskowitz was relieved since he was "politically suspect because he was personally independent." Chester Wilmot, *The Struggle For Europe*, (New York: Harper & Brothers, Publishers, 1952), 538.

62. Pogue, *Supreme Command*, 304.

63. Weigley, *Eisenhower's Lieutenants*, 340.

64. S.H.A.E.F. Digest 226, 18 January 1945, Allied Operational and Occupation Headquarters, W.W. II, Supreme Headquarters Allied Expeditionary Forces (S.H.A.E.F.), General Staff. G-2 Division, Operational Intelligence Sub-Division, Intelligence Reports, 1942-1945, R.G. 331, N.A.

65. MS#B-516 (Sodenstern), R.G. 338, N.A.

66. Strategicus (Pseud.), *The Victory Campaign (May 1944-August 1945)*, (London: Faber and Faber, 1947), 28. "Strategicus" was the pseudonym for Herbert Charles O'Neill.

67. Pogue, *Supreme Command*, 229.

68. Wilt, *French Riviera Campaign*, 162; Weigley, *Eisenhower's Lieutenants*, 340.

69. Bryan Perrett, *Knights of the Black Cross: Hitler's Panzerwaffe and Its Leaders* (New York: Dorsett Press, 1994), 207.

70. Wilt, "Wehrmacht in Retreat," 9.

71. Blumenson, *Duel For France*, 410.; Hinsley, *British Intelligence*, III, Part 2, 390; Westphal, *German Army in the West*, 170.

72. MS#B-800 (Blaskowitz), R.G. 338, N.A.

73. Ibid.

74. Hinsley, *British Intelligence*, III, Part 2, 274-277, 375-377 and 391-392.

75. Steuben, "So blieb er ohne Marshallstab,". 11-12.; Möller-Witten, *Mit dem Eichenlaub zum Ritterkreuz* ("Der Feldherr Ohne Marshallstab"), 213.

76. WO 208/4412, P.R.O.

CHAPTER XIV

DEFEAT

AT HOME IN DRESDEN, once again relieved of command, Blaskowitz had no influence upon events. Little is known about these days in his life. He spent them with his wife, sometimes trying to help friends locate missing relatives in the army,[1] sometimes corresponding with old friends.[2] On 28 October Hitler received Blaskowitz in Berlin and presented him with the Oak Leaf Cluster to the Knight's Cross.[3] There is no record that Hitler offered a "solemn apology." The announcement of Blaskowitz's removal from command was not made publicly in Germany until nearly the end of November.[4]

If Blaskowitz studied the situation of his last command during these months he may have been moderately encouraged, autumn had been twice as rainy as usual and the Allied advance had virtually stopped.[5]

Wehrmacht morale, however, was predictably not at its best by November of 1944. According to one study by the S.H.A.E.F. Psychological Warfare Division, only fifteen percent of German P.O.W.s captured the previous month still believed in the possibility of German victory and a compromise peace. Remarkably, however, over fifty percent still expressed some measure of devotion to Hitler.[6] The war naturally continued under circumstances such as these.

On Christmas Eve, 1944, Blaskowitz was suddenly called to Berlin and given a new command.[7] He received his new assignment on the mutual "insistence" of both von Rundstedt and Jodl at *OKW.*[8]

Ironically, Blaskowitz was appointed to fill the very position from which he had been removed only three months earlier—commander of Army Group G.[9] He reported to Hitler that night, finding him obviously burdened and feeling the after-affects of the assassination attempt of 20th July as well as the cumulative effect of years of heavy responsibility: "Hitler's left shoulder drooped and the hand trembled, but he seemed as alert as ever when he talked and at such times apparently forgot his ailments."[10]

On 16 December, a week earlier, the German attack in the Ardennes which became known as the "Battle of the Bulge" had been launched. That day the Army Group G commander, General Hermann Balck, had opened a sealed envelope whose contents told him about the attack and ordered preparations for an attack by Army Group G to support the attack in the Ardennes.[11] On 22 December General Balck was suddenly transferred to special duties and Generalleutnant Hans von Obstfelder assumed temporary command of Army Group G until Blaskowitz arrived. That same day the Army Group Chief of Staff was ordered to plan an attack.

The Chief of Staff proposed an attack westward from the Saar-bruecken area in the direction of Metz. Another suggested operation was an attack southward toward Strasbourg with the aim of eliminating the flank threat to Nineteenth Army troops in the Colmar pocket.[12] Hitler rejected both plans but accepted a third plan proposed the following day which was far more ambitious, calling for a joint operation by First Army under Army Group G, and Nineteenth Army under Army Group Oberrheim. Army Group Oberrhein was commanded by *Reichsführer SS* Heinrich Himmler, so Blaskowitz would be a partner to his erstwhile enemy in the last German offensive of the war on the Western Front. It was named "Operation Northwind."

Operation Northwind called for First Army attacks southward and westward from the areas of the Saar and the Rhine in conjunction with Nineteenth Army attacks northward from the Colmar Pocket. Saverne was to be re-taken and First Army linked with Nineteenth Army, re-conquering Alsace and annihilating enemy forces there in the process.[13] It was a plan which was well-conceived strategically, but which had the singular weakness of being impossible to execute. The German Armies with which Hitler planned to attack "did not have the potential to execute such an undertaking."[14]

It was clear that an attack on Saverne could only be carried out by First Army through the lower Vosges Mountains, east of Bitsche. When the plan was presented on 24 December by Blaskowitz, Hitler insisted on altering it to include two attacks, one through the Vosges and the other west of the Vosges. The dictator's changes did not recognize either the condition of the troops or the essential requirement for a single center of gravity in the attack to provide some hope for success.[15]

Blaskowitz's troops in First Army were a collection of units which had been battered in varying degrees in earlier fighting. It included units such as the 416th Infantry Division which was nicknamed the "Whipped Cream Division" because of the special diets the older men of the division required.[16] On paper the 17th SS Panzer Grenadier Division, with 90 self-propelled assault guns and a full complement of personnel, was Blaskowitz's strongest unit. The reality, however, was that the division was made up of eastern European *Völksdeutsche* of dubious dependability.[17] All of the attacking infantry units except the 17th SS Panzer Grenadier Division lacked tanks and self-propelled guns and were short of artillery ammunition. Army Group G had absolutely no reserves and could count on no Luftwaffe support against an enemy who dominated the sky.[18] Hitler's attack plans were better suited to a fantasy than to the situation in the Alsace area.

On 28 December Blaskowitz, Rundstedt, Keitel, Jodl and Hitler discussed the proposed attack at Rundstedt's Adlerhorst headquarters.[19] Himmler arrived there late. Later that day the officers were told to attend a special briefing where Hitler would deliver a speech. One officer recalled:

> We were, ... all stripped of our weapons and briefcases, loaded into buses and then driven about the countryside for about half an hour. Finally we were led into a large room which was surrounded with SS Guards who watched our every move. Then Hitler arrived accompanied by Fieldmarshal Keitel and General Jodl. Hitler looked sick and broken....[20]

Hitler harangued the officers with a speech that reviewed the entire war and emphasized the critical nature of this offensive for Germany's destiny. Announcing the New Year's Eve attack deadline, he concluded: "In German history New Year's night has always been a good military omen." Rundstedt answered for the assembled commanders, promising that everything possible would be done to assure success.[21] There was not to be any real success.

Blaskowitz had been ordered to command an attack in which battle-weary troops without numerical superiority against the enemy, poorly supplied, "living hand to mouth" with severe rationing even for ammunition and gasoline, were to execute a hastily planned operational assault without any air cover in difficult terrain, in deep snow and over ice-covered roads.[22] It was an assignment with little chance for success but he had been ordered to carry it out and would do his utmost. As one military historian later assessed him, "Blaskowitz was a general who continually reappeared in critical commands, despite his notorious coolness toward the Nazis, on the simple ground of his military competence."[23] Nevertheless, it would take more than proficiency to be victorious in this attack. Much like the troops under his command, Blaskowitz was true to his sense of duty and fought bravely, but had inadequate means to win victory: "Even the greatest will to fight could not gain a victory over [American] material superiority."[24]

The attackers enforced strict orders for radio discipline, permitting no transmitting of orders by radio.[25] For the second time within a month Ultra failed to warn of a German attack.[26] The Germans nevertheless did not attain complete surprise. German prisoners taken on 31 December revealed the hour of the attack to their American captors.[27] Already on 26 December Eisenhower had anticipated the German plan, or perhaps he had only shortened the bulge in his own line of defense, but the result was the same. He had given orders to prepare rear defense lines and to withdraw if necessary in the event of an attack in northern Alsace—exactly where the German First Army planned to attack.[28] The element of surprise—perhaps Blaskowitz's strongest weapon—had been compromised. So had the attack.

Blaskowitz established a command post at Massweiler in a bunker on the "West Wall." He wanted to supervise the attack closely. First Army had its headquarters in Massweiler also and was linked to Blaskowitz by telephone. Coordinating the attack would not be unduly problematic with arrangements such as these.

Some troops in Blaskowitz's command toasted that New Year's Eve to a "New Year full of question marks ...."[29] The offensive itself was really a question mark. Would it force the Americans to transfer troops from the "Bulge" sector, fueling renewed success there? At 2300 hours the attack spearheads began the assault without preliminary artillery bombardment.

After some initial success the attack bogged down.[30] Combat strength among the attacking units, "compelled to fight without rest and live in the open ...," visibly abated.[31] "They won ground, but for that they lay unprotected in unprepared positions, exposed to the enemy and the inclement weather ...."[32] According to one German colonel, "Here at the front the young men ... quickly shed their illusions about marching with Hitler into a 'Thousand-Year Reich.' They ... soon grasped the difference between propaganda and reality."[33] Sporadic tactical successes and territorial gains did not translate into strategic success.[34] No relief was won for their fellow Germans attacking in the "Bulge" despite the "fanatic" efforts made by infantrymen in Operation Northwind.[35]

On 9 January Blaskowitz informed OB West (Rundstedt), in a message also received by the *OKW*, that "Operation Northwind" had ceased to be effective after initial success, simply because insufficient infantry forces were available to occupy the conquered territory, replace casualties and continue the attack. Because of his superior mobility, better equipment and more numerous troops, together with air superiority, the enemy had recovered from the initial shock of the attack, fortified his new front line, and prepared to counterattack if the opportunity presented itself. Blaskowitz proposed to continue the attack in the direction of Hagenau to keep the Americans off balance and requested more tank and infantry divisions as reinforcements.[36]

Reports emphasizing reality were often poorly received by Hitler, who frequently confused the messenger with the message. The truth was that Blaskowitz issued realistic evaluations of situations in his reports, and this upset Hitler, who labeled the reports "pessimistic."[37] By the end of the month the Führer again dismissed Blaskowitz, allegedly because he "did not display sufficient initiative ...." In the opinion of General Siegfried Westphal, "the fact that Himmler insisted upon having a high SS officer as Commanding General of an Army Group was an important factor in Blaskowitz's dismissal."[38] For the remainder of the month, however, Blaskowitz continued as commander of Army Group G. The last German offensive in the west, although no longer called "Operation Northwind," continued as well.

Blaskowitz prepared a plan for a continuation of the attack as demanded by Hitler, but an alternative plan was proposed by *Reichsführer SS* Himmler which shifted the main weight of the proposed offensive to his own Nineteenth Army. Rundstedt preferred Blaskowitz's plan but Hitler sided with Himmler. Continued interference in operations sealed the fate of the unsuccessful attack. It had no further success at all; the front became stabilized.[39]

The Germans had made only an insignificant "improvement in their over-all situation."[40] According to one source, the attack had really only had "nuisance value."[41] Further compounding the already difficult German military predicament, on 21 January Hitler issued a directive which held commanders responsible for reporting in advance to him all decisions pertaining to operational movements, even down to the tactical level.[42] This order reduced all German commanders to the role of Hitler's local chiefs of staff.[43]

It was a critical time for the moribund and disintegrating Third Reich. The Russian winter offensive against Army Group North had overrun Blaskowitz's birthplace in East Prussia. In both the east and the west the fight had reached German soil.

On 27 January 1945, between 4:20 A.M. and 6:50 P.M. at Hitler's headquarters the question of command organization along the western front was raised by Generaloberst Jodl. The question was whether to replace Generaloberst Kurt Student, commander of Army Group H along the northern Rhine, with Blaskowitz, transferring Blaskowitz there from Army Group G.

Generaloberst Student, a well-built man, 55 years old, just over six feet tall, looked more like "a successful business executive rather than the intrepid leader of all German parachutists." He had a "dominant forehead, thinning hair, pale face and [a] high pitched voice ...."[44] He had been largely responsible for the creation of the German parachute forces and was famous for his airborne capture of Eben Emael in May 1940 and his conquest of Crete in 1941.[45] By this late time in the war he thought of himself as Hitler's "trouble-shooter."[46]

Nevertheless, von Rundstedt considered Student's capabilities inadequate for such a high position as Army Group H commander. He made a special request for Blaskowitz's appointment to the position.[47]

Hermann Goering, who attended the conference that night at

Hitler's headquarters, defended Student against reports that he was "worn out" by arguing that he was "still one of our staunchest and most steady men, one who will hold tight when it gets tough again."

The discussion continued with Goering defending Student:

> GOERING: He is a tenacious guy. He may not be a genius in other respects, but he is staunch and straightforward and he knows that his troops must hang on....
>
> HITLER: ...I'm not sure what to do. Is Blaskowitz tenacious like that?
>
> GOERING: No, he's much more pliable. Student's little toe is worth more than all of Blaskowitz.
>
> HITLER: That's just the question.[48]

Despite such discussion, Hitler decided to grant Rundstedt's request and to transfer Blaskowitz to Army Group H, removing Student from command. The dictator did not know it, but he had been tricked by his "faithful" servant, Field Marshal Keitel.

It was Keitel who had received Rundstedt's request to transfer Blaskowitz to command of Army Group H. Keitel, however, did not go directly to Hitler with the request, but instead reported to Hitler that Student was sick, probably because he did not think that Hitler would appoint Blaskowitz. Keitel knew that Hitler had a special liking for Student. The ruse worked, Blaskowitz was appointed. The story did not end here, however, for Hitler eventually learned the truth.[49]

At 1200 hours on 29 January Generaloberst Hausser took command of Army Group G from Blaskowitz, who took command of Army Group H immediately. Blaskowitz's new assignment was a dismal one. He faced the British under Montgomery for the first time. His responsibility was to keep "Monty's" British, Canadian and American troops from crossing the Rhine, but he was without the means to do so. In less than two weeks Canadian Intelligence learned that Blaskowitz had been visiting the key points on Army Group H's front and concluded that he had replaced Student. "Blaskowitz, recognized as an able field commander if not an equally good Nazi, may have been given the field appointment ...," concluded the Canadians.[50] So it was, and it led to Blaskowitz's brief adventure in intrigue.

February, 1945 was a time when involvement in any intrigue could easily prove terminal. Drastic preventive measures had already been taken by the Nazis. Since the attempted assasination of Hitler on 20th July "*Sippenhaftung*" had been practiced in the Fatherland. It meant that relatives were held responsible for "treasonous" acts. Punishment might mean anything from confinement in a concentration camp to confiscation of property and the relative's ration cards, tantamount to starvation.[51] Despite the extreme danger, Blaskowitz took the risk. It is nevertheless not an episode that does not qualifies as one of Blaskowitz's more noble moments.

In mid-December 1944, Alexander Constantin von Neurath, German Consul in Lugano, Italy, and son of the former German Foreign Minister, met Gero von Gaevernitz, who worked for the U.S. as an OSS agent in Switzerland. Gaevernitz was interested in establishing candlestine contact with German Army Commanders on the western front with the aim of negotiating a termination of resistance by the German armies in the west. The OSS chief in Switzerland, Allen Dulles, and Gaevernitz had tried without success to find a German commander on the western front with the courage to act. They later wrote:

> They were all surrounded by agents of Himmler's Gestapo. They were terrified and subdued by the brutal ... massacre of the Generals following the July 20th affair, and were disposed to hide behind their oath of allegiance to the Fuehrer—German or rather Prussian military abhorrence of "Eidbruch" (breaking the oath) played a sinister role during those days.[52]

Neurath was convinced that the war was lost and that it was criminal to continue it. At considerable personal risk, he was prepared to help arrange an early end to the war. He knew many of the highest ranking German officers personally and was willing to approach Field Marshals Rundstedt and Kesselring, Colonel-General Blaskowitz and General Siegfried Westphal, Rundstedt's chief of staff.[53]

In January, 1945 young Neurath visited Field Marshal Kesselring in Italy to discuss the possibilities of local surrenders in Italy and on the western front. Kesselring arranged for Neurath to meet with Blaskowitz and Rundstedt's chief of staff, Lieutenant General Westphal, on 10 February at a secret rendezvous in a small village inn near Stuttgart. Blaskowitz and Westphal travelled in mufti to avoid notice by the Gestapo.[54]

All three agreed that continuation of the war was hopeless; Germany had been defeated. Neurath suggested that they work together to open the western front to the Allies. The generals noted that it was difficult to do this in the light of the fanaticism of the SS and the state of mind of their army troops. Their armies included large numbers of Germans from East Prussia and eastern Germany whose homes had been overrun by the Russians and who felt they had nothing to lose. Their fighting spirit was unshaken and they were ready to fight to the end.

Westphal and Blaskowitz wanted assurances that generals cooperating in the scheme would not be included on any war criminals list and might have an opportunity to demobilize the *Wehrmacht* themselves. Neither general had "definite suggestions," but Neurath reported to the OSS that the two generals "might be approaching the point where they would carry through a capitulation."[55]

The OSS pursued these negotiations and they led to a local surrender in Italy shortly before the war's end. But in northwest Europe they led to nothing. On 1 May SS Obergruppenführer Karl Wolff, who negotiated the surrender in Italy, again contacted Blaskowitz, who had by then been transferred to the command of Twenty-fifth Army in Holland, and attempted to persuade him to surrender. Blaskowitz took only a moment to tell Wolff that he would not get involved.[56] Shortly after the end of the war Wolff explained to an SS Sturmbahnfuehrer while both were Allied P.O.W.s, unaware that their conversation was being recorded:

> Another iron we had in the fire, with the aid of a middle-man to Kesselring—Blasgowitz (?) [sic] had also failed, because he was too cowardly and clumsy and too interested in his own gain, to have the strength and courage to get Kesselring on our side.[57]

Wolff's judgment of Blaskowitz in the sole episode of intrigue in Blaskowitz's life is certainly severe. It is particularly harsh when it is realized that Blaskowitz, known to some in Germany as a "pronounced anti-Nazi," was likely to be under close Gestapo scrutiny.[58] Nevertheless, despite the obvious mitigating factors, there remains an element of truth in such a judgment. Traditional military doctrine, as stated by Napoleon, proscribed such conduct as "infamous."[59] It is less clearly so in Blaskowitz's case. What is most regrettable—although understandable—was his interest in gaining an exemption for himself personally. The episode adds nothing to the generaloberst's honor; if anything it diminishes his stature. Perhaps, however, he only made this effort due to the insistence of his old friend von Rundstedt.

Four days after the meeting between Blaskowitz, Westphal and Neurath—14 February 1945—Allied Air Force bombers began the systematic incineration of Dresden, Blaskowitz's last home. His house survived the bombing as did his wife and daughter. He knew that they had gone to Bad Kissingen only a few days before the terrible firestorm left Dresden in ashes.[60] It was a narrow and precarious escape. The bombing did not add to the Allies' fund of honor. If anything, it gave some apparent credence to Nazi charges that "The allies and Russia are united on one thing, to annihilate and destroy the German people totally ...."[61]

Blaskowitz's assignment as commander of Army Group H provided no cause for optimism. His arrival in Holland was not to be confused with the "wonder weapons" Hitler had promised. Charged with the responsibility to defend the northern Rhine River against crossing attempts by Montgomery's 21st Army Group, Blaskowitz ordered all possible defensive measures, but realistically "looked to the future with great anxiety."[62]

He had no strategic and practically no tactical reserves, expected no Luftwaffe support, was low on supplies and acutely short of mobile anti-tank weapons; he commanded an army group that was a hodge-podge of units that had been continually battered since June 1944. Many of the "troops" were Naval and Luftwaffe personnel without any training in their role as ground troops. Reserves were limited to the 34th SS Division (Netherlands). Fuel supplies were scarce! Reinforcements were needed desperately but were unavailable because of heavy fighting further south and in the east. "In spite of the situation, Army Group [H] was resolved to the last man to defend every inch of soil and to render as difficult as possible the enemy attempt to thrust towards the Ruhr area ..., Germany's last armoured forge."[63]

The fighting along Army Group H's front during the autumn had left the Allies in control of a line that ran roughly from the North Sea along the Maas River eastward as far as Nijmegen, the northeastern most point held after the end of Operation Market Garden. From Nijmegen southward the front roughly followed the German border as far south as Strasbourg. Army Group H was responsible for the

Fortress Holland

September 1944 - May 1945

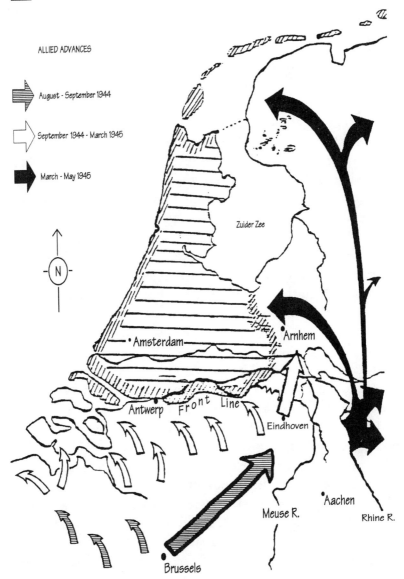

German Defensive
Positions

German Occupied
Northwest Holland

ALLIED ADVANCES

August - September 1944

September 1944 - March 1945

March - May 1945

N

Zuider Zee

Amsterdam

Arnhem

Antwerp Front Line

Eindhoven

Aachen

Meuse R.

Rhine R.

Brussels

defense of Holland north of the Maas River and from the Nijmegen area southward as far as Roermond (west of Dusseldorff). The Twenty-fifth Army under the command of General Gustav von Zangen, guarded the Maas River line while the First Parachute Army, commanded by General Alfred Schlemm, defended the Rhineland.

During December 1944 Army Group H's front was comparatively quiet since all German and Allied energies were concentrated upon the Battle of the Bulge further south. By the middle of January, however, the Allies had decided to clear the Rhineland by attacks all along the front virtually from the North Sea to the Swiss border.[64]

Generaloberst Blaskowitz located his headquarters just east of Zutphen (northeast of Arnhem) on the Ijseel River in Holland, about mid-way on the "hinge" or "joint" which connected Twenty-fifth Army with First Parachute Army.[65] Although his Army Group was in relatively better condition than Army Groups B and G further south on the German border,[66] there was little solace to be found in this fact.

Blaskowitz and his immediate superior, Field Marshal von Rundstedt, who was once again OB West, were agreed on the strategy they thought the Allies would follow. Both expected the Americans to launch the main attack across the Roer River, followed by an Anglo-Canadian (21 Army Group under Montgomery) diversionary attack a few days later further north. An attack developed along these lines would enable the Allies to envelop the Ruhr, the Americans on the southern wing and the Anglo-Canadians to the north. It was a classic strategy.

German military intelligence was so discredited by January 1945 that Rundstedt and Blaskowitz anticipated the Allied attack and made their own defensive dispositions according to their conception of how the attack would transpire. There was almost no aerial reconnaissance, few army patrols due to the many rivers and inundations, and thus nothing to contradict their own conceptions.[67] Unfortunately for the Germans, neither Rundstedt nor Blaskowitz was clairvoyant.

The Allied plan of attack was code-named "Operation Veritable." Contrary to the expectations of Rundstedt and Blaskowitz, "Veritable" was not aimed at the Ruhr, but instead simply at clearing the west bank of the Rhine of German forces. It did not include an attack northward into Holland but instead was a two pronged attack. First

Canadian Army would attack southeast from the Nijmegen area while the U.S. Ninth Army would attack northeastward to meet the Canadians. The aim was to capture so many Germans in the net that it would be impossible for the Germans to mount a strong resistance against the leap across the Rhine which was to follow "Veritable."[68]

The attack began on the morning of 8 February supported by over one thousand Allied artillery pieces, the "heaviest barrage hitherto experienced and by heavy attacks of strong formations of four-engine bombers ...."[69] In addition to this, the 2nd Tactical Air Force provided close support for ground troops with a thousand fighters and fighter-bombers. When the artillery and air assault began at 5 A.M. that morning there was such a constant flash of gunfire that it was light enough to read a book; it was the greatest artillery barrage in British history.[70]

Nevertheless clouds overhead limited Allied tactical air support and water and mud slowed the ground assault. Both sides needed webfeet and waterproof skin. Four Allied divisions attacked from the direction of Nijmegen toward the Reichswald, a forest which was sometimes called the "side door to the Ruhr."[71] The Germans added to miserable conditions by opening dike sluices selectively, flooding critical areas. Despite the benefit of tactical surprise, the First Parachute Army recovered quickly and fiercely contested every yard of the difficult ground. It was some of the bitterest fighting in all of World War II.[72]

General Schlemm screamed for reinforcements which Blaskowitz released the next day, after receiving them himself from Rundstedt. The OB West reserve was the XLVII Panzer Corps; the 116th Panzer Division, the 15th Panzer Grenadier Division, and later also the *Panzer Lehr* Division, which were sufficient to stall the Anglo-Canadian assault east of the town of Cleve, northeast of the Reichswald, and at the eastern edge of the Reichswald itself. These reinforcements, however were inadequate to firmly halt the Allied attack.

When Blaskowitz realized the need for further reinforcements he could turn only to General Günther Blumentritt, who had replaced General von Zangen as commander of Twenty-fifth Army a few days before Operation Veritable began. Blumentritt was a Bavarian officer, intelligent and friendly, who gave the impression of balance and good judgment.[73] He no sooner arrived in Holland to take command of

Twenty-fifth Army's defense of the Maas River when Blaskowitz ruthlessly stripped his front, transferring the 6th Parachute Division, then the 2nd Parachute Division, the 361st Infantry Division and finally a regiment of the 346th Infantry Division to First Parachute Army.[74] Twenty-fifth Army became a skeletal force capable only of "observation" of the Allies across the Maas River.[75] Holland was virtually without defense but continued to be "occupied" by the Germans under Allied observation.

The U.S. Ninth Army, which was supposed to be the southern pincer of the attack, code-named Operation Grenade, was supposed to attack across the Roer, turn north to meet the Anglo-Canadians, and sweep the lower Rhineland free of Nazis. It did not turn out to be so simple. General Schlemm anticipated Ninth Army's assault, scheduled for 10 February, by disabling the discharge valves on the Schwammenauel Dam. This was even more effective than blowing up the dam since the flood tide was released steadily. Within hours the Roer River rose five feet and overflowed its banks. The flood conditions created by Schlemm's canny tactic postponed Ninth Army's attack until 23 February.[76] The Rhineland was not cleared of German troops until 5 March, except for a few small bridgeheads.

The Germans fought with "utmost obstinacy," according to the 43rd Wessex Divisional historian,[77] but overwhelming superiority of numbers, an armada of amphibious weapons, complete control of the air, and massive artillery superiority all took their toll. The terrain and weather had aided the German defense. Eisenhower later stated, "Probably no assault in this war has been conducted under more appalling conditions of terrain."[78] But this only delayed the inevitable.

When the U.S. First Army, which fought opposite the German Fifteen Army (part of Army Group B) in the area of the Rhineland opposite the Cologne-Koblenz region, successfully shattered the right wing of Fifteenth Army, the left wing of Schlemm's First Parachute Army was without flank protection. The time for further difficult decisions was at hand.

Although the west bank of the Rhineland had been virtually cleared of German troops, the First Parachute Army still held small bridgeheads at Wesel, Homberg, Duisberg and Verdingen. General Schlemm, commander of the First Parachute Army, or rather what was left of it, directed the defense of the Wesel bridgehead. Behind the bridgehead at Wesel, as well as each of the other bridgeheads, was a bridge across the Rhine. There were also a number of ferries working on the river. Naturally, Hitler took special interest in these bridges. On 3 March Hitler personally issued orders that the bridges were not to be blown up until the very last moment to enable supplies to reach the troops in the bridgeheads and to permit industrial machinery evacuated into the bridgehead to be transferred to the east bank of the Rhine.[79]

Hitler also forbade, by a second order, transfer to the east bank of the Rhine even a single soldier, weapon, or vehicle without his personal permission. Finally a third order insisted that no bridge was to be allowed to be captured intact, or Schlemm, would "answer with his head." "Since I had nine bridges in my army sector," said Schlemm, "I could see my hopes for a long life rapidly dwindling."[80]

Hitler's orders meant that each shrinking bridgehead, supposedly held to keep the Rhine free from shelling, became a concentration of men without military purpose, crushed together with damaged and useless equipment, staffs without troops, artillery without ammunition, tanks and trucks without fuel, all packed together within range of Allied artillery and pounded from the air.[81] These orders amounted to military insanity. First Hitler had demanded the army defend the west bank of the Rhine, saw his army smashed, then he refused to allow it to retreat in good time so that a true defense of the east bank of the Rhine could be made. On the contrary, Hitler forbade the construction of defensive fortifications on the east bank of the Rhine until the last moment.[82]

Already in January Rundstedt had protested to Hitler that "staying too long west of the river would increase the danger of the enemy's following closely on the heels of the German troops." Hitler replied, "with an Olympian detachment and finality, that he saw no point in merely transferring the catastrophe from one point to another."[83] Now General Schlemm could forsee disaster in the Wesel bridgehead and appealed to Blaskowitz to intervene with Hitler. So it was Blaskowitz's turn to try and persuade the "greatest commander of all time" to release the men and machines to retreat across the Rhine.

On his own authority Blaskowitz ordered the gradual transfer of non-mobile fortress artillery behind the Rhine. In addition supply troops were sent to the east bank of the Rhine, formed into alarm units, and assigned to areas. First Parachute Army had about fifty thousand men without weapons at its disposal in the Wesel bridgehead. They were to be transferred to the east bank of the Rhine and put to work under the direction of engineers to build defensive positions. Blaskowitz could not persuade Hitler to revoke his orders but he did convince the dictator to modify them.

Hitler agreed to permit damaged weapons, useless vehicles and soldiers suffering from battle exhaustion to move to the east bank.[84] Hitler insisted, however, that each commander had to sign a paper certifying that "no men potentially capable of fighting" were being evacuated. Schlemm had also suggested to Blaskowitz that the time to abandon the Wesel bridgehead was at hand, that if Hitler did not agree, he might send an officer to see for himself and report to Hitler what he saw.[85] Blaskowitz did exactly that when he conferred with Hitler via *OKW*. A lieutenant-colonel was immediately dispatched from Berlin.

In the meantime, the fighting in the bridgehead became "increasingly desperate." Blaskowitz thought holding the bridgehead was justifiable only if it were to be used as a staging area for a counterattack. There was no prospect of a counterattack, especially after the Allies captured the bridge across the Rhine at Remagen, much further south, on 7 March. In Blaskowitz's view, after the Allies had seized the bridge at Remagen the Wesel bridgehead was nothing more than a dangerous trap to the troops who held it. Its retention was actually rendering a good turn to the enemy. The troops in the bridgehead were putting up a "fanatical resistance," the British saw "little sign of disorder' in the bridgehead.[86] In spite of this, Blaskowitz believed it was only a matter of days before they would be annihilated.[87]

Hitler relented. The lieutenant-colonel he had dispatched to the bridgehead was "a dapper officer all fresh and crinkly in his best new uniform, replete with broad pink stripe down the pant-leg." Schlemm, a "rather short" man, who had "a broad Slavic face, large bulbous nose and dark almost chocolate skin ...," was not exactly a "representative Aryan," but nevertheless had a keen tactical sense and could be a very cunning man when he chose.[88] "I made him get down on the ground ... and crawl forward with me to our furthermost positions, amidst one of your intensive bombardments." The lieutenant-colonel agreed that the position was hopeless and that the bridgehead should be withdrawn.[89] *OKW* gave permission on 6 March for evacuation of the bridgehead by 10 March. After the last troops had been withdrawn, the bridge was blown up on the night of 10 March.[90]

The British paid tribute to German "pluck and toughness, even if we now know that their desperation was that of suicide on a national scale."[91] The British verdict was that the German "defense was skilfully conducted right to the end [which] once more served to remind us of their martial qualities, even in defeat."[92] Blaskowitz knew better. He wondered why the British and Americans did not immediately attempt a daring thrust across the Rhine, wherever they reached it, before the Germans had time to build new defense positions.[93]

While the final withdrawal from the bridgehead was underway another withdrawal took place behind German lines. Field Marshal Rundstedt was removed from command as OB West for the final time. When he had resumed command in the west in September British 21st Army Group Intelligence had drolly written:

> The return of von Rundstedt is reminiscent of the description of the role of cavalry in modern wars: "to add distinction to what otherwise might be a vulgar brawl."[94]

The defeat of the German armies west of the Rhine River "was the occasion of a *coup de grâce* to a distinguished [military] career."[95] What remained was merely a "vulgar brawl."

Field Marshal Albert Kesselring was appointed to replace Rundstedt as OB West. He arrived at his headquarters, greeting his chief of staff, Siegfried Westphal by sardonically announcing, "I am the new V3!"[96] Kesselring knew he was no "wonder weapon," nevertheless, even in those difficult times, he had not lost the sense of humor that had earned him the nickname, "Smiling Albert."

Kesselring met with Blaskowitz and General Schlemm on 11 March in the late afternoon at Schlemm's headquarters on the east bank of the Rhine, opposite Wesel. Kesselring gathered from the discussion "that the Army Group was fairly sure of itself if it were allowed at least another eight or ten days to re-equip, prepare positions, bring up supplies and rest. They liked their task of defending the Rhine."[97] Kesselring was a notorious optimist, but it is highly doubtful that he could have had any genuine optimism about Army Group H successfully defending the Rhine.[98]

The Germans received a two-week respite during which the Allies organized their assault across the Rhine. Two weeks of quiet along the front, fourteen days in which to prepare the defense.[99]

Blaskowitz directed a feverish pace of arming and reorganizing the surviving troops, constructing field fortifications, preparing counter-measures against probable Allied parachute assaults, transforming static divisions into mobile divisions and moving virtually all flak units from the defense of Holland to an anti-tank role on the east bank of the Rhine. Additionally, all important enemy objectives to the rear of the Rhine defenses were prepared for demolition. On 14 March OB West, Field Marshal Kesselring, approved all the measures which Blaskowitz had taken.[100]

Despite the undoubted improvements in Army Group H's fighting power Blaskowitz nevertheless "realized that they were insufficient to prevent the crossing of the Rhine by the enemy."[101] During the next days the signs mounted that the Allied offensive was imminent.

One of the recognizable signs of a pending Allied attack that the Germans might have learned to expect by March of 1945 was systematic air attacks upon German command posts. On Sunday 18 March, it was Blaskowitz's turn. During the early daylight hours British Typhoons and Spitfires of the R.A.F. 2nd Tactical Air Force attacked Blaskowitz's headquarters in a country house and adjacent buildings near Deventer, Holland with one thousand pound bombs, rockets and incendiaries. The daring pinpoint attack on the house, which was guarded by heavy, medium and light calibre anti-aircraft guns, was made from only two hundred feet and resulted in two direct hits.[102] The British planes dropped a half-ton of explosives on Blaskowitz's headquarters alone. Although the headquarters was destroyed, both Blaskowitz and one of his staff officers, Major-General Paul Reichelt, escaped without injury.[103] If this were not enough, the R.A.F. bombed Blaskowitz's new headquarters again twelve days later. Again, they missed Blaskowitz himself.

Blaskowitz estimated that Montgomery's attack would strike between Emmerich and Dinslaken (seven miles south of Wesel). He correctly guessed that the Americans would strike at Wesel. On 20 March he ordered the troops under his command into a state of alert.[104]

The Rhine was a formidable barrier between four and five hundred yards wide along the front where Montgomery's 21st Army Group attacked. The current was about three and one-half knots.[105] Nevertheless, crossing it was well within Allied capabilities. The Allies code-named it "Operation Plunder."

Five thousand Allied artillery pieces began a thunderous barrage at 9 P.M. on 23 March. At 10 P.M. specially trained British commandos crossed the Rhine while the R.A.F. heavily bombed the east bank of the Rhine in what Montgomery called "the final assault on Germany." An Allied newsman named Howard K. Smith, later an achorman and commentator for NBC Television News, reported what he saw opposite Wesel on the U.S. Ninth Army radio transmitter:

> I watched that assault from an observation post on the Rhine, and it was the single most terrifying spectacle I have ever seen. The entire town was smothered, red and yellow flame, and smoke billowed thousands of yards up in the sky.[106]

March 24 was a gloriously beautiful spring day along the Rhine, especially so for the Allies. The German garrison at Wesel resisted fiercely. First Parachute Army, in reality already reduced to the size of a corps even before the battle got underway, nevertheless offered a determined defense on the British left flank. On the Canadian sector, too, the Canadians reported, "the enemy fought like madmen."[107]

The paratroop operation (comparable in scale to Operation Market Garden in the autumn), code-named "Operation Varsity," was also roughly treated by the flak units which Blaskowitz had transferred from Holland to the east bank of the Rhine. Although the defenders made the airborne assault expensive in blood, it nevertheless resulted in the successful seizure of all objectives in a matter of hours.

"There was no real fight to it," noted First Lieutenant Whitney Refuem of Company B, 117th U.S. Infantry Division, "The artillery had done the job for us."[108] History's "most elaborate river crossing operation" was a major triumph.[109]

Naturally, a major Allied success was a German defeat. There was little Blaskowitz could do. He had exhausted his reserves before the end of the day.[110] These amounted only to a total of thirty-five tanks for the entire army group.[111] Even on the northern part of the front, where Montgomery's left flank sputtered before the surviving contingents of Lieutenant-General Eugen Meindl's II Parachute Corps, the

German situation was precarious. Everywhere else on the Rhine a German disaster was unfolding.[112]

Further to the south in the sector of Army Group B the Americans had the great good fortune in early March to seize the Ludendorff Bridge at Remagen and had built up a bridgehead on the east bank which had acted as a magnet to the defending Germans, leaving few other defenders elsewhere in this sector. It was even worse for the Germans further south on the Army Group G front where the Army's Chief of Staff wrote: "This [is a] shadow of an army," in which the morale of the troops varied "from suspicion to callous resignation." He continued, stating that "the officer corps lacked confidence and wondered just what were the demands of duty." Concluding, he called it an army that "could only pretend to resist."[113]

Even OB West, Field Marshal Kesselring, later admitted there was little hope. "I felt like a concert pianist who is asked to play a Beethoven sonata before a large audience on an ancient, rickety and out-of-tune instrument." He even admitted his own impotence: "events were moving too swiftly for me to have time to influence them much."[114]

In the days following the unsuccessful defense of the Rhine, while the Allies built up their bridgeheads and began to make penetrations eastward, Blaskowitz lost his most talented subordinate, General Schlemm. On 21 March Allied fighter-bombers destroyed Schlemm's headquarters in an early morning attack, seriously wounding Schlemm. Although he attempted to remain at his post, this proved impossible.[115] Blaskowitz ordered General Blumentritt to report to him at his headquarters.

Blumentritt arrived at Blaskowitz's headquarters on 28 March and was quickly informed that he was to replace Schlemm. Blumentritt concluded that both Blaskowitz and his Chief of Staff, General Rudolf Hofmann

> were of the opinion that now that the Rhine had been crossed the German position was beyond repair. Everyone seemed possessed of the secret hope that the Anglo-American forces would advance so swiftly into Germany that the war would be brought to a speedy conclusion.[116]

Indeed, the Allies began their deployment eastward into central Germany that very day. Montgomery promised that the Allied armies would "crack about in the plains of northern Germany, chasing the enemy from pillar to post."[117]

Kesselring retrospectively criticized Blaskowitz's dispositions and actions during the Rhineland defense. He added; "Army Group H accepted the inevitable with a certain fatalism which was obvious to me at every conference." Schlemm's loss "was very noticeable." When the Americans switched forces to the British right-wing it was clearly the signal for the assault. Instead of moving his own headquarters into the threatened flank "Army Group North moved its headquarters north." Moving into the threatened flank would have been "acknowledgement that much, indeed everything, depended on its standing firm."[118] Kesselring was too accomplished a soldier to casually make remarks such as this in fits of personal pique; it was uncharacteristic of him. On the other hand, he had reason to be angry with Blaskowitz.

Kesselring saw Hitler personally four times between 20 March and 12 April. He claimed in his post-war memoirs that "In spite of our serious defeats he never uttered a word of reproach, certainly because he appreciated that *the situation in the west had deteriorated too far to be effectively remedied.*"[119] Nevertheless, when, on 28 March Blaskowitz, together with Hofmann and Blumentritt, formulated what Kesselring called "an entirely supererogatory account of the situation," and forwarded it to *OKW* on Blaskowitz's authority, with a copy sent to Kesselring after the fact, Kesselring was infuriated. He thought it a "psychological blunder," a "perfect example of the way to rouse Hitler's wrath." Kesselring wanted Blaskowitz removed from his command.[120] Indeed, Hitler took it as "insufferable arrogance."[121]

As Kesselring saw it, Blaskowitz had told Hitler "that he was not capable of grasping the operational picture."[122] Blaskowitz informed *OKW* that since the Allies had broken through Army Group B to the south it was a matter of days before they could swing around the flank of Army Group H and be in its rear. Holland and the Ruhr would be sealed off as "pockets" by the Allies and the best troops would be trapped in these "pockets." Since the "pockets" were no longer of decisive importance, and since there were no troops to defend the Weser River line and bar access to central and northern Germany, Blaskowitz suggested that *OKW* abandon Holland and the Ruhr and allow the troops there to retreat to the Weser River and build a defensive line. He requested orders to initiate the retreat immediately.

Hitler's response was a rejection of all the proposals and "strict orders never to submit a similar evaluation of the situation again." Army Group H was to stand and hold firmly with all available means.[123] Hitler instead planned to send Generaloberst Student to "assist" Blaskowitz in carrying out a counter-attack southward from Holland into the Allied flank and rear. It was a calculated insult to send a junior officer to "assist" a man of Blaskowitz's stature. "Displeased with Blaskowitz's handling of the situation, he thought to remove an imagined lethargy by the appointment of Student." At *OKW* Generaloberst Alfred Jodl told Hitler; "you may send up a dozen Students, mein Führer, but it won't alter the situation." Even Kesselring agreed that the counterattack was an impossible fantasy.[124]

On 30 March the American spearheads broke through north of Lippe and the Germans were compelled to withdraw as Blaskowitz had suggested. It made a mockery of Hitler's "hold firm" orders.[125]

OKW repeatedly sent orders to Blaskowitz to begin an attack southward without delay with all available forces in order to cut off the Allies advancing into Germany. Army Group H responded that an attempt to execute this order would not even meet with initial success, let alone succeed in penetrating sixty kilometers. Blaskowitz informed *OKW* in a radio message promptly intercepted and decoded by Ultra that the infantry strength of 7th and 8th Parachute Divisions was about 200 each, II Parachute Corps had 13 assault guns but no tanks, ammunition was nearly exhausted.[126] Army Group H was in dire straits.

OKW reproached Blaskowitz as a *pessimist* and announced Student's dispatch and role. Within hours of his arrival, however, Student was convinced that Blaskowitz was correct in his evaluation of the situation. The reality was that Blaskowitz was truthful and accurate in his reports as he had always been;[127] Hitler resided in a megalomaniac fantasy in which his divisions were fresh and at full strength. Only local counterattacks followed. A few days later Student was withdrawn and assigned the task of building a defensive front on the Weser River.[128]

When the Allied armies crossed the Weser River on 6 April the result for Blaskowitz was the virtual severance of communications with OB West, Field Marshal Kesselring. Consequently, the next day *OKW* reorganized their forces in the northwest. Army Group H was renamed OB Nordwest and placed under the command of Field Marshal Ernst Busch. Blaskowitz was shifted to command of the German forces in the northwestern Netherlands, OB Nederland, responsible to Busch as his immediate superior, a further indication of "Hitler's continuing disenchantment with Blaskowitz ...."[129]

Ernst Busch was a professional soldier, two years younger than Blaskowitz, and was one of the many that Hitler had promoted to the rank of field marshal while by-passing Blaskowitz. Busch was the son of an orphanage director in the Ruhr and his common background probably appealed to Hitler.[130] During World War I as a captain he had been a company and battalion commander in the west and had been awarded the House Order of Hohenzollern, The Iron Cross First Class and the coveted "Pour le Merite." He had occupied a series of line and staff positions in the Weimar and "Nazi Peace" years. During the Polish campaign he had led a corps, and then in the French campaign, an army.

It was his personal tragedy that he did not retire at that time. He had already been promoted beyond his abilities, probably because he had been so devoted to Hitler and the Nazi Party.[131] Perhaps as a result, Hitler appointed Busch to replace Field Marshal von Kluge as commander of Army Group Center in October 1943, after Kluge was injured, despite the clear evidence that Busch had performed with mediocrity as an army commander in Russia. According to several historians, he proved a "thoroughly incompetent army group commander .... [there] "[132]

Under Busch, Army Group Center headquarters became a "mindless instrument for transmitting the Fuehrer's will."[133] The result was the destruction of his army group in the Russian summer offensive in 1944, after which Busch was replaced by Field Marshal Walter Model. Thereafter Busch did not speak often of the destruction of his army group that summer, but when he did, "He said, with something close to awe, that after one single Russian attack thirty-six of the forty-eight divisions .... completely disappeared leaving hardly a trace of their previous existence."[134] It was a disaster greater than the more famous Stalingrad debacle. By the time of his appointment as Blaskowitz's immediate "superior," Busch was "a tired old man suffering from heart trouble."[135] Busch's incompetence mattered little in the circumstances of early April 1945. It is doubtful that a genius could have transformed the situation.

Blaskowitz's final command was unenviable. Northwest Holland was the triangular region north of the Maas River, east of the Atlantic coast and west of the Zuider Zee, the most densely populated part of Holland. Between the southern limit of the Zuider Zee and the Maas River Blaskowitz organized the Ijseel and Grebbe Lines to protect "Fortress Holland's" eastern land front. The innumerable rivers, canals, and dikes were utilized "with his customary professional skill to compel the Canadians to work hard ... [against] as stubborn a defense as any at this stage of the war ...."[136]

Blaskowitz's "troops" included the remains of Twenty-fifth Army, much reduced to defend the Rhineland during the previous month, numerous German air force personel serving in a ground role, contingents of naval and marine troops also in a ground role, and scattered remnants of both German and Dutch SS. There was no air support available, virtually no armor or heavy artillery. He had, however, more than 120,000 Germans under arms, often organized in *ad hoc* battle groups.[137] The 2nd Canadian Corps facing Blaskowitz's troops reported "myriad identifications" of German units on their front, but, nevertheless added that:

> Although the terms 'hodge podge, odds and ends, scrapings,' etc., are accepted epithets for such an order of battle ... on our front, the skill and fighting spirit of individual units has often been to the standard of elite troops. They are fanatical and brave.[138]

It is no wonder then, that at least some Dutch thought Blaskowitz "very capable." One Dutchman added: "In the last four weeks of the war ... he showed himself an energetic and ruthless leader."[139] The bitter German resistance "testifies to the strong grip and discipline which Blaskowitz kept."[140]

Perhaps, however, it would be more historically accurate to qualify the estimate of the German defense made by the 2nd Canadian Corps. The experience of Canadians in the I Canadian Corps when they met the German defenders of Holland was probably more representative:

> Disorganized in their administrative areas, the remnants of a

hundred regiments of infantry, SS, Jaeger, Luftwaffe troops and many otherwise fighting now with a fierceness one step removed from manic fury. Knowing the war was lost, they fought with a puposeful savagery—or, and the numbers were about equally divided, they dropped their weapons and walked out to meet and hasten the inevitable end. There was no way of knowing what they would do. Machine gunners who could have massacred a Canadian platoon fired no shots but walked into captivity from behind their silent guns. Then there were those individuals who, by-passed by the advance and swallowed by the victors in a foreign and hostile land, snatched up a rifle and sniped at the backs of passing soldiers until they themselves found death.[141]

Generally the paratroopers under Blaskowitz's command, "as usual were handling their anti-tank and self-propelled guns and their aggressive Panzerfaust teams with skill and obstinacy."[142] The SS, as always, was a separate case:

> Each Nazi SS trooper knew well what his fate would be when Germany was gone, but for the renegade Dutchmen who had joined the SS, that fate would be even more terrible. And so they fought this, their last battle, with the particular savagery that only civilized men who have abandoned civilization can achieve.[143]

Despite bitter German resistance and the defensive advantages of the landscape, Blaskowitz could accomplish little more than delay of the inevitable defeat, combined with some satisfaction in tying down Allied troops that might otherwise have been utilized in the main Allied attack into central Germany. Nevertheless, Canadian contingents attacking northeastward along the eastern bank of the Zuider Zee reached the North Sea on 16 April thus isolating Blaskowitz's troops in "Fortress Holland." Another Canadian corps took Arnhem on 14 April and by 18 April had turned westward toward "Fortress Holland" and crossed the Ijsselmeer line after vicious fighting.[144] First Canadian Army advanced to the Grebbe Line by 17 April. Then Field Marshal Montgomery intervened.

Blaskowitz was intent upon continued resistance. Commanders in the field could do nothing less than resist, even in so-called "hopeless situations." On 13 April in a message intercepted and decrypted by Ultra, Field Marshal Busch ordered "Ruthless use of flooding for the defense of Fortress Holland."[145] Therefore Blaskowitz issued orders for the emplacement of two unexploded American aerial bombs in the two to five hundred kilogram range in the Wieringermeer Dike. This was accomplished by 15 April. The destruction of the dike would result in the flooding of the Wieringermeer Polder, land below sea level, a great defensive advantage. Residents of the area were warned to evacuate.

On 17 April as the Canadians began to cross the Ijsselmeer Line, the dike was blown up, flooding 18,000 hectares of what became "No Man's Land."[146] A few days later Montgomery issued his halt order.

According to Montgomery, "Little use could have been served by further advance at this stage." He ordered First Canadian Army to halt offensive operations against "Fortress Holland." Montgomery reasoned that the Germans in the "Fortress" were cut off from any hope of reinforcement or relief, and were entrenched behind formidable defensive barriers improved by artificial flooding of lowlands. An Allied offensive would have required significant resources unavailable in this sector and better used in the attack in Germany. In addition considerable suffering would have been inflicted on the already desperate Dutch population.[147] The Canadians halted. Sporadic firing continued.

Despite the respite gained by the temporary halt of the Canadians, Blaskowitz was still fully occupied with a multitude of difficulties in Holland. Complicating these problems was the fact that he shared power with the civilian head of the German government of northwest Holland, Reichskommissar Artur Seyss-Inquart.

Seyss-Inquart was an Austrian Nazi, devoted to Hitler, who had served as temporary head of Austria after the *Anschluss* and then as deputy governor-general to Hans Frank in occupied Poland until appointed *Reichskommissar* for Holland in May 1940, where he remained until the end of the war. He was a tall, thin, bespectacled man who walked with a pronounced limp from an old mountain climbing accident.[148] Hitler described Seyss-Inquart as "an extraordinarily clever man, as supple as an eel, amiable—and at the same time thick-skinned and tough." His vapid face seldom revealed his capacity for ruthlessness.[149] Nevertheless, Seyss-Inquart and Blaskowitz were able to cooperate to some extent.

In mid-March Hitler had issued "scorched-earth" orders for territory lost in the west to the Allies.[150] In addition to widespread flooding, industrial and power plants, mines and transportation and communications facilities were ordered destroyed. Although Seyss-Inquart could never be described as a humanitarian, he was sympathetic to the Dutch as one of the Germanic peoples, especially since it was obvious that the war was lost and could last only a few more weeks.[151]

On 2 April Seyss-Inquart had met with the Reich Minister of Armaments and War Production, Albert Speer. Seyss-Inquart surprised Speer with his admission that he had opened communications with the Allies to prevent the large-scale flooding, destruction of industry, and senseless demolitions which Hitler was planning.[152] They agreed not to carry out such orders in the civilian sphere and to approach Generaloberst Blaskowitz regarding military floodings and demolitions. Blaskowitz "told him that orders were orders, but if a way could be found to avoid this order he would be ready to do so."[153] There were no further demolitions or inundations.

Participation in a conspiracy to circumvent the Führer's orders— "scorched earth" or otherwise, was potentially lethal business in April 1945. In Berlin Himmler was announcing the execution of an SS colonel and a police director named von Salisch for desertion and also a Colonel von Hassenstein for unauthorized retreat. On 15 April Hitler ranted about the "Jewish-Bolschevik" attempt to "destroy Germany and exterminate our people." The "old men and children are murdered and women and girls are reduced to army camp whores. The remainder go to Siberia."

On 21 April Berlin was declared a "front line city."[154] The German press had repeated General von Bülow's remark to the Swedish Crown Prince in August 1813 as "significant today": "Our bones will bleach in front of but not behind Berlin."[155] "Sieg oder Siberien" (Victory or Siberia) became the prevalent propaganda slogan. The Anglo-Americans were called "Slave-drivers for Siberia."[156] Some German soldiers continued to fight only because it was better to die in battle than "for the rest of my life ... to chop wood in Canada or Siberia ...."[157] The fanatics knew that their last moments of "glory" were at hand and they made the most of the Nazi version of the "Ride of the Valkyries."

There were innumerable "*Ost-truppen*" and foreign refugees in Holland, an obviously explosive element. In the lunatic atmosphere of the war's final days anything could happen and sometimes did. On 16

April one garrison of "Germans" mutinied, crossed the Allied lines, and surrendered to the Quebec Armored Regiment. It turned out that the surrendering garrison was mostly Russians and Poles who had killed fifty of the sixty actual Germans in their unit before crossing the line to surrender.[158]

Added to the chaotic mix in Holland was the Dutch Resistance, ready to unfurl their orange and white flags, and to seek revenge against Dutch collaborators and the hated "Rot-Moffen," as they called the Germans.[159] Nevertheless, collaborators were everywhere, still cooperating with the Germans. Indeed, according to one report the Dutch SS was holding together wavering German morale behind the Grebbe Line. *The New York Times* called the situation in Holland "comparable to what might have happened in the United States if the Capone gang had seized ... control of the country during prohibition days."[160]

Perhaps, however, the most immediate problem facing Blaskowitz, Seyss-Inquart and the Dutch in west Holland was the food situation. West Holland was one of the most densely populated parts of Europe. Its food supply was located in Holland east of the Zuider Zee. Because of a railway strike by the Dutch Resistance originating in September 1944 when the Allies had advanced to the Dutch border, west Holland had been cut off from its food supply. By the end of January the food ration had been reduced to 18 oz of bread and 2 lbs, 3 oz of potatos per week. This translates into 2 1/2 oz of bread and 5 oz of potatoes per day, a starvation level.[161]

In some "parts of western Holland the daily ration for a civilian was less than that of a concentration camp inmate in Germany." In Amsterdam alone, it was estimated at the end of March that five hundred people were dying per week from privation.[162] With rations reduced to 400 calories per day in some parts of western Holland, it was estimated that 3,500,000 Dutch faced starvation.[163] Some Dutch understood that the Canadians had halted to avoid destruction and civilian casualties, but others asked cynically: "Is it better to die of hunger in undamaged towns?"[164] The Germans too were alarmed, and signaled the High Command on 26 April that food for the civilian population "would not last beyond 10 May."[165]

Even before Blaskowitz had been appointed OB Nederland (C-in-C Netherlands 7 April), Seyss-Inquart had begun to explore a solution to the food shortage. On 2 April he had invited the Dutch Secretary General of Economic and Agricultural Ministries, Heinz Hirschfeld, for a talk.[166] Seyss-Inquart hinted to Hirschfeld that a separate surrender might be possible if the Netherlands could be isolated, that he was himself prepared to act independently. Hirschfeld passed the information on to members of the Dutch Government-in-Exile in London.

In further secret discussions on 12 April Seyss-Inquart revealed that he had had discussions with Generaloberst Blaskowitz and that Blaskowitz would not permit a separate surrender. Seyss-Inquart, apparently with Blaskowitz's concurrence, "declared his willingness to prevent further destruction and to open ... Rotterdam for food transports, provided the Allies would stop at the Grebbe Line."[167] The Dutch Government-in-Exile referred the matter to Winston Churchill, who turned it over to General Eisenhower.

The negotiations were awkward, confused and halting, despite the urgency of the situation for the Dutch people.[168] Between 25 and 28 April Blaskowitz sent out many wireless messages in English to the First Canadian Corps: "the senior German Commander" asked that "food be sent to the starving Dutch and guaranteeing a fair and just distribution through the Dutch Food Ministry."[169] The information was forwarded once again to Eisenhower and the Allied governments. "It was obvious that the German's hints offered the means of reconciling the requirements of strategy with those of humanity ..." was the way an eminent Canadian historian officially described what had transpired.[170]

On 27 April Eisenhower sent a message to Seyss-Inquart requesting an immediate meeting between him, Blaskowitz, the senior German Naval officer and Allied representatives the next day. It announced that the military advance into Holland would be halted and that no further bombing would take place. The Russians were notified by Eisenhower to conform to previous agreements about no separate surrenders.[171]

The next day, 28 April, Brigadier M.P. Bogert of the 2nd Canadian Brigade made contact with a German delegation under white flags between the forward defense lines. The German spokesman was the senior *Wehrmacht* judge-advocate in Holland, Ernst Schwebel. Lieutenant-General Reichelt represented Blaskowitz at the meeting. In accordance with the previously agreed arrangements, the Germans were blindfolded and driven by a circuitous path behind the Allied lines to the village of Achterveld.[172]

The Achterveld village school had been quickly refurbished by a work party of Princess Patricia's Canadian Light Infantry. In the schoolhouse, now divided into conference rooms, there were two entrances, one for the Germans, the other for the Allies. Representing the Allies was Major-General Francis De Guingand, Montgomery's Chief of Staff, who described the atmosphere as one of "subdued excitement."

The German convoy arrived with white flags flying, the blindfolds were removed, and the head civilian, Schwebel, and the head soldier, Reichelt, stepped into the schoolhouse, saluted and offered their hands for a handshake. General De Guingand ignored the proffered handshake, returned the salute, and examined the German's credentials. He quickly explained to the Germans that food was available for the Dutch, but it must be certain that the food would reach the Dutch and not be consumed by the Germans.

Across the table from De Guingand sat Schwebel, Seyss-Inquart's representative. De Guingand thought Schwebel was "one of the most revolting men I have ever seen. A plump, sweating German who possessed the largest red nose ... at the end of which was like several ripe strawberries sewn together." Schwebel agreed with De Guingand's assessment of the situation, but revealed that he was not empowered to make definite commitments. De Guingand then adjourned the meeting, demanding another soon, since "there was not a day to lose" if the Dutch were to be saved from starvation. Either Seyss-Inquart and Blaskowitz must attend the next meeting or send someone empowered to act in their stead.[173]

Two days later, 30 April, a second and much better attended conference was held by mutual agreement. Prince Bernhard of the Netherlands, a Russian delegation, Lieutenant General Foulkes representing the Canadians, General De Guingand from Montgomery's staff and Eisenhower's chief of staff, Lieutenant General Walter Bedell Smith all represented the Allies.

The German delegation was headed by Seyss-Inquart with Blaskowitz represented by Lieutenant-General Paul Reichelt. A number of minor officials followed in their wake. Both parties sat at a table and discussed in "cold, matter of fact language, the points connected with food distribution ...." After about ninety minutes General Smith held a smaller conference with Seyss-Inquart.

Sandwiches were brought out for all present. Smith poured a stiff glass of gin for Seyss-Inquart and then proposed a German surrender in Holland. Seyss-Inquart told him that surrender was a question for Blaskowitz, not for him. He had no authority to surrender and Blaskowitz would not do so while resistance continued in Germany.

General Smith then dropped all of his reserve, and, turning to Seyss-Inquart, stated: "You have lost the war, and you know it. And if, through pigheadedness, you cause more loss of life ... you will have to pay the penalty." "I wonder if you realize that I am giving you your last chance ...." "Yes, I realize that," Seyss-Inquart replied. Smith added: "The consequences to you yourself will be serious. You know what your acts have been here. You know the feeling of the Dutch people toward you. You know you will probably be shot." To which the Reichskommissar replied: "That leaves me cold." Smith retorted: "It will!" According to De Guingand, Seyss-Inquart then said, "rather quietly and slowly, I am not afraid—I am a German.'"[174] The negotiations were over for the day. The temporary truce continued in force. Food deliveries to the Dutch began immediately.

Dutiful to the very end, but not to a fault, Blaskowitz informed the remnants of the High Command the very next day that negotiations for the delivery of food had been successfully completed.[175] Clearly the end of the war was at hand. In Berlin the Russians were closing in on Hitler's headquarters. Blaskowitz did not know it, but Hitler had already commited suicide in Berlin the previous day.

Events rushed forward rapidly in both Germany and the Netherlands. Already on 29 April the R.A.F. had used Lancaster bombers to drop tons of food to the Dutch.[176] The U.S. Eighth Air Force followed R.A.F. efforts with almost four hundred B-17 "Fortresses" dropping seven hundred tons of rations on 1 May. The "Mighty Eighth" pilots reported it was "The pleasantest missions we ever flew."[177] As agreed during the negotiations, German anti-aircraft guns everywhere remained silent. The food was dropped at low-levels, planes sometimes flying at only three to five hundred feet. In the Hague the Dutch could be seen dancing in the streets, waving orange flags.[178] "Thank you boys" and similar messages were spelled out in white linen sheets in the fields of the Dutch countryside.[179] The food deliveries were clearly another "definite milestone ... on the road to Nazi surrender."[180] In Germany there was no such rejoicing.

Much to his surprise, Grand Admiral Karl Doenitz learned on 30 April that Hitler had appointed him his successor.[181] Doenitz reluctantly accepted the responsibility of bringing the war to a conclusion while simultaneously preventing as much bloodshed as possible. The war would be continued for a few days solely to allow both the refugees and armies fighting the Russians to retreat quickly westward in order to surrender to the western Allies.[182]

Despite his announced intentions, Doenitz hoped to arrange a "partial surrender" in north Germany to the British under Montgomery. Doenitz had a conference on the following day, 1 May, with Field Marshal Busch, who commanded the remaining German forces in northwestern Germany, and who was also Blaskowitz's immediate superior. Busch wanted to attack the superior British forces advancing toward Hamburg.[183] It was pure bluster in the spirit of the dead Führer. Any attack would have been suicidal. Busch was directed simply to do everything possible defensively to keep open the path to the west for the retreating refugees and soldiers.[184]

Busch then proceeded to inform the Allies through Stockholm that he was prepared to surrender, but not until British forces had reached the Baltic Sea, so that he would be cut off from the Russians and also from the possibility of reinforcements by the SS, which he feared might insist upon the continuation of hostilities, or even seek revenge upon him personally. He sought Allied protection against the SS.[185]

Busch's fears of the SS were neither unusual nor unrealistic. Some Allied soldiers even thought that "From this time until the end of the war we were fighting the SS and not the *Wehrmacht*." Indeed, "the SS were terrorizing members of the *Wehrmacht* and civilians who showed any inclination to surrender."[186] Military failure and "indiscipline" (expression of views contrary to the official line) had been cause enough for some time already on all fronts to "justify" hangings, shootings and imprisonment of officers, especially General Staff officers. Officers "were actually being hanged on lamp-posts and trees ... as examples to others." It was the barbaric climax of the reign of terror begun in 1933.

"General officers, even field-marshals, trembled for their lives, for the whole world had gone mad around them."[187]

Despite the SS fury, German attempts to hold back the British and Americans were futile. On 2 May the British reached the Baltic at Wismar and Lubeck. Doenitz's efforts to keep open a channel of retreat for Germans fleeing westward before the advancing Russians were now at the mercy of Field Marshal Montgomery. Consequently, Doenitz dispatched General-Admiral Hans von Friedeberg to Montgomery's tactical headquarters on Luneburg Heath, to surrender German forces in Holland, northwest Germany and Denmark. The instrument of surrender was signed at 1820 hours on 4 May, to be effective at 0800 hours on 5 May.[188] Three days later the Germans surrendered formally at Rheims, Eisenhower's headquarters. In the meantime Blaskowitz had to make the necessary arrangements for the local surrender.

Already on the previous night the BBC had announced the German surrender and implementation of the cease-fire for the next day. The German troops along the Grebbe Line "showed their enthusiasm by firing off into the air all their verey lights and tracer ammunition. Much singing could be heard along the German Front." Schnapps-happy parties developed and many Germans crossed the lines attempting to surrender only to be sent back by the Canadians who explained that "such conduct was not on' as the war did not end until 0800 hours the following morning."[189]

Blaskowitz was not as enthusiastic as his troops on the Grebbe Line. Dutch partisans who had managed to wiretap his telephone overheard him discussing the possibility of delaying the local capitulation until he received assurances that his troops would not be marched into Russian captivity. He was critical of unconditional surrender terms and sought assurances, not for himself, but only for his troops. Despite his personal objections, his sense of military discipline prevailed; Blaskowitz agreed to receive the local terms of surrender at 4 P.M., Saturday, 5 May, at the shell-damaged "Hotel World" in Wageningen.[190]

Promptly at the appointed hour a "very tired and disconsolate Colonel-General [Blaskowitz] and his chief of staff sat under the glare of photographer's floodlights ..." in the long ground-floor restaurant room of the shell-scarred hotel.[191] Both Blaskowitz and Reichelt wore belted grey leather trench coats with their Iron Crosses showing at their throats. They both looked "impassive" according to *The Times* (London) correspondent, who described Blaskowitz as "shortish, sixtyish and thick-set, with a heavy square jaw, his chief of staff taller, perhaps younger and less heavy faced; both clean shaven."[192] According to a Canadian observer, "They looked like men in a dream, dazed, stupified and unable to realize that for them their world was utterly finished." Blaskowitz set the tone for the Germans by adopting an attitude of "dignified gloom."[193]

Lieutenant-General Charles Foulkes, Commander of the First Canadian Corps, opened the proceedings by reading a brief general instrument of surrender in English. Prince Bernhard, representing the Netherlands, sat with General Foulkes, opposite Blaskowitz and Reichelt. The document was then read aloud in German by a German colonel who served as Blaskowitz's translator. One London newsman observed that the "bitterness of defeat" was painfully obvious on Blaskowitz's and Reichelt's faces, with their lips tightly clamped together, [and] eyes staring straight ahead ...."[194] Blaskowitz asked a question here and there without a change of expression. According to one witness to the proceedings, Blaskowitz occasionally peered at Foulkes, "and at such times his clear blue eyes seemed to have a penetrating quality which under different circumstances would have impressed his personality on any audience ..." "Those glances were rare, his eyes being directed to the papers on which were written ... the conditions which he was required to fulfil [sic]. He never smiled.[195]

The Times (London) observer thought that far from the surrender of a "once mighty, arrogant and cruel military tyranny, listening to their conquerer's conditions," the atmosphere "was irresistably suggestive of a well conducted business board meeting." General Foulkes, however, made his "relationship" to Blaskowitz crystal clear when he declared:

> I want it made quite clear that in the Netherlands now there is only one authority, and that is myself. I will issue orders to General Blaskowitz and he will pass them to those concerned. There will be no German civilian orders from now on.[196]

Blaskowitz expressed his concern for the fate of his men at the hands of the Dutch patriots and asked permission for his troops to be allowed to retain their weapons for protection.[197] Foulkes later agreed to this request. In turn, Blaskowitz undertook to disarm the Dutch SS, to see that demolition charges on all the dikes were removed, and to demolish minefields. Ceremonies were thus at an end. Blaskowitz and Reichelt saluted and departed in the well-worn and dirty little Volkswagen which served as their staff car.[198]

The return trip to Blaskowitz's headquarters went through the Dutch town of Leersum, where a firefight had just taken place between the local German troops and the "BS," the Dutch Army of the Interior. The Germans had arrested some thirty civilians after the skirmish and had lined them up for execution by firing squad. Fortunately for the captured Dutchmen, Blaskowitz intervened, ordering the execution cancelled.[199] The rest of the journey to his headquarters was uneventful. It had been a more than full day.

Notes for Chapter XIV

1. MSg 1/1814, BA/MA.

2. File SII/9256, Stadtarchiv Konstanz.

3. NOKW 141, M-898, Roll 28, R.G. 238, N.A.; "Hitler Decorates Blaskowitz: A Belated Report," *The Times* (London), 7 November 1944, 2.

4. "Blaskowitz Out, London Informed," *The New York Times*, 25 November 1944, 6.

5. Essame, *Patton*, 212; John Bookman and Stephen Powers, *The March To Victory* (New York: Harper & Row, Publishers, 1986), 284-285.

6. S.H.A.E.F. Weekly Intelligence Summary For Psychological Warfare, November 1944, 350.9, Special Staff P.W.D. Executive Section Decimal File, 1944-45, Entry 87, R.G. 331, N.A.

7. NOKW 141, M-898 Roll 28 R.G. 238, N.A.; Blaskowitz Interrogation, 28 July 1945, CCPWE#32/DI-43, WO 208/3154, P.R.O.; Blaskowitz Interrogation Report, 5 June 1945, First Canadian Army Intelligence Periodical No. 4, Vol. 10,655, File 215C1.023, R.G. 24, P.A.C.

8. Westphal Interrogation, 17 December 1947, M-1019, Roll 79, R.G. 238, N.A.

9. Westphal, *Erinnerungen*, 299.

10. Blaskowitz Interrogation, 28 July 1945, CCPWE#32/DI-43; WO 208/3154, P.R.O.

11. MS#B-095 (Wilutzky), R.G. 338, N.A.

12. First Army and Nineteenth Army which together had made up Army Group G during the summer of 1944 had been divided into Army Group G which commanded First Army and Army Group Oberrhein which commanded Nineteenth Army. Blaskowitz's Army Group G command in December included only First Army, but it controlled five Corps and 17 Divisions by the end of January, 1945. MS#B767 (Hold), R.G. 338, N.A.; MS#B-095 (Wilutzky), R.G. 338, N.A. See also: Magna Bauer, "*Army Group G*, January 1945" R-91, Office of the Chief of Military History and the Center of Military History, Washington, D.C. The author wishes to express his indebtedness to the U.S. Department of the Army, Chief of Military History, and the

Center of Military History, for providing a copy of this unpublished study for his research.

13. Bauer, "*Army Group G*, January 1945" (R-91); MS#B-767 (Hold), R.G. 338, N.A.; MS#B-095 (Wilutzky), R.G. 338, N.A.

14. Bauer, "*Army Group G*, January 1945" (R-91), 11.

15. MS#B-767 (Hold), R.G. 338, N.A.

16. Mitcham, *Hitler's Legions*, 269.

17. MS#B-767(Hold), R.G. 338, N.A.; MS#B-095 (Wilutzky), R.G. 338, N.A.; Roger Bender and Hugh Taylor, *Uniforms, Organization and History of the Waffen SS* (San Jose, California: Bender Publishing, 1986), 5 Vols., IV: 131,139 & 143.

18. MS#B-767 (Hold), R.G. 338, N.A.

19. Adolf Hitler Papers, "Discussion of the Fuehrer with Colonel-General v. [sic] Blaskowitz, 28 December 44, Fragment Page No. 40, U.S.A.M.H.I., Carlisle Barracks.

20. Gilbert, ed., *Hitler Directs His War*, 219.

21. Ibid., 241.

22. MS#B-095 (Wilutzky), R.G. 338, N.A.

23. Weigly, *Eisenhower's Lieutenants*, 552.

24. MS#B-767 (Hold), R.G. 338, N.A.

25. MS#B-095 (Wilutsky), R.G. 338, N.A.

26. Hinsley, *British Intelligence*, III, Part 2, 264.

27. MacDonald, *Mighty Endeavor*, 395.

28. Ibid, 396; Weigly, *Eisenhower's Lieutenants*, 552; *Seventh U.S. Army Operations Report*, II: 560-561; John Eisenhower, *The Bitter Woods* (New York: G.P. Putnam's Sons, 1969), 397-399.

29. Luck, *Panzer Commander*, 179.

30. Bauer, "*Army Group G*, January 1945" (R-91).

31. *Seventh U.S. Army Operations Report*, II: 575.

32. MS#B-767 (Hold), R.G. 338, N.A.

33. Luck, *Panzer Commander*, 178.

34. MS#B-095 (Wilutzky), 38.

35. Lockhart, *T-Patch to Victory*, 213.

36. Jacobsen, ed., *Kriegstagebuch des Oberkommandos der Wehrmacht*, Vol. IV, No. 2, 1350-1352.

37. Stahl, "Johannes Blaskowitz," 44.

38. Westphal Interrogation, 17 December 1947, M-1019, Roll 79, R.G. 238, N.A.

39. *Seventh U.S. Army Operations Report*, II: 584-590; Bauer, *"Army Group G,* January 1945"(R-91); MS#B-095 (Wilutzky), R.G. 338, N.A.

40. MS#B-767 (Hold), R.G. 338, N.A.

41. Ziemke, *Stalingrad to Berlin*, 419.

42. Trevor-Roper, ed., *Hitler's War Directives, 1939-1945*, 203-204.

43. Messenger, *Last Prussian*, 204.

44. Student Interrogation Report, 15 December 1945, Liddell Hart Papers, King's College, London, LH 9/24/143.

45. Barnett, ed., *Hitler's Generals*, 474.

46. Letter, Student to Liddell Hart dated 3 May 1949, Liddell Hart Papers, King's College, London, LH 9/24/81.

47. Westphal Interrogation, 17 December 1947, M-1019, Roll 79, R.G. 238, N.A.

48. Gilbert, ed., *Hitler Directs His War*, 166-167.

49. Westphal, *Erinnerungen*, 277-278. When Hitler was visited later by Student, who was obviously not ill, Hitler confronted Kietel, who blamed Westphal for the report of Student's "sickness." See note 124.

50. First Canadian Army Intelligence Summary Number 245, 2 March 1945, vol. 10,654, File 215C1.023 (D17), R.G. 24, P.A.C.; Bauer, *"Army Group G,* January 1945" (R-91).

51. Appendix "B" to 2 Canadian Corps Intelligence Summary No. 163, vol. 10,812, File 225C.023(D39), R.G. 24, P.A.C.; First Canadian Army Intelligence Summary No. 149, 26 November 1944, Vol. 10,653, File 215C1.023(d11), R.G. 24, P.A.C.; Weekly Intelligence Summary for Psychological Warfare, 350.9, Special Staff, P.W.D. Executive Section, Decimal File, 1944-45, Entry 87, R.G. 331, Records of Allied Operational and Occupation Headquarters, World War II, N.A.

52. *Report* on the Sunrise-Crossword Operation, Feb. 26-May 2, 1945, May 22, 1945, "Sunrise Operation", Entry 110, R.G. 226, N.A.

53. John Toland Collection, Library of Congress, Madison Library Manuscript Division, *John Toland Papers*, Box 9, "Operation Sunrise", File No. 4, Letter dated February 25, 1945 from Gaevernitz to Brigadier-General Siebert, G-2 Section, 12th Army Group.

54. Ibid; Memorandum of Information for the Joint Chiefs of Staff, 26 February 1945, U.S. Joint Chiefs of Staff, Geographic File, CCS 387 Germany (9-21-44) Sec. 1, R.G. 218, N.A.; Allen Dulles, *The Secret Surrender* (New York: Harper & Row, Publishers, 1966), 48-49, Bradley Smith & Elena Agarossi,

Operation Sunrise; The Secret Surrender (New York: Basic Books, Inc., Publishers, 1979), 61.

55. Ibid. (All of the above).

56. Smith, *Operation Sunrise*, 166.

57. CSDIC/CMF/X168, 26 May 1945, I.D. File 926537, R.G. 319, N.A.; In *Operation Sunrise* Bradley Smith refers to this conversation as found in R.G. 331, AFHQ (Allied Forces Headquarters Mediterranean Records), Reel 21M.

58. CSDIC (U.K.) SIR 1417, G-2 Divisions (MIS-Y Branch), R.G. 165, N.A. The description of Blaskowitz as a "pronounced anti-Nazi" was Lieutenant-Colonel Friedrich Freiherr von der Heydte's in March 1945.

59. Chandler, ed., *Military Maxims of Napoleon*, 77-78.

60. Gert Steuben, "So blieb er ohne Marschallstab," *Das Neue Blatt*, 24 Februar 1953, 11-12. *Collection Koepcke*, Copy in author's possession. The Russians had advanced to within fifty miles of Dresden, prompting Frau Blaskowitz and her daughter to abandon Dresden.

61. Jay Baird, *The Mythical World of Nazi War Propaganda, 1939-1945* (Minneapolis, University of Minnesota Press, 1974), 248.

62. MS#B-147 (Hoehne), R.G. 338, N.A.

63. Ibid.

64. Pogue, *Supreme Command*, 407-422.

65. MS#B-365 (Blumentritt), R.G. 338, N.A.

66. Pogue, *Supreme Command*, 418-419.

67. W. Dennis Whitaker and Shelagh Whitaker, *Rhineland: The Battle to End the War* (New York: St. Martin's Press, 1989). 6-7.; Milton Shulman, *Defeat in the West*, (New York: E.P. Dutton & Company, Inc., 1948), 264-265.; Jeffrey Williams, *The Long Left Flank: The Hard Fought Way to the Reich, 1944-1945* (London: Leo Cooper Ltd., 1988), 198-200.

68. Hugh Darby and Marcus Cunliffe, *A Short Story of the 21 Army Group* (Aldershot, England: Gale & Polden Ltd., 1949), 106-107.

69. MS#B-147 (Geyer), R.G. 338, N.A.; Colonel Rolf Geyer was Blaskowitz's operations officer. James Lucas, *Storming Eagles: German Airborne Forces in World War Two* (London: Arms and Armour Press, 1988), 159.

70. H. Essame, *The 43rd Wessex Division At War 1944-1945* (London: William Clowes and Sons, Ltd., 1952), 204.

71. Whitaker, *Rhineland*, 7.

72. Michael Glover, *That Astonishing Infantry: Three Hundred Years of the History of the Royal Welch Fusiliers (23rd Regiment of Foot) 1689-1989* (London: Leo Cooper, 1989), 234-236.; Bernard Fergusson, *The Black Watch and the King's Enemies* (London: Collins, 1950), 292.

73. WO 208/4178, P.R.O.

74. Blumentritt Interrogation, 22 May 1946, Canadian Military Headquarters, Entry 427, R.G. 407, N.A.

75. Ibid.; MS#B-147 (Geyer), R.G. 338, N.A.

76. Williams, *Long Left Flank*, 199-200.; Whitaker, *Rhineland*, 72-74.; Pogue, *Supreme Command*, 421.

77. Essame, *43rd Wessex Division*, 220.

78. L.F. Ellis, *Victory in the West*, Vol. II, *The Defeat of Germany* (London: Her Majesty's Stationery Office, 1968), 275.

79. WO 205/1020, P.R.O.; Shulman, *Defeat in the West*, 268.

80. Ibid.

81. Ibid.

82. Charles MacDonald, *The Last Offensive* (United States Army in World War II: European Theater of Operations, Washington, D.C.: Office of the Chief of Military History, United States Army, 1973) 178.; MS#B-147 (Geyer), R.G. 338, N.A.

83. John North, *North-West Europe 1944-5: The Achievement of 21st Army Group* (London: Her Majesty's Stationery Office, 1953), 202.

84. Kurt von Tippelskirch, *Geschichte Des Zweiten Weltkrieg* (Bonn: Atheneum Verlag, 1954), 549.

85. WO 205/1020, P.R.O.; Shulman, *Defeat in the West*, 270.

86. Ellis, *Victory in the West*, II: 277.

87. MS#B-147 (Geyer), R.G. 338, N.A.

88. WO 205/1020, P.R.O.

89. Ibid.; Shulman, *Defeat in the West*, 270.; North, *Achievement of 21st Army Group*, 202.

90. MS#B-147 (Geyer), R.G. 338, N.A.

91. George Blake, *Mountain and Flood: The History of the 52nd (Lowland) Division 1939-1946* (Glasgow: Jackson, Son & Company, 1950), 154.

92. Captain the Earl of Rosse and E.R. Hill, *The Story of the Guards Armoured Division 1941-1945* (London: Geoffrey Bles, 1956), 215.

93. MS#B-147 (Geyer), R.G. 338, N.A.

94. Messenger, *Last Prussian*, 204.; Shulman, *Defeat in the West*, 177.

95. Ellis, *Victory in the West*, II: 277.

96. Macksey, *Kesselring*, 225.

97. Kesselring, *Memoirs*, 240-241.

98. MacDonald, *Last Offensive*, 302.

99. MS#B-414 (Geyer), R.G. 338, N.A.

100. Ibid.; MacDonald, *Last Offensive*, 301-302.

101. MS#B-414 (Geyer), R.G. 338, N.A.

102. CL. 2198, I.W.M.; "R.A.F. Blasts 3 German H.Q.'S Opposite Monty's Front," *Daily Express* (London), 19 March 1945, 1.; Christopher Shores, *2nd Tactical Air Force* (Reading, England: Osprey Publications, Ltd., 1970), 80.

103. "Two Nazi Headquarters in Holland Smashed by Low-Flying Strikes by Fast RAF Bombers," *The New York Times*, 20 March 1945, 4.

104. MS#B-414 (Geyer), R.G. 338, N.A.

105. Darby and Cunliffe, *21 Army Group*, 116-117.

106. *From D-Day Through Victory in Europe: The Eye-witness as Told by War Correspondents on the Air* (New York: Columbia Broadcasting System, 1945), 142-143.

107. C.P. Stacey, *The Victory Campaign*, Vol. III, *The Operations in North-West Europe 1944-1945* (Ottawa: The Queen's Printer and Controller of Stationery, 1960), 539.

108. MacDonald, *Last Offensive*, 305-306.

109. MacDonald, *Mighty Endeavor*, 444-448.

110. MS#B-414 (Geyer), R.G. 338, N.A.

111. MacDonald, *Last Offensive*, 301.

112. Ibid., 314-315.

113. Ibid., 301.

114. Kesselring, *Memoirs*, 259.

115. William Breuer, *Storming Hitler's Rhine; The Allied Assault: February-March 1945* (New York: St. Martin's Press, 1985) 202-203.

116. Blumentritt Interrogation, 22 May 1946, Canadian Military Headquarters, Entry 427, R.G. 407, N.A. Eisenhower agreed with Blaskowitz's assessment: "The March 24 Operations sealed the fate of Germany."

117. MacDonald, *Mighty Endeavor*, 446.; Breuer, *Storming Hitler's Rhine*, 203.

118. Kesselring, *Memoirs*, 257.

119. Ibid., 264 (Emphasis added).

120. MacDonald, *Last Offensive*, 338.

121. Kesselring, *Memoirs*, 257.

122. Ibid.

123. MacDonald, *Last Offensive*, 338-339.; MS#B-414 (Geyer), R.G. 338, N.A.

124. Kesselring, *Memoirs*, 280.; Field Marshal Montgomery agreed with Blaskowitz's assessment: "it was clear that if he [Hitler] decided to continue the

struggle, he had no option but to withdraw the remnants of his forces as best he might, with the hope of forming an improvised front further to the east." Bernard Montgomery, *Normandy to the Baltic* (Boston: Houghton Mifflin Company, 1948), 327.; General der Flieger Karl Koller was apparently one of those individuals who can find humor even at the most desparate times. He had this conversation in a P.O.W. camp after the war with Generalfeld-marschall Hugo Sperrle:

> SPERRLE: It's all such a lie! It's impossible that such orders could have come from the FÜHRER, as if he knew nothing whatsoever about the situation.
>
> KOLLER: (laughs) Sir! That's not true, unfortunately. The FÜHRER gave ridiculous orders even when he was informed about the situation. He had such extraordinary ideas that all one could do was to clasp one's head. JODL sometimes opposed him fairly vehemently. I remember one recent instance of that (laughs). The FÜHRER had ordered that the RUHR district was to be attacked southwards from Dutch territory, and said that the enemy thrust towards the east could be neutralised by such an attack. Then JODL said: "There are no forces there at all, that's impossible." Then the FÜHRER said: "That's it, it just depends on who I'm dealing with" and sent for STUDENT and saw him. The next day he kicked up a frightful row about the C-in-C West, Feldmarschall von RUNDSTEDT and WESTPHAL, saying that they had told him that STUDENT was a wreck. an old man no longer able to do his job, who had been dismissed for that reason. "That's another dirty lie", Hitler said. "I've seen STUDENT now. He is an absolutely fresh, lively, highly intellectual man. He is going there now, and he will carry it out!" I was standing behind JODL. His bald patch was slowly going red, and when his bald patch went red it was a sure sign that something was going to happen. I knew that. Then JODL repeated what he had previously said. Then the FÜHRER again said: "That's quite immaterial, that's not true." So JODL's bald patch went even a shade darker red, then he suddenly shouted: "You can send nine STUDENTS there if you like, but it won't do you any good, there are no troops there!"
>
> WO 208/4170, P.R.O.

125. MacDonald, *Last Offensive*, 338.

126. Hinsley, *British Intelligence*, III, Part 2, 688.

127. Stahl, "Johannes Blaskowitz," 44.

128. MS#B-414 (Geyer), R.G. 338, N.A.

129. MacDonald, *Last Offensive*, 385.; MS#B-414 (Geyer), R.G. 338, N.A.; The reorganization orders were immediately intercepted and decoded by ULTRA. Hinsley, *British Intelligence*, III, Part 2, 725.; Trevor-Roper, ed., *Hitler's War Directives, 1939-1945*, 208-209.

130. Franz Kurowsky, "GFM Ernst Busch zu seinen 25. Todestag," *Deutsches Soldatenjahrbuch: 1970* (Munich: Schild Verlag, 1970), 21.

131. Blumentritt, "Stellungnahme zur dem buch Offizier Gegen Hitler,'" Unpublished essay of November 1946, papers of Sir John Wheeler-Bennett, St. Antony's College Archives, Oxford University.; Brett-Smith, *Hitler's Generals*, 196-197.

132. Samuel Mitcham, *Hitler's Field Marshals and Their Battles* (London: Leo Cooper Ltd., 1988), 272.; Brett-Smith, *Hitler's Generals*, 197.

133. Ziemke, *Stalingrad to Berlin*, 316.; Brett-Smith, *Hitler's Generals*, 197.; Wistrich, *Who's Who in Nazi Germany*, 35. According to Wistrich Busch "proved incapable of resisting his [Hitler's] spell."

134. Student Interrogation, 15 December 1945, B.H. Liddell-Hart Papers, King's College, London, LH 9/24/143

135. Blumentritt Interrogation, 22 May 1946, Canadian Military Headquarters, vol. 20,438, File 981.023(6), R.G. 24, P.A.C.

136. Weigley, *Eisenhower's Lieutenants*, 721.

137. Ellis, *Victory in the West*, II: 420., North, *Achievement of 21st Army Group*, 232.

138. 2 Canadian Corps Intelligence Summary Number 153, 6 April 1945, vol. 10,812, File 225C2.023(D39), R.G. 24, P.A.C.

139. Walter Maass, *The Netherlands at War: 1940-1945* (London: Abelard-Schuman, 1970), 228.

140. Brett-Smith, *Hitler's Generals*, 52.

141. Farley Mowat, *The Regiment*, (Toronto: McClelland and Stewart, Ltd., 1955), 301.

142. Williams, *Long Left Flank*, 288.

143. Mowat, *The Regiment*, 304.

144. MacDonald, *Last Offensive*, 460-461.

145. Hinsley, *British Intelligence*, III, Part 2, 726-727.

146. *I.M.T.*, VI: 396-398.; *I.M.T.*, XVI: 229-234.; The explosive charges were set up at the top of the dike, destroying it only to a level somewhat lower than the surface of the water. This may partly explain the rapidity of repair. By 1946 the dike was repaired and the land pumped dry for cultivation. See: N.W. Posthumus, ed., *The Netherlands During German Occupation* (Philadelphia: The Annals of the American Acadamy of Political and Social Science, 1946), vol. 425, 50-54.; See also: Jacob Zwann, "De Wieringermeer En Het Verzet," Unpublished article by retired archivist of the Rijksinstituut voor Oorlogsdocumentatie, kindly provided by D. van Galen Last, Librarian. Copy in author's possession. The U.S. General Walter Bedell Smith judged

the destruction of the dike a "military necessity." See *I.M.T.* above. According to "several high ranking Germans," they had no aircraft and no tanks, only one remaining weapon, and that was water. See: L. DeJong, *Het Koninkrijk Der Nederlanden in De Tweeds Wereldoorlog, Deel 106, tweede helft, Het Laatste Jaar II* (S'Gravenhage: Martinus Nijhoff, 1982), 1273. The author wishes to thank Colonel John Pelt (Netherlands-Ret.), former Dutch Military Attaché to the U.S. for providing a translation.

147. Montgomery, *Normandy to the Baltic*, 336-338.

148. Burton Andrus, *I Was the Nuremberg Jailer* (New York: Coward-McCann, Inc., 1969), 22-23. Hitler had certainly judged Seyss-Inquart's intelligence correctly. His I.Q. was 141 according to tests administered by the Allies in post-war captivity. Ibid., 102-103.

149. H.R. Trevor-Roper, ed., *Hitler's Secret Conversations, 1941-1944* (New York: Farrar, Straus and Young, 1953), 279.

150. Trevor-Roper, ed., *Hitler's War Directives, 1939-1945*, 206-207.; Speer, *Inside the Third Reich*, 476-477.

151. Eugene Davidson, *The Trial of the Germans* (New York: Collier Books, 1966), 460.

152. Ibid., 479.; Speer, *Inside the Third Reich*, 541.; *I.M.T.*, XVI: 12-13.

153. *I.M.T.*, XVI: 214-215.; In September 1945 Lieutenant-General Reichelt told his Canadian captors that Blaskowitz had repeatedly tried to avoid carrying out demolition orders and that he had proof of this in his notebook. WO 309/643, P.R.O.

154. Baird, *Mythical World of Nazi War Propaganda*, 252-253.

155. Supplement No.11 to FATHERLAND No.25, 5 April 1945, S.H.A.E.F., R.G. 331, N.A.

156. "Berne" (Via Radiophone), Entry 88, November 1944, Restricted "In" (#235-#245), R.G. 226, N.A.; Ibid., 16 March 1945.

157. Hastings, *Overlord*, 185.

158. "Mutiny Hits Germans: Impressed Russians and Poles Kill 50 Wehrmacht Soldiers," *The New York Times*, 17 April 1945, 6.

159. Williams, *Long Left Flank*, 280.

160. "8000 Dutch SS Men Make Germans Fight," *The New York Times* 1 May 1945, 3. On 24 April the SS and Police Commander in Fortress Holland reported to Himmler the "daily deterioration" and "poor German morale." Hinsley, *British Intelligence*, III, Part 2, 727.

161. J. Boolen and J. Van Der Does, *Five Years of Occupation: The Resistance of the Dutch Against Hitler-Terrorism and Nazi Robbery* (N.P.; The Secret Press of D.A.V.I.D., n.d.(circa 1945), 114-115. To support the Allies Dutch Railway workers went on strike. In an attempt to break the Dutch rail strike the

Germans would not allow food to be shipped until the Dutch gave up their strike. The Dutch refused to yield and the food situation worsened. Werner Warmbrunn, *The Dutch Under German Occupation: 1940-1945* (Stanford, California: Stanford University Press, 1963), 16-17.

162. Williams, *Long Left Flank*, 283-284.

163. "3,500,000 Reported Starving in Holland," *The New York Times*, 22 April 1945, 27.; The British Official History reports that a large proportion of the Dutch in western Holland had lost an average of 45 pounds in weight.; F. Donnison, *Civil Affairs and Military Government, North-West Europe, 1944-1946* (London: Her Majesty's Stationery Office, 1961), 147-148.

164. Norman Phillips and J.N. Kerk, *Holland and the Canadians*, (Amsterdam: Contact Publishing Company, N.D. circa 1946), 26.; The Dutch Prime Minister visited Montgomery's headquarters to hasten the attack on Holland, but was taken aback when he learned the extent of the destruction anticipated: "I felt he expected soldiers to fight without damaging his beloved country." Francis De Guingand, *Operation Victory* (London: Hodder and Stoughton, 1947), 439-440.

165. Hinsley, *British Intelligence*, III, Part 2, 727.

166. *I.M.T.*, XVI: 16-17, 229-230.; Maass, *Netherlands at War*, 236-237. One of Seyss-Inquart's deputies was almost simultaneously approached along similar lines.

167. Ibid.

168. CCS 387, Germany (9-21-44) Sec 2, U.S. Joint Chiefs of Staff, R.G. 218, N.A.

169. "Brief Historical Outline of the Occupations of N.W. Holland By 1 Canadian Corps," undated, circa May 1945, Background Papers for *The Supreme Command*, R.G. 319, N.A.

170. C.P. Stacy, *The Canadian Army, 1939-1945: An Official Historical Summary* (Ottawa: King's Printer, 1948), 267.

171. CCS 387, Germany (9-21-44) Sec 3, U.S. Joint Chiefs if Staff, R.G. 218, N.A.

172. G.R. Stevens, *Princess Patricia's Canadian Light Infantry, 1919-1957* (Griesbach, Alberta: Hamilton Gault Barracks, 1923-[1958]), III: 242-243.; G.R. Stevens, *The Royal Canadian Regiment*, Vol. II, *1933-1966* (London, Ontario: London Printing & Lithographing Co., Ltd., 1967), II: 192.

173. De Guingand, *Operation Victory*, 446-447.

174. Ibid., 450-452.; Walter Bedell Smith, *Eisenhower's Six Great Decisions* [Europe 1944-1945] (New York: Longman's Green and Co., 1956), 197-199.; "1 Canadian Corps intelligence Summary No. 290," 6 May 1945, War

Diary, General Staff, 1 Canadian Corps, Appendix 43, Vol. 13, 691, R.G. 24, P.A.C.

175. Jacobsen, ed., *Kriegstagebuch des Oberkommandos der Wehrmacht*, Vol. IV, No. 2, 1469.

176. Desmond Hawkins, *War Report*, 426-428.

177. Roger Freeman, *The Mighty Eighth: A History of the Units, Men and Machines of the U.S. 8th Air Force* (New York: Orion Books, 1970), 230.

178. "With the Canadian Troops in the Netherlands," *The New York Times*, 1 May 1945, 15.; "Allies Double Air Delivery of Food to the Netherlands," *The New York Times*, 1 May 1945, 15.

179. Freeman, *Mighty Eighth*, 230.

180. "Allies Feed Dutch Under Nazi Permit: Safe Conduct is Guaranteed Sea, Air Supply—The Hague and Rotterdam Fed First," *The New York Times*, 2 May 1945, 14.

181. Karl Doenitz, *Memoirs: Ten Years and Twenty Days*, trans. R.H. Stevens (New York: World Publishing Co., 1959), 441.

182. Ibid., 445-446.

183. Speer, *Inside The Third Reich*, 583-584.

184. Doenitz, *Memoirs*, 449-452.

185. Montgomery, *Normandy to the Baltic*, 346-347.; Ellis, *Victory in the West*, II: 333-334.; Seaton, *German Army*, 250.

186. Lockhardt, *T-Patch to Victory*, 280.

187. Seaton, *German Army*, 249-250.; Goerlitz, *German General Staff*, 498.

188. Montgomery, *Normandy to the Baltic*, 348-9.; Ellis, *Victory in the West*, II: 339.

189. 1 Canadian Corps Intelligence Summary No. 289, 5 May 1945, War Diary, General Staff, 1 Canadian Corps, Appendix 43, Vol. 13,691, R.G. 24, P.A.C.; "Brief Historical Outline of the Occupation of N.W. Holland by 1 Canadian Corps," undated, Background Papers to *The Supreme Command*, R.G. 319, N.A.

190. L. De Jong, *Het KoninKrijk Der Nederlanden in De Tweede Wereldoorlog*, Vol. 2, *Het Laatste Jaar II* (S'Gravenhage: Martinus Nijhoff, 1982), 1394-1396.

191. 1 Canadian Corps Intelligence Summary No. 289, 5 May 1945, War Diary, General Staff, 1 Canadian Corps, Appendix 43, Vol. 13,691, R.G. 24, P.A.C.

192. "Freedom for Holland; Surrender by Blaskowitz, Meeting with General Foulkes," *The Times* (London), 7 May 1945, 4.

193. The Surrender of Colonel-General Blaskowitz 5 May 1945, War Diary GSHQ, 1st Canadian Corps, Appendix 43, Vol. 13,691, File: 1 May-45 to 31 May 45, R.G. 24, P.A.C.

194. "What it feels like to be a German," *Daily Express* (London), 7 May 1945, 1.

195. 1 Canadian Corps Intelligence Summary No. 289, 5 May 1945, War Diary, General Staff, 1 Canadian Corps, Appendix 43, Vol. 13,691, R.G. 24, P.A.C.

196. "Freedom for Holland; Surrender by Blaskowitz, Meeting with General Foulkes," *The Times* (London), 7 May 1945, 4.

197. *Ibid.*; "Brief Historical Outline of the Occupation of N.W. Holland by 1 Canadian Corps," undated, Background Papers to *The Supreme Command*, R.G. 319, N.A.

198. 1 Canadian Corps Intelligence Summary No. 289, 5 May 1945, War Diary, General Staff, 1 Canadian Corps, Appendix 43, Vol. 13,691, RG. 24, P.A.C.; "Freedom for Holland; Surrender by Blaskowitz, Meeting with General Foulkes," *The Times* (London), 7 May 1945, 4.

199. De Jong, *Nederladen in De Tweede Wereldoorlog*, Vol. 2, *Het Laatste Jaar II*, 1,411.

CHAPTER XV

THE END

WHEN GENERALOBERST BLASKOWITZ put his signature on the instrument of surrender on 5 May it symbolized not only the German capitulation, it also represented a personal hiatus. Life as he had known it had come to an end. Indeed, his world had come to an end. That he had foreseen this end could not have been a source of solace.

The local surrender agreement Blaskowitz signed on the afternoon of 5 May became effective at 8:00 A.M. local time the following day. Almost immediately however, the jubilant Dutch learned of the surrender and flocked into the streets of the cities and towns across Holland to celebrate. In Rotterdam, Utrecht and Dordrecht there were reports that Dutch SS troops and a few German soldiers had opened fire on the crowds, killing and wounding an unspecified number of Dutch civilians. Prince Bernhard of the Netherlands called it a "last minute orgy of murder...." Blaskowitz ordered the Dutch SS rounded up, disarmed and jailed.[1] Further incidents had to be avoided.

Allied-controlled Netherlands Radio announced at 8 A.M. local time that "the surrender of [the] German occupation [forces] comes into force at this moment and that 'The country of the Netherlands is free again.'"[2] For many Dutch, literally on the verge of death by starvation, the news was nearly too late.

The Allies recognized that the ordeal endured by the Dutch people after September 1944 "was incomparably more severe than that suffered by any other country liberated in the west."[3] Accordingly, the Allies focused their efforts upon providing relief for the starving Dutch. But the Germans were not forgotten.

417

Montgomery decided to work through the existing German command structure to accomplish the goals of "Operation Eclipse," which aimed to return German troops to Germany."[4] It meant that Blaskowitz received his orders from a British Field Marshal. There was no time to waste. The Netherlands was a very dry powder keg. German soldiers still carried arms, as did the Dutch resistance and the small number of Canadian troops entering the Netherlands. The army of foreign workers was also part of the mix. Doubtless, many still felt they had old scores to settle.

Generally, however, the Allies found the German officers efficient and cooperative, "as though they still were under the command of the Reich." The German officers were so scrupulously "correct" that they sometimes gave the Canadians the impression of "a board of directors attending at the liquidation of their assets" instead of the leaders of a defeated army. It took some time for the Canadians to adjust to their recent enemies moving about freely in their midst. The realization that it had become the duty of the Canadians to protect the Germans from Dutch seeking revenge took longer still.[5]

The weapons that the flotsam and jetsam of the Reich in Holland surrendered to the victors was a motley collection of British Bren guns and Lee-Enfied rifles, American Garand rifles, French rifles, Thompson submachine guns, sten guns and a mixture of every automatic weapon produced in the countries the *Wehrmacht* had overrun.[6] With a kind of poetic irony, it suited the hodge-podge remnants of the once glorious *Wehrmacht*.

Blaskowitz was ordered to parade all persons under his command, army, navy, police and some civil staffs and to produce all individuals in Allied "automatic arrest" catagories. Blaskowitz's compliance produced ninety per cent of those wanted, including "complete Abwehr and SD units, Dutch Quislings and SS, and all SD and Gestapo officials up to major-general...." They were arrested and escorted to a German camp in Holland under Canadian guard.[7]

Even in moments of triumph and tragedy, there is occasionally still room for humor. The Canadian 48th Highlanders were assigned to move into the Hague and guard a large contingent of SS and Gestapo. After a tumultous welcome by the Dutch, the Highlanders began to encounter wandering German formations in search of some authority to whom they could surrender and who would provide them with food and prison lodging. Together the Highlanders and the SS encircled an area with barbed wire, disarmed the ranks and left the management to SS officers armed with lugers (which some used for suicide). Just as the Dutch were about to begin lobbing grenades over the wire the Canadian guards intervened. In response the SS began singing defiant Nazi songs at night. After some days had passed the SS officers demanded that the Canadians remove twenty-eight Dutch prostitutes from inside the compound. The "problem" was passed through channels to Brigade for "consideration and disposal."[8]

The mixture of German troops was incredible. In some instances German units marched proudly into capitivy, "heads held high and in good order. Almost every man (or boy) was carrying either a *panzerfaust* or a schmeisser as they marched in to end their war. They looked neither defeated nor dispirited."[9]

In other cases the impression was the diametric opposite. One German column making the return march to Germany "presented a very ragged and solvenly appearance." They marched by wagon convoys which looked like "gypsy processions" in camouflage paint. Along with them were about a hundred motor vehicles, in poor condition, carrying "sloppy looking officers." The lazier prisoners had abandoned their personal kits.[10] They made an altogether unfavorable impression—truly a defeated army.

In some cases even dispirited remnants of elite paratroop units—on their "involuntary *Drang Nach Osten*"[11]—were assaulted by rock-throwing Dutch civilians. "*Vae Victi*," woe to the vanquished.[12]

In such an immense undertaking as the return to Germany of her defeated armies amid the chaos of war torn Europe, it was surprising that there were so few "incidents." In part, the credit for this in Holland must be attributed to Generaloberst Blaskowitz. Aware of the tensions and dangers of the circumstances, and undoubtedly determined to avoid the worst of what took place in November 1918, Blaskowitz kept a firm grip on his subordinates down to lowest ranking soldier. Fully aware that unprecedented amounts of blood had been shed already, Blaskowitz was determined to see that German discipline in Holland remained strictly "correct."

On 17 May, Blaskowitz borrowed ten rifles and one hundred rounds of ammunition from the First Canadian Corps for the execution of ten German soldiers who had attempted to desert in civilian clothes. They had been given a summary trial and found guilty of desertion. According to Canadian headquarters, German discipline was consistently high and Blaskowitz's cooperation "generally satisfactory." There were still 98,000 Germans in captivity and approximately one thousand German headquarters and security troops were still fully armed.[13]

It was mid-June before the bulk of the Germans in Holland at the time of the capitulation had been marched to the Wilhelmshaven-Emden peninsula sector of northwestern Germany.[14] Blaskowitz naturally moved his headquarters there as well, but by that time his personal circumstances had undergone significant transformation.

6 June 1945 was a fair and warm day at Delden, Holland, where the First Canadian Army Headquarters was located. It was the first anniversary of D-day and, in commemoration, the day had been declared a holiday. It was no holiday for Blaskowitz, however; he was arrested as a war criminal and placed under guard as a prisoner by the Royal Montreal Regiment.[15] His arrest signaled the next step in his personal post-war odyssey. Until 14 June, Blaskowitz was kept prisoner under close arrest in a tent within a barbed wire compound. Charges against him were not specified,[16] and his arrest was due simply to his falling within the "automatic arrest" classification as a high-ranking German and past member of the General Staff.[17]

Ironically, little more than a month prior to Blaskowitz's arrest, a British Army officer had asked several captive German officers, Major General Siegfried von Waldenburg, Panzer-General Otto von Knobelsdoff, Lieutenant-General von Kleist, and one civilian prisoner, Franz von Papen, once the deputy chancellor in Hitler's first cabinet, to suggest for Allied consideration a suitable man to lead the reconstruction of Germany. Each of the men had named Blaskowitz, "a fine man" who had "avoided the dirty dealing in Poland.[18]

Blaskowitz was headed not for a position of power in the construction of the New Germany, but instead for a most unexpected "re-union" of Hitler's underlings at a place appropriately code-named "Ashcan" by the Americans, "Dustbin" to the British.

"Ashcan," alias "Dustbin," was more commonly called CCPWE #32, Central Continental Prisoner of War Enclosure number 32, by those few who knew of its brief and top-secret existence. That is before the worldwide press discovered it was Mondorf-les-Bains.[19]

Mondorf was a pleasant though small spa just on the Luxembourg side of the Franco-Luxembourg border. Founded more than a thousand years earlier by the Romans as a place to "take the waters," it had developed into a picturesque health resort with numerous inns, hotels and a clinic. The dominant feature of the town in the summer of 1945 was the Palace Hotel, a four-story luxury structure where Europe's elite had taken their holidays. It was a pretty and peaceful town on the Moselle River.

The Allied command had conceived of the Palace Hotel at Mondorf as a site where the elite of Nazi Germany would be gathered together under close guard and interrogated in secret. Reichsmarshal Goering, Albert Speer, Keitel, Jodl, Ribbentrop, Seyss-Inquart, Hans Frank, Doenitz, Rosenberg, Streicher and a host of Field-Marshals and Colonel-Generals were assembled—The whole hierarchy. Blaskowitz arrived there on 13 June.

Speer called it a "ridiculous memory" and "The only time I ever saw what was left of the Reich government assembled together ..."[20] He thought it a "ghostly experience" to find the relics of the Reich reunited.[21] The prisoners soon nicknamed "Ashcan" "das Prominent lager," the camp of the prominent people.[22]

Top-secret for obvious reasons, entry to the hotel was permitted only with a pass issued by General Eisenhower's headquarters, and signed by "Ike" himself.[23] When Lieutenant John Dolibois, U.S. Army Military Intelligence Service, who had been assigned by Military Intelligence to work at "Ashcan," first reported to the guard at the front gate he asked, "What kind of place is this? What's going on in there?" The guard responded, "Hell Lieutenant, I don't know. I've been here two weeks and I haven't been inside yet. To get in here you need a pass signed by God, and then somebody has to verify the signature."[24]

On 4 June SHAEF, Supreme Headquarters Allied Expeditionary Forces, had issued an order that "Luxury Furnishings will be removed if hotels are used for accomodations [for high-ranking German P.O.W.s] and there must be nothing which would suggest that special privileges are being accorded Germans or that they are being treated as guests."[25]

Already in late April, forty-two German P.O.W.s, including a barber, a dentist, a doctor and even a hotel manager had been moved into the Palace Hotel to prepare it for its high-ranking "guests." The fancy furniture had been relocated and replaced by folding army cots and straw mattresses.[26] The crystal chandliers were removed from the Hotel lounges as was the luxurious carpeting. A stockade was built around the hotel with four watch towers occupied by soldiers armed with machine guns. Barbed wire was stretched on the top of the stockade, and a camouflage screen was hung around the hotel to keep the Germans out of the gaze of any public that might try to observe them. Eventually, all 1600 glass window-panes were removed and replaced with shatter-proof plexi-glass and metal bars.[27] Ironically, when the glass-panes were broken (prior to replacement with plexiglass) the "inmates" laughed and called it "Kristallnacht."[28]

Replacement of the glass windows was taken as a suicide prevention measure. It was only one among many such measures. Pesonal property was searched and razor blades, scissors, shoe laces, neck-ties, suspenders, watches, walking sticks, canes and batons were confiscated.[29] Before their captivity ended the German P.O.W.s, Blaskowitz among them, doubtless became accustomed to such security measures.

Even during meals, security came first, knives and forks were banished. All meals were eaten with spoons, a particular source of grievance since, in Germany, "criminals" suffered such restrictions. Meals met the sixteen hundred calories per day prescribed by the Geneva convention; they were prepared by German P.O.W. cooks supervised by U.S. personnel. A typical day might include a breakfast of soup and a biscuit; dinner might be soup, hash, potatos, mashed peas and beet salad with coffee; supper might include a bean stew, bread and coffee.[30] It was not exactly a gourmet's delight, but it was suitable to sustain life.

The commandant of CCPWE #32 ("Aschcan") was an American army Colonel, Burton C. Andrus, who worried about the threat of fanatical Nazis trying to rescue the inmates, or furious anti-Nazi citizens of Luxemburg seeking revenge.[31] When a U.S. Department of State Mission led by George Shuster arrived at "Ashcan" to interrogate some of the German P.O.W.s Andrus told them "he knew how to keep these S.O.B.'s in line ...."

According to Ken Hechler, an American army officer involved in duties at "Ashcan," Andrus "was not a sadist, but he had a little mind and exercised his command through many petty demonstrations of "I am the boss now!"[32] For example, Andrus insisted that all German P.O.W.s come to attention whenever he appeared. The clever Germans, however, began to play games with such orders, springing to rigid attention and chanting "Guten Morgan Herr Leutnant" whenever any lieutenant entered their room. Eventually these matters settled down on both sides, the Germans abandoned their burlesque and Andrus restrained his "Chaplinesque figure of authority."[33]

The German inmates soon developed three cliques. The first was the generals: Keitel, Jodl, Walter Warlimont (Jodl's deputy at *OKW*), Kesselring, Blaskowitz and others. Later Rundstedt, Blomberg and Guderian joined them. They wanted as little as possible to do with the other prisoners and generally were quick to denounce them under interrogation. Most of them denied knowledge of Holocaust.[34]

The second group was made up of the Nazi Party Bosses, the "Bonzen:" Robert Ley, Julius Streicher, Hans Frank, Alfred Rosenberg, Seyss-Inquart and, of course, Hermann Goering. They blamed the generals for losing the war and the generals avoided them with disdain.

The third group was the bureaucracy of the Nazi Reich: Otto Meisner, Franz von Papen, Hans Lammers and Hjalmar Schacht. They tried to be "helpful" sources of information to the Allies and the only two of these brought to trial—Schacht and Papen—were acquited.[35]

During their time at "Ashcan" many of the inmates were repeatedly interrogated, sometimes by the Americans, on occasion by the Russians, now and then by others. Blaskowitz, however, was "neglected" at "Ashcan." The "Weekly Roster of Ashcan Internees" always had a place for "remarks;" Blaskowitz's place for remarks was commonly left blank.[36] Little of importance seemed to take place for him at Mondorf-les-Bains.

On 20 July 1945, a Major Ken Hechler, who had been assigned to establish an historical organization to tap the German military viewpoints on the war, arrived at "Ashcan." He finally called Blaskowitz for an interrogation about four P.M.

Blaskowitz went to the interrogation in full uniform. Initially, he made a less than favorable impression; "he was a short, rather comical looking, bald-headed character whose speech was handicapped by the lack of teeth. [Blaskowitz had lost his dentures in the Allied air raids on his headquarters in the spring.] Despite the unfavorable first impression of a comic figure, however, "he was deadly serious about everything he said and did, I slowly began to build up a respect for him and his knowledge of military tactics." The "interview" with Blaskowitz contrasted sharply in Hechler's perception, with that of Field Marshal Keitel, who had punctuated his "interview" with bows and scrapes and other despicable gestures ...."[37] Even in captivity, apparently, character could remain consistent.

Blaskowitz had been interrogated on the day prior to his arrest by the Canadians, and was interrogated again on 28 July, this time by the Americans. On another occasion he was taken to Wiesbaden temporarily for an interrogation.[38] Otherwise, he seems to have been neglected. He apparently endured the neglect with patience, probably utilizing the Bibles made available to all inmates at "Ashcan." And if he had not received mail from his family recently, he at least could take comfort in the knowledge that they had escaped the bombings of Dresden and had moved on to Bad Kissingen safely.[39] They had escaped the Red Army, but how would he ever find them?

By late July however, "Ashcan" had outlived its purpose. The world press had discovered it and clamored for photo and interview opportunities with those in captivity. The decision to move the prisoners to different locations followed. Since Colonel S.L.A. Marshall, head of the U.S. Army Historical Project, had received official approval of his plan to utilize the captured German officers to write their side of the war, it was a natural place to which to transfer Blaskowitz.[40] The site of his new "residence" was the Military Intelligence Service Center, United States Forces, European Theater (MISC-USFET), at Oberursel near Frankfurt.[41]

Oberursel had served during the war as a Luftwaffe Interrogation Center for American and R.A.F. fliers who had been shot down and whom the Luftwaffe had chosen to "sweat" for information. After the war some Americans thought it would be a "cute trick to give some of the same treatment to German prisoners."[42] Most convenient! Albert Speer spent one night at Oberursel, called it a "notorious Interrogation camp," and recorded that the sergeant in charge had greeted him with "crude mocking jokes" and a "thin, watery soup with which I nibbled my British biscuits."[43]

In the prison building the cells were dark, "hot and dirty;" comparable to a "telephone booth" with a double-decker wooden bunk without mattress or pillow. It was barely possible to stand up without bending slighty and the latrine was located at some distance from the cell. It was altogether unpleasant.[44]

Fortunately for Blaskowitz and a number of other German officers, there were other facilities which were not infamous. These were "Florida" House and "Alaska" House, where so-called "blue-ribbon" inmates, those cooperating with U.S. Army Intelligence or those such as Blaskowitz, who had been selected to work for the Historical Section compiling a History of German General Staff Corps, were housed. These "blue ribbon" P.O.W.s received preferential treatment in the form of soft beds, more food and exercise, and generally more comfort. Blaskowitz and the other "blue ribbon" prisoners had virtual freedom of movement within the Oberursel compound. They could wear their uniforms, but had to remove all badges of rank or merit.[45]

Blaskowitz was moved to Oberursel in the middle of the second week of August. The Americans had selected Walter Warlimont to be the temporary German leader of the German P.O.W.s working on the History of the German General Staff and Blaskowitz worked closely with him. Most of the Germans welcomed the opportunity to be involved in the project and were excited by it. At the very least, it would help pass the time as a P.O.W.[46]

The more low-key atmosphere at Oberursel among the "blue ribbon" P.O.W.s permitted the re-emergence in some of them of that exaggerated sense of self-importance which inevitably worked to their own detriment. Blaskowitz was not one of them. U.S. Army Captain John Dolibois, who transferred from Mondorf to Oberursel with the German P.O.W.s, later recalled that Blaskowitz was a very quiet, unassuming personality. He "spoke only when spoken to...," unlike some of the more blustering, arrogant members of the G[eneral] S[taff] C[orps]. "He impressed me as a competent tactician." According to Dolibois, Blaskowitz's opposition to SS and Police Actions in Poland when he was military governor there were part of his Prisoner of War Record and this information helped him considerably. Captain Dolibois was even told that Blaskowitz had described the atrocities in a memorandum "sent directly to Hitler" in which he had made some devastating charges of SS brutality which he was powerless to stop.[47]

Despite the comparatively moderate circumstances of his captivity, Blaskowitz was naturally worried about his family. The war had been over for four months and Blaskowitz had not received word from his wife since February. He had spoken to his daughter in early April, but had not received a word since then and was naturally feeling concerned. On 27 September he wrote to his old friend Koepcke, to his sisters and to his wife and daughter's last known address at Bad Kissingen, trying to make contact once again. His letter to his wife read in part:

> God grant you health and strength, to wait for me in faithful confidence. We three [including his daughter]will remain united happen what will.... I try to imagine with worry how you will be getting along, for I have almost no idea about the world outside. Healthy and with equanimity, I let pass over me all the difficult things of life unknown to me till now, more and more firmly believing in the Bible. Stay firs [sic], we will see each other again in our faith. All mentioned be heartily greeted, you two especially. Your daddy, who is provided with everything.
> —Johannes Blaskowitz [48]

Before he could receive a reply, before he could become too accustomed to the P.O.W. historical team at Oberursel, it was time for Blaskowitz to resume his journey. The victorious Allies had adopted the London Agreement on 8 August 1945, declaring their intention to bring to trial as major war criminals those individuals and organizations named in the indictment of the International Military Tribunal. One of these organizations was the "General Staff and High Command of the German Armed Forces." The Office of the U.S. Chief of Counsel for the Prosecution of Axis Criminalty, Robert H. Jackson, officially requested that Blaskowitz be brought to Nuremberg on 2 October 1945, for "interrogation and/or prosecution."[49]

In October of 1945 Nuremberg was a "gigantic rubble-heap" of burned-out and bomb-blasted houses. Albert Speer, Hitler's architect and Minister of Armaments and War Production, had known Nuremberg well in pre-war times, but found the city so shattered on his trip to Nuremberg for trial that he "could only guess where streets had once been." In the middle of the devastation the Nuremberg Palace of Justice stood, damaged, but nevertheless, still stood. Speer thought the building's survival a miracle with "deeper meaning"[50]

The Palace of Justice had been damaged by the bombing but was under repair. Hundreds of German P.O.W.s, many of them still wearing Waffen SS insignia on the uniforms, did the repair work on the Court and prison complex which had once served as the State of Franconia's prison. The SS men working on the prison repairs were considered dangerous by Colonel Andrus, who had taken over command of the Prison and court complex.[51] Surprisingly, however, Andrus seemed unconcerned about the German P.O.W.s who worked preparing meals, then delivering them. Perhaps he was not worried about them because, as he wrote later in his memoirs, "These men have been checked and double-checked. They are mostly Wehrmacht conscripts and are above suspicion. Already they are part of a team that has a common purpose."[52]

In Nuremberg the Palace of Justice building, on Further Street, was quite large and impressive. The prison itself was behind the main building, completely surrounded by a thirty foot high stone wall which formed a semi-circle. The central wing of the prison served as the chapel with four larger wings running from it, two at right angles almost like a cross and the other two at forty-five degree angles from the top of the chapel wing almost (when seen from a plane above the prison) like the blades of windmill. Witnesses for the trials were housed in the two wings running from the main chapel wing at right angles.

In the two wings where those on trial were held the prisoners were kept in solitary confinement. Each cell was nine feet long by thirteen feet wide and had a heavy wooden door with a small opening through which food and drink were passed and by which prisoners were kept under observation. One guard was present for every four cells. Each cell had a small barbed window. In each cell there was a metal cot which hung from the wall, a flimsy table and a straight chair. There was a small toilet—set in a niche in the wall for privacy—and a lavatory bowl. Even Colonel Andrus had to admit that the "Eerie stillness gives a strong impression of a abject loneliness as though time has stood still ... The very air feels imprisoned."[53] The atmosphere itself may actually have closed in on the prisoners to some extent. Speer recalled the penetrating odor of an American disinfectant wherever he was a prisoner.[54] Forty years later one of the guards from the First U.S. Infantry Division-the "Big Red One"—a Private Joel S. Parris, still remembered most vividly that the prison was "cold and clammy and depressing." He had to watch the prisoners very closely, never allowing them to put their hands under their blankets at night—presumably to prevent suicide.[55]

Wilhelm Keitel, one of Joel Parris' responsiblities to guard, thought conditions in the prison "less than eviable." He had lost substantial weight and claimed that his "nerves and frame of mind ..." had deteriorated. The interrogations were "wearying" and the solitary confinement a "burden." He complained that the "uncertainty over my fate" had taken a toll which he felt had resulted in "unchecked physical and mental decline."[56]

The guards contributed to the torment of some of the prisoners by having bright lights rigged to shine through the peek holes in the cell doors and then making little nooses out of string and dangling the nooses in front of the light so that a large shadow of a hangman's noose was cast on the wall at the back of the cell.[57] Try as they might, the authorities seemed powerless to stop such indignities.

Prisoners were permitted to have family photos, writing materials and personal toilet articles. Extra clothing, too, was allowed, as were showers once per week. Actually it was a "trickle bath" with hot water supplied by a wood stove fed by German P.O.W.s who were also watched by the guard supervising the prisoner taking the shower.[58]

Fortunately for Blaskowitz, he avoided the worst aspects of incarceration at this time because he was "treated as a willing witness for the prosecution."[59] This meant that instead of being held in the wings of the prison where those on trial were held, such as Keitel, he was housed in the witness wings. He had far more freedom. In fact, in the witness wings the cells were never locked. The prisoners were free to circulate and visit each other.[60]

The official opening session of the Tribunal was held at Berlin on 18 October 1945. It was a genuine "business" session; the indictment of charges was made. Preliminary hearings were held on 14, 15, and 17 November and the actual first session was held on Tuesday 20 November 1945. These Major War Crimes Trials lasted until 1 October

1946. Blaskowitz was held in Nuremberg in the witness wing from 2 October 1945 until May 1946.[61]

The American officials at Nuremberg kept very careful records of prisoner interrogations during the trials of the Major Criminals. Blaskowitz was interrogated only occassionally, filled out a few af-fadavits and questionaires and was once again largely neglected.[62] Fortunately, he continued to work on the General Staff Corps Histori-cal Project even while at Nuremberg.[63] Naturally, after late November 1945 when the German postal system began to function once again, he was able to renew correspondence with his family and friends, even providing some money for his wife's support by transferring funds to her with the assistance of the Prison Commandant, Colonel Andrus.[64]

On 14 March 1946 Blaskowitz wrote a letter to his old friend from World War I, Johannes Koepcke. Koepcke had recently written to him to remind him that he and his wife and daughter were always welcome to stay at Thomashof, Koepcke's farm. It was a welcome reminder. A new refugee law was about to go into effect and Blaskowitz hoped that his role as godfather to Koepcke's son Hans would legally make him eligible for release from prison to move to the farm. He asked Koepcke to please renew his release application. He continued:

> Your words were such bells in my ears, when you said: "be welcome here in my house." I hear it now .... Spring is on its way, I am well endowed with news from the family, I feel good and my body is well.... I wish also to say thank you and say hello to your family, with all my heart. Now, my dear friend, this is your old, but stable "captain."[65]

Blaskowitz admitted to Koepcke that he had "begun to contemplate a little on my past and think a little on the future." It was not easy for him to be homeless and without means, and to have to "seek shelter." He proposed to repay Koepcke by working on the farm; he had pushed himself physically, all of his life, and felt "strong and tough." His head worked well also," he asserted.[66]

The trial of the Major War Criminals dragged on through the spring of 1946. In April Blaskowitz was interrogated on three occasions.[67] Each interrogation had to do with the trial of the "General Staff and High Command of the German Armed Forces" still underway at Nuremberg. On 26 April the "High Command defense counsel, Dr.

Hans Laternser, attempted to introduce into evidence the very thorough and scientifically prepared report made by Blaskowitz..." to show that the High Command and General Staff had "always taken a stand against cruelty ... and to prevent atrocites ...."[68]

U.S. Justice Jackson, however, ruled that, "if what counsel says about General Blaskowitz is true, that is a defense for him, and I am right to say that General Blaskowitz did defy this Nazi conspiracy. And if that fact is ever verified, he certainly should not be subject to penalties for the acts which he stood up against." He continued, however, ruling that "the report which one particular general made does not tend to show that the group was either innocent or criminal." Therefore, Jackson ruled on 6 April that "what was contained in that report is not admissable."[69]

Whether there was any connection between these events and surviving but unexplained documents appears impossible to establish. What is known is that, some time prior to 28 March, the Prosecution requested that Blaskowitz and five others (Erich von den Bach-Zelewski, Bogislaw von Bonin, Adolf Heusinger, Hans Roettiger and Walter Schellenberg) be segregated from other prisoners held in the witness wing. The Prison Commandant, Colonel Burton Andrus, was unhappy with the segregation, "for reasons not known to this office, and which may have ceased to exist ...." In a memoradum, Andrus continued: "the present crowded condition of the jail makes it impossible to continue this segregation, and it will have to cease on April 1st."[70]

Two days after Andrus wrote this memo, and four days after Justice Jackson had ruled that testimony by Blaskowitz about his "Poland Memorandum "was not admissable in the General Staff and *OKW* trial, Blaskowitz proceeded to address a memorandum to Colonel Andrus requesting to see the German Defense Counsel, Dr. Laternser, "to clear some questions and to receive necessary explanations."[71] This request was followed on 5 April by a similar request again regretably without detailed explanation.[72] The unusual measure of segregating Blaskowitz and five others could only have been for their protection, but there is no further evidence.

What is established is that Blaskowitz was transferred, along with fifty-two others internees, from Nuremberg to the infamous PWE #29,

Dachau.[73] Dauchau, of course had become notorious as one of the earliest Nazi concentration camps; it was used by the Allies as Prisoner of War Enclosure number 29, and as a location for further War Crimes Trials.

Blaskowitz was transferred to Dachau on 30 April 1946. It was not the last he was to see of Nuremberg and the Palace of Justice. The transfer order itself hinted at this when it directed that the British Delegation to the International Military Tribunal be notified of Blaskowitz's transfer and further noted that Blaskowitz's name appeared on CROWCASS (Central Registry of War Criminals and Security Suspects) Wanted List No. 8 by Poland for Murder.[74]

There seems to be agreement in the surviving testimony of those who knew Blaskowitz well that his time as a prisoner "in Dachau and the conditions there caused him much distress."[75] Indeed Blaskowitz's faithful WW I comrade, Koepcke, later wrote that Blaskowitz's time at Dachau was the "harshest" of his entire life.[76]

Blaskowitz himself left no explanation as to why the period spent at Dachau was so difficult, but it can be fairly surmised. Dachau had primitive living conditions and had been known as a camp for "criminals;" he certainly did not think of himself as a criminal. Neither could the living conditions have been easy to accept. Further complicating his circumstances, perhaps, was the fact that, at that time, Dachau was inhabited overwhelmingly by SS men. On 16 May, roughly two weeks after Blaskowitz arrived at Dachau, the infamous Malmedy Massacre Trial commenced. The trial continued until 16 July when forty-three SS men were sentenced to death by hanging. A number of others received lesser sentences, for example, the SS leader that Blaskowitz had tried unsuccessfully to have arrested in Poland in 1939—Sepp Dietrich—received a life sentence.[77]

Imprisonment in a concentration camp alongside those whom he had tried to bring to justice could not have been easy to endure, or perhaps even to survive. Generaloberst Alexander von Falkenhausen, who was imprisoned at Dachau with Blaskowitz described the treatment as "worse than from the Gestapo. One is fully without rights."[78] Falkenhausen knew the Gestapo intimately from personnel experience. They had arrested him for complicity in the 20 July assasination attempt and put him into a concentration camp.

During his stay at Dachau other difficulties began to emerge for Blaskowitz, though he may not have known it. In the dossier of Blaskowitz's papers kept by the Allies, papers called his "201 File," there was an "Indentification of Prisoner" form which had a sub-section headed "Incident." Entries had read "witness" on Blaskowitz's "Identi-fication of Prisoner" form when he arrived at Dachau. Thereafter the "Incident" subsection had "witness" crossed out and "CROWCASS #7—Murder Civilian Poland" appeared. Then followed the statement: "This prisoner is a possible War Criminal and/or witness to a war crime and should not be released without notification and approval by this organization [Judge Advocate Section]."[79]

On another form Blaskowitz was listed as "cleared for extradition to Poland as a war criminal on 17 September 1946.[80] On still another form, this time dated 27 November 1946, he was described as "of No War Crimes interest to the U.S., but of possible War Crimes interest to the Polish authorities."[81]

Despite the difficulties of his situation at Dachau, Blaskowitz continued to write letters filled with strength to his relatives, encour-aging them to be strong. Ironically, Blaskowitz gave comfort to his relatives rather than the other way around. Even at Dachau itself, he was a "model of calmness and composure for his comrades." Despite his harsh situation, he never lost his nerve.[82]

Finally, in January 1947, Blaskowitz was transferred from Dachau to Allendorf near Marburg.[83] Blaskowitz was the senior ranking German P.O.W. at Allendorf, succeeding Field Marshal Wilhelm Ritter von Leeb in this role.[84] Blaskowitz was again put to work for the U.S. Army Historical Project, this time writing a report on the retreat of Army Group G in 1944. After his time at Dachau, the transfer to Allendorf must have been a relief.

Behind the scenes, unknown to Blaskowitz, there appeared to be yet further relief. The Netherlands, which had filed charges with the United Nations War Crimes Commission,[85] decided on 3 March 1947 that it had no objection to Johannes von Blaskowitz [sic],"who appears on UNWCC-List No. 42 [as] No. 56 as wanted by the Netherlands [,] being handed over to Poland for the trial."[86]

According to a memorandum sent out by the British Army of the Rhine five months earlier, the British had no interest in Blaskowitz either.[87] Later that month, the British requested that Blaskowitz be transferred to their custody temporarily as a witness in the trial of General Kurt Gallenkamp relative to events that had taken place near Poitiers, France in early July 1944. The British, however, apparently did not follow up their request and Blaskowitz did not appear as a witness at that trial.[88]

When Blaskowitz had been at Allendorf for nine months, he was given a leave from prison upon his word of honor that he would return in two weeks time. It was not an unusual privilege at this date, for "blue ribbon" P.O.W.s.[89] His leave began on Wednesday, 3 September 1947. He spent it at the home of his oldest and most loyal comrade from WW I, Johannes Koepcke, where his own wife Anna had been staying since shortly after the end of the war.

Blaskowitz found solace and comfort with his wife of forty-two years and his best friend at Thomashof in Bommelsen. Koepcke spoke positively to Blaskowitz:

> Captain, do not worry, very soon, very, very soon everything is going to be normal again, and we can iron out those few wrinkles left ....[90]

On Sunday morning, 7 Semptember 1947, Blaskowitz and his wife Anna were awoken by a serenade by the Bommelsen Trumpet Choir, a distinguished local choir which had been sufficiently distinguished to perform at Potsdam in former days. Koepcke, coincidently, was the chief of the choir, whose performance clearly was a moving one for Blaskowitz. After the concert, Blaskowitz agreed to say a few words to the audience that had come from the surrounding farms and villages to greet him:

> There will be a day, and the day is coming soon, where I will be free and I will be able to join you in Bommelsen. I want to be here, with my old friend Koepcke, who is the one and only faithful and loyal friend to me, and who is my brother forever. I want to help build up Germany again, make it mine and yours. Make it into our homeland again. Germany, our fatherland, will rise again.[91]

Koepcke continued to be optimistic: "Captain, very soon you will be with us for good. Your attorney says that you cannot be harmed and brought to trial because they cannot find anything on you ..."[92]

At the end of his two weeks leave Blaskowitz said goodbye to his wife, who showed the strain of the circumstances, and to everyone else at Thomashof with great bearing, with pride and dignity. According to those present, he showed no visible signs of sadness.[93] His friends were in awe of him because he did not become cynical or sarcastic, but simply continued to do what he knew what was right.[94] He returned as promised to Allendorf.

Blaskowitz was transferred upon his return to Allendorf to the nearby camp at Neustadt, also close to Marburg.[95] He resumed work on the historical project there. Once again in confinement, Blaskowitz immediately took the opportunity to write to his old friend Koepcke:

> Now I am back here by myself, alone and yet peaceful, for I have the memories, I have the full feeling of being loved, and thought of, and when I look at the destruction that the war has caused I remember the days with you and I am in heaven. Each time I am with you, I am refreshed, reborn, remade, redone, reincarnated, ready to pull through again.[96]

He ended his letter, declaring, "You have made me happy when I visited because you are a healthy and a happy man! As long as I know that you are alright, more than alright, I will be alright too."[97]

While Blaskowitz was at Neustadt, he was visited by the Reverend Ernst Froese, who had served for a time as Chaplain to First Army at Bordeaux. Froese concluded from the visit with Blaskowitz that the Generaloberst "had not lost any of his integrity and wholesomeness that I had known him to have. He had no knowledge of what was awaiting him in the future, but his conscience was clean and he was fearless. We had a good conversation."[98]

Blaskowitz had been at Neustadt for only a month when the Office of the Chief of Counsel for War Crimes, Mr. Telford Taylor, requested that Blaskowitz and a number of other Germans be brought to Nuremberg for interrogation. The memorandum still classified Blaskowitz as a "witness."[99] Two days later, 17 October 1947, Blaskowitz's status was changed to "Defendant."[100] When Blaskowitz returned to Nuremberg, this time it was to the defendant's wing.

On 2 November the Generaloberst wrote again to Koepcke, this time to thank him for a Biblical quotation which he had hung on the wall of his cell. It was Romans 12:12, "Rejoice in hope, be patient under trial, persevere in prayer."[101] Two weeks later, in another letter, Blaskowitz wrote to Koepcke, "I am doing well under the circumstances, I have pretty much adjusted to my way of life here."[102]

On 28 November Blaskowitz and thirteen other Germans including three Field Marshals (Wilhelm von Leeb, Hugo Sperrle and Friedrich von Küchler), nine generals (Hermann Hoth, Hans Reinhardt, Hans von Salmuth, Karl Hollidt, Karl von Roques, Hermann Reinecke, Walter Warlimont, Otto Woehler and Rudolf Lehmann), and one admiral (Otto Schniewind) received the indictment. It was indeed a formidable document.

The indictment handed over at four P.M. on 28 November was couched in the sweeping terms which had become familiar since the trial of the "Major" War Criminals: Count One—Crimes Against Peace; Count Two—War Crimes and Crimes Against Humanity: Crimes Against Enemy Belligerents; Count Three—Crimes Against Humanity—Crimes Against Civilians; and, Count Four—Common Plan or Conspiracy.[103]

Paradox and tragedy surround both Blaskowitz's indictment and the remainder of his life. He who had been a spokesman for decency and Human Rights in occupied Poland; he who, on his own responsibilty, had issued orders in contradiction to Hilter's for the treatment of the Maquis, was charged with "crimes against humanity."[104] Despite the difficulties of his own circumstances, however, he seemed to maintain a "very rooted and firm attitude."[105]

On 17 December 1947, for example, he wrote to his loyal friend Koepcke:

> I am confident and I know, that I will have the strength to go the way that God chooses for me to go, and when the time comes, I will be as good as I have to be. In the meantime, you can be sure that during the holidays, I will more often than not have a conversation with you in my thoughts, and I want you to relax as if I were right next to you, sitting there. Please give my warmest wishes to everyone on the Thomashof, and my heartfelt wishes for a Merry Christmas and a Happy New year.
> —Always, your Old Captain [106]

In another letter on 27 December, he wrote;

> I do feel the grace of God, who has guided me this far, and has

never left me, I do feel the strength and love of God, when He leads us through the rocky patch. You know me well enough to be aware that I will not yield to destructive thought and action, that I will cling to my chosen path, the path of God. My belief in God is not shaken. When I am alone in my cell, I feel His strength around me and I am always surprised, how many comrades come to me for solace and comfort, while they are the ones giving me comfort through their belief in me.[107]

It is clear that his deep faith was indeed a mighty fortress, even in prison at Nuremberg. Evidence of this is undeniable, as found in his letter of the following day, 28 December 1947:

I can see how gentle and kind God is and how He knows how to keep us from being hurt when we are getting hurt. I know why God chooses not to let us see our fate. I know now also that this trial will pass, that all I have endured in the past was nothing but a preparation for this, and that it is with the knowledge of these things that I don't despair. It is the knowledge that there are people out there right now that think about me and honor me and will not forget what they shared with me. This is what helps me to go on and carry through.[108]

Deeply faithful in God, Blaskowitz nevertheless experienced those awful, aching spasms of doubt that all men may have at difficult junctures when life may seem momentarily to have been a mistake. This may have been one of those times. His memoranda of protest, written in Poland in 1939 and 1940 had, to his knowledge, not been found and were therefore apparently unavailable for his defense. This caused him to be "very depressed," according to Friedrich Christian Stahl, a German historian who later wrote a sketch of Blaskowitz.[109] Major-General Eckhart von Tschammer und Osten, who might have served as a witness to the events in Poland, had been put on trial for atrocities by the Soviets in January 1946, found guilty, and hanged the same day.[110] General Erwin Jaenecke, who also might have served as a witness, had been tried by a Soviet Court at Sevastopol the previous month, 2 November 1947, found guilty and sentenced to twenty-five years imprisonment.[111] Other witnesses were dead or missing. In these inauspicious circumstances Blaskowitz's trusted friend, Koepcke, began to scramble for affadavits for Blaskowitz's defense. Blaskowitz's court appointed counselor, Dr. Heinz Müller-Torgow, did the same.[112]

Blaskowitz was also troubled by another burden. He worried that "he might cause damage to his comrades by revealing things about them."[113] Having to speak against one's comrades violated every principle of loyalty and comradeship with which he had been imbued since his days as a cadet at Köslin and Gross-Lichterfelde. It was not an enticing prospect to consider; but it was one which had to be examined.[114]

In the meantime, developments continued to unfold. On 30 December 1947, Blaskowitz pleaded "not guilty." When the Allies made up their rosters of defendants and internees confined at Nuremberg on 7 January 1948, there were 116 defendants and 131 witnesses, including Blaskowitz.[115] The jail population had been significantly reduced. This change may have been the result of the efforts of Walter Rapp of the U.S. Evidence Division.

On 30 July 1947, Rapp had addressed a memorandum to Prosecution personnel requesting that every effort be made to transfer to the facility at Dachau all witnesses and defendants not immediately required by the Prosecution. Rapp complained that there were 461 prisoners then held at Nuremberg "which number already is beyond its actual capacity." He continued, suggesting that "A serious shortage of guards, deterioration of health and the letting down of security measures ...," necessitate transfer of some of the prison population to Dachau.[116] Among the security measures which had been allowed to lapse was the inexplicable removal of the security nets which had been streched between the tiers of the prison galleries during the trials of the "major" war criminals to prevent suicide attempts. Prison officials had declared the prison "suicide-proof" at that time. They would no longer make such a claim.

Indeed, much had changed within the prison since the days of the "Major" War Crimes Trials. In January 1947, for example, refugee Lithuanians were reported by Albert Speer as replacing the American guards. "I bade the American guards a reluctant goodbye.," Speer wrote. But he soon came to appreciate their Lithuanian replacements who "even permit us to visit the witnesses for the new trials in the other wing of the prison: generals, industrialists, ambassadors, state secretaries, party functionaries."[117] Even in mid-February 1947, Speer wrote: The Lithuanian guards still have trouble abiding by strict regulations.

They repeatedly allow me to go into the witness wing with a pail and broom. This afternoon I talked there with several generals..."[118]

By the time that Blaskowitz returned to Nuremberg for his trial, the Lithuanian guards had been supplemented by Estonian guards. In fact, there were the 8920th Guard Company, called the "Baltic" Company, presumably composed of Lithuanians, the 4221st Estonian Guard Company and the remaining American guards.[119]

The presence of non-Americans as guards at Nuremberg, according to Mr. David Petree, Director, U.S. National Personnel Records Center, was attributable to U.S. recognition that there were "a vast number of displaced persons in Europe at the end of World War II." Therefore, the U.S. established a Labor Service as a method of utilizing the displaced people. Many of these were organized into units which relieved U.S. troops of certain duties. They were given food, uniforms and housing and were assigned enlisted ranks from Private to Master Sergeant for organizational purposes, but they "were not members of the U.S. Armed Forces, nor were they civilian employees of the United States Government."[120]

These Labor Service Companies have been described as "non-American service auxiliaries attached to the U.S. Army in Germany."[121] Their role was reportedly "to guard POW camps, clear rubble from bombed-out cities, locate graves of casualties, and carry out similar tasks.[122] In any case, some of these Labor Service Companies became guards at Nuremberg during Blaskowitz's final stay there in late 1947 and early 1948. In particular, it was the Estonian guards who are relevant; they were on duty on 5 February 1948, a fateful day for Blaskowitz.

On the 5th day of February 1948 the *United States of America v. Wilhelm Ritter von Leeb et al.*(case XII) began. It has become more commonly known as the "High Command Case." Blaskowitz was one of the fourteen defendants scheduled to appear at 9:30 A.M. before the Tribunal in the courtroom at the Palace of Justice for the commencement of the trial proceedings. All of those scheduled to appear were there that morning; all, that is, except Blaskowitz.

The Associated Press announced that morning that Generaloberst Johannes Blaskowitz, a "64-year old Wehrmacht veteran, killed himself today in a flying leap from the top tier of the Nuremberg prison only a short time before his trial with 13 other commanders was due to open."[123] According to the news release, Blaskowitz broke away from a file of prisoners on the third tier in the prison, climbed up a seven-foot protective wire, then hurled himself over it, plunging thirty feet to the floor below. His chest was crushed, his lungs punctured by fractured ribs, and he died shortly afterwords in the 385th U.S. Military Hospital.[124]

The New York Times provided a bit more detail the next day. According to its story, Blaskowitz and his thirteen co-defendents "were returning in single file from the prison barber shop and had mounted a spiral staircase to the third or top story." Blaskowitz then reportedly climbed the wire netting and dived to the concrete floor below, crushing his chest, although he did not die until three hours later in the hospital.[125]

On the heath of the North German Plain, in the town of Bommelsen, lies Thomashof, the farm where Blaskowitz's life-long friend Koepcke, lived with his wife and son Hans, and where Blaskowitz's wife had resided since shortly after the end of the war. That fateful morning each of the members of the household had risen early as usual. A knock at the door and the delivery of a telegram to Johannes Koepcke Sr., abruptly jolted the day out of the ordinary. The telegram read: German Reich-Post, Telegram, Nuremberg; Frau Anna Blaskowitz, Bommelsen; "Your husband died this morning, please come." [signed] Heinz Müller-Torgow [Blaskowitz's defense counsel] [126]

Koepcke was dazed by the telegram. He understood its contents but simultaneously failed to grasp its meaning. His hands involuntarily shook. He put the telegram into his pocket and walked around the house to a place from which he could see the spot where Blaskowitz, his "captain," had stood a few months prior and thanked the trombonists for their concert. He had promised to join them in Bommelsen soon. Koepcke thought that it just didn't fit, didn't make sense. Something was wrong. He turned around, entered the house and saw Blaskowitz's wife Anna sitting near the window, listening to the radio, as she did every morning, perhaps hoping to hear good news on the BBC.[127]

Koepcke entered the kitchen, where his wife was making breakfast. He showed the telegram to her, her face quickly turning into grief as she began to cry. She asked: "Did you tell her?" Koepcke shook his grey head. "I cannot do it. I am afraid she will die of fright and despair. We have to ...."[128]

Just then Koepcke's young son, Hans, Jr., came in from the fields, and immediately knew from their faces that something was wrong. His father handed the telegram to him. He too turned "ashen." He had worshipped Blaskowitz. Suddenly Koepcke,Sr., said, "the radio—she cannot listen to the news." Young Koepcke ran to the fuze box and took out the fuze. The electricity was off, the radio silent. It was dark.

Frau Blaskowitz entered the kitchen and asked, "What is wrong?" Young Hans Jr. responded, "Nothing much, just a fuze" A candle was lit and they all sat quietly. Frau Blaskowitz was unaware that she was now a widow, but she sensed that something was awry; the Koepckes could not cover up their shock. Tears ran down Frau Koepcke's face and young Hans Jr. bit hard on his lips, fighting back tears. "Something must have happened, talk to me," Frau Blaskowitz said. "For God's sake—is he ill?" Koepcke answered, "Very ill, very very ill ...." His voice became hoarse, he struggled to speak: He is ..., he is ...." He could not say it. Frau Blaskowitz screamed: He is no longer with us?" "We cannot believe it ourselves," Koepcke's son said, "But the telegram from his attorney is clear. It is possible that he was sick and did not want to worry us ..."[129]

The men left the room, the woman remained there weeping, trying to grasp it all. Frau Blaskowitz was "heartbroken and without strength, just crying". The men went to the stables as if to find comfort from the animals. A neighboring farmer entered a short time later. He had heard the news on the radio; it was a suicide. During an unattended moment, Blaskowitz jumped the railing from the third tier in the prison".[130]

Koepcke could not believe it. He wrote: "Nobody knows what happened and what caused his death. One can only guess. Some say it was suicide. Some say it was an accident in the stairwell of the courtyard where he fell to his death".[131] Koepcke had known his old "captain" for a lifetime. He had known the depth of Blaskowitz's religious faith. His "captain would never have taken his own life![132]

The Reverend Ernst Froese from East Prussia, who had been Blaskowitz's First Army chaplain at Bordeaux, and who had visited

Blaskowitz recently at Neustadt just prior to his transfer to Nuremberg, could not believe the news either. "I cannot believe that he took his own life, from the way I know him to be and from the way I found him in Marburg and from everything about him. It does not fit ...."[133]

Koepcke and Frau Blaskowitz went to Nuremberg in the pouring rain to fetch Blaskowitz's corpse. It was a lengthy trip by train, involving numerous changes of route. Koepcke and Frau Blaskowitz traveled in silence, Koepcke re-reading Blaskowitz's letters to try and discover a clue that had been overlooked, something sounding desperate. There was none.[134]

Koepcke and Frau Blaskowitz claimed the body at Nuremberg, purchased a simple black coffin with a silver crucifix on it, and returned in silence by train to Fallingbostel, the nearest train station to Thomashof at Bommelsen. They made the rest of the journey by hearse, travelling slowly down the main street of the village. When the hearse arrived at the Thomashof, Koepcke stepped out and held the widow Blaskowitz closely for support; she was beside herself in tears and grief.[135]

The generaloberst's body was taken to the local church, where a burial service was held on St. Valentine's day, 14 February 1948. Fittingly, but in disbelief, the trumpet choir that had played so recently for Blaskowitz was at the funeral for his final requiem. A number of civilian and military figures attended the ceremonies, along with a number of the local people from Bommelsen. Blaskowitz's window grieved deeply, but with dignity, as did the general's daughter Anne-marie, and Koepcke.

The eulogies often referred to the Generaloberst's warm humanity and his piety, his humility, his sense of duty, his courage in defying the Nazi terror in Poland, his likeness to a knight who always fought for justice. They spoke of his sorrow as he witnessed the destruction of his country during a war which he had long since known was lost. He loved nature. He was a family man and did not seek fame as a general. Neither did he win it. And then the eulogies came to the subject of his death.

There were three men who delivered eulogies, a Herr Schrader, the Superintendent from nearby Fallingbostel, the district's biggest city; Pastor Froese, who had been Blaskowitz's Army Chaplain at Bordeaux;

and a Dr. Gerd Wolff, a local luminary. Each grappled with the matter of "suicide". Each repeated the story then circulating that the charges against Blaskowitz were without substance and the trial a mere formality prior to his release from custody. Herr Schrader then spoke of the end:

> We all know that there were several who could not bear the burden, who chose to go to their own death, at their own time and at their own free will! The burden of imprisonment was geared and intended to wear the prisoners down morally, spiritually and physically. And this it did. Imprisonment was not easy on Blaskowitz. It did not wear him down, but it showed upon his face and in his body posture. Now we are told that Blaskowitz took his own life. We are being told that but we don't know that is true. Nobody saw him take his own life. If we never find out what happened, we will have the assurance that he was with God, that he had found some form of peace of mind in his exasperating and unjust imprisonment. That he was a little tired and maybe this was his time to go.[136]

In his eulogy, Pastor Froese added one most important thought to what Herr Schrader had said: "It is useless for us to argue about what went on while he died. We will probably never know for sure what happened."[137] It is a "conclusion" that has had many echoes.

On his grave, in the churchyard at Bommelsen, under twin birch trees, where he is buried with his wife, there is a simple stone cross. The inscription states, "Durch Kreuz—zur Krone," (Through the Cross to the Crown).

Notes for Chapter XV

1. "Freedom for Holland; Surrender by Blaskowitz, Meeting with General Foulkes," *The Times* (London), 7 May 1945, 4; "Germans Murder Dutch Celebrants," *The New York Times*, 6 May 1945, 9.; "Avoid Incidents Netherlands Told," *The New York Times*, 7 May 1945, 3; Peter Simonds, *Maple Leaf Up, Maple Leaf Down: The Story of the Canadians in the Second World War* (New York: Island Press, 1947), 348.

2. "War Racing to End," *The New York Times*, 5 May 1945, 1.

3. Donison, *Civil Affairs and Military Government, North-West Europe, 1944-1946*, 151.

4. Arthur Smith, *Churchill's German Army: Wartime Strategy and Cold War Politics, 1943-1947* (Beverly Hills, California: Sage Publications, Inc., 1977), 73.

5. Stevens, *Royal Canadian Regiment*, II: 194.; Stacey, *Victory Campaign*, III: 613.

6. Ibid.

7. S.R. Elliot, *Scarlet to Green: A History of Intelligence in the Canadian Army, 1903-1963* (Toronto: Canadian Intelligence and Security Association, 1981), 334.

8. Kim Beattie, *Dileas, History of the 48th Highlanders of Canada, 1929-1956* (Toronto: privately printed,1957) , 762-764.

9. Williams, *Long Left Flank*, 299.

10. Harold Jackson, *The Princess Louise Dragoon Guards: A History* (Owen Sound, Ontario: np., 1952), 277.

11. Stacey, *Victory Campaign*, III: 615.

12. Martin Poppel, *Heaven and Hell: The War Diary of a German Paratrooper*, trans. Louise Willmot (New York: Hippocrene Books, Inc., 1988), 238.

13. "10 Germans Executed by Blaskowitz," *The Times* (London), 18 May 1945, 1.

14. Stacy, *Victory Campaign*, III: 615; Pogue, *Supreme Command*, 503.

15. Royal Montreal Regiment War Diary, First Canadian Army Headquarters Defense Battalion, 6 June 1945, Vol. 15,224, R.G. 24, P.A.C.; R.C. Fetherstonhaugh, *The Royal Montreal Regiment*, 1925-1945 (Westmount, P.Q.: privately printed, 1949), 206.

16. "Blaskowitz Arrested," *The Times* (London), 11 June 1945, 3,; "Blaskowitz Arrested," *The New York Times*, 10 June 1945, 6.

17. C.I.C. [Counter INTELLIGENCE CORPS] Central Registry, IRR Files, Subject File, German General Staff Study, XE001893, Vol. IV, Folder (3), R.G. 319, N.A., Although Blaskowitz was not charged with a specific crime publicly, on his "Military Government of Germany, War Criminal Arrest Report, 6 June 1945, the reason stated for arrest was that his name appeared in Crowcass Wanted List No. 1, P.5, serial 52, dated April 1945." "War Criminal Arrest Report," Headquarters Nürnberg Military Post, 6850th Internal Security Detachment, OCCPAC and OCCWC, 201 files, R.G. 238, N.A.; Crowcass is Central Registry of War Criminals and Security Suspects, SHAEF AGWAR SVC 3067, 15 June 1945, International Affairs Division, War Crimes Bureau, Case 103-1A, R.G. 153, N.A.

18. 6824 DIC(MIS)/X-P3, "Ashcan" Reports and Miscellaneous File, MIS-Y, G-2, World War II, European Theatre of Operations, R.G. 332, N.A. This is a security monitored conversation.

19. John Dolibois, *Pattern of Circles: An Ambassador's Story* (Kent, Ohio: The Kent State University Press, 1989), 96.

20. James O'Donnell, "The Devil's Architect," *The New York Times Magazine*, 26 October 1969, 107.

21. Speer, *Inside the Third Reich*, 594.

22. Leo Kessler, *The Battle of the Ruhr Pocket* (Chelsea, Michigan: Scarborough House/ Publishers, 1989) 148.

23. Leon Jaworski, *After Fifteen Years* (Houston, Texas: Gulf Publishing Company, 1961), 140.

24. Dolibois, *Pattern of Circles*, 84-85.

25. Paraphrase of State Department Cable Information to War Department, NR. 3279, 4 June 1945, International Affairs Division, War Crimes Bureau, War Crimes Case 103-1A, RG. 153, Records of the Office of the Judge Advocate General, N.A.

26. Dolibois, *Pattern of Circles*, 87.

27. Andrus, *Nuremberg Jailer*, 22-23.

28. Dolibois, *Pattern of Circles*, 93.

29. Andrus, *Nuremberg Jailer*, 29.

30. "Ribbentrop nearly got bread and water," *Daily Mail*, N.D., N.P. *B.H. Liddell Hart Papers*, Kings College London, LH 9/24/183.

31. Andrus, *Nuremberg Jailer*, 23.

32. Kenneth Hechler, "The Enemy Side of The Hill: The 1945 Background on Interrogation of German Commanders" (Unpublished), Series 1, Box 12,

The Last Hundred Days, John Toland Papers, Madison Manuscript Library, Library of Congress, 19.

33. Dolibois, *Pattern of Circles*, 95-96.

34. Ibid., 92.

35 Ibid., 92-93.

36. WO 208/4969, WO 208/3183, P.R.O.

37. Hechler, "Enemy Side of the Hill," 37.

38 Dolibois, *Pattern of Circles*, 106.

39. Steuben, "So blieb er ohne Marshallstab", 11-12.

40. S[amuel] Marshall, *Bringing Up the Rear, A Memoir*, ed. Cate Marshall (Novato, California: Presidio Press, 1979), 156-158.

41. Anhang zum Fragebrogan, undated, Headquarters Nürnberg Military Post, 6850th Internal Security Detachment, OCCPAC and OCCWC, 201 Files, R.G. 238, N.A.

42. Martin Middlebrook, *The Nuremberg Raid: 30-31 March 1944* (New York: William Morrow & Company, Inc., 1974), 272-273; Dolibois, *Pattern of Circles*, 134; Hechler, "Enemy Side of the Hill", 122.

43. Speer, *Inside the Third Reich*, 599.

44. Hechler, "Enemy Side of The Hill," 122 & 137.

45. Ibid., 122-123.; Dolibois, *Pattern Of Circles*, 142-143.

46. Ibid (Dolibois).

47. Letter, John Dolibois, Oxford, Ohio, to the author, 10 December 1991. Copy in author's possession.

48. Letter, Johannes Blaskowitz to Frau Anna Blaskowitz, Headquarters Nürnberg Military Post, 6850th Internal Security Detachment, OCCPAC and OCCWC, 201 Files, R.G. 238, N.A.

49. Office of U.S. Chief of Counsel for Prosecution of Axis Criminality, 2 October 1945, Headquarters Nürnberg Military Post, 6850th Internal Security Detachment, OCCPAC and OCCWC, 201 Files, R.G. 238, N.A.

50. Albert Speer, *Spandau: The Secret Diaries*, trans. Richard and Clara Winston (New York: Macmillan Publishing Company, Inc., 1976), 52.

51. Andrus, *Nuremberg Jailer*, 73.

52. Ibid., 84.

53. Ibid., 83-84.

54. Speer, *Spandau*, 7-8.

55. Letter Joel Parris, Shelby, Missouri, 26 June 1986, to the author. Copy in author's possession.

56. Keitel, *Memoirs*, 30-31.

57. Letter, Joel Parris, Shelby, Missouri, 26 June 1986, to the author. Copy in author's possession. see also; The Robert B. Franklin Sr. Papers, Oral History Project 82-III, Colonel Robert B. Franklin, Sr., U.S.A. (Ret.). Interviewed by Colonel Frasche, U.S.A. and Lt. Col. Robert B. Franklin, Jr. (U.S.A.) 1982. The Robert B. Franklin, Sr. Papers, Archives, U.S.A.M.H.I., Carlisle Barracks, PA.

58. Speer, *Spandau*, 16.; Dolibois, *Pattern of Circles*, 148.

59. Letter, John Dolibois, Oxford, Ohio, to the author, 10 December 1991. Copy in author's possession.

60. Dolibois, *Pattern of Circles*, 167.

61. Anhang zum Fragebogen, undated, Headquarters, Nürnberg Military Post, 6850th Internal Security Detachment, OCCPAC and OCCWC, 201 Files, R.G. 238, N.A.

62. See for example: 3706-PS, *N.C.A.*, 6: 417.; See also: Telford Taylor, *The Anatomy of the Nuremberg Trials*, (New York: Alfred Knopf, 1992), 240-241, 251.; *I.M.T.*, 21: 380.; *I.M.T.*, 42: 226-228.; *I.M.T.*, 21: 403-404.

63. Dolibois, *Pattern of Circles*, 184-185.

64. Letter, Blaskowitz to Andrus, Nuremberg, 28 November 1945, Headquarters, Nuremberg Military Post, 6850th Internal Security Detachment, OCCPAC and OCCWC, 201 Files, R.G. 238, N.A.

65. Letter, Blaskowitz to Koepcke, 14 March 1946, Justice Palace, Nuremberg, *Collection Koepcke*. Copy in author's possession.

66. Ibid.

67. Interrogation Record, 10 January 1946, 2 April 1946, 29 April 1946 & 30 April 1946, entry 199, R.G. 238, N.A.

68. *I.M.T.*, XII: 303.

69. Ibid., 303-305. The only evidence to Blaskowitz's protests to Hitler about conditions in Poland in 1939-1940 appears to have been Blaskowitz's testimony under interrogation, which was apparently received, at least by Justice Jackson, with some skepticism. Blaskowitz did not keep copies of his protest memoranda and Nuremberg Document No. 3011 was not discovered and translated until 15 July 1947 according to the internal evidence of the document. Curiously, when the protest memorandum was finally found it was in the records of Heinrich Himmler's office: T-175/237/725985-726011, Records of Reich Leader of the SS and Chief of the German Police, Part III, R.G. 238, N.A.

70. Subject: Discontinuance of Segregation, 28 March 1946, Headquarters, Nürn-

berg Military Post, 6850th Internal Security Detachment, OCCPAC and OCCWC 201 Files, R.G. 238, N.A.

71. Letter, Blaskowitz to the Prison Commandant, 30 March 1946, Headquarters, Nürnberg Military Post, 6850th Internal Security Detachment, OCCPAC and OCCWC, 201 Files, R.G. 238, N.A.

72. Letter, Blaskowitz to Prison Commandant, 5 April 1946, Headquarters, Nürnberg Military Post, 6850th Internal Security detachment, OCCPAC and OCCWC 201 Files, r.G. 238, N.A.

73. Roster of Internees to be transferred to PWE NO 29 Dachau, undated, Entry 199, R.G. 238, N.A.

74. Transfer of Internees, 30 April 1946, Entry 199, R.G. 238, N.A.

75. Stahl, "Johannes Blaskowitz," 44.

76. Koepcke, "Ein Grab in Bommelsen."

77. Messenger, *Hitler's Gladiator*, 180-186.

78. Letter, Falkenhausen, 7 May 1946, Headquarters, Nürnberg Military Post, 6850th Internal Security Detachment, OCCPAC and OCCWC, 201 Files, R.G. 238, N.A.

79. Identification of Prisoner, N.D., Headquarters, Nürnberg Military post, 6850th Internal Security Detachment, OCCPAC and OCCWC, 201 Files, R.G. 238, R.G.

80. C.I.C. [Counter Intelligence Corps] Central Registry, I.R.R. Files, Subject File, German General Staff Study, XE001893, Vol. IV, Folder (3), R.G. 319, N.A.

81. Dachau Detachment 7708 War Crimes Group, 27 November 1946, Headquarters, Nürnberg Military Post, 6850th Internal Security Detachment, OCCPAC and OCCWC, 201 Files, R.G. 238, N.A.

82. Dr. Bettenhausen, "Thomashof in Bommelson: Gedenkworte in Trauerhaus," *Collection Koepcke*, Copy in author's possession.

83. Anhang zum Fragebogen, undated, Headquarters, Nürnberg Military Post, 6850th Internal Security Detachment, OCCPAC and OCCWC, 201 Files, R.G. 238, N.A.

84. Leeb, Wilhelm von, *Tagebuchaufzeichnungen und Lagebeurteilungen aus zwei Weltkriegen*, ed. George Meyer (Stuttgart: Deutsche Verlags-Anstalt, 1976), 80.

85. *United Nations War Crimes Commission Index of War Criminals*, 1942-1948, Germans A-Cz Reel, file 3628/Ne/G/206.

86. WO 309/643, P.R.O.; The Dutch did bring Blaskowitz's predecessor to trial. see: *Het Process Christiansen* ('s- Gravenhage: Martinus Nijhoff, 1950), passim.

87. WO 309/643, P.R.O.

88. WO 309/643, P.R.O.

89. Bemerkenswerte aus dem siebenjahrigen Erleben eines hamburger Ehepaares auf dem Thomashof des Herrn Johannes Koepcke in Bommelsen-Kreis Fallingbostel vom 2 August 1943 bis 30. April 1950," *Collection Koepcke*, Copy in author's possession.

90. Koepcke, "Ein Grab in Bommelsen."

91. Ibid.; "Bemerkenswerte aus dem siebenjahrigen Erleben eines hamburger Ehepaares auf dem Thomashof des Herrn Johannes Koepcke ...." *Collection Koepcke.* Copy in author's possession.

92. Steuben, "So Blieb er ohne Marshallstab," 12.

93. "Bemerkenswerte aus dem siebenjahrigen Erleben eines hamburger Ehepaares auf dem Thomashof des Herrn Johannes Koepcke ...." Copy in author's possession.

94. Möller-Witten, "Blaskowitz," 173.

95. Office Chief Counsel for War Crimes, 15 October 1947, Entry 199, R.G. 238, N.A.

96. Gert Steuben, "Nürnberg: Blaskowitz opfert sich," *Das Neue Blatt*, 24 Februar 1958, 11, *Collection Koepcke*, Copy in author's possession.

97. Ibid.

98. Froese, "Meine Begegnung mit Hans Blaskowitz," 10.

99. Office Chief of Counsel for War Crimes, 15 October 1947, Entry 199, R.G. 238, N.A.; Johannes Blaskowitz, Personal Data Sheet, Office of Chief of Counsel for War Crimes, Headquarters, Nürnberg Military Post, 6850th Internal Security Detachment, OCCPAC nd OCCWC, 201 Files, R.G. 238, N.A.

100. Inter-Office Memorandum, 17 October 1947, Headquarters, Nürnberg Military Post, 6850th Internal Security Detachment, OCCPAC and OCCWC, 201 files, R.G. 238, N.A.

101. Letter, Blaskowitz to Koepcke, 2 November 1947, Justice Palace, Nuremberg, *Collection Koepcke.* Copy in author's possession.

102. Letter, Blaskowitz to Koepcke, 17 November 1947, Justice Palace, Nuremberg, *Collection Koepcke.* Copy in author's possession.

103. Msg 1/2435, BA/MA; *T.W.C.*, 10: 10-48.

104. Möller-Witten, *Mit dem Eichenlaub zum Ritterkreuz*, 223.; Pers 6/20, BA/MA.; Blaskowitz Interrogation, 17 October 1947, M-1019, Roll 6, R.G. 238, N.A.; T-311/139/7183353-54.; T-311/139/7183719.

105. Gies, "Generaloberst Johannes Blaskowitz," 6.

106. Letter, Blaskowitz to Koepcke, 16 December 1947, Justice Palace, Nuremberg. *Collection Koepcke*. Copy in author's possession.

107. "Porträts grosser Soldaten," *Kampftruppen*, Nr.3 (Juni 1967): Msg 1/1814, BA/MA

108. "Blaskowitz: Durch Kreuz-Zur Krone," *Der Seehase*, Nr. 66 (1955), Archiv der Kameradschaft ehemaliger 114er and 14er, Konstanz. Copy in author's possession.

109. Stahl, "Johannes Blaskowitz," 44.

110. United Nations War Crimes Commission, comp., *History of the United Nations War Crimes Commission and the Development of the Laws of War* (London: His Majesty's Stationery Office, 1948), 529.

111. Ibid., 526.

112. Affadavit, Franz Halder, undated, circa 1947, *Collection Koepcke*, Copy in author's possession. See also Msg 1/1814, BA/MA (Affadavit, Hans Gies).

113. Stahl, "Johannes Blaskowitz," 44.; Gies, "Generaloberst Johannes Blaskowitz," 6.

114. The following conversation, secretly tape-recorded in a British P.O.W. Camp, took place between Generalmajor Johannes Bruhn, former commander of the 553rd Volkgrenadier Division and Generalmajor Paul von Felbert, Commandant of Feld Komandatur 560, Besancon.

> Bruhn: I don't mind if they shoot me, but they can only shoot me for stupidity, not for any dirty business. Nevertheless, they must grant me extenuating circumstances, inasmuch as I acted in good faith. You must certainly believe what official representatives tell you. No one would have imagined it possible for a *criminal* to get into the government. Don't you think that our "Armee-Fuhrer' or our 'Heeresgruppen Kommandeure', when reporting about us to Keitel and Rundstedt said: "A last point I have to mention is those massacres in South Poland—shouldn't we protect our Officer-Corps against being blamed for such actions?" Do you think discussions on those matters took place? What did they do about it?
> Felbert: You can see for yourself.
> Bruhn: They've probably given them money and an estate, and tied their hands in that way. Or else people have got annoyed and said: That's nothing to do with me; leave me in peace.
> Felbert: You see it in the case of Blaskowitz. They simply got rid of him.
> Bruhn: Did he actually bring up a thing like that? With whom?
> Felbert: He brought it up in the OKW, I believe. As a result the man was simply sacked; he went immediately.

Bruhn: Then we who are regular officers must advocate that men be shot who are themselves wearing our uniform.

Felbert: Naturally you must.

Bruhn: We must even disassociate ourselves from our own superiors, who are also regular officers

Felbert: Yes because they knew. They knew about it without any doubt.

Bruhn: Well, give me a motive.

Felbert: What do these people call a motive?

Bruhn: To get promotion? That makes it even *worse*. To get a decoration? That makes it worse still. They were so well off that they lacked for nothing—they were even better off than that.

Felbert: These people all miscalculated. They said to themselves: "The war is nearly over anyway."

Bruhn: Yes, but surely I can't miscalculate on question of honor?

Felbert: Oh, *those* people have no honour.

Bruhn: But they must have. We are always preached it. After all we were 'Bataillon' and 'Regiments Kommandeuré.'

Felbert: We have no honour either. We have ambition, filthy ambition, filthiest ambition, but nothing more.

Bruhn: Do you believe then, that, not with individuals but with the mass of people, their ambition is so great that even if they are regular officers—I'm speaking only of these and not of the SS—they shrink from no measures whatever, just serve their ambition?

Felbert: I don't know what was behind it all. Of course, its also possible that pressure was brought to bear on them.

Bruhn: But there was always the possiblity of simulating illness and saying: "I can't do it anymore." Do you really think they soberly said to themselves: "Might is Right" and "We'll win the war and then no-one will worry about that." But in that case these people can have no conscience at all.

Felbert: They haven't.

WO 208/4177, P.R.O.

115. Roster of Internees, 7 January 1948, Roster of Defendants, Entry 199, R.G. 238, N.A.

116. Walter H. Rapp, Memorandum, 30 July 1947, Entry 199, R.G. 238, N.A.

117. Speer, *Spandau*, 38.

118. Ibid., 41.

119. Headquarters, Company "C," 371st Infantry Battalion, U.S. Army, 25 March 1948, Entry 199, R.G. 238, N.A.

120. Letter, David Petree, Director, National Personnel Records Center, St. Louis, Missouri, 24 February 1993, to the author. Copy in author's possession.

121. Ian Sayer and Douglas Botting, *America's Secret Army: The Untold Story of the Counter Intelligence Corps* (New York: Franklin Watts, 1989), 346.

122. Christopher Simpson, *Blowback: America's Recruitment of Nazis and Its Effects on the Cold War* (New York: Collier Books, MacMillan Publishing Company, 1988), 142.

123. MS#B-800 (Blaskowitz), R.G. 338, N.A.

124. Ibid.

125. "Blaskowitz Leaps to Death in Jail Before Start of War Crimes Trial," *The New York Times*, 6 February 1948, 13.

126. Telegram, Heinz Müller-Torgow, Nuremberg, 5 February 1948, to Frau Anna Blaskowitz, Bommelsen, *Collection Koepcke*. Copy in author's possession.

127. "Bemerkenswerte aus dem siebenjahriger Erleben eines hamburger Ehepaares auf dem Thomashof ...." Copy in author's possession; Steuben, "Nürnberg: Blaskowitz opfert sich," 11.

128. Ibid. (Steuben)

129. Ibid.

130. Ibid.

131. Koepcke, "Ein Grab in Bommelsen."

132. Steuben, "Nürnberg: Blaskowitz opfert sich," 11.

133. Froese, "Meine Begegnung mit Hans Blaskowitz," 10.

134. Steuben,"Nürnberg: Blaskowitz opfert sich," 11.

135. Ibid.; "Bemerkenswerte aus dem siebenjahrigen Erleben eines hamburger Ehepaares auf dem Thomashof des Herren Johannes Koepcke ...." *Collection Koepcke*, Copy in author's possession.

136. Schrader, "Feierlickeit anlassich der Beisetzung des Generalobersten Johannes Blaskowitz am 14 Februar 1948 in Bommelsen," *Collection Koepcke*, Copy in author's possession.; Msg 1/1814, BA/MA.

137. Froese, "Ansprache," 14 Februar 1948, *Collection Koepcke*, Copy in author's possession.; Msg 1/1814, BA/MA.

EPILOGUE I

WAR CRIMINAL

BLASKOWITZ'S TRIAL ENDED on its first day with his tragic death. It is impossible to re-examine the evidence in the spirit of the judicial proceeding since the accused cannot defend himself. Nevertheless, an inquiry into the charges and probable defense is appropriate in a biography in which the allegations of criminality and the imprisonment are pivotal in his death.

In the files of the United Nations War Crimes Commission the basis of the Netherlands' interest in prosecuting Blaskowitz is clearly without substance.[1] The withdrawal of charges by that country was fully warranted.[2] Similarly, the Czechoslovakian charges were dubious, apparently based upon the premise that Blaskowitz was responsible for incidents which took place in Czechoslovakia long after his departure simply because he had carried out the initial occupation.[3] Clearly, it was appropriate to fail to include such charges in the eventual indictment. Polish charges, perhaps inevitably, cannot be dispensed with so quickly.

Blaskowitz is listed on the United Nations War Crimes Commission CROWCASS (Central Registry of War Criminals and Security Suspects) Wanted List No. 8 by Poland for murder.[4] Examination of the files of the United Nations War Crimes Commission reveals that Blaskowitz is indeed listed in the index to the files, but that the files which are supposed to contain the Polish charges actually hold only a note stating that the file is "missing."[5] Correspondance addressed to Professor-Dr. Kartimierz Kakol, Director of the Main Commission for the Investigation of Hitlerite Crimes in Poland, nevertheless brought the response that the charges against Blaskowitz could be found in the files of the United Nations War Crimes Commission and in the U. S. National Archives.[6] Inquiries at the U.S. National Archives resulted in the failure to locate the Polish charges against Blaskowitz accompanied by the suggestion that Professor- Dr. Kartimiere Kakol at the Main Commission for the Investigation of Hitlerite Crimes in Poland might be helpful![7] Another route to the facts was obviously required.

Perhaps the most well known book of Polish charges against Germans is Szymon Datner's tome, *Crimes Against P.O.W.s: Responsibility of the Wehrmacht.* It is not surprising at this point, however, that Blaskowitz is not mentioned at all in this book.[8] Rundstedt, Reichenau, Manstein and Strauss are mentioned repeatedly, but not Blaskowitz. The Central Commission for the Investigation of German Crimes in Poland published a book called simply *German Crimes in Poland,* in which Blaskowitz is mentioned once, as having issued on 30 September 1939 a proclamation which was posted in the streets, assuring Jews that they "need have no anxiety about their fate" and "should return quietly to their occupations."[9] Finally, the book *Polish Charges against German War Criminals,* asserts that Blaskowitz was accused of ill-treatment and murder of Polish prisoners of war, which is curious since he is ignored completely in the Datner book (above) about precisely this subject. In any case, the charge apparently is that on 27 September 1939, when Blaskowitz accepted Polish General Juliusz Rommel's surrender, the terms of capitulation were later violated; officers were not treated honorably, many were brutally treated, many later dying in P.O.W camps.[10] No other accusations are presented.

Although Blaskowitz was "cleared for extradition to Poland as a War Criminal" according to the one U.S. document which dated the clearance as 17 September 1946, and a second American document which described Blaskowitz as "of no war crimes interest to the U.S., but of possible War Crimes interest to the Polish authorities ...," Blaskowitz was never turned over to Poland. Many years later Telford Taylor, the American prosecutor who eventually chose to indict Blaskowitz on American charges, did not recall a request made by the Poles to turn Blaskowitz over to them.[11] Although such a request may have been made prior to Mr. Taylor becoming Chief Prosecutor, no record of it has been located. The explanation may be found in politics.

By August 1949, Taylor was stating publicly that Nazi war criminals had benefited from the onset of the Cold War:

> A number of notorious Nazis were held at Nuremberg for eventual prosecution in countries that had been occupied by the Germans. Some of these countries became Russian satellites. 'Owing to developments in the international situation a number of these transfers did not take place and the individuals in question have never been brought to trial.'[12]

Questioned about this many years later, Mr. Taylor recalled that "In late 1946 or early 1947 General Lucius Clay put down a general prohibition on sending any more of our prisoners to Poland or Yugoslavia."[13] The Poles never received Blaskowitz from the Americans. Indeed, it was rescue from an American trial that Blaskowitz required.

The decision to indict Blaskowitz was solely Mr. Telford Taylor's responsibility. Then Colonel Taylor assumed his role as Chief Prosecutor on 1 October 1947.[14] It appears that prior to that time Blaskowitz was not considered a defendant for an American war crimes trial. In fact, as recently as mid-January 1947, when Mr. Walter Rapp composed a memo listing "Highly Probable Defendants in [the] Future Cases of [the] Military Division," Blaskowitz's name did not appear. What seems to have transpired in the meantime however was a British war crimes trial at Wuppertal Prison, not far from Dusseldorff, in the British zone of occupation.

The Wuppertal case involved several Germans, the most important of whom was Lieutenant General Curt Gallenkamp, who had served as commander of the LXXX Corps at Poitiers, France in 1944. LXXX Corps was part of the German First Army at Bordeaux which was under Blaskowitz's command. When Blaskowitz became Commander of Army Group Gustav (G) in the spring of 1944, LXXX Corps remained under his command. This, then, was the connection between the Wuppertal proceedings and Generaloberst Blaskowitz.

It seems that on 3 July 1944, in the vicinity of Poitiers, France 29 members of the British 1st Special Air Service Regiment and one U.S. Army Air Force officer, to which were added three other British SAS men, who had parachuted into the Poitiers area earlier for purposes of conducting sabotage, had performed a number of demolition missions, and were captured by troops from the German LXXX Corps. In accordance with orders issued by Hitler, particularly the so-called "Commando-Order," a detail of troops from LXXX Corps executed 31 Allied personnel outside of Poitiers on 7 July, burying them in a mass grave in a nearby forest.[15]

The Commando Order of 18 October 1942 was the brainchild of the Führer himself. It was issued in response to the "Especially brutal and treacherous ... behavior of the so called commandos .... " The Commandos, Hitler asserted, have themselves been ordered not only to "shackle prisoners, but also to kill defenseless prisoners on the spot at the moment in which they believe that the latter as prisoners represent a burden in the further pursuit of their purposes ...." Thus the Führer ordered that "all enemies on so called Commando missions ... even if they are ... in uniform ... are to be slaughtered to the last man." The order even applied to troops who gave themselves up. Further, Hitler announced that he would "hold responsible under Military Law, for failing to carry out this order, all commanders and officers who either have neglected their duty of instructing the troops about this order, or acted against this order where it was to be executed."[16]

The last part of Hitler's order, threatening the lives of commanders failing to pass on the order or to carry it out, presumably was inserted because the Führer was "aware of the opposition this order would arouse within the Wehrmacht."[17] Execution of uniformed P.O.W.s was obviously a violation of long standing international law; Hitler's desperate attempt to redress the major threat posed by commandos in modern wars. And there was opposition within the *Wehrmacht*. Nevertheless, the order was distributed as ordered.

Brigadier General Telford Taylor and his Deputy Chief of Counsel, Military & SS Division, indicted Blaskowitz as a war criminal in part for the simple fact of his passing on the Commando Order to LXXX Corps on 18 October 1942.[18] Detailed in the indictment also was the incident carried out near Poitiers on 7 July 1944 in which 31 Allied Commandos were executed by soldiers of LXXX Corps.[19]

It seems that between the original distribution of the order in 1942 and the incident at Poitiers for which Blaskowitz was indicted there was only a single incident of the Commando Order being carried out in occupied France. On 11 December 1942 at Bordeaux the German Navy, with the SD present, carried out such executions.[20]

According to the testimony of General Günther Blumentritt, who was Rundstedt's long-time chief of staff, when the Commando Order was issued "it was not possible *not* to pass on this order." Instead, Blumentritt continued:

> The Supreme Command West did everything verbally and by telephone in order to water down so far as possible and to make a difference between theory and practice. I know of no case during my service in which this order was executed.[21]

Blumentritt added that "disciplinary action was never taken against officers for not carrying out this order and inquiries were never made as to whether it was carried out.[22] In fact, Blumentritt elaborated, OB West, Rundstedt, so heartily disapproved of the order that, on his own initiative, he made application to Hitler, demanding that the Commando Order be rescinded.[23] Hitler disapproved the request. Not only did Hitler reaffirm the order, the Führer actually re-issued it on 26 June 1944.[24] The Führer's reaffirmation was sent to OB West, Rundstedt, who, in turn passed it on to Blaskowitz (as commander of Army Group G) and other subordinates in the chain of command. Blaskowitz in turn passed it to the commanders of First and Nineteenth Armies.[25] Several days later the executions took place at Poitiers.

In addition to the records in the War Diary of Army Group G, including the actual order and distribution list, there is also the testimony of the commander of LXXX Corps, General Curt Gallenkamp, that the Commando Order forwarded by Blaskowitz to First Army eventually did reach LXXX Corps and was the basis of the executions.[26] Therefore there was apparently a sound basis in evidence for the Prosecution decision to bring Blaskowitz to trial.

In addition to the charges against Blaskowitz relative to the Commando Order and the Poitiers incident which followed it there were other charges against him. Blaskowitz was charged with using P.O.W.s for the construction of fortifications on 2 February 1945.[27] He was also charged with having distributed on 1 and 10 August 1944, an order to arrest "all able bodied men between 16 and 55 years of age in sectors where resistance forces were observed for deportation to Germany." This, following the prior distribution on 25 January 1943 of "Fundamental Order No.2" which directed that "protection and cooperation" be given by the army to "recruiting commissions" conscripting slave labor in occupied France.[28] There seems to be no question that this additional charge was warranted, but to jump to the conclusion of guilt without Blaskowitz being able to respond is obviously impossible.

Two other charges were leveled against Blaskowitz in the indictment. First, Crimes against Peace were alleged, specifically his role in the Czech occupation, as Eighth Army Commander in the campaign in Poland, and in his brief command of Second Army in the attack upon France in May 1940. Finally, Blaskowitz was charged with participation in a "Common Plan or Conspiracy" (to commit Crimes Against Peace, War Crimes, and Crimes Against Humanity).[29] Since all of those indicted in Case XII at Nuremberg were also charged with "Crimes Against Peace" and "Common Plan or Conspiracy," and all of those who actually went on trial were acquitted on these two charges, it is reasonable to assume that Blaskowitz too, would have been acquitted on these two charges. Therefore, it is desirable to return to the essential charge against Blaskowitz, the matter of the Commando Order and the incident at Poitiers.

Implicit in returning to the Commando Order section of this indictment is the recognition that the charge involving the use of P.O.W.s as illegal laborers in the war as specified in the indictment, while quite serious, does not approach the magnitude of other charges in this and similar trials. Blaskowitz pleaded not guilty to this charge at Nuremberg, but never had the opportunity to defend himself. It is, therefore, impossible to consider this charge further except to note that according to the interrogation of Colonel Horst Wilutzky, a member of Blaskowitz's staff, army groups had only the responsibility of selecting the lines to be fortified. Actual constuction of the lines, including employment of laborers, was the responsibility of Service Command XII, an organization not under Blaskowitz's command, as provided for in Hitler's basic orders.[30] The issue is beyond resolution, but a closer look at the Commando Order charge is necessary.

The most important allegation in the indictment, pertaining to the Commando Order and the Poitiers atrocity, cannot be clarified simply. The starting point may be a story which circulated at the time of

Blaskowitz's death. It was heard at the time by Johannes Koepcke, and repeated later in a news article by the reporter Gert Steuben:

> There had been an incident that was originally going to be held against him and he was going to be charged with it (the incident was the shooting of thirty English paratroopers by the command of LXXX Army Corps).
>
> But later on this had to be removed because of the Wuppertal Trial, where it was determined that the corps had acted on its own volition and not upon orders by the general, nor by First Army Command order, nor by order of Army Group G.[31]

According to this story, an unnamed American prosecutor had congratulated Blaskowitz's defense counsel, Dr. Müller-Torgow, on his good fortune in representing such a lucky man as Blaskowitz, who would therefore be acquited. Blaskowitz himself had been told of this.[32] Mr. Taylor, the chief American prosecutor, however, has no recollection of any suggestion that the indictment might be lifted, and states that any such idea was "incompatible" with the indictment.[33] Other questions remain.

If the testimony at the Wuppertal trial is accepted as true it appears that irony accompanied Blaskowitz throughout his life, even in the atrocity at Poitiers. Blaskowitz's behavior in Poland and again in France (relative to the Maquis and the French civilian population) establishes beyond doubt that he recognized and acted upon the knowledge that Christians cannot remain neutral in a struggle against evil, but that he was realistic in his assessment of what he could accomplish.

A German who found himself a defendent in other war crimes trials, General Alexander von Falkenhausen, perhaps more eloquent than Blaskowitz, cited in defense of his actions during the war no less an authority on ethics than St. Augustine, thusly: "He whose weakness was unable to make goodness triumph must prevent as much evil as is in his power."[34] Blaskowitz clearly had done this in other matters both before and after the Poitiers incident. His army legal advisor in Poland, Otto Schmeidler, who knew Blaskowitz well, wrote in December 1947:

> I believe it is unusual for a man with an intelligent and clear perception to hold on to his beliefs and contain his outrage in the face of blatant violent disorder, military deviance and obstruction of the law. He abhorred the methods of the Third Reich, while loving

the German nation and the German people. He was incapable of violent acts or actions contrary to international law and he would not suffer such behavior in his office.[35]

Günther Blumentritt, von Runstedt's chief of staff, testifed that it was *not* possible *not* to pass on the Commando Order but that it was followed up by telephone calls and verbal "watering-down," to make certain that it was not carried out.[36] He believed the order was never carried out until he learned otherwise after the war.[37] His chief, OB West, Field Marshal von Rundstedt, repeatedly stated that the Commando Order was never carried out by the Army under his command in France.[38] Under interrogation, Blaskowitz too, denied any knowledge of the Poitiers atrocity until the Wuppertal trial.[39] According to the Wuppertal trial records, the commanding general of LXXX Corps General Gallenkamp, had discussed the infamous order with his staff and they all opposed it, themselves beginning the process, previously mentioned and unsuccessful, of appealing the order to Hitler, demanding it be rescinded.[40]

What appears to have taken place is that after the capture of the SAS men and the lone American LXXX Corps attempted every possible delay and obfuscation to avoid carrying out the notorious order. The first three SAS men were captured on 29 June, the remainder on 3 July. According to the Commando Order these were to be executed immediately, with imprisonment under guard strictly prohibited. On 5 July a German Communique originating at the Führer's Headquarters, announced that, "In Central France, a British sabotage party, 43 men strong, which was dropped by parachute, was liquidated. An additional 108 terrorists were shot."[41] But it was not true. The British SAS men and the American were still alive.

The verbal warnings to evade the order, not to carry it out, combined with the opposition to the order by LXXX Corps' staff, temporarily accomplished their goal. Blaskowitz operated in the same fashion according to one of his subordinate officers, Hans Gies, who later wrote: "Blaskowitz tried to be wise and just and fair to the enemy, even when it meant to change an order from headquarters." He elaborated upon this knowledge this way:

> Whenever we received radical orders from Central Headquarters
> in Berlin, ordering drastic measures of revenge, etc., there was a

tendency on the part of the Commander-In-Chief [Blaskowitz] not to take the orders literally to say the least. In other words the Commander-in-Chief had the tendency to change the drastic order into an order of humane spirit and behavior. I have not seen or heard, coming down to me from my Commander-in-Chief ... Any order forcing or enforcing revenge action toward the resistance or the population at large. On the contrary, I only received approval from my Commander-in-Chief, Blaskowitz, when I chose to change an order that could be interpreted more drastically, into an order that would allow for compromise and gentleness toward civilians.[42]

Then what happaned? Why were the British SAS men and the American executed? It appears that when Hitler refused to rescind the Commando Order and reaffirmed the original order with a second Commando Order on 26 June it took several days to reach LXXX Corps because of the poor state of army communications.[43] When asked about this, Rundstedt himself was "of the opinion that it might well have lasted until the 5th July before the order arrived at Poitiers.[44]

When this second and harsher version of the Commando Order reached LXXX Corps it is not surprising that the reaction there was panic and then hasty execution of the commandos. Neither is it surprising that Blaskowitz and Rundstedt were never informed; LXXX Corps reported those dead as "*Killed in Action*."[45] Thus, Rundstedt and Blaskowitz were telling the truth when they stated repeatedly that they had subverted the order and had never heard of a case of the Army carrying it out in France. In fact the attempt to rescind the order may have been what led to the commando's executions; all efforts to the contrary tragically miscarried.

The fact that Blaskowitz and Rundstedt had been threatened with court martial if they failed to pass on the order, their attempts to subvert it and similar orders, and the probability that the executions resulted in part from their attempt to get the repugnant order rescinded may all be mitigating factors in the primary charge against Blaskowitz—the Poitiers Affair. But we shall never know if this is the entire story since Blaskowitz did not have the opportunity to tell the truth—the whole truth. Ironically, years after the trial, the man who indicted Blaskowitz, then Brigadier General Telford Taylor, questioned about Blaskowitz, would reply:

> The evidence against him was not voluminous. I should add that, in later years when I started to write books on the German Army, I learned a good deal more about him and it is an open question in my mind, whether, if I had known everything I came to know later, I would have included him in the indictment. I really can't say whether I would have or not. It certainly would have made me look very closely at what evidence we had, but there was that evidence ... and that was why he was put into the indictment.[46]

The entire truth is known only to God. But one lesson is abundantly clear. Modern war is highly brutalized and all who take part, however decent and respectable, even in the defensive, are likely to be debased to some extent. There is an old German aphorism that seems to sum up Blaskowitz's predicament at Nuremberg: "Mitgegangen, mitgefangen, mitgehangen," or, "went with, caught with, hung with ...." Napoleon had said, "You must remember, Gentlemen, that in war obedience comes before courage."[47] Modern war has perhaps reversed Napoleon's dicta; Courage must come before obedience. Blaskowitz knew this and acted upon it repeatedly.

In his concluding remarks to the Tribunal in the General Staff trial, Justice Robert Jackson said,

> Many of these men have made a mockery of the soldier's oath of obedience to military orders. When it suits their defense they say they had to obey; when confronted with Hitler's brutal crimes, which are shown to have been within their general knowledge, they say they disobeyed. The truth is that they actively participated in all those crimes, or sat silent and acquiescent witnessing the commission of crimes on a scale larger and more shocking than the world has ever had the misfortune to know. This must be said.[48]

These remarks were made about the German General Staff. Acquittal followed. In so far as these comments could be considered an accusation against Blaskowitz as a long-time member of the General Staff, they are indeed enlightening. Blaskowitz did not sit silent and aquiescent witnessing crime; his protests and alterations of orders are a matter of record. When he had to obey he did so, but when disobedience was necessary to uphold honor, he chose the path of honor, at great personal risk. Bitter personal experience in Poland had taught him that forthright protest was pointless in a police state. His conscience nevertheless compelled him to try to secretly sabotage repugnant orders such as the Commando Order. The concurrent appearance of culpability in having distributed the order was a risk which he accepted. That he did not always succeed does not diminish his valor or shade his realism.

Notes for Epilogue I

1. *United Nations War Crimes Commission Index of War Criminals, 1942-1948*, Germans, A-Cz Reel, File 3628/Ne/G/206.

2. WO 309/643, P.R.O.

3. *United Nations War Crimes Commission Index of War Criminals, 1942-1948*, Germans, A-Cz Reel, File 399 99/Cz/G/8,423/Cz/G9,432/Cz/G/11, 463/Cz/G/13.

4. Transfer of Internees, 30 April 1946, Entry 199, R.G 238, N.A; Dachau Detachment 7708 War Crimes Group, 27 November 1946, Headquarters, Nürnberg Military Post, 6850th Internal Security Detachment, OCCPAC and OCCWC, 201 Files, R.G. 238, N.A.

5. *United Nations War Crimes Commission Index of War Criminals, 1942-1948*, Germans, A-Cz Reel, UNWCC/NDX/1, FILE 284/P/G/29.

6. Letter, Professor-Dr. Kartimierz Kakol, 18 November 1991, Warsaw, Poland, to the author. Copy in author's possession.

7. Letter, William Lewis, 9 September 1988, Archivist, Modern Military History Field Branch, U.S. National Archives, to the Author. Copy in author's possession.

8. Szymon Datner, *Crimes Against P.O.W.s: Responsibility of the Wehrmacht* (Warsaw, Zachodnia Agencia Prasowa, 1964), passim.

9. Central Commission for Investigation of German Crimes in Poland, *German Crimes in Poland*, trans. Biultyn Glow Komisji Badania Zbrodni Niemieckich w Polse (New York: Howard Fertig, 1982), 137.

10. Marian Muszkat, *Polish Charges Against German War Criminals* (Warsaw: Polish Main National Office for the Investigation of German War Crimes in Poland, 1948), 136-140.

11. Letter, Telford Taylor, 21 July 1988, New York, N.Y., to the author. Copy in author's possession.

12. Malcomb Hobbs, "Nürnberg's Indecent Burial," *Nation*, 169 (December 3, 1949), 534-5.

13. Interview, Mr. Telford Taylor 02/18/88, New York, N.Y. Copy in author's possession.

14. Letter, Telford Taylor, 10 October 1988, New York, N.Y., to the author. Copy in author's possession.

15. WO 235/293, P.R.O; WO 309/226, P.R.O., WO 309/1549, P.R.O.; The preliminary inquiry into the matter may be found in the following records: Joint Chiefs of Staff, 1942-45, CCS 000.5, War Criminals, (10-18-43) Secs 7& 12, R.G. 218, N.A.; The 29 British SAS men plus the lone American added to the original 3 SAS men captured total 34 men. Three were wounded. These were subsequently executed separately WO 235/293 P.R.O.

16. 498-PS, *N.C.A.*, III: 416-417; *I.M.T.*, IV: 440-445; *I.M.T.*,VI: 350-353.

17. Edward Crankshaw, *Gestapo* (New York: Pyramid Books, 1957), 169.

18. *T.W.C.*, X: 31; Msg 1/2435, BA/MA; Memorandum: James McHaney to Telford Taylor, 20 February 1948. Copy graciously provided to the author by Mr. Taylor. Copy in author's possesssion.

19. Ibid.

20. *I.M.T.*, V: 38-41, 278-279.; VII: 164-165.; Messenger, *Last Prussian*, 165.

21. Statement of Günther Blumentritt, 20 March 1947, Wupperthal, Germany, WO 235/293, P.R.O. Emphasis added.

22. Ibid.

23. Ibid.; Blumentritt Interrogation, 17 October 1947, M-1019, Roll 7, R.G. 238, N.A.; 531-PS, *N.C.A.*, III: 435-437.

24. 532-PS, *N.C.A.*, III: 437-438; WO 235/293, P.R.O.

25. NOKW 213, R.G. 238, N.A.; T-311/139/7183381 (Kriegstagebuch Anlage 325); T-311/139/7183816

26. Gallenkamp Interrogation, 13 February 1948, M-1019, Roll 19, R.G. 238, N.A.; WO 309/1549, P.R.O.

27. *T.W.C.*, X: 33.; Msg 1/2435, BA/MA.

28. *T.W.C.*, X: 38.; Msg 1/2435, BA/MA; T-311/140/7185813; T-311/140/7185501.; T-311/140/7185079, *Anlagen* 353 + 355.; See also, however: Speer, *Inside the Third Reich*, 369-372,382-384,476.

29. *T.W.C.*, X: 13-28, 48.; Msg 1/2435, BA/MA.

30. Wilutzky Interrogation, 27 January 1948, M-1019, Roll 79, R.G. 238, N.A; Wilutzky's testimony is supported by Hitler's order of 24 August 1944 "for the construction of a German defensive position in the West." Trevor-Roper, ed., *Hitler's War Directives, 1939-1945*, 181-184. Wilutzky, however, was on Blaskowitz's staff at Army Group G and by 2 February 1945 Blaskowitz had moved onto Army Group H, the records of which are extent only for January 1945. According to a memorandum graciously provided to me by Mr. Telford Taylor, the following statement suggests the existence of evidence: "our proof showed that Blaskowitz used prisoners of war in labor for exam-

ple, in the construction of fortifications." Memorandom: James McHaney to Telford Taylor, 29 February 1948. Copy in author's possession.

31. Steuben, "Nürnberg: Blaskowitz opfert sich," 12.

32. Ibid.; Koepcke, "Ein Grab in Bommelsen."

33. Letter, Telford Taylor, 9 May 1989, New York, N.Y., to the author. Copy in author's possession.

34. Cassandra (pseud.), "Ungrateful Belgium," *Mirror*, 30/3/51. BH Liddell Hart Papers, King's College London, L.H. 9/24/193.

35. Otto Schmeidler, Oberstrichter a. D., Eidesstattliche Erklärung, 10 December 1947, Villa Dalfrid Billdal, Schwaben, *Collection Koepcke.* Copy in author's possession.

36. W.O. 235/293, P.R.O.

37. Ibid.

38. *I.M.T.*, XXI: 26-27, 44-45.; XXII: 78.

39. Blaskowitz Interrogation, 17 October 1947, M-1019, Roll 6, R.G. 238, N.A.; Per 6/20, BA/MA; Blaskowitz's Operations Officer, Horst Wilutzky concurred. Wilutzky Interrogation, 26 January 1948, M-1019, Roll 79, R.G. 238, N.A.; A search of Army Group G Records for this time failed to locate any such report, thereby supporting the testimony of Blaskowitz and Wilutzky.

40. Gallenkamp Interrogation, 13 February 1948, M-1019, Roll 19, R.G. 238, N.A.

41. WO 235/293, P.R.O.; WO 309/1549, P.R.O

42. Msg 1/1814, BA/MA; Yet by necessity, this was not annouced to those who did not need to know it for obvious reasons. Years later a member of Blaskowitz's staff, Dr. Edward Hay, wrote: "To my knowledge, it is possible and fits with the convictions of Blaskowitz, that he would circumvent orders of that nature, but I did not have direct knowledge that he did." Letter, Dr. Edward Hay, 24/8/92, Königsdorf, Germany. Copy in author's possession.

43. MS# A-954 (Zerbel),R.G. 338, N.A.; Report of the Interrogation #5581, Unnamed German Major, P/W 21G-1266435, 26 July 1945, R.G. 165, N.A.

44. WO 235/293, P.R.O.

45. Ibid.

46. Interview, Mr. Telford Taylor, 02/18/88, New York, N.Y. Copy in author's possession.

47. *I.M.T.*, 22: 69.

48. Ibid., 522-523.

BLASKOWITZ'S DEATH

NEARLY HALF A CENTURY HAS PASSED since the death of Generaloberst Blaskowitz and many of the events of that time have receded into the mists of history. The nature of his death, for example, has still not yet been clarified.

In 1953, the prestigious German publication, *Deutsche Soldatenkalender* wrote:

> Yet, just prior to the trial, the general took his own life, and this must have been the result of some deep and terrifying experience. The general must have lost faith in justice and lost trust in life altogether. His experience prior to his suicide must have taken all the life out of this brave soldier and must have left him with nothing.[1]

Within five years, *Deutscher Soldatenkalender* had changed its views. In a 1958 article on Blaskowitz, it stated: "we will never know for sure whether it was an accident, whether he fell down the stairs of the prison where he was kept—or whether it was suicide." The article further stated that the defense counsel for Blaskowitz made a statement, "After his death ... that nobody could say or do anything against this brave and decent man."[2] In a book a few years later, the same historian, Hans Möller-Witten, who had written for *Deutscher Soldatenkalender* in 1958, had found no evidence which caused him to alter his judgement. He wrote that, "he died in the local Nuremberg court prison, when he fell from the stairwell—whether on his own volition and by his own hand or by another—will probably never be resolved." His defense attorney, Heinz Müller-Torgow, said, "Nobody had anything on him, and nobody could possibly have anything on him."[3]

Representing the opposite position is the German historian Frie-drich-Christian Stahl, who wrote in 1987, that Blaskowitz, "probably following a momentary impulse—jumped to his death in the Nurem-berg courthouse."[4] Stahl's assessment concurs to some extent with that of one of the most prestigious German biographical reference works, *Altpreussische Biographie*, in which the historian Gerd Brausch wrote suggestively in 1975, that, "Blaskowitz took his own life in the stairwell of the prison. There is no witness to this event."[5]

It is not a great distance from this intriguing viewpoint to that of the eminent historian, Gerald Reitlinger, who wrote that when "he committed suicide in Nuremberg prison, his fellow prisoners believed that Blaskowitz had been murdered by SS men."[6] More cautious historians who repeated the allegation of murder suggested that "disgruntled" SS men who had become prison "trusties" were respon-sible. Others called the tale not "substantiated," or of "doubtful authenticity."[7]

It is not surprising then, that in recent books Blaskowitz and the manner of his death are either ignored, overlooked, or mentioned only in passing.[8] The contradictory candor of the soldier's publication, *Kampftruppen*, is preferable when it states: "inexplicably so, Blaskowitz did commit suicide." "His death remains a mystery, which I cannot solve."[9] Preferable, but not satisfying. Indeed, it is not far removed from Frau Blaskowitz's statement little more than two weeks after the Generaloberst's death: "He took with him into the grave the secret of his last step. We will never know. But for every person that knew him there is a certainty that he did not participate in any war crimes."[10]

Since the tragic death of Generaloberst Blaskowitz, however, much "new" evidence has been discovered and some "old" evidence can therefore be seen in a new perspective. Perhaps the place to begin is with public records that have surfaced, but been ignored.

In his article on Blaskowitz's last days at Nuremberg, for example, the journalist Gert Steuben quotes a co-prisoner of Blaskowitz, regret-tably without providing his name. The co-prisoner reports speaking frequently with Blaskowitz those last days, walking to meals together and also walking together in the exercise courtyard. Both lived on the third tier of the prison, so they were neighbors. The co-prisoner found Blaskowitz usually amiable and pleasant, but remembered that "he seemed more subdued and despondent during the last days of his life. He commented on that to me and said that the walk to the tribunal and to court made him anxious."[11] He continued:

> I saw him last on the morning of his death when we walked together as usual. And we met, as we always did at the barber's [in the prison basement]. He left the barber's just before me. While I was walking up the stairs, I saw him suddenly fall over the railing from the third floor down. He must have climbed on the railing and over the wire barrier that was there to prevent such things and then he must have jumped.[12]

If, to this statement is added the testimony of Pastor Froese, who wrote much later, that:

> "One day a telegram came saying that Blaskowitz was dead, that he had died on the day of the trial, and that it had happened while he was supposed to get a haircut at the barber's in the basement, where he always went, and, as always had gone without an escort. It was said he was found dead in the stairwell. What happened and how it happened was never found out. I can not believe that he took his own life ...."[13]

According to the statement by the nameless "co-prisoner" in the news story by the journalist Gert Steuben, Blaskowitz headed back to his cell alone, followed after a brief interval by the anonymous co-prisoner. That Blaskowitz went back to his cell from the barber shop alone was repeated years later by Pastor Froese. Johannes Koepcke's son Hans also remembered his father stating repeatedly that he had been told by "the authorities" in the prison that Blaskowitz had been under guard escort, but that German employees in the prison kitchen had told Koepcke, Sr., that trips to the barber shop were taken, without guard-escort, individually by the prisoners.[14]

These accounts taken together explain to some degree why doubts have lingered, why so frequently descriptions of Blaskowitz's death have ended suggestively with "There were no witnesses." Even the nameless co-prisoner quoted in the Steuben article "Nuremberg: Blaskowitz Sacrifices Himself," did not actually witness the death, merely the last part of the fall and the impact on the floor. But there were indeed witnesses.

In the official inquiry into Blaskowitz's death, which concluded that the death was a suicide,[15] there were four witnesses. Each was an Estonian guard from Civilian Guard Company number 4221, and each wrote a brief report of the events.

Private First Class Koit Tali, from Tartu, Estonia was still only twenty years old on the day of Blaskowitz's death.[16] This is his statement:

> In the morning of 5 February 1948 I was on duty as a super. My job was to escort the prisoners from the CW-1, third tier to the barber shop. Returning from the barber shop with 7 prisoners I walked in front of the group and was placing the first man in his cell when I noticed the last prisoner make a quick turn, climb up the wire netting of the Rotunda and jump over. Several prisoners between myself and the man climbing the wire made it impossible for me to get him fast enough and properly prevent him from jumping. It happened about 0730.[17]

The statement of the other guards corroborates Koit Tali's statement above. Private Kalju Küünal, who was only a few weeks shy of his twenty-first birthday, and who came from Narva, Estonia,[18] testified a few days later that:

> On 5 February 1948 I was on guard on post number 19, stationed in the wing CW-1, third tier. At 0730 I saw one of the prisoners, who was coming back from the barber shop, jumping over the wire net in the rotunda at CW-1, third tier. To stop the attempt of committing suicide was not possible because I stood in the middle of my tier side and locked the cells of the prisoners who returned from the barber shop. The prisoner who jumped down was a man of my post, cell number 97.[19]

Private First Class Richard Kamar, the "elder" of the group of Estonian guards at age 24, came from Virumaa, Estonia. His statement is almost exactly a repetition of Küünal's declaration except that he was at guard post 18 and could not interrupt the suicide attempt because he "stood in the opposite end of my wing."[20]

The fourth Estonian guard to witness the suicide was twenty-one year old Ilmar Elbri, who, like Koit Tali, hailed from Tartu, Estonia.[21] His statement is remarkably reminiscent of Gert Steuben's unnamed German co-prisoner. After placing himself in the rotunda of the prison at the ground-floor level at 0730, Elbri stated:

I was just closing the door to the wing WW-2 when I heard a loud thud. Looking back I saw a prisoner lying on the floor of the rotunda at CW-1. I did not see the prisoner fall. The American wardens took care of him immediately.[22]

According to a "certificate" in the same group of records, the prison doctor, Dr. Standke, arrived on the scene "within a minute." The 385th Station Hospital was notified and Blaskowitz was brought there by ambulance, only to die at 1020.[23] The "certificate" is signed by a First Lieutenant Moffat Gardner, Company "A," 18th Infantry (U.S.), who certified that the death took place in the manner described by the guards. He did not, however refer to himself as a witness, raising the obvious question as to how he could otherwise certify any statement at all in this matter.[24] This question aside, there is yet another document concerning Blaskowitz's death which is of great interest, a statement dated 7 February 1948, by a Dr. Karl Wiedenfeld, presumably another physician assigned to Nuremberg.

Wiedenfeld states that he had been treating Blaskowitz "medically and spiritually" for four months, and during numerous discussions had discovered a "soft and emotional nature" underneath his soldierly character. Blaskowitz had suffered a "multitude of disappointments, difficulties and shocks" during the previous ten years and according to Dr. Wiedenfeld, had reached the point of apathy." After his treatment during the Third Reich, Blaskowitz felt his arrest and imprisonment "completely unjustified," a feeling that reached a climax when he received the indictment. During this time he outwardly "retained his soldierly attitude," and "hardly permitted anybody to look into the depths of his actual feelings." Dr. Wiedenfeld then retrospectively saw a change in Blaskowitz, who remained "quite communicative and hardly showed signs of depression, complaining only of insomnia.[25]

Wiedenfeld then got right to the point in his statement:

> However, during the last few weeks I noticed an increasing inner restlessness combined with hopelessness regarding his future in general and his trial in particular which necessitated more barbituates than before. I kept on trying to get him away, in many long talks, from the situation he was in, but although he was exceedingly grateful, it appears today that the success of such attempts was merely of an outward nature. In view of the approaching commencement of

his trial I noticed that his restlessness was increasing, but as that was quite a natural symptom with all persons of a frail frame of mind, it was not out of the ordinary. For that reason I did not consider his earnest attitude, which was characteristic of him, in any way suspicious on the afternoon of his suicide. [sic]; I rather believe that his resolve to take his own life was not the result of long planning, but a sudden short circuit reaction on the first morning of his trial.[26]

Dr. Wiedenfeld's retrospective summary of Blaskowitz's depression and anxiety plausibly explains the death of the Generaloberst as a suicide. Surviving documents of Blaskowitz's physical condition after the impact on a concrete floor following a thirty foot drop are sufficient to explain the death. But the inconsistancies remain unresolved. The statement of the nameless co-prisoner in the story of Gert Steuben, the German journalist, to the effect that Blaskowitz had told him that "the walk to the Tribunal and to court made him anxious," is especially intriguing in the light of other inconsistencies between the guard's statements and those of the co-prisoner, particularly since in the guard's statements Blaskowitz was under escort but in the co-prisoner's tale Blaskowitz walked alone. Most disturbing also, if the "official" version related by the guards is completely true, is another question.

According to the guards' statements the Estonian guard, Koit Tali was escorting seven prisoners from the barber shop to their cells. If this were the case , why are there no statements verifying the guard/witnesses' reports by German prisoners? And, naturally, were there any former SS members in the prison on the day of Blaskowitz's death? After all, the SS had always done the "dirty work." At the time of the suicide of Hermann Goering it was established that there were twenty-six Germans inside the prison who had access to him.[27] The number having access to Blaskowitz cannot be established. Finally, the question of motive remains, but it is apparently one of the relatively more simple of the lingering questions.

A clue may have been provided by one of the most controversial members of the German resistance to Hitler, Dr. Otto John, who had escaped the Nazi retribution upon those connected with the 20th July conspiracy and eventually got to England where he had made broadcasts to Germany for the BBC. After the war he had worked for the British government in the German P.O.W camps in Britain, "screening"

Nazi from anti-Nazi P.O.W.s so that the latter might be repatriated to Germany quickly. In this way he came to know many high ranking German officers in addition to those he had known from his days in the resistance in Germany. In January 1948, Dr. John found himself at Nuremberg, where the chief prosecutor for the Americans, General Telford Taylor, permitted him to question a number of German generals. Dr. John later wrote that at Nuremberg:

> Senior Wehrmacht commanders found it quite compatible with their consciences, some even thought it their patriotic duty, to make false statements to the Allied Military Courts, even under oath. While in prison in Nuremberg they had concerted their defense tactics and agreed that they would categorically deny all knowledge of the genocide of Jews, Poles and Russians. Rudolf Freiherr von Gersdorff, however, one of the youngest of the senior officers, admitted the truth—that they had all known of these atrocities. He had himself sent reports on the subject to Army Headquarters, but in Nuremberg there was a concerted loss of memory on the subject.[28]

If Dr. John is correct in his declaration that von Gersdorff was the only senior officer to tell the truth about his knowledge of atrocities then another of his statements is of special interest. In the summer of 1946, while Blaskowitz was at Dachau, von Gersdorff found himself at the camp Allendorf near Marburg, where Blaskowitz was to arrive in January 1947. At Allendorf, in the barracks of a former ammunition factory, the Americans had gathered together one hundred senior officers from Halder and Guderian, both formers Chiefs of the General staff, to von Gersdorff and later Blaskowitz, to write the History of the German General Staff and the war through German eyes. Ironically, Gersdorff reveals, "We were assigned imprisoned members of the so called Waffen SS to take care of our needs for services, but we had an unwritten agreement not to use them for anything."[29] So the SS still had a "presence," even inside Allendorf; a tribute to American niaveté.

One summer day Gersdorff walked through the streets of Allendorf, "amazed" to find that his co-prisoners failed to return his greetings. Then one general called him into a barracks, pointing out a newspaper opened up upon a table, with an article marked. It was a book review of Fabian von Schlabrendorff's book, *Officers Against Hitler*. It contained the story of von Gersdorff's attempt to assassinate Hitler in

March of 1943. Gersdorff read the part which dealt with him, turned around, and found himself facing a group of officers who had silently surrounded him. Courageously, he said, "Well, it looks like this is what really happened and how it happened. This was done pretty much in the way it really was." Then he turned and walked out.[30]

Von Gersdorff soon found himself in a sort of internal exile within Allendorf. Other than a group of loyal comrades from his regiment, no one would speak to him. He prepared a short essay declaring that he stood completely behind the description of events in the book and then went to the senior German officer at Allendorf at that time, with the intention of requesting that he agree to read it to the assembled German officers at the next camp roll call. The senior German officer at Allendorf during the summer of 1946 was Generaloberst Karl Hollidt, who would later be indicted as a co-defendent with Blaskowitz in the High Command Case, and who went on trial at Nuremberg on the very same day that Blaskowitz was to have appeared.

Gersdorff went right to Hollidt with his text and his request. Hollidt replied:

> I don't think that you are aware of your situation. I recently had a group of generals visiting the camp who were insistent on having you removed from the camp. I was told that otherwise they would tell the SS men present in the camp to kill you.[31]

Gersdorff courageously replied that both the Americans and the SS men had been aware of his past deeds for quite some time and that he had nothing to fear. He knew better. Some SS men had received his story "very well," but there were certain SS "unteachables" who clung to their beliefs and were hostile to him. A truce could not be reached. He could only hold his head high and be a "walking target."[32]

Blaskowitz arrived at Allendorf himself in January of 1947, taking over as senior officer among the Germans from Field Marshal von Leeb, who himself had replaced Generaloberst Hollidt the senior officer who had refused to intervene on behalf of Gersdorff. Hollidt nevertheless remained at Allendorf until the end of June 1947, so he and Blaskowitz had six months in which to renew their old acquaintanceship.[33]

Karl Hollidt was the son of a *gymnasium* professor at his birthplace, Speyer on the Rhine. He was a Protestant, a graduate of Spayer's Humanities Gymnasium and eight years younger than Blaskowitz. He had joined the Army in 1909, become a lieutenant in 1910, and spent World War I exclusively on the Western Front. He was a professional soldier retained by the Reichswehr and served in a number of command and staff positions in World War II, mostly on the Russian Front, until finally promoted to Generaloberst in September 1943. In April 1944 he had been transferred to the Führer Reserve and was without an active command for the remainder of the war.[34] According to the "Watch List of German Generals in the British and U.S. Zones of Germany and in the U.K." Hollidt was a "Keen Nazi."[35]

Field Marshal von Manstein, generally thought to be the most gifted of Hitler's commanders, thought highly of Hollidt, describing him in an official evaluation during the war thusly:

> Firm personality, radiant and confident though not sweeping one off one's feet. He leads with surety and even in difficult situations he considers matters and commits his own person. Suitable for Commanding General.[36]

By the end of the war, however, some of Hollidt's colleagues thought he was exhausted, as Generalmajor Gerhard Franz's comments in late April 1945, make abundantly clear: "Nothing more can be done with Hollidt; he has worn himself out. His spirit has been completely broken recently. He is a clever and decent man, but he no longer has the robust strength to make something of it again."[37]

Whether the Allies were correct and Hollidt was a "Keen Nazi," or if he was exhausted and incapable of resistance, or, whether he indeed feared for his own life, Hollidt apparently supported those firm SS "believers" who opposed von Gersdorff. Not only is this important because Hollidt was in Allendorf with Blaskowitz and also later a co-defendant with Blaskowitz at Nuremberg, and therefore in a position to try to "influence" Blaskowitz. It also may explain why Blaskowitz was so concerned that his testimony might harm his comrades. Beyond the matter of loyalty to comrades was the matter of personal safety, given Hollidt's seeming willingness to apply "pressure" as he had done to Gersdorff. But there was more.

Coincidentally, Hollidt had been appointed as chief of staff to Blaskowitz in early November 1939 and had served in that role until May of 1940 when he became Chief of Staff of Ninth Army for the invasion of France—an army briefly under Blaskowitz until Hitler forced Blaskowitz's removal.[38] In other words, Hollidt may have been one of the few who had witnessed Blaskowitz's struggles against the atrocities in Poland, his repeated protest memoranda to Hitler, and who had survived and was in a position to support Blaskowitz by his testimony—if his memory had not failed him.

If Blaskowitz were to be interrogated publicly before the Tribunal at Nuremberg in the High Command Case in which he was indicted he would certainly have referred to his protest memoranda in his defense. The obvious implication of such a line of defense would have been to make it a matter of record that the High Command and General Staff had not only known about the atrocities, but had known about them as early as 1939/40. Indeed, in the March 1940 meeting with Himmler, no one had dared to support Blaskowitz officially. If Blaskowitz proceeded in his testimony to name the inevitably well-known names of his colleagues, it would be more than a public humiliation of his comrades. Certainly it was a reason for Blaskowitz to worry about his own testimony and perhaps to consider alternatives.

Without doubt, it was also a source of alarm to those threatened; to protect their "honor" was a strong motive in dealing with any perceived threat including even one by a member of the caste. It is a small step from motive to method. According to the rumor circulating in the prison after Blaskwitz's death, SS "trusties" in the prison murdered Blaskowitz. The manner by which the SS may have gained access to Blaskowitz that morning is shocking at the very least.

Richard Kamar, the oldest of the four Estonian guards who witnessed Blaskowitz's death at Nuremberg, according to the SS Personnel Records found in the Berlin Document Center, "was evaluated on 14 January 1945 in Frankfurt/Main in connection with an assignment to the 'Legion' (presumably the 20th Waffen SS Grenadier Division—Estnische No 1)"[39] Although the document does not indicate that Mr. Kamar actually became a member of the unit, it is clear that very few able bodied men were being rejected by the Waffen SS in January of 1945. Since the surviving records of the Waffen SS unit for which he was being evaluated are indeed very fragmentary, however, it is not possible to establish beyond a doubt that this was the case.

Among the records of the Estonian Waffen SS that did survive, however, are some of very great interest. Most important are two surviving lists of SS personnel for the 20. SS Waffen—Grenadier—Division (Estnische Nr. 1). These SS personnel lists provide name, date of birth, rank, military unit, and profession of personnel. Regrettably these two surviving personnel lists are themselves undated. On both of these surviving lists appears the name Ilmar Elbri, a second of the guards who witnessed Generaloberst Blaskowitz's death. He is listed as a "student," born 31 August 1926 and serving in SS Artillery Regiment 20 as an artilleryman.[40] An Erich Elbri is also listed.

Interestingly, there is also a Karl Küünal, born 22 June 1925, on the list, but no one named Kalju Küünal who was born on 24 February 1927.[41] Neither does the name Koit Tali (born 27 November 1927) appear on the surviving SS personnel lists of the 20th Waffen SS Grenadier Division (Estnische Nr.1), but there are both a Hendrik Tali (born 13 November 1923) and an Erwin Tali (born 2 September 1902).[42] Finally, in the U.S. National Archives "List of SS Officers, T-Z," there is a Juhan Tali (born 5 January 1902) listed.[43] Regretably, it has been impossible to establish that those Estonians on such lists with the same family name are related in any other way. It may merely be a coincidence.

There does appear to be far too many connections between the four Estonian guards who witnessed Blaskowitz's death and the 20th Waffen SS Grenadier Division for the explanation to be "coincidence." Indeed a closer examination of the Labor Service Companies in which the Estonian and Lithuanian guards were enrolled is warranted.

According to one source the U.S. Army recruited 30,000 Russian and East European Waffen SS veterans,[44] according to a second source there were 40,000 such men.[45] If these sources are correct, recruiting of former Waffen SS volunteers began as early as 1946. In some cases "Latvian, Lithuanian and Estonian labor units found themselves serving under the same officers ... as they had earlier in the SS.[46] In the case of at least one Latvian Labor Company, the commander, Vodemars Skaitlauks, was a former SS general and all six of his top lieutenants were Waffen SS veterans.[47] By 1950 these units had apparently been trained to play a role as pro-western guerrillas in Eastern Europe after any U.S.—Soviet Russian nuclear exchange at the outbreak of World War III.[48] Numerous other stories surround these labor companies, but they stray far from the death of Johannes Blaskowitz's death at Nuremberg.

Tracking down these Estonian guards who were witnesses to Blaskowitz's death almost fifty years after the incident is highly problematic. Richard Kamar and Koit Tali have receded into the historical mists, defying all efforts to locate them. Kalju Küünal died in New York City in 1989, according to the Social Security Death Index. Ilmar Elbri, however, was located and agreed to an interview on 11 December 1993. Not surprisingly after nearly one-half century Mr. Elbri remembers the events only vaguely, asserting that his best recollection is that his witness statement written so long ago is entirely correct. He can suggest no reason why none of the Germans who were reportedly marched with Blaskowitz back to their cells that morning, according to the statements of the other guards, left witness statements supporting the statements of the guards. He did not hear the story that circulated in the prison about Blaskowitz being murdered by SS trusties until the subject was raised in the interview.

When confronted with photocopies of the 20th Waffen SS Grenadier Division (1st Estonian) he responded only that he never served at all in the SS. He suggested that his name may have appeared on the SS personnel list, but that could only be due to the fact that his name had been forwarded by his draft board. He claimed that he had never reported to the unit because he had a broken ankle, was unfit for duty, and was sent to Germany to convalesce. He said he had documents to prove it. The documents, however, only re-stated the story of the ankle injury and convalescence in Germany, in the absence of lost documents, according to Mr. Elbri's statements. Although his name did appear on the SS lists, he asserted that there was no evidence that he ever reported to the Waffen SS.[49] He knew nothing more.

Perhaps Frau Blaskowitz was correct when she wrote shortly after the Generaloberst's death that he took the secret to the grave with him. The existence of a motive for the general's murder and the existence of a rumor that he was killed by SS "trusties," combined with the possibility that at least two of the only four witnesses to the death may have been connected to the SS is strong circumstantial evidence, but not conclusive proof. Motive, means and opportunity do not total murder; they do add up to unanswered questions. Blaskowitz may indeed have taken the secret of his death to the grave with him. But there is evidence enough to leave open the question of whether he died by his own hand.

Notes for Epilogue II

1. "Johannes Blaskowitz," *Der Deutshe Soldatenkalender 1953* (Munich: Schild Verlag, 1953), 19.

2. Möller-Witten, "Generaloberst Blaskowitz," 173.

3. Möller-Witten, *Mit dem Eichenlaub zum Ritterkreuz*, 224.

4. Stahl, "Johannes Blaskowitz," 1: 44.

5. *Altpreussische Biographie*, 1975 ed., S.V. "Blaskowitz, Johannes Albrecht," by Gerd Brausch.

6. Reitlinger, *SS*, 135.; See also: Graber, *SS*, 151.

7. Snyder, *Encyclopedia of the Third Reich*, 29.; Wistrich, *Who's Who in Nazi Germany*, 18-19.; Brett-Smith, *Hitler's General's*, 53.; David Downing, *The Devil's Virtuosos: German Generals At War, 1940-1945* (New York: St. Martin's Press, 1977), passim.

8. Barnett, *Hitler's Generals*, 81.: Samuel Mitcham and Gene Mueller, *Hitler's Commanders* (Lanham,Maryland: Scarborough House, 1992), 167.

9. "Porträts grosser Soldaten", *Kampftruppen*, Nr.3, June 1967); Msg 1/1814, BA/MA.

10. Gies, "Generaloberst Johannes Blaskowitz," 6.

11. Steuben, "Nürnberg : Blaskowitz opfert sich," 12.

12. Ibid. Most regrettably it has been impossible to trace Herr Steuben.

13. Froese, "Meine Begegnung mit Hans Blaskowitz," 10.

14. Interview, Johannes Koepcke, Jr., Bommelsen, Germany, Thomashof, 07/01/92 by the author. Regrettably the tape recording is badly damaged and the testimony is according to the author's careful recollection.

15. "Death of General Johannes Blaskowitz," 6 February 1948, Headquarters, Nuremberg Military Post, 6850th Internal Security Detachment, OCCPAC and OCCWC, 201 Files, R.G. 238, N.A.

16. "Tali, Koit," Headquarters, Nürnberg Military Post, 6850th Internal Security Detachment, Passes for OCCPWC Personnel to Courthouse, American—Allied—Displaced Persons—Germans, R.G. 238, N.A.

17. "Blaskowitz, Johannes," Headquarters Nürnberg Military Post, 6850th Inter-

nal Security Detachment, OCCPAC and OCCWC, 201 Files, R.G. 238, N.A.

18. "Küünal, Kalju," Headquarters, Nürnberg Military Post, 6850th Internal Security Detachment, Passes for OCCWC Personnel to Courthouse, American—Allied—Displaced Persons—Germans, R.G.238, N.A.

19. "Blaskowitz, Johannes," Headquarters, Nürnberg Military Post, 6850th Internal Security Detachment, OCCPAC and OCCWC, 201 Files, R.G. 238, N.A.

20. "Blaskowitz, Johannes," Headquarters, Nürnberg Military Post, 6850th Internal Security Detachment, OCCPAC and OCCWC, 201 Files, R.G. 238, N.A.

21. "Elbri, Ilmar," Headquarters, Nürnberg Military Post, 6850th Internal Security Detachment, Passes for OCCWC Personnel to Courthouse, American—Allied—Displaced Persons—Germans, R.G. 238, N.A.

22. "Blaskowitz, Johannes," Headquarters, Nürnberg Military Post, 6850th Internal Security Detachmnet, OCCPAC and OCCWC, 201 Files, R.G. 238, N.A.

23. 385th Station Hospital, "A&D Sheets" (Additions and Dispositions), 5 February 1945, National Personnel Records Center, Military Personnel Records, St. Louis MO, Copy in author's possession; "Certificate," Moffat Gardner, 6 February 1948, Nürnberg Military Post, 6850th Internal Security Detachmnet, OCCPAC and OCCWC, 201 Files, R.G. 238, N.A.

24. Ibid ("Certificate")

25. Dr. Karl Wiedenfeld, 7 February 1948, Nürnberg, Headquarters, Nürnberg Military Post, 6850th Internal Security Detachment, OCCPAC and OCCWC, 201 Files, R.G. 238, N.A.

26. Ibid.

27. "Nürnberg: Last Laugh," *Newsweek*, 28 (October 28, 1946), 45-47.

28. Otto John, *Twice Through the Lines*, trans, Richard Barry (New York: Harper & Row, Publishers, 1972), 189.

29. Rudolf-Christoph Freiherr von Gersdorff, *Soldat im Untergang* (Frankfurt/M: Ullstein Verlag,1977), 200.

30. Ibid.; 201.

31. Ibid.

32. Ibid.; 201-202.

33. "Basic: List of Time Internees in Case 12 spent in prison or camps, Karl Hollidt," undated, Entry 199, R.G. 238, N.A.

34. NOKW 2442, Hollidt, T-1119/31/0438-0447, R.G.319, N.A.

35. Watch List of German Generals, 3 April 1946, XE049474, R.G. 319, N.A.

36. NOKW 141, Hollidt, M-898/28/0200-0204, R,G, 238, N.A.

37. WO 208/4169, P.R.O.

38. NOKW 2442 Hollidt, M-898/28/0196, R.G. 238, N.A.; NOKW 2442, Hollidt, T-1119/31/0444.

39. Letters, David G. Marwell, Director, Berlin Document Center, 27/01/93 and 22/03/93 including photocopy of Richard Kamar Document, to the author. Copy in author's possession.

40. T-354/160/3805461-69, Elbri is listed as number 53 on the list; T-354/160/3805589-5627 Elbri is listed as number 917 on this list.

41. T-354/160/3805461-5503; "Küünal, Kalju", Headquarters, Nürnberg Military Post, 6850th Internal Security Detachment, OCCPAC and OCCWC, 201 Files, R.G. 238, N.A.

42. T-354/160/3805565; T-354/160/3805820.

43. "SS Officers, T-Z", Handbook, Modern Military Headquarters Branch, N.A.

44. Sayer and Botting, *America's Secret Army*, 345.

45. Simpson, *Blowback*, 142.

46. Ibid.

47. Ibid, 145.

48. Ibid. Sayer and Botting, *America's Secret Army*, 345,; See also: Rein Taagepera, *Estonia: Return to Independence* (San Francisco: Westview Press, 1993), 71.

49. Interview, Ilmar Elbri, 11 December 1993, at Mr. Elbri's home, by the author. Tape in author's possession.

Document NO-3011 from the Office of Chief of Counsel for War Crimes

The Commander in Chief East, Headquarters, Spala, 6 February 1940

NOTES FOR ORAL REPORT by Commander in Chief East to the Commander in Chief of the Army, 15 February 1940, Spain

1. Morale of the Troops
2. Education
3. Health of the Troops
4. Supply Situation
5. Condition of Horses
6. Salvaging of Booty
7. Economic Situation
8. Military Political Situation
9. Guiding Lines for the Employment of Troops in the Event of Revolts and Hostilities breaking out in the Area of the Commander in Chief East
10. Establishment of Forest Police, Works Police, etc.

(handwritten note)
Fraeulein KNOBRAUCH:
In my safe, special file "Gouvernement Poland"
—Initials—4 May,
The Commander in Chief East Headquarters Spala 6 February 1940

MORALE OF THE TROOPS

The morale of the troops and their probable fighting value can be described as thoroughly satisfactory.

The rather non-military bearing shown at first, has meanwhile visibly improved. The people submit to their training willingly and in spite of their advanced age, make a fressh and soldierly impression. The arrival of recruits has a good effect on the morale of the older people.

Offenses, as well as extreme cases of lack of discipline, are few in the area and continue to decrease. Serious offenses and crimes (looting, race defilement, desertion) scarcely ever occur now. The cases on which sentences have been passed so far, or on which sentences are still pending, originate almost exclusively from the time of the fighting.

The publication of the past heavy sentences has served as a deterrent.

EDUCATION

1. Newspapers: Supply of newspapers from home completely in order since Christmas, time taken in transit 2 to 8 days. The Warsaw or Cracow newspaper with soldiers' supplement "Watch in the East", time taken in transit 1 to 4 days. The delivery of illustrated papers has not yet been successful in every case, the same applies to the delivery of the magazine "Wehrmacht".

2. Film Supplies: News reels are regularly supplied. Mobile film units—6—of the Propaganda Offices and Propaganda Squad East are set up in the smaller villages that have no movies. The supply of entertainment films is still short, however, immediate delivery of these by the High Command of the Armed forces is expected. Twelve small film projectors (sound-and silent projectors) will be dispatched after the cold period has abated (are already available). By these means special service can increase its film supply for the troops.

3. The supply of books has for the main part been accomplished. The last transports are on the way.

4. The supply of games has started with the delivery of chess games (3,000). Further supplies of games are expected.

5. In the area of the Commander in Chief East 677 shows have been given during January. In the central and southern area exclusively by "Strength Through Joy", in the north with the support of the civilian theaters in the Reich territory. Evening theater performances; variety cabarets, vaudeville, concerts and folk-dancing, etc. (Volkstumabende).

6. Lecture evenings for officers and suitable enlisted men have begun. So far 10 subjects: "Outlines and Polish History," "The Birth and Death of the Last Polish State, viewed from a military and a political angle," "Germany's Food Situation," "Problems of the Eastern Territories," "Our Propaganda Activities and that of the Enemy."

7. Soldiers' homes and physical welfare: Wherever the troops are stationed, they are nearly always engaged in establishing soldiers' homes, mostly by conversion: in the same way their physical welfare is assured or will be further improved when the weather is better. There is a great shortage of wardens and helpers for the soldiers' homes, repair workshops and laundries. The Red Cross has declared itself ready to take on this task. Negotiations with the High Command of the Armed Forces are in progress. It is to be expected that the management and welfare will be assigned to the Red Cross.

8. "Strength Through Joy" and Reich Office for Propaganda. Cooperation with "Strength Through Joy" is good. The achievements of the "Strength Through Joy" entertainment groups are appreciated by all. Difficulties still arise regarding cooperation with the Reich Office for Propaganda. The Commander in Chief East hopes shortly to be able to remove these through personal discussions; if this should not be possible, a report will follow.

In summarizing, it can be stated that the educational welfare of the troops is already satisfactory. When the improvements in all fields, which are shortly to be expected, have been completed, the troops will be really well supplied.

HEALTH OF THE TROOPS

The health of the Eastern Army can be described as being very good.

Approximately 1.2% sick in January. There is no immediate danger of epidemics apart from the small areas of infection which always exist in the East. The existing typhus epidemic in Warsaw is abating. So far, one doubtful case of typhus among the troops.

SUPPLY SITUATION

1. Food: The food for the men is sufficient, although High Command East (Oberost) on its own initiative reduced the meat ration to 180 mg two months ago and, in addition, substituted a meatless day.

There are no complaints about insufficient food.

The fodder for the horses is insufficient, on account of lack of coarse fodder from home. Orders have been given for fodder substitutes to be used as fodder. Only 1/2 of the coarse fodder ration can be issued.

The supplies which can be drawn from the country by purchase through quartermaster's offices are very small on account of low stocks and insufficient organization of the civil administration. From 1 December 1939 to 10 January 1940, out of the total requirements, only 20% of rye, 100% of sugar, 100% of brandy, 100% of cigarettes, 1% of oats, 1% of hay, 3% of straw and 70% of meat could be procured in addition to 100% of potatoes and some fresh vegetables. For the rest, supplies have to be sent from Germany, and the General gouvernement wishes to dispense entirely with drawing supplies from the country. This, however, cannot be permitted, but the troops were prohibited from procuring rationed foodstuffs in excess of the amounts due.

2. Quarters: Quarters consist for the most part of Polish barracks and are simple but sufficient. Urgent improvements and repairs were carried out partly by contractors and partly by the troops themselves at not very great expense. Raw materials for this work were in no case supplied from Germany. The supply of woollen blankets was adequate, as additional supplies were obtained from Poland in good time. Lodz supplied 250,000 blankets in all.

3. Coal Supplies are difficult on account of the low capacity of the railway.

4. Clothing: So far, the supply of the current requirements of clothing and equipment has been very slow, since orders had to be given through the intermediary of the ...?... An improvement is to be

expected if the authorization is given, as planned, to supply the troops continuously from the army clothing stores. The urgent need of underclothing, in particular, was able to be met by supplies obtained from Lodz. Fur coats for sentries and drivers of horse-drawn vehicles were issued to a proportion of 5% of the men in December and January; 6,000 of those coats were supplied by the home country: and 4,000 were procured from the country locally. Only 4,000 pairs of felt boots could be supplied, and 10,000 were ordered to be delivered from the country locally. So far it has only been possible for 1,000 of these to be delivered on account of the difficulties of procuring raw materials, the remainder is expected in February.

5. Pay: The pay received by the troops is adequate. Generally the troops complain of the differences made between members of the civil administration and those of the Armed Forces. The former receive separation allowance and are also supposed to receive a danger bonus from the Gouvernement; their rate of pay is, therefore, considerably higher, especially in view of the fact that their food is cheap and their billets mostly free of charge.

CONDITION OF HORSES

The position with regard to fodder for the horses is suffering from the lack of coarse fodder. Cases of scabbiness and chest diseases are reported from individual formations. In spring it is planned to organize convalescent centers for horses on a large scale in districts rich in grazing grounds.

SALVAGE OF WAR BOOTY

On the whole, the removal of the booty, with the exception of a few large ammunition depots, has been concluded.

For this achievement most of the credit is again to be given to Oberst DIEHM of the Fz (Transportation Corps?)

The necessary instructions have been given for the remaining stocks still scattered at different places to be collected and also those stocks of arms and ammunition which it has been proved were hidden deliberately.

The arms found by the SS and the Police were not surrendered, but were retained by them for their own use.

ECONOMIC SITUATION

The Generalgouverneur has declared that in the meantime his original order for the destruction and exploitation of the country has been changed and that from now on, all the important and valuable production facilities of the country are to be utilized as far as possible.

The food situation has developed still more unfavorably.

Enormous increases in prices, profiteering and black marketing make it impossible for the mass of the population to obtain supplies.

According to remarks made by the staff of the General-gouverneur, the scale of prices has reached a catastrophic state, and people are of the opinion that if energetic measures are not taken soon, a collapse will be inevitable. The price control section, which had left as a result of a personal dispute, is to be called back again.

It is questionable whether the administration will be able to save the situation at the last moment after having stood by for months on end without taking any action. It is significant that in the last few days, General Buehrmann has come to the fore in all these matters as representative of the Four Year Plan.

The General gouvernement has no coal supplies. It is not necessary to enumerate the effects of this in all spheres, e.g. without coal there is no possibility of threshing. The corn is standing unused in the stacks. The farmers are holding back their produce and are no longer willing to accept Zlotys, as they already have enough and yet cannot buy anything with them. Resorting to barter is a general sign of the times.

It has not yet been ascertained what stocks there actually are in the country. Opinions on this matter differ.

High Command East (Oberost) is of the opinion that sufficient stocks are available and that with reasonable organization, supplies for the branches of the Wehrmacht stationed in the East could, in general, be assured from this country.

High Command East (Oberost) will resist the endeavors of the General gouvernement to order the Wehrmacht to obtain supplies from the home country exclusively.

The purchase of horses is progressing slowly but according to plan. About 10,000 horses have already been shipped back home.

The conversion of the administration and economy for the supplying of fuel from the country's own resources is still in its initial stages.

The reactivation of the armament industry is very slow and is, at present, in its initial stages, so that no relief worth mentioning has so far come from this quarter. Thus the state of unemployment of large sections of the industrial population has not changed much.

These classes of the population are suffering severe hardship and are starving. Their situation, combined with the other circumstances, offers the most fertile ground for the cultivation of anti-German activities.

For details, please refer to the reports of the armament inspection (RUE Insp.). (Major General Barkhausen) The statement made by the bank of issue (Emissions bank), which was to ease the entire stock market, was of no help whatsoever for the time being. The bank cannot work, since the notes will not be ready until the middle of April.

MILITARY POLITICAL SITUATION

For the first time a very extensive resistance and sabotage movement in the industrial area of Kamienna has been discovered. The chief supporters of this movement are members of the former Polish Army. The material which has been found on numerous arrested persons is, at present, still being examined. The State Police is, for the time being, desisting from further arrests, in order to guarantee the destruction of the entire movement at a later date.

The danger likely to arise herefrom calls for a definition of policy as regards to the treatment of the Polish people.

It is a mistake to massacre some 10,000 Jews and Poles, as is being done at present; as this, as far as the mass of the population is concerned, will neither eradicate the idea of a Polish state nor will the Jews be exterminated. On the contrary, the manner in which these massacres take place, causes the greatest harm, complicates the problems, and renders them much more serious than they would have been if the matter had been dealt with more deliberately and methodically. The consequences are as follows:

(a) Enemy propaganda is furnished with material more effective than can be imagined throughout the world. The propaganda hitherto broadcast by the foreign senders, is only a diminutive fraction of the actual events. We must take into consideration that the outcries abroad will increase, and will thus cause most serious political prejudice against us, since the atrocities really happened and can, in no way, be refuted.

(b) The acts of violence against the Jews, which are enacted in public, do not only provoke the most profound disgust in the religious Poles, but also a pity just as great for the Jewish population, towards which the Poles hitherto showed a more or less hostile attitude. This will soon have the effect that our arch-enemies, in the East—the Pole and the Jew, especially supported by the Catholic Church—will join against Germany in every respect, because of their hatred for their tormentors.

(c) We need hardly again point out the part to which the Wehrmacht is subjected by being forced to watch these crimes inactively; the esteem in which they hitherto were held by the Polish population, has greatly decreased and will never be restored.

(d) The worst results, however, which will arise for the German people from this situation, is the immeasurable brutalization and moral depravity, which will very soon spread like a plague among valuable German men. If high officials of the SS and of the Police demand atrocities and brutalities and praise them in public, then soon the brutal man will rule. Surprisingly quickly like minded persons and people of poor character will come together, as is the case in Poland, in order to find in violence an outlet for their bestial and pathological instincts. There exists hardly any possibility of restraining them, as they quite rightly feel themselves authorized officially and justified to commit every outrage. The only possibility to ward off this plague, would be to apprehend the guilty and their followers and put them immediately under military control and jurisdiction.

On 2 February 1940, the Commander in Chief of the border section South, General of the Infantry, ULEX, writes the following to the Commander in Chief East Spala:

> The atrocities of the Police Forces, which have particularly increased of late show a quite incomprehensible lack of human and moral feelings, so that one can almost speak in this case of bestiality. And I am convinced that my office is informed of only a small fraction of the atrocities committed. It appears that the superiors secretly approve of these activities and do not wish to take any steps.

To my mind, the only way out of this unworthy situation, which is sullying the honor of the entire German nation, is to replace and disband all the Police units, including all their higher leaders, and all the officers holding posts in the General gouvernement who have been watching these atrocities for months, and arrange for them to be replaced by complete and honorable units.

—signed ULEX

On 5 February, the General gouvernement liaison officer, Major von TSCHAMMER und OSTEN, states that in Rzeszow and Tschensto-chau, the regular police passes a number of death sentences, which were to be submitted to the Fuehrer for confirmation. In Tschenstochau alone, four officers are said to have been indicted, the battalion commander is said to have been sentenced to death on three counts.

After all that hitherto happened, we shall have to wait and see whether there actually exists the desire to maintain order, especially as more or less all leaders took part in those atrocities, at least supported or permitted them.

We do not know all the details of what happened in Tschenstochau. According to a statement of a police officer, the officers of the police here and in several other places indulged in bloody massacres.

The interrogation of a staff-sergeant, of a non-commissioned officer, and of a corporal of the Inf. Regt. 414, given in Appendix No. 1, prove what brutalities these beasts were capable of. The attitude of the troops towards the SS and the Police alternates between abhorrence and hate. Every soldier feels disgusted and repulsed by these crimes which are being committed in Poland by members of the Reich and representatives of the Supreme Power. He cannot understand that such things, especially as they are committed under his protection, if one can put it thus, are possible without punishment.

Each police search and confiscation is accompanied by looting and plundering on the part of the policemen involved in the action. Apparently it is quite customary that confiscated goods of every kind are distributed among the Police and SS units, or are sold in return for small payments.

Major General BUEHRMANN, the Plenipotentiary for the Four Year Plan, stated in a meeting at the Governor General's, which took place on 23 January 1940, that the clever field office chief, under his

491

command, a certain Rittmeister SCHUH, succeeded in persuading the SS to hand over large quantities of watches and jewelry.

In view of such conditions, it really is no wonder that the individual makes use of every opportunity to enrich himself. And he is able to do so without any danger, for if everybody is stealing, the individual thief need not be afraid of being punished.

There is no doubt that the Polish population who has to look on all these crimes defenselessly or is itself effected by them and driven to despair, will support fanatically every subversive movement for revenge. Large numbers of people who would never have thought of a revolt, will now make use of every opportunity for such a revolt and support it as determined fighters. Especially the numerous small farmers who would have worked for us in a quiet and satisfactory manner if reasonably treated by a competent German administration, are driven, so to speak, forcibly into the enemy camp.

The re-settlement scheme is causing particular and steedily [sic] increasing alarm in the country. It is quite obvious that the starving population, struggling for its very existence, can regard the wholly destitute masses of evacuees, who were torn from their homes over night, as it were naked and hungry, and who are begging shelter from them, only with the greatest anxiety. It is only too understandable that these feelings are intensified to immense hatred by the numerous children starved to death on each transport and the train loads of people frozen to death.

The idea that the Polish people can be intimidated and kept down by terror will certainly prove to be wrong. The capacity for endurance which this nation commands is much too great.

During the last months, approximately 100 death sentences passed under martial law and mainly because of possession of weapons and sabotage, were executed by our troops. The Polish population acknowledge that we are entitled to do this and submits to it. On the other hand they will resist with every means the atrocities, the maltreatment and the looting, as committed by the SS Police and Administrative Authorities.

The older Polish generation knows from its own experience very well all the tried dodges of a skillful conspiracy, which have been applied during hundred years of struggle. It will pass this knowledge on to the next generation, making it an opponent to be taken particularly seriously.

The opinion, frequently expressed, that a small Polish revolt would be quite desirable, as it would furnish an opportunity of decimating the Poles on a large scale, can only be considered very irresponsibly. It can be proved that quantities of arms and ammunition are hidden in the country, so that a subversive movement would certainly involve the loss of much German blood. Apart from that it must be feared that reinforcements from the West would be required to subdue such a revolt, reinforcements which it might be very difficult to dispense with.

There can be no doubt that these activities endanger the military security and the economic exploitation of the East in an irresponsible manner, and to no purpose whatsoever.

From the great number of transgressions and offenses by the Police, SS and Administration, which have come to the knowledge of Commander in Chief East (Oberost) after 9 December a few significant cases are herewith listed on enclosure 2, in addition to the former list submitted.

There has been no change in the relationship between the Governor General and the Police since the visit in Spala. Attempts are being made to create the impression as though everywhere the best relationship existed with the Wehrmacht. More caution is being observed as far as the troops are concerned. The position of the troops has no doubt been strengthened. Transgressions against them are not likely to be repeated.

In compliance with orders resubmitted to Generalleutenant von BOMHARD, after copies of excerpts had been made.

(signature) DR. LEBUS (initial: B)

Re-submitted to the General of the Police, DALUEGE.
All necessary steps will be taken.

25 April

(signature) BOMHARD (initial)

Dg

26 April

1. On 28 October 1939, a short distance from Krosniewice, SS men threatened a Pole with their pistols: they took away his truck, although he had shown them a trip ticket of the Warsaw garrison headquarters, (Kommandantur).

2. On 29 October 1939, SS aspirant Franz POROBATSCH searched apartment No. 3 at Radom, Mickiwica, and took this opportunity to steal playing cards, a pocket-watch two purses, etc. He was arrested by an officer of the Regional Defense Guards (Landesschuetzen Regt. 2/IV) and handed over to a SS Sturmbannfuehrer.

3. On 23 November 1939, Polizei-Oberleutnant (1st Lieutenant of the Police, ALTENDORF started a campaign against Jews at Parzew in the course of which, his men (men of the Police Battalion 102) looted and destroyed a great number of shops, subjecting the civilian population to ill treatment. Allegedly stocks kept by Jews were supposed to be searched for hoarded goods. Even an SS officer of the Security Police considered this action of the police intolerable and reported it to his superior headquarters at Lublin.

4. On 10 December 1939, three SS men completely drunk broke into the apartment of a Polish woman in Radom and destroyed her furniture. When arrested, they had to be taken to the local headquarters by truck as, owing to their drunkedness, they were unable to walk. Allegedly they were men from the 11th SS death-head division at Radom.

5. At the beginning of November 1939, the Kreisleiter of Sokolow, WALLADE, requisitioned horses, which were allegedly to be used for ethnic-Germans by unharnessing them from carriages of farmers, who were engaged in the harvest of sugar beet. The receipts he issued, which were illegible in most cases, were not redeemed. Despite complaints to the Kreisleitung (district administration) the same occurrence was repeated twice. The harvest of sugar beets, which had only been set in motion through the initiative of the Wehrmacht, was severely handicapped by these incidents and could only be reverted to its normal function after troop units were made available for employment.

6. In Opole, a SS squad, under the leadership of SS Obersturmfuehrer BERGER and accompanied by an armed ethnic-German, ULLRICH by name, attempted to raise 100,000 zlotys from Jews; this money was said to be used for wages which became due for the manufacture of fur coats for the SS. No previous notice had been given to the local headquarters.

7. On 31 December 1939, at Czenstechew, about 250 Jews were dragged (written marginal notation illegible) into the street at night in bitter cold weather. After some hours waiting they were taken to a school where they were searched for gold, as it was pretended. Also, the women had to undress completely and were searched by policemen, even in their genitals.

8. The Jewish actress Johanna EPSTEIN in Warsaw, formerly living in the rear building at Poznansta 12, occupies together with SS Untersturmfuehrer, WERNER under the new name of PETZOLD and now as an ethnic-German, the front-house apartment of a fugitive Englishman.

9. On 8 December 1939, members of the Police Battalion 72 looted a Jewish shop at Czenstochow. On this occasion, quantities of leather were seized which were being worked up there, also, for the troops. After investigation had been made by the troops, the owner's wife, Frau BARMHERZIG, was arrested and killed by the Police as an incriminating witness.

10. On 29 December 1939, at Anin, two sergeants of the Construction Battalion 538 were killed by two professional criminals, whilst they attempted to arrest the latter. They were only escorted by a Polish policeman and had neglected to take with them a sufficient number of men. The Police battalion 6 which was rushed to the site of the crime by the administration, upon notification of the murder, had the innkeeper hung in front of his establishment where the crime was committed and 114 Poles from the residential quarter Anin, who had nothing to do with the crime, were shot. According to a statement of the Warsaw Kreishauptmann (district prefect) three members of the district office (Landratsamt) and 2 ethnic-Germans, were supposed to have been among the Poles who were shot.

The shooting particularly aroused bad feelings among the Poles because the murder was not caused by acts of hostilities on the part of the population, but was a pure criminal offense. All the more so as the population itself had reported the professional criminals to the Construction Battalion 538 and thus tried to help to arrest them. The action of the Police Battalion 6 was particularly praised in a regimental orders of Police Regt. 31 and represented as being unobjectionable and energetic. Every member of the battalion had to be notified of the commendation. This case was reported by the BBC in London on 11 February 1940.

11. On 11 January 1940, Inf. Rgt. 414 at Tomaszow handed over three Poles, suspected of having looted a Polish vehicle, to the 2nd Comp. of the 91st Police Battalion. The prisoners, when they were handed over, were severely maltreated by Police Captain SCHMUCKLER and 1st Sgt. of the Police (Polizeimeister) THOMKE in the presence of members of the Wehrmacht. Without any cause, the Captain hit one of the Poles with his fist and aiming at both his carotid arteries, so that the Pole tumbled onto a box and was unable to rise again. After further ill-treatment, the Poles were shot immediately without any sentence having been imposed on them. The regiment refused in future to hand over to the Police people who had been arrested, because this automatically would result in their being shot, and thwart any further investigations or trials.

12. On 19 January 1940, 1st Lt. BOCK, leader of the 1st Comp. of the Police Battalion 102, before his departure, had the Jewish population of Kasimierz, men and women, maltreated in the worst possible manner, so that "they won't forget us so easily" as he said himself. (illegible marginal notations)

13. On 22 January 1940, by order of Kreishauptmann (prefect of the district) DR. EHAUS at Rzeszow, 30-40 Jews were publicly whipped by the Police on the market place. (Ilegible marginal notation)

14. On 16 December 1939, ten people who had been sentenced to death, were shot by Police Battalion 63 near Rzeszow. After the condemned had dug their own graves—hereby one of the Poles had already been shot for trying to escape—half of them were shot, not having been blindfolded, but facing the riflemen while the others were waiting.

The Major of the Reserve (Medical Officer) (Oberstabsarzt der Res.) who was present at the execution, gave the following detailed report:

After the sentence had been pronounced, the ammunition was handed to the 10 riflemen who, in turn, had to fire at each man's head and chest. When the volley had been fired, the men who had been hit, fell into the pit without death occurring immediately in all cases. One of them called out loudly, asking to be killed: hit by a grazing shot in his head and lungs, he had fallen across two other men. Likewise, in the 2nd group, one of the condemned in the pit who had been hit pointed with his hand at his head begging to be shot. Subsequently, gun and revolver shots were fired which caused death beyond any doubt.

15. On 1 December 1939, two men in SS uniform and one civilian took one lady's fur jacket, five fur waistcoats and two skins from the apartment of the Jew Chaim NIEWIEDOWICZ at Glowne, Mosciesky, and left in a car (allegedly No. 44 208 082) in the direction of Lodz. The Jew had been given a commission for these articles from an office of the Wehrmacht; he showed a voucher to this affect.

16. At Radom, on 8 January 1940, 2 SS men searched the apartment of Mrs. BUGACKA, wife of a Polish official, residing at 4a Moniuskistrasse, and robbed her of linen, cutlery and two savings bank books.

17. On 8 January 1940, two SS men driving in a car, trade-mark Hansa, No. 03 73, stopped a truck, No. 01 737, about 10 Km before Garwolin (in the direction of Warsaw), took away the identity papers of the Polish driver, forced him to leave the vehicle, and drove the truck towards Lublin.

18. On 18 January 1940, members of the SD (Sicherheitsdienst—Security Service) broke a window pane in the quarters of the 2nd Comp., military Police Battalion (Feldgend. Abt.) 531 at 1, Piasowskastrasse, Petrikan and most rudely insulted the members of the military police (Feldgendarmerieleute). We were able to establish the identity of one of the men only; he was Heinz Friedel HEUER, member of the SD (Security Service) 14 Leononska, Petrikan. The superiors of the SD men, SS Sturmfuehrer KULLER and his deputy, refused to name the persons involved. We did not hear about any punishment having been inflicted.

19. In December 1939, Police Sergeant (Polizeiwachtmeister) WERNER, from the 1st Company Police Battalion III, Warsaw, assaulted a military policeman of the motorized battalion 531 and

threatened him with his pistol because the latter wanted to settle a quarrel between members of the Police Force in an inn. Recommendation for punishment was forwarded to the tribunal of the Warsaw garrison headquarters.

20. In December 1939, the Police Sergeants (Polizeiwacht- meister) and KRAMES, 1st Company Pol. Battalion III, Warsaw, threatened Polish civilians with their pistols—on this occasion, KRAMES shot at an unknown Jew—and annoyed women in an inn in Warsaw. A military policeman (Feldgendarm) who interfered, was seriously offended by him and a n.c.o. of the Military Police Battalion was threatened with a pistol. Both Police sergeants were arrested. Recommendation for punishment was forwarded to the tribunal of the Warsaw garrison headquarters.

21. On 17 January 1940, SS Untersturmfuehrer WALDNER, Chief of the Security Police, branch office Lukow, had some of the Lukow vicarage sealed up, although he knew that the building was situated in a block of houses reserved for the Wehrmacht and the rooms would be wanted again as billets for the Wehrmacht. WALDNER did not comply with the request to break the seals. The Higher Police Leader (Hochere Polizeifuehrer) promised to make investigations.

22. Towards the middle of November 1939, members of the Police forced their way into the office of Director MALINOWSKI, who was appointed by the Deputy Chief of the Army Archives in Warsaw. When they were shown a decree signed by the Commander of Warsaw, to the effect that members of the Wehrmacht, Police, etc. were not allowed to enter this office because important documents were being filed there. They stated that the general had nothing to do with them, and that they only accepted orders issued by the Chief of the Police. This decree was removed from its frame by members of the Police and taken from another building where documents were also stored. When charges were made by the Chief of the Army Archives, the Senior Police and SS Group Leader (Hoehere Polizei und SS Gruppenfuehrer) MODER urged the assistant Police Sergeant in question to apply "more restraint".

23. On 5 December 1939, a certain Oberscharfuehrer HILLIGES at Tedlina, in the district of Radom, forced three Poles, by holding his pistol in front of them, to sell to him some pigs at a low price; allegedly

for the Security Police at Radom (price 60-70 Gr. for one kg instead of 3 Zloty). According to the statement of a butcher from Radom, two German soldiers, wearing a black uniform, came daily to the slaughter-house at Radom and bought up pigs. As the SS is fed by the Army, double rations were drawn from the country.

24. On 22 January 1940, four members of the SS at Warsaw took away goods at a total value of RM 5000; from the wineshop and delicatessen shop ALEJE Ujazdowskie 34; maltreated the grandchild of the owner and forced the owner to sign a document which he did not understand. He received the sum of 300 RM.

25. On 3 February 1940 members of a SS unit stole 50 qwts of coal out of a railway truck containing coal for the soldiers' home at Radom. They used truck LSS-19 121.

26. On 25 January 1940 an SS leader of the local headquarters in Miedzyrzec reported that he had been ordered to seize stocks in textile shops. The decrees ordering the seizure were not stamped, and signed by SS Untersturmfuehrer GLAESSNER at Miedzyrzec.

27. On 31 January 1940 Police Assistant LUCHT and HOSPO-DARSCH, employee of the Criminal Police, both from the SIPO (Sicherheit- spolizei—Security Police) and SD (Sicherheitsdienst—Security Service) head-quarters at Radom both in SS uniform) took away food and spices of various kinds from six Jewish shops at Kosienice, mainly without payment. On this occasion they stole two rings. The number plate of their car was completely concealed. They stated that they had to take care of food supplies for their headquarters.

28. The Jewish tanner Elias RAPPAPORT from Zarki, who had to supply leather by order of the Oberfeldkommandantur (military government area headquarters) in Tschenstochau, was stopped by a police official and searched and maltreated at the quarters of 1st comp. /Police Battalion 72 at Tschenstochau; all of his money, amounting to 1102 Zloty, was taken from him. He had gone to Tschenstochau to buy tannic acid. Due to the energetic action taken by the *new* C.O. of the Police Battalion and the *new* Chief of the above mentioned company, the money, which had been stolen, was secure and handed to the Oberfeldkommandantur (millitary government area headquarters).

29. Three members of the Wehrmacht (1 S/Sgt. (Ufdwb.), 1 Sgt.

(Uffz.), 1 Pfc. (Gefr.) toward the middle of January 1940, wanted to be present at the execution under the martial law of two Poles; the execution was carried out by the 2nd Comp., Police Battalion 91 at Tomaszow/Lublin, and the following statement was recorded by the members of the Wehrmacht: "When we approached Police quarters we noticed several people—soldiers and policemen—standing behind the building on the open grounds in front of sandhills. Furthermore, we saw two civilians who were digging a ditch. We asked the Police officials for information who were standing around, and heard that one of the civilians, a man, allegedly had shot somebody, and the second civilian, a woman of about 22 years of age, was supposed to have hidden cartridges behind the low neck of her dress. No trial of the case had taken place so far: but they were to be shot in any case. The Captain had not come back from a hunting party; he still had to sign the order. Preparations for digging the grave were supervised by two police guards wearing steel helmets and rifles. All other people standing there were spectators. The place was not fenced off. The ground there, however, is situated in such a way that if one stands behind the pit, which is to be dug, one cannot watch the proceedings opposite, whilst on the other hand, there are occupied houses at the back to the left and half way to the right, from which the following proceedings could easily be watched.

In our opinion, the two civilians dug eagerly and took pains. The pit might already have been dug down to 3/4 meter. Meanwhile, a policeman with a steel helmet and belt and without an overcoat, came towards the pit from the police barracks, which are surrounded by a wooden fence. Then there were shouts from the crowd of onlookers: "Here comes the right one." Apparently this policeman was already known from previous executions. Remarks were also heard concerning the woman who was to be executed. The crowd said she did not look so bad, but on the contrary seemed harmless. Whereupon the policeman who had arrived by that time answered: "She is worse than the man, you don't need to have any pity for her." Soon he added, "I only want to know whether she is still wearing her panties. Well, we shall see. They will get their treatment through me anyway." And, "Light a good fire in the stove." We thought then that they were going to be tortured on the burning stove.

In response to a shout from the crowd that the two still needed a good "rubbing down", the same policeman went towards the male civilian, picked up a spade from the ground and hit him on his back so that the blade of the spade came off at once and flew into the pit. The civilian thereupon fell to his knees, and when getting up, picked up the blade in sheer fright. Thereupon, the policeman hit the civilian a second time on his back with the spade handle. The civilian then fell to his knees again and only got up very slowly. Nevertheless, he went on digging.

Now there were shouts that the woman was much worse—this woman, by the way, was thought to be the wife of the civilian. Thus incited, the policeman went around the pit and hit the woman with all his strength on her behind. The woman screamed softly and said in Polish in a whining and complaining tone: "Please, sir, I am doing my best." Thereupon the policeman jumped into the pit in front of the woman and hit her face with the back of his hand, which was clad in a leather glove, with such violence that it sounded like the report of a bullet. The women fell down immediately; as she was standing in front of the pit which she had dug, she fell backward on her behind, with her knees apart. At the same time a great stream of blood came gushing out of her nose and mouth.

At first she was unable to move. Gradually, however, she moved and wiped her face with the back of her hand. The policeman shouted at her several times to go on working. Then, in order to force her, he drew his revolver and pressed it against her breast. The woman, however, was completely apathetic and did not comply with the order to go on digging, which was repeated several times. Thereupon the male civilian went to the woman in order to help her get up. As she still was unable to do so, she opened her legs and lifted her skirts so that one could see that her underwear was completely soaked with blood, almost down to her knees. The agitation must have caused her to menstruate. The policeman who was standing before her at the pit then said: "Now she has got her menstruation—there will be no fucking now." Thereupon the policeman jumped out of the pit. This incident shook us deeply, so that we almost felt sick. As the shooting was not to take place until the afternoon, we left again then. On our way we discussed those incidents and all of us were indignant at these things.

In the afternoon, the Unterfeldwebel, together with other members of the 19/414 went back to the police barracks in order to watch the further developments of this affair. There he was told that at lunchtime the policeman at the station had ordered the two civilians to kiss each other in their presence for five minutes. This order too was obeyed by the civilians. In the course of the afternoon it became known at the station that the woman would not be executed because of a mistake made in the process of identification. This was confirmed in the late hours of the afternoon. At about 5:30, one male civilian was shot at the place of execution. He had to take off his shoes beforehand and had to walk to the place of execution with only rags covering his feet. Because he had tried to escape, he had been struck in the face. Afterwards he was unable to get up again.

He had to be dragged to the pit and then, too, he could neither stand nor sit up, but fell into the pit face downwards. As he was lying in such a way that the back of his neck was exposed, he could be killed in this position with three pistol shots in his neck. Thereupon the woman who had been discharged had to fill in the man's grave with a spade, which was pressed into her hands.

One of the soldiers took a photograph of the incident. The negative, which is with the original, shows the two Poles, the man and the woman, digging the grave.

30. At the beginning of January Obw. (Oberwachtmeister police sergeant) KRAUSSE of the First Company of the Police Battalion XI in Pultiek, broke into the home of a Polish family while drunk. (Illegible handwritten marginal note.) At the point of the pistol, he forced the daughter to accompany him to the tavern. When the two left the tavern, the girl called for help to a passing military patrol. The latter separated the official and the girl, whereupon the official soon afterwards fired a shot after the patrol. When arrested, he denied having had a pistol, however, the latter was found in a doorway. The matter has been referred to a court martial.

31. Shortly before Christmas, 1600 Jews were to be expelled from Nasielek. (Handwritten marginal note: Where is this?) The police locked them all in the synagogue and there beat them with dogwhips. Some were shot there and then beside the synagogue. When the greater part was being taken to the station next morning, they were forced by

blows of the whip to traverse a mire, known as the "red moor". 24 Jews, who later returned secretly, were given five bread-rolls between them as their daily ration, and were locked in an ice cold room, the windows of which were boarded up. The Police took away their coats and left them locked up at a temperature of 9 degrees below zero. The screams and wails of the freezing Jews, who included some women, is said to have been heard several streets away. The commander of the troops stationed in Nasielok had to bring the matter before the competent Landrat and Kreisleiter GAEBLICH, before the deportation of these Jews could be affected. The matter was brought to the attention of the competent Gauleiter.

32. On 3 February 1940, Stabsingenieur DIETRICH, acting on behalf of the Generalluftzeugmeister, informs the liaison officer of the Armament Inspectorate:

When travelling in the company of a Polish director of an airplane factory near Warsaw, he had learned that, that same day, a truckload of SS men had stopped at a Warsaw furrier's and "confiscated" the entire stock of the finest furs, including even furs which had been brought in for repair. They neither paid nor made out a receipt for the goods confiscated. The matter was brought to the attention of General UDET.

33. On 18 February 1940 in Petrikau, two police sergeants (Wachtmeister) (handwritten, marginal note: 181 19 February), of the 3rd Company, Battalion 182, with raised pistols, came to take the 18-year-old Jewess MACHMANOWIC and the 17-year-old Jewess SANTOWSKA from their parents' home. They took them to the Polish cemetery, where they raped one of the girls. They told the other girl, who had her menstruation at that time, that they would come back in a few days and promised her 5 zloty.

CERTIFICATE OF TRANSLATION
15 July 1947

We, ANNETTE JACOBSOHN, No. 20146, HANNAH SCHLESINGER No. 20081 and I. MONICA WELLWOOD, E-00525, hereby certify that we are thoroughly conversant with the

English and German languages and that the above is a true and correct translation of Document No. NO-3011.

(signatures)

SOURCES

ARCHIVAL COLLECTIONS

National Archives of the United States, Washington, D.C.
    Record Group 242. Captured German Records.
        Microfilm Series T-77, T-84, T-175, T-311, T-312, T-354, T-501, T-580, T-989.
    Record Group 238. World War II War Crimes Records.
        Office of Chief of Counsel, Administrative Records.
        Microfilm Series NOKW T-1119.Pretrial Interrogations.
        Microfilm Series M-1019, M-1270.
    Record Group 59. Diplomatic Records.
        Microfilm Series M-679, M-898.
    Record Group 38. U.S. Naval Attaché Records.
        Microfilm Series M-975.
    Record Group 38. Records of the Chief on Naval Operations.
    Record Group 153. Records of the Judge Advocate General (Army), General and Administrative Records, 1944-1949.
    Record Group 165. Records of the War Department General and Special Staffs.
    Record Group 226. Records of the Office of Strategic Services.
    Record Group 238. World War II War Crimes Records.
    Record Group 319. Records of the Army Staff.
    Record Group 331. Records of Allied Operational and Occupation Headquarters, World War II, General Staff G-2 Division Intelligence Reports, 1942-45.
    Record Group 332. Records of U.S. Theaters of War, World War II.
    Record Group 338. Records of the United States Army Commands, 1942.

United States Army Military History Institute, Carlisle Barracks, PA.
    Office of the Chief of Military History Collection.
    The Army War College Collection.

United Nations Archive, New York City
    United Nations War Crimes Commission Records.

Franklin D. Roosevelt Presidential Library, Hyde Park, New York.
    John Toland Papers.

Library of Congress, Washington, D.C.

Madison Manuscript Library.
John Toland Papers.

Maxwell Air Force Base Historical Research Center, Alabama
World War II German Air Force Papers.

Ohio University Archives, Athens, Ohio
Cornelius Ryan Papers.

Canadian Public Archives, Ottawa
Record Group 24. Records of the Department of National Defense.

B.H. Liddell Hart Centre for Military Archives, King's College, London.
B.H. Liddell Hart Papers.

Imperial War Museum, London
Nuremberg Interrogations.
Mason-MacFarland Papers.
Diary of Generalfieldmarshall Erhard Milch.

Public Records Office, London
War Office Records 208. German Officer Interrogations.
War Office Records 235. Judge Advocate General's Office: War Crimes Papers
War Office Records 309. War Crimes Group Case Files(NWE)

St. Antony's College Archives, Oxford University, Oxford
Sir John Wheeler-Bennett Papers.

Churchill College Archives, Cambridge University, Cambridge
Sir Malcolm Noel Christie Papers.

Generallandsarchiv Karlsruhe, Karlsruhe.
Kriegstagebuch Infanterie Regiment 111.
Kriegstagebuch 75 Reserve Infanterie Division.

Stadtarchiv Konstanz, Constance.
File SII/9240.

Bundesarchiv-Militärarchiv, Freiburg im Breisgau.
MSg 1/1814, MSg 1/1669, MSg 2435, Pers 6/20.

Institut für Zeitgeschichte, Munich.
IFZ, ZS-237.

Collection Koepcke, Bommelsen, Germany
Private Papers of Johannes Koepcke

H.R. Trevor-Roper Papers, Oxon, England
Private Papers of H.R. Trevor-Roper, the Lord Dacre of Glanton

PRIMARY WORKS

Andrus, Burton C. *I was the Nuremburg Jailer*. New York: Coward-McCann, Inc., 1969.

Baur, Hans. *Hitler At My Side*. Translated by Lyndel Butler. Houston, Texas: Eichler Publishing Corporation, 1986.

Below, Nicolaus von. *Als Hitlers Adjutant 1937-45*. Mainz: V. Hase & Koehler Verlag, 1980.

Bibliotheca Rerum Militarium. Quellen und Darstellungen zur Militarwissenschaft und Militargeschichte. Vol. 15 *Stellenbesetzung im Reichsheer vom 16 mai 1920, 2 Oktober 1920, 1 Oktober 1921*. Osnabruck: Biblio Verlag, 1968.

Blücher, Princess Evelyn. *An English Wife in Berlin*. London: Constable, 1921.

Blumentritt, Guenther. *Von Rundstedt: The Soldier and the Man*. Translated by Cuthbert Reavely. Long Acre, London: Odhams Press Ltd., 1952.

Campell, Gerald. *Verdun to the Vosges: Impressions of the War on the Fortress Frontier of France*. London: Edward Arnold, 1916.

Chapman, Guy. *A Passionate Prodigality*. New York: Faucett Crest Books, 1967.

Ciano, Galeazzo. *The Ciano Diaries: 1939-1943*. Edited by Hugh Gibson. New York: Doubleday & Company, Inc., 1946.

Detwiler, Donald, Editor. *World War II German Military Studies*. 24 volumes. New York: Garland Publishing, Inc., 1979.

Deguingand, Francis. *Operation Victory*. London: Hodder and Stoughton, 1947.

Dolibois, John. *Pattern of Circles: An Ambassador's Story*. Kent, Ohio: The Kent State University Press, 1989.

Duff, Shiela Grant. *A German Protectorate: The Czechs under Nazi Rule*. London: MacMillan & Co., Ltd., 1942.

Engel, Gerhard. *Heeresadjutant bei Hitler: 1938-1943 Aufzeichnungen des Major Engel*. Edited by Hildegard von Kotze. Stuttgart: Deutsche Verlags-Anstalt, 1974.

Foucault, Marquise de. *A Chateau at the Front, 1914-1918*. Translated by George Ives. Boston: Houghton Mifflin Co., 1931.

Gersdorff, Rudolf-Christoph Freiherr von. *Soldat im Untergang*. Frankfurt/M.: Ullstein Verlag, 1977.

Geyr von Schweppenburg, Freiherr. *The Critical Years*. London: Allan Wingate, 1952

Gilbert, G.M. *The Psychology of Dictatorship*. New York: The Ronald Press, 1950; reprint ed., Westport, Connecticut: Greenwood Press, 1979.

Gisevius, Hans Bernd. *To the Bitter End*. Translated by Richard and Clara Winston. Westport, Connecticut: Greenwood Press, Publishers, 1975.

Goebbels, Joseph. *My Part in Germany's Fight.* Translated by Kurt Fiedler, New York: Howard Fertig, Inc., 1979.

_____. *The Goebbels Diaries: 1939-1941.* Edited and Translated by Fred Taylor. New York: G.P. Putnam's Sons, 1983.

_____. *The Goebbels Diaries: 1942-1943.* Edited and Translated by Louis Lochner. Garden City, New York: Doubleday and Company, 1948.

Goerlitz Walter, Editor. *The Kaiser and His Court. The Diaries, Note Books and Letters of Admiral Georg Alexander von Muller, Chief of Cabinett, 1914-1918.* New York: Harcourt, Brace, Inc., 1961.

Groscurth, Helmuth. *Tagebücher eines Abwehroffiziers: Mit weiteren Dokumenten zur Militäropposition gegen Hitler.* Edited by Helmuth Krausnick and Harold C. Deutsch. Stuttgart: Deutsche Verlags-Anstalt, 1970.

Guderian, Heinz. *Panzer Leader.* Translated by Constantine Fitzagibbon. Washington, D.C.: Zenger Publishing Co., 1979. *Erinnerungen eines Soldaten.* Heidelberg: Kurt Vownickel, 1951.

Halder, Franz. *The Halder Diaries: The Private War Journals of Colonel-General Franz Halder.* Edited and translated by Arnold Lissance. 2 volumes. Boulder, Colorado: Westview Press, 1976.

_____. *The Halder War Diary, 1939-1942.* Edited by Charles Burdick and Hans-Adolf Jacobsen. Novato, California: Presidio Press, 1988.

Hassell, Ulrich von. *The von Hassell Diaries: 1938-1944; The Story of the Forces Against Hitler Inside Germany, As Recorded by Ambassador Ulrich von Hassell, a Leader of the Movement.* Garden City, New York: Doubleday & Company, Inc., 1947.

Hawkins, Desmond. *War Report: A Record of Dispatches Broadcast by the BBC's War Correspondents with the Allied Expeditionary Force, 6 June 1944—5 May 1945.* London: Oxford University Press, 1946.

Hedin, Sven. *With the German Armies in the West.* Translated by H. De Walterstroff. New York: John Lane Company, 1915.

Hitler, Adolf. *My New Order.* Edited by Raoul de Roussey de Sales, New York: Octagon Books, 1973.

Jodl, Luise. *Jenseits Des Endes: Leben und Sterben des Generaloberst Alfred Jodl.* Munchen: Verlag Fritz Molden, 1976.

Jaworski, Leon. *After Fifteen Years.* Houston, Texas: Gulf Publishing Company, 1961.

Juenger, Ernst. *The Storm of Steel: From the Diary of a German Storm-Troop Officer on the Western Front.* Translated by Basil Creighton. London: Chatto & Windus, 1930.

Kabisch, Ernst. *Deutsche Siegeszug in Polen.* Stuttgart: Union Deutsche Verlagsgesellechaft, 1940.

Keitel, Wilhelm. *The Memoirs of Field-Marshal Keitel*. Edited by Walter Goerlitz; Translated by David Irving. New York: Stein and Day, 1966.

Kesselring, Albert. *The Memoirs of Field-Marshal Kesselring*. Translated by Lynton Hudson. London: William Kimber, 1953.

_____. *Kesselring; A Soldier's Record*. Translated by Lynton Hudson. New York: William Morrow & Co., 1954.

Kessler, Harry. *In the Twenties: The Diaries of Harry Kessler*. New York: Holt, Rinehart and Windston, 1971.

Leeb, Wilhelm von. *Tagebuchaufzeichnungen und Lagebeurteilungen aus zwei Weltkriegen*. Edited by George Meyer. Stuttgart: Deutsche Verlags-Anstahlt, 1976.

Luck, Hans von. *Panzer Commander: The Memoirs of Colonel Hans von Luck*. New York: Praeger, 1989.

Ludendorff, Erich von. *Ludendorff's Own Story*. 2 volumes. New York: Harper & Brothers, Publishers, 1919.

Manstein, Eric von. *Lost Victories*. Edited and translated by Anthony G. Powell. Chicago: Henry Regnery Company, 1958.

Mitteilungsblatt der Zentral Kartei der Konigliche Preussischen und Konigliche Sachischen Kadetten, N.p.,N.d., Nr. 42.

Mellenthin, F.W. von. *Panzer Battles: A Study of the Employment of Armor in the Second World War*. Translated by H. Betzler. Edited by L.G.F. Turner. New York: Ballantine Books, 1971.

Montgomery, Bernard. *Normandy to the Baltic*. Boston: Houghton Mifflin Company, 1948.

Morgan, J.H. *Assize of Arms: The Disarmanent of Germany and Her Rearmament (1919-1939)*. New York: Oxford University Press, 1946.

Nagel, Fritz. *Fritz: The World War I Memoirs of a German Lieutenant*. Edited by Richard Baumgartner. Huntington, West Virginia: Der Angriff Publications, 1981.

Nazi Conspiracy and Aggression. 8 volumes. Washington: United States Government Printing Office, 1946.

Nowak, Jan. *Courier From Warsaw*. Detroit: Wayne State University Press, 1982.

Paget, Reginald. *Manstein: His Campaigns and His Trial*. London: Collins, 1951.

Patton, George. *War as I Knew It*. Boston: Houghton Mifflin Company, 1947.

Poppel, Martin. *Heaven and Hell: The War Diary of a German Paratrooper*. Translated by Louise Willmot. New York: Hippocrene Books, Inc., 1988.

Raleigh, John. *Behind the Nazi Front*. New York: Dodd, Mead & Co., 1940.

Reichswehrministerium, Heeres-Personalamt, Editor. *Rangliste des deutschen Reichsheeres nach dem Stande vom 1 Mai 1930*. Berlin: E.G. Mittler and Son, N.d.

René, Henry. *Lorette: Une bataille de douze mois, octobre 1914.* Paris: Librairie académique, 1916.

Report of Operations: The Seventh United States Army in France and Germany. Three Volumes. Heidelberg: Heidelberg Gutenberg Printing Company, 1946.

Röhricht, Edgar. *Pflicht und Gewissen; Erinnerungen eines deutschen Generals, 1932 bis 1944.* Stuttgart: W. Kohlhammer Verlag, 1965.

Rückerl, Adalbert. *The Investigation of Nazi Crimes: 1945-1978. A Documentation.* Translated by Derek Rutter. Heidelberg: C.F. Muller, 1979.

Ruge, Friedrich, *Rommel In Normandy: Reminiscences by Friedrich Ruge.* Translated by Ursula R. Moessner. San Rafael, California: Presidio Press, 1979.

Schadewaldt, Hans, Compiler. *Polish Acts of Atrocity Against the German Minority in Poland.* 2nd edition. Berlin: Völk und Reich Verlag; New York: German Library of Information, 1940.

Schaumberg-Lippe, Friedrich Christian Prinz zu. *Zwischen Krone und Kerker.* Wiesbaden: Limes Verlag, 1952.

Schell, Adolf. *Battle Leadership.* Columbus, Georgia: The Benning Herald, 1933.

Schlabrendorff, Fabian von. *The Secret War Against Hitler.* Translated by Hilda Simon. New York: Pittman Publishing Corporation, 1965.

Schmidt, Paul. *Hitler's Interpreter.* Edited by R.H.C. Steed. New York: The MacMillan Co., 1951.

Schramm, Percy, Editor. *Kriegstagebuch des Oberkommandos der Wehrmacht (Wehrmachtführungstab): 1940-1945.* Volume 2, 1942. Frankfurt am Main: Bernhard & Graefe Verlag fur Wehrwessen, 1965.

Schroeder, Hans. *A German Airman Remembers.* Translated by Claud W. Skyes. London: Greenhill Books and Aeolus Publishing, 1986.

Speer, Albert. *Infiltration.* Translated by Richard and Clara Winston. New York: MacMillian Publishing Company, 1981.

_____.*Inside The Third Reich.* Translated by Richard and Clara Winston. New York: MacMillan Company, 1970.

_____. *Spandau: The Secret Diaries.* Translated by Richard and Clara Winston. New York: MacMillan Publishing Company, 1976.

Stahlberg, Alexander. *Bounden Duty: The Memoirs of a German Officer 1932-1945.* Translated by Patricia Crampton. London: Brassey's, 1990.

Stammliste des Konigliche Kadethauses Culm-Coslin (1 Juni 1776-1 Nov. 1907). 2 Volumes. Berlin: Hermann Walter Verlags- buchandlung, 1907.

Student, Kurt. *Generaloberst Kurt Student und seine Fallschirmjager: Die Erinnerungen des Generaloberst Student.* Edited by Hermann Gotzel. Friedberg: Podzun-Pallas Verlag, 1980.

Sulzbach, Herbert. *With the German Guns: Four Years on the Western Front 1914-1918*. Hamden Connecticut: Archon Books, 1981.

Sweet, Paul, Editor. *Documents on German Foreign Policy 1918-1945*. Series D. Volume 8: *The War Years*. Washington, D.C.: 1954.

Taylor, Telford. *The Anatomy of the Nuremberg Trials*. New York: Alfred Knopf, 1992.

Tippelskirch, Kurt. *Geschichte Des Zweiten Weltkrieg*. Bonn: Atheneum Verlag, 1954.

Trial of the Major War Criminals before the International Military Tribunal; Nuremberg 14 November 1945-1 October 1946. 42 volumes. Nuremberg, Germany: 1947-49.

Trials of War Criminals before the Nuernburg Military Tribunals under Control Council Law No. 10. 15 volumes. Washington: United States Government Printing Office, 1951.

Truscott, Lucien. *Command Missions: A Personal Story*. New York: E.P. Dutton and Company, Inc., 1954. United Nations War Crimes Commission.

Compiler. *History of the United Nations War Crimes Commission and the Development of the Laws of War*. London: His Majesty's Stationary Office. 1948.

United States War Department, General Staff, *Histories of 251 Divisions of the German Army Which Participated in the World War (1914-1918)*. Washington: Government Printing Office, 1920.

Warlimont, Walter. *Inside Hitler's Headquarters: 1939-1945*. Translated by R.H. Barry. New York: Frederick A. Praeger, Publishers, 1964.

Westphal, Siegfried. *Erinnerungen*. Mainz: V. Hase & Koehler Verlag, 1975.

_____. *The German Army in the West*. London: Cassell and Company, Ltd., 1951.

Westman, Stephen. *Surgeon with Kaiser's Army*. London: William Kimber, 1968.

SECONDARY WORKS

Abshagen, Karl. *Canaris*. London: Hutchinson and Company, Ltd., 1956.

Addington, Lawrence. *The Blitzkrieg Era and the German General Staff: 1865-1941*. New Brunswick, New Jersey: Rutgers University Press, 1971.

Allen, George. *The Great War-The Wavering Balance of Forces*. Philadelphia: George Barrie's Sons, 1919.

Altpreussische evangelische Pfarrerbüch von der Reformat bis zur Vertreibung im Jahre 1945. Volume I. Hamburg: N.p., n.d.

Amort, C. and I.M. Jedlica. *The Canaris File*. London: Allen Wingate, 1970.

Asprey, Robert. *The German High Command at War: Hindenburg and Ludendorff Conduct World War I*. New York: William Morrow and Company, Inc., 1991.

Barnard, Henry. *Military Schools and Courses of Instruction in the Science and Art of War in France, Prussia, England, and the United States.* New York: Greenwood Press, 1969.

Barnett, Corelli. *Hitler's Generals.* New York: George Weidenfeld & Nocholson Ltd., 1989.

Bartov, Omer. *The Eastern Front, 1941-1945, German Troops and the Barbarisation of Warfare.* New York: St. Martin's Press, 1986.

_____. *Hitler's Army: Soldiers, Nazis, and War in the Third Reich.* New York: Oxford University Press, 1991.

Bayles, William D. *Caesars in Goose Step.* New York: Harper & Brothers Publishers, 1940.

Becamps, Pierre. *Bordeaux sous l'occupation.* Rennes: Ouestfrance, 1983.

Bekker, Cajus. *The Luftwaffe War Diaries.* Translated and Edited by Frank Ziegler. Garden City, New York: Doubleday & Company, Inc. 1968.

Berton, Piertre. *Vimy.* London: Penguin Books, 1986.

Bethell, Nicholas. *The War Hitler Won: The Fall of Poland, September 1939.* New York: Holt, Rhinehart and Winston, 1972.

Bethge, Eberhard. *Dietrich Bonhoeffer: Theologian, Christian, Contemporary.* Translated by Eric Mosbacher, *et. al.* London: Collins, 1970.

Binion, Rudolf. *Hitler Among the Germans.* New York: Elsevier, 1976.

Blumenson, Martin. *Breakout and Pursuit.* United States Army in World War II: The European Theater of Operations, Washington, D.C.: Office of the Christ of Military History, 1961.

_____. *The Duel for France: 1944.* Boston: Houghton Mifflin Company, 1963.

Brand, Karl-Hermann Freiherr von and Eckart, Helmut. *Kadetten Aus 300 Jahren deutscher Kadetten Korps.* Two Volumes. Munich: SchildVerlag Gmbh, 1989.

Breitman, Richard. *The Architect of Genocide: Himmler and the Final Solution.* New York: Alfred A. Knorf, 1991.

Brett-Smith, Richard. *Hitler's Generals.* San Rafael, California: Presidio PLress, 1977.

Brissard, Andre. *Canaris: The Biography of Admiral Canaris, Chief of German Military Intelligence in the Second World War.* Translated and Edited by Ian Colvin. New York: Grosset & Dunlap, Publishers, 1973.

Broszat, Martin. *Nationalsozialistische Polenpolitik: 1939-1945.* Stuttgart: Deutsche Verlags-Anstalt, 1961.

Brownlow, Donald G. *Panzer Baron: The Military Exploits of General Hasso von Manteuffel.* North Quincy, Massachusetts: The Christopher Publishing House, 1975.

Burdick, Charles. *Germany's Military Strategy and Spain in World War II*. Syracuse, New York: Syracuse University Press, 1968.

Burton, Pierre. *Vimy*. London: Penguin Books, 1986.

Carsten, F.L. *Essays in German History*. London: Hambledon Press, 1985.

_____. *The Reichswehr and Politics: 1918-1933*. Berkeley, University of California Press, 1973.

Carter, Kit and Mueller, Robert. Compilers. *The Army Air Forces in World War II: Combat Chronology*. Office of Air Force History, Air University, 1973.

Chandler, David. *The Campaigns of Napoleon: The Mind and Method of History's Greatest Soldier*. New York: MacMillan Publishing Co., Inc., 1966.

Churchill, Winston. *Blood, Sweat, and Tears*. New York: G.P. Putnam's Sons, 1941.

Citino, Robert M. *The Evolution of Blitzkrieg Tactics: Germany Defends Itself Against Poland, 1918-1933*. Westport, Connecticut: Greenwood Press, 1987.

Cole, H. M. *The Lorraine Campaign*. United States Army in World War II: The European Theater of Operations, Washington, D.C.: Historical Division, Department of the Army, 1950.

Coombs, Rose E.B. *Before Endeavors Fade: A Guide to the Battlefields of the First World War*. London: Plaistow Press Magazines, Ltd., 1976.

Cooper, Matthew. *The German Army, 1939-1945: Its Political and Military Failure*. New York: Stein and Day Publishers, 1978.

Craig, Gordon. *Germany, 1866-1945*. New York: Oxford University Press, 1978.

_____. *The Politics of the Prussian Army: 1640-1945*. Oxford: Clarendon Press, 1955.

Craven, Wesley, and Cate, James. *The Army Air Forces in World War II*. Volume III. Washington, D.C.: Office of Air Force History, New Imprint, 1983.

Datner, Szymon. *Crimes Against P.O.W.S.: Responsibility of the Wehrmacht*. Warsaw: Zachodnia Agencia Prasowa, 1964.

Deist, Wilhelm. *The Wehrmacht and German Rearmament*. Toronto University of Toronto Press, 1981.

DeJong, L. *Het Koninkrijk Der Nederlanden in De Tweeds Wereldoorlog, Deel 106, tweede helft, Het Laatste Jaar II*. S'Gravenhage: Martinus Nijhoff, 1982.

Delarue, Jacques. *The Gestapo: A History of Horror*. Translated by Mervyn Savill. New York: William Morrow & Co., Inc., 1964.

Demeter, Karl. *The German Officer-Corps In Society and State: 1650-1945*. London: Weidenfeld and Nicholson, 1954.

D'Este, Carlo. *Decision In Normandy*. New York: E.P. Dutton, Inc., 1983.

Deuel, Walter. *Hitler and Nazi Germany: Uncensored*. N.p.; n.p., 1941.

Deutsch, Harold C. *Hitler and His Generals: The Hidden Crisis, January-June 1938*. Minneapolis: University of Minnesota Press, 1974.

_____. *The Conspiracy Against Hitler in the Twilight War* Minneapolis: The University of Minnesota Press, 1968.

Diehl, James. *Paramilitary Politics in Weimar Germany*. Bloomington, Ind.: Indiana University Press, 1977.

Donnhauser, Anton and Drews, Werner. *Der Weg der 11. Panzer* Division. N.p. 11. Panzer Division, 1982.

Duffy, Christopher. *The Army of Frederick the Great*. London: David & Charles, 1974.

_____. *The Military Life of Frederick the Great*. New York: Atheneum 1986.

_____. *The Military Experience in the Age of Reason*. New York: Atheneum, 1988.

Eksteins, Modris. *Rites of Spring: The Great War and the Birth of the Modern Age*. Boston: Houghton Mifflin Company, 1989.

Elbe, Rolf. *Die Schlacht an der Bzura im September 1939 aus deutscher und polnischer Sicht*. Freiburg: 1975.

Ellis, John. *Eye-Deep in Hell: Trench Warfare in World War I*.

Baltimore: Johns Hopkins University Press, 1989.

Ellis, L. F. *Victory in the West*. Volume III. London: Her Majesty's Stationery Office, 1968.

Endres, Franz Carl. *The Social Structure and Corresponding Ideologies of the German Officers' Corps before the World War*. Translated by S. Ellison. New York: Works Progress Administration, 1937.

Essame, H. *The Battle for Europe, 1918*. London: Batsford, 1972.

_____. *Patton: A Study in Command*. New York: Charles Scribner's Sons, 1974.

Fattig, Richard. "Reprisal: The German Army and the Execution of Hostages during the Second World War." Ph.d. Dissertation. University of California at San Diego, 1980.

Fraser, David. *Knight's Cross: A Life of Field Marshal Erwin Rommel*. New York: HarperCollins Publishers, 1993.

Friedrich, Otto. *Before the Deluge: A Portrait of Berlin in the 1920's*. New York: Harper & Row, Publishers, 1972.

Frischauer, Willi. *The Nazis at War*. London: Gollancz, 1940.

Gansberg, Judith. *Stalag U.S.A.: The Remarkable Story of German P.O.W.'s in America*. New York: Thomas Y. Crowell Co., 1977.

Geffen, William, Editor. *Command and Commanders in Modern Warfare: The proceedings of the Second Military History Symposium, U.S. Air Force Academy, 2-3*

May 1968. Office of Air Force History, Headquarters USAF, and U.S. Air Force Academy, 1971.

Gellately, Robert. *The Gestapo and German Society: Enforcing Racial Policy, 1933-1945*. Oxford: Clarenden Press, 1992.

Geschichte des Infanterie-Regiments von Grolman (1 Posenschen). 2 volumes. Berlin: Ernst Siegfried Mittler and Son, 1913.

Goerlitz, Walter. *History of the German General Staff: 1967-1945*. Translated by Brian Battershaw.New York: Frederick A. Praeger, Inc., 1957.

_____. *Paulus and Stalingrad: A life of Field-Marshal Friedrich Paulus with Notes, Correspondence and Documents from His Papers*. Edited by Walter Goerlitz. New York: Citadel Press, 1963.

Graber, G.S. *History of the SS*. New York: David McKay Company, Inc., 1978.

Gray, Randal. *Kaiserschlacht 1918: The Final German Offensive*. London: Osprey Publishing Ltd., 1991.

Gudmundsson, Bruce. *Stormtroop Tactics: Innovations in the German Army, 1914-1918*. New York: Praeger, 1989.

Guttzeit, Johannes. *Ostpreussen in 1440 Bildern*. Ostfriesland: Verlag Gerhard Rautenberg, 1972.

Harrison, Gordon. *Cross-Channel Attack-The United States Army in World War II, The European Theater of Operations*. Washington, D.C.: Office of the Chief of Military History, Department of the Army, 1951.

Hart, W.E. [pseud.]. *Hitler's Generals*. Garden City, New York: Doubleday, Doran & Company, 1944.

Hastings, Max. *Das Reich: The March of the 2nd SS Panzer Division through France*. New York: Jove Books, 1986.

_____. *Overlord: D-Day, June 6, 1944*. New York: Simon and Schuster, 1984.

Heimatbuch des Kreises Wehlau. Leer: Gerhard Rautenberg, 1975.

Hermann, Carl-Hans. *Die 9. Panzer Division, 1939-1945: Bewaffnung, Einsatz, Manner*. Friedburg: Podzun Pallas Verlag, 1976.

Hilberg, Raul. *The Destruction of the European Jews*. New York: New Viewpoints, 1973.

Hinsley, E. Thomas, Ransom, C. and Knight, R. *British Intelligence In the Second World War*. 6 volumes. London: Her Majesty's Stationery Office, 1979-1988.

Hirschfeld, Gerhard, Editor. *The Policies of Genocide: Jews and Soviet Prisoners of War In Nazi Germany*. Boston: Allen & Unwin, 1986.

_____. And Marsh, Patrick. Editors. *Collaboration in France: Politics and Culture during the Nazi Occupation, 1940-1944*. New York: Berg Publishers, 1989.

Hochman, Elaine. *Architects of Fortune: Mies Van Der Rohe and the Third Reich*. New York: Weikdenfeld & Nicolson, 1989.

Hoffmann, Peter. *Hitler's Personal Security.* Cambridge Massachusetts: M.I.T. Press, 1977.

_____. *The History of the German Resistance: 1933-1945.* Cambridge: I.M.T. Press, 1977.

Höhne, Heinz. *Canaris: Hitler's Master Spy.* Translated by J. Brownjohn. New York: Doubleday Company, Inc., 1979.

_____. *The Order of the Death's Head: The Story of Hitler's SS.* Translated by Richard Barry. New York: Balantine Books, 1977.

Horne, Alistair. *The Price of Glory: Verdun, 1916.* New York: Penguin Books, 1978.

Humble, Richard. *Hitler's Generals.* Garden City, New York: Doubleday & Company, Inc., 1974.

Hughes, Daniel. *The King's Finest: A Social and Bureaucratic Profile of Prussia's General Officers, 1871-1949.* New York: Praeger, 1987.

Irving, David. *Göering: A Biography.* New York: William Morrow & Co., Inc., 1989.

_____. *Hitler's War.* 2 volumes. New York: The Viking Press, 1977.

_____. *The Rise and Fall of the Luftwaffe: The Life of* Field Marshall Erhard Milch. Boston: Little, Brown and Company, 1973.

_____. *The Trail of the Fox.* New York: Avon Books, 1978.

_____. *The War Path: Hitler's Germany 1933-1939.* New York: The Viking Press, 1978.

Jackel, Eberhard. *Frankreich in Hitlers Europa: Die Deutsche Frankreich Politik in Zweiten Welkkrieg.* Stuttgart: Deutsche Verlags-Anstalt, N.D.

_____. *Hitler in History.* Hanover, New Hampshire, University Press of New England, 1984.

Jacob, Berthold. *Das neue deutsche Heer und seine Führer: Mit einer Rangliste des deutschen Heeres und Dienstalterliste.* Paris: Editions du Carrefour, 1936.

John, Otto. *Twice Through the Lines.* Translated by Richard Barry. New York: Harper & Row, Publishers, 1972.

Jones, Nigel. *Hitler's Heralds: The Story of the Freikorps, 1918-1923.* London:John Murray Publisher's, Ltd., 1987.

Keegan, John. *Six Armies In Normandy: From D-Day to the Liberation of Paris, June 6th—August 25th,m 1944.*New York: Viking Press, 1982.

Kennedy, Robert. *The German Campaign in Poland (1939).* Washington, D.C.: Department of the Army, 1956.

Kershaw, Ian. *The "Hitler Myth:" Image and Reality in the Third Reich.* New York: Oxford University Press, 1990.

Keilig, Wolf. *Das deutsche Herr 1939-1945, Gliederung, Einsatz, Stellenbestzen.* Bad Nauheim: N.p. 1957.

Krammer, Arnold, *Nazi Prisoners of War In America.* New York: Stein and Day, 1979.

Krausnick, Helmuth and Wilhelm, Hans-Heinrich. *Die Truppe des Weltanschauungskrieges: Die Einsatzgruppen der Sicherheitspolizei und der SD, 1938-1942, Volume 1: Die Einsatzgruppen vom Anschluss Österreichs bis zum Feldzug gegen die Sowjetunion Entwicklung und Verhältnis zur Wehrmacht.* Stuttgart: Deutsche Verlags-Anstalt, 1981.

Leed, Erich. *No Man's Land: Combat and Identity in World War I.* London: Cambridge University Press, 1979.

Lehmann, Rodolf. *The Leibstandarte.* Translated by Nick Olcott Volumes 1 and 2. Winnipeg, Canada: J.J. Fedorowicz Publishing, 1987.

Lewin, Ronald. *Hitler's Mistakes.* London: Leo Cooper, 1984.

Lewis, Samuel. *Forgotten Legions: German Infantry Policy, 1918-1941.* New York: Praeger, 1986.

Liddell Hart B.H. *The Real War 1914-1918.* Boston: Little, Brown and Company, 1964.

_____.*History of the First World War.* London: Book Club Associates, 1973.

Lockhardt, Vincent. *T-Patch to Victory: The 36th Infantry Division from the Landing in Southern France to the End of World War II.* Canyon, Texas: Staked Plains Press, 1981.

Lucas, James. *Das Reich: The Military Role of the 2ND SS Diviston.* London: Arms and Arms and Armour Press, 1991.

_____. *Hitler's Elite Liebstandarte SS,1933-1945.* London: MacDonald and James, 1975.

Ludtke, Franz. *Ordensland.* Berlin: Verlag Erwin Kintzel, 1943.

Lukacs, John. *The Last European War: September, 1939-December 1941.* Garden City, New York: Anchor Press/Doubleday, 1976.

MacDonald, Charles. *The Last Offensive.* United States Army in World War II: European Theater of Operations. Washington, D.C.: Office of the Chief of Military History, United States Army, 1973.

Macksey, Kenneth. *Guderian; Creator of the Blitzkrieg.* New York: Stein & Day, 1976.

_____. *Kesselring: The Making of the Luftwaffe.* New York: David McKay Company, Inc., 1978.

Maier, Klaus, et al. *Germany and the Second World War.* Volume 2. Translated by Dean McMurray and Ewald Osers.. New York: Oxford University Press, 1991.

Manvell, Roger and Fraenkel, Heinrich. *Himmler.* New York: Warner Books, Inc., 1972.

Mastny, Vojtech. *The Czechs Under Nazi Rule: The Failure of National Resistance, 1939-1942.* New York: Columbia University Press, 1971.

Masur, Gerhard. *Imperial Berlin.* New York: Basic Books Inc., 1970.

McKee, Alexander. *The Battle of Vimy Ridge.* New York: Stein and Day, 1967.

Messenger, Charles. *Hitler's Gladiator: The Life and Times of Oberstgruppenführer and Panzergeneral-oberst der Waffen-SS Sepp Dietrich.* London: Brassey's Defence Publishers, 1988.

_____. *The Last Prussian: A Biography of Field Marshal Gerd Von Rundstedt, 1875-1953.* London: Brassey's, 1991.

Messerschmidt, Manfred. *Die Wehrmacht im NS-Staat: Zeit der Indoktrination.* Einführung von General a.D. Johann Kielmansegg. Hamburg: L.R.V. Decker's Verlag, 1969.

Middlebrook, Martin and Everitt, Chris. *The Bomber Command War Diaries: An Operational Reference Book, 1939-1945.* New York: Penguin Books, 1990.

Mitcham, Samuel. *Hitler's Legions: The German Army Order of Battle, World War II.* New York: Dorsett Press, 1988.

Möller-Witten, Hanns. *Mit dem Eichenlaub zum Ritterkreuz.* Rastatt: Erich Pabel Verlag, 1962.

Mosley, Leonard. *The Reich Marshal: A Biography of Hermann Goering.* New York: Dell Publishing Co., Inc., 1974.

Mueller, Gene Arnold. "Wilhelm Keitel: Chief of the Oberkommando Der Wehrmacht, 1938-1945." Ph.D. Dissertation, University of Idaho, 1972.

Müller, Klaus-Jürgen. *The Army, Politics and Society in Germany; 1933-1945.* New York: St. Martin's Press, 1987.

_____. Das Heer und Hitler: *Armee und Nationalsozialistiches Regime;1935-1940.* Stuttgart: Deutsche Verlags-Anstalt, 1969.

Murray, Williamson. *Strategy For Defeat: The Luftwaffe, 1933-1945.* Secaucus, New Jersey: Chartwell Books, 1986.

Muszkat, Marian. *Polish Charges Against German War Criminals.* Warsaw: Polish Main National Office for Investigation of German War Crimes in Poland, 1948.

Necker, Wilhelm. *The German Army of Today.* East Ardsley, England: E.P. Publishing, Ltd., 1973.

Niepold, Gerd. *Battle For White Russia: The Destruction of Army Group Centre, June 1944.* London: Brassey's Defense Publishers, 1987.

North, John. *North-West Europe 1944-5: The Achievement of 21st Army Group.* London: Her Majesty's Stationery Office, 1953.

Nothaas, J. *Social Assent and Descent among Former Officers in the German Army and Navy After the World War.* New York: Works Progress Administration, 1937.

Nowak, Jan. *Courier From Warsaw.* Detroit: Wayne State University Press, 1982.

O'Neill, Robert J. *The German Army and the Nazi Party, 1933-1939.* New York: James H. Heinemann, Inc., 1966.

Ose, Dieter. *Entscheidung im Western 1944: Der Oberbefehlshaber West und die Abwehr der Allierten Invasion.* Stuttgart: Deutsche Verlags-Anstahlt, 1982.

Padfield, Peter. *Himmler: Reichsfuhrer SS.* New York: Henry Holt and Company, 1970.

Paget, Reginald. *Manstein: His Campaigns and His Trial.* London: Collins, 1951.

Paschall, Rod. *The Defeat of Imperial Germany: 1917-1918.* Chapel Hill, North Carolina: Algonquin Books, 1989.

Perrett, Bryan. *A History of Blitzkrieg.* New York: Stein and Day Publishers, 1983.

Pitt, Barrie. *1918: The Last Act.* New York: W.W. Norton, Inc., 1963.

Platt, Grover Cleveland. "The Place of the Army in German Life: 1880-1914." Ph.D. Dissertation, State University of Iowa, 1941.

Pogue, Forrest. *The Supreme Command: The European Theater of Operations.* Washington, D.C.: Office of the Chief of Military History, 1954.

Poliakov, Leon. *Harvest of Hate: The Nazi Program for the Destruction of the News in Europe.* Westport, Connecticut: Greenwood Press, 1971.

Post, Gaines. *The Civil-Military Fabric of Weimar Foreign Policy.* Princeton, New Jersey: Princeton University Press, 1973.

Pryce-Jones, David. *Paris in the Third Reich: A History of the German Occupation, 1940-1944.* New York: Holt, Rhinehart and Winston, 1981.

Rangliste Des Deutschen Heeres 1944/45. Compiled by Wolf Keilig. Friedberg: Podzun-Pallas Verlag, N.D.

Read, Anthony and Fisher, David. *Kristallnacht: The Nazi Night of Terror.* New York: Random House, 1989.

Reiss, Curt. *The Self-Betrayed: Glory and Doom of the German Generals.* New York: G.P. Putnam's Sons, 1942.

Reitlinger, Gerald. *The Final Solution.* New York: A.S. Barnes Co., Inc., 1961.

_____. *The SS: Alibi of a Nation, 1922-1945.* Englewood Cliffs, New Jersey: Prentice Hall, 1981.

Reynolds, Francis. *The Story of the Great War.* New York: P.F. Collier & Son, 1916.

Reynolds, Nicholas. *Treason Was No Crime: Ludwig Beck, Chief of the German General Staff.* London: William Kimber, 1976.

Rich, Norman. *Hitler's War Aims.* New York: W.W. Norton & Co., 1973-1974.

Rings, Werner. *Life With the Enemy: Collaboration and Resistance in Hitler's Europe, 1939-1945.* Garden City, New York: Doubleday and Company, Inc., 1982.

Ritter, Gerhard. *The German Resistance: Carl Goerdeler's Struggle Against Tyranny.* Translated by R.T. Clark. Freeport, New York: Books for Libraries Press, 1976.

Rossler, Helmut. *Biographischer Wörterbuch zur Deutschen Geschichte.* Volume I. Munich: Francke Verlag, 1974.

Rothfels, Hans. *The German Opposition to Hitler: An Assessment.* Translated by Lawrence Wilson. London: Oswald Wolff (Publishers) Ltd., 1970.

Schall-Riacour, Heidemarie Grafin. *Aufstand und Gehorsam: Offizierstum und Generalstab in Umbruch. Leben und Wirken von Generaloberst Franz Halder, Generalstabschef 1938-1942.* Wiesbaden: Limes Verlag, 1972.

Schell, Adolf von. *Battle Leadership.* Columbus, Georgia: The Benning Herald, 1933.

Schlabrendorff, Fabian von. *The Secret War Against Hitler.* Translated by Hilda Simon. New York: Pittman Publishing Corporation, 1965.

Schlachten des Weltkrieges. Vol. 17: *Loretto.* Berlin: Gerhard Stalling, 1927.

Schoenbaum, David. *Hitler's Social Revolution: Class and Status in Nazi Germany, 1933-1939.* Garden City, New York: Anchor Books, 1967.

Seaton, Albert. *The German Army: 1933-1945.* New York: St. Martin's Press, 1982.

Selle, Gotz von. *German Thought in East Prussia.* Marburg: Elwert Grafe, 1948.

Showalter, Dennis. *Tannenberg: Clash of Empires.* Hamden, Connecticut: Shoe String Press, 1991.

Shulman, Milton. *Defeat in the West.* New York: E. P. Dutton & Company, Inc., 1948.

Siegler, Fritz Freiherr von, Editor. *Die Hoheren Dienstellen Der Deutsche Wehrmacht: 1933-1945.* Institut fur Zeitgeschichte: N.P., 1953.

Smith, Bradley and Agarossi, Elena. *Operation Sunrise: The Secret Surrender.* New York: Basic Books, Inc., Publishers, 1979.

Stacy, C.P. *The Victory Campaign,* Volume III. Ottawa: The Queen's Printer and Controller of Stationary, 1960.

Staiger, Jorg. *Ruckzug durchs Rhonetal: Abwher und VerzogerungsKampf der 19. Armee in Herbst 1944 unter besonderer Berucksichtigung des Einsatzes der 11 Panzer- Division.* Neckargemund: Kurt Vowinckel Verlag, 1965.

Stein, George H. *The Waffen SS: Hitler's Elite Guard at War, 1935- 1945.* Ithaca, New York: Cornell University Press, 1966.

Streit, Christian. *Keine Kameraden: Die Wehrmacht und die sowjetischen Kreigsge-fangenen, 1941-1945.* Stuttgart: Deutsche Verlag-Anstalt, 1978.

Stumpf, Reinhard. *Die Wehrmandt-Elite: Rang und HerKunftsstruktur der Deut-schen Generale und Admirale 1933-1945.* Boppard am Rhein Harold Boldt Verlag, 1982.

Sulimierskiego, Filipa and others. *Slownik Geograficzny Krolestwa Polskiego.* War-saw: Wieku Nowy-Swiat, 1882.

Sweets, John. *Choices in Vichy France: The French Under Nazi Occupation.* New York; Oxford University Press, 1986.

Sydnor, Charles, Jr. *Soldiers of Destruction: The SS Death's Head Division, 1933-1945.* Princeton: Princeton University Press, 1977.

Taylor, Telford. *Munich: The Price of Peace.* New York: Vintage Books, 1980.

_____. *Sword and Swastika: Generals and Nazis in the Third Reich.* New York: Si-mon and Schuster, 1952.

Thomas, Joseph. *Lippincott's Gazetteer of the World.* Philadelphia: J.B. Lippincott Company, 1893.

Tolischus, Otto D. *They Wanted War.* New York: Reynal and Hitchcock, 1940.

Toland, John. *Adolf Hitler.* Garden City, New York: Doubleday & Company, Inc. 1976.

_____. *No Man's Land: 1918, The Last Year of the Great War.* Garden City, New York: Doubleday & Company, Inc., 1980.

Tournier, Michael. *The Ogre.* Translated by Barbara Brey. New York: Dell Publish-ing Co., Inc., 1972.

Tuchman, Barbara. *The Guns of August.* New York: The MacMillan Company, 1962.

Uetrecht, E. *Meyers Orts und Verkehrs Lexikon des deutschen Reich.* Leipzig: Bibliog-raphische Institut, 1912-1913.

Umbreit, Hans. *Der Militarbefehlshaber in Frankreich: 1940-1944.* Boppard am Rhein: Harold Boldt Verlag, 1968.

_____. *Der Militarische Besetzung der Tschechoslowakei und Polens.* Stuttgart: Deutsche Verlags-Anstalt, 1977.

_____. and Muller, Bernard. *Das Deutsche Reich und Der Zweite Weltkrieg.* Vol-ume 5, Stuttgart: Deutsche Verlag Anstalt, 1988.

U.S. Adjutant General's Office. Military Information Division. *Military Schools of Europe And Other Papers Selected for Publication.* Washington, D.C.: Govern-ment Printing Office, 1896.

Vizetelly, Henry. *Berlin under the New Empire.* 2 volumes. New York: Greenwood Press, Publishers, 1968.

Waite, Robert. *Vanguard of Nazism: The Free Corps Movement in Postwar Germany.* Cambridge, Massachusetts: Harvard University Press, 1952.

Wallach, Jehuda. *The Dogma of the Battle of Annihilation: The Theories of Clausewitz and Schlieffen and Their Impact on the German Conduct of Two World Wars.* Westport, Connecticut: Greenwood Press, 1986.

Watt, Richard M. *Dare Call It Treason.* New York: Simon and Schuster, 1963.

Weigley, Russell. *Eisenhower's Lieutenants: The Campaigns of France and Germany, 1944-1945.* Bloomington: Indiana Univesity Press, 1981.

Weingartner, James. *Hitler's Guard: The Story of the Liebstandarte SS Adolf Hitler, 1933-1945.* Nashville: Battery Press, N.D.

Weintraub, Stanley. *A Stillness Heard round the World: The End of the Great War: November 1918.* New York: E.P. Dutton, Truman Talley Books, 1985.

Wheeler-Bennett, John. *Hindenburg: The Wooden Titan.* New York: St. Martin's Press, 1967.

_____. *The Nemesis of Power: The German Army In Politics, 1918-1945.* New York: St. Martin's Press, 1953.

Wilmot, Chester. *The Struggle For Europe.* New York: Harper & Brothers, Publishers, 1952.

Wilt, Alan. *The French Riviera Campaign of August 1944.* Illinois University Press, 1981.

_____. *"Das Oberkommando des Heeres during World War II: An appraisal."* Unpublished Paper delivered to the Western Association for German Studies Convention at Madison, Wisconsin, 1 October 1983.

Young, Desmond. *Rommel: The Desert Fox.* New York: Harper & Row, Publishers, Inc. 1950.

Zahn, Theodore. *Das infanterie Regiment Markgraf Ludwig Wilhelm (3. Badisches) Nr. 111 in Weltkriege 1914-1918.* Wiesbaden: Matthais Grünewald Verlag, 1936.

Zaloga, Steven and Madej, Victor. *The Polish Campaign, 1939.* New York: Hippocrene Books, Inc., 1985.

PERIODICAL LITERATURE

Altpreussisches Biographie. 1975 Edition. s.v. "Blaskowitz, Johannes Albrecht." By Gerd Brausch.

Assmann, Kurt. "Hitler and the German Officer Corps," *United States Naval Institute Proceedings.* Volume 82, May 1956.

Bartov, Omer. "Soldiers, Nazis, and War in the Third Reich," *The Journal of Modern History.* 63: March, 1991. 44-60.

"Blaskowitz, Johannes," *Der Deutsche Soldaten Kalender 1953,* Munich: Schild Verlag.

SOURCES

Bülle, German. "Das Königliche Preussische Kadetten Korps," *Deutscher Soldaten Kalender.* (1962), 208-218.

Delarue, Jaques. "La Gestapo En France," *Historia hors serie,* circa 1972.

Devers, Jacob. "Operation Dragoon: The Invasion of Southern France," *Military Affairs.* Volume X, No. 2, Summer, 1946.

Die Tradition: Informationen Fur Militaria Sammler. July: 1992 Edition S.V. "Das Königlich Preussische Kadetten Korps."

Froese, Ernst. "Miene Begegnung mit Hans Blaskowitz," *Der Seehase.* Nr. 122. 1976.

Gaudig, Hellmut, "Im Gedenken an Generaloberst Johannes Blaskowitz," *Wehlauer Heimatbrief.* Hanover: Rudolf Meitsch. 1980.

Geyer von Schweppenburg, Leo Freiherr. "Invasion Without Laurels," *An Cosantoir: Irish Defense Journal.* Parts I & II, December 1949-January 1950.

Gies, Hans. "Generaloberst Johannes Blaskowitz," *Der Seehase.* Nr. 93/94: 1965.

Gollwitzer, Hellmut, "Der Uberfall", *Zeit Magazin.* Nr. 13, 23 March 1984.

"Kommt auch Blaskowitz an die Riehe?" *Nachrichten fur die Truppe,* Nr. 83, Sonnabend, 8 Juli 1944, Band 1, Nos.1-190.

Kurowsky, Franz. "GFM Ernst Busch Zu Seinen 25. Todestag," *Deutshes Soldatenjahrbuch: 1970.* Munich: Schild Verlag, 1970.

Krannhals, Hans von, "Die Judenvernichtung in Polen und die 'Wehrmacht,'" *Wehrwissenschaftliche Rundshau,* 15/1965: 570-592.

Krausnick, Helmuth. "Hitler und die Morde in Polen: Ein Beitrag zum konflikt zwischen Heer und SS um die Verwaltung des besetzten Gebiete," *Vierteljahrshefte für Zeitgeschichte,* 11: (April, 1963), 196-206.

Möller-Witten, Hanns. "Generaloberst Blaskowitz," *Deutscher-Soldatenkalender: 1958.* Munich Lochausen: Schild Verlag, 1958.

O'Donnell, James. "The Devil's Architect," *The New York Times Magazine.* 26 October 1969.

Porch, Douglas. "Artois, 1915." *Military History Quarterly.* Volume 5, No. 3, Spring, 1993.

"Portrats grosser Soldaten," *Kampftruppen.* Nr. 3, June, 1967.

Rothfels, Hans, ed. "Ausgewählte Briefe von Generalmajor Helmuth Stieff," *Vierteljahrshefte für Zeitgeschichte,* 2: (1954), 291-305.

Seiz, Gustav. "Durch Kruez-Zur Krone," *Der Seehase.* Easter, 1955.

Sprung, G. "The Mentality and Ethos of the German Army," *The Army Quarterly,* 56 (1948), 46-59.

Stahl, Fredrich-Christian. "Johannes Blaskowitz." *Bädisches Biographien.* Stuttgart, 1987.

NEWSPAPERS

Chicago Sunday Tribune. 1939.
Daily Express (London). 1944-45
Militär Wochenblatt. 1938.
The New York Herald-Tribune. 1939.
The New York Post. 1939.
The New York Times. 1915-1918, 1936, 1939-1940, 1944-1945, 1948.
The Times (London). 1914-1918, 1939, 1944-1945.
Völkischer Beobachter. 1939-1940.

INTERVIEWS AND CORRESPONDENCE

Blaskowitz, Anne Marie
Brandner, Hans
Deutsch, Harold C.
Dolibois, John
Elbri, Ilmar
Hay, Edward
Kakol, Kartimierz
Koepcke, Johannes Jr.
Lewis, William
Marwell, David
Parris, Joel
Taylor, Telford
Von Curland, Prince Friedrich Biron
Von Mach, Nikolaus

Index